TIME RUNNING OUT

Dad set down the dill pickle he was about to bite, peered over his trifocals. "You okay, son?"

That pissed me off. "'Okay'?" I snarled. "I'm friggin' dandy."

"Now, son —" he swiped both ends of his mustache with a crooked finger — "if it *is* breast cancer, it *is not* a death sentence, there's hope today. Improved chemotherapy, radiotherapy, and a soon-to-be-approved drug, taxol, which has incredible anti-cancer qualities available soon."

"When?"

"Next year!"

I slammed my fist down hard. The salt shaker fell over. "That might be too damned late."

Professors wield so much power over college kids it makes them think their hold on them is real, and they possessed all the answers. They're so insolent and unflappable any criticism befalling them rolls off their backs like water off a duck. Maybe that was what was infuriating Mom.

"What the hell can be done for Anastasia *today*, Dad?" I snarled.

"Go to Ginsburg's office. Listen to him, find some taxol, and get it into her ASAP."

"Swell," I said and shuddered. I felt queasy. I thought I'd throw up.

Get a grip, I told myself, took some deep gasps, and said, "Look, don't say a word. I'll tell Nastia at home."

But I never had the chance.

THE
TAXOL
THIEF

The Heist That Killed Millions of Breast Cancer Victims

Ceylon Barclay

Also by Ceylon L. Barclay
Red Rum Punch
An Easter Charade

Nonfiction with Co-Authors
An English Course For Chinese Graduate Students—Liu Hong-shang
Images of America: Ormond Beach

Edited by Ceylon L. Barclay
Famous English Articles About Philosophy and Life by Yi Yin-liang
Twenty Years in Beria's Hell

boldventurepress.com

The Taxol Thief
by Ceylon Barclay

First Edition
November 2016

Audrey Parente, Editor
Rich Harvey, Design

Copyright © 2016 by Ceylon Barclay. All rights reserved.

This novel is a work of fiction. Names, characters, places,
and incidents are either the product of the author's
imagination or are used fictitiously, and any resemblance
to actual persons, living or dead, business establishments,
events, or locales is entirely coincidental.

ISBN-13: 978-1539454441
Print edition $16.95
Available in eBook edition

All rights reserved. No part of this book may be reproduced
or transmitted in any form or by any means without express
permission of the publisher and copyright holder.

Printed and bound in the United States.

**To the shining
memories of all those
the Emperor
of All Maladies
summoned early**

For three decades, the FDA denied the approval of a first-in-class drug, taxol, condemning hundreds of thousands of breast-cancer victims to certain death. This is a story of one couple's attempt to evade that fate by smuggling taxol from China.

ONE

Winter Park, Florida
Noon, November 22, 1991

"Say, Nastia," I said, "you spilled Gatorade on your tennis top."

My eyes darted from the Margarita Drive cul-de-sac to the coaster-sized blotch over the left breast of Anastasia's hot-pink tennis shirt then back to the luminescence sparkling off Waunatta Lake like strobe lights on the day after Thanksgiving.

"It's sweat," she said dismissively. She didn't look down and tilted her long blonde locks into the wind stream. "It's nothing."

"Really?" One of my hairy blond eyebrows shot up.

"Must've brushed it with a sweaty wristband."

"Sure you did." I always try to tell the truth. It saves stumbling recalling my flaky dodges.

I hooked a right on Helena Drive and a left onto bumper-to-bumper Hall Road. Nastia stroked my hand resting on the shifter and blew off my skepticism with a little lift of an eyebrow and a bantam shoulder hunch. She dabbed her forehead with a stretchy pink wristband and drew it over her left breast — demonstrating — then draped the banded wrist out the BMW rag-top to blow dry. With her hot pink outfit and my neon-yellow T-shirt, aboard the robin's egg blue roadster we looked as colorful as two Easter eggs in an Easter basket.

Her reply sounded fishy, but I was not about to impugn it and spoil a fantastic day that had me beginning to believe in divine retribution: *I'd thrashed her at tennis for the first time!*

Anastasia, like world-ranked Maria Sharapova, had been coached in Moscow by a champion, Martina Navratilova. When Martina sent Maria to Nick Bolletieri's tennis camp in Bradenton, Florida, Nastia returned to her native Tver, Russia, to perfect her game.

And yrs truly had never had a tennis lesson! So vanquishing the reigning Winter Park Tennis Club's Champ had sent me dancing victory laps around the court. Adding to my elation was Nastia snagging a job teaching high school math; it meant the doubling of the gravy train and emancipation from our two-by-four, fourth-floor, walk-up efficiency. So, on this gorgeous late November day under a beamy sun, frisky breeze, and temperature still balmy enough for toplessness — the BMW 325xi, not my bride — it was a perfect day for tooling around seeking a wreck to rehab into our dream home. Oh, and finally, my spirits were buoyed by my parents' turkey day visit. They'd flown in from Blowing Rock, N.C., blissful their son and daughter-in-law was gainfully employed, happily married, and house hunting. Their liberation at long last!

I'd been daydreaming of all these positives in my life when I spotted the blemish on Nastia's Bolle Palermo tennis top, (one of my two marital gifts). And that's how this tale began, with a smudge on Nastia's hot-pink top that I hadn't noticed during our tennis match or, afterward, when dropping off a copy of her CV at UCF or sharp-elbowing through Black Friday hoards for a phony Yuletide fir.

It took Nastia forever to fess up that day, and the saga nearly ended with the Bering Strait demise of your humble scribe, who having been christened twenty-two years ago Igor Vladimirovich Fetisov, was adopted at seven and rechristened Troy V. Locke. I am now the upbeat, jocular, head-honcho of the Winter Park McDonald's and the only undergrad in Colby College's 188-year history to be expelled graduation day.

I slid the BMW's shifter knob down-and-in for a tire-squealing curve at Lake Nan, lost for a jiffy in the rapture of driving finely-tuned wheels that still gave me heart palpitations, feeling the frictionless clutch glide over the five-speed tooth-cogs as smoothly as a NASCAR driver gearing down for turn four at Daytona. My raptured abruptly ceased when Nastia pinched my hairy leg. Yes, my bride of six months really does that.

I yelped, "For God's sake, Nasty, what is it?"

"Americans," she scoffed, "are so petrified of a daub of sweat they hide it with sticks, sprays, and roll-ons until they smell like Parisian floozies."

What a dodge! She'd detoured my wet boob perception into American's cornucopia of perspiration alleviates. Fortunately, I'm a sunny lad whose stein is always half-full, and skepticism is always short-lived. I am also a stickler for veracity and precision in the spoken word. What ten-cent philosopher isn't?

"Whoa there, Cupcake," I said. "How would you know how French bimbos smell? *I* am an Arrid-using American and *you've* never been to France in your life."

"You're a *naturalized* American," she fired back then kissed my cheek lovingly. Her typical response, a sting trailed by a smooch. She scrubbed the wet spot with her spongy pink wristband ferociously and added, "Say, when *am* I'm getting that Parisian honeymoon?"

"Same time I do."

She placed a tanned finger under my mandible, turned it, and planted a smackeroo on my lips so sensuous I gasped. She fluttered her eyelashes and danced her fingertips up my bare thigh.

"This century, Honeybuns?" she cooed.

"Keep that up and we'll jet off tonight." A kiss like that is a promise of goodies to come.

We grinned at each other in secret understanding. Wisps of blonde hair baked pale by long hours whacking fuzzy yellow balls in swampy Florida heat grazed her Nordic face, the perfect picture of vibrant health. She folded the strands into a creamy spill, looped by a pink headband, snapping in the wind-stream perfumed by orange blossoms like a bottle of Chanel No. 5.

I pointed at a Prudential Realty office on Hall Road and lifted my chin.

Anastasia shook her head.

"Don't forget Paris wouldn't fit on my credit card," I said, vindicating my paltry marital gifts and turning onto Amber Oak Drive. Amber intersected with North Landmark on a meager spit between two kidney-shaped sinkholes called, collectively, Lake Burkett. There were no For Sale signs, and I made a U. My second gift, a titanium, tungsten, graphite, and carbon-fiber Head racket, was a gigantic step up from her laminated wood-framed paddle, interestingly pioneered by the misogynist Henry VIII.[1] Though tennis harks back to 11th Century French monks who popularized the game in rope-split courtyards shouting, *Tenez!* — Take — when serving, it only grew trendy in Russia with the 1985 elevation of Mikhail Gorbachev to CCCP [2] Top Gun.

"So get another credit card, nobody uses cash today," she snipped. Problem solved.

"Just pile on plastic debt?" I scoffed. "Never!" A vow I would break that very afternoon.

Nastia shot me a snarky scowl. *Everyone else does; why not?* She was correct, of course. Banks securitized a third of their massive credit card receivables by tapping domestic and international capital markets to fund America's plastic fix. But I returned her scowl with a wry smile and a look of incredulity. Aggrieved innocence was one of her better roles when she hid something. I narrowed my eyes. Nothing appeared amiss, and yet, I was sure there'd been no blot on her tennis top during our match. And she had not, like me, slobbered Gatorade on herself replenishing electrolytes to preempt wilting as my chopshots, scorching serves, and McEnroe-like cunning gave me my first-ever victory: 6-3, 6-2, 6-0, which might explain her dour disposition. I'm a klutz at tennis, and, for that matter, the tango. Rugby's my game.

"Let's zip down Aloma and look for a fix-me-upper closer to town, maybe the Sylvia/Osceola Lakes area," I suggested. "It's a quiet area, and you can tell me what's upsetting you?"

"Why not?" she replied.

On four-lane Aloma traffic thickened. Parents headed to the mall to Christmas shop without their broods, unaccompanied kids unloaded on Disney. Walt's a great babysitter.

"Troy, you immigrated here at seven when your long-widowed Mom remarried," she began.

"So?" I said.

"So you're used to sticky-heat," Nastia said in heavily-accented but syntactically-perfect English. "I left Tver in May for our *real* wedding, and then you just had to drag me to swampy Florida. I sweat. Get used to it."

"Yeah, you do," I agreed and wondered if the sticky heat had goosed her five million eccrine glands into working overtime … *but only on her left breast?* "Want the top up and air on?"

"Nah, it's cool when we move, leave it hatless," she said flippantly.

I smiled. "Heat's the price tag for living in Florida."

"Life always extracts its price."

"It does, but this is a mecca of snowlessness, a land of the brave and home of the free."

"Oh, yes, I'm so delighted to be here, Troy." There was bitterness in her voice.

Anastasia, raised in thousand-year-old Tver, only knew long, dark winters and broiling, short, white-night summers, light years from Florida's sizzling heat and humidity. Tver, sitting on the same rung of latitude as Juneau, is located at the confluence of the Volga and Tvertsa Rivers and home to five colleges. Nastia graduated from Tver State and put her Ph.D. in math from Moscow State University to work at Akademgorodok, a research center of 25,000 scientists Stalin squirreled away at invasion-proof Novosibirsk, the capital of Siberia.

"May I use your handkerchief, *pul-lease*?" she asked. The corners of her mouth were turned down. There was more than a flicker of impatience in her voice. She had slid to the far side of her seat, and her voice had fallen into an alto's husky range.

"Sure." I pulled the unused square out of my shorts, handed it to her, and started to say Winter Park only broiled ten months a year, and Blowing Rock hadn't seen swamp heat since *Tyrannosaurus rex*. But even bridegrooms know there are driving forces at work within Venuses that will forever remain mysteries to Martians, either that or her love-hate relationship with Russia had raised its head again. I opted for a conciliatory, "Our Moscow *brackocheetanie*—civil-ceremony—did lack much charm."

Anastasia's eyes pop open. "'*Much charm?*'" She shook her head, wiped her brow with my handkerchief, and attacked the damp spot with guttural determination and an eye roll.

Candor often does that to me. I was used to it.

"I never felt married until our ceremony *à l'eglise ravissante en* Blowing Rock," she griped, nailing the point in French, a display of her trilingual dexterity that pops out *de temps en temps*.

"Me either," I acknowledged, bamboozled by her jitteriness set off by her tennis defeat.

She was referring to the alluring stone sanctuary, Saint Mary of the Hills Episcopal Church on the corner of Main and Chestnut Streets in Blowing Rock, just down steep Chestnut from the home of my parents, tenured professors at Appalachian State University in Boone. My stepdad, the proverbial dour New England Puritan, ever-so-polite, erudite, parsimonious, and stolid, and my Mom, an ascetic Universalist, had fled the wilds of Appalachia to join us for turkey — my treat. I was shocked to see Mom brazenly flaunt scarlet nail polish on her fingers and toes. With their tenures had come a comfortable lifestyle, a tony pad in posh Blowing Rock, his-and-her Volvos (his white, hers red), plus five months off a year.

But I digress. In our six months of marital bliss, I'd found it hard for Nastia, when discontent, not to reproach the one closest to her — *me* — for her irritability. She was not at fault. It was her culture at fault. Svetlana Stálina (the daughter of Stalin[3]) wrote, *The ugliest feature of Soviet life was the double-facedness infused in Soviets from schoolroom days.*[4] Add Soviet lawlessness, lies, and aching scarcities lorded over by corrupt, dissimulating, iron-fisted despots, and people discover a cobra curled in the pit of all their stomachs. Naturally, when Soviets hear of America's carnival of freedoms: independence from tyranny, inalienable rights, and the pursuit of happiness, out pop their fabrications. My heart weeps for them, their frustrations with lives of discouragement, isolation, anguish, and existential abandon, with never the time, money, or freedom for the music of life, the moments of insouciance that add color and joy to living.

I stole a glance at Nastia. Something nerve-racking was going on. But what it was, I hadn't a clue. She stopped scrubbing, dabbed at a filmy mist on her cheek, and glanced back at me. Then she wiped my handkerchief on her damp breast, slid it inside her bra, and blurted out, "Tell me, again, why the hell we left Blowing Rock for friggin Florida."

Substitute teaching had expanded her vocabulary.

"No work in Boone," I soothed. "And you wanted a one-season climate, Nastusha,"

"I had a one-season climate in Russia."

What a straight-man line! I couldn't resist giving it a whack. I waggled my eyebrows like the unhinged Groucho Marx and let it fly, "Yeah, Siberia!"

In a lightning-fast mood change, Anastasia smiled and elbowed me in the ribs so hard I grunted. "Better than sweating twelve months a friggin year," she joshed.

We laughed out loud. The game was on.

"'Friggin?'" I teased. "Do Russian Ph.D.'s have their own language?"

"Bet your ass."

"Lyrical, too. Who taught you that?"

"Eighth graders."

"Glad we can teach a Russian Ph.D. something."

"You wouldn't believe the terms I know for sexual congress." Nastia nibbled a hangnail on her thumb nervously. "Is that the word?"

"If you're talking to Grammy Locke, screwing's fine for me."

We broke out in giggly snickers. Two kids again. In my commitment to a life of joviality, I recommended no worries and one good chuckle a day. It's better for you than chicken soup.

On Aloma, Anastasia looked left and right and back at two block-houses built almost two inches apart. "Couldn't we buy those toy-houses, tear them down, and build a big new one?" She had picked up her tennis racket and aimed it like a shotgun at the shacky twins.

"*If* we qualified for a construction loan," I said and pointed at another wreck. "Hey now, that chintzy, cinder-block cutey could be a money-making starter and not far from your school."

The thousand-foot hovel had a moldy window air-conditioner grinding diligently and sat far back on a sandlot beneath a sprawling live oak draped with Spanish moss. Bucolic.

"Sure, under that big, buggy tree. Close in the carport, parquet the floors, swat mosquitoes, and watch the neighbors' junks rust. Lover, Aloma is too damn trashy, let's hit O-B-T."

She was kidding, of course. Her reference was to Orange Blossom Trail, a hotspot of drugs, prostitution, and strip clubs set among cabbage palms and dumpier houses. A dream of all callow fellows my age is to marry a dream girl and unearth a love-nest overlooking one of Florida's 30,000 sinkhole-spawned lakes. Our complex abuts such an oasis, and I often hear that mantra from the cliff-dwellers.

"You know, there's not enough glue in America to keep my ass stuck to a teacher's seat very long," Nastia said. "Joseph Silney of Coral Gables has authenticated my dissertation's, and I *will* teach college, *get* oodles of time off, and *earn* serious bucks."

"I'm sure you will," I said. "Full-time public school teaching's tough."

We turned off Aloma onto Sylvan Drive. The homes looked pricey; few had For Sale signs.

"Then pray for me," Nastia said and crossed herself and cast beatific eyes heavenly.

"I will. Once you're a college prof, the kids will enrich your vocabulary exponentially."

"Oh boy." Anastasia looked left and right. "These homes are too damn ritzy."

"We'll keep looking; the Goldilocks' house awaits."

"Wonderful." Her voice descended into a depth only a flounder could love.

It seemed a good time for a conversational hiatus, though I commiserated with her hostility. I goosed my premature college graduation present. I was booted out of Colby but kept my parents' graduation gift: a brand new, 1991, Beemer-325xi convertible with AWD, a 168-HP inline-6, a Getrag 260 5-speed gearbox, and a brawny sound system. Nastia seemed as if she needed romance, so I tuned in a station and got a gung-ho DJ playing the driving strains of *I Got Rhythm,* the Gershwins' oldie but goody (circa 1930; music by George, lyrics by Ira) our octet sang at Colby. I snapped my fingers and hummed my part to bass thumps vibrating the seat as we wound through lakes close to downtown Winter Park. The burg is a resplendent cradle of trees, meadows, flowers, and well-heeled-transplants; it sits in the middle of Orange County, a municipality of fifty percent Hispanic and twenty percent blacks center-pieced by a nineteenth-century WASP fantasy that was one hundred percent neither.

"Your geek brick's ringing," Anastasia said, pointing between my legs at my new phone.

I hadn't heard it. "I didn't hear it."

"Tinnitus ringing badly?" She twisted the radio down so low I couldn't feel the bass.

"Like those 203-milimeter 110-howitzers. I'm surprised you can't hear them."

Tinnitus, an incessant ringing in the otitis media, was a gift of the big guns G. H. W. sent over to soften up the invaders. Bush forgot the ear protectors. I slowed down and drifted to the side of Sylvan near Harris Circle. The homes were two-story with big yards of coarse Bermuda grass studded with oaks and palms. Kids played baseball, hide-and-seek, and kick-the-can.

"I'll get it," Anastasia said and slid her hot palm down my hirsute leg.

"Don't stop!" I gasped. Why does nonsense keeps rolling off my tongue?

She ignored me, punched a button, and said, "Ah-low." Her shalom dripped with enough borscht to cast her forever a émigré. "This is she." She listened. Unlike me, Nastia had perfect grammar in Russian and English. She could even spout the tenses of verbs by name. Do you know the Future Perfect Progressive tense of the verb lust? Me neither.

"You'd better tell him." She handed me my brand-new, analog, second-generation, IS-136 cell phone, the size and weight of a brick, and said, "It's Big Kahuna."

I rolled to a stop, slid it in neutral, and set the brake. "Hey, big guy, what's happening?"

Anastasia leaned over to eavesdrop. Soviets snoop.

"Gees, Boss," my assistant manager whined. "We got slammed at breakfast;

we're in the weeds, and the damned tourists keep flooding in. We're running out of — "

"Fantastic, Kahuna! Proof Yankees yearn for our sugary, fatty, salty sustenance."

Anastasia made a phony laugh. "You call that crap *sustenance*?"

I ignored her and listened to Kahuna. "I know, I know, Boss, 'We're killing 'em with heart attacks and cancer.' But now we're almost out of English muffins. What am I gonna do?"

There was desperation in his voice.

"What do I do when we're low on buns?" I said patiently. We'd had this conversation before.

"You call José at his bakery and get a special order 'delivered lickety friggin split'."

"Because?"

"Because 'We're his biggest customer, and he wouldn't want to lose us and starve to death in threadbare Oviedo.'"

I grinned. "And where's Rafael's number kept?"

"You keep it right here — " WHACK! Kahuna smacked the wall next to the phone.

"Suppose you can give Rafael a call, Kahuna?"

"That's a ten-four, Boss. I'll get 'er done!"

"No more problems?"

"Nope, none. And don't you worry; you guys enjoy lunch with your folks."

"Thanks, big guy; see you Sunday afternoon. Adios."

At six-six and two hundred twenty pounds, Kahuna was my Man Friday and a Poster Boy for McDees. He had the face of a romance novel cover, chiseled features, shoulder-length blond hair, wasp waist, and biceps the size of my thighs. He ate like a refuge, was loyal, rode herd on our dropouts and potheads, kept our retired staff awake, and bagged our grease-juicy burgers with panache. He was not Einstein. And he called me way too often.

Anastasia smiled. "Handsome but a tad slow, huh?"

"Someday he'll put a wife in a padded cell."

"Poor girl. I hope I don't know her."

I set the cell phone on the floor and pulled back onto the road. Traffic was heavy. Peregrines were looking for winter nests; Florida building to its winter frenzy. I was growing upset with Nasty.

"Nasty," I said peevishly, "that wet spot's getting bigger on your shirt; *stall eta*—what is it?"

When serious we often spoke in our native Russian.

Anastasia shot me a puzzled look, nibbled her hangnail again, and remained tongue-tied.

Soviet silence does not fool Sherlock; it's the way Soviets get when vexed, finding shelter in reticence and shutting down. Over turkey and pumpkin pie at Miller's Ale House last night, Mom dabbed Cool Whip off the corner of her mouth with a frayed napkin and explained, "*Every* Soviet family had a friend or relative sentenced to the Gulag[5] like both yours grandfathers. Most were never heard from again. We learned only the silent survive." My stepdad, aka Doctor, who had appeared lost in philosophic cogitations — or bewitched by the vast array of slinky-curved, young waitresses — seconded Mom. "Gorbachev laments, 'After six years of *glasnost* [6] and *perestroika* [7] Soviets still bribe, steal, lie, and hang medal on each other for those lies.'"

"*Well?*" I prodded, figuring something big was hatching. Motherhood? At that thought, my pulse quickened. Fatherhood made butterflies flutter in my belly. Having known Anastasia twenty years, long enough to know her every trait and predilection, especially to secrecy, it left a tension between us, particularly when I knew she had something locked away and inaccessible.

I stroked her arm and coaxed, "*Eta moloko mama*—Is it mama's milk?"

She stared at me with a forced grimace. "It's not *moloko mama*. I told you, 'It's sweat.'"

"Nastenka, are you pregnant?"

Her head flew back, and she roared with laughter. I never knew another woman who laughed as she did, loudly, brashly, with a joyous ring.

"Are you crazy?" she cried. "Of course not. Why would I lie to you?"

"Because that's what Soviets do?"

"I know that, but look at this tummy!"

She yanked the seatbelt off her breast, sat up straight, arched her back, and stuck out those juicy cantaloupes. I wished she hadn't done that. An adoring smile spread across the clear, smooth lines and gentle curves of her face. Her blonde eyebrows arched questioningly over intent blue eyes thicketed with long blonde lashes. She pulled her tennis shirt tight against her belly. I wished she hadn't done that. I've been the victim of salacious satyriasis since I was 14. Wild women are no anodyne for my affliction. Nastia's belly was as flat as a grill. If I hadn't known her from the sandbox to the scabbed knees of tennis to our marriage vows last May, all the accumulated experiences that make her, her, I would have believed her. But I remained suspicious. However, to keep peace, I tossed in the towel on finding the truth of her breast wetness.

"I once hiked a mountain range in Jackson Hole like those," I joked. "*La Grand Tetons.*"

"The Big Tits." Anastasia blinked. "Do Americans really use that slang for a name?"

"We do, and it would be infinitely pleasurable if you'd cuddle yours this way." I tilted my noggin at my right arm.

She tossed her head, heave-hoeing my suspicions, and snuggled my arm between her *Grand Tetons*, sending me to horny heaven. Extra helpings of vasopression and oxytoxin, two sexual hormones, explains what turned me into such an insatiable hound.

I never knew my biological father; he died while I was still in the womb, but his brother, Ivan, an Aeroflot pilot on the Sheremetyevo[8]-to-JFK run, told me while we downed vodka shots and drooled at Russky babes at a Brighten Beach Disco, Papa had been a rascal at Tver State University. Add that to my stepdad's roving eye and you get a nature-nurture double whammy that vindicates my carnal proclivities.

Houses grew stately as we approach the heart of Winter Park. On our port side were tree-arched canopies effulgent with leaves shading jewel-box gardens and velvet expanses of lawns that looked like Bay Hill putting greens engulfing stately mansions at the end of crushed-shell drives. The architecture was nouveau Tara. The manses were probably lorded over by owners as stern-faced as Easter Island megaliths who had voted conservative since Calvin Coolidge. Pools and colonnades led to altars, and sprinklers busily thuped-thuped-thuped watering grass while lowering Florida's aquifer. Sunshine through their mist made fleeting rainbows of iridescence. Orange and grapefruit trees studded Bermuda-grass in backyards the size of hunting preserves running down to Lake Sylvan. An offshore breeze kicking up made light-diamond-sparkles between frothy whitecaps where robins, full of mortician-dignity and memories of Archaeopteryx, worked the shoreline looking fat and happy.

I suspected there was more to Nastia's wet-breast yarn but had no clue why she was so evasive. Maybe the lousy fix-me-uppers we'd seen were depressing. A three-month deployment in Iraq taught me always to be circumspect; desert rats do that to you, Soviets, too. I also knew Anastasia had to convey things at her pace. I glanced at my golden Timex. We had a few minutes before meeting my parents for lunch, enough time for her to explain. A big city girl, Nastia knew only minuscule apartments, pot-holed streets, concrete expanses, and the choking belch of chemical factories. She loved American metropolises and adored suburbs. She probably had her heart set on a glamorous home. Naturally, Soviet disinformation portrayed all American families living in crumbling, burned-out, South Bronx slums. Soviet citizens knew better: all Americans lived in mansions. I liked driving around, too; it calms the restlessness stalking me slinging burgers and dreaming of my chain of cantinas.

I teed up some charm and tapped her arm with my fingertips. "Nastenka, honey," I murmured, "I'd like to hear about your wet spot."

Her chin came up in a gesture of skepticism and pride. "You want to know, do you?"

I gave her a clumsy smile. "Yes, Nastusha, I *really* do." Finally, the truth!

She paused, probably searching for the right English words or another dodge. Seventy-four years of communism taught Soviets never to reveal their feelings.

"Come on, Nastenka," I urged. "Let's have it."

Icy silence.

Nastenka is one of the diminutives of Anastasia, a name that means *reborn* in Russian. Its pruned versions convey feelings lost in other languages. When wanting curtness addressing an Anastasia, use Naska; tenderness, Nastenka or Nastyona; caring, Nastusha; haste, Nastia; cuteness, Nasty. A shortened version for every mood. It gives a kid plenty of warning when a whack is coming.

Anastasia slipped off her headband and tilted her hair into the slipstream, jumbling her golden locks. For a moment, she appeared lost in thought, and then she sat erect, forked back her hair with splayed fingers, and gave me a sensual, almost erotic, smile that I felt in my gut.

"Honey," she said lovingly. "It's nothing. So don't fret about it, okay?"

Her words did not comfort me, and I figured I was headed for trouble, but said, "Okay."

Unexplainably, her mood swung voluptuous. Her face flushed. Her eyes went Marilyn Monroe droopy. She made a low-pitched vocalization of a cat's meow and nibbled my earlobe setting a python stirring in my shorts. How quickly catnip gets me off track.

I crooned, "Who could ask for anything more?"

Anastasia glanced down. "My, my, is that a snorkel, Troy?" she purred with a little lift of an eyebrow, a little tilt of scimitar lips.

She knew English well. Her inflection was thick as cabbage soup. Her tongue darted about in her mouth; her breathing was a little harder. Nasty thinks men's penises are a structural defect the Creator should recast as a breathing apparatus.

"It's Cupid's Arrow," I said, pant, pant, pant. "Mind riding with a guy with an erection?"

She made a raunchy growl. "Not if he keeps it caged; some women love earthy, carnal men."

"Earthy and carnal, that's me."

She canoodled her hot wet tongue deep into my ear, helpless under my ambrosial spell.

"A Q-Tip does that better," I reflected flippantly.

She shoved me away and feigned a pout. "Be serious, Troy!"

"I can't be." And that was gospel. "*You* be serious and tell me what's going on."

"You mean about this?" Anastasia touched her damp left breast.

"Yes. And it's not just that that bothers me. I've got a funny feeling."

She huffed out a long weary sigh. "Oh, alright, Troy." Her fingers weaved down my arm. "You know I love you." Her habitual prelude to a grudging admission.

"I know you do, Nastenka. And I love you, too, have ever since Cupid fluttered his silken wings in our sandbox." My habitual reply. I leaned over to hear her.

Nastia smiled tenderly. Her eyes focused on mine fleetingly. Her total engrossment always made peace between us and redoubled the happiness in our love. Her faculty of intense concentration, particularly when in conversations with others, always made them feel what they said was not only relevant and critical but fascinating and mesmerizing. And yet that attribute never prevented confrontations from recurring between us, often frequently for unexpected, insignificant reasons. Maybe that's the fate of all newlyweds, keenly aware of the chain that binds them and equally alert to what drives them apart.

"Ginsburg said *eta moloko ved'my;* or did he say *moloko prividenie*?" she said.

Every muscle in my face twitched at that bomb. "*Who* said *what?*"

"Doctor Abraham Ginsburg said my left breast was dripping witch's milk or ghost's milk; I forget which. *Les petites miséres de la vie humaine* — the little miseries of human life."

"Then it's not a sweat gland problem or *moloko mama*?"

"Not a chance." Nastia's voice was firm but humble, eyes soft, tone candid and low with a remote, coddling quality. She sounded like a teacher telling kindergarteners about Goosey Gander, expecting neither comprehension nor rebuttal. Butterflies rumbled in my stomach.

"Ginsburg, witch's milk, ghost's milk, you?" I repeated.

"*Yes, Igor Vladimirovich Fetisov,*" the bomb-thrower quibbled. "*Me!*"

What vehemence! Nastia had spit out my baptized name *always* used by Russkies to show respect and *never* used maliciously. Dread swept over me, but it didn't stop me.

"Who's Ginsburg?" I challenged.

"Doctor J. Abraham Ginsburg," Anastasia shot back.

My mind ran over my OB/GYNs acquaintances for a J. Abe Ginsburg. Zip, zero, zilch. Abe Lincoln, I remembered, said, *Men who part their names in the middle had things to hide,* but I was so miffed I let it go.

"I've never seen you look for obstetricians in the Yellow Pages."

"No, you haven't. Ginsburg's not an obstetrician."

I slammed my hand on the steering wheel. "What the hell *is* Abe, Nastia, a neurologist, an endocrinologist, a pulmonologist? What?"

"He's a specialist to whom my physical exam doctor referred me."

My jaw dropped open. "Your physical-exam-to-teacher doc sent you to an unnamed specialist. Why? When? Where? You never mentioned a — "

"I never mention lots of stuff," she interrupted. Her eyes narrowed as cold-blue as a malamute's. She had not named J. Abe's specialty. Was that by design or oversight?

"What kind of stuff?" I dared and slowed for a Century 21 sign askew in a mound of sodded-over sugar-sand. The manor sat in the jagged-fingered shade of towering royal palms. It was in perfect shape: Lots of bucks. I hit the gas for the umpteenth time. "Well?"

"Such as the pittance I make driving all over Timbuktu to substitute teach," she snapped.

"Don't forget your driving to pick me up after work," I added, reminding her of that sacrifice.

"And driving to Blockbusters for old movies to fill lonely nights, driving to Publix for groceries, driving to the cleaners, driving for oil changes, driving to — "

"Okay, okay, I capeesh. You drive."

"And *you* used to wine and dine me, and we spent days in bed."

"That was in Russia after our *brackocheetanie.* Champagne was cheaper than bottled water, and I had dysentery. Married men can't keep up that level of charm; we'd have strokes."

Anastasia smacked her forehead with the heel of her hand. "So that's the reason."

That was total malarkey, of course, but it illustrated the perpetual strain of independence and evasiveness in Nastia, as there was in me, that kept us apart and kept us so devotedly together, able to transform trivial quarrels into insignificance and write them off as drivel. But doubts lingered. I glanced at her belly again. Snug and tight and flat as a pool table. The moist spot over her left breast had grown. My heart reached out to her. I slipped an arm around her shoulder, drew her close, and joined Bing crooning a few bars of *White Christmas.*

"Nastusha," I said, "I think you need some loving."

She relaxed, nuzzled my neck, and let out a deep sigh.

"When you feel you can, tell me more, Nastusha," I began and soon as those words crossed my lips I knew the truth. Her Russian birth control pills had bombed. She was pregnant. *Nah, impossible,* I told myself and shoved that worry aside. I'm good at that.

Anastasia rested her head on my shoulder lovingly, or contemplatively. One of her slim, tanned hands fell languorously atop the leather-encased gearshift. The other slinked up my Nike shorts. *Way up.* Fingers as subtle as vine tendrils started kneading those long, thick, adductor muscles, pressing and stroking like a diligent genie, eliciting groans. *Gesta non verba.* Bliss. Probably another dodge, but a blissful dodge. She must have had second thoughts and stopped abruptly. She moved to the corner of her seat, leaned forward, elbow on knee, and chin on knuckles like Rodin's Thinker. She studied me.

I knew the look: ready to spill the beans. For truth, neither sun nor moon can hide. She smiled knowingly. Dimples cavernous enough to hide pearls creased both cheeks. "You want every last detail, don't you?" She dipped her chin to her bosom, leaned back, and held her knee.

"Yes," I empathized. "It will help me understand."

"I doubt it, but okay. Just don't worry or take this too seriously."

The seriously rolled off her tongue with the trilled-r Russkies use, like Latinas. I lost mine in second grade, lose it or be bullied to death at Blowing Rock Elementary where memories still lingered of rancid steam pipes, funky floor cleaner, and red-neck taunts over my two-word English vocabulary: Ice cream.

"Take it seriously?" I echoed. "Never! Life's too short to be taken seriously."

"I've heard that." She smiled broadly, revealing peat-stained teeth, a malady of tannin-brown drinking water in northwest Russia seeping out of a million square kilometers of peat bogs.

"That's my favorite aphorism."

Anastasia whistled softly. "Aphorism. Pretty snazzy word."

"I'm a pretty snazzy guy."

"Sure you are, for a guy booted out of Colby graduation day."

I ignored her reference to the only blot on my escutcheon, my graduation day expulsion by President Cotter. The man was so nasty he probably sold coeds with 3.9 GPAs into prostitution. It had poured on our commencement processional wending to the green below Miller Library. Yrs truly, band director, goosed Pomp & Circumstance to a Sousa tempo and detoured the ensemble to Johnson Pond where I divested of *all* my duds, except for my mortarboard-cap and tassel, and streaked into the pond to frolic with swans to the cheers of peers and consternation of Pres. C who de-sheepskinned me on the spot. Luckily, my folks, wending home from Vladivostok via the Trans-Siberian Railroad from Kunming, China, did not witness the plight of their son and heir.

"There's oodles of time for gravity after we croak," I opined. "About the 'witch's milk'?"

I took both hands off the wheel and made those annoying curly-fingered quote things Dad makes during philosophy lectures to grad students at Appalachian State and slowed to turn onto Aloma. A sad little cinder-block abode with a sign out front sat patiently awaiting a buyer near Osceola Lake.

Anastasia said, "Doctor Ginsburg said — "

A soccer ball flew out of nowhere, a gang of kids in pursuit.

"The wheel!" Anastasia screamed. "Grab the friggin wheel!"

An old black Lincoln convertible, top down, shot across four-lane Aloma aiming for one humungous sinkhole.

I grabbed the wheel and stomped the brake. We fishtailed. Skid. Screeched to the edge of a very deep, sour-smelling abyss, missing it by a great big two inches. Troy Petty saved the day.

The skid killed the engine. It started making tinkling sounds.

The Lincoln's front wheels disappeared in the sinkhole, impaling on the undercarriage. Its nose stuck over the edge of the hole like a hound sniffing its territory. Millions of sinkholes, swallets and dolines, formed by overdrawn aquifers, pockmarked the Sunshine State. Once water-filled, these caverns have now been drained and are unable to support the weight of 962 people-a-day flooding in. Broken water mains, rotting sewer lines, and flushed chemicals help.

A chauffeured man in the Lincoln's backseat jumped up and started swatting the driver.

The dust settled. I turned the key. The engine coughed, whined, and started.

I pulled around the Lincoln and pulled over at Alberta and Aloma for a deep breath. I got a scent of honeysuckle as sweet as a bride's garter and glanced in the rearview mirror at the classic car.

"The guy in the back, swatting the old dude driving, looks like Number 41."

"Exactly like him," Anastasia agreed. "A brown-skinned Bush."

The black, four-door, 1961 Lincoln convertible was driven by a chauffeur wearing a spiffy white uniform cap. The swatter wore a short-sleeve white Gueyabera. His arms were as brown as a Navajo. The swattee appeared some-what familiar as he ducked blows.

"Poor driver probably fell asleep at the wheel of that old chariot," Anastasia commiserated.

"Septuagenarians are a damn menace," I said. "That inexhaustible supply of wrinkly assed old peregrines who make the sixteen-hour drive down from Newark in a day, hit Orlando, and turn our roads into demolition derbies."

"And keep cash registers ringing, hospitals full, and morgues busy. Don't put them down. Those bored, baggy-pant grumps keep you in business," she said sharply. A bite.

"They do," I agreed. "And my heart weeps for them, locked in frail bodies, gravity tugging everything south. They only go nuts when patronized by pompous clerks while frittering away their final chapters keeping juices flowing by swimming, shelling, and shuffle-boarding."

"Thank God they eat junk food like spring bears," Nastia said, ruffling my hair. The lick.

"Stoking up to find those empty, white-sand beaches they saw on TV."

"You'd think after the first winter of finding only postcards of those beaches they'd never return."

"The hidden fear of us who've repainted, rehired, and repriced in anticipation of their arrival."

I looked both ways and turned on busy Aloma, aka SR 426.

Anastasia hunched her shoulders. "What can you do?"

A stream of Jeeps, Broncos, and pickups with oversized tires and tinted windows towed bass boats to Lake Jessup. While wives and girlfriends shopped Black Friday deals, anglers stalked bream, largemouth bass, black crappie, and, with the densest population of gators in the state, gator-hides for their Florida Room walls. Aloma soon doglegged left and became Brewer. The snaky thoroughfare changes names as often as a chameleon changes color as it wound into the heart of the ritzy, lily-white, urban-oasis of Winter Park, now growing rowdy with tourist traffic.

I decided to try again. "Let's hear details of the witch's milk."

Matter-of-factly, Anastasia said, "Doctor Ginsburg said 'lots of women have it.'"

"That sounds fatalistic."

"Like something your Dad might say."

That was a stretch. My Dad is a closet *bon vivant* and the image of rectitude and intellectual probity … except for his roving eyes. It made me wonder what Ginsburg had said. Nastia looked far from happy. Maybe she'd heard unwelcome words. Or maybe my clever *zehna* — wife — had woven Ginsburg's words into words she wanted to hear, something I often do myself.

"My beautiful *zehna*," I began endearingly, "is there *anything* more you want to share with your *moosh* — husband?"

Anastasia hesitated. She laid her silky hand on mine atop the shifter. "Well, yes. Ginsburg said 'life is what it is, random, and luck plays a role.'"

"Now, that sounds exactly like Dad. He says, 'The spiritual find the illusion of God's order in the universe comforting when *life, in fact, is random.* It's as simple as that, Nastia.'"

"But randomness doesn't help me accept my fate, Troy."

That sounded ominous. I wondered if there was more and figured an anecdote might provide soothing. "Dad says, 'there's no grand divine plan at work, no blueprint that could apply to five billion earthlings simultaneously. The idea that a person's lousy karma is a payoff for violating designs of a vengeful God is absurd. We *can* change the hand we're dealt; otherwise, we'd still be dying of bubonic plague, smallpox, diphtheria, and polio.'"

"Ginsburg said my breast milk was from a genetic mutation," Anastasia said sheepishly, "something out of my control. Still — " her tone was low, humble, defeated — "I know it's my fault and not random. If I'd been to church more …." Her chin dropped to her chest. Her voice trailed off.

"Sophistry, Nastia, pure, unadulterated sophistry!" I pontificated. "Your witch's milk is a hiccup, a miscue in a chromosomal regulator in one of your body's seventy trillion cells!"

Anastasia smiled sweetly, wanting to lighten up. "For a philosophy major you know lots of chemistry."

"I do."

"Don't bullshit me, Locke. I met Shaw at our wedding. He told me about holding court at that Waterville watering hole of yours and your fraternity's dopamine addiction."

I ignored her reference to my frat brother, Brad's, tipsy outpourings. The chemical nature of KΔR's sexual scaffolding, blathered at Onies, was not up for discussion. Philosophers can do that.

"Look, Nastia, any of your cells could've misfired on life's Roulette Wheel. Being a prince or pauper, healthy or sick, it's all *random*! And that's the very heart of your bad luck delusions."

She rolled her eyes and quibbled, "Why does that sound suspiciously unlike you?"

"*That's* common knowledge among the enlightened," I said, raising the shield of sarcasm.

"Well," she huffed, "the Russian Orthodox Church taught me if I had good health I earned it, and I'd be punished if I wasn't godly." She crossed herself.

"*Naïve!*" I howled. "You can't possibly believe your breast milk is God's punishment?"

"That's precisely my belief!" she extolled with a sheeple's seriousness.

"I've loved you for twenty years, but it doesn't make me blind to your screwy thinking."

"Are you calling me irrational?"

"Sometimes, but never uncertain."

Anastasia smiled, pensive, silent, unswayed by logic, intent on cozening the yokel and entrusting in God's vengeance as her sky was falling. For her, deific certitudes clenched in Rottweiler convictions withstood the light of science and tide of unbelievers. It left her terrified that life is, indeed, random. There is a cause but no design.

Sometimes in her silent hiatuses, Nastia searched for English terms to explain her convoluted thoughts. Sometimes, unable to strike gold panning for articulate justifications, she displayed the scourge-of-silence that plagues Russian women to this day, a real Klondike for their men. And sometimes she portrayed a fierce, innate, religious sentimentalism, prepared to mitigate her guilt with a blood sacrifice, unmoved by logic and accepting of all pain.

Was that what was going on now?

I hadn't the foggiest idea. But I felt the calamity's shadow looming.

***

TWO

Downtown Winter Park:
The Truth Revealed

Anastasia had to come clean. "Well," I said impatiently, "what's the story?"

"*Pro moloko* — About the milk?" Anastasia asked.

"*Daaaaa,*" I said, drawing out the Russian yes in multi syllables.

Nastia shifted in her seat and stared at me appraisingly as if guessing my weight. We were winding through Winter Park's rarefied world of opulent homes, impressive even for WP, castles set far back on manicured lawns the size of the Louisiana Purchase. They looked like the empty set of Homes of the Rich and Famous. Nothing moved. No dogs, no cats, no latchkey kids, no one disembarking from stretch limos. You could strafe it with a machine gun and not hit a soul.

"This place is as deserted as the Tunguska Crater," Nastia said, referring to a horrendous, Siberian disaster caused by the minutia of Mother Nature.

"Always is," I groused. "Only a few people have the money to buy these châteaux."

"The 'glitterati, respectable thieves, and professional ball players'?"

She's heard it before. "Only Tiger, Shaq, drug dealers and their ilk make the oodles needed to buy these places … while many teachers qualified for food stamps."

Traffic thickened on Brewer Avenue and clotted to stop-and-go at Henkel Circle where Brewer changed its name to Osceola.

"About the *moloko*?" I prodded.

"It's — " Anastasia began and stopped. She gave me a look that begged indulgence, voice solemn, tone resolute. I'd heard that humbling quality when she described the fearsome power of nature unleashed by that Siberian asteroid. Little Boy's *two pounds* of uranium-235 dropped on Hiroshima generated the energy of *thirty-two million pounds* of TNT, and the Tunguska Crater, carved by a 120-foot-wide asteroid exploding at a white-hot 44,500 degrees at 33,500 mph, had the energy of 185 Hiroshimas and devastated an area the size of Rhode Island.

I dreaded the analogy she was about to relay and gulped some air. In the *Apology*, Socrates maintained the unexamined life was not worth living, but tread gently, you truthseekers, sometimes you get what you ask for.

"It's what, Nastenka?" I asked.

Anastasia sat up straight, stretched her neck as if looking for Polaris, lowered her chin determinedly, and blurted out, "Ginsburg said a *malenkee massa* — a small mass — caused my beast milk. Now you have it all! He said 'it's nothing to worry about,' so don't."

I doubted that, but discovering a breast mass had to be terrifying. "*Eta anam* — Like a cyst?"

"*Da, da, da.* That's what he called it, a cyst."

"And he said it was 'nothing to worry about?'"

That was stupid. Certainly it was something to worry about; it might even be lethal.

"Ginsburg said, 'Lots of women have them.'"

Traffic stopped. I reached over, brushed aside strands of damp blonde hair, and kissed her lips gently. "Nastenka, that's wonderful news, then you've nothing to worry about." I did not believe a word of that and wondered out loud, "Say, why haven't I felt that cyst."

"Because you've never held your fingers together and pressed down like this."

She jammed three finger pads into my thigh hard enough to hit the femur and made quarter-sized circles in a saucer-size area. It hurt.

"That hurts!" I said, rubbing my thigh. Traffic moved. I was in first and let out the clutch.

"It's supposed to hurt. If you were to do it like I showed you, you'd feel a lump like a sharp rock on a sandy beach."

That was a nifty use of the subjunctive, but I kept that observation to myself and soothed, "I'll do that, Nastenka. Now, did Ginsburg say anything else about the cyst? The kind, size, cause?"

Anastasia gazed at her knees and lapsed into silence, a reticence that pervades Russia to this day. Acquiring personal information from a Russian is nearly impossible. They rarely discuss their problems. They do not rebel or take to the streets. It allows anarchy to reign and dictators to flourish. Dad attributes it to a mindset rooted in the infallibility of Bolshevism: *The most vicious regime the world has ever known that displaced entire populations, constructed five hundred Gulags, and murdered forty million in a horror that still petrifies the country.* Mom agrees: *Everyone remains silent, when honest citizens are imprisoned in sham trials.*

During Tver's bitterly cold winter of 1974, Mom complained to our building's Communist manager that our ninth-floor pipes had frozen. He shut off the building's heat for a week. Mom landed in jail for a month for hooliganism. Fear has leveled the social equilibrium of Russia down to a chaotic state of silent stasis, a societal paradigm of the Second Law of Thermodynamics.

"Nastenka," I said affectionately, "I love you, always have, and always will. But I want to know what's happening to you. An uninformed husband's worthless as a rock. Now, tell me how Ginsburg did it."

"You're persistent aren't you?"

"I never give up on anything." Portentous.

"That's not always an asset." She snapped her head a couple of times, focusing. "Under local anesthesia, he did a fine-needle core aspiration. He drew out fluid, snipped off a rice-sized cyst, and sent the tissue in for a biopsy to determine its cause, infection or injury."

"Ouch!" I winced. "Where'd he do it?"

Careful to avoid touching her breast — demonstrating a malady on your body makes it happen, according to Russian folklore — Nastia pointed two inches above her left nipple. "He numbed here, dabbed it with alcohol, and, with a hollow needle guided by ultrasound, snipped the cyst."

I hissed through clenched teeth. "That had to have hurt."

"Not much, like the needle-prick for our blood test. Millions of women get it done."

"Results?"

"Soon," Anastasia said, treating the procedure casually.

I tried to emulate her heedlessness as we proceeded along Osceola. Homes gave way to businesses and lots of real estate offices. Traffic stopped. I stared at Nastia and wondered if that were the *entire* truth. It sounded like a cancer biopsy, but she hadn't used those words. I abhor my cussed skepticism, always presuming there's more, but partial truths and twisted truths are an idiosyncrasy endemic to Russians, especially when they claim to be spilling the beans and not. I looked at Nastia again and only saw her beauty and health. Cars moved. The road changed names again to East Fairbanks. An eighteen-wheeler roared up behind us, grinding gears and downshifting noisily. He sounded like a NASCAR driver at a Daytona caution flag. His load was probably rush orders of Mickey ears, Pluto Frisbees, and Little Mermaid T-shirts that drive Orlando's GDP. The big rig stirred up a whirlwind of fast-food debris. An Arby's flyer plastered my windshield. I flipped on the wipers. A couple swipes scraped it off, but it couldn't scrape off my lingering doubts. I narrowed my eyes like Hercule Poirot and said, "There's more, isn't there, Nastia?"

"No, that's it," Anastasia asserted, her big, button-blue eyes flashing wide, her smile fading into a look of incredulity. "*Pravda* — truly — that's everything."

Maybe. But a sense of understanding was building inside me at the terrifying plight she had faced alone. I squeezed her hand tenderly. "Nastia, honey," I said, "sometimes you forget, everything you told me was filtered through a mind so brainwashed with Communism it has the holes of a colander. Maybe it's colored your judgment. All our lives we've accepted lies as truths and corruption as its yardstick."

"*Us?*" she squealed. "*Me*! And what choice did I have? You lived in Kalinin until your mom snagged an older American and fled to a country untouched by lies and ugliness. I lived in that pig sty until six months ago."

"You did, Nastusha," I admitted. "Neither of us had a choice."

"I guess you're right," she subsided. "The world is what it is; but there's nothing to worry about, Ginsburg said. I believe him. It would help us if you did too."

"I'll try. But we can't help our childhood. Mom was a pregnant widow when Papa was killed in Kābul; nothing I can do about that. At thirty-six, she was seen as desirable by an older American, married him, and we bolted. Nothing I can do about that. You lived in the Soviet Union until six months ago when we married, and now you see how it affected you. Nothing we can do about that either but try and understand it."

I was trying mightily to convey the air of a man who had cut his teeth on totalitarianism and matured enough to know it well. Lenin's 1917 coup transmogrified Russian life. He seized all banks, factories, businesses, and property and provided lousy health care, selective education, and dinky apartments. He outlawed religion, confiscated art, criticized literature, and ended freedom of speech and freedom of movement, which set the stage for Stalin's Reign of Terror. Still, most Soviets thought they were *free*. The millions landing in Gulags knew better.

Anastasia shrugged. "Communism affected me, sure, but I'm a survivor and not naïve."

"No, you're not," I agreed. "But old habits linger. Your childhood was spent huddling in the Armageddon predictions of Leonid Brezhnev. You still carry that baggage, and it makes you glum, disbelieving, and distrustful." Sigmund Locke.

"So I've been told." Anastasia shot me a treacly smile. "Often."

"Well, it's the truth, Nastia. You're often cynical and construct elaborate fabrications."

"Only for self-preservation." She sighed. "How can you love me with all this baggage?"

"I'm stuck on Russian P-h-Ds."

She relaxed. "I guess I could mention a couple of other things, but they won't help."

"Let me decide," I said, knowing I was not qualified to make medical assessments.

"Ginsburg said fibrous growths in breast glandular tissue, sometimes from genetic mutations, usually cause young women's cysts. Are those the right words?"

"They are, but you'll never find them in a Dick and Jane reader."

She smiled. "We discussed my family history, menstruating early, birth control pills, breathing second-hand smoke, hydrocarbons in fried meat, and lack of carotenoids — "

"Carotenoids?" I shot her a puzzled look and let out the clutch as traffic moved.

"Carrots, squash, melons. The lack of them and external factors can cause lumps."

Traffic stopped for a jaywalker at Locinar Street. Nastia's belly growl as loudly as our golden retriever puppy, Leftovers, does when he's locked in mortal combat with his teddy bear. Locinar is a shortcut to downtown where my folks waited. Five county DOT guys in hard hats and beer-bellies draped over their belt buckles leaned a detour sign against a sawhorse, blocking our shortcut.

Slouching on their shovels, they assessed a pothole the size of a gallon of milk.

"Why potholes?" Anastasia griped. "If I don't eat, I'm going to gnaw this leather seat."

I glanced at my Timex. One o'clock. "We ate five hours ago. I'm starved, too."

"*We*? *You* ate like a refugee. Orange juice, barrels of coffee, two bagels schmeared with butter and cream cheese, and an Everest of lox, eggs, and onions."

One of the DOT geniuses unplastered himself from his shovel. A decision had been hatched.

"Sweetie," I said, "I was slaked and ravenous from our three gymnastic sessions. Pickles Deli's the only eatery on the planet that can refuel me *and* goose my libido simultaneously."

"Nice to have two reasons."

Anastasia, clearly wanting to divert the subject from the cyst, dwelled on our bacchanalia, and joked, "But Pickles Deli is Jewish, darling." She added an ingratiating smile and a thigh squeeze. "You're not, are you?"

"My twenty-first appendage has undergone their *rite de passage*."

Anastasia laughed coyly. "Circumcision's why a Russian *goy* craves a Jewish deli?"

"Sometimes we stray." I squirmed. "Say, you're really superb at that."

"Of course, I am. I have a Moscow State University education."

"They have courses in stimulation?"

"Courses in everything but cooking."

Cooking for Anastasia was popping a TV dinner in the microwave.

At the intersection of Fairbanks and Park Avenue, the traffic light turned yellow. I stopped, law-abiding as always. When it turned red, a bevy of leggy Rollins co-eds sauntered across the four-lane in slow carnal cadence, Apache-brown legs scissoring, hips switching, sun-streaked hair bouncing, confident and at home in their eighteen-year-old bodies as young lionesses. Wearing Ray-Bans, crop-tops, and skin-tight short-shorts, they looked like glitzy Parisian models with their teeny-breasts, pouty-lips, flashing eyes, rounded glutens-maximus, and perfectly-disheveled blonde hair atop perfect faces, perfect bodies, perfect everything. They looked so much alike they should have worn numbers on their sides like race horses. Trailing behind them swaggered boys as tall as NBA players. I wondered if they could read. Just then reality struck. Nastia had just divulged she had a worrisome cyst, and my feeble brain had wormed right back into the saga of girly delights. Why am I so cursed?

I tried to ignore the girls, but one vixen turned her Bambi eyes on me. She battered long lashes embellishing bedroom eyes and added an attractive smile. She reminded me of a girl I'd had a fling with in Lauderdale. I thought of that night and the hot sandy beach and the silky maiden and felt pheromones and dopamines ping-ponging in my brain. I grit my teeth and tried to ditch those ape-like wants. Why would a beneficent, omnipotent, loving God set such a sneaky trap for the world's men? I smiled at Anastasia innocently and popped the clutch. The car jumped.

"Watch out for the girl on the bike!" Nastia shrieked, clasping my arm with prehensile force.

"I see her." I was stupefied by her outburst and figured she could read minds. I glanced at the bike chick and back at Nastia. She was glaring at me with a look that would remove varnish, sending an energy-wave of hard-assed attitude my way.

"Of course, you see her," Nastia seethed. "You'd never miss a tight ass in short-shorts."

I threw up my hands. "Rich girls wear short-shorts; can I help it?"

"And that one's got the same golden ass Olga Askenova had," she taunted.

"That was three years ago in Tver, how could I possibly remember?"

"The phone tête-à-tête I overheard didn't sound forgettable."

"Olyushka's[9] brother was in the hospital."

"Oh-ho," she said bitterly. "So it's *Olyushka*, is it?"

"Good heavens, Nastia!" I yowled. "Your attitude's unworthy of you."

"And you've known *Oylushka* all your life, buster."

"Her brother was in a terrible accident. He could have died."

"Did you ever see golden-ass Olga again?"

"Only at the hospital."

That was not true. I did *see* Olga again. Our first kiss was magic, the second erotic, and when I peeled off her shorts, it was like peeling a golden apple, but that was not something I wanted to confess. There is no refuge between lovers after never-forgotten sexual confessions.

I had crossed my fingers surreptitiously and felt a blush inch up my face. To avoid eye contact, though, I stared at my hands, nicked and welted with scars from too many hours in a kitchen crammed with knives, slicers, toasters, and fryers and ruminated on my infidelities. I admit I am a hypocrite, but I *have* turned that page.

Nastia had every right to be angry, but I said, "Olga's history, so let's drop it, huh?"

"Sure, if you'll keep your lecherous eyes on the road and *both* hands on the wheel."

"Do I detect a touch of jealousy?" I teased with faux innocence.

She looked at me coquettishly. "Why lover — " she added with a fake southern drawl — "I'd just hate for my handsome, horny hubby to get in a wreck daydreaming about romping some Florida chickadee." Anastasia kissed my cheek and added, "Learn not to blush when you lie."

That made me blushed even more. I couldn't help it. As a kid, Mom could take one look at me with her X-ray vision and know I stole the cookies. I figured I'd outgrow it. I was wrong.

The Rollins vixen stopped at the far curb, turned, and stood poised, hipshot pelvic thrust forward, shoulders tilted back, and widely-separated unconfined breasts hammocked so as to display her tank top's bounty. One hundred and fifteen pounds of energetic, healthy, unblemished, arrogant girl fearing to be alone more than fearing to be be owned. A girl looking for a keeper to ride like a horse on which to use all of her half-educated voluptuousness. Bridle-him with innovative sex and punish him with big mortgages and car payments until he croaks from ulcers and coronaries.

With gutsy flirtation, she eyed me and caroled, "Nice ride, cutey!"

Her voice had that tight-jawed, WASPy, monied-drawl that elocution lessons, generations of dough, and Boston private schools instill. I wondered if it's me or the car that made her lustful, so I sat up straight, rolled my shoulders back, sucked in my gut, and ignored her. I was lauding my sterling character and waiting to hear the fanfare of trumpets. They didn't.

Nastia glowered at her and sneered, "Disgusting isn't she?"

"Yes, indeed," I agreed and continued to hone my observation skills. God gave me the ability to undress women with my eyes.

When Nasty turned her daggers on me, I figured it was a good time to change the subject. "Years ago," I began, "this land was a seabed of silt, sand, fossils, and limestone. Surface water carved underground rivers and caverns, and then ten years ago, right *here* — " I jabbed at the ground — "a limestone aquifer turned into a massive sinkhole. Town fathers plugged it, filled it with water and christened it Lake Rose."

"Probably where those chickadees you're undressing are going to skinny dip."

My jaw dropped open. "Is it my fault I'm a chick magnet?"

Anastasia snickered despairingly. "Do tits and asses spike all men's dop-emine?" Her eyebrow shot up. Her mispronunciation of dop*am*ine bore the effect it had on this dope, me.

"Some men's, but not all." I flipped my hand back-and-forth.

"And you?"

"Desperately so." I leaned over and kissed Anastasia's cheek as the light changed.

"Just drive," Nastia said and rammed the shifter into first.

I turned right on swish Park Avenue. Winter Park's main drag was the de-marcation line dividing east and west, like Berlin, without The Wall, which fell on November 9, 1989.

"Are you still pissed about getting tromped at tennis?"

"You didn't have to tap-dance around the court," she pooh-poohed. "You could have fallen on your ass."

We crossed Lyman Street and stopped for a swarm of jaywalkers on New England Street. Lots of Oakley wraparounds. Lots of sunburns. If I were a skin oncologist, I'd hang out my shingle here in Florida's bellybutton.

Anastasia said, "Damn it, Troy, you know I hate being woken at dawn for your frolics and to play tennis." She rammed her snout in the air. "It was no time to eat raw salmon and the day was hot enough to melt the court's No-vacrylic."

I flashed a beguiling smile; I can do beguiling. "I was just trying to keep you in shape."

"*Me*? How about you, chubby?"

I made a clown's rubbery-faced grin. "That's fair. My shorts *are* getting a tad snug."

"If you want to play tennis that early again, put up strobe-lights, it'll look like I'm moving."

Anastasia loved to sleep and hated Florida's hot, clammy heat. Siberia has a sixty-day summer, mid-June to mid-August, otherwise, it's as cold and dark as a meat locker and why 'Russkies guzzle more booze than any other people,' Dad says. Unlike him, I'm not a heavy thinker. I never fume over man's endless ills. I take life in little bites. Hit a snag? Fix it.

Traffic unsnarled. Horns beeped. I stayed in first gear and tapped the gas.

At 307 South Park Avenue, in the very heart of Winter Park, next to the Amtrak Station, rose the posh Park Plaza Hotel where my parents were bunking. Guests had no trouble hearing the music of the passing train barreling through at midnight and vibrating the earth like tectonic plates shifting.

"Want to keep house-hunting after lunch, climb aboard the property road to riches?" I asked.

"I guess. Your folks will be at the Morse Museum, but shouldn't you check in at work?"

"Nah, Kahuna's got me covered until Sunday."

"Kahuna told me we needed a big down payment to buy a house."

"The big guy's wrong. Banks finance anyone who can fog glass. Plus its time. You lived in a one-room efficiency in Russia."

"Ha!" Anastasia unloaded, "I live in one-room efficiency in America."

"But it's a spacious one-room efficiency. You're moving up in the world."

"Not by much."

"Next week you'll be teaching; we'll be rolling in dough and able to buy a mansion."

"Like the Biltmore?" she mocked and gave me a gotcha look.

"Maybe not quite that châteauesque," I hedged. Our two-night honeymoon in Asheville, NC, included a Motel Six and visit to America's largest private home, George Washington Vanderbilt II's extravagant Biltmore, a two-hundred-fifty-room, 178,000-square-foot castle, big, but only a quarter the size of Liz's Buckingham Palace.

"How much loan will we qualify for?" Nastia asked, shifting in her seat. Her skort crept up, exposing all of her long, lean, tan thighs.

"Probably three-hundred-grand. Enough to buy a place with an office, library, four bedrooms, entertainment room, and bathrooms galore. Everything you've ever dreamed of."

"Sounds fantastic." Anastasia's eyes glistened. She clung to my arm and shuddered with delight. Meanwhile, my fingers tap danced up her thigh, drawn like a compass needle to heat emanating from beneath her bantam skort. When dressed, the clothed Anastasia cast a reserved, elegant, erogenous air. In the buff, she morphed into a jolly, erotic, lascivious goddess, and my lungs felt the weight of her glow. It changed my breathing. I was pondering why bachelor predilections throb so in my veins when Anastasia snapped, "Knock it off!"

"There's not another damsel in the world with your legs; they leave me helpless."

Baloney keeps rolling off my tongue. It must be genetic. Papa must have been a fast-talker to snag a looker like Mom. Of course, Mom's heart must have leapt, too, chosen at thirty-six, a time most women think their time for being desired has passed.

Anastasia sighed. "Good God you're hopeless, Troy Vladimirovich." She used my patronymic the way Saint Vladimir intended when he introduced Byzantine ways to pagan Russia in 988 and snuggled the delicious warmth of mellow breasts against my arm. "See, you *can* be serious."

"About boobs? Never." I shook my head. "Boob seriousness is Margaret Mead saying big bazooms propagate the species, or Madison Avenue hyping slick ads with big jugs, or — "

Anastasia jabbed me. "Jesus, cut it out! The more I learn about men, the more I love dogs."

"So it's Leftovers and not me?" I referred to our two-month-old, shelter-purchased *canis familiaris* with a preponderance of Retriever.

"The puppy for sure," she said. "You're still a question mark."

I gave her a hurt look — I can do hurt. "You don't love me," I moaned.

"You idiot." She smiled a crooked smile. "I've loved you since you were three."

"Of course, you did and showed it by biting me."

"Only after you smashed my Anastasia doll. They should've locked you in Lubianka." [10]

She was kidding and closed her eyes to see the memory, laying her head on my shoulder in the delicate act known as *le-newt* in Russian.

Traffic moved a car length and stopped at Morse Boulevard. With a balmy breeze kissing my cheeks, I leaned over and gave her a smooch, inhaling greedily and getting a whiff of *Opium* intertwined with the orange bouquet of citrus blossoms and the leathery scent of the Beemer, a few of the trillion different odors the schnozzle can detect. Married men must savor life's ephemeral moments, right? Life was good. Well, except for Anastasia's worrisome cyst and my expulsion from Colby, but even those had a bright side. Getting booted out of college forced me to grow up and realize how short life was. After Colby, armed with youthful defiance, I'd enlisted in the Army and served in America's 100-hour ground war, Operation Desert Storm. I'd taken one in the butt (literally) and recovered in enchanting Heidelberg under (figuratively) the TLC of a comely *hausfrau* before receiving a purple heart and a medical discharge.

"Your geek brick's ringing," Anastasia said, motioning between my legs. "I'll get it." She picked up the cell phone and leaned my way so I could hear. "Ah-low."

I heard screaming and BANG! BANG!

"He's right here, Kahuna!" Anastasia exclaimed and passed me the phone.

I moved a car length and stopped. Heat waves danced off the pavement and blurred the sooty, rumbling exhaust of a '65 Malibu in front of us packed with hooting teenagers and five surfboards lashed to the top. Probably headed to Cocoa Beach.

"Yo, Kahuna," I said. "What's up?" Maybe the paychecks hadn't arrived. Like me, Kahuna was rapturous to receive his weekly bite of burger bucks.

"Boss, we *just* got hit!" he screamed.

"Not again," I moaned, banging the steering wheel with the heel of my hand. "Tell me it's April Fools' Day and not Black Friday." Black Friday is the shop-fest day after Thanksgiving that retailers hope will catapult them into the black for the year.

"It's April Fools' Day," Kahuna repeated obediently. "But Boss, it ain't April."

Kahuna was somewhat of a bubblehead and an exception to the rule of Natural Selection. Ten thousand years ago he would have been an easy snack for a Florida saber-tooth tiger.

In the background, kids screamed, BANG, BANG, BANG!

I turned the heist over in my mind, probing its facets, injuries, losses, claims. Where to begin? *Begin at the beginning;* the king told Alice.

"Anybody hurt?" I asked.

"Roger, that's a ten-four, Boss; slug winged my thigh," Kahuna said staunchly then chortled, "not my ass like you. I ain't bleeding bad. Boss, we gotta pack heat."

"Jesus, Kahuna, no guns! The joint's not exactly awash in blood."

"Go ahead, joke, I'm the one's bleeding. They're gonna hit us again, you know."

"Sure they will. And we'll fork over the dough as we always do. How'd it happen?"

The facts, get the facts, insisted Dr. Watson.

The office chair creaked. I could see Kahuna leaning back. Big greasy fourteens up on the desk smearing suet on the DSR — Daily Sales Report.

"Perp comes into the kitchen through the back door," Kahuna said. "José slipped on a ketchup wrapper scrambling out of his way, hits the pistol, it fires, and slug gets me. The perp was shocked. I think he said, *Mierda.*"

"'*Mierda,*' huh? You get a good look at him?"

"I could pick him out of a line-up ten miles long," Kahuna boasted. "But it ain't gonna help."

"Why?"

"Cause he was President Bush."

I mulled that over a sec. I was confident G. H. W. wasn't robbing McDees, even though his reign had inspired Democrats to disguise themselves as '*No good*' Republicans. "A disguise?"

"Ten-four. A George Herbert Walker plastic mask."

"Now, Kahuna, think. Was the trigger finger white, black, brown, red, or yellow?"

Traffic budged. I elbowed Anastasia, and she slid the shifter into first. The Briarpatch restaurant appeared on the right. There was no breeze. Sweat was breaking out on us. How could such a beautiful day crash so fast? A worrying cyst and my assistant manager wounded in our ninth robbery this year.

"Hey," Kahuna said, "the prep's arms were brown as a berry. Is *mierda* Spic for shit?"

"Now you're cooking," I said. "Every hopped-up, spaced-out cokehead with a nose full of candy stops at Disney on the way to Miami for a coke refill. Was the masked bandito solo?"

"Until he snatched old Buck. Said he needed a driver."

"Right, and yes, *mierda* means shit," I said, answering his hanging question.

"What's your twenty, Boss?" Kahuna loved cop-speak.

"Park Avenue at Lincoln. Been riding around, before lunch with my folks."

"Castle-hunting again, huh?" Kahuna's cackle could probably be heard up on I-4.

"We need a house."

"You need a down payment." Anastasia adored him.

"Hey, Boss," Kahuna said, "you'll love the prep's M.O. He hid behind the Dumpster and waited for old Buck to climb out of his wife's car — Jeannie still drives him in mornings — and the prep comes into the kitchen with a gun poked in Buck's ear."

"Yeah, that's great."

Buck was seventy-four, half-blind with diabetes, had two bypass surgeries, a foot amputated, can't hear anything quieter than a jet, and takes so many pills he regularly blacks out. Naturally, this being the Sunshine State's Mecca for the sunset gang, Buck had a driver's license.

"Oh," Kahuna recalled, "*El Bandito* stole a navy guy's dress-hat, gave it to Buck, and told him to chauffer his old ride."

"A black, sixty-two, four-door, Lincoln ragtop, top down like JFK had that day in Dallas?"

"How'd ya know that?"

"I know everything."

"Hey, I 'member something else. The guy sounded Mex. That's one, two, three, four greasers," Kahuna counted, "three spades, and two gringos this year."

"I suppose the registers were full of loot?"

"Two grand was there; then it was gone."

"You call nine-one-one?"

"They're on the way. I called 'em as soon as the bandito jumped into his ride and Buck screeched off. I thought they was going for I-4, but Buck rocketed — "

"East on Fairbanks."

"How'd ya know?"

"Got spies everywhere, too."

"You coming in?"

"After being robbed nine times this year, do you truly need me?" I scoffed.

"Nah, I know the drill. Call the cops, secure the scene, call Bill Allen, District Honco."

"Listen, Kahuna," I enunciated carefully. "When the fuzz gets there, tell them the get-away car and perp are knee-deep in a sinkhole at the corner of Aloma at Brewer, near Alberta. Tell them Buck's a good guy and not to shoot his ass and if they hustle they'll make a collar."

"Far out!" Kahuna shouted. "Maybe I'll get my picture in the *Sentinel*."

"Sure you will," I said. "Surfing queens will be crawling all over you."

What a crock! With twenty thousand murders, rapes, robberies, burglaries and thefts in Orlando last year, fast food heists were never news. Stolen get-away cars are as good as Get Out of Jail Free Cards. Why Oak Brook (corporate

McDee's), won't mount rock-hurling catapults on the Golden Arches was beyond me. Why America doesn't wall our southern border was unconscionable. We gladly open our door to the legally *tired, poor, and huddled masses*; Miss Liberty never said send me your crooks, too. Dad worries about America's naïveté: we must persevere, discover, invent, and find innovative new ways of doing things more easily, quickly, and profitably. He says we're too accepting, too gullible, too unread, and must ditch the jejune collections of nostrums and clichés of wonderment about our democracy, freedoms, open markets, and the rule of law. Of course, I don't give a rat's. When out of the salt mine, Nastia and I head for Ormond Beach. America's knee-deep in doo-doo, folks. Don't believe me? Ask Dad.

"Oh, Boss," Kahuna added, "a Betty called from a doctor's office. Said it was wicked important he see you guys today at three. Both yous."

A nauseous feeling hit my stomach. I engaged the clutch.

We finally passed Lincoln Avenue and the Briarpatch with its long, hungry line of customers.

I snapped my head to clear the fog and mustered a terse, "Thanks, Kahuna, aloha."

I pressed the off button and set the phone on the floor pan.

Anastasia touched my arm gently. "Another robbery?"

"Yeah."

"Anybody hurt?"

"Kahuna got a leg wound. The thief got away with a sack of dough."

"That's it?"

"Un-huh."

Anastasia shot me a quizzical look. "Why do you look so worried?"

"That's our ninth robbery this year," I said, omitting the doctor's call.

"Shouldn't you go in and be seen? Remind your District Manager you're always on the job, indispensable and ready for a promotion?"

"That's the Soviet way, Nastia. In America, we're not afraid of taking a day off. Kahuna's got it handled."

That was pure b/s. Two fundamentals of American business culture: be working when the boss appears and be there to take his calls whenever he calls.

My cell phone rang again. I picked it up and said, "Locke."

"Bill Allen here. Where the hell are you?"

"Downtown Winter Park, about to have lunch with my parents."

"You've just been robbed for Christ's sake! Don't you think you should be tending the store?"

"I've got it covered."

"Covered my ass! I hope the hell you do, or you'll be looking for work."

"That was our ninth robbery this year, Bill," I explained. "I've found the robber. Cops are arresting him as we speak. Everything's cool."

"Terrific, now you're a private dick?"

"When I have to be. The store's fine; the loot's being returned; enjoy your golf game." Bill severed the connection.

"I told you so, smarty-pants," Anastasia said.

Admitting she was right would lead to a discussion I did not want to have. And I sure as hell did not want to bring up our doctor's appointment before lunch. Two can play the secrecy game, especially if my worst worry was correct. It was.

***

THREE

Briarpatch Restaurant,
Winter Park, Florida

Golden sunshine bathed the heart of the very posh and pleasant burg of Winter Park. The absence of fast-food eateries, gas stations, and big box stores harkened back to a Norman Rockwell-time, when villages were charming, homey, and congenial — a time before bottom-line-driven corporations churned out cut-rate junk for deal-addicted customers, coring America's towns and cities, leaving them to rot in lawless abandonment.

Anastasia gazed this way and that, inhaled a deep, deep breath, and let out a long weary sigh. "If only Kalinin looked like this, shiny, spotless, bustling, and bright."

I was stuck in a cancer-fear muddle but managed to scoff, "Huh! Stylish-dressed adults, laughing kids, brick-paved streets in Kalinin? Never."

Anastasia shrugged. "Tver's changing, there's even restaurants serving borscht at midnight."

"You've never eaten borscht at midnight in your life."

"But it's there."

"Good for the beet growers. Look at that quaint train station over here, the picturesque old cemetery over there — " I was lost in the moment and pointed left and right — "Kalinin's been dreary since Stalin turned its cathedrals into repair shops and parks into junk yards. Kalinin look like *this*? Never."

"It's getting better. Gorbachev re-renamed Kalinin Tver last year."

"Calling a pit-bull a lap-dog doesn't dull its fangs or curb its appetite. Look

…." I was trying to illustrate my remarks and swung my arm in a wide arc to take it all in. "There's a two-story buildings glistening with paint, upper façades railed, roofed, and festooned with ivy. Here's are trendy signs branching off storefronts snagging money passing beneath in streets full of peregrines in vivid T-shirts, shorts, and sandals schlepping between boutiques, bistros, and swanky shoppes. And over there, in the park, wiry, sunbaked, out-of-control kids flinging Frisbees in Central Park, active, cute, and savage as weasels. Sweetheart, in Tver you never see dotty pensioners doling out peanuts to squirrels, or jack-booted cops rousting homeless off park benches under live oaks draped with Spanish moss and trimmed into topiaries." Pastoral.

Nastia nodded. "You're right; this is a beautiful town. But it's as hot as Hades."

"Only ten months a year. December and January you might need a sweater evenings."

"There's a spot!" Nastia yipped, pointing beyond Canton Street. "In front of the Morse."

A couple of blocks from the Briarpatch, nestled beneath camphor trees, rose a white-sided, red-roofed monolith with a dearth of windows and no sign identifying it as the Charles Hosmer Morse Museum of American Art. It looked as charming as Alcatraz and as out of place as a thistle at an orchid festival, but it housed the world's largest collection of Tiffany stained glass and for that we can be thankful. Two testy old duffers, locked in a fender bender, snarled traffic at Cole Street and glared through their steering wheels, faces red with distaste, eyes blinking like lizards. I did a quickie U-turn and snagged the cherished spot by the Morse.

I set the parking brake, glanced skyward, and said, "No thunderheads, leave her topless?"

"Sure, Locke, but lock the tennis gear in the trunk," the fledgling wordsmith said, looking at me for a smile. I gave her a great big beamy one.

We bounded out and stowed gear. Anastasia shouldered her purse, and I grabbed my brick-sized cell phone. Robbery 10 awaited. Preparation is *de rigueur*. On the sidewalk swarms of honey bees were carrying on an extensive collection operation from a candle bush's showy yellow bracts. Teens on skateboards roared by, weaving through shoppers, food-lovers, and lay-about *flâneurs*. Bees kamikazed Anastasia for her *Opium*.

She ducked and zigzagged and shouted, "Ouch!" and scrubbed a sting.

I shooed bees away and guided her by the elbow off the sidewalk. "The street may be safer."

She rubbed the sting. "My hero."

On the macadam, the orange blossom breeze was laced with the residual stench of a flotilla of clown-colored cars twinkling and inching up Park Avenue. As we stood, starving, and waiting to dash, we watched Park Avenue's ant-farm of activity. Sweaty, sunburned snowbirds, decked out in flamboyant T-shirts, Bermuda shorts, and Dockers — Florida's three piece suit — duck between shops to pump bucks into the local economy. They nearly trample each other to death in their glassy-eyed stampede for rubber alligators and Goofy junk that adds one more shekel at a time to the thirty million Walt pays C.E.O. Mickey Eisner. God bless them all. May they get back safely to Bangor, Burlington, and Boston.

A quartet of blue-haired, full-bodied condo-ettes, wearing moo-moos and smelling musky, shuffled up beside us. One, a hands-down septuagenarian with alligator skin nearly masked with lilac powder, was snapping her fingers and swinging her hips in time with music only she could hear. She squealed, "We're celebrating a bridge slaying at that nifty Italian restaurant — " she pointed across Park Avenue — "veal scaloppini and Kahlua-and-cream shooters all afternoon. Is that where you're going, handsome?"

I shook my head. "Sadly, no. Maybe for dinner, we're just not very hungry."

Anastasia shot me a sassy smile and swiped her nose with a finger, insinuating Pinocchio.

"Well, good-looking, we might just still be there at dinnertime," the condoette said, resuming her rumba. "Don't you wish you could swing your toosh like me?"

I smiled sweetly. "You're really doing that marvelously."

Anastasia shook her head and raised her eyes toward heaven.

A red, 1964½, Mustang convertible — a museum-quality gem among an arcade of present-day generics — top down, radio cranked up, stopped. The driver had the forlorn eyes of resigned acceptance of a local. The six of us scurried past. I heard a fragment of Kenton's *Take Five* drifting from the Mustang, a jazz tune in 5-4 time, turned and gave the guy thumbs up.

He beamed. His look said *Stan's still The Man at seventy-nine.*

"Did you ever see such pasty-skinned fatsos?" Anastasia said. "In moo-moos, for God's sake! Florida needs a dress code. Oh, damn, look at that friggin line! We'll never eat."

"Sure we will, Nastusha," I comforted. "And be entertained."

We stepped past two testy old farts; cigars clenched in ashen teeth, beer-bellies covered by Sea World T-shirts, and bald heads helmeted by Red Sox and Yankee baseball caps nose-to-nose and going at it strong. With plastic bats swinging, rheumy eyes glaring, and voices snarling, they were yapping about Gladdin's hit in the bottom of the tenth in game seven that gave the Twins the World Series. Nastia brushed aside their stale air spawning clouds of additives. Urea, potassium sorbate, ammonia, glycerol, and diammonium came to mind as their saggy waddles trembled, a testament that skin loses elasticity with age, desiccated wrinkles proliferate, and smoking gooses the aging process. She looked over her shoulder, captivated by their craggy faces screwed into expressions of distaste in their pretend kerfuffle.

"Darwin got it wrong," she said. "Men didn't evolve from apes; it's the other way around."

"Nah," I said. "They're just fussing. They really love each other."

"Sure they do. Next thing you know they'll be picking off each other's lice."

The lunch line was long, extending halfway to Lincoln Avenue. Lots of school teachers, secretaries, and retirees. Some women flock to Florida dreaming of romance and beach bums and turning wild enough in a week to fill dreary lives with Buddy and the kids for another year. Retirees come to golf, bask in the sun, and enjoy hell out of the Golden Years. Many struggle into restaurants in walkers and wheelchairs dragging oxygen tanks hooked to cannulas jammed up their noses. Thousands get sick, confused, and land in hospitals with ALS, COPD, gout, osteoporosis, diabetes, dementia, and cataracts and are treated with I.V.'s, catheters, and colostomy pouches. Each winter, five thousand croak, are crated up, and shipped back to Toledo for the long dark sleep.

"There're your parents!" Nastia yipped, whacking my butt and darting. "Halfway to the front of the line, come on!"

There they were, indeed. Dad, about as thin as a wire and taller than Italy is long, towered a foot over everyone. He and Mom looked tanned, fit, tailored, and especially spiffy today, garbed in the full dress of academic power, ready to wing off to Wimbledon[11] to see Steffi Graf whip Martina Navratilova.

As always, seeing my beanpole Dad aroused a feeling of disappointment in me. I forever imagined him the swashbuckling entrepreneur I hoped to be, and it takes me a minute to accept him as he is. Not having lived with him, Nastia thought him God-like, character flaws notwithstanding. Having lived with him, I can attest, with abundant assurance, he was not. But Dad was a talented, introverted man with the continence of the dedicated academic. At six-eight and 195 pounds, he had a long-boned, earnest face, high wide cheekbones tapering to an uncompromising mouth, and a pointy chin, large, bright, honest eyes, and a drooping right eyelid that bracketed a slightly hooked Roman nose usually stuck in a book searching for philosophy's invisible truths. At ASU he donned potentate attire: rumpled chinos, button-down oxford shirt, regimental tie, scruffy loafers, and threadbare Harris Tweed coat with elbow patches. Long ago he smoked a pipe. As we approached, I saw he sported a blue seersucker suit, dashing pink shirt, and racy (tasseled) white Florsheim loafers. Dad's overflowing zeal found an outlet in running, and his marathoner-frame reflected both the stamina of the consummate athlete and the concentration of the relentless academic. He often radiated a standoffish bookish-introspection amplified by a mop of white hair, bushy white eyebrows, trimmed white beard, and horn-rimmed specs that gave strength to his austere face. He smiled, returning his attention from misty distances and giving him the impression of a snowy-haired Abe Lincoln, reading *The Wealth of Nations*, no doubt. With the ardor of St. Paul wrestling with Atonement, Dad scoured seminal oeuvres for the etiology of poverty and a universal palliative. Over his half-slice of pumpkin pie last evening, he announced he was up to 1776, the year Smith published his *magnum opus*. Like many tenured professors, Dad was published in a vanity press, remained hopeful, and continued writing. When he'd glanced at us, a frown etched his forehead and circles under his eyes indicated unmistakable anxiety that gave me a sinking feeling. Was it his high blood pressure and stents inserted at Wake Forest Baptist Hospital in Winston-Salem?

At his elbow, Mom, Irina (ee-REE-na), known by a pint-sized moniker, Ira (EE-ra), wore her wavy golden hair short, a match for her perennial perky personality. Like Dad, Mom was a hiker and marathoner with the determined personality to go with it and not one speck of body fat. Mom could eat one potato chip at a faculty retirement party (occasionally tenured faculty retire before they expire). She'd live to be one hundred. Talented, saintly, and self-sacrificing, my tough-cookie Mom hailed from a well-to-do Soviet family. She was the only child in her youthful circle to have her own bedroom *and* her family owned a country dacha. They'd holidayed in Yalta once, attended the Bolshoi once for caviar, Tchaikovsky, and glimpses of Kremlin tyrants and, once, took an excursion to Sofia, Bulgaria. After graduating from Tver State University and the appropriate number of socials and picnics, Mom married *a*

clever, outgoing, cocky, spunky, plucky, strawberry-blond who was soon con-
scripted and sent to Kābul where he was killed by Taliban, shattering her dreams
of happiness — her words. She returned to Tver, earned a Ph.D., and, after
mourning five years, in lieu of my ardent requests for her to remarry a Russian
and secure for us an apartment with a bedroom for me, she snagged an older,
holidaying American and we fled Communist horrors that obliged me to learn
English. America was Mom's elixir, and today, dressed in a tailored outfit of
royal blue, she was in an animated *tête-à-tête,* in French — Soviet elite's second
language — with an elderly, crinkly-skinned woman with the bluest veins on
earth who appeared to have been kiln-dried in Québec. Mom was waving her
arms like a line judge arguing an umpire's call, punctuating polemics with flying
hands as Italians were wont to do, probably arguing our Thanksgiving dinner's
debate: whether tenured professors should be required to teach at all if a book
they wrote actually sold.

Unlike Mom, Dad, aka Troy Locke IV and addressed as Doctor, was every
inch the doctor of philosophy right down to his proclivity for prolixity and
Socratic smile. As we approached, his blue-gray eyes sparkled and his face
broke out into a lofty, slightly-ironic beam that revealed the flawless, blinding-
ly-white ivories his parents paid a Beacon Hill orthodontist a ransom for when
No. 35 (JFK) was a senator. Movie-star teeth, Dads were that perfect.

On August 8, 1974, the day No. 37 (*I'm not a crook* Nixon) resigned, Mom
and I arrived in Blowing Rock high atop the Blue Ridge Mountains of North
Carolina. Two weeks later, she stepped into the traces at Appalachian State
University in Foreign Languages, and I was condemned to second grade with
my vast, two-word English vocabulary: ice cream.

"Hi, kids," Dad sang out with a beamy smile, looking up from a book he
held in long-fingered hands. He stretched out an octopus arm to shake my hand
— our relationship was that of most professor fathers-and-sons, open affection,
an embarrassment, was shown by a word or skinny handshake — and embraced
Anastasia. "Hungry, Nastia?" he asked.

"Famished," Anastasia replied exasperatingly. "Think we'll eat before
sunset?"

"Don't let this line bother you," Dad said humorlessly. "It's moving steadily."

"So do glaciers," she said.

"Steph'll seat us quickly, guaranteed," I said and eyed Nastia's left breast.
It was wetter.

My comment brought an inquisitive frown to the squire's brow. I did not explain who Steph was. Ahead of us, the lunch line was a haphazard queue of retirees, Joe Six-packs, teachers in Oakley wrap-arounds, teenagers, and gym-set mothers toting babies. They looked like grandparents, parents, students, conventioneers, and cherubs as they milled around like rhinos at a watering hole, salivating from aromatic pastrami contrails wafting from kitchen fans. Clever owner.

Dad said, "You two appear dehydrated, here, have some water." He pulled a bottle of Zephyrhills finest from his backpack, and we drank thirstily. "Now, tell me, who won the post-Turkey-Day Shootout; Anastasia?"

Dad was a hyper-articulate heavyweight. His speech had the hard, nasally-affluence of a Kennedy. Money bought the diction. Pilgrims left the accent. Colby and Yale nurtured the question that bordered on screed, but Dad had given me a new life and educated me, and for that I was rarely judgmental.

"No, sir," I said, putting my arm around Nastia's waist. "I won for the first time ever!"

"Yeah," Nastia said and made a throwaway gesture. "My game was *ochen ploho* — very bad."

"That's uncharacteristic," Dad opined, bombastically. "None of us has ever vanquished you."

"My luck hit a wall and — " she tipped her head at me — "Jimmy Connors was hot."

I pushed her out to arm's length and shot her an owlish look. "Not that hot; your game was way off."

"Tell me about it," she said, dropping her voice and the subject.

Excusing herself from Mattie Megabucks, Mom touched Dad's arm, undaunted by his gangly height, and narrowed her eyes at his tome in a silent, unyielding reprimand that I had never seen before. I wondered if they had had a spat. His tome reflected his innermost self, one of ardor, zeal, determination, conservatism, and piety, and his didactic posture reflected his lectern stance. He closed Smith, bookmarking it unhurriedly, moving at one speed, more decelerate and deliberate than languid and slow.

"*Pree-vet* — Hello — Nastenka Yevgenyevna," Mom said in a chirpy tone, using the respectful Russian greeting that included a patronymic reference to Nastia's Papa, Eugene. Mom's cheery tone defied a worrisome sadness in her eyes that stirred a nauseous feeling in my gut. Despite the intolerance, conceit, and self-assurance I possess in abundance, I felt a growing angst, first Dad's washboard frowns, and now Mom's maudlin eyes.

"*Pree-vet, Mamoska*," Anastasia replied bubbly and leaned forward.

They exchanged three, air kisses, which I thought a bit much. They hadn't seen each other for what, thirteen hours? But, turning a new leaf, I refrained from criticizing, silently bearing their smooches that a wave of Swine Flu had drastically curtailed in France.

"Hi, dear," she said to me and lifted a velvety cheek to be kissed, adding a light touch to my forearm with an affectionate squeeze.

"We're so glad you flew down, *Mamoska*, but you shouldn't have spent all that money for, ah — " Nastia said, pausing in search for the word.

"Next-day tickets?" I suggested, making myself excruciatingly helpful.

"Yes, next-day tickets," Anastasia said.

"*Nechewo* — It's nothing — Nastusha Yevgenyevna; *dva dnja platit* — two days' pay." Mom flicked her hand and the reproof vanished like a fly heading for the borscht. She spoke English with the regionlessness of Johnny Carson but preferred speaking in her native Russian.

"*Dva mesetsa platit' v Rossii* — Two months' pay in Russia," Anastasia countered, jamming her hands on her hips and adding in Russian, "In Tver I had to wring kopeks out of trashcan bottles to buy beets for borscht."

"*Dabuska* — Ladies," I objected. "You sound like *babushkas* — grandmas — squabbling over market prices. English, *pashalseta* — please."

Mom placed her hand on her heart. "I'm so sorry, dear," she said to Dad with a genuine smile. "From here on, it's English and no more market prices."

Dad said, "Irinka, don't worry about it, I grasped most of it."

"Flying hands and facial contortions are ringers," Mom said and turned to Nastia. "Nastenka, you'll never have to worry about money again, *ever.* For anything, I swear."

I thought that an odd vow. Mom must have been thinking of her father's ten years in the Gulag and her family's decade of poverty as tears glazed her eyes. The two women embraced again and exchanged more kisses.

I placed a hand on Mom's back and kissed her cheek again. "Mom," I said, "we're delighted you tore yourselves away from the Athens of Appalachia for a visit."

Mom gave me a cheerless smile and forlorn look. "Igor Vladimirovich, it *is* nice to get back to civilization." Sometimes she forgot and used the name she gave me the day I arrived, the afternoon of the day Neil Armstrong climbed down from Eagle and took his *Small step and giant leap* — July 20, 1969, in case you've forgotten.

"How much did you wager on today's match, Nastia?" Dad asked.

"The usual dollar," Anastasia said.

I hooked an arm around her shoulder and reeled her in close. "Winning was such a delight, though, I took this former champ shopping." *Nearly maxing my credit card*, I didn't add.

"You'd do that, son," Dad said.

To his precise diction and rumbling voice, he added a smile and a nod, which, for him, was the equivalent of a *Croix de Guerre.* He bent over and slid his weighty book into his backpack.

As he did, I noted a hint of tonsure in his thatch of white hair. His white mustache and trimmed white beard were still full, outlining a chiseled face weathered by flannel-shirt hikes on Blue Ridge footpaths to reacquaint with woodsy natives, furred, feathered, and finned. A rigid diet of creatures that swam or flew and daily workouts at the ASU gym kept his cholesterol level low, tummy taut, and quadriceps toned to those of Edmund Hillary. Sadly, his regimentation was no offset for a lousy family history of leaky aortic values that required cleaved breastbones to repair his.

"I'll retake my tennis crown," Anastasia pledged. "Though I don't know when, I start teaching high school math Monday and Troy always works weekends."

"There's always Ingrid," I said, referring to Anastasia's friend and tennis partner, a Rollins student and part-time waitress here.

Mom quickly looked aside. Dad studied his size fourteens. I grew suspicious.

Anastasia touched Mom's arm. "Get your Christmas shopping done?"

"Your gifts," Mom said smiling awkwardly. "And a dazzling lump of coal for Doctor."

We all laughed on schedule. I spotted a weatherworn hostess swinging through the Briarpatch door.

"Hey, there's Stephanie," I said to them and yelled, "Hey Steph! Hey!"

Tourists turned to stare at the lunatic flapping his arms. Steph looked up the line and spotted me. She had a wonderful, spontaneous childlikeness about her, the amiable, open, giddy, eager manner of a womanly child ardent for approval. She wore Ben Franklin glasses, a black skirt, and a red polo shirt with a bunny darting from a briar patch emblazoned on the pocket. At her waist, there was a slight bulge where her girdle stopped. Her legs were thin, the kind women admire and men don't, that made her body look like a beer keg on stilts. She had an armful of menus, schmoozed with regulars, bobbed her head at some tourists, and pulled a pencil from gray-hair shellacked into a sixties beehive.

"Lis'en up," she bellowed in a gravelly Maine twang. "I gotta itty-bitty table by the bathroom doe-AH (door), perfect for newlyweds!" Her deep, Down-East shibboleth had a two-pack-a-day timbre. She waved her pencil back-and-forth, seeking newlyweds.

"We're newlyweds!" I shouted back.

A dozen people turned and looked at us. A few smiled. Some glowered.

"Then get down hee-AH!" Steph yelled, blocking the entry with hands on Rubenesque hips.

I tugged Anastasia's hand. "Come on before some geriatric bride beats us."

We wormed through the crowd. As we approached Steph, I saw a smile cross her risible face tanned one shade lighter than nutmeg from untold hours spent tending her posies. After returning from Desert Storm and ascending the throne at McDee's, Steph, or her lead waitress and Nastia's tennis pal, Ingrid, and I have, on occasions, swapped sacks of burgers her illegals crave for deli sandwiches my over-the-hill gang preferred. As we pushed through the crowd, a Canadian cursed at me in French, the baseball aficionados snarled obscenities, and an old lady smiled lovingly at an old man with memories of her virginal night twinkling in her eyes.

Steph beamed as we got to the head of the line. "When was it you kids got hitched?"

Anastasia bent close and whispered, "Memorial Day, an unforgettable week for Russians."

Steph looked perplexed. "Why was that?" She sounded like a lobster-man.

"Commie hard-liners jailed Gorbachev, Yeltsin squashed a coup, and capitalism was born."

"Oh, sure (sho-AH)," Steph said. "Saw that on TV."

"And Strike-The-Gold won the Kentucky Derby and was retired to stud," I let fly.

I stepped aside for two groups leaving. The first, a quartet of sun-burned road crew, were rubbing bellies that looked like beach balls hidden beneath twill shirts. Behind them strutted three, chalk-white women with bodies slithering like Anacondas breeding. In the Sunshine State, conventioneers stick out like Dalmatians on a fire truck. One said, "I'm not heading back to that barn of an OCCC [12] to hear more teacher yap."

"Amen!" her pals seconded. Below skimpy tops, doing a commendable job of revealing their bounty, the three's long legs dropped out of short-shorts. They sounded like teachers but looked like Vegas showgirls and unlike any teacher I'd ever had in hillbilly school.

After the conventioneers passed, Step said, "Ay-uh, saw that horse race, too."

"Lucky nag," I said.

"Sex, Steph," Anastasia joshed. "That's all he thinks about. He should be kept in a stall."

"Women need men like horses need gills," Steph said, nailing the point with flapping menus.

"But think of the unborn!" I howled.

Despite their reference to caponizing me, I gave them a rapscallion grin and patted Nasty on the toosh lovingly. It felt firm enough to dent an oak chair.

Steph drilled a finger into my chest. "Take good care (kay-AH) of this pretty thing, Romeo, or she'll can your sorry ass and wing back to Moscow."

I shot Steph a discrete bird just as my folks stepped up and made hasty introductions.

"Folla me," Steph said in a proprietary tone and turned, her heels squeaking on entry tile. We followed her motionless hair over the marble threshold, dished from long use, into a bright, cheery, narrow oasis crowded with diners, big-band sounds and scents of meats, cheeses, pies, cakes, and yeast breads in loaves larger than shoeboxes. We swooped beneath a spidery-legged, hula-hoop-sized, Christmas-cactus ablaze with taillight-red blooms beside an antique soda fountain and dessert case stuffed with cakes towering a foot high and pies gleaming with mountains of sugar diamonds. Plastering the far wall were sepia-photos of Winter Park in horse-and-buggy days. Towards the rear, Steph stopped at a table beside a busy bathroom door and dealt out menus. The table, immersed in a perfume of fragrances, mostly deli smells and indigenous disinfectants, was sated with silverware rolled in paper napkins, Tabasco sauce, Dijon mustard, salt and pepper shakers, and a rack of Sweet and Low. I drew the gunslinger seat, handy for spotting desperados, and pulled out chairs for Mom and Nastia. Dad peeled off his suit-coat, draped it over the back of his chair, adding a thin sour smell of sweat to the potpourri of perfumes. He folded his giraffe-frame onto the facing chair and craned his long neck around to hone his observational skills on the abundance of short-short-clad waitresses glowing with, apparent, all-over tans that keep the dudes coming back.

Steph studied Dad's face and then mine. "Troy looks just like you, Doctor Locke. Not your white and his reddish-blond hair, but the nose, cheekbones, and eyes."

Mom bristled and held up her menu like a shield. "Well, he should, Steph, he's his father."

"He sure is," Steph said, straightening the condiments. "Spittin' image."

I leaned over, grazed Mom's ear with my lips, whispering, "I'm adopted, Mom."

"Sometimes I forget," she murmured.

Anastasia kissed my cheek. "What a precious moment *entre mère et fils*."

Mom shifted in her chair and pulled the hem of her skirt down as if she could cover her knees, which she couldn't. She was preoccupied and ignored Nastia's mother-and-son remark; maybe worried about ASU canning the Russian program? Not much Russian spoken in Appalachia.

"Get to Orlando often, Doctor Locke?" Steph asked and brushed off some table crumbs.

"First time," Dad said. "With your traffic, probably the last."

"Didn't use to be this way," Steph said. "Disney. Say, if this is a celebration, may I suggest a *têtes de cuvée*, perhaps Mumm's René Lalou?"

Dad bolted upright. Mom said, "We're professors, Steph, not oligarchs buying wine in gilded bottles. Mumm's way too pricey." Mom was still smarting from the Colby ransom.

"I understand," Steph said. "Ingrid'll be here as soon as she finishes the table I just sat her, so I'll send over something for you to nosh on." She hustled off to bus a table.

"I need a toilet," Anastasia said and picked up her purse. Occasionally, she provided a bit more info than needed and often tripped over English articles. But she moved with quick, sure, steps, and her long golden legs scissored and her hips flexed as she opened the bathroom door and disappeared. My beautiful *zehna* was as unabashedly sensual as a hula dancer.

The instant the bathroom door closed, Mom dropped her menu with a clunk. Her evanescence vanished. Her lips tighten. Her eyes fell on her wedding ring's thirty-six big diamonds, her age when she remarried, large enough to make her arm weary.

"*Poor Anastasia*," Mom lamented.

"'*Poor Anastasia*,'" I echoed. "What are you talking about?"

Mom's face took on an elegiac countenance, and she remained silent, lost in some internal debate. She clutched my arm as she had in scraped-knee-days when I'd howl up nine flights to our one-room flat in a forest of clones overlooking the Volga River — she didn't snuggle me to her breast. That was long ago, a time when the world waited, hushed and silent, for me to grow up, long before the need for school, work, and marriage. As a city kid, I had few chores and ample time to scrape knees climbing trees or wondering about stuff sprawled out on the clover-sweet banks of the Volga with my cloud-friends, wispy elephants and popcorn Caspers, or relish life in the grass roots below timothy-crowns swaying in soundless shadows and crawling with life that directed my phantasmagorias as the Caspers drifted off the edge of my world. But that was long before the laws of life brought the needs of the world crashing down upon me to shatter those dreamy, dawdling days of pachyderms and apparitions and skinned knees.

Mom looked at Dad and then looked at me. Their faces would have depressed a mortician.

My mouth went dry. "Well, Mom? For God's sake, tell me."

"Troy Vladimirovich," she hushed, "Your Nastuska has a big problem."

A chill licked my neck hackles. "Is it serious?"

"*Da, da, da, ochen*—Yes, yes, yes, very."

I gasped. Mom must have details that Kahuna had not had, and her words knifed into my heart. Bile rose in my throat. I'd suspected as much; hell, I knew as much. But good old Troy Locke had refused to face it.

"Please, Mom, what is it?" I pleaded. "What's Nastia's problem? Tell me."

"Her doctor's office called while we were at the apartment to walk Leftovers. A woman said, 'Is this Mrs. Locke?' and, without thinking, I said, 'Why, yes it is.' Then she blurted out, 'This is Betty at Doctor Ginsburg's, and your mammography came back wicked bad. He's wantin' ta see you and the mister today at three o'clock.'"

"Cancer!" I blurted.

I let out a gigantic sigh and slumped back in my chair. My shoulders drooped. My head bowed. My legs flopped out wide apart. Realization shot through my head. I felt blood pound the top of my skull. I closed my eyes and saw the future:

Anastasia departing our rich world of tennis, restaurants, dancing, beach walks, and love. Gone forever.

Mom hugged me. Her tears gushed over my cheek. "I'm so sorry, Troy; I didn't mean to — "

Dad set down the dill pickle he was about to bite, peered over his trifocals. "You okay, son?"

That pissed me off. "'Okay'?" I snarled. "I'm friggin' dandy."

"Now son —" he swiped both ends of his mustache with a crooked finger — "if it *is* breast cancer, it *is not* a death sentence, there's hope today. Improved chemotherapy, radiotherapy, and a soon-to-be-approved drug, taxol, which has incredible anti-cancer qualities available soon."

"When?"

"Next year!"

I slammed my fist down hard. The salt shaker fell over. "That might be too damned late."

Professors wield so much power over college kids it makes them think their hold on them is real, and they possessed all the answers. They're so insolent and unflappable any criticism befalling them rolls off their backs like water off a duck. Maybe that was what was infuriating Mom.

"What the hell can be done for Anastasia *today*, Dad?" I snarled.

"Go to Ginsburg's office. Listen to him, find some taxol, and get it into her ASAP."

"Swell," I said and shuddered. I felt queasy. I thought I'd throw up.

Get a grip, I told myself, took some deep gasps, and said, "Look, don't say a word. I'll tell Nastia at home."

But I never had the chance.

***

FOUR

Lunch at the Briarpatch Restaurant:
The Taxol Story

With quick light steps, Nastia returned from the ladies room with a touch of fresh lipstick, a dab of new eyeliner. Her long slender fingers patted blonde hair brushed straight down, but not enough to hide sharp blue eyes sparkling with life. She looked as fresh as a garden of daffodils. Her primping stopped, and she threw her arms out proudly in a *voilá* gesture.

"The new me!" she exclaimed and smiled broadly.

With her back straight and head high, she appeared cheerful and confident and radiated the unabashed vigor that shouts: *LIVE!* so persuasively she could convince the pope to rumba. She stepped behind me and placed her hands on my shoulders. I craned around and looked up at those clear, honest eyes and saw the magic intensity that bound us together ever-closer in love, a paralyzing intensity that I nearly missed at that particular moment I was so overcome with anguish.

Her eyes caught ours. She sensed something amiss. Her eyes darted from Mom's weepy face to Dad's pensive mien then my morose mug. Then, in a silent auto-hypnotic flash, her face, already piqued with curiosity, transformed. From some distant corner of the backwoods of her mind, she gathered the instantaneous insight that filled her with comprehension. Any other woman could not have done so and would have looked pallid in her penumbra.

"Ah-ha," Anastasia discerned and punched the air with an index finger. "Ginsburg called."

She bent down and set her purse on the oak floor, deeply stained with corned beef and pastrami spatters. She straightened and withdrew her hand from my shoulders. Her face was aware, composed, and affable, but neither expectant nor anxious.

"Well?" she said amiably. "Someone speak." Anastasia plaited her fingers together, steepled the index fingers, and pressed them to her lips, waiting.

My heart was beating so loudly I could hear it and wondered how she'd take the news. "When my folks were at the apartment to walk Leftovers, Ginsburg's girl called," I said. "Mom answered the phone. He wants to see *us* this afternoon at three — *both of us*." I joggled a finger back-and-forth.

"It sounded urgent," Mom volunteered.

Without looking directly at either Mom or me, Anastasia, unruffled, addressed a spot halfway between us and said consolingly, "As I expected."

Mom's eyes popped open. Her hand flew to her face.

I flinched, wretched with a feeling of cautious doubt. "You *expected* him to call today?"

"We'd talked about it, if my test came back lousy. He'd said he'd want to see us."

"A trifle you didn't think I'd like to know?"

Anastasia hunched, elbows pinned to sides, palms raised. "I didn't want you to worry."

"Jesus, Nastia," I grumbled, "Ginsburg's not inviting us to a Hanukkah party."

Mom reached across the table and touched Anastasia's hand tenderly. "Nastusha, this has to be the scariest thing you've ever faced."

"And you're trying to do it alone," I interjected, fingers nervously drumming the table tile.

A smiley grimace crossed Nastia's face. "The truth? It *has* been hard. But awaiting bad news always is." Her grimace faded. Her eyes turned empathetic and swept over us and were quickly shadowed by a charmingly-calm, enigmatic, beamy smile that warmed her loving face. "Which is standard fare for a Soviet woman raised on repression by a corrupt government and a two-faced church."

We exploded in edgy laughter; such was the tension, so welcome the relief.

Anastasia slipped onto her chair with the grace of the collapsing prima ballerina at the curtain of Swan Lake. She smoothed her skort over smooth thighs. I felt a toe run up my bare shin. She gave me a quick, saucy look, arched her back alluringly, edged forward in her chair, and transformed her face again, this time into a tranquil, stress-free mask.

But all her Mona Lisa-calmness did not remove the knot in my stomach. "A little while ago you said you'd told me *everything*," I griped. "Now you're saying — "

"Easy, dear," Mom interrupted, squeezing my hand caringly. "Nastenka's lots on her mind."

"So much she can't tell me there's something wrong going on?"

Anastasia spread her napkin across her lap and pat my stubbly cheek. "Sweetheart, we know you want to be Sir Gawain, but you're four hundred years too late."

"Six hundred," I said robotically. She frowned. "The Round Table was six hundred years ago, and chivalry had nothing to do with it. Love is devotion, need, understanding, respect, trust, caring, honor, *and sharing*."

"That's a lot of things for a little word. I thought love meant deep affection."

"Too narrow!" I said, dismissively. "Love is much broader."

"So like Humpty Dumpty you can make a word mean what you choose it to mean?" Nastia shook her head. "Aren't you the guy who bragged that love was taking, using, and scoring, the guy who said boys made goaty conquests so they could strut around like tin soldiers?"

I turned and gave her my disparaging look. "That was yesterday's definition."

Nastia smiled solicitously. "Right. Well, keep me posted, we've lots to discuss." She set her palms on the tabletop. Her fingernails were lacquered pink. The one teensy-weensy diamond in her engagement ring gleamed. I felt a lecture coming. It came.

"Millions of women are diagnosed with breast tumors every year," Nastia said. "Some serious, most not. I know this was a shock to hear. It was for me. But it's my body, my worry, and if it's the worse, well, it leaves me with lots to do. A real job to find, a family to start, a life to live. I cannot — *I will not* — sit back and cry about something I can't control any more than if it were a broken fingernail. So let's drop it until we know more; then we'll make plans, okay?"

I swallowed hard and nodded grudgingly. "Sure, Nastia." She had used the words *if it's the worse*, unable to say the word cancer, but that's what she meant.

"But please don't forget, Nastenka, love is about sharing *joys and woes.*"

"I know, I know, Troy, and I love, worship, and adore you for caring." She reached over and tousled my hair lovingly as if that made everything okay. "Hey now, don't look so worried."

Just then, José, a short, skinny, Mexican busboy (and MacDee's aficionado), hurried up to our table. He plunked down a big bowl of sliced dill pickles that filled the air with a tantalizing garlicky aroma then dealt out little bread plates. Anastasia passed them around and dove in.

José grinned, and in a thick accent out came, "*Aqua, Señor Troy?*"

"*Si,* José," I replied in my best Puerto Vallarta Spanish. "*Quarto, por favor.*"

José's mustache arched high over his broad white teeth. "*Si, Señor;* Ingrid come pronto."

"*Gracias.*" I took a dill pickle slice and bit into its crunchy coldness. "Yum, yum."

Anastasia took a second pickle, scoffed it down hungrily, and took another. Just as she was about to take a bite, without preamble, Dad, in his well-ordered, Simon Legree voice said, "Tell us about your Doctor Ginsburg's visit, Anastasia."

Anastasia scowled. Mom sighed. I thought his query terribly brusque for a man bred on Beacon Hill. Unlike Americans, Soviets are taciturn and usually offended by public questions about personal issues. To my amazement, Nastia set down her unbitten pickle, wiped dill-juice off her fingers onto the napkin, cupped her left breast in left hand, and, with her right index finger, tapped a spot two inches above the nipple.

"Ginsburg put me under general anesthesia, made an incision right here — " she tapped the spot — "and with a little probe snipped out the cyst then stitched me up. It was a piece of cake."

"I've heard it is," Mom seconded. "A colleague said so."

"Oh, there'll be a little cut," Anastasia said, shyly, "but it'll be inside my bra, and no one will ever see it. Ginsburg said there might be more tests."

Dad looked over the tops of his bifocals. "Staging tests?"

"Yes, that's what he called them, staging tests."

I didn't know what a staging test was, but Operation Desert Storm, (O.D.S.) — the repelling of Iraq's invasion and annexation of Kuwait — taught me staging for battle. Coalition forces from thirty-four nations gathered on Iraq's southern perimeter while U. S. forces readied, unexpected and undetected, on its western border. Five weeks of aerial bombardment softened up Saddam's troops. Shrewd staging pinpointed their location and capacity, which made O.D.S. the world's second shortest, effectual, war: 100 hours. The Anglo-Zanzibar War of 1896 lasted 38 minutes. Staging: Plan ahead and know your target. I figured that was close.

Mom stroked Anastasia's arm lovingly. "You'll be all right, dear, just fine," she said, turned her head and looked at me. "Are the pickles tart, son?"

My mouth was so full of dill pickle I could only nod — that or splatter her with relish.

Mom picked up a slice and crunched it noisily. "Mmm, we Russians love our pickles."

I swallowed and grinned. "Usually with vodka."

Mom smiled at a memory and kept on chomping.

Dad leaned forward, forearms sprawled on the table's polychromatic tile and laced together his long bony fingers. He studied them a sec then looked at Nastia questioningly. "If it is *the worse*, did Doctor Ginsburg relay the chemicals he'd use in treatment?" Characteristically, Dad plowed on, priming the prolegomenon, tact be damned. His question produced another sigh from Mom and a slight scowl on Anastasia's face that quickly softened.

"Cytoxan was one," she replied. "There were others, but he spoke so fast in a heavy New York accent and, well, honestly, I wasn't tracking so well."

"Of course. Cytoxan's the trade name for Cyclosphosphamide, a powerful drug." Handing out pieces of gratuitous information was Dad's way. With time on his hands from his tenure-light academic load, his research into the etiology of poverty had led him to the fortune Americans spend on health care and alternative medicines used by the world's poor.

Anastasia's eyes narrowed, wonderingly. "Is Cytoxan powerful good or powerful bad drug?"

Dad looked at her carefully to weigh his response. "Both, really. It's most effective used in conjunction with chemotherapy; however, it makes some women infertile."

Mom caught her breath; she wanted grandkids, but first I wanted Nastia healthy.

"Not good," Anastasia said, shaking her head. "Ginsburg mentioned methotrexate, but it's not available, and another, said it would be approved soon, tax something or other."

"Taxol, perhaps?" Dad proposed helpfully.

"That's it! Taxol. He said it's had incredible trial results for decades."

Dad beamed. "Yes, it's been a newsmaker for thirty years."

"I've never heard of it," I scoffed, taking a fourth dill pickle. Tasty.

Anastasia shot me a squinty-eye look. "You folks better grab a dill before they disappear."

Mom took another dill pickle demurely.

Dad held up his hand and plowed on, "Taxol has a two-thousand-year history."

"Oh, dear," Mom fretted, "we need some wine." Mom was confident and at peace within her skin and not shy about speaking her mind. Her conversational indolence probably stemmed from being raised as a child prodigy and achieving academic success that gave her the self-assurance of a she-lion.

"Wine sounds fine to me," I said amiably.

"I've no objection," Anastasia agreed pleasantly.

Dad, oblivious to irony, said, "In *vino* there is *Veritas.*"

I piped up, "If you can figure out which facet of it that you're hearing."

Mom looked around for a wine cooler. "Think the Squirepatch has champagne?"

"*Briar*patch, Mom," I corrected. "It does, if you like Cold Duck."

"Kendall-Jackson makes a lusty Sauvignon," Dad said.

"I've seen that," I interrupted, rising half-canted in my chair to look for Ingrid. "Where *is* our waitress?" Deli traffic was wall-to-wall. I couldn't see her and decided to give her a couple of minutes and slid out of that awkward position onto my seat.

Dad continued, "As to taxol's history, Nastia, it's extracted from the yew tree, a conifer in the *Taxus*-family. Roman scribes recorded the Cantabrians, a Basque Region people, chewed its poisonous seeds, *Taxus baccata,* in twenty-two B. C. rather than submit to Julius Caesar's slavery. His soldiers used taxol wood to make deadly arrows."

"That's incredible," I marveled. "Is the entire tree lethal?"

"Everything but the aril, the fleshy red seed casings," the Squire said. "They're delicious."

Nastia looked puzzled. "If the Romans knew of the tree's toxicity — and folklore prods science — why did it take two thousand years for science to find a use for taxol?"

"The short answer?" Dad said, professorially, "an over-abundance of toxic plants. In nineteen thirty-four, a Belgium doctor named Dustin extracted the alkaloid colchicine from crocus seeds and proved its antimitotic effect on animal cells."

I cocked my head. "What's an *antimitotic effect*?"

"Interfering with mitosis, or cell division," Nastia explained. "*You* studied chemistry?"

"I read a lot." That was gospel. I did read a lot in college: Playboy, Hustler, and Esquire. My chemistry was at a Waterville bar-room school taught by a Beantown, frat brother, Brad.

But Dad, the unshakably dilettante, was intent on clarifying taxol's muddy history. "Dustin, using the new electronic microscope, watched colchicine dissolve the spindle microtubules found during cell division. Thirty years later, improved microscopes allowed undergrads like me — " he tapped his chest — "to see microtubules move, walls convergence, and microtubules vanish."

"That was ages ago," Anastasia said and swiveled around. Her eyes bounced over the deli, but she didn't see her tennis partner. "Where *is* Ingrid?"

Nastia was starved, and I was trying hard to stay interested. Fortunately, months serving the public at McDonald's had begun to teach me patience. "So if Romans knew the yew was poisonous," I said, "and Dustin discovered it stopped cell division, why didn't he try colchicine … hey, there's Ingrid." I lifted my chin at the knockout, chatting affably as she was delivering frosty drinks and meaty sandwiches to a four-top three tables away.

In today's *laissez-aller* world, anything goes. Waitresses dress as provocatively as Hollywood starlets slinking across the Red Carpet, and Ingrid was the deli's Lorelei, enticing customers and flirting brazenly to keep them coming back. She was outgoing and friendly and treated customers with the allure that implied their arrival just completed her day. With an abundance of ensorcelling confidence, dished out in a narrow range of behaviors between obsequiousness and rudeness, she knocked down scads of dough. She had an apple-pie appeal and looked like Anastasia's clone. Same killer smile, furtive look of smoldering sexuality, honey-tan, flawless-skin, a long-limbed, blue-eyed knockout, and an amalgam of Carmen and Mother Theresa. Ingrid was noticed, admired, and the focus of all men's attention, and they reacted to her as if they'd been kissed by Marilyn Monroe. Her head was crowned with a casual ruff of corn-silk hair over a trim, taut, intricacies of curves, hollows, and textures, a tiny waist, and glow of golden legs below bubblegum-pink short-shorts. I wondered if she were tanned all over. Men would throw themselves to their knees in homage, panting to take her for a test drive. Thank God I'm a married Christian, who, though occasionally suffering illusive faith, has intractable guilt. One day Ingrid will shower her acquirer with her exceptional beauty, mobile lips, eager hips, and hardy laugh. Her bottomless blue eyes were the portal to an animated, driven, wild, wondrous gift of brio to the strongest alpha male in the pack. On a later day, she will be middle-aged and invisible and cast off for a newer model. I felt a wave of guilt. Why was I even thinking of Ingrid? Why was I not concentrating on Nastia? Is it me or the swirling world men live in that seeps into our veins and clouds our vision?

Mom tapped my hand. "Excuse me, dear, when that girl you're staring at gets here get us a bottle of Kendall-Jackson."

I tugged my wandering eyes back. "You bet."

I returned my eyes to Ingrid and willed her to look at me. When she did, I beamed brilliantly and beckoned with a come-here-wave of the hand. She brushed silky strands from her forehead with a cutesy flip of fingertips and responded with a saucy, melt-titanium smile and a finger held a quarter-inch from her thumb in a just-a-sec purlicue. Ingrid smiled quickly, but she thought carefully and had a full set of curves that nobody could improve on. I shuddered, undetected, and turned my eyes away, lamenting their cussed libidinousness, convinced their philandering was a genetic flaw. I noticed Dad fingering crown hair to conceal the bald spot as he admired Ingrid's legs, swing of hips, narrowness of waist, and flex of calves.

Ingrid finished serving sandwiches, provided extra napkins and headed our way on lithe legs and a dancer's light-footedness. Everyone eyeballed her, women for her generous spill of flaxen hair, men her bounty of breasts, hips, and legs. Pink sneakers and a matching polo shirt with a Briarpatch rabbit embossed on the escutcheon completed her ensemble. Ingrid was a Dean's List, English lit-major-student/waitress at Rollins College, which had floored Anastasia. Soviet propaganda showed Americans living in abject poverty. Soviet people knew better: all Americans were rich.

"Love your pink outfit and gorgeous tan, Nastia!" Ingrid exclaimed with a beamy smile. "You look radiant, the picture of health!"

Ingrid's upbeat voice was laced with an echo of Finnish articulation as smooth as sherry filtered through silk. Her body couldn't stand still. She slipped her order pad beneath her belt in back with one hand, and, with her other hand, touched Nastia's arm. Hipshot, she shifted her weight from one foot to the other and back, swaying like a willow.

"Wish I felt radiant," Anastasia carped.

"Bad day?"

"Not the best, Ingrid." Nastia elbowed me. "McEnroe, here, beat me for the first time."

"You beat your wife?" Ingrid howled. The pretend accusation was loud enough to draw attention from the next table. Ordinarily we have a bout of chivvying before ordering, but I hoped Ingrid noted our somberness and quietly shrugged. The poor girl had probably made reckless by my charming allure and didn't deserve the caustic snippet sitting on the tip of my tongue like a poisoned dart.

"Mom, Dad," Anastasia lilted. "This is our good friend, Ingrid, my tennis partner."

"Hi," Ingrid said, smiling warmly. "Nastia and I play Saturdays while Super Chef slings Egg McMuffins."

"We heard," Dad said, glancing at his ancient Rolex — his father's bequeath — with a worried frown that knotted his face and made him older. He quickly flipped open his menu to the salads.

"We'd like a chilled bottle of Kendall-Jackson Sauvignon Blanc, Ingrid," I said. "Got one?"

"We do!" Ingrid enthused. "Peek at your menus; I'll be back in a flash." She wheeled around and disappeared, her hair spiraling out like a comet's tail.

Mom opened her menu but watched Ingrid. "With all that hair she could play Lady Godiva."

Naturally, that set Dad to yammering to Nastia about that munificent Anglo-Saxon's charity occurred before the Norman Conquest. I stared at my hands, folded on the table, patiently awaiting the Godiva lesson to end.

"So back to taxol," Dad transitioned, "Dustin watched colchicine bind to the protein tubulin-forming microtubules, and for years his work was the standard for measuring the mitotic effects."

"In other words, he found the missing link between plant compounds and anti-cancer drugs?" Nastia probed, setting aside her menu. She was a swift decision maker.

"Yes, which launched a massive search in the fifties for other *Vinca* alkaloids."

I snapped my head. "*Vinca*?"

"Glossy evergreens of the genus *Vinca*," Dad explained. "One of those, taxol, had made headlines since nineteen sixty-seven when a North Carolina

Doctor Wall announced it stopped cancer and published its molecular structure, a scientific *shot heard round the world* that set world scientists clamoring for taxol. Animal trials began, women were tested, and papers blossomed like May flowers until a problem surfaced." He glanced at Mom studying her menu. "Find something, Ira?"

Mom closed her menu and set it aside. "The seafood salad sounds delicious. Want one?"

Dad nodded, and I asked him, "Was the problem not enough yew trees?"

"Exactly. The shortages exacerbated in the seventies when Susan Horwitz, a molecular pharmacologist, explained how taxol paralyzed cell division. World biologists flooded the NCI with taxol requests, and, overnight, a complex organic molecule became a political lightning rod, object of hope, bone of contention, and subject of greed."

Anastasia nibbled her pickle. "So where does this miracle tree grow?"

"Our taxol comes from the bark of the Pacific yew, *Taxus brevifolia,* but — " he scowled miserably — "the distressing fact is its sluggish development is mostly due to supply problems that caused millions of deaths and pilfered our treasury."

I raised a hand as a student. "Let me guess, agency infighting and low bidders?"

"Yes!" Dad exclaimed, clapping his big paws. "The promised taxol was never delivered."

Anastasia shook her head. "So all those women who waited decades died?"

"Tragically, yes." Dad shook his head despondently. "The one-woman-in-eight succumbing to breast and ovarian cancer is an astronomical number. But there is hope. Ten months ago the N. C. I. gave up on taxol and gave it to Bristol-Meyers Squibb — *our* — half billion dollars of studies, inventory, and research."

Mom cocked her head at Dad like a one-eyed hen inspecting a bug. "In exchange for what?"

Dad threw up his hands. "For nothing, bringing it to market! BMS will make billions."

"Lemme see if I got this," I said disparagingly. "It took the government thirty years to realize it didn't have the know-how to bring a life-sustaining product to market, is that about right?"

Dad's nodded, his face twisted into a grimace. "It is. Their cure for breast and ovarian cancer was abandoned and gifted to BMS with nary a soul held responsible for incompetence."

Anastasia's face blanched into appalled incomprehension. "Didn't relatives of dead women sue? I mean everyone sues everyone in America, right?"

"Of course," I agreed. "In America shysters multiply like rabbits. Oh, there are a few genuine ethical attorneys advocating for the rich *and* the poor, but most are scoundrel with ears pinned to the ground, listening for victims, ready to cut corners to pilfer fat fees."

"Usually with one foot barely inside the law," Dad said, hunching his shoulders. "Then the government did what governments do best. It assigned a commission to study the SNAFU, and four months ago Congress launched an investigation into NCI's gift to BMS. It looked at bidder deals, the revolving door between the NCI and BMS, and why no one explored the shift to synthetic taxol."

Nastia looked weary. "In other words, nothing will be done. Is BMS still cutting yew trees?"

"Not at all," Dad said. "And they fired the Boulder outfit, Hauser, supplying them and moved into the study of synthetic taxol." He took Nastia's hand and squeezed it. "Another sad reality is synthetic taxol was also developed by an NCI grant to FSU. But the NCI's left hand never knew what its right hand was doing."

Just then Ingrid appeared with four wine glasses, corkscrew, frosty bottle of Sonoma County's finest grape, coddled in a napkin, and a plastic ice bucket that looked as cheesy as a plastic weekend wedding ring. She went into her sommelier act: twist corkscrew, withdraw cork, pass cork to the squire, gurgle a splash in his bowl-mounted stemware, step back, smile.

Dad snuffled, rotated, studied, sipped, and nodded. Benign enough to drink. Amen.

Ingrid decanted dollops around the table, wiped a dribble off the bottle, and plunked it into the bucket. We clinked glasses, held eye contact for a sec, and hailed, "*Za vashe zdorovie!* — Cheers!" and sipped.

"Ready?" Ingrid said pen posed.

Mom set down her glass. "The clam, oyster, and shrimp salmagundi salad, please, and no dessert. Oh, and unsweetened ice tea." Her ice tea was a concession to decades of southern living; most Russians prefer hot tea.

Dad looked up, his eyes lagging as they made their way to Ingrid's face. "Ditto," he said, waggling a finger back-and-forth between himself and Mom.

Anastasia looked up. "What are you pushing today, Ingrid?"

"Spinach salad with arugula, endive, and grilled scallops."

"Sounds good. I'll take it and water no — "

"No ice," Ingrid said. "Gotcha."

The ground in northwest Russia is tiered like a layer-cake with peat moss. Some have smoldered since Napoleon burned Moscow in 1812, a year immortalized by Tchaikovsky and boomingly memorialized by Americans every Fourth of July. Burnt peat turns potable water and teeth brown, so most Russians forgo brown ice. Would you drink a vodka martini on the rocks the color of Johnnie Walker? Me neither.

Ingrid looked at me. A plethora of anxieties churned in my stomach. I wondered if I could eat or if the meal would lie in my stomach like a dead cat. But I needed sustenance. "The usual." Fast food managers do not eat well. Our 'balanced' diet is fries, shakes, and cheeseburgers *with* lettuce, tomato, and mayo.

Ingrid recited, "One corn beef-pastrami combo on grilled rye, side of slaw, kosher dill, and a Doctor Brown Celery Cream Soda." Observant.

When I passed her my menu, our fingers touched. I felt a tingle of excitement. An awareness of her smoldering sexuality magnified tenfold. I looked at her, and her pale glance was fleeting. From a closet in the back of my noodle, a voice screeched: *You fool! Not now! Not ever!* With a head flick, Ingrid tossed her long hair back and vanished.

Anastasia, repulsed by my lunch, snipped, "Think that might hold you, Rambo?"

"With all the major food groups covered, let's hope," I said.

"Red meat is *sooo* bad for you," she said, making it a guilt trip.

"It's the fuzzy green meat that's bad for you."

Heaps of dead meat disgusts cholesterolphobes. Let them survive on fish tidbits or chicken nuggets sprinkled on rabbit food and celebrate their sacrifice. If I wanted to live on chicken and fish, I'd eat a penguin. I am more of an epicurean than a gourmet or gourmand and have never learned to enjoy leaving the table hungry. And I love veggies. Carrot cake, zucchini bread, pumpkin pie. We should take pleasure in the *now* of life, in the edacious pleasure of chewing tender morsels of filet, sipping a fine single-malt Scotch, listening to Itzhak Perlman, driving a well-tuned machine, and I wonder how those insipid souls always sniffing the reductions survive. Homo sapiens have had incisors since Lucy and until recently used them. Left unused, in a few millennia, we'll turn

Darwin on his head and revert to the toothlessness of turtles. If God hadn't intended us to eat bovine, why had He created incisors to tear into them?

Dad leaned back and laced his long fingers behind his neck. "July's congressional hearing unearthed the revolving door between NCI and Bristol-Myers Squibb and its failure to stipulate pricing guidelines, recovering costs, or solve the fate of the spotted owl."

"I've heard about that owl," I recalled. "What's the revolving door?"

"According to *The Wall Street Journal*, Robert Wittes, N.C.I. Director of Cancer Therapy, left three years ago to become the senior VP of cancer research at BMS. Within months, the NCI awarded BMS the gift of *our* taxpayer research, results, and inventory, and he returned to the NCI three months ago in what Congress called, 'The Great Taxol Giveaway.'"

"'I'm shocked, shocked, to find corruption going on,'" I said, mimicking *Casablanca's* Captain Renault. "Were there others?"

"Oh, yes, John Douros, Stephen Carter, and others."

"At least American corruption's more subtle than Russia's," Anastasia said, unfazed by the blatant double-dealing. She sensed movement and looked up. "Lunch."

Ingrid made her way through the deli, juggling four platters, three running up her left arm like dominoes and my massive combo held out front like a snowplow. She set the combo before me and dealt out humongous salads bowls that impressed my parents. My sandwich had a heap of potato chips I had not ordered and the slaw I had ordered. I ate a chip, shame to waste them, and sprinkled Louisiana Tabasco Pepper Sauce on the pastrami.

"Good God, do you have a death wish?" Anastasia needled, stabbing a juicy grilled scallop.

"We used hot sauce in Iraq to force confessions." I crunched a big chip.

"Then why do you eat it?" She popped another scallop into her mouth and jabbed a third.

"I love hot food," I said and winked, "hot women, too." I took a jaw-stretching bite of my double-decker, trying to keep the peripheral from dripping on my shirt, scarfing hungrily, and eyed the assortment of pies in the rack. Plan ahead.

Dad tied a napkin, apron-like, around his neck and forked a dripping oyster. Between chews, he said, "One thing you can't lose sight of is America's taxol fascination began forty years ago after the National Cancer Institute and the Department of Agriculture vowed to solve the riddle of cancer." His Adam's apple worked like a sleeve of snakes as he swallowed. He toyed with some lettuce and speared a clam. "The NCI began by testing thirty-five thousand plants for antimitotic effectiveness. In nineteen sixty-two, the Harvard-trained botanist, Arthur Barclay, and his grad students, stripped, dried, bagged, and tagged paper-like bark from the Oregon yew tree and shipped it in for analysis. It had taken a few years before lab tests revealed its anti-cancer properties. Wall, a chemist at the Research Triangle, working the compound, isolated the molecule, and named it taxol — tax from the tree, *Taxus brevifolia*, and ol as it was alcohol-based. Then the rush-to-market began. It ended with taxol selling for fifty-nine hundred dollars a gram or eight hundred thousand a pound."

"So they investigated lots of plants and taxol's expensive," Anastasia said munching on some endive. "So what happened?"

"Throughout the eighties, the media regaled taxol's astonishing successes with breast and ovarian cancer and hammered government's supply problem — cutting and peeling the bark off hundreds of thousands of yew trees. Politicians panicked, environmentalists marched, and women kept dying of breast cancer. There were predictably demands to save the forests and the spotted owl, but the government never harvested enough yew bark to acquire the taxol needed for clinical trials, yield was *that* minuscule. And the endless low-bidder problem. For a decade, low-ballers couldn't deliver the tons of bark contracted for, and yet our government would only deal with them. Myopia. And NCI's failure to stay in touch with the synthetic taxol program delayed clinical trials for years."

"Causing hundreds of thousands of deaths," Anastasia said.

Dad forked out a shelled clam. "And only *after* world labs proclaimed taxol a miracle drug did they give up — knowing it an elixir! — and toss in the towel on taxol's lethal history."

Mom ate her shrimp and oysters. She heard the story and appeared bored. Nastia looked incredulous. I was livered but not enough to stop me from eating my double-decker sandwich. The corned beef was incredible.

"So," I said, mouth full, "what was the outcome of last July's congressional investigation?"

"Are you kidding?" Dad joshed. "Investigating itself, the government found it did no wrong."

"Naturally," I said. "Silly me." I moved onto the cold slaw. It had too much mayo.

Mom said, "One of our Kunming, post-doctoral, writing student's dissertation was on the second source for taxol."

"And knows all about the extraction process and how taxol works," Dad said.

"You two have met him," Mom added, "Song Lin and Mim were at your wedding."

Anastasia's eyes squinted, searching memory. "The Chinese couple who spent the afternoon on Canyons' balcony in Blowing Rock gazing down at the Blue Ridge Mountains."

"Probably homesick for Kunming," Mom said. "Song visited us Wednesday evenings with his little girl, Lori, for Spoken English Night."

I drummed my fingers on the table tile, thought carefully, and said circumspectly, "His name means Pine Forest, the double-doc doing cancer research."

Dad smiled. "M.D. and Ph.D., good memory, son."

At times, I am baffled at my Dumpster's capacity for names. What groom would remember the meaning of a Chinese name at his wedding? For that matter, who'd remember the name Harry Carney, Ellington's saxophonist for five decades and the driving force in Duke's powerful swing-piece, *Take the "A" Train*, written the year Dad was born, 1941, that we sang at Colby?

"We have a copy of Song's dissertation," Mom said, stabbing her last oyster with finality.

That astonished me. "*You* read a chemistry exposition?"

She smiled and pointed the forked-oyster at me. "I scanned it after a stop in Blagoveshchensk to see your uncle on that seven-day, Trans-Siberian-odyssey, Vladivostok to Moscow. *A Study of the Chemical Constituents of Taxus Yunnanensis* is light years beyond my specialty."

"What's that?" Anastasia asked pleasantly, pushing her arugula aside.

"Twentieth-Century Russian lit," Mom replied.

"Yikes!" I gasped. "I thought it was tennis."

Mom kissed my cheek. There was a faraway look in her eyes as if she were kibitzing with a ghost. "Tennis, dear, has become my passion."

"I bet you give esoteric lit lectures with the same éclat you wield a racket," Anastasia said.

Mom laughed and rocked her hand in a *comme ci comme ça* manner. "Well—"

"Wasn't your *Solzhenitsyn's Aesthetics in One Day in the Life of Ivan Denisovich* published by Moscow State University?" Anastasia asked.

"Surely something that hot will be a New York Times Best Seller," I threw out.

"You're sweet, Troy, but you jest," Mom said.

Anastasia appeared puzzled. "Didn't Solzhenitsyn write *Denisovich* after eight years in the Arctic's Solovki Gulag?" She was referring to the mother of all Gulags, the ancient monastery buildings on the Solovetsky Islands, in the White Sea.

"Actually," Dad said, visibly tiring of our persiflage, "Aleksandr Isayevich was imprisoned in several Gulags, but mostly in Ekibastuz in Kazakhstan."

"Solzhenitsyn used the Special Purpose Camp or *Solovetsky Lager 'Osobogo Naznachenia*," Mom explained. "The acronym SLON, Russian for elephant, was the embodiment of evil.'

"Aesthetics in the Arctic's an oxymoron," Dad said. A lesser man would have made some bilious outburst at our educational braggadocio. Not Dad, he plowed on with the taxol story and the last of his salad. "I grasped an overview of taxol from Song's dissertation on that forever-train-ride; it was in English, after all."

"With page after page of pentagons, hexagons, heptagons, and octagons with little numbers scrunched in the corners," Mom said. "Too much for me."

"You don't have to understand something's chemical structure, Irinka, to grasp its nature. Dad's voice was tender, and he'd used Mom's affectionate diminutive.

"I thought you studied chemistry at Tver State University," I said to her.

"I did. It was an eight o'clock class. I dozed a lot."

"Me, too. Must be a family trait."

Anastasia looked at us and shook her head. "So, Dad, is there anything new with taxol?"

"Not a thing. The only source is the bark, needles, and stems of yew trees from the Pacific Northwest. Song's work isolated seventeen new taxoids found in the roots of *Taxus Yunnanensis,* the yew from Yunnan Province in southwest China."

"But taxol's still a big deal?" I said and winced at Dad's expression of distaste.

"Calling taxol a *big deal* is like saying Salk's polio vaccine helped succor the afflicted."

"Gotcha." I felt like a jerk.

Anastasia looked puzzled. "Aren't those locales much different? The Pacific

Northwest and southwest Yunnan, I mean latitude, longitude, and climate?"

"Not really; the yew thrives in moist, temperate climates," Dad explained. "Yunnan's on Key Largo's latitude, but it isn't hot and sticky year round due to its high elevation."

"Spring year round," Mom said and dabbed some salad dressing off her fingers onto her napkin. She held out her hands, palms down, and raised one. "Like Kābul and no other major city in the world, Yunnan is six thousand feet above sea level and always cool. Chinese call it the City of Eternal Spring. Vegetation is lush year-round; imagine, fresh berries in February."

Anastasia said, "And no one ever studied the yew's root before?"

"Not until Song," Dad said. "Now China is hurriedly planting yew trees next door in Burma."

My eyes popped open. "To harvest in a century? We wouldn't wait a century for anything."

"Different view of time," Dad said, smiling enigmatically. "The Chinese are an old, patient civilization. They know to lower costs supply must increase and the next generations will prosper even if the present one does not. They're also keenly aware of our environmentalists stopping the cutting of Oregon yews to preserve the Spotted Owl."

"The Spotted Owl oughta be preserved in formaldehyde," I said and licked pastrami juice off my fingers and picked up the last chip. Someone had to eat it.

Anastasia asked, "What about taxol's price?"

"Expensive," Dad said. "It'll *not* be free as the polio vaccine was, and, with one woman in eight needing it, there'll be enormous demand and make it the most lucrative drug in history."

Mom pushed her plate aside. "But, Doctor, wouldn't not making it free and widely available be an egregious oversight on governments' part and misanthropic greed on industry's?"

Dad stroked her hand. "Of course. Maybe our legislators and BMS will see taxol as vital to the world as Jonas Salk's vaccine was in nineteen fifty-four with free inoculations."

"Fat chance," I insisted. "There's no line on a corporate balance for social consciousness."

Dad agreed, "Leaving victims stuck with the bill."

Dad was a rare breed of professor, a conservative. You'd need a Geiger counter to find one at today's colleges. And yet, he was a typical professor, too, with the inane intellect that never dwelled on the cost of producing anything.

If money is needed for the greater good, he subscribed to the liberal dogma: raise taxes, soak the rich and let the five percent paying eighty-five percent of the tax load pay more and the fifty percent paying no tax continue their free ride.

"Still, taxol sounds terrific," Anastasia avowed. "If I need some, I'll buy it no matter the cost." Her outlook had jumped orbits, and shining at the center of her new universe was taxol.

"Amen," Mom said. "Here's to taxol!" She raised her glass of wine.

I thought I saw a tear gleam in the corner of her eye. Was it worry for Anastasia or her mention of Kābul, the city where Papa was killed? The skeptic in me wondered if all this taxol-cure talk was the cause of being so cheery; if taxol was so hot, why had it taken our FDA thirty years *not* to get it to market.

Anastasia looked reflective. She reached across the table and touched Dad's hand. "Have you read of taxol's clinical results?"

"A little." He sipped some wine. The wine was regenerative for him, enlivening, making him less professorial … sometimes. "Taxol's been effective in sixty percent of the women in clinical trials, which means you may be the beneficiary of this wonder drug if — and I emphasize *if* — it works in your body, *and if* you get the right dose as soon as possible."

"What do you mean *if*? Why wouldn't my taxol work?"

"Taxol kills cancer cells, but that doesn't mean it works for every woman. Some have an intrinsic resistance to the proteins in taxol. But ask Song. I called him this morning. He'd like you two to call him at home this evening."

"You do go on and on, Doctor," Mom said pertly and glanced at her microscopic wristwatch.

Dad noticed and popped the last jumbo shrimp in his mouth. "Is your doctor's office close?"

"Fifteen minutes," Anastasia said.

"Longer today," I cautioned. "Walt's packing them in this weekend, which reminds me, we got robbed for the ninth time this year this morning. I gotta call Kahuna." I picked up my brick.

"You have burglars at your store?" Mom asked with alarm.

"Robbers," I replied. "But fewer than last year." I took the last bite of my combo, started chewing, picked up the cell phone and danced fingers over the keypad.

Tom Rowe, an assistant manager, answered. "Kahuna's gone to the hospital."

"Maybe we won't be robbed again today," I said.

We finished lunch. Dad caught Ingrid's attention, made a scribbling motion, and she scurried over with an eager smile and Superwoman eyes that could count money in your wallet. Dad glanced at the bill, scooped some change out of his pocket, set it on the table, and covered it with two twenties from his wallet. Ingrid scooped it up so swiftly I swear the hairs on Old Hickory's head fluttered.

"Now, Nastusha," Mom ordered, "don't look so worried. Things'll work out. You focus on what you need to do, your home, husband, work, tennis — all the things that bring you happiness and contentment. We've spoken with a Boone, oncologist friend. He *will* help you."

Steph weaved through the tables to us. "Well?" she said, hands raised, eyebrows arched.

"Wonderful lunch," Mom enthused. As soon as we stood, Steph snatched our plates. The restaurant was packed; the hungry gawked in the windows. We hurried out through the crowd, anxious to hear Ginsburg's verdict.

Worries of how I would come up with the taxol ransom had been flashing through my head. And, just then, up popped a solution. Four maxed-out credit cards. Better make that six.

No matter how smart you are, it's always good to have insurance.

***

FIVE

Dr. Ginsburg:
Diagnosis

Lengthening palm shadows rested on the BMW as Nastia and I said *da-sveda-nia* — goodbye — to my parents. We watched them cross Canton Avenue, hand-in-hand, heading for an afternoon at the Morse Museum. No one had stolen my wheels, and we saddled up.

"Ouch!" Anastasia cried out. "This leather seat's on fire."

"Another day in paradise," I said.

We edged onto Park Avenue, turned right at Fairbanks, and wedged aboard I-4. Black Friday gridlock, a four-lane, bumper-car jumble as far as the eye could see was punctuated by flatulent Harleys weaving in and out. Lots of Jersey plates. Most heading back to motels for naps; some wouldn't sleep.

Fifteen minutes of bottlenecks and I pulled into our apartment complex, a sprawl of five-hundred-fifty-two cubes stacked six-to-the-floor in twenty-three, four-story units. They encircled an empty parking lot next to an algae-green sinkhole we labeled Paradise Lake.

I snagged a cherished spot in an acre of shade beneath a massive live oak big enough to house the Swiss Family Robinson. A squirrel scolded us with cheeks ballooned with acorns, then he bound along a guano-streaked limb, leaped to a higher branch and vanished into a chink. In the squally western sky, a flock of seagulls wheeled in from Clearwater, harbingers of an approaching storm carrying rackety kettle drums, suggesting I raise the top. The swampy air was a song-fest of trilling frogs and leg-rubbing grasshoppers, spreading that news. We dismounted, raised the top, and, hand-in-hand, dashed to dodge the first fat splatters.

The click of the key in the lock of our fourth-floor aviary triggered ecstatic yips from our burglar alarm. Leftovers, a neutered, creamy-gold male of four months, vaulted against the door as I eased it open. There was no sign of break-ins. My Rembrandts were safe. Anastasia headed for the fridge for cold, bottled water. I turned down the thermostat, set on eighty; it was a lesson Mom had instilled to save moola. A distant drone propelled wintry air into our efficiency and fluffed Leftovers' silky mane. He scrambled back-and-forth, tail wagging ferociously, whines emanating from deep in his puppy throat, professing, politely enough, he wanted a love pat. He clambered up my leg, licked my thigh, and sniffed my crotch as I'd taught him not to do. I held his downy face, stroke his head, and explained some etiquette. He seemed to understand — they do, you know — alighted, and bound over to stand ceremoniously beside a suspicious yellow puddle on the cracked linoleum and barked proudly. We knew that bark.

"*Ne pisai*! — No peeing!" Nastia scolded, intent on making the Golden a bilingual pooch. She ran her hand down his spine and swatted his butt. Russky tough love.

Leftovers sat, cocked his head in puzzlement, and raised a paw. With his Russian-as-a-second-language skills still in development, he was undoubtedly confused over the *pisat,* gerund for peeing. He grasped the verbs pee, моча́ — *mocha* —in both languages. I gave his ears a robust scratch, noted a flicker of intelligence in his big chocolate eyes, and said, "*Mochit'sya* is a gerund, old boy, the noun form of the verb *mocha.*"

Undressing, Anastasia watched the grammar lesson, hands on hips, head shaking back-and-forth. "Why in the world are you talking to that dog? They're stupid, you know."

"Not this one."

"Because he's so handsome and intelligent?"

"Just like me."

"Are you intelligent enough to wipe up his *mocha*?"

Leftovers smiled and scrambled off to the doormat for a nap, and I reeled off some paper towel and went to work, and then I heeled off my sneakers. I left them beside the mutt and the soggy paper towel on a worn spot in the linoleum with the brown backing showing. Echoes of infancy. In northern Russia, snow blankets terra firma nine months a year. Grungy footwear is doffed at the doorways of dank, drafty *Stalinkas*, the nine-story, pre-cast-concrete beehives Stalin threw up for the tens of millions he dehoused in collectivization. Leftovers didn't like the position he'd taken, stood, stretched, turned around three times, and flopped down in the exact spot.

"Close the drapes," Anastasia said, peeling off her bra.

I went to the window and gazed out at the apartment sprawl. Cozy as Mesa Verde on a rainy day. Only the burglar bars spoil the view. I pulled the drape cord and dropped my shorts.

"If we shower together we can be ready faster," I said, voice as thick as hot fudge.

Anastasia turned around and glanced down warily. "No way, buster."

My bottom lip jutted out. "But what about … "

"That thing jumps up at green lights."

She spun around and closed the bathroom door. After showering, we dressed casually. Nastia slipped on a sleeveless, red, scoop-neck blouse, white linen slacks, frilly red sandals, and started on her makeup. I donned a raspberry-striped polo shirt, henna shorts, and hauled my favorite scruffy Bass sandals from the closet.

"Those shoes are so sixties," Anastasia declared. "Something your dad would wear."

"Old stuff's cool," I said, "I'm a retro guy. I want some coffee; you want some?"

"Not now." In an absent-minded way, she said, "How are we going to find the taxol money?"

"I've devised a way."

She looked at me suspiciously. "We are *not* asking your parents, Sherlock."

"Think plastic."

I zapped some cold morning coffee in a Blue Danube cup, part of a Czech-set Anastasia brought from Russia that went with our apartment décor like cocktail onions on pancakes and plopped down on our queen-sized hide-a-bed (my parents' marital gift) to explain.

"How many credit cards do you have?" I asked, knowing the answer.

"None," she said. "You know that."

"I have one. *One*! Most Americans have dozens."

"So?" She sounded mystified and peered into her wallet mirror to outline on some eyeliner.

"We're flooded with credit card offers. It's time we became plastic-plenti-ful. We'll each open two checking accounts simultaneously at two different banks and apply for their Master and Visa cards that same day. Banks are fast but not fast enough to catch us. Then, we max out the four cards, pocket twenty grand, and buy the taxol, just like that!" I snapped my fingers.

Anastasia looked at me apprehensively. "Is it legal?"

"Of course. Our economy's based on credit."

"So we'll get the taxol and pay for it next year?"

"You're a fast learner."

I sipped my leftover Maxwell House Instant — Zowie! — and planned the strategy while eyeing stuff around the efficiency that needed upgrading ... if we had a windfall from a boosted credit limit. Out with the ratty, olive-green sofa that matched the refrigerator and microwave and clashed with the rickety card table from Goodwill serving our dining, computer, and storage needs. Ditto two weathered orange-crate bookcases, heisted from an Indian River grove and stuffed with Mexican recipe books flanking two ratty, maroon, overstuffed recliners and a plastic sego palm purchased at garage sales in Ocoee for a dollar. One big heave-ho of the honeymoon elegance. No more sleazy-motel look for us. Time for pictures on the walls, photographs on a coffee table, a shelf of Russian nesting dolls. Payback would be no sweat. We both had jobs.

I looked at my golden Timex, a Rolex-looking rip-off. Two-thirty-five. "Ready?"

"About." Anastasia brushed a smidgen of toast-shaded stuff into her eye-brows, did the lipstick-rolling-lips thing women do and blotted them on a Kleenex while I shuffled through overdue bills. I picked up the checkbook, glanced at the balance, and slipped it in my hip pocket.

Anastasia asked, "Much left?"

"Less than a million."

"I start teaching Monday. That'll be a second three thousand a month."

"What will our creditors do without us?"

Leftovers nuzzled my leg and howled. He knew he'd be orphaned again.

"Maybe we should get him a sister," Anastasia said. "Poor thing's lonely."

"Aren't we all?"

I gave him an ear-scratch and filled his blue enamel bowl with fresh water. He approached it slowly, lapped loudly, and hunched into the noisy ceremony of crunching Purina nuggets, making a final futile whine as the door was locked.

We stepped into intense mustard rays of mid-afternoon sun radiating heat like Vesuvius. The parking lot steamed with evaporating rain and bustled with Black Friday winding down. Robins looked for worms on the edge of swampy Paradise Lake. Seagulls swooped into the parking lot looking through the garbage. From the sound of it cocktail hour was cranking up. Cliff dwellers live on pizzas, burgers, and fries and toss incorruptible Styrofoam containers into the parking lot that will be there long after the last Homo sapiens has gasped his last polluted breath.

"Oh, shit," I moaned as we scampered down the stairs. "The Beemer's got chicken pox."

In the checkered shade of the live oak's massive arms, my ride's shiny hide, the pride of Leipzig and template of everything German, was speckled with ashen scat of diarrheic robins.

"Bird turd washes off," Anastasia mocked. "Quit squawking."

I smiled at her flippancy, her first touch of insouciance in hours. "Watch your handle, that robins' white is not a good match for your slacks."

Anastasia dug in her purse, unearthed a Kleenex, and warily opened her door. Then she tossed the soiled tissue into the parking lot, a pointillist-touch of jetsam to complement the Styrofoam, our species plastic spore that dot parking lots from coast to gleaming coast like endless fields of Matisse flowers. Today's parking lots are tomorrow's middens.

I cranked up the Beemer, eased back a prudent distance, lowered the top so fresh exhaust fumes could dispel the hot air, and nosed into the afternoon as hot and steamy as a Turkish bath. I-4, heading west, was not its usual clot of frantic drivers, honking, stomping, braking, and gunning and motorcycles sla-loming around cars and slaloming back. Anastasia sat rigidly silent, marble eyes fixed straight ahead, her face a tenacious mask of dogged resolve.

All too soon we reached Ginsburg's exit. "Turn there," Nastia said.

At an oak-shaded street, she lifted her chin at doctors' sign. "Turn here."

The Ginsburg Oncology Center sign listed six doctors, three medical on-cologists, two radiation oncologists, one surgical oncologist — all board-cer-tified specialists in distaff. Impressive credentials. I wondered if they treated patients as well as the cancer. I swung into the parking lot studded with royal palms and groomed with oleander shrubs fringing spaces for three dozen cars set in a swampy hammock that the breeze had obviously jumped over. In the rear, stood the most unusual doctors' building I'd ever seen. With its massive-ly-elaborate Spanish mission gingerbread, it reminded me of Tucson's San

Xavier del Bac, looking impressive, if misplaced, as if Benito Juárez had just worshiped within. Tall, arched windows radiant with stained glass marched down its stuccoed-sides and rose two-stories into a campanile, a two-foot projection dappled in light- and dark-rose. Fantastic for pouring hot oil on Seminole Indians. The pantiled roof, capped with burnt-sienna, S-shaped, interlocking-barrel-tiles, reinforced the place-of-prayer feel so tangibly that I recited a silent supplication. I spotted an open slot and pulled in between a black Bentley and a '72 Malibu low-rider in green and purple. The cars represented the top and bottom rungs of America's economic ladder, which provides two cars for every three Americans and clogs our air. Wait until the billion-plus Chinese with one-car-per-ten-thousand attain those numbers. That much smog will be a sun-proof blanket to halt photosynthesis like the asteroid did at Chicxulub, Yucatan. That explosion had the force of three million nuclear bombs detonating simultaneously sixty-six million years ago. It turned day into icy night for three years, which snuffed out the dinosaurs' 135-million year reign. Could it recur? You bet.

I held up a hand to ward off the sun. No black clouds. "I'll leave it topless."

"How do you like Ginsburg's ride?" Anastasia said, lifting her chin at the Bentley.

"Love it." I stepped into breathlessness and danced fingertips over eighteen layers of hand-rubbed walnut paint. "This car was handmade by four thousand people in Crewe, England and sells for over one hundred grand."

"More than I'd have made in fifty lifetimes in the Soviet Union."

"Oncology is a money machine."

"That's Ginsburg up there, watching those glitzy birds."

There was a nervous twitch at the corner of her mouth as she stared at a short, thin, narrow-shoulder man standing in the belfry window in the green-shadowed appendage. He was gazing at two fire-engine-red macaws with blue and yellow wings that looked like they'd been shot from flamethrowers.

Anastasia took my hand and pulled me into the shade of a date palm to see them better. I leaned a haunch against the Bentley's hot metal fender and slapped a mosquito on my arm. They're the deadliest creatures on earth, killing millions with malaria, Yellow Fever, Saint Louis encephalitis, West Nile, Ebola, Zika, and the Dengue Fever that I suffered in Iraq. High overhead, in a clump of palm fronds rattling listlessly, Daddy Macaw flapped his wings and shrieked like a chicken with laryngitis at his mate. Probably wanting her to do a bug run.

"They're screechy but oh sooo beautiful," Anastasia swooned.

"Not as beautiful as you," I said and slid an arm around her waist. Everyone needs a hug.

The puckish and volatile psittacines, like some people, communicated emotions in strident tones, probably discussing their Disney escape and flight back to Ecuador. When their argument settled down, they touched beaks and clicked tongues. Daddy Macaw had a bug in his hooked snout and disappeared into a hole. It reminded me of the truth as old as caveman that Lenin failed to grasp: The great engine of human wellbeing is self-interest. People want the freedom to own things, homes, cars, or macaws. In Communist countries, shops are lined with empty shelves or shelves with goods so shoddy no one buys them. When *all* property is state-owned, the state can ignore consumers' niggling demands; production is dictated by its *very visible* hand. What you get is Adam Smith turned on his head, comrades so poor they never splurge on anything. Extra rubles are hoarded under mattresses, which leaves the Politburo flummoxed. How can Westerners, living in an economy guided by the invisible Hand of Demand, give consumers countless selections and function so well with no one in control? Naturally, the Left has the goal of abolishing it.

I tapped the Bentley's fender with a knuckle. It rang richly. "Come on, Nastenka; it's time."

"Yes." Her voice quivered on the brink of control. "Time for the dénouement."

I opened the clinic's massive door. The dusky heart of the Mission of Oncology felt like a funeral parlor and smelled of incense. It was ringed with closed doors leading to unknown offices. Soft strains of Mozart waltzed in the blaze of spotlights focused on an ornately-carved oak table with a waist-high, filigreed, Chinese vessel stuffed with fresh, tropical flowers in splashy colors. Anastasia's frilly sandals slapped against the terracotta tile, counter-pointing my sandal's leathery clicks, a syncopated swish-click, swish-click that ended when we stepped aboard the carpeted, mahogany-paneled Otis. Our truncated jaunt of fourteen feet was just long enough to identify Wolfgang's *Concerto in C Major for Flute and Harp* before the door opened to a second-floor reception area and another incongruity. British Empire splendor.

The foyer reminded me of the mahogany-and-leather Gentlemen's Bar at the Saint Andrew's Hotel in cool, high Nuwara Eliya, Sri Lanka (formerly Ceylon), where we'd taken pre-combat R & R, strolled Queen Victoria Garden, sailed Lake Gregory, and stood in awe at Devon Falls. In the heart of tea country, endless four-foot tea-hedges sprawled over hill and dell plucked by swarthy-skinned Tamils with leaf-baskets lashed to foreheads, babes sheathed to breasts, pockets jingling with ten-cent-a-day wages. Here, Amadeus danced among the leathery scents of armchair-hides stained a bottle green bordered by wainscoting of burled walnut bisecting forest-green walls counterbalanced with gold-framed oils of English hunting scenes: foxes, hounds, horses, and riders in red riding caps, red jackets, jodhpurs, and Wellington boots. What fun! Oscar Wilde called it the unspeakable pursuit of the inedible.

We stepped through the thick carpet to a tiny window, a postern in the castle's wall. A grossly obese, acedia-plagued woman sat on a swivel chair slouched over a desk engaged in the *National Enquirer*. She had a faint mustache, ink-black hair with a half-inch nimbus of gray roots, and, on the right side of her nose, just above her scarlet mouth, a charred wen with a protruding long black hair. It looked like a mini radio transmitter and antenna, and I tried not to fixate on it as I started to speak. Her nametag rested on a massive breast read Betty. When she looked up, there was contempt in her spit-green-eyes. Most of her patients were rich. Not us.

I stuck my head in her window. Her right eyebrow shot up nearly to the shadowy halo.

"Nice Belushi trick," I said of the eyebrow feat John mastered on SNL, God rest his soul.

"Who's that?" she barked.

"Skip it," I said and hooked an arm around Nastia's waist, drawing her in.

Betty glared at Anastasia. "Name?"

"Ahh, Anastasia Locke."

Nastia often remarked how friendly Americans were. Betty was a boorish exception.

She scowled, dragged her pudgy finger down the list, and snapped, "Ya ain't here."

"But you called this morning and spoke to my mother-in-law," Anastasia said.

"Sweets, I caint 'memba everybody I call. Look." She whipped the schedule around. "See, you ain't here. Gimme your name again."

"Anastasia Locke. L-O-C — "

"Do I look like I caint spell? You sound foreign. We don't take refugees. You got insurance?"

"Yes, I *am* a foreigner, and no, I do not have insurance."

"Yet," I interjected. "Anastasia's teachers' insurance kicks in Monday."

Betty glared at me. "That's three days off, buster. How ya gonna pay today?"

"Can't you move today's date ahead three days so the insurance will cover it?"

"No can do. We got ethics."

"Sure you do," I replied, putting on a phony grin and pulling out my checkbook. "A check?"

"Make it to Ginsburg PC for two hundred bucks and give me a credit card in case it bounces."

"Bounces?" I acted so flabbergasted I could barely scribble. "It's good as gold."

"Sure it is. Son, you got a bad case of the clevers, just gimme the check and grab a seat."

Anastasia shot me a skeptical glance. She knew what we had in the checking account and that I got paid at month's end. She didn't know of America's friendly Pay Day Advance bandits, opened holidays and weekends to rescue the impoverished for a mere forty percent vig.

I finished writing the check, handed it to Betty along with my Master Card, and we turned, me mumbling over my shoulder, "'Away you scullion!'"

Anastasia head cocked. "*Scullion?*"

"Childhood poetry lessons from *Henry the Fourth*."

"No *Baba Yaga* for you?"

I shook my head. "Would my Mom waste time on witch tales with Willie around?"

"Never!"

We took seats in the waiting room, far from Betty. A dozen older couples, looking like zombies, leafed through tattered magazines.

Anastasia looked preoccupied and grim and needed an escape.

I said, "I hate holidays, help nosedives."

She said, "Think that's why Ginsburg hired such a nasty woman?"

"Probably. The world's full of mean, embittered, petty bastards like Betty. They inflate their self-esteem by stomping on others. They're nobodies locked in dead-end jobs who affirm themselves by being nasty because you need them. Betty is so aware of being a nobody, it's soured her. I'd bet her husband split years ago; she's raising the kids alone, and she's always worked lousy jobs. If I were King of the World, I'd roam my kingdom incognito, give gold to people friendly to me, and round up all the snotty checkout-clerks, receptionists, Help

Desk workers, and ship them to Parris Island for a year of basic training."

"Betty giving me crap to show her power over me makes her feel good about herself?"

"I think so. Dad disagrees. He says it's more pervasive as many of his peers are disgruntled with their career choices. They earned Ph.D.s in esoteric subjects no one gives a hoot about, and they think they're Einsteins. They express their disgust by turning radical leftists to tear down the system that feeds them. Dad may be right. But in Betty's case, I'd guess Ginsburg hired her for the same reason I hire druggies and dropouts."

"The fifty-three thousand Disney employ, anyone who can smile?"

"Which leaves zilch unemployment in Central Florida and employers scraping the bottom of the barrel for dregs then hiring guys like big Kahuna to keep them in line."

"There's no deterrent like fear," Nastia said. "That's the Soviet Way."

We picked up old magazines with name and address labels snipped off. Nastia thumbed through last Christmas's issue of *Southern Living;* me, *Newsweek* and Bush's February 27, 1991, speech, 'Kuwait is Liberated, Iraq's Army is Defeated.' My war. Ten minutes later, a nurse in a starched white uniform with a nametag, Janice Chicoine, swooped into the room. She smiled broadly and sang out, "Lockes" in a chainsaw voice as piercing as a drill sergeant, probably from interacting with the deaf. Janice was a jolly woman of medium height, shoulder-length pepper-and-salt hair, and a pleasant manner. We stood, and she stepped between us, hooked our arms, and escorted us into the inner sanctum.

"Glad you could make it, Troy," she said to me in her gravelly voice.

"A nuclear strike couldn't have kept me away," I replied.

After a few steps down a long hall, Janice dropped my arm and guided Anastasia into an alcove and onto a vintage Fairbanks scale. "Slip off those gorgeous sandals, dear. Here, let me hold your purse."

"That scale's old enough to have been built by Thaddeus," I said.

Janice shot me a befuddled look.

"Thaddeus Fairbanks. He launched Fairbanks Scale in Saint Johnsbury, Vermont in 1830."

Janice's eyes sparkled. "Doctor Ginsburg did buy the antique during his medical school days."

"Dartmouth?"

"How'd you know?" Janice said, tapping the indicator to the right. She had long graceful fingers glistening with clear-polished nails. She tapped it right some more.

"A gang of us visited the Saint Jay museum the day we got iced out of Killington."

"Smart," Janice said. "Ice-skiing breaks arms. Your sandals are darling, Anastasia."

"There're comfortable, too," Anastasia said.

"They look it," Janice said and noted Anastasia's weight on a buff-colored chart. "I'd love some; mine are so frillless. Ski much, Troy?"

"Alas," I lamented, "not since I was spoken for."

Janice laughed. What a bubbling sweetheart she was, keeping two conversations going. She had used one of the few English words with three identical successive consonants and made a ripple-free shift in hortatory mood that set us both at ease.

Anastasia tried to read the chart upside down and couldn't — a skill I perfected in the army. Janice noticed and said, "One-twenty-nine."

"Up," Anastasia said, stepping off the scales and sliding red-painted toes into red, strappy sandals.

"Doctor's ready." Janice ushered us down the hall to the end, swung open the corner office door, and announced, "The Lockes, Doctor Ginsburg."

Ginsburg's chamber was striking. There was an oak floor almost hidden by a buttery Oriental rug, mahogany paneling, oil landscapes in gilded frames (one, an original Bierstadt), leathery smells, and a view of the parking lot and wedge of I-4. Ginsburg, standing stiffly erect at the window, turned. He was an olive-skinned man, as thin and short as a racehorse jockey, dressed in fashions finest.

"Hello," he said brusquely with the slightest touch of wintry smile. He glanced from a medical file in his hand to sixty grand of Rolex Pearlmaster on his thin wrist as if late for a T-off. We nodded and mumbled salutations, in dazed preoccupation with the upcoming verdict,

"I'm *Doctor* Ginsburg, a board-certified, surgical, oncologist," he said to me through perfectly shaped teeth so remarkably white they gleamed like a new bathtub. His fingernails gleamed, too.

I tried to smile and considered bowing. Was he so insecure he had to highlight his CV? I considered retorting, *I'm Restaurateur Locke, burger boss at the apex of a local totem pole*," but gave him a terse, "Troy Locke," instead.

Dr. Ginsburg's manner was as cold, impersonal, and as grim-faced as a death row inmate and in stark conflict to his affable appearance and the welcoming aura of his office. He looked like a bug-eyed, cricket-sized barker outside a Bourbon Street bordello. His kinky hair, unkempt, fell over lemon-yellow, Mickey Mouse glasses that matched his cotton shirt accented with wide, blue stripes and French cuffs. He wore a silk, pink paisley tie with fat commas of chartreuse, gray slacks with razor-sharp creases, and polished Italian loafers with tassels. When you're around death and dying all day, it must make you dress like a court jester.

Ginsburg motioned at two client chairs in front of his enormous desk, and we sat.

He looked up and almost smiled. He must have worn braces to have such perfect teeth. He jutted out his chin and leveled his intent gaze at Anastasia.

"You have cancer," he said matter-of-factly, like a dentist saying you have a cavity.

"Akh!" Anastasia gasped. A deep frown drew her eyebrows together. She leaned forward from the waist, breathing hard and rapidly, stunned by confirmation of the suspected news.

In that instant, everything in the charged atmosphere changed. Everything seemed to stand out distinctly and vastly important in the hypersensitive, surreal moment. All my automatic responses became acts of will. I felt as if I could take nothing for granted. I wasn't conscious of how Ginsburg's words hit me. It felt like it was forever before I slowly came out of it before I felt my toes dig into the carpet, my jaw went kerplunk. I reached for Anastasia's hand and tried to speak, but I couldn't find my voice. I felt dizzy. Sick. Guillotined. I wondered why the tactless son of a bitch was still alive. The pronouncement cancer didn't ring true. Cancer was for old people, not healthy young women. Ginsburg's three words, "*You have cancer*," would change our lives forever. Oh, I'd tried to accept the idea of cancer, had half expected it, actually, but could not. Hearing Anastasia had a malignancy eating her alive was so onerous, so dreadful, so traumatizing it was inconceivable to grasp, impossible to accept.

I brushed Anastasia's cold arm with my fingertips. "Nastenka," I finally managed to murmur, "we'll get through this together."

She didn't respond.

"Look at me; I said, 'together.'"

Anastasia was in shock. Adrenaline was charging through her trembling body. When she did turn, she stared wide-eyed at me. She looked emaciated. Her vitality was gone; her face was as gray and deadened as a convalescent. Ginsburg's words had stripped life from her, stolen her lilt, her modulation, her color and left her eyes deep-set and as lifeless as ball bearings. Tiny lines appeared around her mouth. Snail-track tears ran down her cheeks.

I felt my face flush, shoulder muscles clench. I was furious. Furious at Ginsburg's shabby treatment, furious at cancer, furious with Nastia for not telling me. I wanted to leap over the desk, grab Ginsburg by his scrawny neck, and clobber the little bastard. The tactless son of a bitch was talking to my wife. I gripped the arms of the chair and fought with myself to shove that yearning away. I stared at my hairy calves, knobby ankles, and toe nails that needed cutting.

It seemed like hours but was probably just seconds when slowly, steadily, stoically, Anastasia's continence rebuilt. The animal panic in her face tempered to a stunned, boggled, bewildered look. She was scared speechless by the black hole that lay ahead of her. The muscles at her jaw hinge were clenched. A tic in her left eyelid fluttered. Without seeing me, she reached over and clamped fingernails into my arm above the elbow. The force of her clasp hurt. She stared at Ginsburg with the full-focus-concentration that made her such a great listener. The heat of it was visceral. When she concentrated on anything long enough it would smolder.

"I have cancer," she repeated, her face twisted in a gargoyle grin.

"Yes," Ginsburg said.

"I suspected it." Anastasia's voice quivered, but not much.

"I'm sure you did." Ginsburg slapped a film onto the wall view-box, flicked on a light, and pointed at a thin, white line a half-inch long. "There it is. I've got a surgery slot open Monday."

"Whoa!" Anastasia yelped. "I'm thinking about doing nothing."

Ginsburg's palms smacked the desk, shocked. "But you *must* want it out?!"

"I've lived with uncertainty all my life; why do you want to rush things now?"

"Most of my patients, when told they have cancer, consider it a death sentence and act."

"Well, I'm Russian, Doctor," Nastia countered. "I'm *not* hardwired to treat cancer as the beginning of the end or convinced it's urgent. Aren't there many kinds of cancer?"

"Oh, yes," he replied in a resonant voice. "Hundreds! Many simultaneously."

"So the word cancer should never be used as if it were one disease?"

"No, it's a limitation of language. Cancer is hundreds of heterogeneous diseases lumped together and defined by the growth and spread of cellular mutations. The dissimilar maladies affect various parts of the body, separately or simultaneously, but with one shared characteristic, the uncontrolled growth and spread of abnormal cells that invade and damage healthy tissue and organs."

"So what kind of cancer do I have?"

"Ductal carcinoma in situ, or DCIS.," he said. "A cluster of cancer cells in the milk duct." He illustrated by tapping the white line on the viewer of Nastia's left breast. It's common in eighty percent of women whose breast cancer starts with DCIS."

"I understand. But couldn't mine be a false positive?"

I straightened abruptly. She'd never used that term before.

"Sometimes in mammograms," Ginsburg said. "Never in a biopsy."

"Can't cancer be unpredictable, stabilize, and nothing happens," Nastia pushed on.

"There are many unknown progressions of DCIS that's noninvasive."

"Haven't many oncologists held that they've long over-treated slow-growing tumors?"

"Yes. But given your biopsy, mammogram, and ultrasound, the malignancy in your milk duct is confirmed; it should be removed immediately. And I think this — " he tapped on a faint, walnut-sized shadow — "is another tumor."

Anastasia flinched. "*A second tumor*! You never said anythi — "

"I didn't know." Ginsburg raised both hands as if defending himself. "Radiographic images reflect the ability of the tissue to impede the passage of X-rays. Like most young women, you have dense breast tissue, which make whiter images. The image of a breast composed of a predominance of fatty tissue is black, and that allows fibrous strands and glandular essentials to stand out — white against black. White flecks of calcified tissue can be easily diagnosed in fatty breasts." He tapped on the white spot. "These are easily missed in dense tissue."

"I see." Anastasia slumped back into the chair, hands dangling from the armrests. "I have dense breast tissue and, probably, *two* tumors. Would that explain this weighty feeling?" She sat up, placed her cupped right hand beneath her left breast. Her hand shook.

"You'd not mentioned a weightiness," Ginsburg said. "Describe it, please."

"It feels like something's yanking on my breast all the time." Anastasia's cupped hand formed a claw beneath her breast and yanked downward. "How big *are* the tumors?"

"The first is this tiny line—" he tapped the film— "the second may be this shadow and has grown to two centimeters. That might explain the sensation of weightiness."

"How fast did those grow?"

"Some double in size in weeks; some months; some years."

My heart was racing at their endless confabulate. I reached over, took Anastasia's hand, and laced our fingers together and prayed, *Get to the cure!*

Ginsburg picked up a file and studied it for a horrifying minute. His second tumor verdict settled around us like a black silk shroud. The news had rattled Anastasia. It had floored me. I am the emotional side of our marital equation, the partner who wears his feelings on his sleeves, the mouthy, out-spoken, shoot-from-the-hip side. Ginsburg's words went through me viscerally, shimmered along the nerve roots and jarred me as nothing had in my entire life as far back as memory reached. As a kid of six, I watched Anastasia devotedly practice her flute then her ballet moves singing: *plié, tendu, bouree, frappé, demi-pointe,* and *relvé,* until the toes of her slippers were bloodstained. She never complained. I'd see her bloody toes and fling myself on the couch like Raskolnikov, wondering, *why was she punishing herself so?*

Anastasia dropped my hand and twisted her wedding ring around and around. Her forehead shone with perspiration. What was she thinking? In the parking lot, looking at this mission-like building, I'd prayed Ginsburg would use the words Woody Allan calls the most beautiful in the English language: *It's benign.*

"Doctor," Anastasia said hesitatingly, "do you think both are … "

"Malignant? I'm positive of the first," he stated in a clear, Richter-scale revelation. "I won't know about the other, or others until I operate and perform more biopsies."

"*Others*!" She clenched my hand and sat unnaturally still. I watched her raise her eyes and fix on Ginsburg. In a hushed voice, barely audible, she repeated his assertion, "You're positive about the first, the second might be, and there may be others."

The reality of her suffering produced a flood of silent tears as Anastasia wept.

Ginsburg pushed a box of Kleenex across the desk. Anastasia took one and blew her nose. I took one and dabbed my eyes. Ginsburg straightened his cuffs.

"Pathologist's biopsies are conclusive. We'll have to wait to know about any other tumors."

Anastasia shivered. "How long have these *things* been growing inside me?"

"Six months or longer."

"Can you cut them out?"

"Surgery is our first line of defense. And" — he checked his surgery schedule — "I have a slot open early next week."

"Cut to cure," Anastasia concluded, regaining some composure. "I've read breast tumor surgery is trial and error and usually ends in radical mastectomies."

"Unfortunately, yes. For too long, heuristic shortcuts have been used, and the saga of breast cancer is more notable for iatrogenicity and expanding doctor knowledge than patient benefit. But we *are* learning, and after a generation, we're adapting and changing. There's a tendency in breast cancer today of fewer mastectomies and more lumpectomies."

"But you don't want to wait to operate?"

Ginsburg shook his head. "No."

I was perplexed by Ginsburg's verbosity. The word periphrasis came to mind, but I said nothing. Sometimes I'm guilty of verbal diarrhea, too. Words are the lifeblood of our species, helping to circulate thoughts, ideas, and dreams. They can nourish, soothe, cure, mend, and heal like medicine, but the wrong words can also wound, cut, and make us seethe. Nastia had said Ginsburg seemed kind, and what he lacked for in warmth he compensated for with sincerity. To me, the timbre of his voice was orotund and his message as impersonal as a Florida weatherman's describing another hurricane. Maybe his was a matter of survival. Ginsburg was a cancer surgeon. His job was to cut out tumors. He must not empathize too much with his patients. It might interfere with his cutting. He had to think of people under his knife as globs of meat. Sympathy would be a distraction. I wondered if he had testicular cancer if his attitude would change.

As for now, Anastasia needed me. I stood on quivering legs, placed one hand on her back, and knelt. As our foreheads touched, I set the other hand on one of her clenched knees and kissed away a salty tear with my lips.

"Nastusha," I said slowly, "everything will be okay," and then my voice picked up speed. "It *will* work. You'll see. I'll help." But in my heart, I didn't believe it. I knew Anastasia didn't buy it either. A cancer verdict is the worst news in the world.

She ignored me. "But, doctor, there's no pain. None." Her voice had demurred into the sad, halcyon tone of a Soviet who'd known nothing but a lifetime of misery and grief suffering. "It doesn't hurt even a little," she insisted. "And I know suffering."

I wanted to scream! Russians have lived with pain and anguish for a thousand years, from the intertribal slayings of Slav on Slav to Genghis Khan's brutal tyranny to three centuries of heartless rules by the Romanovs to the Bolshevik's bloody reign and the birth of Communism. Yes, Russians knew pain. And they never did anything to stop it. There had never been a people-power revolution, a Red Spring — even after the fall of Communism last summer. When Anastasia immigrated to America, all she wanted was a simple life, a decent job, happy marriage, and an absence of trouble with authorities. Not an unusual dream but all too often an unusual attainment. She loved fresh raspberries on her oatmeal in November, shopping in supermarkets with overloaded shelves, zipping on a superhighway to Ormond Beach weekends, landing a high school math job at thirty times the money she earned in Tver, and life devoid of spies reporting her every move to party bosses. And yet Anastasia never linked the dots to ask why Russians continued to suffer in silence.

Ginsburg cleared his throat. "I understand your breast doesn't hurt, Mrs. Locke. Cancerous cysts rarely do. But they *must* be removed immediately." He shuffled some papers.

"*How immediately?*" Anastasia inquired.

"Monday morning. You'll check in Sunday afternoon."

Anastasia snapped her head in disbelief. "In *two days?*"

Ginsburg nodded. "Yes. During the lumpectomy, we'll biopsy the second cyst. If it's malignant I'll remove it and look for others."

"Under local anesthesia?"

He smiled. His pearly teeth shone. "Oh, no, to remove the breast lump and biopsy the second cyst, you'll be administered a general anesthesia. Depending on the type of cancer and amount of tissue expunged, the procedure could take several hours."

"*Hours!* I had no idea." Anastasia looked puzzled.

"You'll be started on intravenous chemotherapy before discharge Wednesday with radiation beginning in two months to reduce the risk of a recurrence."

"Chemotherapy, radiation, both now?"

"Chemotherapy as an adjuvant treatment first, yes. After the initial treatment, there'll be eight sessions of chemotherapy, one every two weeks, then radiation."

"Does that means losing my hair and getting deathly sick and tired?"

Anastasia fingered her long soft tendrils the color and texture of corn silk. Since childhood, she'd taken great pride in her thick locks of shiny pale-blonde hair. People thought she bleached it and were surprised to discover she did not.

"There're many drugs used in chemotherapy," Ginsburg monotoned. "They're determined by the type of cancer cells being eradicated. For you, we'll use Cisplatin and Cytoxan. Most women lose their hair during chemotherapy, but hair grows back. Some drugs are more toxic than others, and all people react to them differently. Frankly, most women suffer nausea, fatigue, low blood count and get very sick. But I'll prescribe medications to help with that. Also, Cisplatin and Methotrexate have little effect on fertility." Cancer 101.

I wondered how many times Ginsburg had given the speech.

"I understand," Anastasia said charily and suspiciously. "Will I keep my breast?"

Ginsburg's eyes rested on the oak floor. "I won't know until I operate, biopsy the second cyst, determine if there are other cysts or if cancer has metastasized."

"So I won't know anything until I wake up?"

"I'm afraid not." Business-as-usual.

I was furious as hell and wanted to do a Krakatoa on Ginsburg's snout. He was talking to my wife. When someone makes your loved one suffer, he must be struck. I took a few deep breaths and realized I was angrier at cancer than the doctor. Angry for what it was doing to Anastasia's life, our lives, and not irate at the messenger for bearing the dreadful news. Most of us wander through life with an unknown death some distant tomorrow. Anastasia now had a good idea what might kill her someday. I worried if a cure might happen, now, in 1991. For a while, Anastasia might seem okay, but cancer often recurs, and when it metastasizes to vital organs, it will kill her. I tried hard not to weep and watched an image of Roseanne Roseannadanna flash across my silver screen. Gilda Radner was one of my favorite comics. She had died of cancer two years ago. I'd heard about it and wanted to read her book, *It's Always Something,* written just before her last curtain call.

In the hushed office, I said, "What about this new cancer drug available soon, taxol?"

"Taxol has had remarkable success," Ginsburg enthused.

"My Dad mentioned it at lunch," I said. "He said phase two trials were complete, and the drug will be approved next year."

Ginsburg sat back in his chair and folded his hands over his flat stomach. "Taxol appears to be nearly through the FDA's decades-long approval process. Presently, scientists are investigating over nine hundred other remedies, including ablating tumors with microwaves, some are in clinical trials. Remember, though, cancer is not a single disease like a kidney stone. It *is* insidious. There can be dozens of different cancers within a single tumor fueled by numerous, often redundant, genetic anomalies. These aberrant molecules may contain fifty to one hundred different mutations that require an equal number of different treatments. When a drug is discovered that blocks one cancer, it is exhilarating, but it's only a first step. Think of trying to stop all the traffic on Interstate Four with a roadblock at the intersection of Fairbanks and Park Avenue. You'd stop some of the six-lane there with an artery roadblock, but only those cars coming from downtown Winter Park going onto I-Four. The rest, those drivers coming from Daytona or Tampa or Gainesville, would breeze through."

Anastasia said, "So my cancer cannot be stopped with one drug."

"Probably not," Ginsburg said. "It means two women can have 'breast cancer' and yet have very different diseases at the molecular level. Similar treatments can result in one being effectual and the other powerless. Still, taxol is the most promising drug I've ever seen. The FDA is slated to approve it as part of a comprehensive chemotherapy treatment next year in conjunction with carbolate treatment. But until then — " he threw up his hands — "you can't buy it."

Astonished, I blurted out, "*Anywhere?*"

Ginsburg almost grinned. "It's a big world, Mister Locke. Taxol's been studied in Europe and China, and they're ahead of us. But for now, no, you cannot purchase taxol in America."

"But I don't understand," I said. "Science has known of its unique ability to kill cancer for three decades. Are you saying Anastasia has no right to help herself? That makes the FDA the judge, jury, and executioners of women desperate for it."

"That's a political question. But it's all we can do for now. I recommend you two go home and get some rest. A cancer diagnosis is difficult. Mrs. Locke is facing daunting treatments."

Anastasia sobbed. I tightened my arm around her back.

She stared at the doctor with tears streaming down her cheeks, gulped and snuffled. "You mean the chemo?"

Ginsburg pushed out his chin again. "Chemotherapy *and* radiation, yes."

Then, out of nowhere, a low, mournful "Ahaaa," emanated from deep within Anastasia's chest, a guttural wail, more animal than human. A woeful lowing. A heifer herded into a blood-splattered abattoir. A sound without inflection, without gesture, a sound so simple and so complex it linked the timeless efficacy of death's anguish and a supplicant's imploration for mercy.

I shuddered and squeezed her hand hard. I closed my eyes, bowed my head, and pressed a knuckled fist against my teeth, trying to think of something bolstering to say. "I'll find some taxol for you, Anastasia," I vowed. "You will be okay. Say it; *I will be okay.*"

Anastasia frowned at me and started moving her hand in slow circles over her belly, struggling to choke back tears that overwhelmed her. "Don't you understand, Troy?" she sobbed. "You can't make me okay? No one can. I'll *never* be okay. Those treatments will wreck me." Her eyes narrowed with a concentration and intensity I'd never seen. "And it *will* kill our baby."

I gasped. Her words lasered through me and struck my soul. "*Our baby?*" I closed my eyes and saw the tiny embryo, incapable of giving her a kick, but with the potential to, tunneling into the uterine wall, blood flowing nutrients and oxygen to it. When I opened my eyes, Doctor Ginsburg had sprung up from behind his desk, his nifty complacency visibly shaken.

"You're pregnant, Mrs. Locke?" he blurted.

Anastasia wiped tears from her eyes with the back of her hand. "I'm three weeks late. I've never been late in my life. I think so, yes."

Ginsburg stepped around his desk. "That'd explain the difficulty seeing the other tumor. Pregnancy causes vast hormonal changes in a woman's body. High levels of estrogen engorge the breasts and make them tender, lumpy, and challenging to map, often obscuring early cancer."

"But if I *am* pregnant could the mammogram have hurt my baby?"

"Oh, no," Ginsburg said. "You had a lead apron over your uterus, and mammograms emit small doses of radiation. Yours was focused far from the fetus." He straightened his cuffs, did that push-out thing with his chin some more, and returned to his chair. "There are no reports of fetal harm in the literature attributed to mammograms."

"Regardless, Doctor," Anastasia said, raising her hand to emphasize the point, "I will not, repeat, *will not* have radiation for nine months. Is that clear?"

"Crystal clear," Ginsburg said. "But I'd strongly advise you to reconsider. You're young with years ahead to have children. There's always the risk of a relapse and potential side effects of the estrogen."

"*No radiation*," Anastasia insisted.

"Fine. And what about the lumpectomy Monday?"

"What will anesthesia do to my baby?"

Doctor Ginsburg looked so concerned he appeared human. "There's slight risk to either of you. I think you'll both be fine. The literature supports this extensively."

Anastasia looked at me.

I hunched my shoulders. "Sounds safe."

"Okay, doctor," she said. "A question: can I give cancer to my baby?"

Surprisingly, Ginsburg smiled. "No. Cancer cannot be transferred from mother to child."

"How about all those chemicals in chemotherapy?"

"That's another matter. Those chemicals will enter your blood stream and be transferred to the fetus. They'll have the identical effect on both of you. However, because of the large size of your tumors and the fact you could be in your first trimester, your primary goal must be to control cancer. Chemotherapy could be withheld for nine weeks, until your fetus's internal organs, currently undergoing rapid development, develop sufficiently to proceed. In fact, at *this* time, I would insist you wait. Chemo next week would put your baby at great risk. Studies of late-pregnancy cycles indicate few birth defects or stillborns from later chemotherapy."

"That's too iffy!" Anastasia snapped. "Why not inject the tumor with chemo poisons and not my whole body?"

"We're incapable of doing that today, but it's an idea that's being studied."

"So cut these damn tumors out of me," she directed, pointing at her left breast. "And if I am pregnant, I'll wait until *after* the baby is born to start chemo and radiation. That's final!"

"Mrs. Locke," Ginsburg said, "I implore you to reconsider. Delaying chemotherapy and radiation for nine months will exacerbate the chance of recurrence, hasten the growth of any remaining cancer cells, and put your life at great risk. I do not recommend you postpone treatment. If you wait eight weeks to begin, you'll place both of you at less risk and the baby probably would survive without any serious defects."

"Let me understand you," Anastasia said. "If I have chemotherapy next week, it will probably kill or disfigure my baby. If I wait on chemotherapy and radiation eight weeks, it will be of little risk to us but might result in birth defects. If I have no chemotherapy or radiation for nine months, it might kill me. Is that about right?" She looked hard at me and then at him.

Ginsburg nodded. "Those are the choices."

"Lousy choices," she said dismissively.

Anastasia's pregnancy was good news and horrible — it left me feeling hopeless. I placed a hand on her stomach and said, "We'll beat this, Nastusha, I swear to God we will. And you *will* be fine." As soon as I said it, I knew how dumb it was. Guaranteeing someone's future was as futile as trying to undo the past. You can't give destiny the finger.

Anastasia's eyes zeroed in on mine. She clutched my arm so hard I wanted to yell.

"Didn't you hear me?" she snarled. "Didn't you hear him?"

She sounded like she was talking to a moron. She was. But I did what came naturally and larded up my response. "I heard you both, but Ginsburg doesn't know you, and he sure as hell doesn't know me. I'm a happily-married, Russian-born, father-to-be in love with a wife who I'm willing to do anything for."

Anastasia stared at me in fading disbelief. A faint smile crossed her lips. Determination slowly built behind her pale blue eyes. The muscles in her jaw started working again. She rolled her shoulders back and sat up straight. She cleared her throat, in full control again. Maybe she believed me. Maybe she didn't. But, regardless, she had made a decision.

"A final question, doctor," she said, "how much does a lumpectomy cost?"

"Surgery, hospital?" Ginsburg replied. "About six thousand dollars. Have you insurance?"

"Not yet," Anastasia said. "My teaching job starts this Monday, November twenty-fifth."

"Orange County School District?"

"Yes."

Ginsburg looked at me. "Will your insurance cover her?"

I shook my head. "It barely covers me."

Ginsburg sat back in his chair, cradled his chin in a palm, and closed his eyes. After a minute, he yanked open a desk drawer, took out his Surgery Planner.

"Let's do this; I'll call the hospital and put off your lumpectomy for three weeks until Monday, December sixteenth. That'll give you time to get your feet on the ground in your teaching job. By then your insurance will be in force, and you can take three or four days off to — "

"Hold on!" Anastasia raised both hands and stopped him mid-sentence. "If you scheduled the lumpectomy for Friday afternoon December twentieth, I'd only have to miss a half-day of work; the next week is Christmas break."

"Of course, good thinking, and that will give you ten days to get rested and back on your feet." Ginsburg slapped his desk with both hands. "Consider it done."

"Let's go home," Anastasia said to me and stood.

"Great idea," I said.

As I said that, the démarche became clear. I knew what I must do. For twenty-two years, my life had been a long arc of domination, a yo-yo with someone else pulling the string, winding and rewinding me, scheduling my life. Trumpet lessons, ski lessons, AP courses at Watauga High, college visits. Colby was my first choice in life. Even after Desert Storm, joblessness drove me to a manager's job at McDees, not a free choice. Nowhere in all that programmed life had I ever fulfilled my sense of self and done what I wanted to do. I now had a mission. Like Lochinvar, my white steed waited in the stable, armor heaped in the corner, lance leaning against the wall. I would suit up, tie Nastia's scarf about my neck, and gallop off to save my maiden. It meant putting my chimerical restaurant dreams on hold — hell, McDees was not exactly a path to riches to fund my chain of Mexican restaurants. I'd throw everything aside and scour the planet for taxol. Legitimate or not. No matter the cost. I would wage an all-out battle to save the lives of my wife and child. Only the Mavericks of the world get things done.

I stood and hugged Anastasia. She looked resolute but felt frail. I lifted her chin, looked into her pale blue eyes glassy with fear and kissed her lips. We turned. Arm-in-arm we walked to the door. I turned and said, "Thanks, Doc."

He looked up. "Call the hospital on Thursday the nineteenth for admission instructions."

"Okeedoekee," I said, using a Dad word and my mind jumped to my parents. I wondered about that Chinese taxol he'd mentioned.

In the reception area, Betty waved my Master Card.

I took it from her and gave her my 32-tooth smile. She scowled and stayed silent, nary a *Good luck!* to Anastasia, who needed to be with friends and family, people who had known her and loved her for years. Unlike Russian extended families who stay put, the average American household moves every three years and infrequently visit relatives. Shoptalk, electronic gadgets, and childish jokes with people you've known five minutes have replaced heartfelt conversation. It leaves us with few obligations and emotional entanglements. We join clubs, have fun, make new friends, discard them, and move on. Maybe we should move back to North Carolina to be with family and friends, use the cancer center at Watauga Medical Center, and work at the McDonalds in Boone. Blowing Rock would be a better place to live while Anastasia underwent treatment, and Mom would love to nurse Anastasia back to health and spoil a grandkid.

But the Fates had other plans.

***

SIX

Home after the Verdict: A New and Welcomed Discovery
November 22, 1991

Outside Ginsburg's Oncology Center, dazzling rays of late afternoon sun slanted through palm fronds, littering the scorched pavement with slivers of light and shadows of swords that beaded my brow with sweat and brightened highlights in Anastasia's hair. Wind gusts skittered dried leaves across the parking lot. There was a taste of rain in the clammy air though none had fallen. In the West, a tropical disturbance had pushed in from the Gulf to deposit an anvil cloudbank over Clearwater promising moisture that a whisper of breeze was pushing our way, a rain-engine to break the heat wave. There was the distant hum of expressway traffic. Lightening zigzags shadowed faint grumbles of thunder, guaranteeing relief, and chasing snowbirds off the beaches. In the thick hot air, I felt as if I were suffocating, needing to breathe in more air than I had a capacity for, but I said nothing. Anastasia didn't seem to notice.

The inside of the car was an oven. Sweat stung my eyes. The seats burned, but Anastasia didn't seem to notice that either. She sat wordless and rigid, an automaton clenched in clinched arms, radiating a bilious silence. i looked at her slender waist and left breast that tumors were invading. It is said rust never sleeps, but cancer is worse. Rust encroaches flake by flake in a fender well, but it can be chipped off. Cancer hides like a monster lurking beneath the bed devouring all from within.

Backing out of the parking space, we heard faint peeps. Anastasia placed her hand atop mine atop the shifter. I stopped and followed her eyes. In the overhead palm, a tiny Macaw head popped out of its hidey-hole and looked around for its mother. Mama Macaw, perched on a nearby frond, vigilantly stood guard. Daddy Macaw was out hunting bugs. We paused to watch baby Macaw fluff his feathers to remove sawdust. It drifted down, and the baby turned around to chat with his Mom. Sweet love between mother and newborn.

"I'm living in the *here and now* from now on," Anastasia declared. "Enthralled with birds, approaching storms, and being giddy about the possibility of being pregnant. The world is too complex, Troy, and way too centered on the material. I've overlooked my spiritual, emotional, and psychological side. Doctors like Ginsburg are lost in the cacophony of science. They've drawn a scalpel line between what is real and what is unreal, between the tangible and the intangible, between the empirical and the spiritual. They've forgotten the pain, suffering, and emotions of patients. Much of what he said was just words describing facts, words that don't acknowledge the beliefs, pain, joy, sorrow, spirituality, and inner focus of what it means to be human."

"Impossible not to agree," I said and let out the clutch. "We should all be more in the here-and-now, fathom love, and inner needs. That's what it means to be human."

Anastasia smiled a rueful smile and left her hand on mine as I ran through the gears.

"Speaking of the here and now," I said, "let's start by finding a two-bedroom apartment."

Anastasia didn't respond, apparently lost in the dread of cancer.

Up and into I-4's snarl, I tried again, "Let's paint the second bedroom pink … or blue."

"Umm." Anastasia sat poised, sphinxlike; her stare fixed on a spot out there beyond Venus.

"Look at all these damn cars," I said, trying to engage her with a traffic report. "Tires yelping, horns braying, idiots cutting in and out, families hauling ass for motels before black sheets of rain hit these oil-slick roads."

"Umm."

A traffic report didn't work. Her stare remained fixed, her response nil. I downshifted to fourth gear, tromped down, slid it into fifth, and pulled into the fast lane. At seventy mph, my left arm felt like it was in a blast furnace. Anastasia's hair became a snaky riot. She remained silent.

"Let's call your Mom as soon as we get home, tell her she may be a grandmother," I said.

"Umm," Anastasia equivocated.

Neither speed nor a call to her mom budged her to speak. Usually, when Nastia dropped into a voiceless trance, she was brooding about the Soviet Union, homesick, but never for long. As soon as she dwelled on living there again, she realized her delight in living in America. Dad says it's the Russians' conviction of their metaphysical inequality that has numbed their senses. He says it stems from their turbulent, thousand-year history of rule by repressive troglodytes and Neanderthals who plumbed the vast empire with murders and Gulags and created a mutant race of introspective subservient fixated on death and dying. Mom agrees. She thinks Nastia still sees the world from that glum perspective, and, when you factor in Nastia's innate despondency over her cancer verdict, the result is a horrifying trip through Dante's *Inferno*.

I turned off at our exit and stopped at a red light. A noisy, under-aged, carload of sun-bleached, tank-topped, beer-guzzling surfers pulled alongside. The steely-eyed driver gunned the engine: *bruuum, bruuum, bruuum.* He twisted the wheel ferociously without removing his hands. He appeared drunk or lobotomized. Probably thought he was piloting the spaceship *Enterprise* and needed the radio cranked up so Spock could hear it. His high-decibel racket set my tinnitus ringing, but it jarred Anastasia from her daze, and for that I was thankful.

"That asshole driving was in one of my classes last week!" she shouted above the din.

"You subbed at a school for the deaf?!"

She smiled, and I blasted the horn. Kirk looked over, recognized Anastasia, and waved. I made an exaggerated twisting motion with my hand. He spun the knob. The racket stopped.

Anastasia started to say something, kissed me instead, and then said, "I'm sorry, Troy, my head's so full of black clouds I can't think straight. Cancer growing inside you is the worst thing that could happen to anyone. The seconds tick by and you know you're being eaten alive; you're both a powerless victim and wary observer, watching as your body tries to become a corpse. I'm trying to think deep thoughts about life and dreams, but I'm on a collision course with destiny. I hate to focus on death. I mean, I know we're mortal, but we all push it off and prefer to dwell on caviar and champagne. Death is too bleak to face. And what if I *am* pregnant? What about my job? Will they fire me for missing work? Will I be able to work? For how long? I want to believe in God, His mercy, and goodness, but this insidious growth is strangling my spirituality."

"Or," I said, lightening up, "as Dad would say, 'empiricism is trumping your transcendentalism.' Nastenka, all of us want life to stay fixed, but it won't. To live is to endure change. Life is unconcerned and uncaring. To make sense of it, though, I begin by confronting dilemmas head-on. That's step number one."

Anastasia shifted in her seat to face me. The traffic light changed. Captain Kirk screeched off, zipped through the next red light, and dodged two DOT trucks. I stopped. The county trucks idled roughly and spewed smog. Six beefy men, leaning on long-handled shovels and five-foot pry bars, discussed a bent guardrail.

"So where's the beginning for me?" Anastasia asked, looking at me hopefully.

"We're Russians, raised by a state that owned and directed everything like a queen bee."

"*Tak* — So?"

"So the Soviet state gave us lousy jobs, poor food, dirty water, closet-sized apartments, and inadequate medical care. It taught us life is random and citizens were the state's property."

"What are you saying?"

"Listen to the echoes of history."

"You mean Communists don't value human life?"

"Bingo!" I drummed my fingers on the wheel impatiently. At the guardrail, the DOT conversation had gotten heated, voices raised, arms flayed. Perhaps a decision was about to be hatched, and traffic would flow.

"Soviets citizens exist to further state's wishes," I said. "The reverse of America's view."

Anastasia said spitefully, "And that indoctrination starts early. Our elementary school walls were plastered with pictures of eight kids killed during World War Two. All the teachers praised them for throwing their bodies on German machine guns: *They'd helped save Mother Russia!* For eight years, we listened to that story every day. We memorized their names and sang them anthems. The teachers swore us to follow their example: *Be martyrs, children. Sacrifice your lives for Mother Russia.*"

"Not me," I said, astonished. "If our government tried that, rallies would form, and lawyers would materialize like gunslingers at high noon filing class-action lawsuits. When I was a kid, we slid through class, played cowboys and Indians, and watched TV, learning how to smuggle drugs, rob banks, murder bad guys, and get our laundry twice as white."

The DOT guys decided the guardrail could be bent back in shape. They jimmied the pry bar behind the curved rail. Two public servants pushed; two tugged; two pried. They couldn't bend the steel, picked up their signs, boarded the trucks, and headed for lunch. Traffic moved.

"The Soviet mindset is why Americans discovered taxol. Soviets haven't uncovered one mystery that will prolong life, relieve pain, or make life enjoyable. Imagine this; it took them until nineteen sixty-nine, the month Armstrong walked on the moon, to introduced toilet paper to the Soviet people. China's part of that screwy world. But those billion people have a six-thousand-years-old society with strong family bonds, and kids respect their elders. Because of those ties and their love money, they've developed taxol, beating us to the taxol bazaar."

"I hope you're right," Anastasia said.

"I know I am," I said. "Hey, there's a Wells Fargo Bank, and over there — " I pointed — "a Bank America. Let's go open checking and credit card accounts now."

And so we did. In thirty minutes that Friday afternoon, we'd each opened checking and credit card accounts were given temporary checks and had four, six-thousand-dollar, lines-of-credit.

Feeling flush, I wheeled into the apartment complex and parked far from the Live Oak alive with robins. Fat raindrops splattered down as I raised the top and we jumped out of the Beemer. It started pouring as we sprinted for the stairs. Leftovers barked a greeting, tail wagging like a metronome as we yanked off clothes.

"Relax, boy," I said, patting him affectionately. "We're home."

He barked once more to show he had a mind of his own, licked my toes, and sunk his needle-sharp, baby teeth into the leash, tugging it off the hook. He had a fire hydrant to water, robins to flush, and squirrels to chase, rain or shine. I slid on flip-flops, leashed the mutt, and we bee-lined outside. Despite the downpour, Leftovers saw with his nose what I couldn't see with my eyes and scampered for a live oak. He went on point at a moss-bearded swag. The short, tapered head and blunt whiskered muzzle of a gray squirrel appeared. Their flexible ankle joints rotate, and the rodent descended head first, hind feet splayed flat against the trunk. Its large, bright eyes conveyed an alert demeanor. He flicked his bushy tail and Leftover howled. The rodent leaped, bound along a branch, and disappeared. With prey banished, Leftovers remembered his mission, sniffed the bushes for a particular scent, found the right spot, and hoisted a leg. We returned soaked. Leftovers did a series of full-body trembles, sprinkling the entry. I stripped and toweled dry. Nastia had pulled out the hide-a-bed, sprawled across it, and buried her head in a pillow, sobbing and exuding dread.

I tossed my soggy clothes into the wicker hamper in the bathroom and lay down beside her. We talked. She wept. We clawed around during the warm late-afternoon glow in a darkroom of fear, clinging to each other in the murky shadows, two lovers, one fated for a premature blast-off if I was not successful.

"Having cancer is like being smothered by a poisonous haze," she said.

"I know," I said. "But not for long. I'll find you the taxol."

Cancer stayed with us. The unshakable miasma was dread and sadness, an occlusion that never lifted, a smoky shroud of amorphous shapes that kept us afloat on fear and moving like mindless globs of protoplasm sleepwalking through space. We did what we had to do. We drank when thirsty. Ate when hungry. Cuddled when frightened.

After a while, a subtle change began to happen. Her weeping died. Hysterics ceased. Self-pity stopped. We slipped off our underwear, slid between sheets, and clung to each other. Kisses grew intent. Bodies became instruments of insistent needs. Grieving souls left anguish behind. Though our world was as full of the black holes as a Dostoevsky saga, our clasping gave way to the ancient muffled sounds of sweaty bodies thudding. With hips locked, breathing fevered, yips convulsed with the primal effort of oohs and aahs and slick-bodies-grapplings, the prying, twisting, hunger-to-fulfill that came out of Africa with the hairy primates a billion hours ago found us.

Later, slackened in the post-conjugal glow, I stroked Nastia's silky back moist from exertions. "You gotta love Mother Nature's way of protecting her kiddies from mental breakdowns."

Anastasia turned over, smiled tenderly and danced her fingertips through the slick, damp hair of my underbelly. "She's one smart Lady."

I kissed her forehead. "With no doctorate from Moscow State University."

"That kinda stuff we girls know intuitively."

Leftovers whined. I reached down and scooped him up. He cuddled between us, got up, circled three times, and lay down in the same spot. Sighing mightily, he closed his big brown eyes.

"When Ginsburg told me about the cyst," Anastasia whispered, fingers combing my belly hair thoughtlessly, "all I wanted to do was lash out and get even with the world. I blamed Mom's cooking, God's lack of interest, and you for hauling me to that smoke-filled nightclub, Zebra."

"Most cancers are no one's fault."

"I know. Our bodies have seventy trillion cells, and the plasma membrane around each of them has thousands of swinging doors that let in water and food for cells to function. Similar building blocks, doing many different things depending on programming make up all those cells. Some carry oxygen. Some defend against invading bacteria. Some convert sunlight into food by photosynthesis." She tapped my manhood. "And some transmit signals from wandering eye to pea-brain to the twenty-first finger."

"You got it."

"Each of those seventy trillion cells has a nucleus and twenty-three pairs of chromosomes telling the cells what to do, when to do it, and what to be. Then mutations come along. Genetic defects stop protein being crafted or create proteins that should be destroyed. Cells usually detect mutations and fix them or signal them to die. But if defective cells live, they can become cancerous. Troy, I know all that stuff. Accepting it is another thing."

"Taxol is your solution," I vowed. "And while I find your taxol, you stay mentally and physically strong. Never give up on yourself, or the baby, or me."

She took my hands and kissed them. "I won't, Troy. We're Russians; we will persevere."

I held her face gently between my palms and kissed her lips. "That's my Nastenka. Your God-given hope, grounded in perseverance, is one of the reasons I love you so."

Anastasia brightened. "That same hope kept our grandpas alive in the Gulag: The conviction they could change the world despite their horrors, the hope that gave them the will to survive."

"That, to me, is the God's presence in mankind," I said and rolled Anastasia's full length aboard me. Mother Nature rose to the occasion, and we rejoined.

"Like your presence in me?" Anastasia said.

"I'm but her handmaiden," I breathed.

It was an earthy remark but one that did not leave me languishing in anguish or submerged in angst. I enjoyed every delightful minute of the romp. Later, we heard another thunderstorm arrive to freshen the day. I shut off the air conditioner, opened the window beside the bed, and re-closed the curtains, fluttering in the cool, moist air. We heard desultory bird chirps in the massive live oaks, probably robins. Pigeons cooed and ate junk food in the parking lot. Then, a strange, wild optimism, like hope at the bottom of Pandora's Box, made us giggle and chortle and laugh long and hard and unexpectedly. Our fright took flight, replaced by a giddy lightheadedness, a springboard to creativity, a rise from the depths of depression, and the vague contour of an idea took shape as we drifted off to sleep.

As if on cue, evening rain pounded down hard at six o'clock and washed away our fear like beach sand off a boardwalk. Our panicked passions transformed into tangles of giddy emotions. And wherever He hides that storage bin of bright ideas, whenever there is enough worry conjoined with the right amount of laughter, there comes a *voilá* moment. The mist clears and a passageway through life's underworld is exposed. There is no trace of rationality. You're certain that life is, indeed, the *riddle wrapped in a mystery inside an enigma* the chubby cigar-smoker said it was. Search wherever you will for as long as you want, you'll find no explanation.

You know there's no vile-purposed Designer there dispensing evil and wreaking havoc on five billion bodies hurtling through space, all bearing petty thoughts and wistful dreams in lives spent sailing zigzags and going nowhere. You realize you are alone in the struggle. You know we all seek solutions to postpone the certitude of death. Most of us outsource our cures to doctors never to be confronted, while we partake of life's banquet of champagne and caviar.

Anastasia stirred. Leftovers groaned. He jumped off the bed, his toenails ticking on linoleum. He trotted to his dish for a snack and crunched noisily.

I stroked Anastasia's long soft hair. "Remember, I *will* find the taxol for you."

"I know you will," she said, snuggling. "And remember, I'm a survivor."

"Me too."

"Remember, in your quest, you speak Russian with an American accent, lover."

"You bet your ass. And you speak English with a Russian accent. Speaking of ass — "

She raised up on an elbow. "What if I say no?"

"I'd accept it."

"Good. Your goddess is pooped from making plans not to die some Gandhi-death, quietly and passively as so many cancer victims do." Anastasia referred to Mahatma Gandhi's doctrine of Satyagraha, the passive resistance inspiration he borrowed from Tolstoy.

"I know you won't," I said.

"You said you'd find me taxol, and I believe you. But remember you've been Americanized. Cocky Americans piss people off. It's their innate aversion to servility. Russians don't have it. You're cursed with it, lover. Men like Ginsburg don't affect me the way they do you."

"Ahh," I scoffed. "Don't let American casualness fool you. We're not a happy, classless society full of happy people. There are classes in America as well defined as Indian casts with an upper crust that most of us will *never* be servile to, and here's something else. Just because Ginsburg said the F-D-A hasn't approved taxol doesn't mean we can't buy it in China."

"I know." Anastasia ran her fingers through my hair and smiled shyly, a smile without smugness or affection. Her eyes remained sad, though, struggling to coordinate my words with reality.

"I plan to start with Song Lin," I said.

"I can help you win over Song Lin," Anastasia replied.

"You? How?"

"With my Russian charm. I'll throw in nagging; he's married and will be looking for that."

"You *are* good at nagging." I gave her a big wet kiss on the mouth. "You know, I've been thinking about my Papa's brother, Ivan, who lives in Blagoveshchensk." I pinched my eyes closed and watched an idea take shape. "At my folk's hotel, when we talk to Song Lin, I'll ask him about buying taxol and making the handoff in Heihe, across the Amur River from Blago. I could cross the ice, make the purchase, and zip back to Russia to fly home. Who'd dream of smuggling a life-giving cancer-drug through Siberia?"

"Who'd even care?" she asked. "But, lover, get me a towel and a Kotex."

I lurched off the sheet and stood while my brain processed her request. "You're not — "

She shook her head. "Pregnant women don't flow like the Volga."

***

SEVEN

Park Plaza Hotel, Winter Park, Florida
Black Friday, November 22, 1991, 7:20 p.m.

Later that Friday evening was chilly, dark, and drizzly. Anastasia and I rejoined my parents at their suite in the Park Plaza Hotel, a luxurious, part-vintage, turn-of-the-century inn with rooms adorned with antiques, brick-lined walls, wing-backed chairs edged with lacey antimacassars, and flowered balconies festooned in greenery trimmed with manicure scissors.

"Hi, kids," Dad said, swinging open the door with a cheery smile and woeful eyes. He swooped to kiss Anastasia's cheek. "We're in the sitting room."

He placed a hand on Anastasia's back and guided her over the oak-planked floors waxed to a high gloss, past their big brass bed under a ceiling fan paddling soundlessly, sending dust motes sailing and gossamer curtains billowing, to the parlor, colorfully lit by vintage Tiffany table lamps at the ends of a settee. Mom sat gazing out the open balcony door, bunioned feet's red toenails resting on the coffee table, mind a million miles away. A soft rain came steadily down rinsing the world and splattering off the garlanded balustrade onto potted plants, including a leafy oleander in a clay pot nursing its poisonous pink blossoms. Through the ashy mist silhouettes of stately oaks along Park Avenue rose above a blurry rainbow of umbrellas and fashionable raincoats as tourists scurried to restaurants and the Amtrak Station just beyond Central Park's rose garden. Reflections of distant lightning flickered off window glass followed by thunderclaps but not very loud.

I swiveled around the oak chair from the pigeon-holed roll-top desk to face

Mom and offered it to Nastia. She shook her head. I kicked off my shoes and plunked down. Nastia settled on the hassock between my calves. Dad joined Mom on the settee and placed a hand on her thigh.

Mom said, "Let's hear all about your doctor's visit, Nastenka," voice detached but caring.

Anastasia relayed details of the appointment and stopped when Mom said, incredulously, "My God! Ginsburg just blurted out, '*You have cancer*?'"

"His very first words to me," Anastasia said spitefully. "Not even a hello."

Then, emotionlessly, she told them about her upcoming lumpectomy, possible radiation, and chemotherapy. She nervously rubbed my bare feet as she spoke, her velvety hands warming my tootsies, my thoughts, too.

When she finished, Mom looked at me. "I could use a gimlet. Will you do the honors, dear?"

"Certainly," I said. "'Servants must their masters' wants fulfill.'"

Mom smiled at me for dredging up that childhood lesson, no kiddy books for this kid.

"*The Shrew*?" she guessed.

"Tranio," I replied. "Nursery rhymes are for sissies."

Mom smiled enigmatically. "Discover Goosey Gander with your own kids."

"Oh boy." I tried to look pleased.

Mom frowned, reached over and picked a roasted pecan out of a can of Planter's Mixed Nuts, and popped it in her mouth. Dad replaced his hand on her thigh, but not high enough to be brazen. They sat erect, spines pressed against the back of the antique horsehair settee covered with green silk and set on spindly legs. I was slouched back, cradling Nastia between my calves, watching a soft mist float in through the open balcony door and listening to birds chirping goodnights and distant thunder rumbles that broke the silence.

I put on a happy face and tried to sound upbeat. "Say, anybody else for replenishing electrolytes?"

Anastasia smiled weakly. "Bailey's Irish Cream, if they've got it."

"We do," Dad said ardently. "And I'll have a bit of Scotch."

Dad meant a bit — a half-shot. He was the rare professor who rarely spoke in hyperbole. Most professors are long on education and short on experience. They know everything about nothing and never stop telling you. Not Dad. He was no charlatan. He survived Vietnam. Fifty-eight thousand G.I.s and six million Vietnamese, Laos, and Cambodians did not. I wonder why no one hears of that Asian-Belly Holocaust.

I looked around for the booze.

"Paper sack on the bedroom bureau," Mom said. "Ice and glasses, too."

Dad started to get up. I motioned for him to stay put, twisted a knot out of my neck, and yanked down the legs of my shorts.

Anastasia touched my arm. "Need help?"

"*Apollo need help?*" I scoffed, flexing my biceps like Arnold Schwarzenegger.

"Whoops," she said. "I forgot Olympians were formidable."

"Modest, too."

I kissed her head and got the booze-sack and bucket of ice. Mom moved her feet, and I set up shop on the coffee table. In the bag were four lowball glasses, a package of cocktail napkins, shot glass, lime, Chivas Regal, Stolichnaya, lime juice, and Bailey Irish Cream. Something to please about anyone. I dealt out four napkins, plunked down glasses, plunged my hand into the ice, and clunked three glasses full.

"Buying hooch here," I said. "Boone must still be dry, forcing all those real Christians to drive down the mountain for their booze."

"It is," Dad said. "But there is a movement afoot."

"Boone enter the twentieth century? Fat chance. Fundamentalism's too engrained in Appalachia." I poured two Chivas and stirred them with the closest thing handy, my finger.

Mom smiled. "Good deduction, son."

"With no deerstalker cap and meerschaum pipe. Cleverness must be a genetic gift," I said.

"Your papa was obsessively ingenious," she said. A faraway look flashed in her eyes, and I wondered if she was still in love with him. I often felt she was and merely tolerated Dad.

From the rain-hushed street three stories below, I heard a man singing in the rain that Gene Kelly tune and gurgled out Anastasia's Bailey's.

Dad said, "Volva's brother, Ivan, is certainly adroit with his 'international business.'" He used the diminutive of Papa's name, Vladimir, adding the requisite quotation marks. "He's selling *matryoshky* — nesting-dolls — in China, most gutted and filled with vodka to bolster his skimpy hundred-dollar-a-month military and commercial pilot's pension."

"Ahh-ha," I said. "Craftiness. Another family trait." I was wondering if I might enlist Ivan in my taxol smuggling scheme as I built Mom's drink and saw a way.

"Ivan has married five times," Mom said. "That's *not* a family trait; couples in our family stay together."

Anastasia frowned with wonder. "Why hasn't he settled down?"

"Piloting," I offered. "Too much booze, too many stewardesses, too little sleep. It loused up his biologic clock. His circadian rhythms are out of sync, or at least that's what he told me at a Brighton Beach disco one spring break."

"Maybe his pineal gland is overworked," Dad offered.

"There's always that," I said, with no idea what a pineal gland did.

A wet gust blew into the sitting room, depositing a thin film on the table. Lightning flashed. Thunder grumbled. A hard rain roared in, beating down the bleeding hearts and Anneke-calla lilies that had looked like red trumpets aimed at Zeus. I sprung for the balcony door, closed it, and finished Mom's gimlet: five parts of Roses West Indies sweetened lime juice (instead of the usual three), two shots of Stolichnaya, and dealt out the drinks.

Mom held up a hand. "A slice of lime, too, please." She produced a Swiss army knife from her purse. Professors married to professors are always prepared, though it's a wonder they don't poison each other's herbal tea. To paraphrase Churchill's reply to Lady Astor's query, if I were a professor married to a professor, I'd drink the hemlock.

I placed the lime on a napkin, sliced off both ends, cut a one-half-inch-slit lengthwise, then sliced off a perfect wheel and slid it on the rim of her glass. I held the drink up to the light.

"One cloudy, lime-on-lime shiznit," I said and handed it to her. "No one I know likes gimlets as you do."

"I like them tart enough to pucker my lips," she said and puckered her lips.

"My point exactly," I said.

We lifted our glasses in a toast. Dad said, "I've always liked the Spanish tribute. It covers about everything: *Al amor, salud, dinero y tiempo para disfrutar de ellas* — To love, health, money, and time to enjoy them." We clinked.

Mom and Anastasia sipped their drinks with all the gusto of hummingbirds. Dad looked at his watch, swirled his Scotch, but did not drink. I took a generous slug. The Chivas warmed my throat and immediately triggered hunger pangs. I was starved but didn't take any nuts. I didn't want to seem eager.

"It's seven-thirty," Dad said. "Time to call Song Lin."

He sat back, set his stocking feet on the coffee table, and sipped some Chivas.

"Here's his number, Nastia," Mom said, placing her knobby feet next to Dad's and handing Nastia a yellow sticky note with Song Lin's name and ten-digit number written in her trademarked Palmer Method cursive penmanship in blue fountain-pen ink. She took a handful of nuts from the Planters' can and shook them loose in her hand, the way you shake dice in Vegas, and popped some in her mouth.

"I'll use the bedroom phone; you use that one," Anastasia said in a sepulchral voice and pointed at the desk phone.

I stood, slid a haunch onto the desk, dangled a leg, and watched Anastasia sit on the bed. With real reluctance, she picked up the phone, took a deep breath, and punched numbers. I lifted the extension and heard a bird drone outside. The rain had tapered off. A hummingbird hovered at a cluster of blue Heliotrope. Its stamp-sized wings rotate eighty times a second as it poked its long bill in for nectar while I watch the winged wonder. I listened to phone signals whoosh over wires, computers, switches, fiber-optic cables, and satellites to Hanover, ready to digitize Anastasia's voice into a byte-stream. I wondered when the world's billions of phoneless would get Bell's 1876 invention and sipped some more Chivas. I graduated from beer to Scotch in the army and preferred Glenfiddich's oak flavor to a blend, but any port in a storm.

After three rings, Mim answered. "Har-row."

"Hi, Mim," Anastasia said. "Anastasia Locke here; Troy's on the line. Is Song home?"

"Absolutely — " it sounded like absorootree. "He outside, I'rr get him," she singsonged.

A door opened, a flurry of Chinese in trailing pitch-changes and unstressed syllables followed. WHAM! A door slammed.

Silence. A very long silence. Then, finally, "Hi, guys, sorry for the delay; I was gutting a doe; hit her coming home." Song spoke in English slathered with Dad's Down East twang laced with Chinese intonations, like maple syrup-drenched pancakes eaten with chopsticks.

"Are you hurt?" Anastasia said voice braced with concern.

Song laughed kindheartedly. "No, not at all."

"How 'bout your wheels?" I asked.

"Now that's something else. The right fender was already bashed in." Song cackled. "Mim's smashed all the fenders learning to drive."

"And you're butchering roadkill?" I marveled.

"Don't all Americans?"

"Americans don't eat carrion, only shrink-wrapped, color-enhanced, super-market-protein."

Song hooted. "Gosh, don't squeal on me."

"Your secret's in the vault."

Song's reply radiated the warmth and sincerity my parents spoke of, incredible when you know he and fifty other doctors spent three years in a Mao re-education camp, two years digging a mountaintop reservoir, one year filling it back in. Several colleagues committed suicide rather than bury their toil.

"Doctor Locke spoke with me this morning, Anastasia," Song said. "Perhaps I can help."

"Thanks, Song. He discussed your work; we'd like to hear about taxol, how it works."

"Sure," Song said, and his voice segued into a lecture mode. "You've heard of the N-C-I?"

"The National Cancer Institute, yes."

"In nineteen fifty-five the NCI and USDA established the Cancer Chemotherapy National Service Center, a taxpayer-supported, screening-base to test plants for anti-cancer compounds. They'd known for sixty years of some plants' capability to dissolve spindle fibers during cell division and hired hundreds of chemists and botanists and funded university research across the country. By the late fifties, screening was underway on thirty-five thousand plants."

"That's gotta be all the plants on earth!" I wowed.

"Hardly. There are over a quarter million plant species." Song cleared his throat. "In two years, they investigated one hundred thousand plant extracts. In nineteen sixty-two, botanist Arthur Barclay bagged and tagged bark from the Pacific yew tree, *Taxus brevifolia*. He extracts a thin mixture of its insoluble substance and sent the slurry to Monroe Wall's fractionation laboratory in the Research Triangle. Wall isolated a cytotoxic compound and announced his findings at the nineteen sixty-seven Chemist Society meeting in Miami. He named it taxol, 'tax' from the tree's name, *Taxus brevifolia,* and 'ol' from it being alcohol-based. A few years later he published its molecular structure."

Anastasia sat up straight. "Doesn't cytotoxic means toxic to animal cells, Song?"

"It does," he replied. "Overnight an Oregon trash tree became the forest's most valuable species and made headlines around the world."

"Could world labs scaled-up enough to fulfill all the taxol needs?" Nastia asked doubtfully.

"Not a chance," Song said. "And that was just the beginning of the taxol problems for the NCI. Funding, screening, bark shortages, environmental issues, political uproar, interagency turf wars, and oversite myopia followed. The NCI got it. Clear-cutting forests wasn't a good idea. Accepting taxol shortages for twenty years was utter idiocy, despite the predictable tree-huggers' uproar. Hundreds of books and articles were written about taxol after Wall published its molecular structure, $C_{22}H_{26}O_7$, in nineteen seventy-two. Then *nothing happened!"*

Song's language had vastly improved; he'd probably given the speech often. He paused. I tilted my glass of Chivas up to get the last drop. Small chunks of ice slid down the glass and clicked against my chicklets. Mom noticed, dabbed a trace of lime off the corner of her lip, and came to my rescue.

"It's been twenty-four years since Wall isolated the molecule," I said. "Why nothing?"

"Supply shortages," Song said. "Despite the finite number of yew trees, the NCI's never foresaw the need for synthetic taxol. They kept requisitioning bark and tens of thousands of yews to be cut. Luckily, world scientists were more insightful. They saw taxol's significance, foresaw the environmental and political problems, and searched for a new source. Ironically, *and simultaneously*, under a million-dollar government grant, F-S-U's Bob Holton synthesized the tricyclic taxane ring, a cousin to taxol, and produced *Taxusin*, the first synthesis of a naturally occurring compound from the camphor tree."

"Isn't camphor used in celluloid and explosives?" Anastasia puzzled.

"It is," Song said. "But Holton's discovered a new use: taxol. Montana State discovered a fungus, *Taxomyce andreanae*, growing on yews and produced taxol from microbial fermentation. At Albert Einstein, Susan Horwitz published how taxol worked and described its mechanism in cell stabilization and why microtubules stopped working. Her discovery only pushed the NCI into contracting for even more yew trees that never arrived. Animal toxicology studies were completed in June eighty-two. The NCI applied for an Investigational New Drug Permit to conduct clinical trials on humans, and it took them *two years* to buy enough taxol to begin Phase One Trials in April eighty-four. Phase Two trials started late that year with results showing a thirty percent response rate."

"In other words, because of SNAFUs, millions of women died needlessly over decades because low-bid contracts were never fulfilled, then tree-huggers stopped the cuttings," I said.

"That's the sad reality, yes," Song said, voice dismal. "The media hyped NCI's wanting to buy *three hundred sixty thousand yew trees a year,* and that caused a panic in the northwest and a wake-up call to politicians and environmentalists!"

Anastasia wondered aloud, "Why so many yew trees?"

"Bark yield was unpredictably low," Song said, "about zero point oh, oh, four percent. Phase One Trials were done at seven locations and only administered to terminally ill cancer patients predicted to survive two months. The NCI had to evaluate taxol dosages to determine its maximum tolerated dosage level. One patient died of cardiorespiratory arrest, seven experienced low blood pressure, and all experienced severe shortness of breath. The NCI ordered the administration of taxol altered to a twenty-four-hour infusion with pre-medications given to prevent hypersensitivity. By April 1985, response rates had improved, and the NCI allowed Phase Two trials to restart. Patients were given taxol in continuous intravenous infusion after being pretreated with Benadryl, cimetidine, and an oral steroid to suppress allergic reaction. These trials focused on taxol's efficacy on a broader scale. Hopes were high. Bark harvesting became a matter of national urgency, but the next years became a saga of low-bidders' catastrophes — failure to deliver bark, contract squabbles, budget limitations, forest fires, unstable extraction, purification problems, the adverse effects climate, location, and the yew's brief harvesting-window had on delivering — and the endless bark drying, storage, and shipping problems. When, finally, the NCI grasped how utterly unreliable their purchase and delivery system were they gave up."

I was amazed. "After three decades of research and tests, they just walked away?"

"Taxol supply was so poor, in nineteen eighty-six shortages halted Phase Two trials. Those shortages continued a year. The NCI tried to buy their way out of the problem by requisitioning thirty tons of bark and contracting with another low bidder to cut twelve thousand trees, but no luck. Meanwhile, taxol trials proceeded at John Hopkins and two other institutions with spectacular results with lung, breast, colon, and ovarian cancers. The media proclaimed *Taxol the Next Big Cancer Drug* and overnight cancer victims begged for it. That set off a war with environmentalists and politicians. By 1988, world scientists focused on semi-synthesis and published a flurry of articles. That work, coupled with NCI's problems, forced them to admit their shortcomings in capacity, know-how, and the bark collection, extraction, isolation, formulations, and clinical trials. They considered planting millions of yew trees, pushing synthetic taxol, investing more money, or walking away. By last year, thirty colleges and labs were working on synthetic taxol, and Bob Holton patented his semi-synthetic taxol molecule.

"Then Robert Wittes, head of the Cancer Therapy Evaluation Program at NCI, pushed the idea of giving the taxol program to a pharmaceutical company. In November of eighty-eight, he left the NCI to become a Senior Vice President at Bristol-Meyers Squibb and soon afterward the NCI offered its bark, research, and proprietary rights to all taxol data, to any company that would agree to collect, isolate, fund large clinical trials, and bring taxol to market. Four companies responded. The NCI chose BMS and gave it five hundred million dollars of taxpayer-funded research and materials."

Song laughed. "Dr. Witttes returned to the NCI the following year, and BMS applied to trademark the name taxol to Taxol; approval is expected next year. That application led to a flurry of lawsuits as competitors consider taxol a natural product thus impossible to trademark."

"So BMS hit the jackpot, millions of women died needlessly, and the public got fleeced," I summarized.

Song sighed. "And there's more. The NCI never gave thought to making its gift a collaborative effort or demanding royalties. BMS announced plans to sell billions of dollars of taxol annually and charge patients thousands for treatment. When Congress finally woke up to their hosing and gift of a taxol monopoly, they started hearing."

"Of course," Anastasia hooted, "after BMS looted America's medicine cabinet!"

Song laughed. "And there's was one more. BMS applied for a New Drug Application, and, under the provisions of the Waxman-Hatch Act, were given a five-year exclusivity on marketing taxol. Competitors will file lawsuits, but BMS will have them tied up in court for years."

"For a bright people, Americans are so naïve," Anastasia moaned. "But forget that, can you tell us how taxol works?"

"Sure," Song began. "Two phenomena occur in cell division, an increase in number and an increase in size. In a tightly regulated process controlled by external protein signals, cell growth factors respond throughout life, conception to death, and nothing that interferes with them is good. You've heard of mitosis?"

"Certainly," Anastasia said proudly. "At Moscow State."

"I've *never* heard of it," I admitted. "What philosopher has?"

"That's bull," Anastasia said. "I studied philosophy in college and know mitosis."

"Philosophy? You studied Marx and Lenin."

"Propaganda was mandatory," she said.

Song piped up, "For me, too. We studied communism until my last day in medical school."

"Okay, okay, guys; you win," I said. "What's this mitosis thing?"

"Mitosis," Song explained, "is the formation of genetically identical daughter cells, same chromosomes, same motion as the parent cell achieved via spindle fibers attached to centromeres at the center of the nucleus. Microtubules are the skeleton-like protein structures that look like long tubes that divide, shape, organize, and direct the formation of new cells."

"Weird," I said. "It sounds as if they have a mind of their own."

"How they work *is* a mystery. Microtubules must function properly and remain flexible in the separation of the chromosomal spindles to make an accurate copy of the parents' DNA. They also must send chemical signals to all parts of the cells. For unknown reasons, normal cells know when to stop dividing and do. Cancer cells, using identical microtubules, don't know when to stop dividing and don't. Horwitz showed that taxol interfered with the formation of the microtubular structures by stabilizing them, essentially locking them in place and blocking the opening of the double helix and separation of the DNA strands housed in the nucleus."

"So when microtubules are frozen, cells can't divide," Anastasia summarized.

"Exactly," Song said. "Cancer is, by definition, uncontrollable cell division. Interfering with microtubule binding sites stops cells' division. And since taxol permanently blocks them from functioning, malignant tumor progression is stopped with little effect on normal cells."

"Taxol throws a monkey wrench into the gearbox, grinding it to a stop?" I said.

Song said, "I guess you could look at it like that."

There was a click on the line.

"I'm on the phone, Lorrie," Song said and to us. "Teenagers. Oh, Mim's pregnant!"

"Congratulations!" Nastia said. "Something she'd never be in China."

"Never," Song agreed. "Apartment spies would've dragged her off to an abortion clinic."

I thought about the fear in people's hearts under totalitarian regimes and turned my gaze out the door. The rain had dwindled to a trickle. The streets were dark, shiny, and silent. The air was as thick as mousse. A man wearing a suit and fedora walked by, bent forward, ignoring the drizzle. He was undoubtedly not a spy. In China or Russia, he might have been.

"Yew trees," Anastasia posed, "what do they look like, Song?"

Over the rim of my Scotch glass, I looked at Anastasia. She appeared enthralled. She took a miniscule sip of Bailey's. Her drink had plunged all of a millimeter.

"The yew's a scraggy conifer that grows in temperate climates. They're either male or females — not androgynous — like most trees. The foliage and seeds contain heart-stopping alkaloids that ancients used to kill people and yet the berry's flesh is benign. The bark is reddish, and the yew looks rather like Frazer firs grown for Christmas trees in Watauga County."

"Portentous," I remarked. "We bought a plastic fir tree this morning,"

"Then you know," Song said. "Yews grow in southwest China, and we're planting millions."

"Insightful," Anastasia said. "What about the extraction process?"

"Yews are only cut when the sap is flowing. The bark peels off like a banana and soaked in alcohol for weeks. The slurry goes through an extraction machine, and a thousand pounds of bark might produce an ounce or two of taxol, making it a very expensive drug."

"How much does a woman need for a breast cancer treatment?" Anastasia asked.

Song paused. "Six milligrams in three doses over several days is the standard. For administering, the taxol is blended with five hundred twenty-seven milligrams of purified Cremophor EL — that's polyoxyethylatea castor oil — and forty-nine percent dehydrated alcohol."

"Six milligrams is a bumblebee wing," Anastasia said. "I don't know ounces."

"There're twenty-eight thousand milligrams in an ounce," Song replied.

"And the price?" Anastasia looked worried. She picked up her Baileys and sipped some.

"My former company, Hande's, will sell you that much for fourteen thousand dollars."

"*How much*!?" Anastasia fumbled her drink. Bailey's ran down the bedside table. I whistled through my teeth.

"Think that's high?" Song exclaimed, "Bristol-Meyers Squibb is selling it for *seven — million — dollars — a — pound! Four — hundred — thirty-seven thousand fifty — an ounce*!" No Chinese kid ever put more feeling in a quote from Mao's Little Red Book. "Add the congressional gift of a monopoly to sixty-five countries for the next five years and no price stipulations, even *to the government*, and BMS will make billions."

"And limit taxol uses to the well-heeled," Anastasia sniped snidely.

"A paradigm of a drug driven by expectations of measureless need and huge profits," I added.

"Surprisingly," Song said, "Jonas Salk didn't patent his work thus minimizing obstacles to universal immunization."

"I got it," Anastasia said. "What's that other thing, cremophor?"

"Taxol doesn't dissolve in water. Cremophor is polyoxyethylated castor oil. When it's mixed with a dehydrated alcohol solution, taxol will dissolve for injection. Raw taxol made mice and women deathly sick. BMS solved the problem; Phase Three Trials finished last year."

"Incredible," I deadpanned, "forest to labs in thirty years and still no sales."

"A long time," Song agreed. "But after BMS smelled money, they moved fast and heartlessly. They made a deal to supply yew bark with Boulder's Hauser Chemical and another deal with FSU's Holton last year for his chemistry to synthesize a form of taxol, 10-deacetyl baceatin III, from the needles of the English Yew. They're now converting that into taxol in Germany, bottling it in Ireland. Sales will exceed a billion dollars in nineteen ninety-three — "

"Ninety-three!" Anastasia yelped. "My doctor said taxol would be available in ninety-two."

This was a shock! Anastasia's mouth dropped wide open; her eyes focused in outer space.

"The FDA *just* delayed it for more testing," Song explained.

"But I can't wait two years!" Anastasia howled with a fist punch.

"You won't have to; I'll help you buy taxol in China."

"*You* can arrange it?"

"*I have arranged it*," Song said. "Give me a week, two tops. You or Troy will have to get it out of China, keep it sterile, fly it home, and administer it."

"You mean smuggle it?" Anastasia corrected.

"Yes, of course," Song admitted. "Paying off border guards and customs agents, risky."

"Your life depends on it, Nastia," I said. "Song, you're talking a capsule, I'll get it done."

I felt a cold breeze and looked outside. The rain had stopped. A cold front pushing through rattled palm fronds and sent patches of oak leaves skittering along Park Avenue. A distant train whistled mournfully.

"It is eight Friday night here," Song said, "meaning it's nine tomorrow morning in Kunming. I'll call Zhou at Hande Company now. He works seven days a week and will be having his tea. I'll get back to you with details, but do start making plans. Avoid Shanghai and Hong Kong. The safest border crossing might be in my home city, Heihe, and return through Russia where security is lax and there are no people-scanning machines, drug-sniffing dogs, or wary agents. Your dad said you had an uncle living in Blagoveshchensk, right?"

"Ivan. My father's brother. They grew up there."

"It might be an excellent time for a nephew to make a holiday visit to his uncle."

"Christmas in Siberia," I said. "I can't wait. I'll plan to go through Moscow. I speak Russian like a native and not a word of Korean or Chinese, so will skip Seoul and Beijing."

We confirmed our commitments and said our goodbyes.

I stood, stretched, and had a wild thought. Why not market Chinese taxol to the world's breast cancer victims? By the time Anastasia returned from the bathroom and sat on the hassock between my legs, I'd decided to let that world-wide taxol marketing idea rest.

Dad pulled out a handkerchief and dabbed his eyes in the thick silence. There was no sound in the room, not even the sounds hotels make, the tiny creaks of a building's endless struggle with gravity, the cycling of air condition-ers on and off, the rising and falling of elevators, nothing but thickening silence. And then, abruptly, the stillness was broken. An Amtrak blast announced its arrival next door. The hotel shook like an earthquake had struck. Mom lifted her exhausted glass. I built her a refill, and we sat in silence, sipping and staring out the balcony window, watching rain-beads swell into pendants that squiggled down the panes. A drop of water contains two different fluids. They bond co-valently into a single atom to form the drop. Since the two liquids evaporate at different rates, they have different surface tensions. The slightest change in humidity at their surface causes internal tornadoes to swirl within each drop and make it act as if it were alive, moving up, down, and sideward.

A faint paradiddle of thunder brought Dad out of his trance. "We're like those raindrops," he said, "bonding to join forces to replenish the thirsty flower box below."

"Teamwork solves problems," I said.

Dad placed a finger to lips, mostly hidden by his white mustache, removed his glasses, and looked into the mirror over the desk with a knitted brow as if searching for a shadowy object. He cleared his throat and turned his gaze on Anastasia. "Song committed to helping you, didn't he?"

"Yes," Anastasia said and clasped her hands together, pressed her lips against the joints of her thumbs. "With Song and Troy's help, I may live a long life."

"You *will* live a long life," Dad said. "Taxol will destroy any remaining cancer cells."

Unnoticed, I shook my head. Guessing the future was too iffy for me, but I felt as if I had to brighten their gloom. "Hey, is anyone else starved? There's an Italian place across the street."

"When you make a decision, it certainly galvanizes you into action, doesn't it?" Mom asked.

"Sure does; I head to the nearest restaurant." As I said that, I remembered the condo-ettes we'd seen crossing the street at lunch and hoped they'd weaved their tipsy abundance out.

Mom ignored my comment and said to Nastia, "What would you like to do tomorrow, dear?"

Anastasia tried to smile. "I've had it with all this taxol business. Let's drive to Ormond, see the historical sites, walk the beach, and have lunch at Billy's Tap Room."

"Sounds like a plan," Dad said. "Is it a good walking beach?"

"The best," I said. "Flat, wide, hard, white sand, the birthplace of car racing."

"I'll fill you in on the racing, rum, and Indians who lived in Ormond for fourteen thousand years," Anastasia offered.

"Indians?" Mom said. "That'll be something new. And we'll have the chance to talk over one more thing."

I looked at her. A small frown etched her forehead. I wondered if she had in mind what I had in mind.

She did.

***

EIGHT

Ormond Beach, Florida
Saturday, November 23, 1991

Saturday morning, still damp from showers, Anastasia and I slipped on shorts, T-shirts, and flip-flops, stuffed fanny-packs with frozen water bottles, and picked up my parents at the Plaza Hotel for a day at Ormond Beach. With the top up, there was almost room for the four of us. We stopped to stretch and eat at a crowded Deltona diner: eggs, biscuits, grits — and grilled sausage links for *le carnivore*. We sat at the counter, chatting and watching four waitresses glide through the crush, taking orders, pouring refills, serving bacon and eggs with grits and white toast drenched in margarine. Two cooks stoically took verbal orders, scraping, flipping, and frying a cornucopia of hash browns, bacon, sausages — link and paddy — and eggs scrambled, over, sunny-side up, and puddled into omelets crammed with viands.

Watching the show made me think of opening my own place and all the knife racks, grills, exhaust fans, toasters, fryers, freezers, refrigerators, steam tables, cheese-melters, dishes, silverware, napkins, tables, chairs, and condiment holders I'd need to buy. Better wait. When I began work at McDees, I'd started saving money to repay Mom for Colby. She'd never asked, but I considered it a loan and had stashed the princely sum of $387. Now, I needed her help again and figured a stroll beside the vast Atlanta would put her in an expansive mood.

As we drove east on I-4, I worked the pedals and plowed through foggy scallops of light, mulling over every compelling reason I could muster to support my request, though my heart, like my feet, felt ankle-deep in molasses. My psyche wanted to skip ahead a year to Anastasia cured, but that couldn't be done; I was chained to the now. Nastia was chained to an insidious beast eating her alive, but after being given the taxol she'd be okay. Without it, well, I refused to think about that. I'm good at that. My folks had been delighted to hear Anastasia would start teaching Monday, and her teachers' insurance would cover the lumpectomy. Would their joy turn into generosity for the taxol? They seemed happy and well off, but was that a mirage?

Mom and Anastasia sat in back, heads together, speaking softly in Russian. Dad glanced back, leaned a bony elbow on the console and tilted my way. "Song did advocate purchasing taxol from his former employer, Hande, in Kunming, did he not?"

"He did so advocate," I said. Sometimes when we speak I slide into Dad-lingo.

"Did he recommend the most advantageous route?"

"Not really," I hushed. "But going via Russia would be easiest."

Dad's eyes narrow, trying to read my mind. "But would it be the safest?"

I hunched my shoulders. "Who knows? I've got dual citizenship; no need for a visa."

"China Southern Air has a non-stop, L. A. to Beijing, with connections to Harbin and Heihe. You know our government forbids employees flying Russian airlines as deathtraps?"

"I'll gamble. I don't speak Chinese; don't have a visa, and don't have time to get one."

"It *did* take us three months to obtain ours, and that was with sponsorship, but still — "

"Look, Nastia doesn't have three months, Dad," I pressed on quietly. "Plus the Chinese might think my taking a one-day, Christmas holiday in Heihe fishier than StarKist."

We remained silent for a few miles, chewing our mental cud, then Dad drew a deep breath. "Troy," he said, "the Soviet Union's disintegrating. Lithuania declared independence fifteen months ago, Latvia, Estonia, Belarus, and Ukraine three months ago. They're giving capitalism and a new judiciary a try, but things are in chaos, nothing is predictable and safe."

"What choice do I have, sir?"

Like many professors, Dad was afraid of living. Safer is best. He'd never take a chance on anything, never wander the globe or have a moment of insane wastefulness. He would stay on the hamster-wheel until he retired at seventy and moved into assisted living (aka assisted dying). Dad thought me reckless, but I'd never failed at a thing I'd set my mind to do. I had the dogged tenacity of a Russian and the boundless optimism of an American. I could conquer all.

Dad seemed to accept my choice and he moved on to my favorite subject: moola. "Did Song mention taxol's price?" he asked with quiet persistence.

I clenched my teeth and whispered, "BMS's charging seven million bucks a pound for it."

"*Seven million a pound!*" Dad brayed, eyes wide, mouth one great big O.

My seat jerked backward. Mom rammed her face between ours. She twisted her head back-and-forth between us like she was at a tennis match. "What's seven million a pound?"

"The price of BMS's taxol," I said. "Chinese taxol will be cheaper."

She rammed her nose about an inch from mine. "By how much?"

Anastasia edged her nose into the fray. "I need three injections. They'll cost fifteen grand."

"How are you kids coming up with that kind of money?" Mom cried out.

"I've got a plan." I did not say she was the key to my ongoing ailment: Lackamoola. Her agony over spending dough was a problem I'd never experienced.

"Oh swell," she said and flopped back in her seat in a pregnant silence. Dad appeared to be fuming as well. He gets quiet and red-faced when in a slow burn figuring he'd be tapped again.

I-4 outbound traffic was light. The fog had lifted by the time we got to the coast, the day bright, breezy, and nippy, as always. I circumvented Daytona's tawdry honky-tonk of bars, hot-pillow motels, drive-ins, shabby shops, tattoo joints, tackle-huts, shell factories, used car lots, T-shirt outlets, and massage parlors — Florida's Parthenon of Sleaze — by turning north on I-95 and east on SR 40. In 1903, Vanderbilt, Ford, Stanley, and Olds raced cars here. Then, Daytona was a sleepy seaside village of 1,690 and cabbage palms and live oaks bearded with Spanish moss bordered its hard, flat, white-sand beaches. In 1948, Bill France launched NASCAR and built the International Speedway. Crowds came. Strip malls, fast-food joints, seedy motels, hotels, and condos followed. Downtown decayed. Sleaze moved in. Eight million visitors a year arrive in Daytona for the Daytona 500, the 24-Hour endurance road race, Firecracker 400, and Bike weeks in spring and fall, making going from Winter Park to Daytona like going from Paris to Dakar.

I turned off I-95 at SR 40 on land Indians once planted with maize and beans for 10,000 years. "Sam" was laying block for a new Super Center. Progress. "Welcome to Ormond *Beach,*" I said, punching the word *beach* to get them thinking broadly. I slowed for an eighteen-wheeler groaning under a load of block for a new Denny's going up across from the new Wal-Mart; suckerfish clinging to the shark.

Mom sat up and looked left and right. "Where's the beach?"

"Five miles down Granada Boulevard," Anastasia said, pointing into the sun.

"Beautiful," Mom said deferentially. "That reminds me, we'll not be seeing sunrises much longer." I looked in the rearview mirror. A passive smile tweaked the corners of her mouth; there was a resignation in her voice but no sadness. Life is what it is, indifferent and unfeeling. "ASU's in a budget crunch," she added. "Cutting foreign languages. Who speaks Russian in Appalachia? They're obsessed with Chinese and Arabic. Plus it's passed-time we sold the house. Blowing Rock's 1,300 residents grow to 8,000 when the well-heeled second-homers arrive weekends and holidays to clog streets and balloon prices."

Dad said, "We're looking at condos at Bass Lake, Chetola, and Banner Elk."

"With no grass to mow or hedges to trim, what'll become of your weekends?" I asked.

Mom laughed. "Gee, tennis, hiking, shopping, concerts, theater, visiting a son and wife ... "

"Leaving the Villafuertes, next door, chained to lawns and flower garden, won't you feel guilty?"

"Not a bit," Mom said. "Francesca is always nagging me to plant roses like hers."

Traffic condensed. We passed gated communities, strip malls, and new businesses. At a new Ruby Tuesdays, a Superior Signs truck from Roswell, Georgia was hoisting a bright shiny sign that disguised the fact that eight-out-of-ten new businesses were destined for downsizing or bankruptcy. Did professors share that destiny? Were they ever downsized?

"What a jumble of eateries, banks, and shops in these beautiful oaks," Dad said.

I knew Anastasia couldn't leave that one alone, and, on cue, she said, "Where yesterday's sugarcane grew, and Indians planted corn, squash, and beans for ten thousand years."

Mom piped up, "Is there no village of Ormond Beach?"

Anastasia edged forward. "Not since the Timucuas (te-MOO-kwas)."

For most of the trip, Anastasia had remained silent, lost in the dread of cancer, and I was delighted to hear her enthusiasm. After our first trip to Ormond Beach, I'd mentioned Indians had lived in northern Florida for 14,000 years and grown to number 300,000 by the time Columbus sailed past. A few days later she hit the library and looked up Paleo-Indians and their descendants, the Timucua, Ais, Calusa, Tequesta, Mayaca, Jororo, and Creeks. She checked out books on the Paleocene Epoch of the Tertiary Period with the riveted tenacity of the consummate intellectual. She studied the giant ground sloth, mastodon, mammoth, bison, saber-tooth-cat, and elephant that inhabited Florida until 10,000 years ago, noting their characteristics at a time when the peninsula was cooler, drier, twice its present width and the sea level was three hundred feet lower. Indians hunted those massive beasts in hardwood forests, built villages, fired pottery and developed horticulture long before Homer wrote the Iliad. Nastia found contentment in research. One afternoon, while tanning and reading at ocean side, she'd said, "Man's so arrogant imposing kingdom, phyla, family, and orders on plants and animals who could care less what we call them." A baby turtle, the size of a silver dollar, appeared, hoeing his tiny flippers toward the ocean. She cocked her head and said, "Hey, little guy, you're *Testudinidae* of the *Testudines* order, a Giant Tortoise; did you know?"

When I laughed, she said, "Well, we're the only creatures on earth that know our name. It couldn't possibly matter to that baby sea turtle what we call it."

In the car, Anastasia said, "The Indians had a civilization while Europeans lived in caves."

"I'd love to hear more, Nastusha," Mom said in her teacher's voice. "Go on."

"Sure," Anastasia said. "When Ponce de Leon landed at Saint Augustine in fifteen-thirteen there were three-hundred-thousand Timucuas in North Florida! Two centuries later, when Europeans settled Ormond, their wars and diseases had killed all but eight hundred Indians."

I knew what was coming and watched in the rearview mirror as Anastasia's hands framed an imaginary picture. Surprisingly, Dad was snapping his head as if he had a terrible headache.

"From drawing by a Spanish artist, Jacques le Moyne," Anastasia said, "we know the Timucuas were a tall, handsome, muscular people who worked naked.

The height of NBA players, they had the bodies of gymnasts and towered over their Spanish discoverers. The natives taught the Europeans, sweltering in body armor, to shuck oysters, cultivate corn, smoke alligator, fish, and lizards. Sadly, the only things left of their civilization are monumental oyster-shell middens three-stories high that protected settlements from storm surges and trapped fish at high tide. There's one next to Ormond City Hall with pots, arrowheads, and skeletons."

"Manifest Destiny," Dad said, "America needed space to grow and become self-sufficient."

"Not Manifest Destiny," I said. "The Nazi's jingoistic *Lebensraum* a closer fit."

Dad mulled that. "You're right; *Lebensraum* does express the expansive aggression better. Ours was far from a benevolent expansion directed by a string of presidents immune to guilt who shamelessly brokered false treaties. History *is* the saga of ridiculous kings and queens, ignorant presidents and generals, the flotsam and jetsam of world currents, and, unfortunately, the thinkers, probers, and creators like Edison, Curie, Bell, and Ford are seldom mentioned if at all."

At the intersection of Granada Boulevard and U. S. 1, the original link between Key West and Canada, I hit the light green and zipped through. On the north side were a gas station, Mexican restaurant, Ormond Funeral Home, miniature golf course, and ruins of England's first contribution to area economics, the Three Chimneys Rum Distillery.

"Look in the jungle, there," Anastasia said tapping her window at a snarl of cabbage palms, greenbrier vines, punk trees, and live oaks. "That blond kid's excavating America's first rum distillery built in seventeen sixty-five by slaves and Indians."

My tongue circled my lips. A rum would taste good right about now. I knew Anastasia would fill space with chatter to avoid cancer talk and watched her nervously rub her breast as she spoke. I pulled off onto the grassy shoulder. Mom scooted forward to get a better look, and I got a whiff of her Estee Lauder.

Anastasia said, "It's a long, sad story, let's stop on the way back. We can walk the ruins, and I'll tell you about King George and the four countries that claimed Florida — Spain, France, America, and the Confederate States — and the Indians, slaves, and sugarcane."

Dad twisted around to face Nastia. "My knowledge of sugarcane is limited to its triangular role in colonial days: West Indian sugar, molasses, and rum sailed to New England, profits used to buy English manufactured goods shipped to West Africa for more slaves."

Anastasia said, "Sugarcane's a tall perennial grass, like bamboo, with thick stalks and buds every six or so inches first recorded in New Guinea eight thousand years ago. It was brought to Egypt in six hundred forty AD and made it to Syria, Sicily, and Cyprus after the Muslim conquests of people fascinated with the *reed that produced honey without bees.*' A Portuguese Prince brought the cane to the Madeira Islands in fourteen-twenty, and Columbus sailed it to Haiti on his second voyage. In George Washington's day, sugar sold in Europe for an incredible fifty dollars a pound! It was so treasured, the French swapped Canada, which they called *a few acres of snow*, to Britain for the return of the cane-growing islands of Guadeloupe, Martinique, and Saint Lucia after the Seven Years' War. In Ormond Beach, there's nothing left but distillery ruins; it's too cold and the growing season too short for the cane to flourish."

After that spiel, Anastasia fell silent. Each time she'd spoken, it seemed to take her away from the cancer brooding she tried to hide. She recognized she was responsible for her fate and could not bury it under idle chatter.

I pulled onto the boulevard and, in a half mile, slowed and pointed out the police station to the south and bank across the street that had been robbed several times by never-nabbed thieves. There were shops, clinics, and city hall adjacent to the Indian midden. On the northeast corner, abutting the Halifax River, the steeple of the little Pilgrim's Rest Church poked through cabbage palms at the foot of the Intracoastal Waterway Bridge. The Halifax River is a brackish confluence of drainage-basin creeks that form part of the channel dredged from Miami to Norfolk. Spanned by a towering bridge, tall yachts glide beneath. At the summit, I pulled into the breakdown lane and stopped. Dad leaned forward, nose to glass, peering at the thickly-oaked sliver of peninsular directly below us and the Atlantic a half-mile beyond, now as still as lime Jell-O. At the shore, boxy hotels and six-story condos, shaped like boomerangs, rose cheek-by-jowl. Between them, narrow slices of sand glittered like shark's teeth scrawled with sluggish surf breaking along the shoreline speckled with people-ants speed-walking dutifully in their endless quest for cardio wellbeing. The condos, retirement fantasies, were uncleverly named Seawind, Sunrise, Seascape, Breakers, Atlantic, and Aquarius and extended north toward Flagler Beach. Motels, hotels, and condos-clones stretched southward twenty-five miles to Ponce Islet. Peeling paint, rusting railings, and drunken seawalls awaited hungry seas and hungrier

hurricanes that would batter structural-pilings, demolish walls, and refill subterranean garages with megatons of soft white sand. When the worlds' oceans rise
three feet in fifty years, one hundred million seaside dwellers around the globe
will scramble for higher ground. But, today, the sea's lazy swells mirrored the
peacock-blue-green sky and ran far, far out to a deep cobalt blue fringed with
white-laced breakers that faded into the horizon.

"See that deep blue out there where heavily laden tankers are riding north?"
Dad asked, pointing at the horizon. "That the Gulf Stream. Europe's
furnace."

"Excuse me?" I said.

"The Gulf Stream's a sixty-two mile-wide, half-mile-deep, warm-water-
river flowing northeast at eight billion gallons a second and five miles an
hour."

"One hellacious lot of water," I said, impressed.

"One million cubic meters of water — or two hundred sixty-four million
gallons — flowing past a point in one second is called a Sverdrup. All the fresh
rivers on earth equal one Sverdrup. When the Gulf Stream merges with the
North Atlantic Drift off Newfoundland that's formed by the ocean's clockwise
flow off Africa, it becomes a staggering one hundred fifty Sverdrups."

Dad, a Logical Positivist, is a stickler for details. I stored that tidbit in the
vault, but I knew I'd never use the word. How wrong I was.

"Isn't that caused by the Coriolis effect, a function of rotation and latitude?"
Anastasia asked.

"It is," Dad said. "And the Stream's forty billion gallons-a-second of warm
water hastening to northern Europe is why there are palm trees in England at
fifty degrees north latitude."

"Imagine that," Nastia said, "like palm trees growing in northern Russia,
fascinating."

"What's fascinating," I said, pointing below us, "is if you'd bought that
peninsular ninety years ago you'd be as rich as Rockefeller. That's the old
wizard's winter home on the river."

Beneath us, on the peninsula's leeward side, were John D. Rockefeller's
winter home, The Casements, city tennis courts, and the Ormond Beach Historical Society's MacDonald House. On the north side, along John Anderson
Drive, rose the seedy remnants of the once-grand Hotel Ormond that John
Anderson managed winters.

Anderson was one of America's first peregrines. In summers, he managed the Mount Washington Hotel in Bretton Woods, NH, site of the 1944 international monetary conference that gave us a monetary system and the IMF.

The historical society has a picture of Harriet Beecher Stowe chatting with Henry Flagler with John D. in the background doling out dimes to squealing kids you can almost hear in a scene reminiscent of a Currier and Ives engraving.

"What a spectacle!" Mom enthused. "Maybe we should consider retiring here."

"You should," I said. "That's the Casement below. Rockefeller died there in nineteen thirty-seven at age ninety-eight; he was and still is America's richest man." A reference to mortality.

Dad shifted around to speak to the ladies. "J. D. was an extraordinary thief and oil magnate who left an inflation-adjusted fortune of one-third of a trillion dollars in nineteen thirty-seven! Born in eighteen thirty-nine — a century before me and thirty years after Lincoln's birth — Rockefeller was in business when Fort Sumter fell in eighteen sixty-one that started the Civil War. With Henry Flagler, he launched Standard Oil, which grew through mergers, acquisitions, and intimidation until it controlled ninety percent of America's oil refineries. He started his first refinery at age twenty-four, and for the next forty-eight years expanded it until — "

"Until the Supremes ordered its dissolution on May fifteenth nineteen eleven," I said. "We studied their court decision and Sherman Antitrust Act in philosophy class. Say, speaking of closures, that's the Ormond Hotel, across the highway," I said. "It's being razed for condos."

Dad sighed. "One of the triumphs of progress is it makes me nostalgic for the Indians."

"Indeed!" Anastasia piped up, "Indians had no taxes, no debt, endless fish, women worked the gardens, and men hunted. Ten thousand years later white men appeared and *improved* life."

"What's that dilapidated, shingled, turrety thing in the swamp?" Mom tapped her window.

"The hotel's cupola," I said. "The only thing remaining of Florida's first winter resort."

"It looks so forlorn," she said, "like a rosebud at a weed show."

"Not for long. The city's dredging the channel, filling the swamp and making a park for oldsters so they can watch sunsets, swat mosquitoes, and dream of immortality."

"Well, I approve progress," Mom huffed. "I've had a lifetime of restoring relics in Europe. Their cultures can't shake loose of their history; spending fortunes restoring old castles and cathedrals is absurd. There's no money left for innovation, always looking backward to glorify their past and never looking forward. And the Soviets are the worst! They continue to restore relics with never a kopeck given to Gulag victims or their families!"

"Yeltsin outlawed the Communist Party two weeks ago," Dad soothed. "Maybe he'll bury Lenin's dream and Russia will begin righting old wrongs and aim for the future."

"Not a chance," Mom said. "Russians will never bury Lenin or be given the freedom to act."

"Give Yeltsin time," Dad said. "Like Reagan, he'll get government out of the way, handle incompetence and graft; the economy will flourish." How wrong Dad was!

The Intracoastal Waterway Bridge sloped down to a three-block-bustle mislabeled the village of Ormond Beach — one long strip mall. The light was green at the intersection of Granada and Ocean Shore Boulevards, or A1A, and I drove through and down a ten-foot embankment, parking on the broad, hard, white sand. There would be sand and salt in the BMW's fender wells, but I felt reckless today.

"May you just park on the beach like this?" Mom asked.

"Sure," I said. "And drive south on it for the next twenty miles."

I slipped off my sandals, opened the door, and stepped onto the cold, damp sand. I turned and pulled the seat forward for Anastasia to slip out.

"Leave your shoes here," she instructed and tossed her frilly sandals in back.

Dad stepped out, pulled the seatback forward for Mom, and took off his Florsheims. He tied the laces together and dangled them over his shoulder. "Last time I walked barefoot on Waikiki Beach I got blisters," he said. "I'm bringing these along."

"Not me," Mom said. She slipped out, draped her purse over her shoulder, bent down and pulled off the high-heels, exposing raw, red bunions and flashy red toenails. She set her shoes in the car and shivered in the cool breeze and weak sun. Goosebumps popped out on her arms.

"You need a bear hug," I said and gave her one.

"Put this on," Anastasia said, pulling her pink tennis sweater from a canvas beach bag with a palm tree-seaside scene. Mom took it. Nastia slung the bag over her shoulder by a drawstring of heavy cotton cord strung through brass grommets. Mom slipped on the sweater and split for the ocean in long, unwavering strides. Resolve. When you've known a person all your life, their walk expresses their mood. Without breaking stride, she hopped over a high-tide garnish of party balloons, flags, a tampon applicator, cigar stubs, crepe paper, and seaweed.

Down the littoral, the incline of hard wet sand between low and high tides, periwinkles, tiny bivalve mollusks in numbers too vast to count, crunched underfoot but didn't hurt. A small nibbling of immature waves lazed in on the outgoing tide. A flock of short-legged sandpipers skittered ahead of us so fast their legs made frantic blurs. They paused to stab needle-bills into the wet sand to eat things too small to see. When we got too close, the sandpipers took off on long, flat, pointy wings, circled wide across the water, and landed directly behind us to resume their hungry teetering search. In a swale, an egret speared minnows. A wedge of pelicans roller-coastered by, precise as a bomber formation, just above the creamy lips of breaking waves. Three hundred yards out a man paddled a kayak. A few clouds drifted across the sky, making islands of shadow on the ocean. Further out, dolphins arched through a ten-acre roil of baitfish. Seagulls dive-bombed its perimeter. Far, far out, beyond empty, high-riding tankers steaming south, bucking the Stream, the deep, blue-black sea shirred with whitecaps to where the horizon met infinity.

There was just enough cool breeze blowing off the Atlantic to keep all but the most dedicated walkers inside. Except for a boy straining coquinas at water's edge, the beach was deserted, all the Yankees holed up in rental condos awaiting the sun to do its job. It is always cooler at the beach than it is in Orlando. The sea is too vast and too deep to store heat as land does, and when the sun sets it always takes a few degrees with it.

Mom looked north and south. Five miles south, near the Daytona pier, a man appeared to be fishing on his knees; the beach was so flat here, his feet were hidden by earth's curvature. Hook, kill, and grill is a favorite pastime of many snowbirds.

"Daytona's that way," I said, pointing toward the amputee.

"Let's go north," Mom suggested, side-stepping a glob of cruise-ship jetsam. "Are there alligators in these tidal pools?"

Dad chuckled. "No, Irinka, you're thinking of saltwater crocodile. Neither are here."

"Sharks?" Mom tried again.

"Nope," I said. "Sharks feed at Ponce Inlet, twenty miles south where the Halifax runs into the Atlantic." I didn't mention the kid nipped by sharks in the knee-deep water *right here*.

Dad looked north, south, and north again. "A seven-forty-seven could land here — ouch!"

He winced and hobbled and pranced on one foot. He pulled his right foot up to his knobby left knee and plucked a sand spur from his big toe. "Knew I should've worn shoes," he said, brushing off his feet and pulling on his Florsheims.

Mom looked east and cradled her chin in her palm pensively. "The sea's so vast, it's hard to see where the horizon ends and heaven begins," she said wonderingly. "Suppose not being able to discern it means we go on *forever?*"

Dad, tying his shoelaces, looked at her, flabbergasted, at her reference to immortality. "If that's an ontological assertion, dear," he said, compassionately, "it sounds too optimistic to me. The end of life *is* the end of us. If it's a universal avowal, it doesn't mesh with science. The universe will end one day in the Big Crunch." He rose and brushed sand off his pants.

Mom touched his arm. "Whatever *are* you talking about, we know the universe's infinite?"

"That's wrong." His face grew red. No one questions the Doctor. "The universe's ninety billion light years wide and expanding at nearly the speed of light. With light traveling seven trillion miles in a year, it makes the universe six-hundred-thirty-septillion-miles wide — that's ninety billion times seven trillion."

Mom stopped strolling to look at him, puzzled at his impatience. "Well, I've never heard of a septillion before."

"It's a number with twenty-four zeros," Dad explained.

"Wow," I blurted out. "To think God created all that in *one* day."

"I believe He did," Anastasia countered. "Genesis is true."

Dad had a snarky look on his face, repulsed by that chatter. I figured a conundrum might prove to him that his son had something besides pudding for a brain. "That's a spacious universe, Dad; it makes me wonder why we are even here; what do you think?"

Dad bit. "Put earth's four-billion-year history on a twenty-four-hour clock, and man's only been here *four seconds*. I think mankind is an evolutionary fluke destined to die out in the next cataclysmic meteor strike. That is, assuming we don't chock to death on our air and water or kill each other off in religious wars directed by forgotten gods."

"Dad," I said, "Aristotle said, *Happiness is the meaning and purpose of life, the whole aim and end of human existence.* Was he wrong, sir?"

"No, he wasn't wrong. What else is there for us to live for but happiness?"

Anastasia started to argue and stopped, so I picked up the ball. "Think we're alone here?"

"Of course not." He kicked sand into the air. "There are more celestial bodies in the universe than grains of sand on earth. Billions of suns circled by planets with water and atmospheres. Odds are there is life on hundreds of planets. Can we drop this and enjoy this lovely beach?"

Dad's face was red, his blood pressure at the boiling point over pointless chitchat.

"Look at this," Mom said, spotting a keepsake in a windrow of seaweed. She poked the shell with her big toe, bent down and picked up the bubblegum-pink home of a dead mollusk. She spied a flaw and tossed it.

We stopped at a swale. Mom stuck her feet in the half-inch tidal pool to sooth her knobby bunions. Soviets shoes never fit. "This feels delicious," she said.

I stepped in, steeped my tootsies, and ambled on. Dad stopped to examine a cannonball jellyfish, shiny and slithy and very dead. He bent over, picked up a little flag pole with the red and blue Haitian-colors still attached and jabbed the jellyfish with the cruise ship flotsam. "These gelatinous invertebrates are the oldest creatures on earth," he said. "They've survived six hundred million years with a nervous system but no brain, a gut but no anus."

"Are you saying only the brainless survive," Mom said, dryly and shook her head.

That didn't slow down the Doctor. "Jellyfish were here two hundred and fifty million years before the dinosaur, and those enormous creatures only lasted one hundred and sixty-five million years, dying off sixty-five million years ago," he asserted. And then, suddenly, he said, "Ahd, nea, bah sheda, ceil." His voice sounded like the crackle of an old record on a hand-crank Victrola. He teetered, wobbled, and collapsed.

Mom grabbed for his arm, caught his hand, and she was dragged to the sand.

"What's happening?" Anastasia cried out and dropped to her knees beside them.

I fell to my knees too. The sand was wet. I pressed three fingers against Dad's long thin neck and felt the carotid artery pulse beat slowly ... very, very slowly.

"Barely a pulse," I cried. "He needs a doctor!"

Mom didn't respond. I looked at her and was stunned by the expression in her eyes: Absolute coldness. A bleak, uncaring apathy. The look disappeared the moment she noticed me noticing her. If I'd been a cartoon character, a light bulb would have appeared over my head. Her monumental impassiveness was her secret. Probably the result of her sacrificial marriage on my behalf. I'd always wondered about her years of overly tender love, caring, and smiles around Dad. It often felt as phony as lilac toilet freshener. Had it always been a sham? Was she wondering if he'd live through this and hoped he wouldn't? Did he even have a clue?

Nastia lifted Dad's confused head onto her lap.

Mom said, "He's having a mini-stroke, a T-I-A."

Anastasia was frantic. "What can we do?"

"It's a transient ischemic attack, a brief symptom of poor blood flow affecting his brain. He's had two this year and will be better in a few minutes but dizzy a few days. His cerebellum's left hemisphere, the half that controls the motor nerves for the right half of his body, has temporarily deadened his functions. An MRI scan of his head and CTA scan of his head and neck showed a partially blocked carotid artery and plaque buildup. Nothing can be done about it."

"But shouldn't we rush him to the hospital?" I implored.

"I rushed him to our hospital in Blowing Rock twice. He had blood tests, scans, EKGs, and MRIs. The doctors gave him baby aspirin. I have some stronger pills in my purse. Don't look so worried. The T-I-A will resolve itself in a few minute."

Mom opened her purse and dug out a brown pill bottle. "Run to the car for water."

I hightailed it and was back in a flash. Mom put a pill in Dad's mouth, tilted the water bottle to his lips, and gurgled in enough to wash down the pill. "All we can do is wait until the brain fixes itself," she said. "Paralysis is temporary. His speech will be back. Confusion and loss of balance will fade."

Dad looked up and blinked; rather, his left eye blinked. His right eye was closed. He stretched his neck as if he were gagging. "Nat gud beha mohe," he said. The right side of his mouth drooped. He tried to reach for his head and swayed like a swami.

"It's caused mostly by a dreadful family history," Mom said.

"But didn't you say you exercise *every* day, Mom, watch your blood pressure, and stay on a low-cholesterol diet?" I asked.

"We do, and sometimes he takes clopidogrel to keep his blood thin and flowing."

We knelt in the sand for twenty minutes, watching Dad. When he finally stirred again, both eyes were opened wide. He snapped his head and said, "I couldn't say what I — "

"You had another T-I-A, dear," Mom said, softly, brushing white sand from his white hair.

"Long?"

"Twenty minutes."

Dad gave her a cockamamie smile. "Maybe it's time for the carotid Roto-Rooter."

We all made the expected edgy laugh and remained kneeling in the damp sand.

Ten minutes later, Dad rose, shakily, and pointed at a sprawling home of stone with trim weathered silver around tinted glass. Mom brushed off his pants. He slurred, "Whose castle's that?" His inquisitive self again.

"Ron Rice's," I said. "Owner of Hawaiian Tropic, a sunscreen company."

"Strange, Ormond's neither in Hawaii nor the tropics." Dad appeared in full control.

"It's a marketing gimmick. Who'd buy Ormond Oils?"

"Touché," he said to me, and to Mom, clinging to his arm with both hands, "You don't have to hold me, dear, I'm okay." He fixated on Ron's castle. "Let's walk closer."

"Are you up to it?" Mom asked.

"I think so." Dad struck out, weaving and smirking. The smirk was lopsided.

Thirty yards northwest, a hurricane surge had sliced off the beach five-feet above the high-tide line leaving a sand cliff. Twenty feet beyond that, shielded by an eight-foot-high cement groin, Rice's spread rolled out over Bermuda-grass mounds studded with cabbage palms, clusters of sea grapes, and scatters of seven-foot sea oats fluffing in the breeze. They added a touch of quaintness to a beachfront shoulder-to-shoulder with mansions and seven-story condominiums angled to give owners a glimpse of the Atlantic from some corner.

While walking a few hundred yards further, I counted forty-seven dead cannonball jellyfish the size of softballs bobbing on weak waves before the sand turned spongy and we turned back. Mom brought up the cost of the lumpec-tomy, insurance, taxol, airfare, and bribes, and we arrived at a total of twenty thousand dollars needed. Dad said the Dow Jones stood at twenty-nine-thirty-two, up two thousand points in ten years, and Mom said not to worry, they'd help.

Anastasia jabbered about Ormond history, reboarding the BMW. We headed back to Winter Park, skipping lunch at Billy's Tap Room and Grill where the décor was plain, the tables had tablecloths, and old pictures graced the walls. Most diners were gray-haired, tri-focaled, and had hearing aids in both ears. Monk Nell, maître d', also owned the always-crowded Billy's.

"Sorry we can't stop at Billy's for some real food," I said.

"No caramelized turnip purée drenched in fresh mango dressing?" Dad said with a nutty smile. He was trying hard to act normal.

Returning to Winter Park, Anastasia and Mom slept. We dropped my parents off at the Park Plaza, and I went to a Friendly Finance Company for a 30-day loan to cover the hot check I'd given Betty at Ginsburg's. We skipped cocktails — Dad was that woozy — had a light, early dinner, and we dropped off my parents at eight o'clock. They had an early flight to Charlotte Sunday morning. Anastasia started teaching Monday, and I started working doubles to cover my week in Russia.

But I never made it to McDonald's for work that Monday.

***

NINE

The Boone Morgue
November 24, 1991

In the thick, predawn, Sunday morning, Anastasia and I picked up my parents at the Park Plaza Hotel for their seven o'clock flight to Charlotte. On the way to OIA, Mom raved about Ormond Beach, and Dad seconded her volubly. By the time we pulled into the Departing Passengers lane, they'd concluded that panegyric and were kibitzing about us all skiing at Christmas in Blowing Rock, delighted it had snowed over Thanksgiving and blanketed the slopes for skiing to begin. We laughed when Dad lamented flatlanders would be up in Biblical numbers, eating turkey, clogging roads, and whamming into one another.

"Finals finish December ninth; then I'm off!" Mom enthused. "When do you finish, Nastia?"

"The nineteenth. My lumpectomy's the next day, Friday. We can leave Saturday if Troy can get it off — " she elbowed me as I started to open the car door. "Can you?"

"No problem," I said, getting out and picking up their carry-on.

Dad stepped out and stretched his gangly arms into the stratosphere, trying not to weave.

"I leave for Russia on Sunday, the twenty-second of December: Charlotte to New York to Moscow, arriving the twenty-third and continuing to Blagoveshchensk that evening, arriving early on the twenty-fourth. I'll buy the taxol in China that morning and leave the next, putting me back in Charlotte on Saturday, six days total. And then we'll all hit the slopes!"

"Sounds great." Mom took their carry-on. "Nastia can stay with us that week, and I'll dig out our skis this afternoon," she added brightly. "Mine will fit Anastasia, or we can rent some and all ski ... if Doctor feels up for it."

And so it was agreed. We hugged and kissed and embraced in a family hug. Mom clasped me a final time, kissed my cheek and whispered, "Igor; as soon as I step into the house, I'll make out that check to you for twenty thousand dollars."

I kissed her velvety cheek and remained silent, fearing I'd spoil the gift with the wrong words. Mom took both our hands and squeezed them hard. "Now, don't forget to call your babushkas, today. I'll give you a call as soon as we're home."

Anastasia and I swore we'd call our grandmas — a Sunday ritual — and we were still waving as they looked over their shoulders and stepped through the rotating terminal door. The balance of the day turned into a roller coaster, climbing slowly before swooping into a depth so horrid, so monstrous, it's hard to recall and will remain forever painful.

We remounted the chariot and galloped into town, stopping at Pickles Deli for breakfast. Me: lox, eggs, and onions, but skipping the cream cheese on the bagels. The waistband of my shorts had shrunk. Anastasia: dry wheat toast and tea with honey — Russkies love their *mëd*. We laughed and schmoozed about this and that, and, after trying not to think about work, I gave up, dug out a pen and flipped the paper placemat over to doodle on the Managers' Schedule. We were open seven days a week, nineteen hours a day. Making a schedule was a finicky chore trickier than the D-Day invasion. I planned on Fridays and Sundays off and needed six double-shifts to cover my upcoming days in Blagoveshchensk. I had to dovetail six assistant managers' five consecutive workdays with no overlapping, except noon to two most days. I soon gave up — I'm good at that — and waded into the five-pound Sunday *Orlando Sentinel* shrieking about getting your Christmas shopping done early. I rarely read ads and editorial vomit, and was only doing so when I run out of things to hate, loath, and despise when my cell phone rang.

"Troy Locke," I said, glancing at my Timex. Nine-thirty. Too early for another robbery.

"Not disturbing you am I?" The silky voice had a slight Finnish intonation.

"Nah. We're just sitting here at Pickles, plowing through the Dead Sea Scrolls."

She laughed. "Want to play some mixed doubles?"

I covered the receiver and lifted my chin at Anastasia. "Ingrid. Up for tennis?"

Nastia lowered the *Sentinel's* thin book section. "Sure, I've gotta win back my crown."

"In your dreams," I said to her, and to Ingrid I challenged, "You're on."

"Fantastic! We'll pick you up at twelve, your place."

"*We?*"

"Me and my new squeeze."

"Ah, huh. Do I know the poor cur?"

"Not the way I do."

That made me wonder who he was. "We'll have some post-match hors d'oeuvres, something only millionaires can afford, for just us and no beautiful people we don't know."

Anastasia and I stopped at Publix's for the post-match snacks of Coors, hummus tahini, toasted pita triangles, and a small, pricey tin of Beluga caviar — our baby-step into high society. Arriving at the Taj Mahal, we were joking about Ingrid's mystery man when I opened the door. Leftovers leaped on us, barking excitedly, tail wagging. He scrambled under the couch where he'd stashed his teddy bear. He yanked it out, shook it violently until it was dead, dropped it at my feet, and tugged on his leash. I set the victuals on the Formica countertop, next to a gallon of fermenting kvass, and we headed for the nearest palm, which I sometimes used at 5 a.m. if the coast was clear. When we returned, Leftovers dashed to the couch, woofing at Anastasia. I woofed too.

She had laid her tennis outfit on the hide-a-bed, slipped out of everything except her bikini panties, and sat, foot perched on an armrest, breasts swaying, and lacquering toenails fuchsia. She huffed on them, pulled the cotton balls from between her talons, and dropped them in a fuzzy pile. Leftovers pounced on it, sunk his fangs into the downy fibers, and snarled across the efficiency, flinging his kill back-and-forth like the hindquarter of a hippo.

I opened the refrigerator and gazed in hungrily. "We got any munchies?"

"A half-can of Alpo."

I stared at her with the unblinking eye of a shark. "Right. And brown lettuce and green cheese, a real cornucopia. Where're the Doritos?"

"You ate them."

I gave up, opened the hummus tahini container and drizzled aboard some olive oil. I was whipping the thick purée with my index finger when the wall phone jangled. It had to be Mom, probably to kvetch about hitting snow at three thousand feet. I licked off my finger, leaned a haunch against the countertop, and picked up the phone.

The roller coaster took its downward swoop.

"Locke's Bar and Grill," I said flippantly.

"Troy Locke," said a deep, resonant voice I'd never heard, more a statement than a question.

"The one and only," I said, thinking: *Telemarketer hawking timeshares in a Cocoa condo.*

"Relative of Troy and Irina Locke of Blowing Rock, North Carolina?"

"Well, yes, I'm their son," I snapped, giving Anastasia a puzzled look. "If this is about beach time shares, forget it. Not interested."

"This is Sergeant Foss of the Blowing Rock Police Department. I found your number in your mother's purse. Your parents were in an accident."

"*Accident*? Jesus, are they hurt!?" My eyes froze on Nastia. She jumped to her feet and rushed to my side, nude as a Greek statue. Her eyes were two-inch washers, the nail polish bottle dangled from fingertips.

Foss ignored my question. "They were turning left off Main Street onto Chestnut Drive — "

"Our street," I yelped. "Across from the Presbyterian Church."

"Right. Looks like they'd shopped at Food Lion and stopped for ice cream cones at Kilwins."

I prayed Dad wasn't driving, still woozy from the T.I.A. "Were they hurt? What happened?"

"They were turning onto Chestnut when their Volvo got T-boned by an old purple Impala drove by an alcohol-impaired, undocumented, unlicensed male subject, speeding into town on business three twenty-one. I doubt they saw him coming."

"Which Volvo?!" I cried out.

"The subject's old Chevy bashed in the passenger door of the white Volvo — "

"Dad's car. He was driving?"

"He was. And your mother's side got — "

"Is she okay?"

Foss coughed. "The impact crushed her door. The subject's been incarcerated. Your father's banged up bad. Your mother didn't make it."

"'*Didn't make it*?'" my voice quivered and cracked into a falsetto. "You mean — "

"Yes, sir. Your mother's dead."

"Oh, my God."

I tried to process his words and broke out in a cold sweat. Perspiration trickled down my chest. The waistband of my shorts felt cold and wet. I felt nauseous, fear, dread, anger. Robotically, my right hand made the sign of the cross, touching my forehead and the left- and right-sides of my chest. My eyes went to the ceiling as if God lived on the roof and the sign of the cross would bring Mom back. It felt like lightning bolts had been hurled into my gut. I was drowning in grief. I closed my eyes and saw Mom. I felt Anastasia clutch my hand. I tried, but my mind refused to process a picture of Mom dead. It conjured up blissful scenes of us hop-scotching to the Volga River for a white night dip in the slow cool current; us picking fat red strawberries at babushka's dacha; us on the wildly horizontal swings in Central Park.

Nastia snuggled against me. I felt her arms encircle my waist; warm, anguished sobs wet my shoulder. She tightened her grip. The efficiency started to spin. My head throbbed. I felt sweaty, dizzy, and trembly. Tears filled my eyes. I blinked furiously and wiped them away angrily with the back of my hand. I wanted the building to shake. The earth to open. The crevice to swallow me. Life without Mom? God, please say it is not so! Please tell me you haven't taken her! Mom was my life, my light, my joy. I'd die without her. Please, God.

Foss remained silent, and I said, pleadingly, "But she was fine five hours ago, Sergeant — "

"Icy roads and porous border," Foss groused. "Twenty-three wrecks this weekend."

"Porous border? Jesus Christ, Sergeant, somebody's gotta close it!"

"Amen."

I slid down the counter, legs sprawling out on linoleum. Leftovers jumped on my lap and licked my face. Anastasia sat down beside me and tugged him off. He wormed between us.

"Where are my parents now?" I asked, stroking the puppy's fuzzy head thoughtlessly.

"EMTs took them to the Watauga Medical Center in Boone," Foss said. "You know it?"

"Yes. Deerfield Road. Broke my arm skiing App as a kid. Hospital set it." I had a flash. "Why didn't they take them to the Blowing Rock Hospital? It's up the hill from the church. They could've saved Mom."

"No they couldn't," Foss said firmly. "She died on impact. And that hospital doesn't have a morgue or helicopter pad. EMTs ordered your father flown to Baptist in Winston-Salem. He'll be there a while. You got siblings or relatives in Watauga County?"

"No, I'm an only child. All my relatives live in Russia. Dad's from Boston."

"You'll have to identify your mother."

Silence.

Foss said, "You there?"

"I'm here," I said, faintly, trying to visualize mother. "Mom's in the morgue?"

"Yes. It's in the hospital basement."

An unwelcomed picture appeared. Mom naked and supine on a stainless steel table. Body-cutter in a bloody apron carving her up. Rigor mortis stiffening bruised muscles. Blood settling; underside turning reddish-blue; bacteria hard at work; decomposition underway; body starting to stink. I'd seen corpses in Iraq.

"You okay?" Foss said.

"Far from it," I faltered.

"Alone?"

"No, no, my wife's right here." I touched Anastasia's bare leg. She tightened her grip and nuzzled into my neck, her breath sweet, her tears warm.

"You'll need to make arrangements," Foss said. "Funeral, hospital, will, probate — "

"I'm in Orlando," I said hoarsely.

"No rush. I gave the EMTs your parents' insurance cards from their wallets. Your father will be in Winston, and your mother, well, she'll be right there at Watauga Medical Center until … "

"Yes, of course." I searched memory. "What's the name of that Tara-looking place, on the hill near A-S-U?"

"Finley Funeral Home," Foss said. "You want their number?"

"Shoot," I said and thought, that's a dumb thing to tell a cop.

I heard Foss thumb through a Rolodex and made a writing motion to Anastasia. She sprung up and got the ballpoint pen and grocery pad off the countertop. I scribbled the number.

"Got any good friends up here?"

"Not that good."

Foss paused, and I thought about my old friends. In five years since high school, whenever the old gang got together we did so with great expectations but quickly discovered we were total strangers, having grown in different directions. Some had stood still.

"When can you get up here?" Foss asked.

"I'll call Delta now," I said. "There's a two-thirty flight."

"House key?"

"Had one since elementary school." I thought of the Rocket's basketball practice, walks home from school, stops at Kilwins, Mom's hugs and cookies. All gone. Forever.

"Your folks' groceries, wallets, and keys are here at the station," Foss said. "White Volvo's being held as evidence. If there's anything you need, anything at all — "

"I'll call you," I said. "Thanks."

I pushed up from the floor, hung up the phone, and collapsed into the deep armchair, exhaling a long weary sigh. "Climb one mountain and there's always ... "

"A bigger one," Anastasia said, squeezing in beside me. "She was my mom, too, Troy."

We clung and wept.

After a time, I pushed Anastasia out enough to look in her eyes. "It'll never be the same."

"No, it won't," Anastasia said. "Are you scared?"

"No. Yes. I don't know. Mom's in the morgue, just like that." I snapped my fingers.

Anastasia padded to the closet for her robe and slipped it on. "How about a drink?"

"A Stoli would be nice. Mom would approve."

I followed Nastia into the kitchen. She poured vodka in crystal shot glasses we'd brought from Karlovy Vari. I downed my shot in one gulp, dialed Delta, and waited about ten weeks. I tugged the long phone cord to the armchair and Leftovers started chewing on it. Anastasia gave me her vodka and picked him up. She sat on the arm of my chair, rubbing his belly, nestling his head, and remaining quiet. It's good to have a partner not afraid of conversation hiatuses. I closed my eyes and merged into quietness, too. Stillness was everywhere. There were no dog barks, no people laughs, no bird chirps, no distant hum of traffic. It felt as if I were shrouded in cotton batten. I was the last person on earth, holed up in a sound studio. Or a morgue. I yearned for the sound of Mom's voice, the warmth of her embrace. My Mary Poppins, Mother of the Ages, outstanding citizen, magnificent human being, dedicated teacher, accomplished cook, loving wife, and probably a Mata Hari in bed, without her, I was as lonely as an eagle soaring over Mount Everest, lost in a vast nothingness, isolated, quarantined, segregated. All her years of toil, all her gifts, all her sacrifices gone in one instantaneous, preventable, cataclysmic crash.

After an eternity, a chirpy Delta clerk took my reservation for the two-thirty flight to Charlotte and back on Thursday. Anastasia re-cradled the phone and slipped onto the dusty arm of the overstuffed chair and snuggled my head into the perfumed warmth of her violated breast. I thought of childhood when Mom comforted me after lost playground battles. Anastasia had a large, loving, extended family living close to her nine-story *Stalinka.* Mom and I had fought life's battles alone. She'd listen to my triumphs and woes. She'd feed me when we had little to eat, always claiming she wasn't hungry. I foolishly believed her. She'd walk me to school and run to teach at three different universities. I'd wait, alone, for her evenings, hungry for the chicken leg or hunk of cheese she'd buy at the apartment's first-floor grocery. After I'd eaten, Mom would pour boiled water over the morning's steel mesh tea ball for her evening meal. She'd wash my dish and milk glass and insist I do my homework and read Bible stories — Samuel 1:17 (David and Goliath), was my favorite — at our teeny kitchen table wedged between the refrigerator and corner plumbing. Soviets builders found it troublesome to encase water pipes, toilet drains, and steam ducts within walls as the shorty pipes often sprung leaks. Tying rags around trickling pipes was handy when left exposed. While I studied, Mom would sip tea and iron my uniform and explain biblical miracles but never to my satisfaction. She nursed me when sick, attended my soccer games, tucked me onto my thin pad by the radiator and fall asleep correcting papers on her lumpy convertible sofa-bed. She had fallen in love and married an older American — to secure me a better life? — and all her sacrifices bore my name. Now I must square life's circle without her.

"Are you okay?" Anastasia asked, kissing my forehead gently as she would a China doll.

I was numb with reflections and found little solace in her tenderness. "Why are the good ones taken early? Why don't we enforce our laws? What's happening to America?"

"It's a messy world," Anastasia said. "The talented, hungry ones will always find a way in."

"I suppose." As I said that, I felt a renewed conviction, a compelling resolve that trumped my usual slothfulness.

I pulled Anastasia off the chair's arm, snuggled her tightly, and kissed her decisively. I huffed a lock of her hair back and breathed into her ear, "My only purpose in life, my love, is to fly to Russia, buy the Chinese taxol, and rush it back to you."

"Thank you," she murmured. "I'll be waiting."

"Smuggling might be a crime," I said, anger welling up inside me, "but the real crime, the atrocity, is no other agency controls the fate of more people than the FDA. It knew taxol was the elixir for breast cancer for thirty years, and yet it remained impaled on never ending approvals and low-bidder mandates for three, long decades! *The F-D-A is the taxol thief.*"

"Forget the FDA," Anastasia said. "Thanks to you, with Chinese taxol flowing through my veins, I'll live to be a white-haired babushka playing with our grandbabies."

Her remark brought me back full circle to the struggle of coming to grips with Mom's death. "Mom never got the chance to see our kids all because of some goddamn illegal. What a lousy way to die! Killed on your street by a drunk. Why don't they build a wall?"

"From the Gulf of Mexico to the Pacific?"

"Damn tootin'! I'm sorry America screwed the Indians, slaves, and Mexicans for centuries, but we've made restitutions, and all it's done is created dependency, endless poverty, work dodging, and welfare. Borders make the world orderly. Illegals make a mockery of borders and immigration laws. Why should you wait in line? Cheaters get to stay and receive benefits."

Anastasia grabbed my throat with both hands in feigned strangulation. "You know damn well the wretched will always find a way out of their misery; that's Darwinian. Survival of the fittest. *Poverty and political turmoil* is the disease. Drunkenness is its *symptom*."

"Mom always said, 'The poor will swamp us with their numbers.' The First World doesn't have the resources to help all the world's billions of poor. We accept a million legal immigrants a year, but three times that many sneak here. And that's a pitiful fraction of the world's three billion poor. Then, the world has four hundred thousand births a day, one hundred fifty thousand deaths, and increases a quarter million people every day, ten million — a New York City — every forty days.'"

"All mostly dirt poor," Anastasia lamented.

I ran my fingers through her hair and nuzzled my face into its silky fragrance. "Mom said the absurdity is liberals think we *can* conquer poverty by lowering standards, eclipsing education, flouting laws, deserting discipline, and taxing the wealthy. It's absurd. She said, 'If you confiscate all the compensation of all five hundred CEOs in the S&P Five Hundred, six billion a year, and give it to the poor their income would only increase two dollars a year! These ideas are intent on bankrupting us socially, morally, and financially. Dad says we can cure poverty by allowing the poor the freedom to start businesses while respecting property rights, observing the rule of law, and educating everyone as to how wealth is created. These will lift living standards, and foster charity, private capital outflows, and remittances that, in America, total over two hundred billion dollars a year. Once the poor understand the habits, customs, and values of a free people in a free country, they'll demand freedom from anxiety, trouble, control, and gain the security needed to address their common interests. Governments must give people liberty and autonomy, ease off on handouts, and then stay the hell out of the way."

Just then Leftovers began a low throaty growl. He dashed part way down the hall and froze in a point, nose up, tail out straight, front paw raised, growling growing louder.

BURRING. The doorbell set Leftovers off in high-pitched, puppy yips.

"Ingrid and her mystery man," Anastasia said.

Leftovers scrambled for the door at her heels. She eased him aside with a bare toe. A surge of hot, humid air blasted into the room when she opened the door.

Ingrid stepped in wearing faded jean short-shorts and a snug tank top knotted below her billowing breasts. *Save Water, Shower Together* was silk-screened between nippled peaks. A fetching expanse of tanned, exposed midriff made me wonder if she were tanned all over and felt confident she was. She flashed a mischievous grin from her inventory of smirks, pouts, and moues.

Behind her, a mountain of a man stepped into the cave, shadows hiding his face. He was so impeccably dressed he all but glistened.

I did the preverbal double take. "Kahuna!" I said, flummoxed.

"Ta-da," he said, throwing his arms open wide, head back and roaring at my bafflement. Kahuna had that stud-look, a blend of brutality and irony. Bogart had it. It's a seedy, indolent callousness, a primitive wisdom of the fleshiness women sense and accept knowing how casually they'd be used. Kahuna was dressed for Wimbledon in a Sergio Tacchini crewneck tennis shirt of navy blue with red piping, a red cotton sweater tied casually around his thick neck, navy shorts, and red Nike sneakers. His undershorts probably had his initials in red piping, too. He looked as nonchalantly elegant as Robert Redford had in *The Great Gatsby*.

Anastasia appeared struck anew by Kahuna's good looks, smoothed, styled, and tailored by most of his McDee salary. He carried his six-six height with relaxed assurance and his gray eyes — which he knew how to use — held a basic *joie de vivre*. His hair was long and thick with an unruliness that expensive cutting hadn't thoroughly disciplined. It added to his attractiveness by hinting at an untamed individualism far removed from the tedium of the standard male's slick good looks of a Cary Grant.

"Where'd you buy your outfit?" Anastasia asked, setting hors d'oeuvres on an orange crate.

"Good Will," Kahuna said with a lazy smile, bopping into our narrow efficiency, snapping his fingers and looking around. "Say, you guys must rent this sprawl out for conventions?"

Leftovers leaped onto Kahuna's leg and clung like a hairy tick to the Ace bandage around his thigh, straining to sniff his crotch. Kahuna shook his leg. Leftovers stuck like paint.

"Manners, Leftovers," I said and took a second look at Kahuna's wound. A spot of blood had seeped through the bandage. But not much.

"Your mutt listens like our dropouts do," Kahuna said, eyes twinkling.

He leaned his big frame over and extracted Leftovers. Touched noses. Kahuna flicked his long, blond locks magically into place, cradled Leftovers to his burly chest and stroked his belly. The pooch whined ecstatically with all the loyalty of a hooker.

I fought my way out of the armchair, cavernous enough to swallow Texas, hugged Ingrid, shook Kahuna's massive paw, and waved them to the couch.

"Can you play tennis with that wound, Kahuna?" Anastasia asked.

"Ah, this ain't nothing."

He reached for a hot buttery pita bread point dabbed with poor man's beluga caviar, popped it in his mouth, and licked the hummus off his fingers. For the first time, I saw in Kahuna a new and unexpected quality — a quality I knew so well — the good-natured, sly excitement of The Sexual Conqueror. He wrapped a burly arm around Ingrid's waist and drew her to him. She settled in and kissed his cheek. He grinned like an idiot and extended his other arm along the top of the couch. With legs sprawled, he reveled in the self-admiration he was affecting in the two women. I knew the feeling, the glitter of eye, the lazy smile, the self-assured casual arm around a thin waist, the incidental physical contact, the brush of breast. It's the secret language of human cipher men use that seems so accidental, but never is, that we've used since Adam grazed Eve's boob reaching for the apple. But then that nonsense smacked into the car accident and Mom's death.

"You see a ghost, Troy?" Kahuna said at my mercurial change of mood, levity to solemnity.

I snapped my head, attempting to shake off anxieties. "Worse."

Anastasia looked at their anxious faces and said, "You'd better have a drink."

"Sure, it's Sunday and way past time for my Coors-curls," Kahuna said, flexing an arm.

Ingrid uncrossed her legs and fussed with her snug T-shirt. "Got vodka?"

"A Russian home's never without it," Anastasia said and headed for the kitchen.

We sat in silence, me wondering how I'd tell them about my parents, Anastasia rattling Coors cans out of the refrigerator and plunking glasses onto the counter. She opened the freezer, clunk ice into two glasses, gurgled out stiff jolts of Stolichnaya and dealt the drinks. The women sipped vodka. Kahuna and I settled back with Rocky Mountain spring water.

"Let me start by thanking you for covering for me this morning, Kahuna," I said.

"No problem," he said and reached for more hummus. "What's up?"

I inhaled deeply, shuttered. "You covered for me so we could drive my folks to the airport."

"That's what you said."

"Mom told us she'd call as soon as they got home," I said.

"And a few minutes ago we got a call," Anastasia said. "But it wasn't from Troy's Mom."

"It was from the Blowing Rock P.D.," I said. "A cop said my folks were in an accident. T-boned by a drunk illegal." I shook visibly and spit out, "Mom's dead and Dad's in bad shape."

"My God!" Ingrid cried and rushed to my side, kneeling beside the chair and grasping my arm, as if clinging to it would give me strength.

I stared at Kahuna. His mouth was full. He swallowed, coughed, and sat up straight. "Jesus, Troy. You ain't shitting, are you?"

I shook my head.

Ingrid said, "I can't believe it. You all were so happy at lunch Friday, toasting, chatting, and laughing. Now she's gone?"

"She's gone. And they *were* happy," I said. "But that's not all — "

Ingrid stood, studied me, then turned and zeroed in on Anastasia willfully. "Right. You two *didn't* appear so happy Friday; in fact, you looked like you were at wit's end."

"We were," Anastasia said, apologetically. "I should have told you."

"Told me what?" Ingrid turned from Nastia to me and back and picked up her vodka bomb. She tilted it up and took the last swig, wiping her lips with a napkin.

"Two weeks ago," Anastasia began, "I had a mammogram and biopsy. Friday, at lunch, Mom — " she shuttered, mentioning her — "told us she'd taken a call from my doctor's office. He wanted to see us that afternoon. I have a malignant cyst, need a lumpectomy and may require chemotherapy and radiation."

"Oh, my God!" Ingrid cried. "I'm so sorry. Your mom's death and now you've got cancer."

Kahuna leaned forward, palms outstretched. "What can we do, Boss?"

I hunched my shoulders. "Nothing now, Kahuna, thanks."

"You don't have brothers or sisters — right?" Ingrid asked me.

"No," I said. "No aunts, uncles, or cousins in America either. A few in Russia, Ukraine, Hungary, and the Czech Republic I met them once."

Ingrid turned to Anastasia. "My Mom had breast cancer. Mom made it and you will, too. She truly looked forward to the chemo, knowing she'd be getting her life back."

Anastasia looked startled. "Even knowing she'd get deathly sick?"

"You bet!" Ingrid said.

"I'm going to have my chemo sessions on Friday afternoons."

"Best time," Ingrid said and gave Nastia a hug. "You'll have weekends to cope with sickness and be ready for work Mondays; but you, Troy — " Ingrid caringly gripped my hand — "I'm so sorry."

She gave Kahuna a nod to speak. He licked humus off his fingers, washed it down with a gulp of Coors and said, "I'll cover for you as long as it takes, Boss. Me and the guys will manage; don't worry about nothing."

Kahuna may not be the brightest of UCF grads, but he had a big caring heart beneath that brawny exterior. He was a substantial human being, a mensch, sympathetic, understanding, and offering support at a time when we desperately needed it.

"Thanks, both of you," I said, pushing up from the armchair. I went to the closet, yanked my backpack down from the top shelf, and pulled on a flannel shirt. "Ingrid, if you'll stay with Nastia, I'll have Kahuna give me a ride to the airport for my two-thirty flight to Charlotte."

"Sure," Kahuna said. "A backpack's all you're taking? Ain't it snowing up there?"

"I travel light," I said, stuffing underwear and socks into the backpack. "It'll only be a couple of days and — " I held a pair of long-johns — "I'm bringing these."

Kahuna laughed. "They look like peppermint-striped condoms big enough for an elephant."

Ingrid socked him, and Nastia said, "I'll get that L. L. Bean coat Mom gave you last Christmas that you've never worn." She went to the closet, rifled through stuff, and produced the coat still in its plastic bag. "The tag said, GOOD TO -50°, it'll keep you toasty."

"Ladies, I'll be back in a flash," Kahuna said, "and take you to lunch, dining *alfresco*."

"Sounds wonderful," Ingrid cooed. "Do I know the place?"

Kahuna conjured up a fake Italian accent, "*El Patio da McDonald's.*"

Anastasia and I embraced and murmured some words then I followed Kahuna down to his VW van, baking in the scrubbed-sky for my second trip to the OIA today.

And my first trip to a morgue.

***

TEN

Blowing Rock, North Carolina
November 24, 1991

"Hey, man, I'm so sorry about your mother and Nastia," Kahuna said, veering the van off I-4 onto the Beeline Express at the Texas-sized Orange County Convention Center (OCCC), which had finished the job of clogging Orlando's highways.

I gave him a shoulder hunch. What can you say?

The Beeline to OIA and the Space Coast was jammed. Kahuna tromped the gas. A sweltering blast tore in. He weaved around cars, motorcycles, 18-wheelers, and pickups. I rolled up my flannel sleeves and stared down the highway, thinking about the city the Mouse built. Before Walt, Orange County was a sleepy orange- and cattle-town. Now thousands of square miles of arable land have been paved over with asphalt and concrete, more than two million live here, and the heart of Orlando is rotting. It'll cost billions and take decades to smash up all the asphalt and haul it off when Henry Ford's gift to the world is replaced by jetpacks.

"Nastia's too young for cancer, and your mom — " Kahuna ran his fingers through his long blond hair, grimacing painfully — "I never met her, but from what you said … "

Kahuna's lament made me want to bawl. "They're both very special women."

I knew Kahuna wanted to say more, but he had trouble verbalizing, so I helped him by changing the subject. "You know, I never saw you with Ingrid before. How'd you meet?"

Kahuna grinned insouciantly. "Remember when McDees wanted to be Taco Bell?"

"That disaster? Proof of my slogan for success slogan: Know what you are and stick to it."

Kahuna shot me a befuddled look. "Whatever. So one night a gang of Rollins chicks breeze in. The place was half-full of old duffers, dawdling and socializing with anybody who'd talk to them. The girls ordered burritos. They all sat together and started eating. Then one chick screamed, 'These burritos taste like crap!' The old dudes were bamboozled — they only hang around 'cause they're widowers lonelier than beggars. They cleared out. The mouthy chick demanded a refund, or they'd keep on screaming. She winked at me, then yelled at her army to keep on chanting. After ten minutes of war whoops, I gave 'em freebie coupons."

I figured Kahuna's romance wasn't a Gordian Knot. "And the mouth was Ingrid?"

"Yeap and the rest is history. Quite the looker, ain't she?"

"A marquee headliner."

Status symbols work both ways. Ingrid, a gorgeous, one-in-a-million woman was destined for Nob Hill and would never accept failure. And Kahuna *will* fail. Although blessed with movie star good looks, he lacks the mental alacrity and special talents needed for success and expansive living. Ingrid will cut her teeth on Kahuna and toss him away without emotion or regret, hopefully, before they marry or have a kid.

Kahuna pulled into the Passenger Unloading area where a dazzling array of gaudily dressed, turkey-day furloughers were headed back to the wheel. We shook hands and arranged for pick up Thursday evening at eight. I shouldered my backpack, pulled on my Colby ski hat, and slung my Bean coat over my shoulders. Tramping out of the VW, I probably looked like an Eskimo headed for a beach party.

"Thanks for the lift, Kahuna," I called out. "And get your leg looked at; blood's seeping."

"It ain't nothing," he scoffed, jumped in the van, and screeched off.

There was just enough room on my Master Card for the rental car and ticket for seat 32A, last row, port side, non-reclining, Delta Comfort. I hustled to the monorail and ran to the gate. The regional jet left on schedule at 2:30 p.m. and entered the Charlotte landing pattern at 3:50 p.m. that runs north, adjacent to

I-77. I looked out the window at black clouds rolling in from the Smoky Mountains of Tennessee to the northwest. Traffic crawled past Carowinds, the amusement park I first visited the summer we arrived. Hertz had the paperwork ready for a Subaru, and I barreled out of the terminal, heading southwest on I-85 seventeen miles to Gastonia with adequate time to reach the foothill and beat the blizzard arriving from Knoxville before the sun set at 5:12. I'd checked. Thanksgiving traffic was stop-and-go to Gastonia, and I lost precious time.

When I turned off I-85 at Exit 17, there were three 18-wheelers idling at the red light, belching fumes. The light turned green. I gunned it across the bow of one truck, cut across two lanes, and darted between the other two trucks. A wail of air-horns followed me. I was headed north on SR 321 for Hickory, Granite Falls, Hudson, Lenoir, and a vast stretch of mountain loneliness and had gotten all of three hundred yards when I heard the yowl of a siren and saw a flash of blue lights in my mirror.

The cop motioned me over. I pulled into a Texaco station and watched him sauntered up. I lowered the window, reached for my wallet and pulled out my Florida license. He removed his sunglasses and folded them in his pocket. His gaze was as piercing as a power drill.

"Afternoon," he said and produced a ticket pad. "Little late for turkey, are you?"

"No, sir, trying to beat the storm," I said, pointing at the approaching front.

He glanced over his shoulder. "Going to Watauga County?

"Yes, sir."

"License and registration, please."

I gave him my license and opened the glove box for the registration and rental agreement. "Listen, I'm really in a hurry and gotta get — "

"You listen, Mister — " he glanced at my license — "Locke. You take a nice picture, son, but you just broke a few laws."

"I'm sorry." I handed him the registration and rental agreement.

"Rental car, huh?" He glanced at the contract.

"Yes, sir. I used to live in Blowing Rock; Florida now. Would you please write the ticket?"

"What's your rush?"

"I need to identify my Mom. She was killed this morning by an illegal drunk up in — "

"Locke, huh?" He squinted, searching memory. "Sure, I heard about that."

"*That* was my Mom."

"I'm sorry, son, I didn't mean to … Look, seeing's how it's a death in the family, I'm going to let you off with a warning. And here's the warning. We do *not* cut in front of eighteen wheelers in North Carolina, and we frown on drivers mistaking our highways for the back straightaway of the Daytona 500."

"I understand, sir. Thank you. I won't forget. In Orlando, you have to drive seventy-five or get run over by Mouseketeers."

"Thank God this isn't Florida." He smiled and handed me back my papers. "Good luck."

He got in his cruiser and pulled out with his left taillight blinking. He zipped across three lanes and turned in at the red light in front of Dunkin Donuts. I waited, fingers tapping on the steering wheel until he got out, then I goosed it for the mountains shrouded in thick black clouds.

The northbound lanes were empty, driving was mindless. I'd made the trip a million times, and my mind wandered to pleasant memories. Fishing with Mom on Volga River tributaries, thrill rides with her in Tver's Central Park, pleasant walks on white summer nights, blueberry-picking in the forest near the *dacha* that Communist muscle permitted a few comrades to own. Then, abruptly, the happy memories soured. That was then; this was now. I had to become someone different, someone better, stronger, more focused. As if mimicking me, dark clouds enwrapping the foothills north of Lenoir grew thicker and swaddled distant mountain peaks, a harbinger of the approaching snow. The red ball of five o'clock sun dropped into the blackness, a prelude to the end of the day and the end of everything as I had known it. I felt a prickle of fear, raw fear that stayed with me. A relentless jabbing, a mental digging as irritatingly and raspy as Soviet toilet paper. It was a frightfulness I had felt before, in a foxhole, watching Iraqis advance. It was a fear based on fright and anger; no, that's not right. It was not anger; it was more distressed rage than anger. It was an all-consuming furor at our do-nothing government for allowing illegals to pour over the border. A government so impaled on low-bidder protocols that it took thirty years for it *not yet* to approve a cancer cure drug-desperate women died for needlessly. Now, I fumed, the best I could do was to pray to God for help accepting regulatory failures and getting Anastasia her lifesaving taxol. If God proved dead, or dead to me, and our leaders remain apathetic, what else could I do? Who else could I blame but myself? Maybe with tomorrow's sunrise I would find the strength to deal with Mom's death and my taxol rage. Maybe I would discover Mom was blessed with eternal life as The Book promised. Or maybe I wouldn't.

North of Lenoir, the climb up the Blue Ridge Mountains began. Four-laned SR 321 shrank to two-lanes and steepened like a ski jump. Cut out of sheer granite, the road wound like a cobra the final nine miles to Blowing Rock. The southbound lane was bumper-to-bumper with flatlanders hurrying home from a weekend of turkey, skiing, and conviviality. The northbound lane slickened with heightened elevation. Snow intermittently pelted the windshield as the air thinned. There were dozens of vehicles in the ditch; tow trucks were making a killing. I notched up the defroster. Dusk turned into darkness, and between coughs of snow, I saw shimmering light-fingers flicker on the distant Smokies. Their peaks sheened sporadic reflections with underbellies hued with daubs of feathery violet or wispy lilac, deep purple in the shadowed hollows. The summits were as blizzard-blurred as Monets. At the crest of the Blue Ridge, the interplay of color vanished, dying rays slid behind Smokies, and the road flattened. I hit a patch of black ice at Canyons, the cliff-hanging restaurant where we'd held our wedding reception, and fishtailed. Left, right, and left again.

I got it under control and looked back with time to see the phenomenon that gave Blowing Rock its name, sleet blowing straight up rocky ledges like a dyslexic snowfall. Cherokee legend has it on this spot, gods answered a Chickasaw maiden's prayer for the return of her lover and blew him up the precipice from the valley far below into her waiting arms.

My headlights glared on the historic Green Park Inn and then on a sign, Eastern Continental Divide, 3,620 feet. At an abrupt fork in the road, between Hampton Condos and the two-story, log home of Broyhill Furniture, I hooked a hairpin-left onto Business 321. The road sloped downward and serpentine, flanked with homes of cedar and rock with terraced stone walls. The posted speed was 25 MPH. Sergeant Foss said the illegal was going sixty when he slammed into my parents.

When the hill ended, the village began. I pulled over and parked beside Saint Mary Episcopal Church at the intersection of Main and Chestnut. I left the engine running, headlights on, and got out. There was enough ambient light from the halos of streetlights glistening with snowflakes and the floodlights of the Presbyterian Church, across Main Street, to make my breath glow. Traffic had packed the salted snow into a slushy, gray mush. I kicked some aside and searched for skid marks at the last spot mother had been alive. Nothing. I kicked more slush. Still nothing. No tangible sign of Mom. After a time, I gave up, reboarded the Subaru, and followed an invisible compass drawing me achingly up Chestnut Street to the house. The street was unplowed. The AWD spun, dug in, and plowed up the hill. We lived a few hundred yards from the crest and the Blowing Rock Hospital. Close, but not close enough to help Dad.

Like many Blowing Rock homes, my childhood home —my nest, where I fit in, where I was loved, where I belonged — was made of rock-and-wood, two-story, and notched into the side of a mountain curtained on three sides by rhododendrons and Frazer Firs as tall as flagpoles. The back of the house, the living room, faced east and a silent poem of burnt-umber-washed sky bisected by a sliver of moon racing between clouds in raw, gutsy wind. I stepped out of the Subaru into the howl, slipped on my L. L. Bean coat, and grabbed my backpack. I leaped over windrows of snowdrifts and fumbled for the house key long enough for my fingers to grow numb. In the near-blackness, I found the key, unlocked the door, flipped on hall lights, dropped the key in the key dish on the entry chest, and dumped my coat on the hall chair. The entire first floor was alight. Its warmth reminded me that my body had traveled far, but my heart had never left home. But the joy of home lessened as a subtle sense of loss struck. I stared into the silent emptiness of the house buttoned up tight. Everything was silent except for the faint hum of the refrigerator and the distant drone of a snowplow that penetrated triple-paned glass. In *Karenina*, Tolstoy claimed *each unhappy family is unhappy in its own way*. These four walls of deathly silence were my family's unhappiness. Missing were my parents and the halcyon and noisy delight home was when filled with friends, neighbors, students, and, occasionally, faculty. We knew our roles and filled them like three round pegs in three round holes. Most guests did, too. Most faculty did not. Dad often derogated his garrulous colleagues. He said they were, "tedious, seditious, divisive, wearisome, and dreary; wannabe scholars who eschew careful analysis of mega-best-sellers to display ultracrepidarian tendencies filled with endless sciolism; gadflies who filled conversational hiatuses with standardized academic jargon and jejune collections of nostrums rhetorically and dutifully expounding dull conventional theory while remaining hostile to anything challenging pedantic postmodernism by steering the country away from its constitutional republic roots and framework of free enterprise, personal liberty and personal responsibility." His words.

The oak parquet floor creaked when I stepped over to check the thermostat. Whenever my parents left home, they always turned it down to 50°. It read 70°. They'd been home, left to go to Food Lion, and stopped at Kilwins for ice cream cones.

BONG, BONG — I jumped.

The Westminster melody chimed six full-throated times. The grandfather clock was in the living room. It had been seven months since I'd been home. I'd forgotten how jarring it was.

The cavernous size and effulgent grandeur of the house made our Orlando efficiency feel like a cave decorated by Goodwill, which it was. The entryway reflected my parents' cultural polarity: Russian gild and Yankee-stolid. Dad's pilgrim rug, braided with strands of red, orange, and yellow, covered a sizeable portion of the oak floor and blended in with runners secured with brass-stair-rods leading to the second floor. On the south wall, painted a deep forest green, hung Mom's favorite oil, a spotlighted, gold-leaf-framed painting of Saint Isaac's Cathedral looming majestically near the Neva River in Saint Petersburg that Communists use as a Museum to Atheism. Beneath it stood a three-drawer, Russian, Bombe-chest topped with two Blue Danube dishes: large for mail, small for keys. In the corner rose a T-shaped, Shaker coat-tree of hand-rubbed cherry, sparse as a winter tree branch, beside a thigh-high, brass, naval shell Grandpa Locke brought back from the Pacific now stuffed with umbrellas and walking sticks, handy for strolls around Bass Lake, our Walden Pond. These traces of childhood seemed to say: *You can't escape us; you can't be different; you fit in here. You belong here; this is your home, and you will stay the same here with your doubts, dissatisfactions, and discontent, but you'll always return, like the migrating bird you are.* And yet another voice, one in my heart, said: *You need not submit to the past; you will find happiness despite your mother's death; you will find the cure for Anastasia's cancer; you will become your own person.*

I listened to that second voice and stepped beneath the staircase into a mirrored, glass-shelved, wet-bar lined with rows of neat bottles, shining glasses, and folded napkins. The house and my parents belonged to an era that had those things. Catching my reflection, I said in my best Professor Higgins gentrified voice, "I say, old boy, you look like you could you use a spot of Scotch." In a normal voice, I replied, "Capital idea."

From an array of Baccarat crystal, I selected a Harcourt Old-Fashioned Tumbler that cost enough to feed a Kenyan village for a month, plunked in ice cubes, and gurgled out a generous slug of Glenfiddich.

"Good show!" I said and took a princely sip.

With libation in hand, I stepped into the living room, an orderly and traditional space just a little smaller than the Grand Canyon that often rung with laughter and festive conversation. Its dark-red walls hung with oils my parents loved that gleamed under Halogen low-voltage spotlights. On one wall were paintings of Siberian mountain scenes, bulbous onion domes, the twisted turrets of Saint Basils near Red Square, an old, wooden, Russian church in Novosibirsk, and a Volga River dacha set among soaring pines. On the facing wall were oils of Cape Cod dunes, lobstermen working traps, black-shuttered brick homes on a Beacon Hill cobblestone street, and a sea captain's home in Glouster. There were six groupings of chairs and tables, a grand piano, brass lamps, framed family photos, and gilded bric-a-brac. The north wall was a fieldstone fireplace large enough to roast a bison flanked by bookcases lined with scholarly tomes, paperbacks, hardbacks, and a timeworn stalagmite of unpublished manuscripts in five-inch binders, filled with infuriatingly indulgent longueur. The entire east wall was floor-to-ceiling glass-cloaked by red velvet drapes that would have made a majestic coronation gown for Catherine the Great. The emptiness and quietness of the living room underscored how vital human warmth was.

I felt claustrophobic, opened the heavy drapes, and gazed out. The snow had ceased. A slivered moon appeared to be sailing over distant peaks. High stars glittered. In the soundless house, I felt like the last person on earth and wondered whom I longed for most, Mom or my sick Nastusha. How could I say when I needed them both so desperately? But that was wishful thinking. My world, tough as it was, meant adapting to the hand I had been dealt, captaining a changing course. I stood at the window for a long time, jarred by the cavity left in the house. Several times I expected Mom to walk in and ask, *Hungry for something special*?

Having skipped lunch, I headed to the kitchen to inspect possibilities. The lights of Blowing Rock glowed through the west windows festooned with blue drapes Mom had had made in Russia. I switched on the under-counter lights. Glass-fronted cabinets, granite countertops, and a cookie jar — empty — lit up. There was a scatter of paraphernalia compulsory for Twentieth Century American survival: blender, toaster, knife rack, spice rack, and virgin olive oil, and Seventeenth-Century Russia entertaining: a silver samovar, transparent China tea service, and a silver tray ready for the next tsar's visit. Lean Cuisines, onion rolls, dumplings, salmon, shrimp, trout, but no steaks, burgers, or ribs stacked the freezer. The refrigerator held more promise. I set out sliced Monterey Jack, sardines, lettuce, cukes, onion, and a plump red tomato and zapped an onion roll and made a Dagwood sandwich with a smear of mayo.

I took a bite over the sink and heard Mom yip, *Don't crumb up my floor*!

The sandwich tasted as dry as chalk. I dropped it in the garbage and prowled into their office, on the north side of the house. Matching his-and-her, cherry desks stood before two windows the size of a garage door feasting on a canvas of snowy mountain peaks. I don't know what I expected to find in Mom's sanctum-sanctorum, perhaps secret journals written when she was twenty, or photographs of Joseph Stalin, or her father in the Gulag. But her desk was a mess of uncorrected quizzes and stacks of lectures bushy as an autumn maple with orange Post-ums. Dad's desk was his inviolable retreat: an orderly stack of lectures, books, quizzes, and papers.

"I guess I got Dad's obsessive-compulsive behavior," I surmised, guilt-lessly. *Not a bad thing, really,* he always said. *We'd still be living in caves if that DNA hadn't survived in the gene pool.*

Mom's red ballpoint lay atop an ungraded heap of term papers. She'd written: *Too broad!* beside the first one's title, *A Romantic Account of Pugachev's Rebel-lion,* and had stopped, apparently despairing. I pushed the obtuse scatter aside. Next to her lecture notes on *The Captain's Daughter,* there it was: a check made out to me in her signature blue fountain-pen ink for $20,000.00! God bless her. She'd done what she'd promised and written the check the minute she got home.

I called Anastasia with the gratifying news, but she wasn't home, probably at dinner with Ingrid and Kahuna. I was overjoyed, but exasperated, not being able to share the news, and I sat there fuming until it dawned on me, I'd never once in my snoopy life rifled through Mom's desk. With her gone, who could it hurt? Maybe it held secrets. Nosey is my middle name.

Filling the top left drawer were her checkbook, envelopes, Monet stationery, computer disks, pencils, and pens. The deep drawer on the right held an ac-cordion rack of folders: Taxes, Pending Bills, Insurance, Cars, Mortgage, Fidel-ity, Warranties, Dentist, ASU Contract, Journal Articles, Passports, CV, Troy's High School, Troy's Colby, Troy Marriage, My Marriages, Wills … hmmm.

I pulled the drawer out to its stop. In the very back of the drawer, in the six-inch gap beyond the accordion files was a birch box with a picture glued to the top of Renoir's *The Luncheon of the Boating Party.* Inside the box was a jumble of faded photographs. I pulled them out and studied them. A young couple of twenty or so with the notation, October 19, 1968. The woman was Mom. She wore a one-piece bathing suit, flip-flops, and a shy smile. She was slim, almost skinny, her blonde hair tousled. The young man, snickering — ogling? — was tall, slender with strawberry blond hair. He wore a brown, Soviet, army shirt with lieutenant bars over swimming trunks. He appeared self-assured, swaggering, smug, brash, and cocky — just like me. I recognized Papa from his pictures I'd seen at his mother's apartment, but I'd never seen these pictures. Apparently, Mom didn't want the reminder around. Was it a picnic? A honeymoon? One of the photos was of them laughing on a broad sweep of outdoor stairs that looked vaguely familiar. Another was in front of a hotel. A third was on a rocky beach. Mom never mentioned a honeymoon, but surely, she'd had one. A traditionalist, Mom would have insisted on it. I tried to recall the date they were married in 1968 but couldn't. I pulled out the file labeled My Marriages. The top marriage certificate, in Russian, was her most recent trip down the aisle dated January 24, 1974. Stapled to it were apostilled copies of Dad's notarized birth certificate, college diplomas, passport, first divorce, and marriage license — the chain of authentications multiple levels of Soviet bureaucrats require before granting foreigners permission to marry their cherished women. Behind these was a second marriage certificate, in Russian, of Mom and Papa's marriage, dated October 18, 1968.

"*AH-HA!*" I crowed. The day before the pictures in the box, apostilled copies of their birth certificates, and marriage license. I replaced the marriage papers and pulled out the file marked PASSPORTS. The KGB documents all Soviets' movements. Mom had four passports: two Russian Internal Passports, older and newer, and External Passports, Russian and American. The newer of the two Internal Passports was issued on her 45th birthday; the older, tattered one was issued in 1966 on her 18th birthday. It was stamped in Saint Petersburg and Moscow in 1967 for trips she had taken during college. I flipped through pages. One was stamped October 19, 1968, in Odessa, the day after she and Papa married in Kalinin.

The June I graduated from Watauga High, Mom and I flew to Odessa and then Tver. She never explained why we went to the Black Sea for graduation. Now I knew. To relive her past. The three pictures in the birch box were of my parents sitting on Odessa's Potemkin Stairs, in front of the Mozart Hotel, and at the Black Sea. Their honeymoon was at the same sites we visited on my graduation trip.

I turned to the Odessa page in Mom's Internal Passport and looked at the next pages. They bore multiple stamps entering and leaving Bishkek, Kyrgyzstan. The first one was dated August 18, 1969, three weeks after I was born. The five other stamps were dated the first week of June every successive year. Why would she visit Bishkek soon after her teaching ended every June for five years? A colleague? A relative? A boyfriend? Maybe to ski the snow-capped, five-mile-high peaks around Osh? I couldn't think of a reason, returned the passports to the file, and closed the drawer. Maybe Uncle Ivan would know.

I kissed the $20,000 check and folded it into my wallet. I called the operator for Wake Forest University Baptist Hospital's number in Winston-Salem. After speaking with several people, I landed in ICU. Dad had stabilized but would be in intensive care for a few more hours. I told the nurse I would be down tomorrow, and she said that he could go home soon but would need help. I called Watauga Medical Center, asked for the morgue, and was transferred to security. I made an appointment for Mom's identification at eight-thirty in the morning. Finally, I called the Finley Funeral Home, made an appointment for ten o'clock, and pulled out the file marked WILLS.

Surprisingly, Mom's paperwork was as orderly as a CPA and sounded like a lawyer. She had made a copy of her will with a yellow sticky note attached neatly annotated in her blue-ink handwriting: *The original of this Will, of which this is a copy, is in the vault at the State Employee's Credit Union, 1470 Blowing Rock Road, Boone, NC; the key is in my top middle desk drawer.*

I refilled my chalice, put my feet up on her desk, and settled back to read.

Mom and I arrived in Blowing Rock penniless seventeen years earlier. She had fared well. I was broke and desperate to save Anastasia's life. Would Mom help us from the grave? When I read the answer, I went upstairs to my old room and got a full whiff of my youth: football jersey, snowboard, lettered-sweater (W), and pictures. I brushed my teeth, cracked open the window, took King James and the New International versions of Bibles from my bookcase, and climbed into bed. I reread passages I'd dog-eared at Colby when struggling with the idea of immortality in Thessalonians 4:13-18, Philippians 3:20-21, Acts 24:15, Corinthians 5:1-2, Romans 1:23 and 2:7, John 5:24-29, 6:40, 11:25, 14:1-6, and 16:22. Jesus assured us: *This is the will of my Father that everyone that beholdeth the Son, and believeth in Him, should have eternal life, and I will raise him up at the last day.*

I recalled that Mary Magdalene's argument in Mark 16:9 had been deemed fallacious by my professor. Her *logic*: I saw Jesus rise from the tomb; if you don't believe me, there's the empty tomb. It didn't wash and left me unconvinced. Luke 24 claimed the disembodied spirit of Jesus showed his hands and feet to eleven apostles. He materialized, sat down, and ate fish and honeycomb with them before drifting up into the sky for heaven. Same argument: If you don't believe me, look at our empty plates.

My first dog, Rocky, was run over. She never ate again. My buddy, Tink, died from a bullet to the head, standing beside me in a foxhole. He never ate again. Luke, please don't show me an empty plate and say that's proof of anything except something ate everything.

I closed the Bibles, gazed about my room, unchanged since high school, clicked off the light, and did something I hadn't done in ages. At Colby, I had decided I was an agnostic. But in case I was wrong, I knelt beside my bedside, steepled my hands, bowed, and prayed for Mom's immortal soul. When I finished, I recited a childhood prayer, "Now I lay me down to sleep, I pray the Lord, my soul to keep, if I should die before I wake, I pray the Lord, my soul to take ..."

And I slept like a baby — waking every hour — doubting Paul's promise of eternal life and wondering why there wasn't a Biblical mention of the soul's immortality as there was in Plato, Origen, and Augustine. Did Hosanna, Allah, Thor, and Zeus make the same promise? Tears flooded my eyes. I prayed when I saw Mom's body she would give me a sign that her soul was conscious as Plato claimed or at least let me know she was asleep as Thessalonians claimed.

During the night, I wondered about all the astrophysicists harping about how big the universe is. Dad says, in a vacuum, light travels 5,878,625,000 miles in a year, making the universe 156 billion light years wide. Multiply the speed of light — use 6 trillion miles/year — and multiply it times 156 billion. You get that colossal, septillion number with twenty-four zeros, a vast universe and a very big task for God to have created in six days. My final thought that night was of Mom's five annual trips to Osh, Kyrgyzstan. Why had she taken them? That wondering made my chest feel constricted; I couldn't get enough air and got up and opened the window wide.

Finally, I slept.

***

ELEVEN

Morgue: Boone, North Carolina
November 25, 1991

Sunshine drifting through Fraser Firs awoke me as if it had been an alarm clock. I'd slept fitfully, woke disoriented, and looked out the opened window. I sat up, blinked, orienting, and it came to me. Winter. My old room. Monday. Morgue.

A blustering wind had whipped snow out of the sky and powdered the windowsill. I threw off the quilts and shut the window, glancing out at ten inches of fresh snow. Along the ridgeline, the deceptive weight of snow bowed firs to look like supplicants and hunched over Mr. Villafuerte next door, shoveling his drive. My nose streamed. I erupted in a series of Vesuvian sneezes that rocked the wall poster of my high-school idol, Whitney Houston. I snatched a handful of Kleenex from the box on the bedside table, blew my nose, and dove back under the covers, humming the *Greatest Love of All*. I stared at Whitney, thought of Mom, and tried to examine a jumble of emotions. What I felt was a mixture of love, bitterness, and the tremor of raw fear. What I saw were loving images of Mom and me running up the path from the Volga River ferry through daisy-filled fields bordered with hard- and soft-wood tree-crowns packed together like puffballs and dunce caps shimmering with every hue of green: beryl, pea, spinach, chartreuse, emerald, lime, olive, and jade. Us galloping down the lane to babushka's dacha and her waiting at the gate with an icy pitcher of kvass; us in her verdant gardens behind her palatine summer home — the dacha had electricity and a privy; it *did not* have running water.

And then my mind raced to Washington, D.C. I saw bitter images and our do-nothing Congress, incapable of barricading our southern border, and Mom mangled in Dad's white Volvo, and Anastasia grasping for a capsule of taxol just out of reach. I thought of what lay ahead at the morgue and still felt hot with fever, but cold sweat ran down my chest. I grabbed more tissues and swabbed myself but still felt hot with fever. I poked through the medicine cabinets for some Dayquil, found it in the master bath, and took a swig. The day's bitter cold suited my mood, and I took it as an omen. It had been twenty hours since Mom's death. Now I must identify her body. The woman who had given me life, the woman who, even in death, was reaching out to give Anastasia life.

I twisted up the electric heater in the bathroom, showered, shaved, and dressed in shorts, long johns, jeans, T-shirt, flannel shirt, wool sweater, Russian dog-hair socks, and Dad's too-big L. L. Bean rubber-and-leather boots. Down-stairs, I slipped on my new, good-to-fifty-below-zero L. L. Bean coat and dug through the entry chest for gloves and scarf. I pulled on my Colby ski cap, double-checked my wallet, unfolded Mom's check, kissed it again, replaced it, and locked up. I was still humming *Greatest Love* and thinking of Mom as I brushed a foot of snow off the Subaru. I cranked it up, jockeyed it around, and saw Mr. Villafuerte wave with a grim smile. He'd heard. I held up a finger in a see-you-later-sign and nosed the all-wheel-drive Subaru through the snow-covered driveway onto road.

The storm began anew, and snow blew in small, incoherent swirls as I plowed down Chestnut Street. It came down steadily when I turned right onto Main Street and inched into the village. In summer, tourists throng Blowing Rock, but at eight o'clock on a phlegmy winter morning, its trendy shops were buttoned up, second-homers decamped. Just beyond Kilwins ice cream shop, I turned right on Sunset Drive, swooped down the hill past the elementary school gym, and up onto SR 321, turning left, north, on the two-lane. I stopped at Food Lion for coffee and a blueberry muffin took one bite and tossed it at a crow working the Dumpster. No appetite.

Down the hill, past Shops-on-the-Parkway, a scatter of ditched cars colo-nized the breakdown lane along the unplowed four-lane. I made it the six miles into Boone with one spinout and no calamities and pulled into the Watauga County Medical Center at 8:23. For the next five minutes, I sipped cold coffee, stared at the parking lot, and dwelled on the task ahead. Uncontrollably, tears blurred my vision and gave the snow-covered shrubbery the illusionary appearance of a *Trompe-l'oeil* painting. My dreaded task seemed that much more implausible.

And then, inexplicably, my emotions surged. I felt joyful reminiscences, no longer grappling with the haunting doubts of Luke's promise. Mom might be in a *death sleep* and would awaken and be resurrected when Jesus returned. But then I wasn't so sure. Those heart-wrenching qualms left me feeling compassless, in *terra incognita*. I knew I'd stammer and blubber in Mom's identification process and just wanted it over. I gulped the last of the cold coffee and tried to dwell on our good times. We left Moscow and arrived in Blowing Rock on August 9, 1974. The Vietnam War was ending. No. 37 had resigned. Unelected Gerald Ford, No. 38, was president. America suffered from political skepticism and raging inflation, but it was at peace, something the Soviet Union rarely was. Mom said it was a very good time to start a new life in a new country. And it was. Now, seventeen years, three months, and fifteen days later, her life was over. My life was splintering. My lifelong stalwart was gone. I thanked God she had taught me love and perseverance, and I vowed I would never let her down. How could I? In death, she had reached out to help us a final time, providing amply for us in her will. Now it was up to me to save Anastasia's life by going to China for the taxol.

Yanking my ski cap down over my ears, I opened the car door and trudged through the weakening blizzard to the hospital, the gloom outside not half as dark as the gloom inside me. I knew all life must die. Even the 177-year-old Galapagos Tortoise eventually die, and the oldest plant on earth, the snarled and stunted 5,000-year-old bristlecone pine, clinging to life at the summit of the Rockies, will, one day, die. But neither turtle nor tree will return in an afterlife. The criminality is when death strikes before one's time. That is an insult, a shock. The biblical promise of bodily resurrection some far-off day in the hazy future was of absolutely no comfort to me today and sounded silly. If bodily resurrection took place before the sun puffed into a red giant star and boiled our oceans and devoured our Earth, where would all the resurrected live?

The hospital's double glass doors opened automatically. Handy if you had an armful of flowers. I stomped snow onto the mat between the outer and inner doors and puddled the spotless beige carpet approaching the reception desk.

A thin, gray-haired lady in pink looked up and smiled kindly. "Good morning, young man," she said pleasantly. "May I help you?"

"Good morning," I replied with a head full of cobwebs. "I have an appointment to, ah, to identify my mother. Her body."

"Oh, dear. Let me get Chief Amero."

She picked up the phone and pushed some buttons.

Promptly the chief of hospital police appeared and introduced himself. He had a basset-hound face and melancholy blue eyes. Dick Amero was a tall, heavyset man in his late fifties. In high school, he'd probably played defensive end. His hand was smooth, his handshake firm, and when he escorted me to the elevator, his leather belt creaked under the weight of the tools of his trade. We descended one floor. The door opened, and we stepped into a long, glaringly white, corridor lined with unmarked doors. Two doors had windows. I expected the distinctive odor of formaldehyde and the sound of saws cutting bone, but there was neither odor nor sound. The hall was as void of sensory tactility as if we'd just stepped out of Apollo 11 onto the moon.

Halfway down the corridor, Amero head-tilted at a door on our left. He opened it and stepped into a white-tiled room. A chemical scent hung in the air. I looked over his shoulder at a cement floor slanted inward to a center drain beneath a stainless steel table that sloped slightly head to foot. Grooved with herringbone-pattern gullies, it emptied into a deeper slot running down the middle to the foot of the table above the floor drain. Bolted to one end of the table was a stainless steel rack stuffed with hoses, saws, hooks, knives, tubes, injector-gun, and drills. Along the back wall was a large, deep sink and shelves neatly lined with chemicals, equipment, and manuals. To the left was a walk-in cooler. It was large but smaller than the one we used at the restaurant that kept raw meat at 37°. I couldn't make out its temperature.

I tapped Amero on the shoulder. "Where's Mom?"

"In the walk-in," he said, nodding to it. "It holds four. Any more, we stand 'em up."

I thought that an insensitive thing to say and was about to say so when a pleasant looking Latina wearing a starched white uniform and thick white sweater swung out of the cooler and re-latched the bulky door.

"Theresa," Amero said, "this is Troy Locke here to identify his Mom," and to me, "This is Miss Gomez. Let's step into the room behind us." He thumbed over his shoulder and turned, almost running me down. "Wheel her over, Theresa."

"*Si*," she said. Even America's rural hospitals import Philippine help.

Amero opened the door to a small, narrow room and motioned me to a folding chair, one of a dozen lining the left wall. The right wall was empty.

Gurney ready. I sat. Amero leaned against the doorframe, hands in his pockets, eyes resting on the floor. It was unnervingly quiet. We could have been Armstrong and Aldrin on the Sea of Tranquility. We remained silent, as if we didn't know what to say. Except me. I knew precisely what to say, which was absolutely nothing, and I kept saying it with my chin on my chest and my eyes shut. I felt like kneeling and praying, confessing to God my awe at His sunrises and sunsets, blooming flowers, sweet scents, all the phenomenally amazing miracles of life, the orderliness of the universe and lamenting my sins and reservations about an afterlife. But I didn't throw myself to my knees, and my eyes didn't stay shut, and it was not the time for confession. I had to process the sight of Mom.

THUMP! My eyes whipped to the door. The gurney had struck the viewing room doorframe. Amero grabbed one end of it and yanked the gurney in, barefeet first. The duo jockeyed the gurney back-and-forth a couple of times, snugged it against the far wall, and stepped back, giving me plenty of space to faint without whacking my head. Amero resumed his post, hands pocketed, meaty shoulders pressed against the closed door. His rubbery face smiled compassionately. He gave Theresa a grim go-ahead nod. I stood motionless, my legs trembling. I made fists. I felt dread and quivered. How does one explain morgue fear? How can a war veteran, who had seen blood and gore and smelled the sweet-and-sour putrescence of cadavers by the score sprawled across desert sand have an unalloyed fear of death? I had had no death neurosis in Iraq. But this was Mom, her corpse, and it made me shake with fright. Or was it the stark reminder of my mortality and doubt about Luke's promise?

Theresa sought my eyes and held them as she folded back the stiff white sheet in neat narrow folds. I made the sign of the cross. I wanted to fling my arms around Mom. But at that moment, a myriad of doubts filled my head. Who and what would I be embracing? Mom or a soulless corpse? Had it left already? Where does God store souls after they're disembodied? Is there a Soul Warehouse as Socrates claimed? Has this always been the case? Did Australopith, Homo Rudolfensis, and Neanderthal have souls? Did 3.2-million-year-old, hominin Lucy have a soul? Were they all in some overcrowded warehouse somewhere?

Despite my five formative years of Russian Orthodoxy and subsequent years of Episcopalianism, the idea of this corpse having a soul seemed bizarre and out of touch. My faith conflicted with my common sense. A dull, oppressive, insipid, emotionally-draped Christian discipline grounded in creeds, fantasies, delusions, superstitions, and habits of faith had replaced fact and science. Christianity's cold, rigid, unambiguous heirloom of beliefs had been doled out to the judgmental and unquestioning by a dogmatic hierarchy.

Theresa made a fold. Mom's head appeared. My knees weakened at the blood-matted hair. Theresa's eyes stayed locked on mine. She made another fold. More hair. Another. More hair. *Dark* hair. My eyes darted to the feet. No red toenails. No bunions! Another fold and the forehead, eyes, and nose of an attractive, *young* woman of nineteen appeared, emanating life.

"*This is not my mother!*" I cried out in anguish.

Theresa's hands jumped as if the corpse had come to life.

"It's all wrong," I howled. "Wrong feet, wrong hair, wrong face, wrong everything!"

"I'm sorry, Mister Locke," Theresa said in heavily accented English. "The toe tags must have gotten switched. Last night was crazy. Five peoples brought in — "

Chief Amero pointed with his chin. "Who's *this*?"

"Must be that ASU student hit by the snowplow. I be back quick."

Theresa grasped the gurney and yanked it out. There was enough of a delay for her to have stood up the poor girl and wrestle Mom onto the gurney. Theresa returned and restarted the process.

This time, my eyes locked on the bright red toenails, bare feet — knobby bunions alabaster in death — sprawled out shamelessly on the gurney. I stepped closer. Mom's feet were so white and stiff they looked like marble. There was a tag, LOCKE, tied to her big toe. Her heels were purple. No American had misshapen feet like those. My eyes moved up the draped sheet, over the bulge of knees to the wide hips, on to her large breasts that had settled like puddles of pudding. Theresa made more folds. The top of Mom's head was intact, its crown of golden hair curling over the left temple. I stepped closer. Theresa made another fold. Mom's right temple was damp, the hair washed, the temple bashed in by something the size and shape of a two-by-four. Doorpost. Theresa kept folding down to Mom's neck and dropped her hands to her sides.

There was an expression of mild surprise on Mom's face. Her eyes were partial slits. Her lips were opened enough to expose teeth as if she were about to say something pleasant. Whatever she was about to say was frozen ineffably on her lips, halted in the middle of an utterance. Her nose was bent at an odd angle. Her right cheekbone was black. I studied her expression. There was a slight gleam, not a smile, more forced than a smile. Maybe a death-grin, a

Chelsea grin, an involuntary muscular reaction to the deathblow. No, that didn't make sense. It hinted of a demure mien, a hesitant simper, a Mona Lisa smile. A smile of peace and certainty, as if the last thought in her life had been a secret. I felt the urge to utter a goodbye to this stiff, ungainly body, but one cannot speak to someone who was no longer there. It would vulgarize the moment when her spirit, so recently released, hovered above her, outraged at the inquisitive brutality of the coming autopsy, knowing she would be sliced and diced and probed before cremation. I stepped back and felt my sense of continuity, my touch of vicarious immortality, fleeing. My overly-sensitive nose detected the sour stink of decay, a smell I'd known so well in Iraq. It seemed a good place to stop thinking, and I willed myself to stop. I tried to say goodbye but could not. If her smile meant a harbored secret, let her die knowing something no one else will ever know. I stood there a little longer, staring at mom's face, and, naturally, I started wondering about her secret.

I stepped to her side and ran my fingertips down her cheek. Her skin felt stiff, cold, and papery as if I could peel it off. It made her face a poor imitation of her, a bad wax cast. I had had no clue as to what to expect in the morgue. Mom could have been bloody, bruised, and barely identifiable. Theresa had cleaned her up. This body was, indeed, Mom, but it was not her. Her essence was gone and left a shell. And not an accurate one. Her features were true — damaged and bruised — but true. Even with her eyes sunken into her skull a bit, she looked as if she had been relating a pleasant story and fallen asleep. But her body lacked the mobility of expression, the eyes that always sought others, the hands that always gestured when she spoke, the easy respiration, the caring and goodness and glow from within. Without the breath of life, there was no Mom. Her spark, her essence, had vanished. Mom, standing tall, erect, and poised, could step into a crowded room and total strangers would immediately stop talking and turn and stare at her, sensing in her a dignity, grace, and virtue so rarely seen in others. Now her switch had been turned off. Her body had shut down.

You survived immigration, acculturation, and youthful-widowhood and gave me life, I thought and bent down and kissed her ice-cold cheek. Straightening, I was overwhelmed with doubts: Are you aware, Mom? Are you asleep as the Bible teaches? And what about Papa? Am I like him? Am I an apple off his tree? I wanted to ask her which of the conflicting claims of immortality were true. I touched her arm. It was cold and lifeless. I found no peace, no tranquility, in the extraordinary ideas that someday in the far distant future Jesus would reappear and Mom, this corpse, would be resurrected, instilled with a soul and given eternal life when there was no universe in which to live. Mom believed in God and accepted Jesus as the Messiah, who would bring resurrection and a physical life to everyone, even the doubters, and give them immortality. I tried to believe it, touched Mom's cold face the last time, and begged for enough of God's blessing to accept the Bible's implausible ideas.

I had no idea how much time had elapsed during my ellipsis and said, "This is my mother, Doctor Irina Yevgenyevna Locke."

"Thank you," Chief Amero said. He nodded to Theresa.

Theresa gently pulled the sheet over Mom's face and wheeled her out of the room.

"If you need me, Chief, I'll be at Finley Funeral Home," I said and fled.

***

A strong west wind had blown the sky clean, and the bright sun tried to lighten my spirits. I drove to Finley's Funeral Home. I had planned to stop at Mom's Foreign Language Department office and gather her things. But despite offering languages as different as German, Hindi, Spanish, and Farsi, which all came from the same Proto-Indo-European, or PIE, parents, her office was usually a cauldron of animosity, epic ego battles, and bilious outbursts. I opted to let a braver Daniel enter the den.

"My name is Troy Locke," I said at Finley's, "I called last night about my mother."

"Certainly, sir," said a distinguished looking gentleman with a helmet of gray locks parted in the middle, blow-dried, and lacquered in place. He wore morticians' clothes: black suit, white shirt, black tie, black shoes. No color. "I'm Ken Finley. Good to meet you, sir."

"I, ah, need to make arrangements. My Mom's at the morgue."

"Yes, sir. We'll pick her up this morning."

"I've no idea where to start, Mister Finley."

"Most folks don't. Come into my office. Let's start with things you do know." Mr. Finley motioned me into a small room with a window, three client chairs, and a desk. We sat. He took out a form, unscrewed a fountain pen, and looked up compassionately. "What's your mother's full name and address, Mister Locke?"

"Irina Yevgenyevna — " I spelled it — "Locke, nine twenty-two Chestnut Drive, Blowing Rock, North Carolina, two-eight-six-zero-five." I silently thanked him for the gimme question.

"Date and place of birth?"

"August eighteenth nineteen forty-nine, Tver, Russia."

"Social Security number?"

I dug it out of my wallet and read it to him.

"Was your mother a citizen?"

"Oh, yes. We both have been since nineteen-seventy-six."

"Did she leave a will?"

"Copy and an original. The original's in the Credit Union by the Police Station."

"Fine. Will you be employing an attorney?"

"As soon as we finish, I'm going to Allen, Wagner, Coté, and LaPointe on West King Street to see Ms. LaPointe."

"It's a fine firm," he said. "Now, did your mother specify the type of funeral she desired?"

"She did." I took a deep breath. "She wants to be cremated as soon as possible."

"We can do that. Did she specify an urn and place of interment?"

"She wants half her ashes buried here, half in Russia with Papa. He died in Afghanistan at my age. His ashes were returned to Russia and scattered on the Volga. I'll be going back in a few weeks and will bring her ashes with me."

"Certainly," Mr. Finley said. "I understand your stepdad's in Winston; I'm sure you'd like to get down there. I think that'll do us for now. We'll cremate your mother's body and hold her ashes." Then he asked another question. "Will there be a ceremony?"

Russians always hold a *panikhida* — a memorial service for the dead — and I was surprised Mom had not mentioned it in her will. I had attended a *panikhida* as a boy when my friend, Alex, was run over while on his bike. I was sure Mom would want one.

"Most of her colleagues don't teach on Thursdays," I said. "Would that work?"

"Two to four p.m. Thursday's fine. I'll speak with Miss LaPointe and make arrangements."

I asked him two other questions that prompted lengthy replies. And after hearing those, I thanked him and bolted.

I drove to West King Street, Boone's old main street, and made an appointment for ten o'clock Tuesday morning with Mom's attorney. Her paralegal, an officious, short, stout woman with more than a trace of facial hair gave me a list of items to bring to the appointment. And then she reviewed each one of them: Will, Birth Certificate, Marriage Certificate, Naturalization Documentation, deeds, titles to house and car, details of the mortgage, insurance policies, retirement plans, outstanding bills, bank accounts, safety deposit box, credit cards, and two years tax returns. She said her firm would file notices to creditors, compile asset lists, file papers with the County Clerk, obtain a Federal Tax ID number, determine the Kelly Blue Book value of her Red Volvo, post death notices in the *Watauga Democrat* for a month, and maintain all records of disbursements as stipulated by the court. I said Mom had listed her debts as one credit card, Blue Ridge Electric, Skyline Telephone, the local cable company, and a home mortgage. The paralegal asked me to bring a copy of my parents' bank signature card for any joint checking accounts giving Dad the right of survivorship, which meant any balance would pass directly to him. She asked if the house was jointly owned as well. She said, if it were, the house would pass directly to Dad, circumventing the estate and taxes, and concluded by asking about jewelry, clothes, and the memorial service. By then, my mind was so cluttered with her details I could not think. I went to the bathroom, washed my face, and called Baptist Hospital from the receptionist's desk. I learned a few specifics of dad's injuries and that he would be released Thursday. That gave me time to gather all the documents and call Anastasia during her early lunch break in Orlando.

I retraced my path to the Credit Union to cash Mom's check. I'd need crisp new hundred-dollar bills for the taxol purchase. Russians, and undoubtedly Chinese, refuse to accept anything but new bills. Counterfeiting flourishes in Asia. Inside the two-story credit union, five tellers worked a short line. I waited until a teller in a red dress smiled and nodded. I endorsed Mom's check for $20,000 and passed it to the smiley face.

"Brand new hundred dollar bills, please," I said.

The teller returned my smile, studied the check, front and back, looked again at the signatures, and slid off her high stool. "Just a minute, sir, we may not ... " She was gone a long time.

When she reappeared, she was accompanied by a tall, thin, no-nonsense, gray-haired woman in a dark blue suit and blue heels, probably the manager. She looked vaguely familiar, smiled warmly, and motioned me to the far side of the teller line.

"I'm Anita Roy," she said, "Supervisor of Tellers." She offered me her slim right hand. Her left hand held the *Watauga Democrat*.

"Glad to meet you," I said. "Is there a problem with Mom's check?"

Anita held up the newspaper. "We read of her death in today's paper. I'd like to convey our sympathy. I knew Doctor Locke. She was a good customer and a long-time friend. I haven't seen you, Troy, since high school. You and my son played football together."

"Sure, Tim," I said. "Mom always said the bank was kind to her."

"That's nice to hear, but — " Anita raised a cautionary finger — "according to the law, we're unable to cash that check now."

I gasped. "She's got plenty of money in the bank."

"She does. What I mean is no bank can cash her check. Not until her estate has gone through probate. The law is strict; until the legal process concludes, assets cannot be distributed."

My breathing changed suddenly and audibly into inhales and exhales. "But we need this money. My wife's got cancer. This check is buying her a lifesaving drug. You *must* cash it."

Anita shook her head. "I'm sorry, Troy. It will take sixty to ninety days or longer before we can. There's nothing we can do." She handed the check back and turned away.

I felt utterly powerless. The worst feeling in the world. Now, what?

***

TWELVE

Wake Forest University Baptist Hospital, Winston-Salem
November 26, 1991

A sliver of moon was setting in the lifeless western sky when I left Blowing Rock at six Tuesday morning. To get to SR 421, which descends to Winston-Salem, Greensboro, Raleigh, and points east, I took the Blue Ridge Parkway, a CCC [13] project etched into 469 miles of Appalachian peaks from the Shenandoah Valley to the Cherokee Indian Reservation. It took me twenty minutes of careful navigation on the icy two-lane to reach the state road. Driving into Boone would have been safer and faster, but I relished the mountaintop's vast emptiness and needed time to think. Monday night, waves of grief had struck. I had thought they would have passed after two days, coming to grips with Mom's death. They didn't. The stabbing sorrow that she was *truly gone* and being cremated tomorrow haunted me as nothing else ever had in my life. My last two questions to Mr. Finley came after he'd asked if I wanted to witness her cremation. I, foolishly, had asked him to describe the process. He did. In horrific detail.

Mom's decaying body would be placed in a pine box, slid into an oven, and, through a Judas window, I could watch her burn at seven hundred fifty degrees for three hours. The parts of her that wouldn't completely burn — shinbones, thighbones, hips, shoulders, skull — would be shoveled into a Cremulator, a refrigerator-sized machine with steel balls that pulverized bone to six pounds of gritty, black, eighth-inch, flaky ash. The ash would be scooped up and funneled into *a charming, velvet-lined, mahogany box adorned with brass hinges for display at her memorial service.* He showed me the enchanting box, which, after the service, in a back room, would be opened and half mom's ashes poured into a cardboard box for scattering on the Volga.

Cremation horrified me. I thanked him and opted for a standard burial, asking for those details, adding, "And don't omit a thing."

Mr. Finley said mom would be washed with formaldehyde and disinfectants with names like Permaglo, Permaflow, Permaflex, Introfiant, Restorative and Inrseel. Incisions would be cut in the brachial artery, under her armpits to avoid being seen by mourners, and formaldehyde pumped into her veins to preserve and plump-up her body, giving it color and lifelikeness. Mom's intestines, bowel, and bladder would be drained; her internal organs sucked dry and refilled with formaldehyde to avoid stinking. Pads would be inserted into her rectum and vagina to avoid leaking; cotton would be stuffed up her nose and down her throat to stop seepage. A mouth guard, placed between lips and teeth, would plump out her lips that would be stitched shut from the inside and glued tight. Since eyes sink back into their sockets after death, Eyecaps, smooth on the eyeball side and studded on the lid side, would be inserted to clutch the eyelids, giving her eyes an oval shape, and preventing the eyelids from popping open during viewing. A moisturizer applied to her eyelids would keep them from drying and cracking opened. Mom's hair would be washed, nasal and ear hair clipped, nails cleaned and cut (skin retracts after death; nails appear longer), then a little cosmetic touch here and there would be applied to avoid giving her a waxy look.

Cremation horrified me; embalming was gruesomely worse. We proceeded with cremation.

It was with great relief I looped along atop the CCC's long-ago exertion, gazing down at the vast Blue Ridge Mountains, transfixed by their beauty as layered peaks hazed from view. My ears popped, zipping off the Parkway and dropping onto SR 421, which slalomed down the two-lane for seven miles, descending like a ski jump before blossoming into a four-lane as the panorama flattened outside Wilkesboro. I goosed it through raging snow gusts and occasional whiteouts that slowed me some across the Piedmont and crossed the Winston-Salem city limits at nine o'clock, taking Business I-40 into the city. At the Cloverdale Avenue Exit, I took Medical Center Boulevard, turned in at Wake Forest University Baptist Hospital, a sprawling pile of brick and mortar and an outstanding example of why Americans spend more money than any other people on earth to stay alive.

A woman at the pedestrian entrance directed me to Neurology, Reynolds Tower, eighth floor.

Unlike the Maternity Ward at Watauga Medical Center, always staffed by cute nurses cooing over babies, neurology was different. A man wearing a badge identifying himself as Ray Collins, Surgical Nurse, stepped from the hushed privacy of the nurse's station presided over by gray-haired professionals. Apparently, one must attain a certain age and maturity to be sufficiently empathic to tend the cranial afflicted. Ray had an aristocratic face, convincing manner, and British appearance. His voice confirmed it when he made a small, sympathetic smile and a slight bow.

"I'm sorry to hear of your mother's death, Mr. Locke," he said, his eyes studying me carefully. "There is good news, though. Your father had a cerebral aneurysm, and the doctors' prognosis is a full recovery."

"What's a cerebral aneurysm, Ray?"

Sensitive to my ignorance, Ray began, with boundless patience, "An aneurysm is a weakness in the wall of ruptured blood vessel, usually caused by a hypertensive vascular disease."

"You mean high blood pressure?"

"Yes," Ray replied, smiling. "Often thin athletic men have elevated blood pressure. That, the stress of your mom's death and the accident's cranial blow together, or separately, caused the rupture to an already-weakened cranial blood vessel and leakage into his skull. Our timely response and clot-busting drugs averted more brain damage."

I was baffled. "How did you ever guess the inside of his head was bleeding?"

"Symptoms of a conspicuous head injury: slurred speech and pronounced weakness on one side of his mouth. We performed a Computer Tomography Angiogram pinpointing the location of the ruptured artery and rushed him into surgery. After a small cranial incision, the ruptured artery was replaced with a section of artery spliced from his leg. Some of your dad's symptoms will linger, but there is *nothing* to be alarmed at."

I was astounded. "You mean Dad will be okay?"

"He'll have a droopy mouth, slurred speech, and fumble with his right hand for a bit. But he *will* regain all functions in about six months."

"That's fantastic, Ray. When may I take him home?"

"Thursday morning. He'll need help for a month or two, but let me get Doctor Meserve. He's just finishing up in surgery, and that may take twenty minutes. Your dad's in room eight forty-eight if you'd like to see him."

"You bet I do," I replied and struck off down the long hushed hall. I was never as aware of my father's anonymity as I was at then, startled to see abundant versions of him — bespectacled, gray-haired men, heads mummy-wrapped, anxious eyes fixed on opened doors, waiting. At room 848, I steeled myself for the unexpected.

Dad dosed, slouched in his flex-a-bed at a forty-five degrees angle, eyes shut, hair whiter, face thinner. He looked like an imposter inside an octogenarian's body, gravity tugging flesh south, face-bones prominent, wrinkles hollowing. Mom's death, his injury, stroke, no teaching, life's boundless futilities, had changed him in a way easy to spot but hard to label. With her gone and us in Orlando, Dad not only suffered our physical absences, but he was emotionally unemployed as well. He didn't know what to do with himself. No one depended on him. No one needed him. It gave him the gaunt, weary look — the face of the solitude overexposed to life's vicissitudes.

When he heard my footsteps on the glossy vinyl, his eyelids lifted slowly. When he saw me, his face broke into a bright, spontaneous, loopy smile. To the right of his philtrum, the V-shaped vertical groove extending from under-nose to upper-lip, the right side of his mouth sloped down as if someone had stepped on his jaw. Somehow he rallied his ubiquitous *joie de vivre.* It sparkled. With his left hand, he seized my wrist and reeled me in. We hugged.

He pushed me away, studied me, and pulled me back in. He held me tightly against his bony chest. His breath smelled moldy, stale, and sour. "It's good to see you, son," he slurred, patting my back with his good hand. "Are you okay?"

I leaned back out of range. "I will be, Dad. And you?"

One side of his lips curved up. "I'll be okay. My mind's clear. But you look worried."

"It's been rough. Mom, Anastasia, you. Everything's falling apart. Yesterday I had to identify Mom, and then I heard too much about cremation. Did you know she wanted cremation?"

Dad's placed his left hand under my chin and turned my face to his. "We both want it. Mom wants half her ashes buried in Blowing Rock, half scattered on the Volga."

I gulped some air. "I read her will. Her service is Thursday at two o'clock."

"We'll be there." Dad fumbled for the control box with his left hand, snagged it, and pushed a button. The bed groaned; the head rose. When it was eighty degrees, he dropped the box and nodded at a plastic water jug. I picked it up, sloshed ice around, poured some in a plastic glass, and placed a straw between his lips. He took a long sip, wiped his mouth with the back of a hand, and dug heels into the mattress to push up and sit tall, ready to deliver a lecture.

"You look frightened, too, son," he began, words slurred but not enough to be confusing.

"I am," I said, shivering at reflections of Mom. "I don't know what I believe. I thought I did, but I'm at the end of my tether. Religion preaches certainty, but I find murk. Science seems clear, but reconciling the two leaves me swimming in brackish water. There's no common sense. Christianity was based on inscribed tablets handed down by God and conveyed in fishermen tales and explained by theologians. Science is based on factual observation. Ninety percent of Dutch, Germans, and French have dumped Christianity and closed thousands of their churches. The attitude has tsunamied across the Atlantic. Our soaring cathedrals are being sold for skateboard parks, circuses, shops, condos, and bars. And still, despite all that, slick, mega-church pastors are growing and spouting their *logic* to vast numbers of eager congregants."

"Blind faith's hard to accept," Dad said, "but everyone wants to believe in Santa Claus. People are weary of being stuck in old, inexplicable religious ruts they can't climb out of and yearn for certitude. Mega-pastors preach hope. When I was your age, death frightened. Religion bewildered me. They don't now. Everyone and everything dies. Most of us live in denial of this until late in life when mired in sickness. Long ago, I decided there was but one imperative in life I could subscribe to, use your time wisely and add your thin verse to the Book of Life. I refuse to be a hypocrite and attempt to affect others or mislead them. Either there is life after death, or there is not and scream God is dead. Neither can be proven. I've spent my life recalibrating old beliefs, squaring them with new knowledge, and I do believe I am the architect of my life, *the master of my fate, the captain of my soul,* as Hanley says."

"Yes, but faith is a virtue in religion," I said. "It's a vice in science, and the dichotomy is tearing me apart." I looked into Dad's eyes and dropped my head in exasperated resignation.

He squeezed my arm, wanting more. I said, "The Bible's passages about resurrection are incredibly implausible. I saw Mom. *An afterlife for her*? That's crazy. When the electrons in her brain shut down, she died. Period. The idea of her soul stored on some heavenly shelf waiting to be implanted in her ashes like she was a cake-in-a-box awaiting an egg and an oven is absurd. Mom is as dead as road kill."

Dad slurred, "There are events in life that ask questions and there are events that answer them. From the dawn of man, he has refused to accept death as the end of life."

"So, 'mankind built a theological skeleton on which to hang its hopes,'" I said, quoting him.

Dad gave me a loopy smile. "Expressed in the charm of Plato, the logic of Aristotle, or the exuberance of today's millionaire mega-preachers, a shelter *is* provided by an afterlife rationale."

"And is that why immortality is a common thread in all great religions and philosophies extending back to Iran's prophet, Zarathustra, six hundred years before Christianity?"

"Yes." Dad ran his tongue around his dry, cracked lips and motioned. "God creates atoms in minutes, planets in millions of years, and man in five billion years."

I shook the ice in the glass, poured some more water, and tilted it toward him. "Dad," I said, as he sipped, "but the impossible can't happen. Mom wake up? Never."

The water was restorative. "Christians, Jews, Buddhists, Hindus, and Muslims love theological explanations cloaked in philosophic 'logic.' To a religion, they believe the spark-of-life comes from somewhere and goes somewhere, and I think they are correct. Something does, indeed, seem to be immortal, immaterial, and incorporeal at the heart of all this."

"So you took a big leap of faith?"

"Yes, I suppose I did," Dad acknowledged. "A lifetime of questioning has left me believing the soul can exist apart from the body and resides with God until it is implanted at birth or joins an astral body in a nonphysical dimension after death."

I shook my head. "Dad, proclaiming your faith in a fantasy doesn't make it the Truth, only weird. I think Hawkins is closer to the unnerving truth. In a few billion years, our dying sun will go through its death throes. The hydrogen that fuels its nuclear fusion reaction will run out. The sun will swell two hundred times its size and eventually collapse into a tiny white dwarf with immense gravity. Earth will either be swallowed up by the red giant's searing heat that will boil our oceans and burn us to cinders or we'll be pulled apart by the white dwarf, and our solar system will become great globs of frozen carbon. There are paradigms for this observable scenario out there now."

"That's so glum," Dad said. "If life as we know it is to continue what must mankind do?"

"We find a Goldilocks planet. They're hundreds of them trillions of miles away."

Dad smiled that loopy smile again. "Not a great prospect." He turned my wrist and looked at my Timex. "They'll shoo you out in a minute. Did you get Mom's check?"

"I did, but the bank won't cash it. The manager said Mom's estate had to go through probate first."

"That's right. I'll write you another. Now, when must you return to work?"

"After the funeral, Thursday evening."

"Okay." Dad looked around. "One last thing and this will sound strange, do you remember when and where Mom and I honeymooned?"

I studied his face for a clue. There was absolutely nothing there. "I remember your anniversary, January twenty-fourth. I don't remember the year or where you went for your honeymoon, no."

"Because we held off taking it. I flew back to America the day after we married in nineteen seventy-four. Your Mom finished her school year at Tver State University; I finished mine at ASU. Then, in June, I returned to Russia, and we left for Osh, Kyrgyzstan. Son, it's the place your Papa — "

At that very moment, there was a loud rapping at the door.

"Come in, come in," Dad called out in his professor's voice, one big garish sound.

A short, wiry doctor marched into the room, head down, scanning papers fluttering on a clipboard. "Your blood work looks good, Mr. Locke," he rattled off, "now if you've got help at home, you may leave Thursday." He looked up, spotted me, and stuck out a paw. "Didn't see you, son, I'm Bill Meserve." He gave me a firm shake.

"Troy Locke," I replied. "So Dad's good to go?"

"He is," Dr. Meserve said. "Ray Collins will review your discharge instructions, Mr. Locke."

"It's Doctor Locke, actually," I said to the physician. "Dad's a professor."

Dad slurred, "Don't fret titles, Boone village has more Ph.D.'s than parking spaces."

Doctor Meserve laughed heartily. "I bet ninety-five percent Democrats, like all universities?""

"Of course, but caviar democrats," Dad chortled, "like Hollywood. I'm the exception, an endangered species in the incestuous academic ivory tower of ideology groupthink."

"A minefield for conservatives, huh?"

"Ah, yes. Today's Liberal Art's education would be better labeled the Art of Liberalism."

Dr. Meserve chuckled. "I was in school when colleges taught students how to think not what to think." He turned to me. "Troy, you see, your father's doing splendidly. Take him home Thursday, but any hint of trouble — seizures, memory loss, nauseousness, headaches — call me."

"Right," I said. "It'll be ten o'clock before I get down here from Blowing Rock."

"Ten's fine," he said, writing his cell number on a business card. "Hire a companion for him. Don't leave him alone." At the door, he turned. "We'll evaluate you after Christmas, Doctor."

Dad waved him a goodbye with a, "Fine, Doctor." After Meserve had left, I said, "Want me to call your mother's sister, Great Aunt Harriet?"

"Good heavens, *no*! Not that old crank. I'll ask Mrs. V next door. And don't worry about me. I worry about you. You have a job to do and will need to be Sir Galahad."

"Excuse me?"

"Your securing Chinese taxol might open the door for millions of women."

"Oh, right."

"Now, when you come down Thursday, bring down my navy-blue suit, socks, wingtips, white shirt, underwear, and a red tie — Mom's favorite color. We'll go directly to Finley's."

I left the hospital, drove back to Blowing Rock for dinner at Canyons with high school buddies, and I returned on Wednesday to Boone. The community of 13,000 is Watauga County seat and home to Appalachian State University. App State has grown over the decades; Boone has stayed the same. The unchanged, historical, static part of the village, that on West King Street, houses the courthouse, county and town office buildings, dress and art shops, a sprinkling of dentists, accountants, bars, and chiropractors just scraping by, tattoo parlors, bail-bondsmen, and a gazillion lawyers. High-dollar attorneys operated out of multi-storied buildings. Lesser priced counsels had transformed quaint houses into legal battlefields, and some had purchased store-fronts. A few hid on second floors, not doing so well — the kind of lawyers you hope the other guy has. Attorney Marlene LaPointe and her associates were in a nifty storefront next to the fire station. I took a seat at 9 a.m. in the reception area and did not wait long. Marlene had large dark eyes and a soft, rich, honeyed voice, apt for comforting anxious hearts: Your attorney is here, there is nothing to worry about, everything will be fine. She was a tall, no-nonsense, beauty of fifty-five, who, as public defender fresh out of Chapel Hill must have been a looker, but now looked tough as nails. After exchanging pleasantries, she informed me, in a mellow tone, she'd placed the obituary and hours of service in *The Watauga Democrat* and ordered extra copies of the Death Certificate.

"You'll need every one of them," she assured me as her sympathy continued.

"What about her things in Dad's wrecked Volvo?"

"The police have her clothes, purse, and shoes in Blowing Rock. Since she'll be cremated this afternoon, I've placed her name on the Master Death Index and contacted the university, social security, credit bureau, credit card company, Blue Ridge Electric, Skyline Telephone, and filed a claim for her life insurance. Now—" she smiled warmly—"I need you to do a few things, including talking to her ASU chair about removing her books, files, and papers."

"Sure, anything you say," I agreed.

Marlene gave me a list:
1. Complete a change of address form at the Post Office,
2. List and cancel subscriptions to all her magazines and journals,
3. List and cancel her memberships in all professional associations,
4. Obtain copies of my parents' prior two years tax returns to file a final 1040,
5. Close her email addresses,
6. Take the official will to the courthouse to file a probate petition.

Marlene said she had put all the legal wheels in motion to give the town, county, state, and feds their share of Mom's estate. She said the Social Security death benefit was $255. She said Mom had made several specific bequests to cousins, an aunt, uncle, and niece in Russia, but the bulk of her estate went in equal parts to Dad and me. She did not say how much.

Her grocery list of things for me to do took Wednesday afternoon, and that evening, I sorted through old picture albums for photos of Mom for a display board at her remembrance service. I included pictures of her and Papa in Odessa. What could it hurt? Thursday morning, early, I left for Winston-Salem. I helped Dad dress. Ray Collins wheeled him down to the main door while I got the Subaru. Dad stood easily, leaned against the door a sec, got his balance, and backed in.

"Thanks, Ray," Dad said. "You're the perfect nurse."

"You're the perfect patient, Doctor Locke," Ray replied with a warm pat on the back.

The snow stopped as we left Winston-Salem. The day turned cold and bleak, perfect for a funeral. On the way up the mountain, I wanted to ask Dad more about immortality, but he remained silent, staring up Highway 421 pointed straight as a Cherokee arrow at the rising peaks. He started to speak once about their honeymoon in Osh but stopped abruptly and remained silent. I wondered why he'd mentioned Osh but thought it too taxing to ask.

Mom's funeral turned into an event.

We arrived at Finley Funeral Home in time to greet a crowd of mostly strangers who had come to mourn Mom. I never realized she knew so many people. The interminable line shuffled in, stomped snow off their boots, and shook hands to show their respect and look at her pictures. Students, faculty, children, neighbors, shop owners, doctors, even Mom's dentist. No one from Russia made the trip. They knew I was bringing half her ashes back with me in a few weeks for a riverside service on my return from Blagoveshchensk when she would join Papa in the Volga.

Mom's ashes were in the polished mahogany box with shiny brass fittings and sat on a four-foot cherry stand before a photo display of her life. Pictures from childhood, college, first marriage to Papa in his Soviet army uniform, my baby pictures, marriage to Dad at the Moscow Wedding Palace, and our Blowing Rock home. There were more pictures of Mom with friends playing tennis, hiking, and at ASU's Russian Club. The snapshots brightened the day. I have little memory of the afternoon other than it being a heart-wrenchingly time with speakers trying to be solemn and joking, sympathetic and uplifting, extolling Mom's infinite virtues, some of which she had.

At the end of the two hours, Dad stood beside Mom's ashes. He visibly shook and winced as if the pain was shooting through his body. He spoke with slow enunciation and slurred speech. "Thank you for coming," he said and lovingly touched the box, "Irina, your mother — " he looked at me — "your colleague, friend, wife, and mother was a quiet, loving, reticent, clement soul who was never completely comfortable in America. That may surprise you. Coupled with her concerns that her English was never what it should be, she had grave doubts about the direction of our country. She was convinced when she arrived from the Soviet Union in nineteen seventy-six, she had stepped into a Norman Rockwell painting, complete with a Golden Retriever on our front porch."

People laughed politely.

Dad reached to steady himself against the flimsy stand. The mahogany box wobbled. He continued, "But Irina watched as that Golden Retriever was replaced by a Pit Bull and angry coalitions dismantled that Rockwell painting in ugly movements: political, feminist, gay, black, Latino, environmental, uninformed youth, unemployed workers, unions, and illegals by the millions. All were clamoring for their share of the apple pie while our country's values disintegrated. She tried, in her quiet modest ways, to maintain those values, give back to her students and community and country, and bring a modicum of peace to the world." He stopped abruptly and looked around. "Thank you for coming."

At the cemetery, a cold, hard, north wind had whooshed snow off hillside grave markers. I held Dad's arm, steadying him, as we gathered around an unmarked hole in the frozen earth. In Mom's honor, someone placed a rose beside the hole then read a poem, meaningless sounds in the stony stillness with the rhythmic drones of a metronome. During the reading, I wondered if immortality had unveiled Mom, if she was really in heaven or if her ashes were her end. An ASU Spanish professor gave a brief homily; a priest consecrated her grave and commit her spirit to everlasting life, "*In sure and certain hope of the resurrection to eternal life through our Lord Jesus Christ, we commend to Almighty God Irina Locke and commit her body to the ground; earth to earth, ashes to ashes, dust to dust. The Lord bless her and keep her, the Lord makes his face to shine upon her and be gracious unto her and give her peace. Amen.*" Mr. Finley held out a purple velvet bag. I lifted out the mahogany urn, knelt, reached down to arm's length and set the urn in the little concrete vault at the bottom of the hole, and lowered the concrete lid onto the vault. It made a solid, exhausting clunk. And then, using both hands, I scraped icy dirt into the hole, tamped it down with the heel of my hands, and replaced the frozen disc of dead grass, flicking loose dirt off. Several people approached and prayed over the little plot I'd paid five hundred dollars for plus another four hundred for perpetual care.

"The marker," I said to Dad, "where will it go?"

"Right here," he replied and toed a spot three inches above the dirt. "Mine will be next to it. You'll have no trouble finding us."

After I got Dad home and settled, Mrs. V arrived and I left for Charlotte and the flight to Orlando. The world spins on. One must spin with the merry-go-round or step off. And I wasn't ready to do that. The next three weeks were a blur. For Nastia, it was a jumble of algebra, geometry, calculus, and basic math classes taught to new faces, a cultural and economic hodgepodge of teenagers with personalities to learn, dropouts to delete, transfers to add, fights to quell, and all the while burying herself in the triple life of teacher, cancer patient, and wife. The only breathing space in her life was tennis with Ingrid on weekend mornings while I worked double-shifts, building up hours for my week in Russia. Early on those cool mornings, I rose quietly and walked Leftovers to his favorite palm at 4:30 a.m., ten minutes before I rushed to work. I returned home in time to run Leftovers and shower before a late dinner with Anastasia and bed by eleven. As Christmas break approached and the Friday for her operation grew closer, Anastasia became fighter-tough. She talked about the future, starting a family, buying a home, and she displayed more will to live than I had ever seen. She focused on the positive and barely acknowledged cancer's dark side. In some subconscious way, her store of energy invigorated our lives. She grew stronger and more beautiful, ready to meet whatever the future brought, though I wondered how she would face the future when she lost her hair, grew scrawny, and her skin tone turned yellowish-brown from chemotherapy.

I never knew.

***

THIRTEEN

Florida Cancer Center, Winter Park
Saturday, December 23, 1991

Anastasia's eyes fluttered and opened.

"Hi ya, sleepyhead," I said, pushing myself up from the recliner where I'd spent the night as a human heart monitor, listening to her labored breathing. "Welcome back."

Anastasia slowly lifted her head from the starch-stiff pillow. Her eyes slowly focused on me. She cocked her head, puzzled at the strange odors, strange beeping, the IV tethered to her left hand. On the screen behind her, a mechanical monitor's sharp green line blinked peaks and valleys synchronized with her heartbeat.

"Where am I?" she said in a slow hoarse voice. "What day is it? What time?"

"You're in a new room, and it's — " I glanced at my golden Timex — "eleven fifty, Saturday morning, the twenty-third of December, a velvety Florida day with a bright lemon sun, cloudless azure sky, and chilly enough outside to tingle."

Anastasia coughed. She tentatively lifted her right hand to her fevered face. Everything she did was in slow motion as if the circuitry wasn't all connected. Her hair was sweaty and matted. Her color was as gray as her floppy gown, about the color as one of those human-like statues in Pompeii. She smelled like she'd been bathed in antiseptic, which overpowered the fragrance of roses I'd brought that wilted on the windowsill.

I earmarked the Mexican recipe book in my lap, stepped over to the bed, and kissed her lips.

Anastasia's eyes fixed on the window, refocused on me and then circled the room slowly.

"This room's bigger with a view," I said. "Nice, huh?"

Her eyes crept randomly around the stark white walls, silent television, and apparatus panel with blood pressure gauge, oxygen outlets, and spigots for things unknown.

"Yeah," Anastasia said bitingly, "especially the thick, purple drapes."

I lifted her chin with my finger and kiss her again. "Something we can always share."

Anastasia coughed, propped herself up on her right elbow, and nodded at my Diet Pepsi. I supported her head and tipped the can to her lips. She swallowed and lifted her chin for more.

"Mmmm," she said. Her tongue poked out between her teeth and moistened her lips. She blinked and focused on the window, cracked open an inch, and wiped her brow.

I'd spent the night reading Mexican recipes and J. D. McDonald, trying not to doze in the recliner angled to watch her. At dawn, sunlight streaming through the window made a toasty yellow rhomboid on the cold tile floor, warming me enough to slip into a drowsy sleep. The moon makes me snoozy, too, but there wasn't one. The room was silent. We could hear people outside talking in anxious voices, pacing on the brick pavements of the Cancer Institute.

I pushed her over-bed table aside, lowered the side-rail, and edged a haunch onto the mattress.

Anastasia's ashen features were as motionless and strikingly beautiful as the Venus de Milo — with arms, of course. I brushed a sweaty strand of hair aside and kissed her forehead lovingly. She gave me a helpless look for the smooch.

"Women usually tear off their clothes after a kiss like that," I crowed.

She smiled woefully. "I'm trying hard to control myself."

I stroked her cheek with the back of my fingers. "How are you, Cupcake?"

She squirmed and twisted in search of comfort. "Tired, relieved, thankful, overwhelmed, sore, and feeling very, very mortal."

I lifted her chin. Our eyes were locked. "Glad I asked."

Anastasia looked at me steadily; her eyes were open wide and nearly all pupils. Her breathing was quiet, face relaxed, mien resolute. "What's new with your dad?" she asked.

"I called Mrs. Villafuerte. She's got him up walking. He plans to go back to work after New Year. I think Mrs. V is looking forward to us relieving her tomorrow."

Nastia smiled. "Three weeks with a philosopher is a *very long time.* Your mom was a saint."

An efficient nurse in a flowered smock barreled into the room. Her nametag read JULIE. She said, "Hi," checked the monitor tethered to Anastasia and flicked the IV line with a clear-lacquered fingernail. She unfastened the ties on the front of Nastia's gown, opened it, and studied the edges of dinner-plate-sized bandage over the left side of Anastasia's chest. The skin looked puffy, red, and tender; the breast was flat.

"Need anything, Honey?" Julie said.

"Everything," Anastasia replied with a weak smile. "But water, some water would be nice."

"Not yet," Julie said and shot me a look. "And *no* Diet Pepsi either."

I threw up both hands in shocked innocence. "Not me, never!"

Julie's eyes narrowed at me then returned to Anastasia. "I'll have the aide bring in a cup of crushed ice — but don't talk too fast to her."

"Or use big words?" I gibed.

Julie smiled. "Well, if you're not the perceptive hunk. You must be the *better* half?"

"I am, indeed," I said. "One Hunkus Americanus, Troy Locke the fifth."

"Think you can spoon ice into this pretty thing without giving her a bath?"

"Julie, I never spill Pabulum."

"I'd have guessed you too old for Gerbers," she cooed.

"But not for a grilled steak sandwich and side of au jus," I said, smacking my lips. "Perhaps the aide could bring one of those, too?"

"No problemo. Maybe a chilled bottle of Dom Pérignon to wash down the steak?"

"Nirvana! You're a class act, Julie Nightingale."

She smiled broadly. "It's Julie Kowalzyk, and you sound just like an intern, stuffed with pride and bullshit."

"I've got those Deadly Sins covered; another night in that recliner, I'd be intern-qualified."

Julie grinned and closed Anastasia's gown. She pulled the over-bed table into place and vamoosed, leaving the door ajar. Through the doorway, I watched her talk to a chunky aide built like a tree stump who pointed our way and trundled off. Julie then spoke to a dignified looking man wearing a tailored, white, lab coat and designer glasses, probably a cardiologist, with a haircut that cost more than my Bass penny loafers.

Anastasia motioned for my Pepsi. I looked to see if the coast was clear and gave her some.

"You love it don't you?" Nastia said, touching my hand with burning fingers.

"What?" I said.

"The way you attract women, like, ah, what's that bee saying?"

"*Kak med privlehaet pchel.*"

"That's the one. Like bees to honey."

"Aaay! What can I say?" I thrust both hands out in a double-thumbs-up Fonzie pose. "Tell me more, tell me more."

"Well, you do. You draw women like the moon pulls tides. It's your self-confident, wit, vigor, and surety. It's that brooding intensity of yours, a brute and psychic force." Anastasia gripped my hand tightly and looked resolute. "It's more than physical strength or good looks, Troy, and you know it. You convey energy, drive, sureness, resolve, caring, and certainty, qualities rarely seen in men. I know you're a kind, considerate, generous, and loving person, but it's more than that. You're an intact, complete man; it enthralls women. Most guys lack it."

"So I'm hot stuff." I leaned over, kissed her on the lips, and placed the back of my fingers on her forehead. Fever. "I bet you told all your boyfriends that."

"You *are* and always *have been* the only boy in all my life!"

"And you are and always have been the only girl in my life."

Anastasia shot me a long searching look. "Sure I am."

She winced and grit her teeth. "My breast feels like it's been hacked off." She shifted, took my Pepsi, and finished it. "Was I unconscious long?"

"Nah, couple hours tops."

"Glad you were so worried about me."

I hunched my shoulders. "They checked you every thirty minutes. What more can I say?"

"I was wheeled into surgery at eight o'clock yesterday morning," she said.

"I wake up to find you sprawled out in a recliner cluttered with books, Pepsi cans, Snicker wrappers, reading God knows what."

"*The Deep Blue Good-By.*"

"Intriguing?"

"It was. But not thrilling. McGee always wins."

"Wish I did."

There was a bang on the door. The aide ambled in. Stump body, stilt legs, chipmunk cheeks, blank black eyes, two-foot-red-tipped Afro. She reminded me of a red-wing blackbird. She wore the same flowered smock as Julie had, but hers was stained and missed a button. She carried a Styrofoam cup of ice, two packages of saltines, and a packet of French's mustard. The half of her nametag not splattered with spaghetti sauce read — KIMA.

"I'm Tashakima," she barked with a whopping dose of suspicion and contempt. "I'll be yawls' aide today." She set the tray on the over-bed table. There was a plastic spoon in the ice cup. Her finger, too. "Feed her slow," she growled to me, "and no crackers, unnerstand?"

Tashakima's voice was as warm as my eighth-grade teacher, Mrs. McClure's, was when she'd shout, *Principal Eastman wants to see you, again, Troy! RIGHT NOW!*

"Ice spooned slowly, no crackers," I said. "Gotcha."

Tashakima heaved out a big sigh and turned. She closed the door behind her with a whoosh-and-bang with way too much oomph. I spooned Anastasia some crushed ice and wondered how many African-Americans with Zulu names could ever find Malawi on a map?

Anastasia closed her eyes, tilted her head back, and swallowed. "Heaven."

Her breathing steadied as she cherished the ice and I said, "More?"

She nodded, and I gave her some more. She swallowed, opened her eyes, smiled broadly, and glanced at my crackers. "You look starved, Sweetheart, why don't you throw caution to the wind and eat both of them."

"I threw caution to the wind when I married a Soviet woman," I said.

"Yes, but a foxy Soviet woman."

"Should I lock the door?"

She smiled, and I tore open both two-pack packages of saltines, squeezed lines of mustard on them, squished them into mustard sandwiches, and popped them into my mouth. "Hollandaise on Eggs Benedict, yum, yum."

I gobbled down both cracker-sandwiches, which only made me hungrier.

I'd spent Friday morning at the hospital, waiting outside the operating room. I worked the afternoon and late shifts, and never punched out to eat. Nor could I eat at 1:30 a.m. when I dashed home to walk Leftovers and rush to Anastasia's room where I crashed in the recliner's plastic sumptuousness.

Anastasia licked her lips and groped for the push-button gadget they store where it is least likely to be reached. I helped and dug the control box out of the abyss between the mattress and frame and gave it to her. She pressed a button and held it down so hard there was a clear definition of muscles in her forearm. When the bed was nearly perpendicular, she released it and opened her gown to expose both breasts.

I started to say, "TA-DA!" but the reeking antiseptic and Anastasia's grimace stopped me.

"This one's flat as a pancake," she said, looking down, confused.

"Maybe the bandage's too tight."

She shot me a look that would have melted the polar ice cap. "Did Ginsburg say anything?"

"Only 'you'd be fine.'"

Anastasia's eyes narrowed at me. Without words, things were being said.

"Did he say anything about the cysts or if he got it all or how much he butchered, smarty?"

"Not a peep. He said he'd be by after breakfast."

Anastasia swept her hand over her breast. "I've gone from a D cup to a training bra."

"He did say something about 'extending the margins,' whatever that means."

Anastasia pushed another button. The bed whined downward. She pulled the sides of her flimsy gown together, punched the pillow again, and slumped back. "How's Leftovers?"

"Lonesome."

"Me, too. I miss my family so much I ache."

"We'll go back to Tver this summer."

"Sure we will." She didn't believe me. But she did, in fact, return to Tver the next June. Alone. "Did you swap shifts with Kahuna yesterday?"

"I did and did a double. So I don't need to go in today, and Bill okayed me receiving next week off." I did not mention the effort that had taken. Bill Allen's a company man. He knew of Nastia's cancer. His dad had died at the Togus, Maine VA hospital with cancer and signs of dementia, and yet he had given me a hard time wanting to spend time with my wife.

"Would you give me an ice bath?" she asked.

"Love to." I shook ice from the cup into a towel and dabbed Nastia's face, neck, and arms. She closed her eyes, relishing the nippy wetness. When I stopped, she pushed herself up and looked out the window at the tops of oak trees glistening in the midday sun. I kneaded her shoulders and ran the towel down her back.

Tears rolled down her cheeks. "Think Ginsburg got it all?" she sniffled.

"I'm sure he did," I said and wrapped her in my arms. "He's the expert."

She pushed me away and looked at me with intense, watery eyes. "If this were your body, what would you do?"

"Trust intuition. Consider everything, weigh alternatives, and make a calculated decision."

"Which means?"

"You've done all that you can do. I'll find the taxol; you get it into your body lickety split."

Anastasia smiled weakly. "Sounds like my plan."

"Two great minds."

Anastasia considered that. "They discovered taxol works before I was born and are still putzing around not approving it. I need it, now, today."

"The FDA isn't renowned for its efficiency."

"Now Ginsburg said approval could take two more years. Song Lin said chemotherapy and radiation aren't enough. I can't wait for the FDA."

"I'll be getting you the taxol in China next week and be right back. No problem."

Anastasia opened her gown and pulled my hand to her right breast. "Can you be happy with one breast?"

I smiled and ran my fingertips over her breast. "Who needs two when one's so beautiful?"

She hugged my hand. "I needed that."

"You know," I said, closing her gown, "I called Uncle Ivan at dawn yesterday and told him I'd give him a grand if he'd help me, and he said he would. He's retiring to Egypt with his girlfriend the day I leave for home."

"I hate for you to become a smuggler for me."

I took her face in my hands. "Look Nastenka; you couldn't love me if I didn't do this."

"That's right. Now will you kiss me as if you desire me?"

I did. And after that smooch, she pulled a fold-up mirror from the tabletop and poked at her hair. "Get my brush," she said, turning her head this way and that. "Are your plans all set?"

"Yeap." I fetched her purse from the closet. "Song's got everything ready. I leave Charlotte the day after Christmas; that's this coming Tuesday. I get back Sunday, New Year's Eve. Restaurant business will be lousy that week, and Kahuna's covering for me. We'll ski App Mountain a couple of days and then return to Orlando if you feel up to it."

"I will. But you can make it over and back that quickly?" Anastasia said.

I started counting on my fingers. "Three hours, Orlando to JFK on Tuesday. Eleven hours to Moscow, lose eight hours in time change. That puts me in Sheremetyevo at noon Wednesday, the twenty-seventh. Grab a couple of hours sleep at the Aerostar, take the Metro to Domodedova and catch the redeye to Blagoveshchensk. I'll lose six more hours in time-changes and arrive there before dawn Thursday morning. Grab a couple of hours sleep. Uncle Ivan and I load his sleigh and off we go to Heihe, China. Lunch with the Chinese guys. Buy the taxol; start back the next morning, Friday, the twenty-ninth. Regain fourteen hours heading west and hit Charlotte (CLT), Sunday evening at nine, New Year's Eve."

"Sounds great, and I'll pick you up," Anastasia vowed. "How about Biff?"

"We've talked," I said, referring to my oncologist pal. "He'll do the taxol injections free."

"So everything *is* all set?"

"Everything *will* go off like clockwork."

What I hadn't told her — what I wouldn't tell her — is I'd purchased a pistol, a thirteen-ounce, Ruger, 5-shot, 38-Special with a 1.875-inch barrel and rubber grip. Thugs control commerce in Russia. No one was going to stop my return with the taxol. No one.

Anastasia laced her fingers into mine. "*My mozhen eto dlot; spaseba, spaseba!* — We can do it; thank you, thank you!"

She opened her arms, and I bent and kissed her long and passionately.

"*A kak naschiet dengeg?* — But what about money?" she worried.

"Handled. I cashed Dad's check for twenty thousand and now have two hundred, new, hundred-dollar bills. I'll pay him back from my inheritance. The court will probate Mom's will by February, then you and I can start looking for a house, one big enough for a bunch of kids."

Tears fill Anastasia's eyes. As if she were afraid to think that far ahead, she changed the subject. "You'll need warm felt boots and your new coat in Siberia."

"My Bean coat's ready. I've got dog hair socks and, in Blago, will buy *valenki*."[14]

Just then there was a knock at the door.

Anastasia pinched both cheeks, rechecked her mirror, and said, "Come in."

The smell of expensive cologne preceded Doctor Ginsburg into the room. He was reading a chart and appeared poised, confident, and preoccupied. He'd replaced his green scrubs with a Seville Row jacket of buttery tan vicuna cross-hatched with sapphire stripes, sharply creased merino slacks, buffed loafers, and a crisp powder blue cotton shirt with a royal blue paisley tie. He looked like a short, square-faced, protruding-eared Prince Charles, wearing five grand of psychological armor — nothing flamboyant, you understand, wouldn't want to jolt the patients.

He stopped reading, set the chart on the foot of the bed, and settled his hands on the foot-rail. His nails were buffed. He didn't wear a wedding ring. I wondered if he was married or had a girlfriend. Or boyfriend. His long black curly hair never seemed to need a haircut. I wondered if it was colored. It must be.

Dr. Ginsburg looked at Anastasia hard, like a Taliban terrorist-in-training might. I stepped aside to give the expert plenty of room to do battle.

"How are you feeling, Mrs. Locke?" he said, sounding like a caring professional. His eyes were austere and bored, his smile — definitely a smile — was guarded, as if he'd been taught at Dartmouth Medical School that to display emotion signals inadequacy.

"I hurt," Anastasia said. "Badly."

He nodded patronizingly, holding himself and her pain at bay. "I'll increase the pain medications." His words lacked warmth and closeness. When medical school taught 'Bedside Manners 101: *Impress Your Patients with Caring but Don't for God's Sake Stay Remote*,' he'd cut the class. "I'd like to review what we know for certain," he said curtly.

"I'd like that," Anastasia said.

"You've Stage Three invasive ductal carcinoma in situ or DCIS," he said. "Clusters of aggressive cancer cells have gone beyond the milk duct. It's seen in eighty percent of women with breast cancer. Stage three carcinoma means the cancer cells are poorly differentiated and abnormal in both behavior and appearance."

That made me grit my teeth. Though he'd started his explanation in a sympathetic mode, he segued into an emotionless professional faster than Anastasia had said, I hurt.

Anastasia frowned. "So, what, exactly, does all that mean?"

"It means your cancer had metastasized, or broken through the milk ducts and infiltrated other tissue. There were also other smaller tumors not seen on the mammogram. I removed them and a lymph node during surgery where it could have spread. We'll need more tests to check for alkaline phosphatase, or ALP, which is higher in people with cancer in their liver and bones. To be safe, I took an extra margin of healthy tissue beyond the edge of both tumors to ensure all cancer cells were removed. The pathologist found the margins clear."

"Does that mean you got it all?" Anastasia said.

"Usually, no additional surgery is needed," Ginsburg said, tap dancing. "The hormone receptor test will tell us whether you have receptors for the hormones estrogen and progesterone. If you test positive for estrogen, progesterone, or both, they'll likely fuel the growth of new cancer cells. To combat that, we'll lower the levels of estrogen using inhibitors, aromatase, and tamoxifen, or, lastly, remove your ovaries — the primary source of estrogen."

Anastasia gasped. "You mean *sterilize me*?!"

"Only as a last resort, Mrs. Locke. We'll try tamoxifen after chemo. It usually stops the production of estrogen by blocking the enzyme aromatase." Ginsburg picked up the chart, turned to leave, and said, "You start chemo, today, at three this afternoon."

"May I still go to North Carolina tomorrow, Sunday, for Christmas?"

"Sure. You might feel a little sick, but you'll be fine."

His Italian shoes squeaked on the tile as he left, closing the door gently behind him.

Anastasia looked at me. "Can you get us on a plane to Charlotte tomorrow?"

"Already done," I said. "We leave at nine with Leftovers. He'll love the snow."

"Me too." With her face set with a determined look, Anastasia lowered the bed to forty-five degree. "Looks like my fight with cancer may go on for the rest of my life."

"Not a chance. The taxol will stop it."

"Who knows?" Anastasia drew in a deep breath and huffed it out, turning serious. "From here on, Troy, I'm living life like every day is my last day."

"Sounds like a plan. If you want to quit teaching in Orlando, as soon as I return, we'll move back to Blowing Rock. We can help Dad, live in the mountains, and I'll transfer to the McDees in Boone. We can look for a house, and I'll look for a place for my Mexican restaurant."

"Dad needs us, doesn't he?"

"We all need each other."

Anastasia took both my hands in hers and kissed my fingers. "You're bringing Mom's ashes back with you?"

"I am," I said. "On the way back, scattering them on the Volga with Papa's. I've time."

"You be careful in Russia. I worry about you smuggling."

"Me too."

"What happens if Uncle Ivan gets in trouble?"

"I'm big and strong, and I'll take care of him."

"Yes, you would. You're a caring man."

"A catcher in the rye."

We checked Anastasia out of the hospital that evening, and the next day, we flew to Charlotte and rented a car. Leftovers loved the snow. The house was empty without Mom. Dad was in bed most of the time. We had a sober Christmas and on Tuesday, December 26, we returned to the Charlotte airport. I resisted the temptation to say farewell. I mean, I wasn't going off to Vietnam was I? It was a quickie trip to Russia to buy taxol. I would return in a few days with all my limited faculties intact. At least that's what I told myself.

So we kissed and hugged and said I love yous.

Anastasia final words to me were, "*Speshite* — Hurry back."

To which I said, "*Ya eto sdelayu* — I will."

But I didn't.

*****

FOURTEEN

Charlotte to Moscow
December 26, 1991

Two movies east of JFK, dawn's banked fire glowed across the sanctity of space to sparkle off the North Atlantic's shadowy swells. Left and right of Delta 90's stingy aisles, jumbled bodies sprawled, shoes off, neckties off, legs braided in weightless blankets, heads drooping in restless sleep. We are causalities of the Jet Age. Profits obviate comfort and patrons are packed in as tightly as a frat in a phone booth. The airborne leviathan hurtled east over meridians of longitude at six hundred sixty-five mph as the earth rotated faster westward. Iceland's icebergs flashed by at Mach 2. I'd left Charlotte's Douglas International Airport for JFK at two-thirty and left JFK for Moscow at seven-fifty, late due to de-icing three times. We were on a northeast tack — the shortest distance between two global points isn't a straight line — rocketing out of night's blackness on a biting tailwind. Twice, I'd asked the flight attendant for ice water and aspirin. Each time, I drank the water, stashed the aspirin, and gurgled duty-free Glenfiddich over the ice. My first illegal act of the trip. The more Glenfiddich you drink, the mellower it gets. That's probably true of antifreeze. The Glen didn't affect me any more than the snowstorm affected the Atlantic. Sleep escaped me. Worries imprisoned me: Mom's ashes, Anastasia's cancer, and President Bush's address to America last night about Gorbachev's desolation of the Soviet Union. I'd watched his speech at the JFK Chili's, wolfing down a burger and picking my teeth, saving a few toothpicks for later. Toothpicks are a rarity in the Soviet Union; so is toilet paper.

Bush said Gorbachev's Christmas Day resignation ended our decades-long struggle with Communism. *One of the greatest dramas of the Twentieth Century, the nuclear threat was no more, a victory for democracy and freedom ...*

With Russia covering nearly half the globe, I wondered if Gorby's message had made it eleven time zones to the Far East. Will totalitarianism stay dead? I thought I'd escape those worries reading tabloid banalities, the endless accounts of drugs, corruption, murder, greed, and sleaze that lulls most people to sleep, and asked a heavy-eyed attendant for a newspaper.

Weary of my demands, she snapped, in Russian, "Mister, we've got a crumpled, coffee-stained *Moscow Times* in English, and *Pravda* in Russian; which to you want?"

"Both," I said with my cheeriest smile.

When she delivered them, petulantly, I said, "Thank you, dear," and received a big sigh.

Neither Gorbachev's resignation and dismantlement of the USSR, nor James Collins assignment as the *Chargé d'affaires* in Moscow and the usual litany of white collar corruption stories bored me enough to sleep. I dropped the newspapers and poured more Glen. No help. Delta's skinny seats spaced an inch apart didn't help, either. Built for short scrawny bodies, anyone over five-nine is wedged into ribby luxury and paralyzed knees in sclerotic-h while some guy's dragon breath huffs in your face all night. So I twisted and squirmed and fussed with the play pillow and padded the frosty window beside my featherbed, yawned at reruns, and tried not to worry, which, of course, is what I did.

Mom had had a tough life. She joked she'd been born in the Soviet Union before television, penicillin, polio shots, pantyhose, the pill, frozen dinners, dishwashers, and clothes dryers. At App State, students taught her that grass was not something you mowed, coke was not drunk, and pot not something you cooked in. Now her body had been ground up. Three pounds of her were entombed in a mahogany box buried in Blowing Rock, her life a one-line epitaph on a shoebox-sized plaque snugged deeply enough in winter grass to give gang-mowers ample clearance for quick cutting come spring. Her other three pounds were in a cardboard box in my backpack. On my return from Siberia, the layovers at Sheremetyevo gave me ample time to get to Smolensky Station and the Borodinsky Bridge; I'd make a silent homily and sprinkle her ashes with Papa's in the Moskva River. It flows into Mother Volga and discharges, along with all western Russia's excreta, chemicals, and coal ash into the landlocked Caspian Sea, a remnant of the Paratethys Sea, formed when the world sea levels fell drastically five million years ago.

With Anastasia's life in my hands, I worried about the effect Gorbachev's gift of freedom to enslaved Russians meant for border security in a lawless land on the cusp of anarchy. Would I make it safely into and out of China? Would returning with taxol be a problem?

At 10:35 a.m. Moscow time, directly over 1,140-year-old Novgorod,[15] the pilot banked the Delta 10-11 languidly, and a vast stretch of violet-blushed Tiaga appeared etherized by winter's bitter cold and burning peat. The cabin crew made a final pass for cups and newspapers, and we began our descent over my birthplace, Tver, one hundred fifty miles northwest of the capital. Apparently, for xenophobic concerns — or the smoke-laden sky from eternal peat fires — the pilot waited until the last possible moment to drop the landing gear. When the wheels thump into place, he dove so steeply it plugged my ears. We slammed into Sheremetyevo's snow-cleared tarmac, the engines' reverse thrust whipped up an alabaster blizzard, wiping out all vision, and we taxied ever so gently to the gate.

I swallowed to drain my Eustachian tubes, gathered my things, checked my three passports, and was the last of three hundred passengers to step into the accordion umbilical cord to the terminal. To buoy first impressions, Soviets built a quarter-mile-long glass enclosure that circled Sheremetyevo and eventually led downstairs to two of twelve customs operating booths. Sleep-grumpy passengers lined up. I was last.

"Pepsi Cola!" snarled, in Russian, an old man in front of me, a WW II pensioner with ribbons plastered all over his suit coat. "They open a plant near here, pay three times the salary, and the customs agents quit for American pay."

"Damn free enterprise!" I griped back to him in Russian. "Reagan traded Gorbachev permission to sell Stoli in America for Pepsi sold here."

"Da, da, da. Life better under Stalin."

"Da," I said and left that widely held view alone.

When it was my turn, I stepped up to the window. An agent's fierce scowl greeted me, portentous of draconian intelligence methods that lay ahead. I thought it safer to use my Russian passport and slid it to him along with my airplane tickets and entry form. He glared at me, glared at my passport, and glared at me again.

I tried to look shaken.

He picked up my passport, studied the eagle imprimatur, flipped it open, and cringed. "Your name, Troy Vladimirovich Locke, not all Russian," he snarled in awkward English.

I smiled. "I was born Igor Vladimirovich Fetisov and adopted, years ago, by an American."

"What you do in Russia?"

"Visit a relative." I tried to sound as credible as a priest.

"How long time you be here for?"

"Five days."

"Not long."

"Not my favorite relative."

He almost smiled, scribbled on my entry form, slid my documents back, and waved me through Russia's paranoid security protocol. Forty-six minutes later, our bags arrived on the conveyor belt. I slung my backpack over my shoulder, grabbed the suitcase, and exchange one hundred American dollars for fifty-five Rubles. For decades, the Soviets maintained ruble parity with the Pound Sterling, thereby vastly inflating its value. At that time, it was worth less than food stamps and was not a convertible currency. But I didn't care. I only needed enough rubles for food, bus, and subway fare. I tugged on my L. L. Bean coat, Colby cap, gloves, and beelined out the *Nothing to Declare* exit into the numbing cold. Wind groaning through support pillars sounded like ghosts in a churchyard. No one met me, but I was used to that.

The passenger pickup area stunk of exhaust fumes and cigarettes. A gaggle of cabbies milled around, awaiting fares. They smoked Marlboros and wore black fur *shapka-ushankas* — hats with earflaps — black-leather coats, black jeans, and black square-toed boots. They looked like shadows. Tobacco carcinogens may have caused America's coffin-nail sales to plummet, but the rugged cowboy still buffaloes the rest of the world into lighting up.

A cabbie hurried up to me and said, "Hello."

"How much to the Aerostar Hotel at thirty-seven *Leningradsky Prospekt?*" I asked, in Russian.

He remained silent and admired my coat.

"Hey, man, I love your I'm-no-longer-a-proletariat coat. You speak Russian pretty good," he said in English with a broad smile and a flash of silver-amalgam teeth that remind me of Richard Kiel, the steel-toothed goliath in James Bond's *The Spy Who Loved Me* and *Moonraker*.

"Your English is, too," I said. "How much?"

"Ninety-five bucks."

"Whoa! I don't want to buy your *Lada*. I'll bus to *Rechnoi Vokzal* — River Station."

"That's cool. There're plenty of fish to fry."

Taxi drivers, often moonlighting English teachers, know the value of a dollar and enough American slang to fleece tourists. I was just checking. It's better to know than not know.

Sheremetyevo is twenty miles north of the Aerostar Hotel, which is five miles north of Red Square. For five kopecks I took the bus to *Rechnoi Vokzal,* the northern-most Metro station on the Green Line, slalomed through a crowd flushing outside, and for forty kopecks more, bought a weeklong pass on the Metro. Around the station were forests of new, twenty-story apartment buildings, and, further out, old *Stalinkas*, the nine-story, cavernous prefabs with all the architectural charm of shoeboxes. I was starved. For one ruble, I bought two baloney sandwiches and a Pepsi and scarfed them down before descending the escalator to the train. Inbound train announcers are male. Outbound female. When he announced our arrival at *Voykuvskaya Vokzal*, someone bumped into me. Suddenly, a gypsy with a kid in her arms high-tailed it. I padded my pockets. She'd snatched my passports. I jumped over a drunk sprawled on the floor and snatched her at the door. I wrestled my documents away and, still clutching her, stepped onto the platform to look for a cop. None. I shoved her aside and re-boarded. The balance of the ride was uneventful, well, except for pulling in at *Dinamo Vokzal*, two blocks from the Aerostar Hotel, when a drunk threw up on a student reading *Queen of Spades*. Mom and I had seen it as a play at the Vakhtangov Theater. I recalled, walking to the hotel.

The Aerostar is the best value in Moscow. A four-star, Canadian-owned hotel with a plush lobby, multi-lingual clerks, well-equipped gym, sauna, and a bar on the second floor with live music and real hamburgers. I requested Room 314, the room Anastasia and I had honeymooned in after our *venchanize* — civil wedding ceremony — and night at the *Bolshoi*. The inside of the room was so hot I propped open the balcony door with the remains of my Glenfiddich and stepped onto the balcony to cool. Traffic was heavy on the eight-lane *Leningradsky*. No one turned in at craggy, redbrick, Petrovsky Palace across the way. Its gardens, arches, gates, and towers, which resembled pencil-sharp minarets, were a tribute to the degraded landscape of Russia's politics and its intent to conquer Turkey in 1775. The palace was the freshen-up-spot for Sophie Fredericke Auguste von Anhalt-Zerbst, the German princess/tyrant — aka Catherine the Great — when journeying to Moscow from the then-capital, Saint Petersburg.

In 1812, Petrovsky Palace was torched by a frustrated Napoleon after weeks of waiting for the keys to Moscow. Now, 179 years later, repair scaffolding was going up. I wondered if Gorbachev's tardy nod to historic preservation would continue under Yeltsin.

I'd dumped my backpack and bag on the double bed, checked the Ruger — it was there — and reset my watch to noon from 4:00 a.m., Blowing Rock time. Despite the hour, I called Anastasia. As soon as I heard her speak, I knew we'd feel better. There was always color in her voice, overtones of intelligence, hints of passion, the voice of a beautiful woman brave enough to try anything once. Hearing her voice always gave me a sense of completeness. I pulled down the bedspread, heeled off my sneakers, and dialed a string of numbers.

Anastasia answered with a sleepy, "Al-lo."

"It's your long lost Russian lover," I said.

"Which one?" she said.

"Don't be a smartass. Guess where I am? In our *medovyi mesits* — honeymoon suite — at the Aerostar, I dialed twenty numbers and here you are."

"Are you alone?"

"Would a Buddhist monk snag a lonely Delta stewardess for a one-night stand?"

Anastasia laughed. "Not if he valued his life. How was your trip?"

"Long. Snow at JFK, lousy movies, ditto food, and a gypsy snatched my passports on the Metro. How's Dad? How're you?"

"Better and great. He walked outside yesterday. And me? Tennis champs recover quickly."

"Quickly enough to grade all those geometry finals I saw on Mom's desk?"

"Quickly," she said, "not light speed. Those so-called students — "

I laughed. "They're still trying to figure out how many sides on a triangle?"

"They think Pythagoras was a punk rocker."

I slipped off my jeans and lay supine, schmoozing with my wife in Blowing Rock where it was probably 40°. "Moscow temperature is minus thirty-six. But I'm roasting even with the balcony door wedged open." Russians do not use thermostats. More about that later.

"I've moved from the guest room into your old room," Anastasia said, "snuggling under your Colby comforter."

I heard Leftovers bark in one ear and the hum of traffic on *Leningradsky*

Prospekt in the other. "Do you like my bed?" A vision of her naked popped into my head.

"Of course," she said. "Why wouldn't I like to sleep where you used to fantasize about me?"

"Are you naked?"

"As a Playmate."

"Lonesome?" I breathed.

"Not with a hairy male next to me," she said.

"Who barks?"

"Only when he needs to pee."

"Maybe you should tend to that."

"I'll let him out; he sticks around the house. Like me. Three days since my chemo; two days laying around feeling shitty, then, *voilá,* I feel great again."

"Super! I'm grabbing a nap before heading to Domodedova for another all-nighter. My flight's at eight, which gives me the golden opportunity to ride the Metro during rush hour."

"Where you'll get elbowed to death and gag on smoke, beer, sweat, and desperation. Say hello to Uncle Ivan for me."

We vowed our undying love. Anastasia promised to drive to Charlotte Sunday to pick me up.

And I suppose she did.

***

FIFTEEN

Leaving Moscow
December 27, 1991

Harsh arctic winds whirled cold wet air from the Barents Sea into a blinding snowstorm that battered the jagged silhouette of Petrovsky Palace and snarled traffic on *Leningradsky Prospekt*. The wrath howled through the balcony door, wedged open with my bottle of Glenfiddich, but not enough to cool the room, only enough to deaden a persistent tapping at the door. I snapped my head to dispel cobwebs, glanced at my tanned torso sheening with perspiration, and taped with two thin bricks of hundred-dollar bills … and remembered.

My six o'clock wake-up call.

I opened the door to the end of its chain and peered around the edge at a weathered face, nearly as craggy as the palace profile. The woman wore the black dress and white apron of a *dezhurnaya* — floor worker. Probably paid by the KGB to spy of foreigners.

She spoke in a determined, rural Russian, "*Ya gornichnaya; fai'sta vie* — I'm the room cleaner, get up."

"I'll be gone in ten minutes," I replied in Russian.

A surprisingly warm smile creased her wrinkled face. Her searching eyes studied my face, pausing briefly at my bare arm and shoulder to conclude an impression. "We don't see many tans in Moscow this time of year," she said in Russian. "Dress warm; it's cold outside."

I grinned at her insight. "Yes, I wouldn't want to stand out."

A tanned young American in a posh Moscow hotel in December is not an unseen sight in the capital. A bronze-faced young American in Siberia would be. I took ten hundred-dollar bills out of each sandwich bag for bribes and slid them into my wallet. I showered, shaved, re-taped the eighteen thousand to my lower abdomen, and dressed quickly, loading on the layers, shorts, T-shirt, candy-striped long johns, jeans, dog-hair socks, flannel shirt, wool sweater, Colby ski hat, L. L. Bean coat that I left unzipped. I stuffed my Dopp kit and dirty clothes in the suitcase on top of the pistol, slid the Glenfiddich in beside Mom's ashes in the backpack, and stuffed my three passports into an inside pocket. Downstairs, I checked out, paying eighty dollars in cash.

Yowling gusts of a nor'easter pelted my left side as I trudged through the foot-deep snow down Aerostar Lane toward Petrovsky Palace and *Leningradsky Prospekt*. At the intersection, snow pellets, unimpeded by the flat, wide Tiaga, intensified to feel like bullets strafing my face and collar. Turning right, I walked towards Moscow's faint glow and the barely-visible crenellated-roofline of Dinamo Station two blocks south. The soccer stadium's light towers behind Dinamo were invisible. Drivers honked, waved champagne bottles out windows, and screamed *Democracy!* Party time. The seventy-four-year calamity with Communism had ended. Corruption would cease. Democracy would reign; or would it?

Three guards in thick blue uniforms slouched out of the wind on the west side of the Dinamo Metro Station, smoking and talking. A drunk galumphed to the wall beyond them, leaned against it, and urinated. Workers, bundled in so many padded clothes it blurred their genders, cleaned sidewalks. I pushed through the double-doors, unnoticed and unchallenged. Inside, celebrants' babble and traffic honks ceased. Brushing snow off my coat onto slick tiles, I scanned the bustle for KGB, always well-dressed and military-stiff. None. Kiosks sold fresh tulips, American cigarettes, and soft-porn newspapers of nubile women enduring a variety of sexual feats. The latest issue of *Pravda* at a newsstand, displayed a cover cartoon depicting a fearful Gorbachev-looking bear, with his birthmark, straddling the Soviet Union breaking apart. I thought Dad would enjoy it, stepped over one drunk and around another, and bought the paper. Two kopeks. A box of Chiclets, five. I ran my Metro pass through a turnstile slot and joined the silent herd funneling onto two escalators descending into Moscow's bowels and Stalin's splendid gift to commuters. The underground, built with slave labor, was embellished with reflecting marble walls, ceramic tile, massive arches, grandiose chandeliers, and heroic statues that get the minds of ten million riders off their tiny, cramped quarters.

The Green Line ran to city center and south thirty more miles. No one speaks on Russian subways. I read *Pravda* until a woman's voice announced, "Domodedovoskay Station," where I disembarked for a bus to Domodedovo Airport. One of four airports, Domodedovo was the smallest, its rundown buildings the size of Blowing Elementary School, serve Siberia, a land mass greater than the face of the moon. The others two airports, Vnukovo and Bykovo, served Europe and Africa.

In the Sibir Air ticket line, I overheard snippets of conversations. Texas oilmen returning from two-months-on, one-month-off jobs, businessmen, academics, consultants, vacationers (returning from Cyprus), Peace Corps volunteers, and students heading to rural homes for Christmas. Directly behind me, a portly Russian Pepsi-Cola sales rep with a bloated face, slit eyes, and beet-nose kicked his briefcase ahead and snarled in Russian, "Foreigners are buying Domodedovo; they're in for a hell of a shock."

"How so?" I replied in Russian.

"They'll invest millions, build a palace, make a big profit, be accused of tax fraud, and get shaken down and lose it all to Kremlin plutocrats."

"What's new?" I grumbled. "Maybe Yeltsin will respect the rule of law."

"Ha! They steal assets with impunity after lining the pockets of politicians. You don't know Russia." The Pepsi man stared at me. "You speak Russian good, but you sound foreign."

"Been living abroad awhile."

When it was my turn, I set my suitcase and backpack on the scale and handed my tickets and three passports to a fresh-faced woman straight off the collective farm. She smiled sweetly and studied my documents with sharp, hazel eyes alive with hope.

"Troy Vladimirovich Locke, *poucheemo* — why — your name *malinkee* — little — Ruskee?" she puzzled pleasantly in Russlish.

"Adopted at six; my widowed mom married an American," I said in slow, deliberate English.

"Lucky you." Her tone was envious. She compared my American, Russian, and internal passports carefully. "Did you register with police?"

"No, but I will in Blagoveshchensk."

"You must." She stamped my boarding pass, returned my documents, and weighed my bags.

"Sorry," she said. "Bags is overweight seven kilos. Fifteen rubles." Thirty dollars.

The Pepsi rep behind me muttered a curse, and I left the line for Currency Exchange where a dour woman with squinty eyes snapped my crisp hundred-dollar bill a couple of times, ran it through a scanner, and gave me forty rubles. Big fee.

I paid the ransom to the country lass who slipped it into her pocket. Farm girls learn fast.

Grabbing my bags, I entered a maze of dim corridors that led to Domod-edovo's belly and stopped when I heard mumblings and the familiar click of glasses in a shadowy-to-dark bar. I figured a *pivo* — beer — and food might be soothing and hasten Hypnos on my upcoming, five-thousand-mile odyssey so ordered a couple of sausage sandwiches and a *Baltika 3*. The lager had the right amount of alcohol, a strong malt taste from its slow fermentation, and an entic-ing hops aroma; I ordered a second.

Across the way, a door opened, and, unannounced, a clerk began checking boarding passes and internal passports. I gulped the last of my *Baltika*, bundled up, and descended dark stairs to a bus that took us to the far edge of the tarmac and a waiting Ilyusin 11-114, the infamous deathtrap of all Soviet airplanes.

A surly flight crew armed with flashlights rechecked documents and, just as we were about to freeze to death, permitted us to board. I headed for the last row, starboard side. My seat was next to the bathroom that emitted a gagging, eye-watering, hircine stench that grew worse when the cabin door slammed shut. The seat's threadbare fabric was worn shiny smooth but sported a grimy antimacassar. I dumped my gear and dropped into my seat. No one sat beside me, so I sprawled out and shivered. The heat and ventilation systems were off. The ground crew de-iced the wings and ran out of deicer. An hour later, they returned with more deicer, and Murphy's Law kicked in. The engine booster failed. After another hour, a scout found a working booster. The pilot fired up the compressor and turbines, revved the engines, roared down the tarmac, and yanked back so hard on the yoke it felt like he was dodging Chechen SAMs. I looked in vain for Moscow's lights—lost in the blizzard—and checked my watch, two hours and twenty-three minutes late. Would the lateness foil Ivan's plan to leave for China and the taxol? Could the pilot make up the lost time?

We screeched up seven miles on an eighty-degree angle before leveling off to knife through the crystal-black sky eastward toward Siberia, a land mass larger than America and Mexico combined, unimaginably cold, and resource-rich beyond imagination. But I didn't care. I was here on a narrow, desperate mission to smuggle taxol. Siberia meant nothing to me.

A flight attendant pushed a cart through with cold cabbage rolls and Pepsi-Cola. I felt half at home. At one-thirty a.m., beneath a canopy of stars reflecting off the ice-covered Ob River bisecting Russia's third largest city, Novosibirsk, the pilot slammed down at Tolmachevo Airport. Founded in 1893 as a rest stop on the Trans-Siberian Railroad, the Siberian capital floundered until 170,000 refugees of the Soviet Famine immigrated and Hitler's annihilation of European Russia forced Stalin to relocate people, industrial complexes, and *Akademgorodok* — Science City — with its fourteen research institutes and universities where Nastia had worked.

Most passengers deplaned. The ground crew refueled, de-iced, and we departed. I pondered every facet of the smuggling plan. I arrived at so many unanswered questions I did the only thing possible when an answer won't gel; I moved to a three-across-seat, yanked up two armrests and slept.

Hours later, where the Irkut and Angara Rivers meet, the pilot landed at Irkutsk, the Far East regional cultural center populated by descendants of exiled professors, doctors, and merchants. Two Peace Corps volunteers deplaned, and, to my horror, two KGB-looking agents boarded, one short, stocky, pock-faced, and fifty, the other about my height and age. Both wore long, black leather coats and black mink *shapka-ushankas*. The one my age immediately headed for the rear of the plane and me.

I scrabbled upright and pushed my Colby ski hat back off my face. The agent studied my coat and cap with shrewd eyes. "Nice overcoat," he said to me in American English with a *Maine twang*! "L. L. Bean?"

I was shocked. We were light years from Maine. "Yes, how'd you know?"

"Saw one like it in Freeport when I was in high school."

I outweighed him by twenty pounds, but I wasn't going to wrestle him if he wanted the coat. I smiled and said, "You were an exchange student living in Maine?"

"Ah-ya, Boothbay Harba," he replied, mimicking the Down East accent. "Nice tan you got."

"Florida. I studied at Colby College, sixty miles up the Kennebec River from Boothbay."

"I saw the hat." He stepped back to look me up and down. "You wouldn't mind taking off the coat would you?"

"Of course not." I stood and shouldered out of it. "There might be a gun in the lining."

A cold smile crossed his face. He started going through my coat pockets. "Step into the aisle, Mister Locke," he ordered. "Take off your sneakers."

He knew my name! He wanted my sneakers! Greedy KGB agents are as bountiful as snowflakes in Siberia. I stepped into the aisle, leaned against the seat, and watched him examine the coat as I heeled off my sneakers. When he finished checking it for contraband, he examined my sneakers, twisting the soles for a James Bond hidden microchip.

He motioned to his aide-de-camp over and said to me, "Spread your legs."

I sucked in my gut, spread my legs, and stood motionless as his assistant frisked me, running hands up and down both arms, down my sides, down both legs. He didn't touch my genitals or the ever-so-slight bulge in my lower abdomen where I'd taped the taxol money. He removed my wallet, hefted it a couple of times, looked inside, and passed it to his boss.

"How much?" the former exchange student asked, thumbing the nineteen hundred-dollar bills.

"Nineteen hundred plus fifty or so rubles," I said. "For a hotel and dinner for my uncle."

"Aren't you the thoughtful nephew," he mocked. He wet his fingers and counted the cash. "The Lake Baikal Cleanup Project in Irkutsk is funded by a tourist transit tax. During the Soviet era, the pulp-and-paper industry on the shore of the world's deepest fresh-water lake jeopardized the lives of thousands of species of plants and animals found nowhere else on earth, like our freshwater sharks and seals endemic to Lake Baikal."

"Sounds like a noble cause."

"It is. With more fresh water than all your Great Lake, we're preserving many species. We calculate the tax based on a percent of foreigners' cash unless you wish to contest it in court next week."

"Nah," I said hastily. "I'd like to pay the transit tax now and not wait. How much?"

"Three hundred *dollars*." He passed my wallet back, and I took out three hundred-dollar bills and gave them to him. He slipped them into his pocket.

"Hard to say no to a worthy cause," I said.

"Isn't it." The agent and his aide turned and disappeared into the night.

I was flabbergasted at his bribe and the secret exchange of information about me!

Was this the end or just the beginning?

I didn't have to wait long to find out.

SIXTEEN

Blagoveshchensk, Siberia
December 28, 1991

The Barents Sea blizzard that had slammed Moscow and blanketed it with three feet of snow had lumbered east, crossed the steppes to Novgorod and Ufa, leaped the Ural Mountains — the border of Europe and Asia — and battered Yekaterinburg and Omsk. Moscow is closer to New York than to Blagoveshchensk, and by the time the Ilyusin 11-114 banged down hard at Blago's Ignatyevo Airport, the storm had been cut off by an Arctic Express with tornado-like winds bearing temperatures of minus sixty-seven degrees. The pilot parked the plane a quarter mile from the terminal where it trembled on the tarmac like a terrified Siberian white tiger clawing out of a snowstorm.

I glanced at my Timex; five a.m. local time — fourteen hours ahead of Blowing Rock where it was three o'clock yesterday afternoon. Anastasia would be taking dad to physical therapy at Broyhill Wellness Center in Boone. My stomach quivered thinking how the taxol deal might be affected by scouring winds, unbearable cold, and the delayed flight. Would Zhou's five-day journey by train from Kunming to Heihe with the taxol be on time? Would Uncle Ivan's final load of nesting dolls arrive on schedule after their six-thousand-mile, Trans-Siberian journey? Would Ivan stash vodka in the dolls to make extra money on his last run before retiring to Egypt get us caught? Would Ivan's brash, fast-talking style offend the politesse of Chinese culture with its bowing and eye-lowering? Could Ivan even be trusted? I'd only met him once, in New York, and he'd chased Russian women all night. Would my accent disclose who

I was? Would I need to speak Chinese? And what about the KGB? And, if all this worked out, could I keep the taxol sterile until the doctor injected Anastasia?

I touched the slight bulge in my lower abdomen, bundled up like Robert Peary searching for the North Pole and was again the last passenger to deplane. When I stepped onto the push-up stairs, an arctic blast slammed me back against the plane's fuselage, rocked the stairs, and froze my nostrils. The nostril-numbing felt as if had roared out of Tickse with an intensity so cold and so fierce it could be cut into squares and used to build igloos. Tickse, in Yakutia, was seven hundred miles north of the Arctic Circle and the coldest place on earth with temperatures recorded of -96° F.

I clung to the rail, lumbered down the stairs and boarded the bus, scrubbing my nose to thaw passages. Hunched-shoulder passengers, looking like penguins, crowded around a feeble heater as the bus rumbled to the massive Soviet-bleak terminal that served the city of two hundred thousand, mostly descendants of Stalin's exiles. We hurried inside where it was eighty degrees warmer but still below freezing. Through a wall of glass, I saw two dozen people bundled in greatcoats sleeping on benches and three drunks, amidst a litter of bottles, looking like war casualties splayed on the floor. I entered the customs line and stomped snow off my sneakers. That earned me a growl from a stooped ba-bushka in a greatcoat, scarf, and mittens pushing tracked-in-snow into dirty piles with a tree-branch broom. The Airport Café was not open. When it was my turn, I handed my internal passport to the drowsy customs agent with sleep-wrinkled cheeks standing beside an electric heater glowing red. He looked at it, looked at me, and held up the photo to compare.

"Troy Vladimirovich Locke, *pooseemo* — why — patronymic Russky?" he asked in Russlish.

I smiled as if I had never heard the question before and replied in Russian, "I was adopted at six after my widowed mother married an American. I live in Florida and am in Blagoveshchensk for American Christmas, visiting my dead father's only brother."

He gave me a nosey look and said suspiciously, "You speak Russian good but with an American accent," to which I thought, *Wonderful, now, what?*

Just then a tall, distinguished, handsome man observing us behind the counter stepped up. He had a sunlamp tan, expensively-cut, long, wavy, gray hair and wore a pale, blue, pinstriped shirt with French cuffs, an Italian-cut navy-blue suit with a show handkerchief of dark red silk in his outer breast pocket that matched his tie. He looked like a Hollywood Senator and the epitome of Russian chivalry and honor. He glanced at me with all the fascination you'd give a wall clock. In fact, it was so casual, I was apprehensive. I looked at him again to study his watching and waiting eyes, patient and careful eyes, cold, disdainful eyes — cop eyes. My hackles flared.

"Where were you born and where do you live now?" the customs agent continued.

"Born in Tver," I said. "Live in America, in North Carolina, for the last fifteen years."

"Were your parents divorced?"

"No. Papa was killed in Kabul before I was born. Mom remarried."

With an interest that didn't seem so casual, the Senator reached over the agent's arm and picked up my internal passport in long, thin, manicured fingers. He glanced at it and said in perfect English and an unctuous tone, "What was your father's name, Troy?"

"Vladimir Igorovich Fetisov. I've his army picture. Want to see it?"

He held up a hand. "Not necessary. Sorry to hear about his death; how old are you?"

"Twenty-two," I said, smiling — this always got a laugh — "I was born the day Armstrong stepped on the moon, July twentieth, nineteen sixty-nine, three months after Papa died."

The Senator's soothing voice grew icicles. "Did you get Tver police permission to visit Blagoveshchensk?"

"No, sir," I said, "I just flew in from America. I've only a week off work to visit my only living relative. I'll register today if that's okay."

"Sure, that'll be fine," the Senator soothed. "But bring us your stamped internal passport."

"Will tomorrow morning be okay?" I felt my left eye twitch. It always did when I lied.

"Within twenty-four hours will be alright." The Senator gave me a little smirk, but there was a hard-edged timbre of his voice that made me shiver.

"Yes, sir," I vowed, even though I knew that would be impossible. I'd be in China this morning and homeward bound tomorrow morning with the taxol. Stamped passports provide a trail as good as breadcrumbs for Kremlin spies. Fortunately, the Senator seemed to believe my fib, reached over the agent's arm and slid my passport back to me with glistening fingernails.

I thanked them, slung my backpack over my shoulder, grabbed the suitcase, crossed the lobby, and pushed through an inner door into the air lock, built to keep warm, foul air trapped inside Russian building. I took a last deep breath and exited into an icy wind that flash-froze my face. The morning sun was somewhere over Hawaii, the scene far from a vivid, blinding white. In fact, it was gray and black, and the silence whistled and the brief quiet was broken by a fierce shriek of mature Arctic howls sweeping across the wind-swept sprawl of a long hard winter.

On the landing, a dozen people smoked and milled and nattered. The temperature, at minus sixty-seven, didn't need help from wind chill. Two babushkas, swaddled in layers and looking as round as Pillsbury Dough Boys, hawked frozen "homemade pickles," likely purchased by the kilo at open markets to supplement their dollar-a-day social security. A fusillade of ice crystals whipped the parking lot and blurred orbs of light from Halogen lamps, swallowing *Ladas, Volgas, Chaikas,* and *Zhigulis*, the car modeled on the 1965 Fiat-124. I tugged my Colby ski hat down under my collar, clapped gloved-hands together, and studied the androgynous faces for Uncle Ivan. What I saw were dark, furred *shapka-ushanka* — earflaps down — and dark, ankle-length, *shenels* — greatcoats — collars up, cigarettes glowing like fireflies in faces shrouded in beards and scarves. No Ivan.

Again, I wondered, what did I know about him? Ivan might hate my guts for living in a free country, able to come and go at will. Would he be loyal to his dead brother's son who he'd partied with three years ago? Would he even remember meeting Anastasia in Tver ten years ago? I thought of him and stomped my feet when out of a snow swirl I spotted a *Zhigulis* bandit-taxi pull up outside the airport gate two hundred yards away. The blurry shape of a man got out. He leaned into the wind, shoulders hunched, hands pocketed, and came toward the terminal, puffing dragon huffs and plowing through a labyrinth of knee-deep furrows as embracing as quicksand.

He stopped at the foot of the landing, looked up at me, and in a gravelly voice, rasped, "Igor Vladimirovich?"

"Yeah," I said warily.

"It's me."

"Uncle Ivan?" I was taken back. I hadn't laid eyes on him since New York, and what little I could see of him had aged poorly. I couldn't see his hair. It had been red. He had the fair complexion of a redhead with craggy features corroded from a lifetime of fatty food, cheap vodka, and too many women. Those long nights had made his face florid, cheeks hollow and nose a road map of small broke veins. But, in that corroded monument to the Good Life shone inquisitive, pale, blue eyes, young as a child's. He came up the steps, eyes sparkling.

"Jesus, Igor," he said, "don't you recognize me? Your Papa and I looked like twins."

"Of course, I do," I lied. I didn't want to remind him I'd never seen my Papa.

People nearby scowled at us for using a mysterious language. We bear hugged, slapped each other on the back, and skipped the customary double-cheek smooch, shaking hands instead. This close, Ivan smelled like a stable. Wiry and slat-thin with narrow shoulder and big feet that had seen the world, weather had sandpapered Ivan's cheeks to the color of borscht. His shaggy red-gray beard had the consistency and odor of a horse tail and was nicotine-stained around the mouth. The tips of his mustache drooped with thick frost, and beneath his chin his beard hung heavy with a patina of ice growing with every breath and crystallizing instantly. He appeared sober. There was a strong smell of cigarettes but none of booze and neither the slurred speech nor the glazed-eye-look that drunks so magically achieve. When he turned to wave at his taxi, whitish-red hair poked out from under his *shapka*.

"Uncle Ivan," I said, teeth chattering, "you're looking great."

That was a lie. Ivan looked like what he was, a soiled, scrawny, scam artist who bootlegged vodka to China to supplement his $200-a-month retirement from the Air Force, piloting *MiG*-29,[16] and Aeroflot, captaining *Ilyushins* on the Moscow-to-JFK run. Every NYC layovers had been a Gaudeamus, a merry-making haunt of Brighton Beach bars for Russian divorcees, Santaettes he'd ferried over to bring bliss to distraught Americans fleeced by ex-wives. We'd worked the bars together spring break my junior year at Colby, and I knew Ivan was neither as tall nor as old as he looked. His thinness was accentuated by a ramrod posture, giving him the illusion of height. His life in the fast lane made him look seventy, losing the battle to cigarettes, booze, and bountiful babes. But his maverick spirit and *joie de vie* carried the day, and he planned to retire in Egypt with Olga, according to Mom, who knew he had the drive to accomplish it: *Ivan's as driven as your Papa was.*

Ivan thrust his head back and roared heartily. "Igor, you look tan as a mango freezing off its nuts in that fancy thin coat," Ivan said, in grave need of Listerine.

"I am," I said, spreading my arms and looking down at my pricey L. L.

Bean coat. "This rag's insulated with Thinsulate and good to minus fifty degrees."

"But not one degree lower." Ivan laughed. "Not a problem."

"Not if you're wearing a fur-lined bomber jacket and every wool shirt you own. I've never been so cold and hungry in my life. Can we stop for hot eats?"

Ivan gave me a toothy smile. His tea-colored incisors were as large as ape teeth and displayed borders of silver and artistry of Soviet dentists. "Didn't Siber Air feed you?"

"Tepid tea and frozen *pviozhkis* — stuffed rolls — that took me ten minutes to gnaw."

"You're way past tea," Ivan joshed. "Here; Merry Christmas!" He pulled out of his jacket pocket a narrow cylinder swathed in a *Pravda* — Truth — newspaper, the Soviet Union's *NY Times*. He carefully passed it to me as if it were incense headed for the manager.

I ripped off the end of *Pravda*, peeled back the neck of a liter bottle, and acted surprised to find a liter of Stolichnaya. I twisted off the cap, took an anesthetizing swig, wiped off my mouth on my sleeve and held it out to Ivan. With the back of his hand, he flicked ice from the stubble around his lips, almost glowing with horse smells, looked at me steadily and sighed. He half-smiled, the way a man does when he gets a badly needed drink that's first swallow promises a warmer, sunnier, brighter world. His Adam's apple bobbed as he took a slug so long and so deep it would have shot my blood alcohol level into the poisonous range.

"Plasma," he rejoiced and returned the Stoli. He shook a Prema cigarette from a ten-cent pack, struck a kitchen match on his zipper, cupped both hands around the burst of flame, and lighted it on the first try. He turned the cigarette around to see if it were glowing properly, the match still burning. Then he held the match out in the Arctic blast, gazed into the gale, and flicked it away. He took a deep drag and exhaled slowly, peacefully, through both his mouth and nose, and it boiled across his face and whipped skyward. Nourishment for his soul.

He yelled, "*Ede s'uda, ede s'uda!* — Come here, come here!" and waved at his taxi.

"Why'd you park halfway to Moscow?" I asked.

"Airport thieves charge thirty rubles to park closer."

"Gotcha." Like most Soviets, Ivan was frugal and squirreled all his ill-gotten gains under the mattress. "You still retiring to Egypt tomorrow?"

"I am. Flying out in the morning with Olga and my stash. With your payment, I've enough to buy a business … unless the *siloviki* — KGB cutthroats — stumble on the wrong *matryoshkay* on our way to China this morning." Ivan shielded his eyes from the overhead lamp and shouted at his taxi again, "*Ede s'uda, ede s'uda!*"

There was enough ambient light in the parking lot to see the boxy little *Zhigulis* cough and whine and claw its way out of the knee-deep snow like a mini-tank trailed by a cattail of black fumes as it lumbered past snowbanks ten-feet high.

Ivan pointed at the approaching taxi. "That bucket of bolts sure ain't your BMW."

"No, it isn't," I concurred. "It's as ugly as a *Lada,*" referring to the Russian knockoff of the Fiat one-twenty-four that had died twenty-five years ago in Italy and was still the unchanged model of choice for the USSR. "But is the reliable, ugly little beast cheap?"

Ivan flicked ash off his Prema cigarette and said out of the side of his mouth like W. C. Fields, "Not if the gas tank's full. That ugly duckling epitomizes the triumph of Soviet engineering and the tragedy of Soviet marketing. *Avto Vaz* built them like tanks. Heavy-gauge steel and truck shock absorbers for Siberian winters, bad roads, and lack of repair shops. The Kremlin markets them by ignoring demands for colors, comfort, convenience, and class."

"A nineties version of Henry's Model T's," I said.

"Precisely. Like the T, it's been exported to every continent, including Antarctica; hop in."

I opened the back door and wormed into the miniscule seat. Ivan followed. The bandit taxi was marginally warmer than outside but still far below freezing. Ivan took another pull of vodka and passed it to me. The taxi lurched. Stoli slopped all over my new coat.

"You bring the dough?" Ivan asked expectantly.

I nodded at the driver. "Does he understand English?"

"He barely grasps Russian."

"Yes, I've got the twenty grand here, two stacks of hundred-dollar bills, ninety taped — " I opened my coat and pat the left and right sides of my abdomen — "here, the other here; more in my wallet for bribes."

"We'll need it." Ivan opened my coat further. "I can't see the bulge. Good job."

"A stack of two hundred bills is only two-thirds of an inch thick. I measured."

"That's amazing."

"What's amazing is a stack of one trillion dollar bills is sixty-seven thousand, eight hundred sixty-six miles high. Enough to pay America's debt would reach the moon twice!"

"Whatever, we're home free," Ivan said with elation. "My last thirty cases of *matryoshkee* arrived yesterday after their long train ride from Sergiyev Posad." He referred to the spiritual center of Orthodox Russia, and its toy capital, located thirty miles north of Moscow and six thousand miles[17] from Blago.

I took a slug and passed Ivan the bottle. He gulped deeply. Then he wiped off the top on his grimy sleeve, leaned over the seat and tapped the driver's arm. He took the vodka. As he gulped, one of the *Ladas'* headlights scooped wavy holes in the night directly ahead; the other illumined whiteness off to the right that made Ivan laugh. "That headlight's useful for spotting Siberian Tigers, the world's largest cat."

"*Tiger here?*" I yelped.

"Relax. Not anymore. Illegal logging has clear-cut our oak forests for flooring sold to America. Oak nuts fed the squirrels and rabbits the Siberian Tigers lived on. They starved."

I shifted in the seat, trying, in vain, to stretch my legs. "What time are we leaving for China?"

"*We?*" Ivan said.

"Ivan, I have to go."

"You can't go."

"Why not? I've gotta go; this is our lives, plus I've read lots of spy books. I can be sneaky."

"Forget it."

Ivan removed a half-smoked butt from the Prema package in his bomber jacket-pocket. He jammed it in his mouth and struck another kitchen match on his zipper, cupping the flame. "You know shit from Shinola about smuggling, Igor. Sometimes I make great plans and they come off without a hitch. Sometimes screw-ups happen."

"What about today?"

"Haven't a clue." He looked at me and in snazzy my coat. "You're too Americanized."

"But think of the risk of you going alone."

"What risk?" He glared at me. "You've lost your Russian demeanor, kid."

"I can turn it on at will," I said.

"Sure you can. No other sleigh driver uses a co-pilot. It would look suspicious."

"No other driver has his nephew's wife's life in his hands. You might need backup."

"I won't."

"Shit happens, Ivan. Just this once. It'll be insurance for you, me, Nastia, and Olga."

Ivan stared at me a long minute and then pursed his lips. "Oh, for Christ's sake, you might be right." He shook his head. "Your papa would turn over in his grave ... if he was in a grave. But — " Ivan stabbed me with his yellowed index finger, "you gotta do exactly what the hell I tell you to do, no goddamned exceptions, none!"

"You're the boss. You lead, I'll follow." I thought of my Ruger. "Want me to pack heat?"

"Because the egg rolls might be cold? Jesus, Igor, no guns! Just bring the dough."

"That'll work."

With my participation settled, I peered out the window at the frozen black Siberian morning. Like most Russian cars, our taxi's walleyed-headlights had never been calibrated. One aimed low and straight ahead about ten yards, the other lit up endless fields of snow as if it suffered from strabismus. Ivan's mention of Papa made me think about his ashes. Mom had scattered them on the Volga River, the largest of the 130 rivers that dump into the Caspian Sea. The Caspian has no egress; Azerbaijan, Russia, Iran, Turkmenistan, and Kazakhstan encircle it, dumping too. Not many tourists bask on its squalid shores.

"What an endless ocean of snow," I said. "Blago looks so barren."

Ivan leaned over and tapped the window on my side. "There's a building, a dairy."

Barely visible in blowing snow was a structure the size of a cruise ship, glowing with lights.

"We're in the middle of the rich black farmland of a *kolkhozy* — collective farm — twelve miles from Blagoveshchensk," Ivan added. "Blago has metal, paper, and timber factories, and it sprawls along the Amur, one of Russia's four, great, Siberian river systems, and it's our thousand-mile border with China that runs into the Pacific north of Vladivostok. The others rivers, the Ob-Irtysh, Lena, and Yenisey all flow north to the Arctic Ocean."

As we neared the city, huge, blocky buildings spewed great clouds of toxic chemicals. The factories soon gave way to small, wooden houses with decorative shutters and outhouses in back on quarter-acre lots. A few had multiple-parallel-rod TV antennas. All belched wood smoke — as diesel, Ivan said, cost half a month's pension. After a mile or so, the wooden houses had been razed to make room for endless blocks of bleak, Soviet-era, nine-story, precast-concrete apartments, or *Stalinkas*. In the city center, streetlights that functioned, lit shops, restaurants, and gaudy, brick buildings with gingerbread trim that contrasted markedly from the stark, gray, boxy, government buildings lorded over by the all-pervasive statue of Lenin, left arm draped with a greatcoat, right arm flung out in a look-at-what-I-built-for-you gesture. No one was taking his picture. Front-end loaders had scooped snow into great piles at intersections, which artists carved into twenty-foot sculptures. Babushkas pushed snow off sidewalks with shovels made of two-foot-squares of tin nailed to stout sticks. Women with jugs and pails lined up behind farm trucks for raw milk poured from thigh-high cans. At the Museum of Local Lore, renowned for its dinosaur collection, we turned south on a narrow street toward the Amur River.

"The Chinese call the Amur, Heilong Jiang, or Black Dragon River," Ivan said, pointing straight ahead. "It snakes through Siberia twenty-seven hundred miles before reaching the Pacific."

"It feels like we're a long way from Moscow," I said.

"You are. You're now closer to Seattle than Moscow."

A fierce wind shrieked up the street banking snow into six-foot drifts and heeling over ice-coated birch trees like skate-boats sailing close to the wind. A hail of ice shards chattered at crescendo level against the *Zhigulis* windshield so hard they sounded like ball bearings.

"Nice place for a monastery," I said, pointing at a T-shaped, onion-domed church on the left.

"That's the Popov Monastery," Ivan said, "or used to be; the KGB got another use for it."

I wondered about that as the ice racket stopped when the taxi pulled in at the warehouse, shielded by steel double-doors inside a high cement wall. The driver tooted a tinny horn. Ivan craned his head around again, as he had several times. I wondered if he expected to be followed by a GAZ-M1, the infamous, black,

Ford sedan known as a Black Maria that the KGB drove when arresting people.

I turned around as well. "*Siloviki* follow us?"

"Don't think so." Ivan nodded at the warehouse. "*This* is my Ticket to Paradise."

"Smuggling Central," I said. "Gotcha."

"Don't be snotty. This heap of cement is the epicenter of my enterprise."

I sat up for a better look. The weak splay of the left headlight rested on a ten-foot cement-block wall topped with four-foot poles crowned with snow biscuits and stretched with razor wire.

"I'd have guessed it was a Gulag," I said, pulling up my collar. The car was meat locker cold.

Ivan shrugged. "Used to be. When the Soviets built the sixty-mile connector to the Trans-Siberian Railroad, they arrested eight hundred men and kept them locked up here nights." In Russian, he said to the driver, "Blow the horn again, the watchman's deaf."

The driver grunted and pressed both hands on the horn.

"That oughta do it." Ivan tilted the Stolichnaya into the ambient light, noted an inch and polished it off. "So whatdaya think, Igor?"

"I'm impressed." And I was. "Your warehouse's probably what, three hundred yards long?"

"Oh, it's not all mine. Just one, ten-meter-wide space Americans would call an *in-cu-ba-tor.*" He drew out the word, demeaningly. "I traffic in dolls filled with vodka to China; the guy next to me smuggles gold. Chinks love gold."

I shook my head, puzzled. "What I don't understand is with a billion people next door, why don't Russians sell them wheat, milk, and beef?"

"The *kolhhozy* wants to, but commerce is run from Moscow," Ivan said.

"You'd think after seventy-four years they'd discovered that Lenin's premise is flawed."

The steel door screeched open. Ivan lifted his chin. "That's Alex."

The hunched-back watchman stuck out his head. He had a grizzly beard and wore rags for a hat. He kicked aside some snow and pushed the door open wide enough for us to enter. We drove by him. Alex wore rags for a coat and rags for boots, too.

The taxi's lights illumined the one-time Gulag, now a near-tenantless, state-owned, business incubator. "*Kak oi*? — Which one?" the driver asked.

Ivan pointed the empty Stolichnaya bottle at the end unit. "*Posledniy* — The last."

The *Zhigulis* crawled into the yard — where prisoners had once assembled to be counted twice a day, at the beginning and end of work, five a.m. and nine p.m. — plowing through the snow like Rommel's tanks furrowed through Sahara sand. When it stopped, Ivan looked around before pulling up on the door handle. I thought I saw a flash of light in the rearview mirror, probably the reflection of a passing snowplow.

"We'll only be a few minutes. *Wait!*" Ivan ordered the driver in Russian and English, to me, "Let's go."

When I stepped into a knee-high snow, my dog-hair socks kept snow from stuffing my sneakers. The icy-fingered wind penetrated my L. L. Bean coat like a shawl. Ivan trudged up four stairs to the loading dock, unlocked a door-within-a-door, and pushed it open with a rusty screech. Stable stench leached out. A horse whinnied. Ivan turned on a weak overhead light, and I closed the door. My eyes adjusted slowly to the dimness. Another horse whinnied a different sound. I felt snow-powdering my cheeks as it seeped through wall chinks. What space I could see was about thirty-by-sixty: cement block walls, poured cement floor, and cast cement ceiling. Horses in the rear. A grimy Doctor Zhivago sleigh to one side. Ivan was an orderly man. Most pilots are. A neat stack of wooden boxes. A tidy mound of bailed hay. Lined bags of oats. A cot draped with musty army blankets. Toolbox, workbench, nails in baby-food-jars. A big heap of coal. Fifty-five-gallon drum-stove. The stove and eight feet of flue glowed red in a failed attempt to heat the space. The acrid odor of burning coal did not mask the earthiness of horses. I sneezed and snuffled.

"I know, I know," Ivan said. "This place smells like a shit house." He stomped snow off his boots, wrestled out of his coat, dumping it on the cot.

"Those the *matryoshky*?" I asked, pointing at the birch boxes.

"Yes, I didn't want to load the *troika* until we hid the taxol loot." Ivan grabbed a box and motioned for me to get the toolbox. "Give me a hammer and crowbar."

He dug another Prema butt from his shirt pocket and pressed a kitchen match to the red-hot stove. It exploded. Ivan worked the crowbar into a crack between the crate's side and top and taped it cautiously with the hammer. The lid didn't budge. He flicked ashes on the floor, and, careful not to scratch the box top, with brute force jimmied the bar under the lid, twisted, and pried it off. He tossed out some soft Finnish wrapping tissue — Soviets have yet figured out how to make it — and lifted out a brightly painted *matryoshky* five inches in diameter and eight inches tall.

I stepped close to get a better look. "Who's that?"

"Nicholas the Second," Ivan said and passed me the dark-haired, mustached Czar with so many medals on his chest he glowed. "Lenin had Nick and his family murdered on July seventeenth, nineteen-eighteen in Yekaterinburg. Twist Nick open."

I held the superb-looking Czar up in the light. "Sorry, old boy." With a little force, I spun the Czar into two pieces and pulled out Tsarina Alexandra painted in a white gown, tiara, and pearls. "Wasn't she German?"

"She was and the granddaughter of English Queen Victoria, who had forty-two grandchildren, including German Emperor Wilhelm II, King George V, the Tsarina of Russia, and the Queens of Norway, Greece, Romania, and Spain."

I held her up to the light to size her. "Alexandra's too big for dough, Ivan. It'll rattle."

"Try the next one. They had four girls before the hemophiliac, Alexis."

I twisted Alexandra opened and pulled out a girl. "Who's this?"

Ivan glanced at the dark-haired girl. "Anastasia."

"Dead so young," I said, "and as pretty as my Anastasia." A visual image of the murdered family appeared out of nowhere followed by a vision of my own Anastasia struggling with cancer that was so real it made me shiver.

"Yeah, murdered, your wife's age; give her here." Ivan flapped his hand.

I gave him a look. "Jesus, Ivan, don't sound so broken up."

"Hey, don't get sentimental on me. They're dolls for Christ sake. Toss the others in the fire."

"Mind if I look at them first?"

"Be my guest, but hurry; I want to finish before — "

The rusty-hinged front door screeched open. The storm burst in.

I whipped around and froze.

Out of a maelstrom of coal dust and swirling snow plastering the walls with a gray mush, stepped two goons. A hatless, six-foot-seven giant with a crew cut wearing a long black leather coat and his short, potbellied boss in an opened greatcoat and cheap three-piece suit. He clenched the ubiquitous black-and-white baton of Soviet cops.

Ivan's face turned to instant comprehension: Demons incarnate. He became passive and unexpressive, putting on the face of ancient Russia, the product of millennia succumbing to authoritarian rule. The bold person is a rarity in Russia, a land of little hope and abundant fear.

I looked at Ivan for his lead and tried to look submissive.

Three-piece-suit fixed Ivan with the eyes of the desperate schemer. He appeared to be a man driven by greed and dreams of wealth, willing to risk death to see them fulfilled.

"*Vy* — You — Ivan Fetisov?" he snarled in Russian above the wind's screech.

"*Da*," Ivan said.

"You've been smuggling vodka to Heihe!" the short man screamed in Russian.

"That's a lie," Ivan replied and waved off his accusation with his hand.

Ivan moved, stepped to the door to close it. With one hand on the door and the other on the doorframe, he pushed hard against the wind. The door was about closed when the bright silver mussel of an AK-47 emerged between Ivan's hands.

A third agent stepped in. He shoved Ivan back and slammed the door closed. Ivan's fell against the stove. There were a sizzle and stench of burning wool. Ivan jumped.

The third agent jabbed Ivan with his Kalashnikov. "Going somewhere?" he growled.

"Wanted to close the door," Ivan said, flicking his hands in pain. "I just mopped th — "

Three-piece suit smacked him with the baton. "Cut the crap, Fetisov. You're in deep shit." He whirled around and whacked a *matryoshky* box with his club. Then he stepped in front of me, cocked an eyebrow, and said in perfect English, "Who the hell are you, boy?"

Before I could respond, he rammed the end of the baton into my gut. I gasped. "The fancy coat says American!" he screamed. "What's your name?"

"Troy Vladimirovich Locke. I was born Igor Vladimirovich Fetisov, here visiting my uncle."

"Well, ain't you a thoughtful nephew," he taunted in English.

"It's the truth. Ivan's my only family. Papa was killed in Afghanistan in 1969 just before I was born. Mama died in a car accident last month. I came here to — "

"To learn how to smuggle?"

"No!"

Three-piece suit whacked his palm with the baton. "Hiding vodka in *matryoshky* going to China is a profitable business. Or didn't your uncle tell you?"

I shook my head. "Ivan was telling me the Romanov story."

"Sure he was," the three-piece suit said.

"Hey," Ivan said. "This is my last shipment to China. No vodka. It's clean."

"Sure it is," three-piece suit scoffed. He rammed the baton in my gut again. I doubled over, reached up, yanked it from his hand, and felt the cold muzzle of the AK-47 pressed on my neck.

"Go ahead," the third agent snarled, "make my day." Dirty Harry has gone global.

"You, Mister Fetisov-Locke, screwed up," three-piece suit sneered. "You have dual citizenship, but you're a Russian first, and you *didn't* register with the police in Tver *or* Blagoveshchensk."

The prick knew who I was. Probably got a call from the airport Senator.

He snatched the baton from my hand and hit me across the arm.

I winced and grabbed my arm. "Christ, I just got here. I'll register this morning."

"Too late," he sneered.

Ivan said, patiently, "You know I'm a loyal communist and retired Soviet and Aeroflot pilot. After I sell these *matryoshkay* today, I'm retiring to Egypt. Have a cigarette. Relax." He took out his pack of ten-cent Prema cigarettes and offered them around.

Three-piece suit sneered at them and made a gesture to the giant who pulled out a pack of Marlboros and dealt them out. The agents lit up, filling the space with the stench of smoke laced with urine, hay, horse, coal, birch-boxes, burned flesh, and fear.

With great confidence, Ivan blew a perfect smoke ring. "You know I've permission to leave for Hugarta, Egypt tomorrow morning," he said. "I've got your stamped approval right here." He put the cigarette in his mouth, squinted as smoke curled into his eyes and dug in his leather pocket for the police approval document.

"We know that," three-piece said. He turned to the giant, "Get Locke's internal passport; we'll register him." He turned to me. "The fee's one thousand."

"Sounds reasonable to me," I said, amazed at only one thousand rubles. I tried to ignore my stomach pain, took out my wallet and started counting rubles.

"Rubles?!" screamed three-piece suit. He raised his baton and smacked my leg. "Did I say Rubles, Locke? Do I look crazy? *Dollars!*"

"Right," I said and kept my yap shut.

I gave my internal passport to the giant, wet my fingers, and thumbed apart ten new hundred-dollar bills that stuck together as if they didn't want to leave me. "When will I get it back?"

"It'll be at the *Koogobear* office this afternoon," he said, tucking the bills into his inside suit pocket, and, without uttering another word, the trio disappeared.

Ivan plopped down on the cot and huffed out a long sigh. "That was too damn close."

I went to the door. "Bolted it?"

"Damn toot'n, and toss the royal kiddies in the fire. We'll stash the loot before they return."

I pulled out Anastasia's siblings, open the stove and dropped them on the red hot coals. The paint blistered, crackled, and popped. Then I pulled up my sweater, unbuttoned my shirt, dropped my pants and long johns and peeled two stacks of hundred-dollar bills from my underbelly. "Did Zhou stay at the fifteen grand he promised Song Lin?"

"He did," Ivan said. "After I went to Heihe and got him as blitzed as a Saturday-night wino."

"He speak good English?"

"Yes. And the son of a bitch scarfed three plates of snails and guzzled expensive Scotch on my dime, yapping away in Chinglish and telling me about his ten years at Florida State."

"What's he look like?" I asked.

"Shit, I don't know, black hair, black eyes, skinny."

"That could be a billion Chinese."

"Okay, okay. He's real tall, eyes like knives, broken nose, Prince Charles ears, pasty-colored skin, balding with a wart on the left side of this chin the size of an eraser with two three-foot-long whiskers drooping out of it." Observant.

I took a stack of nine thousand dollars, counted out sixty bills and set it on the first stack, total fifteen grand. I counted out his ten hundred dollar bills and gave them to Ivan. He twisted a rubber band around the wad and stuffed into his pocket.

"This'll get us to Hugarta and settled," he said.

Ivan recounted the fifteen thousand, rolled it tight, wrapped it with a fat rubber band, and dropped it into Anastasia. He spun her together, inserted her inside her Mom, rotated her together, and dropped her inside Nicholas. He screwed Nick tight. Shook. The moola rattled.

"Try it without the rubber band, let the dough expand," I said, extending my fingers.

"Okay." Ivan reversed the process. Removed the rubber band, fluffed the dough, placed it inside Anastasia and shook. It did not rattle. Ivan put the dolls together and set Nicholas in the crate. He carefully nailed the lid shut and smudged the top with a coal dust X.

"Let's load," he said. The marked one goes in the very center. Guards always take two boxes off the back for their payoff."

I worked up a sweat burying the moneyed *matryoshky* in the center of the load of heavy wooden boxes. Russian labels identified each box's content of political figures: Mao, Stalin, Reagan, Gorbachev, Kohl, Mitterrand, and Thatcher along with their respective key honchos. We covered the load with a tarp. The horses watched, whinnied, and stomped their hooves. Time for work.

I stepped over to a mare. She nuzzled me with her soft nose. "Are the horses ready?"

"They are," Ivan said. "I gave them extra oats. It made them suspicious. Look, it's seven o'clock, you've got time for some shut-eye at the *Druzhba* — Friendship — *Hotel*. It's ten minutes from here, and the river crossing is beside it." Ivan snapped his fingers. "Oh, like most of our hotels, the *Druzhba's* a hot-pillow joint. A hooker will call you as soon as you hit the room. Ignore her. Blagoveshchensk's trying to be the Las Vegas of the Far East, gambling and pussy galore. I'll stay with the load, grab a nap, harness the horses, and see you at sun-up."

"Which is when?"

Ivan looked at his watch. "In about three hours. About ten o'clock."

"Anastasia would love it here."

"No, she wouldn't."

***

SEVENTEEN

Blagoveshchensk, Russia to Heihe, China and return
December 28, 1991

As the taxi pulled up to the *Druzhba* Hotel, a swirling blizzard veiled the upper floors that rose ten stories above Kuznechnaya Street and the north bank of the Amur River. The whiteout and night's eighteen-hour blackout concealed the mile-wide Sino-Soviet border. The few lights visible in the *Druzhba* looked as gappy as jack-o-lantern teeth.

On the brief taxi ride, I saw a tall woman in a gray-leather-hooded greatcoat on *Ulitsa Lenina*, Blagoveshchensk's deserted main drag. With her back straight and brisk walk, she reminded me of Anastasia, and I let myself think of her and choked up. Tears stung my eyes. I told myself the tears flowed from exhaustion, but they sprung from sensory overload, lonesomeness, fatigue, and KGB fears. I felt as weak as a broken back. I cursed myself for being half-hearted and swiped my eyes on my sleeve. Let the cabby think they watered from the cold. I missed Anastasia's voice, her smell, her presence, and her lithe caresses when we touched. I missed how she nibbled her lower lip when puzzled, how she scribbled grocery lists in Russian but forgot them when going to Publix. I hadn't wanted to leave her, but what choice did I have? I had to buy the Chinese taxol for her to live. How else could I save her life? That rationalization did not lessen the pain in my heart, pain as intense now as it was the Black Friday Ginsburg told us of her cancer. And dummy me just had to insist Anastasia live in Orlando for a better life and a decent job, a life without family and friends, the support system she so desperately needed. She was my responsibility, mine alone.

Pulling off my gloves, I took a twenty dollar bill from my fat wallet, gave it to the bandit cabbie, dismounted, and glanced up at the hot-pillow *Druzhba.* Tear tracks on my cheeks flash-froze into loge-runs before I'd opened the door to the hotel's airlock where it was a smoky eighty-five degrees. The tear spumes vaporized in the stale heat and vanished by the time I said, *"Prevet,"* to the coat-check woman who stared at me as if I were a Martian. Was it my accent? The L. L. Bean coat? The tan?

Across from her booth, through an open double-door, cigarette smoke and boozy hoots billowed from a casino swarming with Chinese high-rollers wagering at horseshoe tables and guzzling freebies dished out by tall, busty, blondes in skimpy Vegas outfits. The room looked like an upside down wedding cake. Polished poker tables ringed the upper-level perimeter, roulette table down a ledge, and a half-dozen 21-tables in the pit manned by yawning dealers under twinkling chandeliers. Drowsy girls plastered the upper walls. From the shadows, an ebullient peroxide approached, tall, thin, blue-eyed, wide-mouthed, and very attractive. She motioned, coaxing me in with a come-here look blandished with a tantalizing display of her ample chest. I shook my head. Her shoulders sagged and she shrugged: *your loss.*

Carrying my bags, I continued down the dim hall, around a corner, past the Sibir Air Office, past a gift shop, and into a high-ceiling lobby bursting with an incredible scene. There, in the middle of Siberia rose a sumptuous, tropical garden. All plastic. Phony palms rose above bogus banana trees, heavy with fruit. Fake flowers, in dazzling colors, quivered in the volcanic forced-hot-air. A scarlet tulip tree towered above two *babushkas,* one scrubbing floor tiles with a rag-on-a-stick, the other dusting a garish Ginger Lily in gaudy red.

The all-plastic lobby triggered a memory of Saint Monique in the Lesser Antilles. During Christmas break senior year at Watauga High, Dad, Mom, and I had flown down to stroll its black-sand beaches and hike its soaring piton. Dad explained that tropical flora required plentiful sunlight, rich soil, and abundant water. Saint Monique was incredibly suited for abundance, and a place I vowed that day, I would live.

A short, beefy man with a crew-cut and no neck was reading a newspaper under a nutmeg tree aglow as a Christmas tree with peach-colored fruit. Something was off. Under the left arm of his K-Mart suit, there was an ominous bunch. He shook a Marlboro from a pack, lit it, and casually flicked ashes on the gleaming floor. He glanced at me surreptitiously and diverted his eyes to the *Pravda* he was reading. Upside down. KGB are an easy spot.

The registration desk was deserted. I set down my bags and dinged a bantam silver bell.

A tall, scrawny bellboy with a beamy smile and twinkle in his eye stepped out of a curtained doorway, shuffling cautiously on slick tile. A woman followed, rubbing her eyes. The boy half of the bellboy appellation was a stretch. He had to be an octogenarian. But his face glistened with the *joie de vivre* of a teenager on his first date. He wore a threadbare uniform in faded peacock-blue adorned with gold-braided epaulets that hung from his bony shoulders like a grain sack draped on a broomstick. But it was neither soiled nor grungy, and all the gold buttons gleamed, polished and buttoned. He smiled, and his dark black eyes glowed with intelligence that exuded a warmth rarely experienced in Russia.

"Top of the morning to you, sir," the old fellow sang out in perfect British English, bowing from the waist for my bags.

So much pleasantness put me on guard. I raised a hand, declining his offered help. "I have a reservation," I said. "Troy Locke."

"Yes, sir. We've been anticipating your arrival. I say, how was your trek from America?"

"Long, thank you."

"You appear exhausted." He turned to the desk clerk, *"Eto Mister Lokk."*

He squared his shoulders proudly and clicked his heels. "My name is Alexis Romanov, sir, bellman, guide, and translator, should you require my service."

"Thanks, Mister Romanov," I said. "You've excellent English, but I speak some Russian and am here visiting an uncle who speaks English."

Alexis smiled and hesitated as if expecting an observation, so I gave him one. "Your surname is certainly revered in Russia." Historian Troy Locke.

"Once upon a time it was," he said, then wrinkles of chagrin crinkled his face. "Lamentably, few youngsters today recognize the significance of the Romanov name."

"Were your people related to the Czar?"

Alexis rolled his shoulders back and stood tall. "My good man, I *am* the hemophiliac son of Czar Nicholas the Second."

Wacko! I thought and studied him closer. He looked sharp, shrewd, believable, old enough, and entirely batty. Every Russian school kid knows the Czar and his family were murdered on Lenin's order on July 17, 1918, in Yakaterinburg. That would make this Alexis the right age. Russians also know when they interred the family in Saint Petersburg's Peter and Paul Cathedral eighty years later — *to the day* — no one ever found the bodies of Alexis and Anastasia, a girl immortalized by Ingrid Bergman in her 1956 Oscar-winning performance.

"Sir, study my visage," the Czar-in-waiting said. He turned to afford me full profile and raised his bushy black eyebrows so high they nearly disappeared.

I squinted. Alexis's face had the unexceptional eyes, forehead, nose, mouth, and chin of every Homo sapiens on earth. He did not look like the Alex doll I'd just burned.

"Striking." I did not want to prick his bubble.

"Isn't it? Now, sir, if you'd be so kind as to give us your American passport, driver's license, and a credit card, we'll make the requisite copies."

"Sure."

I wondered why Alexis had not asked for my residency permit and internal passport. Did he know the KGB had taken them? Was he an informer? I gave him the documents, and he gave them to the desk clerk and disappeared through a curtained doorway. He reappeared with a silver salver crammed with a bucket of ice, rattling against a liter of Beluga vodka and crystal snifter big enough to hold a cantaloupe, a hard sausage, knife, and tin of toothpicks.

"You might find a bite of sausage and potation of vodka soothing," Alexis said, juggling the tray.

What a line! "It certainly will be," I agreed, feeling like a death row inmate getting his last meal and nightcap — or morningcap if you're a stickler for temporal accuracy. Alexis had a Czar's silky way with words and nose for money, obviously having heard of Americans' proclivity for generous tipping. Still, I was starved, and a drink would settle my nerves and hasten sleep after two days of airborne catnaps and dog food.

The desk clerk completed my registration card and spun it around. I signed it in Cyrillic cursive. She compared my signature to that in my Russian passport, approved, reached beneath the counter and extracted a crisp, synthetic, bath towel the size and weight of a dishcloth and thin enough to read through. Air-drying is imperative in Soviet hotels.

The tray rattled when Alexis reached for my suitcase. "Allow me, sir."

"No, no, Alexis," I said. "You're carrying quite enough, I've got it."

He smiled pleasantly. "Then follow me, sir," and he struck off through the tropical garden.

I stopped at the elevator, but Alexis continued to the stairs. When he turned and looked over his shoulder at me, I said, "Is there a problem with — "

"I regret to say, the lift's awaiting German parts. It's only six flights."

"I need the exercise." What a lie!

We trudged up marble stairs covered with a fake Oriental runner so loose and slippery I knew I'd snag a foot and go flying, but we made it to the belfry unscathed. On the sixth floor, the *gornichnaya* — a housemother posted at a desk on each floor, next to the elevator — gave me a squinty-eyed look. *Gornichnaya* possess all room keys, spy on guests, run prostitutes, and tongue-lash maids.

"*Medovyi meists clouche, spaseba,*" Alexis said to her.

"*Registraseeah,*" the *gornichnaya* growled at him.

Alexis showed her my registration card and said to me, "Did you understand that, sir?"

"Some," I said, waggling a hand. I knew what she'd said, of course, but I thought it prudent to hide my proficiency.

"I asked for the key to the honeymoon suite, and she asked for your registration."

"Ahhh."

We walked down a dim hall to a corner unit. Alexis unlocked the door and swung it open. The temperature in the room approached the surface of Venus. The air was stale and overladen with disinfectant. It would take an hour before it would be cool if the a/c worked.

Alexis flicked on a light. "This is our most elegant suite. When the sun rises, you'll have a splendid view to the south of the Amur River, known as the Heilong Jiang, or Black Dragon River, in Chinese."

A solitary bulb dangled from a long cord and cast a red glow in the room, reflecting the plush, red-velvety wallpaper, which, in places, had loosened by condensation and curled down the walls like wood shaving. The carpet, also red, was soiled. The two single beds jammed together cast lumpy shadows from a thick comforter beneath a silk dustcover embroidered with fierce dragons stained with bodily fluids old enough that Stalin might have made them. Czech crystal crammed the credenza. The ornately-carved armoire held a nine-inch television and radio. A miniature fridge stood between two overstuffed armchairs big enough for sumo wrestlers upholstered in red velvet that matched the wallpaper.

"It's a bit stifling in here," I said pleasantly.

"I'll remedy that straight away before you deliquesce," Alexis said poker-faced and noticed my puzzlement. "Liquefy," Alexis said authoritatively. I smiled and nodded a thank you, and he set the goody tray on the two-foot-wide window ledge that ran the length of the room. He stepped onto an armchair and up the ledge and shuffled along its length to the corner. The wall of windows was six-feet-tall and ice-covered. Directly above the head of the bed was a *fortochka,* or window-within-a-window, two-by-three feet. Alexis banged the *fortochka* and pushed it out into the shrieking blackness.

A rush of cold air whistled into the room, its tone modulating with the blizzard's intensity.

"We don't use thermostats here," Alexis said. "When it gets too warm open the *fortochka.*"

"Of course," I said. With the world's second largest oil reserves and all output owned by the state, Soviet heat is willfully wasted. Thermostats are never used. Too hot? Fling open a window. Too cold? Turn up the heat, which repulsed my nurture-bred sense of thrift.

Alexis climbed down, and with a burst of enthusiasm flung open the bathroom door. "In addition to a refrigerator and television with *two* channels, you have an *Italian* Jacuzzi!"

"Great!" I enthused. "Just what I need to limber up."

"Well," Alexis began, hanging his head, "unfortunately, it's not hooked up as of yet, but will be. Wrong parts sent from Milano. You do have water, though."

"Hot?"

"Evenings between seven and eight."

"Let me guess," I said. "The central steam-line to this part of the city froze?"

"Last month," Alexis said. "But there's hot water in the basement whenever the sauna is working. Oh, and two bottles of Baltika in the frig."

I licked my lips and glanced at my watch. "Thanks, Alexis. Ask the *gornichnaya* to wake me in two hours. Promptly at nine, please." I gave him a crisp, new, twenty-dollar bill.

He looked at it and looked at me. His eyes glazed. "Thank you, sir. Your act of generosity is — " he stammered — "more money than I've seen in six months." Teary-eyed, Alexis left.

I closed, chained, and bolted the door. I turned on the television, poured myself a hefty shot of vodka in the crystal snifter, sliced off a hunk of hard salami, flipped on the TV, and munched, watching Soviet farmers bundle wheat shafts and sing patriotic songs. I flipped to the second channel and watched Soviet soldiers herd German POWs and sing patriotic songs. I clicked off the TV.

After finishing my snack, I undressed and tiptoed over icy bathroom tiles to the tub for a frosty shower. When shivering wet, I slathered on lye soap that smelled like sanitizer and made my eyes water. I'd just started to rinse off when the phone rang. Ivan and a glitch.

I sprang out of the tub and rushed to the phone. "Hello," I said anxiously.

"*Utro seks* — morning sex — you wish, *neit*?" a girl hushed in breathy awkward Ruslish. "Me, Olga, beautiful and not fat."

My breath quicken, high and shallow. My shoulder muscles hardened. I felt an engorging of the droopy muscle. Blood and oxygen drained from my head in a feeding frenzy that left me rationalizing like a pimply-faced adolescent. I needed to reduce stress, sleep, soothed my nerves, build self-esteem, and calmed the ape within me. What harm would it do? No objective harm at all. Olga was no hesitant virgin, and there'd be no emotional significance. Just a quickie and restful snooze before a challenging day. *But Locke,* I told myself, *you'd know, and you must live with yourself ... and Anastasia.*

Overflowing with righteousness, I said, "No doubt you are lovely, Olga, but no thank you. I'm happily married."

I hung up and returned to the shower, proud of my steely resolve, but far from satisfied. When one considers the survival of humanity, it is essential to its continuance the arrogant ape rises in men at the least incitement; he has plunged his primordial dagger in so quickly and so well for so long it has pre-served the species since we descended from the trees. Was that bountiful self-deception? I think not. Man's lusty desire, far from being a character flaw, is a manifestation of that primal urge, a biological stirring of the juices that, on oc-casions, causes momentary mental lapses. I suspected I was fribbling myself again and said aloud, "Cut the crap, Locke, dry off, crack open the fortochka, and jump into bed."

The *fortochka* had done its job. The room was a nippy sixty-five degrees and perfect for sleep. I closed my eyes and heard the wind gust, a car door slam, a man growl, a girl tittered. I rose, slammed the *fortochka* shut, and jumped back into the lumpy sack, snuggling under the *perena* — the foot-thick com-forter — encased in the dragon dustcover, or *pododeal'nik*, and turned onto my left side, right arm under the pillow, and closed my eyes. The last thought I had in non-REM sleep was of Anastasia fourteen thousand miles away. Then I clenched my eyes tight and willed myself to sleep. Just as I was waltzing into the deep, peaceful, bone-building, immune-strengthening, tissue-regenerating REM sleep, there was a faint knock at the door that hastened consciousness.

Ivan had a problem.

I grumbled, pulled on shorts, stumbled to the door, and peeked out the Judas hole.

There stood a tall, gorgeous, raven-haired girl no more than seventeen, pink-cheeked, hip-shot, in a long, thick, fawn-colored mink coat that reached to her ankles.

I cracked open the door. "Yes?"

"Me, Olga," she said in a throaty, melodious voice. Her smile was shy and her long dark hair curved smoothly about her face lightly made up with mascara, eyeliner, eyeshadow, and lip gloss ranging from pink to bronze. Her lashes fluttered innocently. She was an arm's length away and looked like class merchandise, a celebrity's top-dollar girl on tall heels, all fresh and fragrant and resilient. "*Van nravitsya* — You like?"

Her eyes were the deepest purple-blue I'd ever seen. Her cheeks were high, wide, and dimpled. Her chin narrow and strong. Her lips full and ripe. Her teeth snow-white and perfect. I stared at her greedily and forced myself to think of the winter I broke my leg skiing App Mountain and how much that hurt. I thought about getting shot in Iraq and how much that hurt. I thought about blizzards and snowbanks and icicles and, finally, got it under control. I unbolted the door and unhooked the chain. I opened the door wide to refuse the poor beauty's offer. She stepped back as the door swung open, and, before I could speak, she stepped closer.

Olga gave me a warm and knowing smile. She had the aroma of expensive perfume. She unbuttoned her fluffy fawn mink with a flagrant looseness. Nothing I thought of could stop my sweaty hands from reaching up and pulling apart that thick silky coat. She wore white pearls and red heels and nothing else. Heat radiated from her young, taut body sun-lamped to a golden tinge. It looked as solid as a masthead. She made a pirouette with effective grace, displaying the promised goodies, eyes cool in speculation and evaluation. A supple bronze thigh nearly hid the soft, smoky smudge of triangular fuzz. She was elegant and sleek as a seal. She had small firm breasts crowned with pink rosebuds, a long narrow waist, and long and shapely legs. The tip of her tongue circled her lips suggestively. She glanced down at a bulge in my shorts. Her eyes said forget your troubles, vows, and dignity and hurry into the fragrant warmth of my clover patch for a zipless ride.

"You ready, *nyet*?" she breathed. "Everything I do for you, one hundred dollars."

Capitalism had caught on fast in Blago.

Because I gave a damn about what I do, because I had to live with an image of myself, because I did not want to smear that image or my vow to Anastasia, I told myself, *Locke, you noble son-of-a-bitch, don't get caught up in the sophistry that casual, consequence-free sex doesn't matter, because it does matter. Tell the girl no thanks, lock the door, and go to bed.*

I cleared my throat and said, "No thanks," slammed the door, shot the bolt, and rattled the brass door chain into its fastener. Officially prostitution does not exist in Russia. Neither does the Mafia, corruption, nepotism, and payoffs. I was satisfied with my resolve.

Being satisfied is not the same as being happy. Both are judgments about life and what matters is something we each decide. Too often we make appraisals with regret, acceptance, and resignation, like a Rio slum dweller looking down from his scruffy *favelas* at Copacabana Beach, satisfied with the roof over his head but far from happy, seeing all those gleaming breasts baking in the hot salty sand.

In the vast and lonely emptiness of a howling Siberian night, I eventually found sleep.

***

WHAM! WHAM! WHAM!

"*Suichas d'evia; vstavaite!* — It's nine o'clock; get up!"

From a hard sleep, it took me a sec to process: the *gornichnaya* beating on my door.

"Okay, okay!" I yelled. I lay nude and supine on the bed. I looked at my tanned torso sheening with perspiration. The *perena-pododeal'nik* had slid to the floor. The *fortochka* had slammed shut. The honeymoon suite was ninety-five degrees. The scalding had not relieved stiffness from the thirty-six-hour marathon Charlotte-to-Blagoveshchensk, and my old ski injury throbbed. Better than a barometer, it let me know when the weather was to change. I clicked on the radio. An announcer proclaimed in Russian, "The Novosibirsk Symphony will play Mozart's Symphony No. 40 in G Minor. It's a mood-evoking piece that displays the adult genius of a child wunderkind, his creative, complex, and dynamic intensity."

I wasn't ready for that much knowledge and switched off the genius.

I rolled up the stiff, napless towel like a burrito, sawed at sweat running down my back, and went to the gargantuan window. The two dead spaces between three panes of wavy glass did not curb cold from radiating. With surprising speed, chest hairs flash froze to brittle noodles and sweat trickling down my face settled on my jaw and hardened into chinicles. Goosebumps appeared like leopard spots on my arms bronzed from blissful hours whacking fuzzy yellow balls with Nastia. I worked my left thumb pad into ice as thick as plate glass and dissolved a half-dollar-size aperture just as my thumb went totally numb. I put my lips to the hole and huffed. Edges liquefied. The peephole cleared enough for a Cyclops-glimpse, and I peered out with one steel-blue eye.

In the breaking day, I saw horses, sleighs, and an Arctic blast screeching over the Amur River. Aeolus had opened his leather bag and let loose winds filled with snow that hammered the riverfront with pellets and made a kaleidoscope of frosty hues that alternated as tempos modulated. Huge black-and-white crows soared in on the wind and wheeled down to forage for oats in the muck. Everything beyond the tree skeletons rimming the riverbank to the south was an indistinguishable blur. There was a long line of sleighs, awaiting processing at the crossing. Its end vanished in the whiteout. Incongruently, out of that snowy smudge, between snowbanks so high they looked like a luge run, jogged the Blagoveshchensk soccer team, huffing and puffing like Chinese dragons. The men wore sweatsuits, cleats, gloves, and woolen caps. They rounded a corner and disappeared. Ice reclaimed my peephole. I melted it again and looked for Ivan — not there. I dressed. When finished, I looked again and made out the silhouette of his troika five sleighs back.

I rechecked my wallet for bribe funds, tucked the Ruger under the mattress, locked up, and placed a linty toothpick from JFK's Chili's restaurant between the door and frame. Better to know than not know. In the lobby, Alexis was chatting with the desk clerk. The KGB agent stood under the tulip tree engrossed in *Pravda,* still upside down. The Sibir Air ticket office had opened. The coat check lady had closed. The casino was empty. Old women, on hands-and-knees, scoured carpet of whiskey stains in the boozy, halitosis stench of the parlor of fun and games.

Outside, the wind had eased. Bitter cold bathed in an acrid stench remained. Far to the east, somewhere beyond the Sakhalin Islands, long lazy rays of weak winter sun burned through cloud cover to etch the whiteness with a jumbled calligraphy of shadows. Sprawling the vast sprawl of white-slate were trees skeletons stretching from horizon to horizon on both sides of the mile-wide glimmer of ice. The monochrome felt soothing. The Sino-Soviet, border guards patrolling mid-river did not.

Ivan was second in line at Checkpoint Charlie perched atop the riverbank a towering two feet above the Amur River. He appeared ready to go dashing through the snow in his three-horse open sleigh pyramided with *matryoshkay*, one hiding Anastasia's taxol loot. He was armored against the cold with thick gloves, fur-collared bomber jacket, layers of woolen pants, felt boots, and an expensive bobcat *shapka*, earflaps down and tied snuggly beneath his chin.

I wore everything I owned, shivered from cold prying at seams, greeted Ivan with, "*Prevet* — Hi," and climbed aboard, worming one leg under the seat and dangling the other over the side.

"*Prevet,*" Ivan replied, eyes slits in the dazzling brightness. "This has gotta be the coldest damn day I can remember."

"You bring antifreeze?"

Ivan smirked and tapped his pocket.

A chunky guard approached, and stopped, hands on hips, face twisted into a look of gloomy annoyance. He reminded me of Nikita Khrushchev. Same short thickness, sad black eyes, meaty face, and hound-dog earlobes drooping from his military *shapka*. He glowered at Ivan in silence. His eyes said, "Screw you, you swashbuckling hypercapitalist in your pricey *shapka* and fur-lined bomber jacket, clothes as unknown as ermine-trimmed surplices in Blagoveshchensk."

Nikita pointed to the load and growled something to Ivan that gave me the willies.

Ivan pursed his lips, scowled, and then pulled a *Pravda*-wrapped liter of Stolichnaya from under his seat. Khrushchev snatched it, wolf grinned, and tore opened the newspaper.

"How much?" I snooped without moving my ventriloquist's lips.

Ivan mumbled out of the side of his mouth, "Three bucks. Nothing."

Khrushchev headed for the warming hut, and I agreed, "Cheap. Stoli's expensive at home."

"Ours is made in a state-owned Soyuzplodoimport. American Stoli is distilled in Latvia in a Gorby-Reagan deal: Pepsi for us; Stoli for the Yanks."

Guards waved on the sleigh in front of us, and the driver whipped his trio of nags. They strained at inertia and started to descend the river bank, bracing when the payload crested the lip and propelled them onto river ice. The payload gained speed and shot onto the ice, jostling the troika and rattling the milk cans when it hit the ice brim that looked like a pie crust and known as an ice moraine. The upper crust of China's classless society would have fresh milk with their baozi [18] for breakfast.

Ivan clucked. Our trio whinnied, shook their manes, and rammed into their collars. A frozen blast off the river pelleted our faces with ice darts as the load shifted and we moved forward. Ivan turtled into his fur collar. I covered my face and peeked through gloved fingers at long rays trying to scorch lingering fog. What had looked like tree stumps mid-river morphed into outhouse-sized, warming huts, remnants of a 1969 dust-up that incited the communist foes to scramble two million soldiers and one thousand aircraft to the Amur Region to threaten each other with nuclear annihilation. The storm lessened enough that I could see across the river at Heihe, China, or *Khitai*—the Tartar and Russian word. The city of a half million rose at the convergence of the Zeya and Amur Rivers.

A Soviet guard waved us forward. He had enough gnarled facial hair to pass as a werewolf — lycanthrope. Ivan flicked the reins. The mares didn't budge. He slapped the reins hard against the flank of the alpha horse. She shook her head and jumped. The *troika's* runners, buried in knee-deep snow, squeaked pulling up to a cluster of intimidating looking guards wearing long, gray *shenels* — greatcoats — and armed with Kalashnikovs, bayonets fixed. Three guards stepped forward and went to work. One lifted the tarp. Two slithered beneath the troika, bellies to the ground like wolves. Ivan watched in stoic silence, the passive, alienated way Russians faced with adversity display, as they searched for contraband.

Smiling morosely, Ivan muttered to me, "They'll never find the *dengi*."

Ivan used the same word Tartars used for money and bribery, *dengi*, that Genghis Khan gave Russia seven hundred eighty years ago, a legacy still as prevalent today as *balalaikas*, *matryoshkas*, and caviar. The red-haired Mongolian emperor conquered half the known world, Seoul to Kiev, Lhasa to Novgorod, and for two-hundred-fifty-years Mongols reigned supreme. Khans and their hordes annihilated cities, diverted rivers, peopled deserts, slaughtered men, and raped women while in Western Europe the Renaissance flowered and humanism spread. Mom claimed Papa and my reddish-blond hair came from a Khan.

A fourth guard shouted, "*Zadat*! — Wait!"

He stepped over a snowdrift, hoisted a foot onto the runner, and observed, in Russian, "This is your third load this week to the *gang-jae* — he used the derogatory term for Chinese, akin to calling them Chinks. What do you suppose the almond-eyed do with all your *matryoshkas?*"

"Beats me," Ivan replied. "Maybe they like toys."

"They got toys. All those country girls the city-boys snatch when they're horny."

"Maybe when they finish, they give *matryoshkas* to the girls. Who knows?"

The guard leaned closer to Ivan. The wind howled; I couldn't make out what he said.

The day suddenly brightened. In the lemon rays glistening in from the Pacific, the guard's bayonet flashed like a wolf's fang. The AK-47M is the modernized version of the real assault rifles Mikhail Kalashnikov, a tank sergeant, developed after WW II and not the rip-off brand with which pirates flood the Third World. It blasts ten rounds a blazing second at a muzzle velocity of 3,088 feet per second or 2,100 mph. Now, the guard and Ivan were in a heated discussion, and from its tone, Ivan was protesting, or pretending to gripe, for the guard looked pissed, ready to stab or blast him, but Ivan kept on talking.

From deep within riverside white birch, I heard the eerie faraway howl of a wolf working the peripheries of Blago for breakfast. It dredged up a memory of my paternal babushka, Valentina. Ivan had relayed the tale that bawdy night we'd worked Brighten Beach discos three years ago. Valentina had left her two young sons, Ivan and Vladimir, my Papa, at her mother's apartment and drove her husband, Igor, my namesake, to the Novoaleksandrovka train station for induction into World War II. Igor had told his sons the story after he returned from a German POW camp in June 1945 when the boys were old enough to understand what happened to their Mom. On her return to Blago from the train station, her car had struck ice, slammed into a birch tree, and a door flew open. The basket-sized engine shot through the firewall and pinned her legs to the transmission. She was alive when the wolves gnawed all the flesh from her body, except for her ankles and right foot, which remained, untouched, under the dinky engine block. Seven months later, Grandpa Fetisov was arrested for having been captured by the Germans. He, like millions of young Russian POWs, never was issued a rifle at the front and was executed for having been taken captive; their maternal grandparents raised Papa and Ivan.

A deal hatched between Ivan and the guard. He said, "*Spaseba*—Thanks," lifted the tarp, removed two birch boxes of *matryoshkas,* and accepted a bottle of Stoli.

I grabbed Ivan's arm. "Jesus, you had me scared to death. Were you in deep shit?"

"Nah," Ivan chuckled, "just making my reluctance believable."

I twisted around to study the line of troikas. It extended two blocks and dissolved into long black shadows of nine-story apartments, most with *fortochka* open spewing steam. Earlier north winds had cleared the poisonous murk hanging over Blagoveshchensk and pushed it south beyond Heihe to North Korea.

Ivan flicked the reins. "Let's go!"

The trio snorted, surged, and scrambled, sliding down the river bank. I grabbed the seat back and braced a leg on the *troika's* outside runner as the half-ton load smacked into ice hard enough to send a tremor through us. The cargo shifted, but nothing fell off and then the horses were off, galloping at over twenty-five miles per hour. In a few hundred yards, the alpha horse slowed to a two-beat trot, and I could see the crystal clear ice below. I hunkered down. The wind sandblasted my face, and the troika's runners made harsh scraping sounds like fingernails on blackboards. The ice was thick and clear as rink-ice after reglazing with a Zamboni resurfacer. My Colby chemistry pal, a hockey aficionado, once told me the Zamboni was a WW II-era invention that shaved ice off rinks, collected the shavings, washed them, and spread a thin coat of fresh water on the ice. Except for horseshoe half-moons etched in its glassy surface, clumps of scat, and some fishermen gopher holes, this river ice looked exactly like that mirror at Colby's Alfond Area.

"Will the ice hold us?" I asked as trio trotted carefree, as if on a spring outing.

"Six feet's plenty," Ivan said. "We're safe, and those toothless, thirteen-foot, Sturgeon are, too, until spring when runoff, raw sewage, overfishing, and poaching start."

"I thought sturgeon were salt water fish from the Caspian and Black Seas?"

"Some are," Ivan said, "sort of." He flipped a gloved-hand back-and-forth. "The monsters are born in brackish waters at the mouth of Amur a thousand miles downstream from us. The fingerlings feed on chum salmon, herring, smelt, and shrimp. When they're big enough, their DNA tells them to swim up here to live to be one hundred … if the ammonia, iron, manganese, zinc, and poachers don't kill them first."

Guard huts marched up-and-down the middle of the Amur-Heilongjiang as far as the eye could see. White and black. Chinese and Russian. Phone-booth-sized spaced one hundred meters apart. Russian guards in blue. Chinese guards in white. Neither paid us heed in the desultory snowflakes drifting down. The troika's runners hit some rough spots nearing China. Ribby dogs appeared out of nowhere and circled and snarled like their primordial kin.

One mange mutt leaped at my ankle. I shrieked, "Jesus, Ivan, they're attacking!"

"Ahh, he won't eat you," Ivan said. "But watch out for Amur tigers. They will."

I did a three-sixty. No wild cats. I wondered if that was BS. "You're kidding?"

"Not in the least. Mitochondrial DNA proves they're here, relatives of the Caspian tiger."

"Great." The horses slowed, and I thumbed at the *matryoshkay*. "Where's the doll store?"

"The Hailan Jie section, Heihe's all-Russian street, only one in China selling our treasures."

"Where'd you set up the Zhou meet for the taxol buy?"

"See that white, fourteen-story hotel coming up with the top floor lit?" With his chin, Ivan pointed at river's edge. The building jutted high above the skyline and looked like a wedding cake for Goliath. "That's the Heihe International. Zhou and Bao will meet us there at noon."

"Why are so many floors dark?"

"Not many tourists in Heihe."

"Gotcha. Heihe sure isn't Miami Beach. Think our meeting will be a piece of cake?"

"I'm sure it will be," Ivan said.

And it was. For a while.

***

EIGHTEEN

Heihe, China: The Taxol Buy
December 29, 1991

Approaching China, the Amur River's southern shore became rough; snow-blown windrows of wind-whipped snowbanks sent the horses hurdling, the troika airborne, and Ivan and me scrambling for hand-holds. Here, poised on the edge of two snow-bound worlds, the Siberian Far East and the Chinese Far North, I felt estranged, isolated, and alienated. Neither of these worlds was mine. I'd left the Soviet Union as a kid. Winters in North Carolina were short and trivial, and Orlando never saw snow. This was an Eskimo world that Sino-philes call beautiful, mysterious, exotic, and enticing. But where was the allure? Nowhere could I see. It made me wonder if we ever grow up enough to live with the plethora of choices we make, even choices made under compulsion, coercion, or duress. The core of our lives is a long series of good and bad choices we make and the consequences we suffer.

This close to China, the howling wind had pushed the smog bank further south, but it had not diminished the nose-clogging, eye-watering stench of Chinese sweatshops kicked into high-gear cranking out monstrous piles of cheap goods for a waiting world. The cold, snow, and stink only underscored the foreignness I felt in this altered world and triggered logjams of fears: fear of failure, fear of busted plans, and fear of a KGB arrest. Maybe Anastasia should have stayed in Russia, the home she knew. But no, she'd trusted good old Troy when I insisted she emigrate. Had Orlando's sub-tropic climate triggered her cancer? Had marriage and Americanization frets triggered it? It's always the questions that can't be answered, the what-ifs, should-haves, and might-haves that confound thought and snare dreams in titanium cobwebs. Lord, if you hear me, help me make good choices and live with the choices I make.

"Welcome to China," Ivan said, yanking back hard of the reins. He surveyed the steep river bank, snapped the reins, and clucked. The alpha mare snorted, shouldered into her yoke and the trio lurched up the bank, sending the troika rocking.

The white-tiled Heihe International Hotel was refulgent in morning's glaring rays. We galloped through its near-empty parking lot and around the front of the structure. Its height shielded us from the bitter wind, and the day felt marginally warmer, maybe a balmy forty below zero. In front of the hotel, a neon sign blinked Russian in Latin characters, **LOGHEES OCHEN,** which made me laugh. "Get laid well?"

"Picture-words are tricky to translate," Ivan chuckled. "It means sleep well."

A Volvo bus bearing a red hieroglyphic sign pulled up to the covered portico, and out of the hotel scurried a horde of Chinese in quilted overcoats, knee-boots, watchcaps, and gloves. They flicked cigarettes in the driveway and bulldozed aboard, elbowing as frantically as New Yorkers boarding at the Times Square-42 Street Station, America's busiest.

"Except when boarding subways and buses, the Chinese are a courteous people," Ivan said.

"I can see," I said. "What's the hen scratching say?"

"General Motors and something about Heihe is its cold-weather testing ground."

"They got that nailed." I looked around and noted a startling absence of police. "No cops?"

"The Heihe-Blagoveshchensk region's a free-trade zone. When it's not snowing, buses cross the ice; in summer, boats. There's visa-free travel for both countries. Russia uses guards to keep the army employed and the public edgy." Ivan laughed derisively. "But, thank God, that's no longer me. I'm history tomorrow." He tugged the left rein.

Heihe's snow-covered streetscape came into view as we trotted into the city. Shops, galleries, restaurants, and crowded alleyway-threaded neighborhoods. "This place's a clone of Anytown, America! Buildings, shops, alleys, everything, looks the same."

"What'd you expect, pagodas?" Ivan grumbled.

"Well, not eight-story apartment buildings with glassed-in balconies and river views."

Ivan looked at me disgustedly and shook his head. "There *are* differences, kid, language, writing, people. You'll never see so many black-haired, black-eyed people anywhere."

"No half-breed, blue-eyed, strawberry-blonds like us?"

Ivan cuffed my head.

We headed east down an endless street into long rays of the low sun and a ground-hugging, sulfur-smelling fog as translucent and thick as theatrical smoke. To create stage fog pump ethylene glycol — think car antifreeze — into heat exchangers until it vaporizes and forms low-hanging haze. Coal stoves, millions of them, cause this opaque fog.

Ivan raised his chin at a street sign. "This is Tongliang Road, the Hailan Jie Section."

I scrubbed my eyes and coughed. "Everybody's sneezing, hacking, and masked."

"Four thousand Chinese die every day from their filthy air. One day a billion Chinese will gasp for breath, grab their throats, and keel over dead."

I blew my nose, spit, and gawked around open-mouthed. "Will I need to speak Chinese?"

"Nah. Zhou speaks English well, or he did till he got blitzed yesterday. But it's nice to know the basics: hello, goodbye, and thank you: *nihao, zaijian, xiexie* (sha-sha). Growing up in Blago, your father and I learned enough to buy *báijiǔ*, which they call, infelicitously, white wine, and chase Chinese chicks before leaving for college in Tver."

Ivan smiled at the memory. He'd mentioned Papa again, something Mom never did. I always wondered why and was anxious to learn more about him. But not with all this to see. Kids dressed for school plodded through the eye-burning miasma like an army of dwarfs burdened by fluorescent-dyed backpack bouncing off their butts. They wore boots, ski pants, ski parkas, hats, and masks tied so high on their faces all that was visible were the tops of clown cheeks and slanty black eyes.

"School's called off when temps hit fifty below zero," Ivan said and returned a kid's wave. "Never for snow."

Another kid spotted Ivan's face and shouted in Russian, "*Prevet*--Hello!"

Ivan returned his greeting in Chinese, "*Nihao*!"

The kid's buddy scowled at us, yanked down his mask and sneered, "*Wàiguó rén!*"

Ivan pointed an index finger at him and cocked his thumb. "That little shit called us barbarians; its three-character[19] means foreigner."

"But barbarian and foreigner aren't synonymous," I said. "Barbarian's an insult."

"Ah, but this is the Middle Kingdom. Chinese live halfway between heaven and earth."

"Everyone else is a barbarian. Gotcha. Look, those kids are bowing to a statue!"

They bent deeply and devotedly at a twenty-five-foot bronze statue of Mao Tse-tung marked 毛泽东.

Ivan shook his head in wonder. "Bowing to that sorry son of a bitch cat. That's what Mao means in Chinese, cat (猫); sounds the same but with subtle tonal changes and different characters."

"What's the big deal?" I said. "Americans are taught to love that slave-holder George Washington, so the Chinese love Mao and Soviets Lenin, all country founders."

"Cherry-tree George never murdered millions like those guys."

There wasn't anything I could say to that and remained silent.

Between two wide streets, on a broad paved divider scraped clean of snow, clusters of people in thick gray coats did morning exercises in the graceful synchrony of Tai Chi Chuan's[20] gradual movements, fighting ghosts only they could see. Couples danced with the sophisticated grace of Astaire and Rogers, swooping and twirling to tunes only they could hear.

In the Hailan Jie Section, commerce was frantic. Signs in Chinese bore Russian subtitles, some with American flavors: Beach Boy Ice Cream and Beer Bar, Heihe Napa Valley Wines, Hard Yak Café. Shop windows overflowed with Christmas trees, Santa Clauses, gift wrapped presents and from one tinny speaker, Bing Crosby crooned *White Christmas*, reminding me of Black Friday a month ago when Anastasia and I tooled around Winter Park, and I'd warbled the tune to her.

Street cleaners had done an outstanding job scraping macadam bare. The sleigh's runners screeched over the frozen asphalt, dodging women in stocking feet jammed in flip-flops wearing layers of pajamas and scurrying from one plastic tarp selling rice and noodles to another selling hot omelets and dumplings off barrel-top coal stoves. The smog was thick and sharp and laden with arsenic, lead, molybdenum, uranium, mercury, and all the other coal carcinogens that scorch trachea and wreck alveoli, pleura, and cilia. Iron out your lungs and they're the size of a tennis court. We breathe seventeen thousand times a day, six million times a year. Coal keeps ninety percent of China's lights on and rooms warm for the price of a billion pairs of lungs coated with crud that destroys sinuses, tracheas, and lungs in every gasping, stinging, poisonous breath.

Gaunt men pedaled rusty bicycles swaying with plump ducks and geese tied to handlebars in a squawking, honking, flapping cacophony. Old women pushed bicycles lashed with twin fifty-five-gallon-barrels, aka 'honey pots,' listing precariously, slopping feces and urine destined for garden plots to spread humanure and hepatitis A to a billion people with every leafy meal. Lean, wiry men pedaled bikes bolted to fat-tired carts brimming with cages of live rats and food-dogs and teetering twelve-foot stacks of mattresses, tires, furniture, cages, and carcasses of things unknown. There were ribby little horses pulling carts heaped with coal. Thousands of men commuted by bicycle — wife on the back, side-saddle, kid on the crossbars — all riding in absolute silence as if to laugh or joke in this gas chamber were a crime. Above the street congestion, apartment windows brimmed with bonsai, geraniums, and caged canaries. A few windows were open, and women hung out laundry to freeze-dry. Lower floors were alive with people scurrying inside brick buildings whose arched windows reminded me of Boston's Back Bay beside a rip-off Starbuck's sign bragging, in Russian, *Our Coffee Goes Right Through You.* We didn't stop for a cup of Joe.

We sleighed further into Hailan Jie and an astounding vista of nine-by-fifteen-feet stalls appeared, selling *valenki*, gum, fur *shapkas*, faux mink stoles, T-shirts, pencils, mittens, gum, greatcoats, shawls, dog-hair socks, candy, underwear, bear-carvings, icons, ivory scrimshaw, gum, Hollywood's not-yet-released movies, books, frozen hens, hunks of frozen meat and oil paintings and more gum. In tiny spaces between stalls, artisans plied their trade at mini-tables, open-air dentists offering plier-extractions, cobblers, barbers, tailors, and a knife sharpener grinding a meat cleaver on his wheel. An old woman mended socks while-you-wait at a short-legged table, sitting on a three-legged stool, her baby-sized, once-bound feet stretched out, trying to inflate.

Stall-owners hovered over their wares, chatting with customers and casting watchful eyes on tots swaddled in blankets on cots behind them tended by wives and grandmas. Grandpas hunched over gallon-jug-sized coal stoves, heating water, and smogging air.

Ivan said, "Three-generational families of five or six live, sleep and work in these stalls."

"You're kidding?" I said in disbelief. "They're the size of a king-sized bed. Where's the kitchen, toilet, and laundry?"

"Communal privies, one closet with a hot plate and sink shared by twenty families in back."

Ivan yanked back hard on the reins at a stall displaying political *matryoshkay* worked by a short, thin man about my age. He wore a thick black watchcap, padded gray coat, and padded gray pants. He looked up and smiled. His teeth were green. The horses snorted and stamped and woke a baby. It howled. Grandma, all four-foot-five of her, bundled up in probably everything she owned, picked up the imp to cuddle. Gramps, an inch taller, unfazed, poured boiling water into four pickle jars layered with two inches of green tea leaves and set them on the counter beside the *matryoshkay* to steep.

"*Nín hǎo*, Yan!" Ivan said to the young man and me, "This is Yan Zue, my *matryoshkay* outlet, his parents, and son. Yan's wife died last year after a forced abortion."

"*Nín hǎo ma* — Hello, how are you — Fetisov?" Yan replied, smiling and addressing Ivan by his surname, both the Chinese and Soviet custom.

"*Hěn hǎo, nǐ ne??*" From Ivan's broad smile that had to mean, "Fine. And you?"

"*Hěn hǎo, xiexie,*" Yan said and looked at me with curiosity. "*Nǎlǐ shì tā cóng?*"

"He wants to know where you're from," Ivan said. "Tell him, *Wǒ cóng àolánduō.*"

"*Wǒ cóng àolánduō,*" I repeated and stepped down from the troika, pulling off my glove to shake Yan's extended hand. His grip was firm.

Yan smiled. "*Wǒ yào xuéhuì shuō yīngyǔ.*"

Ivan said, "Yan says he'd like to learn English. Let's unload. Stick *the* crate under my seat."

Yan set the family cots on end, pushed the steaming bottles of tea and display *matryoshkay* aside, and stacked the boxes I set on the counter on the frozen pavement where the cots had been. Gramps offered me a pickle jar of green tea.

"*Xiexie,*" I said, accepting it between gloved hands and sipping.

He bobbed his head repeatedly and smiled, revealing khaki-green teeth.

The hot tea warmed my hands and tasted strong and delicious. My stomach growled. I tried to remember my last meal as I unloaded the *matryoshkay* pyramid. Ivan pulled a sack of oats and three feedbags from the troika and fed the horses, giving them snow to wash it down. The sleigh of crates soon disappeared, though where Yan and his family would sleep tonight, I hadn't a clue.

I slid the container with the smudge and loot under the troika seat. "This box is for my wife," I explained to Yan, pointing at the box and pulling off my glove to show him my wedding ring.

He understood and said, "*Qīzi*," and gave me a sad green smile that made me wondered what I would ever do without Anastasia.

With uncanny timing, Ivan finished tending the horses just as I set the last box of nesting dolls on the counter. Yan and Ivan huddled, Rubles changed hands, we said *xie-xie* and *zaijian*, shook hands and left.

I wondered aloud how Yan would ever find another supplier of vodka-bearing-*matryoshkay* to support his family. Ivan responded, the guy he'd sold his business would take care of Yan since he was his sole outlet.

By eleven thirty we were back at the Heihe International Hotel. The sun and blue sky had dissolved into one big cement-gray splotch. A strengthening north wind carried a prophetic message, or so said my old broken leg. The parking lot was half-full, deal-making was picking up. Ivan tied the horses to a willow tree in the building's lee. I took the Nicholas doll wrapped in tissue out of the birch crate, and we hustled through the double front doors.

The hotel lobby was August hot and the size of five tennis courts paved with slabs of gray granite the size of refrigerators scattered with rugs in gray and brown and tables of plastic flowers. Drab. The architecture was functional, the maze of shops, bars, and restaurants surprising. Clusters of Chinese and Russians drank tea and made deals. In remote corners, nooks, and crannies, workers swept, polished, and dusted, restoring luster to that of an aging queen. Ivan stopped at a shop for a box of *Belomorkanal* cigarettes, a ten-cent-a-pack Russian brand embossed with a blue map of northern Russia with the White Sea Canal annotated in red. This is a tribute to Stalin's Arctic canal that he ordered 126,000 Gulag prisoners to dig (12,000 died), aka the Belomorcamels, or White Sea Camels. Russky slang. You could pave a road with *Belomorkanal's* tar. Ivan peeled off the cellophane, dropped it, tapped a filtered cig out, and lit it with a kitchen match. He inhaled greedily and coughed savagely. We tracked across the spotless floor to the concierge desk where an attractive woman with oval eyes and a tiny nose worked on a stack of papers. She rose and gave us a mechanical smile, smoothing her tailored blue suit over long shapely thighs.

She wore blue heels, a white silk blouse, white cultured pearls, and had *Лора* — Lara — on her name tag.

"Doctor Zhivago's lover is still popular here," Ivan said under his breath.

Lara's black eyes appraised us knowingly. "*Prevet,*" she said to Ivan in accent-free Russian.

"*Dobroe utro* — Good morning," Ivan replied.

Lara smiled and glanced with uncertainly at my L. L. Bean coat, waiting for me to speak.

I made it easy for her. "Hi, Lara, I'm Troy Locke. We're looking for Doctor Zhou." I held up the tissue-wrapped *matryoshkay* and smiled. "Time to exchange Christmas presents."

"Herro, Rock," she said. "Zhou waits you in dining room." She turned and with a sweep of the arm, motioned us to the room behind her. "Merry Christmas, Rock."

"*Xie-xie*, Lara, and Merry Christmas to you," I said, tucking the doll under my arm.

"You're wercome. Not many Americans come Heihe."

"Not many Americans have friends in Heihe."

The dining room's yellow-and-brown décor was draped with Chinese art, crowned with shimmering chandeliers, and buoyed by Frank Sinatra belting out *New York, New York;* diluting the room was a crucible of dirty ashtray and stale grease stenches hanging over two dozen massive, round tables swathed in white linen and bull's eyed with lazy-Susans the size of washtubs and corralled with ten sturdy chairs stained in burnt-umber. The north wall was solid glass overlooking the featureless Amur River and Blagoveshchensk's fading skyline, dissolving in the looming front. Two tables were occupied. One by a well-dressed Russian man and Chinese woman huddled over tea and cigarettes in the far corner, the other by two Chinese men in black suits laughing over tea in a cigarette haze next to the window, backs to the cosmic panorama. We headed for their table. When the suits spotted us weaving their way, they rose. The shorter man smiled brightly, snapping his fingers in time with Blue Eyes and a smile so dazzling he looked like a college fund-raiser climbing that greasy academic pole. Maybe he was snorting monosodium glutamate. I wondered if he had the taxol, and my heart raced. His shoulder-length, black hair hung over his pale white complexion, long straight nose, and a shelf of chin. I did not see one iota of Chinese heritage in his face.

"You gotta be Troy Locke," he said in English. There was a trace of southern grits in his accent, and he rammed out a hand. "I'm Doctor Zhou Yan; this is Doctor Bao, my associate. Bao means bun in English — " Yan laughed — "and he doesn't speak a word. You love Sinatra?"

"I do," I said, and we all shook hands.

Yan turned to Ivan. "You survived yesterday's pub crawl, Ivan?"

"I did, indeed, and that is the last time I'll ever drink," Ivan vowed.

"Ha!" Yan laughed and eyed Ivan doubtfully. *New York, New York* ended, and Frank move into a wistful *September Song*.

Bao was six inches taller and forty pounds thinner than Zhou. He had a small flat stubby nose, shoulder-length gray hair, and the squinty-eyed-look of a research chemist who spent too many hours peering into microscopes at infinitesimal things.

"Heihe's weather's got me longing for Tallahassee," Yan said. "I'm from Kunming."

I nodded my head and poked my thumb into my chest. "*Wŏ cóng àolánduō.*"

Bao's eyes popped open. He started to say something and Yan held up a hand.

He grabbed my arm and laughed heartily. "Got another sentence in your Chinese répertoire?"

"Nope, that's it," I confessed. Bao looked confused; Yan didn't explain.

"Kunming's as warm as Orlando," Yan boasted. "Song Lin said your parents taught there."

"One year," I said, "and loved it."

"So how are my old friends, the Lins?"

"Song and Mim are terrific. They attended our wedding last May and are expecting a kid."

"Good for them; second children aren't allowed in China."

The entire world knew that, but I figured Yan didn't need the reminder and said nothing.

Ivan stubbed out a cigarette and lit another. "Song mentioned you have a daughter," he said, impatiently, and picked up the *matryoshkay*. "Think she'd like a nesting doll?"

Bao pulled out a box of Marlboros, shook one out, and fired up with a flame thrower. Yan's eyes narrowed, and he scanned the room. A waitress stood at her station near the bathroom doors. The rest of the restaurant was vacant except for the Russian guy tête-à-tête with the Chinese chick. The fever of love knows no borders.

Yan took the *matryoshkay*, tore a corner open, and appeared cautiously enthralled at it.

"If you twist the head open," I explained, "you'll find more unusual things inside."

"Really?" Zhou's eyebrows shot up, acting surprised. He twisted Nicholas open and set his head on the table. "Well, I'll be," he exclaimed, pulling the Czarina out of Nick and setting to work. He twisted Alexandra open, set her head on the table and shook out Anastasia. Glancing at the headless parents, the scientist held Nick's first daughter in his hand, questioningly.

I lowered my voice. "That fifteen grand's inside Anastasia; now where's the taxol?"

Yan placed the *matryoshkay* in his lap, twisted off Anastasia's head, peered in, and poked it with his index finger. I heard the faint ruffle of bills being shuffled.

"Well I do believe it's champagne time," Yan said, eyes joyous.

"I've no objection," Ivan said, reneging on his minutes-old vow of sobriety.

"First, we need the loo," Yan said. "I'll order bubbly on the way." He twisted Anastasia's head back on, and, palm up curled a forefinger repetitively at Bao in a come-with-me motion. With doll in hand they left. Yan paused to speak to the waitress. She went into action. The happy duo entered one of two curiously mismarked bathroom doors, the one beneath the universal silhouette of a woman with the Chinese characters — 个膏剂and the Russian word Джен-тельмен — Gentlemen. Beneath both signs were the same order, in Russian, *Povysheniye posle gadyat, i zhaluyas'*— Rise Out After Shitting and Pissing.

"Confusing sign, but very explicit instructions," I remarked.

"Yeah," Ivan said. "That hen-scratching, *Yīgè Gàojì*, means Men's Room. The Chinese words for he and she, *tā*, sound about the same. Easy to get 'em mixed up."

Within seconds, a procession coiled our way. The waitress carried a shiny black tray of crystal champagne flutes. Shadowing her was a busboy carrying a pricey silver ice bucket and stand; it reminded me of the cheap plastic one Ingrid had used at our Squire Shop lunch on Black Friday. Trailing him, a sommelier, haughty nose in the smelly air, clutched to his breast like baby Jesus a bottle of Krug Grande Curvé, a pricey French vintage. They set up shop, stood at rigid attention, and awaited Yan's return. When the happy duo was seated, the sommelier popped the cork, wrapped the champagne in white linen, and tilted it over Yan's flute, pouring a tad and twisting the bottle just right to catch the last drop.

He stepped back to await a pat on the head.

Yan swirled it, smelled it, and tasted it while the sommelier squirmed. Yan said, "*Hǎo*—Okay," and the sommelier filled our glasses.

When the convoy left, Yan opened his briefcase and lifted out a package wrapped in a soft musty purple cloth. "This is a crystal salt and pepper shaker for your wife. I know she'll love it." He unfolded the cloth with the tender reverence of unveiling a chalice and exposed a four-inch box wrapped in crinkly gold paper. He placed it in my hands. The box had a substantial heft. Without tearing the wrapper, I eased out a stiff corner, peeked in, and saw twin shakers. I tilted the box into the north window's ambient light. The pepper shaker was black. Pepper. The salt shaker was white. Salt. Ordinary, white, granular salt.

I felt sick to my stomach. "Where's the taxol, Zhou?" I demanded.

"Give it a shake," Yan said.

I shook it, turned it upside down, and shook it again. A twinkle reflected off a plastic capsule. Buried in the salt and filled with what looked like more finely ground salt glinted the Star of Bethlehem. For Anastasia, it was more precious than gold, myrrh, and frankincense.

"That sealed capsule is the sterilized taxol," Yan whispered.

I wanted to throw up my arms, shout, dance and do cartwheels. Anastasia's lifesaver was finally in my hands! "My wife and I thank you more than you'll ever know," I exclaimed.

Ivan stood, refilled our glasses, and said, "Now, a toast!"

We hoisted flutes. Zhou and Bao said, "*Gānbēi*," Ivan said, "*Za vashe zdorovie*," I said, "Cheers!"

We drained our glasses and flipped them upside down, the Chinese custom. Macho.

Yan, humming along with Sinatra, *It Was A Very Good Year*, said, "Got time to eat?"

"You bet, Yan," I said, rubbing my stomach. "Three days of plane yuk, I'm hungry as a spring bear, and I *love* Chinese."

Yan squinted his narrow black eyes at me appraisingly. "This won't be American Chinese, egg rolls and sweet and sour pork."

"Whatever," I said dismissively. "Order this and that. I could eat a skunk."

Yan smiled enigmatically and motioned to the waitress. She trotted over.

Literally. He rattled off a string of Chinese, repeating one word several times.

After she'd scurried away, I said, "What's *go raw*?"

"*Gou rou* is dog brain soup," Yan said.

I thought I'd retch but mastered the reflex. "Glad I asked."

Yan gave me another of those unfathomable Chinese smiles. "After the *gou rou*, we'll have dog liver with fresh veggies from our state-owned, geothermal-heated, hydroponic greenhouses, fried eel, goat lung with hot red pepper, baked rat, black scorpions, dung beetles, bumble bees in tempura batter, sturgeon, and skewers of seahorse." He leaned over close and said in a stage whisper, "Seahorse is better than Viagra." Yan had a severe case of halitosis.

I returned his smile with an inscrutable one of my own. "Wouldn't know, never needed it."

We finished the Krug Grande Curvé before the fizzle flattened and made a sizable dent in a bottle of Glenlivet Archive 21, an elegantly-smooth, velvety-flow of flavors, fruit and honey and rum and oak before our wait staff reappeared with steaming dishes exuding a potpourri of pungent odors. The crunchy fried eel and crusty bumble bee were mouthwatering, but even with a slight buzz from the two-hundred-dollar-a-bottle of single malt Glenlivet, I couldn't gag down the dog liver and baked rat. With clumsy chopsticks I poked them around and buried them under slimy rice noodles while Yan regaled us with his Tallahassee heroics and spit fish bones on the carpet, a feat I thought disgusting but deemed well-mannered in China. He suggested I market taxol worldwide and make a fortune, and I told him I'd think about it. I didn't tell him that I had already planned to take on BMS.

We interrupted Frank crooning, *Strangers in the Night*, with a final *gānbēi*, *za vashe zdorovie*, and cheers, bundled up, and left.

I clutched the golden box of life-preserving taxol to my chest. Bao did the same with the *matryoshkay*. I said goodbye to Lara and held up the purple-wrapped present, and we went out into the cold gray day. At the troika, we shook hands, bowed, and said goodbye at last, but not for the last time.

That came five years later.

The alpha mare was pawing snow with her iron-cleated hoof, scraping the macadam noisily, anxious as a racehorse at the starting gate to go home. We climbed aboard; Ivan flicked the reins, and the trio burst forth. The load-free troika slammed and banged and bounced over the parking lot and down the river bank into the solid whiteout. Unable to see ten feet, Ivan gave the horses free rein, and they plunged into the murk, brailing through the fog for the far shore at breakneck speed. Icy darts stabbed my face, and I covered it with gloved hands, peeking through finger slits at fog, praying that the wooly steeds had bloodhound noses. It seemed like seven hours but was more like seven minutes when the horses slowed, and the ghostly shape of the Druzhba Hotel materialized. The trio slowed to a walk and shook their heads at the scent of garbage and open-sewer scat at river's edge. Ivan clucked and flicked the reins hard, and the horses scrambled up the knoll to the Check Point and halted at the raised hand of the short, round guard, Khrushchev, as he hurried out of his warming hut, panting up to us as if we were the czar.

"Why so late?" Nikita asked in stertorous Russian.

"Stopped for a couple drinks and lunch," Ivan replied in kind.

"Bring anything back?"

Ivan shook his head.

"I did," I volunteered. "A queasy stomach."

Khrushchev laughed. "*Chainik* — teapot — food will do that to you."[21]

I acknowledge that, and Ivan kicked my foot with a can-the-bullshit intensity.

Khrushchev laughed some more, "And there's no tax on *Kutaėcy*[22] chow." He waved us on.

Once out of earshot, Ivan said, "That was risky as hell what if he — "

"It was a joke," I interrupted. "Christ, Ivan, cops are people."

"They start out people. Time will tell if he stayed that way."

"Aren't you the cynical one on our last afternoon in Russia?"

Ivan grunted and flicked the reins.

At the warehouse, Ivan pounded on the steel outer door until the old watchman swung it open. He closed the double doors and climbed onto the back of the sleigh. The horses knew they were home, rammed sweaty shoulders into collars and barreled through snow up to their bellies for the back door where they stopped, snorting impatiently. I jumped down into deep snow that filled my sneakers, opened the double doors, and Ivan drove in the team. The watchman started mucking the stall, and I closed the door. The space was below freezing, but not by much, and it felt as glowingly warm and embracing as a February day on Miami Beach. Ivan fed and watered the horse and told me to shovel enough coal onto the fire's glowing embers to bank it for the night. Then I sat down on his dusty cot, pulled the golden package from my pocket, and studied the taxol capsule inside the salt shaker and thought of Anastasia's delight.

"I gotta be back here at nine," Ivan said, scooping up a bucket of oats, "to close the deal for this goldmine."

"Is the buyer buying your contacts?"

"There's only one."

"So he'll supply the dolls and vodka to Zhu?"

"He'd be stupid not to."

Ivan checked the bolt on the back door, and the old watchman followed us out the front door. Ivan locked up, and I kicked a snowdrift off the loading dock, found its edge and dropped into the Gulag yard. Last night's blizzard had deposited two feet of fresh snow. I broke trail for the three of us in the crotch-high powder. It reminded me of the day I skied Vail's back bowl, The Outer Mongolia, a thigh-burning experience only for the intrepid. At the steel door, Ivan grabbed the old watchman's arm, put his mouth next to his ear and shouted, "I'll be back at nine o'clock."

"I'll be here," the sentry said and clanged the steel door shut behind us.

The night was still. There was no howling wind. There was cold, bitter cold, and the blackened sky twinkled with first stars. I heard the screech of steel-on-steel as the old watchman rammed the rebar through its cradles, bolting the outer door.

Ivan said, "Hey, here's an idea, since you've got Anastasia's taxol in your pocket, and I leave for Egypt in the morning, and you leave for home, how about a celebration?"

"Fantastic idea!" I yelped. "You got a favorite watering hole?"

"I do. It's within walking distance, and you'll love it."

And I did.

I hit the hay just before midnight for a good night's sleep, which ended in the wee small hours of the morning by something I would never have guessed could happen.

***

NINETEEN

Victory Celebration and the KGB
December 29, 1991

We were slogging through unplowed snow on River Street, heading for the center of Blago, when I glanced diagonally across the snowbanks from the warehouse, down a tree-lined lane at the Popov Monastery. The cross-shaped onion-domed church was cut from the same cloth as all Russian Orthodox churches. A narthex, or vestibule-portico, nave, chancel, apse, and altar comprised the body of the cross, the north, and south transept were its arms.

The church had a dozen cars parked in front.

"Odd time for a church service," I said, "late on a Thursday afternoon." I jammed my hands deep into my pockets, checking to see if my *cojones* had frozen off. It was that cold.

"Huh!" Ivan scoffed. "Hardly a service. The Popov Monastery's KGB headquarters. Step on it, Ulitsa Lenina is four blocks north, and I'm freezing my nuts off."

I picked up the pace, and within minutes, we turned left on Lenin Street. Most of the shops on the main drag were closing. At the Telephone Exchange, the big and little hands on the window clock pointed at six and five. Five-thirty. The exchange was busy. One Russian in five hundred owned a telephone. The sidewalk on Lenin Street was pitch dark, the sun long since set. The sidewalks were scraped clean. In four places dark abysses had been dug for repairs, craters abandoned, no caution signs, no barricades. In Russia, no one sues the city or state. Women bundled in fur-trimmed hooded, ankle-length, leather coats and men in greatcoats and *shapkas* — flaps down — carried armfuls of groceries and scurried to their miniscule, drafty apartments.

"Ivan," I said, "it looks so strange, everyone grocery shopping and lugging stuff home."

"Tiny refrigerators," Ivan explained, "if they even have one, and only one person in sixty owns a car, which isn't so bad. In China, one person in ten thousand owns wheels."

I whistled in disbelief. "That explains all those bikes in The Middle Kingdom."

"You better believe it." Ivan slapped me on the back, jovially. "Which reminds me, that bluff to the fat guard about your feeling sick was the same kind of bullshit your father would've pulled."

I was astonished. No one ever brought him up. "Was he a good bullshitter, Ivan?"

"The damned best! He was a trumpet player who never had a lesson; a singer who never studied music; an English speaker who learned it by memorizing tons of Irish ditties, a great footballer, salesman, and soldier. Your Papa had an aura about him of being able to do anything. Swarms of women chased him until Irina snagged him out of their grasps."

"And then he got himself killed in Kābul."

Ivan stopped, placed a glove on my chest, and looked at me curiously. "Who told you that?"

"Mom. She said his life ended in Kābul."

Ivan took his hand off my chest, put both hands on his hips, and stared at me.

After a minute, he said, "Yeah, Igor Vladimirovich, that's right. His life *did* end in Kābul."

Ivan started walking in silence. I thought he might add something, but he didn't, and I didn't want to nag him with details so we continued into the heart of Blago. He didn't speak again until we stood shivering in front of a dimly-lit bar called the *Tequila Grill*. The sign, in English, was scrolled over a Mexican cartoon character snoozing under a cactus, sombrero tilted over his eyes.

Ivan bent from the waist and made a sweeping motion with his arm. "Might I entice you into, let's see if I can say this in Spanish, *mi abrevadero favorite* — my favorite watering hole — for a celebratory libation?"

"Damn tooting," I said, "my belly's screaming for a burrito. Why's the name in English?"

"Why not?"

"Who the hell even knows what tequila is in Blagoveschensk for starters."

Ivan laughed and shoved me through the outer door, crowing, "We hicks are cosmopolitan."

"Sure you are. Is the Mexican food recognizable?"

"What Mexican food?"

"Margaritas?"

"Ha!"

I yanked open the stubborn portal into the airlock and pushed in the throbbing door, reverberating with Mexican strains, to the stench of booze and cigarettes. Two armed guards with meaty shoulders and grim faces blocked the entry. One patted us down.

"*Net pushki* — No weapons," he announced, disappointedly, and noted my L. L. Bean coat. "*Nemetskiy* — German?" he asked.

I shook my head. "*Frantsuzskiy* — French," I lied. Better for him to not know than know.

He said something to his buddy, and he nodded permission for us to join the merrymaking.

Speakers, the size of refrigerators, pulsated *La Bomba,* mariachi trumpets blaring, acoustic guitars purring restrained counter-claims. Platoons of ardent couples humped bumps and grinds in the smoky heat, gyrating bodies thrashing, women driving heels into the floor in syncopated rhythms usually heard in Acapulco. I unzipped my coat, and we edged through the dancers and waitresses balancing their careful way with trays of beer and vodka and fixed smiles servers learn to wear. There were eight booths running down both walls. Center tables pushed aside. Bar in the rear. Kitchen beyond. Walls plastered with smoky Mexican posters of haciendas, burros, señoritas, and a mission that looked rather like Ginsburg's office building.

We sidled onto the last two seats at the bar. There was no barkeep. A sign, in Russian, announced the day's special, *Shot and Beer Twenty Rubles* — one dollar. Above the top-shelf's liquors was a television playing a contraband movie, *True Grit*, John Wayne's 1969 Oscar-winning western. Duke was speaking Russian. I glanced at the bar patrons. No one was drinking white wine spritzers. An attractive blonde bartender in skinny jeans and a very tight, *Tequila Grill* T-shirt appeared.

"*Prevet*, Leda," Ivan said. "You're looking sexy tonight." He fished out his squished pack of *Belomorkanal,* straightened one and fired up. He elbowed me.

"What'll it be, Amigo?"

I was thinking of Anastasia and staring at my mug in the mirror behind shelves of Tanqueray, Grey Goose, Johnnie Black, and Kahlua and saw nothing but a pair of sooty half-moons drooping beneath my anxious eyes. I yanked off my hat, stuffed it in my pocket beside the taxol, and, ignoring Ivan, said, in Russian to Leda, "A white wine spritzer, please."

She shot me a quizzical look. "What's a white wine spritzer?"

Ivan slapped my back and made an instant and unjust assessment of me. "You nut!

"Leda," Ivan said and waggled his index finger between us, "we'll have your special vodka-shooter and beer, twice." Then he yelled over the noise at a man backing out of the kitchen with his padded hands full. "Hey, Slava!"

The stocky man held his hands out straight with steaming platters. Slava was a short, heavy, hairy man with a yard of shoulders, mobile face, and an aw-shucks hickey look. He grinned big and friendly at Ivan. He wore a flannel shirt, jeans, a half-apron with a dirty rag draped over the belt-string, and the ubiquitous square-toed black boots worn by all Russian men. He raised his chin in a just-a-minute gesture and stepped around the end of the bar. The oval platters bubbled with a steamy mayonnaise gunk. They smelled like yeast bread.

"One minute," Slava said in a deep, rich, resonant voice. "Hot stuff, hot stuff!" he yelped and elbowed into the crowd.

"What's he's peddling?" I asked Leda.

"Pizza."

"With mayo? Where are the nachos?"

"What are nachos?"

I drummed my fingers on the bar and squinted at the dish. She looked flustered.

"Well, I *have* heard of them," Leda said defensively. "But we don't how to … say, do you know how to make them?"

"Nachos, I certainly do; and burritos and margaritas," I stated humbly. "Tell Slava Santa Claus is here."

Slava delivered his mayo-slathered pizza and stepped behind the bar just as Leda shoved aside two overfilled ashtrays and plunked down our vodka-and-beer specials. The grungy ashtrays earned her a nasty look from the boss. She snatched them up and headed for the kitchen, saying over her shoulder, "Slava, the cool guy in the cool coat says he's Santa Claus."

Slava twisted off the cap of a Baltika, guzzled some, swiped sticky drink circles off the bar with his dirty rag, and said, "She's a great lay but lousy help." He took another long pull of plasma and rested his hirsute paw on the bar. His fingers were short, chunky, and bushy down to the first knuckle. He eyed my coat covetously and asked in Russian, "French?"

"American," I replied.

"So, Santa, where'd you get your tan, Cyprus?"

Ivan threw his arm around my shoulder. "This is Igor, my brother's son from Florida."

"Well, shit, I thought I saw your rotten family resemblance," Slava said. "Genghis Khan's red hair, slanty eyes, warrior build. I hope he didn't inherit your crazed marauder inclinations."

On cue, Ivan laughed. "Nah, he's harmless, your Leda's safe."

"Good to meet ya, Slava," I said, ramming out a hand, "my name's Igor Vladimirovich."

"Just what the women of the world need, another Fetisov." Slava's hand-shake was powerful.

Ivan offered Slava a *Belomorkanal*. He refused. Ivan took another, tapped some loose tobacco back into the pack, and struck a kitchen match. In the crowded bar, the flame smelled refreshing; the smoke smelled like dog shit.

Ivan said to me, "Slava and I flew fighter jets together protecting Mother Russia from Yankees aggressors."

I shook my head derisively. "Just what all America dreams of, annexing Siberia."

"Your uncle lies, Igor," Slava said. "What we did was nail pussy and drink vodka."

"Oh, come on, Slava, you glorious son of a bitch, we never had the spare parts to keep our jets airborne for long," Ivan explained. The name Slava means glorious in Russian.

Slava raised his chin at Ivan. "You make your final trip today?"

"I did," Ivan said. "We just returned, on time and on schedule."

"I went over with him, Slava," I offered. "Just to make sure things went smoothly."

"So no smuggling," Ivan said, downing his beer and wiping the foam off his whiskers.

"Hey, you're not drinking beer and no vodka," Slava told me.

"I've got to be clear-headed for my trip back home tomorrow," I explained.

Slava growled, "You know, Ivan, it's not fair. You pay bribes in dolls and vodka and get to flee to Egypt; Igor flies to America, and I pay hard cash every Monday and get a city liquor inspector who robs me to stay in business."

I was astonished. "Can't you report him as a thief?"

Slava's eyebrows shot up. "To who? They're all on the take." He plucked the rag from his apron string and wiped our bottle rings off the bar. "Want another?"

Ivan nodded at the special, and I shook my head.

"Russia," Slava said as if the word explained the bribes. "You two hungry?"

"Starved," I said. "Dog brains and seahorse didn't do it."

Ivan tussled my hair. "Seahorse will stiffen your dick and get you ready for your bride."

"That's been frozen since I hit Siberia. What do you have to eat, Slava?"

"Pizza and pelmeni," he said. "Like all Russian restaurants."

"No burritos or nachos?"

"Don't know how to make them."

"Hot damn, and I'm in a burrito mood." I winked at Ivan. "Slava, do you make beef pelmeni?"

"Of course, what Russian restaurant wouldn't?"

"So you've got flour, yeast, milk, oil, sugar, beef, and onions?"

"Naturally."

I slapped the bar. "Slava, this is your lucky day, Santa Claus is going to make you rich."

Slava's eyes popped opened. "You know how to make burritos?"

"I know how to make all the Mexican stuff. I'm going to franchise this planet."

We downed our drinks and banged through the kitchen door. Ten people of various ages and nationalities scurried about in the steamy heat, washing dishes and making pizza dough and scooping globs of mayonnaise on top of cooked pizza shells. I picked up an almost clean rag, wiped the dust off the top of the refrigerator, and rolled up my L. L. Bean coat and taxol into a papaya-sized sausage for safe keeping. For the next four hours the world of cancer, smuggling, guards, and aeronautic-fables ended and jovial kitchen dynamics began: Making tortillas, nachos, beef burritos, green chili sauce, and the best margaritas on the planet. What fun!

I composed a shopping list for the dishwasher duo to fill at the farmers market: pork loins, green peppers, limes, lemons, green chili peppers, tomatoes, fresh eggs, and Arabic chili spices. Slava made an urgent call to his wife, Zhanna,[23] and when he said her name I thought of my one-legged employee, Buck. His wife's name was Jeanne. Slava told Zha to get a sitter for the kids and bring the video camera ASAP; an 'oracle had appeared with Mexican know how!' Really, he said it; I heard it. Within twenty minutes, the slim, dark-haired beauty, with Oriental eyes and a ready smile came through the back door, stomping snow off her boots. She slung her full length mink coat on the office desk, fired up her camera, and, stepping on my heels videotaped my every pronouncement and culinary revelation like today's version of the biblical Matthew.

Slava cubed beef and pulled two babushkas off pizza-dough-duty and conscripted them for tortilla making. I explained and exhibited how to stir yeast into warm, sugary milk, let it work five minutes, and then mixed with oil, salt, and lots of lukewarm water and knead it into flour dough until it was spongy. The grandmas caught on quickly, shoved me aside, cut the dough into one-ounce chunks, rolled them into dough balls, and set them on cookie sheets beside the gas oven to rise. Then, while one babushka kept making tortilla dough and balls, the other roller-penned out the spongy dough balls into eight-inch disks.

"What're you doing with all those puffy little disks," Zhanna asked as the tape rolled.

"Watch," I said and demonstrated to Zha and Anatoly, the prep-cook. "First, we'll pan-fry the flour disks in a lightly-oiled frying pan until dotted with a leopard's brown spots on both sides." I cooked one tortilla, tore it apart, and gave them a taste. "Once the tortilla stack is three inches tall, we'll cut them into two-inch strips and cut them again into the strips diagonally, like this" —I drew lines and two shapes, ∧ and ∨. "Then we'll drop the tortilla chips into the electric fryer heated to a perfect temperature of 360° F and stir them until golden brown."

I cooked a handful of chips, sprinkled them with salt, and gave one crisp, golden chip to Zha and Anatoly. They gobbled them up and raved, "фантастика — Fantastika!"

"Okay, now we arrange the fried chips on a plate, cover them with grated cheese, and pop them in the oven to melt for a couple minutes. Voilà, nachos!"

Slava finished cubing a 30-pound round of beef, and we scooped the beef-pile into a big pot, flavored it with minced onions, garlic, diced green chili, salt, pepper, crushed tomatoes, and brought the mixture to a slow boil. Meanwhile, the grated hard yellow and soft white cheeses, which tasted like Cabot Cheddar and Monterey Jack, were blended. The dishwasher duo were back, and we pureed a bushel of green peppers and basket of mild green chilies. A basket of limes and lemons were crushed and mixed for the margarita mix, adding tequila, sugar, and, lastly, two, raw egg-whites to give the drinks a frothy head when whipped in a blender.

"Zhanna," I said over my shoulder as I cracked an egg, "watch. Selling an inch of egg-white foam on margaritas three hundred times a night will buy you a new Mercedes!"

For the green chili rue, I browned two cups of flour in melted butter, added the pureed chilies and peppers, and set it aside to cook. When it had, I drizzled green chili sauce and sprinkled a generous handful of blended cheese over four platters of golden tortilla chips and popped them in the oven to melt. When they were ready, I exclaimed, "*Nachos con queso y chili,*" and the kitchen crew and waitresses feasted. Next, we cubed five pounds of lean pork, poured three number ten cans of unsweetened crushed tomatoes into a big pot, and added a gallon of pureed green chilies and tomatoes for the best-tasting green chili sauce in all Asia. By seven-thirty, we spooned spiced cubed beef atop flour tortillas, rolled them into burritos, drenched them with spicy green chili sauce, sprinkled them with grated cheese, and popped them in the oven to melt. The burritos smelled heavenly. I cut six eight-inch beef burritos into one-inch-bites, dotted each with sour cream, pricked them with toothpicks, and told the waitresses to waltz around the dance floor, handing out samples. Customers loved them and clamored for more! With cooks trained and patrons shelling out fistfuls of Rubles for burritos, nachos, and margaritas, we graduated from kitchen duty and resumed our seats at the bar, drinking Courvoisier V. S. and laughing until 8:50 when Ivan left to sell his business.

At eleven, when Slava began counting the till, I said goodbye. His last words to me were: *Call me if you ever need help with anything; you've given me a fortune.* I swore I'd call, and in the dark, cold, cellar of night, I took a taxi back to the *Druzhba* for a short night's sleep before my 5 a.m. marathon to Moscow, New York, and Charlotte. On the drive back, I poked through the mental boxes strewn around my mental cellar, laying out the bad times and the fewer good times and mostly regretting remembrances of my infidelities and damn few boldnesses ever boxed. Of course, the exercise made me feel guilty, and I stopped at the gift shop for a red box of my bride's favorite **Красный октябрь** — *Krasny Okyabr,* Red October — chocolates. I said goodnight to

Alexis, the bellboy, glanced at the agent still smoking under the nutmeg tree, and drudged up six flights to my suite, leaving a wake-up call for three a.m. with the ever-vigilant floor lady.

It felt like I'd just crawled under the *perena* — comforter — and closed my eyes when there was a pounding at the door, and a male voice shouted, "*Otkroi dver!* — Open the door!"

I pressed the stem on my Timex. The face lit up. Two-ten. The room was stifling. The *fortochka* had slammed shut. I'd kicked off the *perena*. There was enough ambient light to see sweat gleaming on my torso. Was the hotel on fire?

"*Otkroi dver!*" the voice shouted again, and then, in English, "Open the door, Fetisov!"

"Okay, okay," I said, pulling on my shorts and wondering how a fireman knew English, but what happened next shocked me.

I cracked the door open and looked directly into my eyes of the airport Senator. He wore an expensive gray *shineli* — overcoat — that matched his meticulously coiffured gray hair. Panic!

"Whatdaya want?" I said, trying desperately to curb fear by sounding gruff.

He jabbed a manicured finger at me. "Open the door, Fetisov," he snarled. "NOW!"

I unchained the door. It burst open as if it had been on a spring. The lobby newspaper agent shoved past me like a storm trooper. The Senator followed and whipped around. His arms whirled. His swirling *shineli* exposed his silk shirt and a holstered pistol under his arm. It looked like a Smith & Wesson Bodyguard 380 with a 2.75-inch barrel. The newspaper agent, six inches shorter than me and fifty pounds heavier, grabbed my arm and stared into my eyes with the penetration of laser beams. He slammed me against the door.

My head whacked the frame. I saw stars. I snapped my head to clear it. "Whatdaya want?" I spit out.

"Shut up!" the Senator snarled through perfect teeth and to the agent, "Search everywhere."

The agent did. He yanked open drawers, looked for false bottoms, eyed the empty closet, felt the top of high shelves, pushed the bed out of place, flipped mattresses, ripped bottoms out of overstuffed armchairs, pulled out wall prints to see behind them. He looked behind the television. Opened the toilet tank. Rifled through my dirty clothes and found my Ruger. He waved it in my face.

Growing impatient, the Senator, to my horror, opened my backpack. He pulled out the cardboard box of Mom's ashes. He tore it open, and quick as a flash, poked in a finger, and swirled it around, searching for contraband.

"Jesus Christ!" I shouted. "Those are my mother's ashes!"

The Senator's hands flew apart. The cardboard box hit the rug. It split open. Three pounds of gray ashes sprinkled the red carpet creating a gritty pink splotch.

"Have you no respect?" I yelped and dropped to my knees to rake up her ashes.

The Senator booted the pile. Ashes billowed and coated my sweaty arms. "Forget her," he growled. "You Americans steal our women and repay us with illegal drugs. That 'good neighbor policy' makes me sick. Get some clothes on, you're going for a ride."

"No way!" I yelled. "I'm leaving Russia in a few hours."

"I don't think so," the Senator said arrogantly. "I'm the juggernaut in your life. I'm going to crush you for possession of illegal drugs and violating Russian law."

"I don't have any illegal drugs!"

"Oh, but you do, Fetisov, and you violated an essential law. Get dressed!" The newspaper agent, wearing a gray overcoat and mink *shapka*, yanked me up and shoved me to the bureau. I wiped ashes off my arm and yanked on my long johns, jeans, T-shirt, shirt, and socks while he ground Mom into the red carpet. Just then the wind shifted, and the *fortochka* flew open. Icy wind whistled in. The Arctic blast neither cooled my nerves nor slowed my pounding heart.

The Senator flipped an armchair upright and sat. He lit a Marlboro, took a deep drag, exhaled, and said, in English, "You've got big problems, Fetisov."

I cinched my belt and raised my hands, palm up. "Please tell me, what big problems could I possibly have?"

The Senator looked smug. He reached over, picked up my wallet from the windowsill, and went through it. "Did you have your papa's permission to leave the Soviet Union in nineteen seventy-four?" he asked.

I made a sick laugh. "Now how in hell could I do that? He was killed in Kābul in 1969, three months before I was born."

"Who told you that?" The Senator counted out my last two thousand dollars onto his knee, scooped it up, and slid it into his suitcoat pocket. My wallet went into his overcoat pocket.

"My mother," I said, not believing he was brazenly stealing my money.

"She lied." The Senator leaned over and picked up my L. L. Bean coat with long manicured fingers. He rifled through the pockets and pulled out the package of *taxol*!

"My mother never lied to me," I insisted categorically. "Papa died in the Afghan war. What are you doing with my wife's present?!"

"Did you get this in China?" He raised the package and pulled an end open.

"You know I did." I was horrified. My body went tense. I felt as fierce and resolute as a wolf, ready to bare fangs to protect Mom's name and snatch Nastia's taxol.

The Senator pulled the salt and pepper shaker out of the wrapping and bounced it on his knee. "Our Military Archives say your papa survived Kābul with both legs and one hand blown off by a landmine. He was flown to a military hospital in Osh, Kyrgyzstan and stayed there until he died of gangrene six years later. His body was cremated and ashes were flown to Moscow and scattered on the Volga by his brother, Ivan, you know, the man you went to China with, the vodka smuggler uncle you said you came to visit."

I was dumbfounded, speechless, and furious.

The Senator smirked. "Ask him. Look at his internal passport. He and your mother flew to Bishkek and bused to Osh every June. She was a polygamist, which means you left the Soviet Union without your father's permission — *and that, Fetisov, is a crime*!" He pushed out of the deep armchair, stepped to the windowsill and examined my three passports. "That makes these passports invalid under the fictitious name, Troy Locke. Then, yesterday, you smuggled into Russia an illegal gun, undeclared cash, *and this* — " he tapped the salt-and-shaker package — "What do you suppose it is?"

"Look, I was a seven-year-old kid in nineteen seventy-six," I insisted. "I knew nothing. And that box is a crystal salt and pepper shaker for my wife!"

The Senator shook his head ever so slowly. His charming face took on an evil grimace. "Fetisov, your stupidity is understandable; your ignorance is no excuse. We've combined the charges against you into a single violation of Article Fifty-eight of the Criminal Code: Anti-Soviet agitation. Now — " he waved the taxol box at me — "our joint Chinese-Russian police taskforce has had you under surveillance since Moscow. We knew you were coming. After you and your uncle had left the Heihe International Hotel after lunch, we arrested Zhou and Bao and confiscated fifteen thousand dollars in new American hundred-dollar bills from a *matryoshkay.* Now, where do you suppose two Kunming scientists found all those new hundred-dollar-bills? Perhaps the numbers on these dollars are sequential; I wonder where that evidence will take us."

"I've no idea what you're talking about," I stammered.

"Sure you do." The Senator pulled out the salt and pepper shakers from the box and held them up to the light. He twisted off the top of the pepper, dumped it into his palm, sniffed, and huffed it onto the ash-pink carpet. Then he held up the salt shaker to the light. A blind man could see the taxol capsule.

"Well, well, well," he said, tapping the shaker and seeing the capsule glitter. *"What's this?"*

My knees went weak. I felt overwhelmed, defeated, crushed. My body felt as if it would collapse in on itself.

"It's a crystal salt and pepper set for my wife," I muttered.

"Sure it is." He twisted the top. "Let's see what we have inside … "

"Please don't," I pleaded. "I beg you, don't open it. It's a sterile capsule of a cancer drug!"

The Senator twisted off the top, turned the salt shaker upside down, and picked the taxol capsule out of the salt with his carefully manicured fingers. He huffed the salt onto the rug and started flipping the plastic casing up and down, backhanding it in the air like he was snatching houseflies.

I had to save Nastia's taxol. I couldn't wait. If Truth is the first line in the Poem of Life, Freedom from coercion is the second. I had to try.

"No, the capsule isn't salt," I admitted. "It's taxol, an anticancer drug to save my wife's life. She dying of cancer. Give it to me, please!"

The Senator grinned evilly, shook his head, and tossed the taxol capsule up high.

I sprang, knocked the Senator's right hand with my left hand, and snatched the lifesaving airborne pod with my right hand. Gripping the prize, I drove my left fist into the Senator's handsome face. He groaned and slumped into the overstuffed chair. I bent enough to slam my right elbow into his sternum. He let out a huff of breath and doubled over. I hit him in the face again with a right uppercut so hard it lifted him off the chair. In those few seconds, the newspaper agent sprang into action. He pounced on my back. Fists flayed. I whirled, spun him off, and rammed a knee in his crotch. He hit the carpet, howling. I grabbed his arm, cocked my hip, and heaved him over my shoulder. He walloped the windowsill hard, gasping, and moaning. The Senator pushed up. I chopped his throat at a pressure point. His eyes fluttered and rolled back in his head, his face a pulpy ruin. Blood caked his wavy gray hair. His silk shirt was torn and exposed gray-haired shoulder. One eye was swollen shut. Blood and saliva-ropes ran down his chest from his split lip. The newspaper agent pushed up and came at me again. He grabbed my head and whacked it. I elbowed him in the throat. He rocked backward, went down, and jumped up. He smashed the side of my head with his fist. I got the heel of my hand under his nose and jammed. He screamed. I thrust my right fist, still clinging to the taxol capsule, into his gut. He lay motionless. I rolled up to my feet, grabbed my hat, coat, and gloves. I was making a run for the Tequila Grill. Slava was my only hope. I darted out the door.

Footsteps thundered down the hall. I spun around. No place to hide. Breathing hard and coming fast, another big agent went into action. He pointed a revolver at my head. The hammer snicked back. I ducked under it and rammed a fist into his gut. The gun fired. He shook off my gut blow and got an arm around my throat. He yanked my head back and whacked down with the pistol butt. The newspaper agent scrambled into the hall. They both pounded me with body blows. I felt another blow to the head. I couldn't move. I saw a white-and-black baton and felt its thump.

I went down. And out.

When I slogged awake, I was in the backseat of a Black Maria, sandwiched by two beefy agents. Stuffed between my legs were my L. L. Bean coat, suitcase, and backpack. The Senator sat in front, dabbing his bloody face with his silk pocket handkerchief. The newspaper agent drove. Blago city lights brighten and darkled rhythmically as my vision sharpened with each systolic thrust of my pounding heart.

I shook my head at a whirling confusion, clung to the taxol capsule, and asked, "Where're we going?"

"To church," the Senator snarled.

"The Popov Monastery," the newspaper agent added.

Oh my, God, I thought, *KGB Headquarters*!

TWENTY

Popov Monastery/Prison
December 29, 1991

Turning left off *Ulitsa Lenina* onto *Ulitsa Reeka* — River Street — gale-whipped ice-pellets chattered like rivet guns against the Black Maria's windshield. Inside the sedan, the four KGB agents, snug in their greatcoats, gloves, and hats, smoked in daunting silence, layering the car with Marlboro miasma, while two goons squashed me between them freezing. They ignored my sneezing and shivering dressed in tattered shirtsleeves and my torn pant legs.

Four blocks down *Ulitsa Reeka*, the car's cockeyed headlight sliced through crenulated snowbanks six- to eight-feet-high and played off the steel door to Ivan's warehouse/barn. I wondered if he'd been arrested and concluded, maybe, for aiding and abetting. Or maybe not if he'd made a payoff.

Across from Ivan's barn, the newspaper agent turned left on a birch- and fir-lined-lane, *Pereulok Monastyr* — Monastery Lane, and banged over potholes and plowed through snowdrifts to Popov Monastery, priests long since jailed, church appropriated by the Kremlin. On both sides of the lane, thick boughs swayed sorrowfully. Some had busted off under snow's sly weight. Some pirouetted on Arctic squalls. The white birch stood as motionless as cadaver bones. The withered monastery was nestled on the slopes to the Amur River, looking abandoned and derelict like all those Stalin had padlocked, its towering onion-domes observing all like faithful sentries.

The Black Maria whacked bottom on a lunar-sized pothole prompting a barrage of *govnos* and *yobs* — shits and fucks — from the agents, sending hands flaying at sparks shooting like fireworks. We slid to a stop at the portico lit by one weak, stoop lamp. My guards flung open their doors and jumped out, brushing ashes off their snazzy *voyennyye shineli* — military overcoats — and *norkovyye shapka* — mink hats.

Finally, with elbow room, I started wrestling on my L. L. Bean coat when the Senator stuck his bloody face back in the car. His *shapka* stunk like burnt flesh.

"Bring your bag, Fetisov," he crowed. "Always nice to have fresh undies."

I shot him a cold stare: *How endearing.* "I won't have time to change my underwear."

"Oh, but you will." He sniggered.

I had one arm in my coat sleeves and brailing around for the other when the portside agent thrust in a foot and rammed my side. Simultaneously, the starboard agent reached in and snatched my arm. One kicked the other jerked and I flew out, grasping at my stuff and hitting ice. The suitcase opened. Clothes scattered. With one arm in my coat sleeve, the other hand free to scramble for things, I landed on my hands and knees and snatched at T-shirts and underwear swirling into the gale. I was still grabbing for them when the KGB dragged me over their goal line, the portico. I turned just as Anastasia's picture whirl into the dead of night. The church door opened. I was shoved inside, stumbled into the narthex, and slammed into the Senator. He was looking for anyone.

"*Prevet* — Hello!" he shouted into the towering void. Wind howling through the cupola swallowed his faint echo. The Senator looked left and right and into the nave.

No one was on duty in the wee hours.

I tried to stand still, but, shivering uncontrollably, couldn't. It was not twenty degrees. Where celebrants once stood to worship — Russians don't use pews during their two-hour-long services — the space was a muddle of vacant desks under barren skyhooks long ago pilfered of silver chandeliers and empty wall hooks fleeced of silver candelabras. They now shouldered strings of electric cords and flickering lights draped wall-to-wall that swayed in wind gusts and reflected off Pepsi cans twinkling on flagstones. Splotches of wall icons had been plastered over in khaki, giving the space the dead look of a planetarium's version of when a meteorite's dust-cloud smothered planet life and annihilated T-Rex and cousins. The iconostasis — the triple-door, icon-bearing partition separating the body of the church from the sanctuary — was stripped bare, its doors chain-sawed into a garage-sized opening.

"*Prevet!*" the Senator tried again.

At the far end of the church, his shout finally produced a blond, solid, ordinary-looking man in a blue uniform bearing sergeant's stripes. He looked like a sleepy insurance agent, but he didn't sound like one when he boomed across the emptiness, "Close the fucking door!"

He stepped around the latticed chancel, the screen at the rear of the nave, and sat in a swivel chair at a tall raised altar, now a desk, and the cockpit of Blagoveshchensk law enforcement.

"Up here!" he shouted, waving both arms robustly as if he were gating an Antonov An-225, the world largest airplane.

We wound through the desk clutter to the altar. Where the nave intersected with the transepts forming a cross, two guards were sprawled out on benches, snoring. One farted. I made a silent vow: *Jesus, help me out of this, and I'll go to church every Sunday the rest of my life, I swear!* On the dais, a knee-high heater glowed red and baked the stench of dirty ashtrays.

"Up here with him," the sergeant shouted again. He yawned and jabbed a nicotine-stained index finger the size and color of a tamale at a spot two feet in front of his altar/desk. The backs of his fingers had tufts of blond hair down to his fingernails.

The newspaper agent shoved me forward with an extra dose of virulence.

From three feet away, the sergeant had a cop look, direct, skeptical, narrow, and full of weary wisdom. I didn't need an interpreter for that. A tanned, young foreigner in a fancy coat arrested in the wee hours of a raw Siberian night offended his sense of orderliness. Cops don't believe in coincidences. They find it impossible to believe that such a man had not committed a crime in their lovely city.

I braced myself, stood stiffly, and focused on the old, scarred altar — so decrepit Noah might have found it on Ararat. I kept my eyes downcast, trying to look as guiltless, trustworthy, and loyal as a Boy Scout — Soviet or American — their mottos are the same, Будь готов! — Be Prepared! I wondered if the Russian penal code stated that I did not have to incriminate myself. Fat chance. Russian law wasn't found in law books, and these clowns knew it.

The sergeant swiveled around in his chair enough to set his square-toed boots on the corner of the altar, ankles crossed. He shook a Marlboro out, tapped the filter on his thumbnail, and fired up. His caterpillar eyebrows jumped as he looked at me. I looked at him.

"Who's this?" he growled contemptuously. He stared at me with loathing. His vivid blue eyes were as cold as a galactic meteor. He looked German: Eyes, fair skin, blond hair. His grandfather had probably been a Stalingrad POW.[24] Millions of German, Czech, and Ukrainian POWs were never permitted to return home after VE[25] Day.

"This is Mister Sunshine, a Russian-American hooligan with two names. We're using his birth name, Fetisov," the Senator said and wiped a blood spoor off his cheek.

The sergeant frowned at me, his eyebrows touching as he squinted. He blew a perfect smoke ring at me and said caustically, "Summer tan, nifty clothes, haughty attitude, Yankee for sure."

"I am an American from Florida," I said stoutly. "And a dual citizen."

"He was born in Tver," The Senator explained, pulling my three passports from his pocket and fanning them over the desk.

"I have the required passports and a return plane ticket," I said, hopefully, not surprised he'd failed to mention pocketing my two grand cash. Soviet bureaucrats, like Illinois governors, have a rich and ignominious history of fraud, bribery, theft, corruption, and racketeering. Unlike Land of Lincoln honchos, though, they never land in jail.

I set my suitcase and backpack on the floor and wondered if my luck was going to hold or if it were about to run out. I knew it would run out one day, but *plu-lease*, Lord, not tonight!

The sergeant picked up my passports with long, stained fingers. My Soviet internal passport was five years old, my American passport two, the Soviet passport was valid another five.

"Let's have a look," he said, and his eyebrows arched up.

The sergeant, a rangy man of forty, had a guardsman mustache the size of a shoe brush that twitched as he studied my American passport and froze when he looked at my smudged, old, Soviet picture flawed by time and lousy photo equipment. He held the two out at arm's length and studied both full face shots. He looked at me, at the shots, and me again; his caterpillar eyebrows wormed together as he cogitated, and then they relaxed. He nodded approvingly and set them down. He picked up my plane tickets and scowled at them, trying to decipher the English.

"What do these say?" he asked the Senator.

"They're in English," the Senator explained. "This one is for the flight Blagoveschensk to Moscow on Sibir Air. This one is Delta Airlines, Moscow to New York to Charlotte, a city in the American south. Fetisov is scheduled to leave — " he looked at his diamond-studded Rolex — "in four hours."

The sergeant laughed and twisted the end of his mustache hard enough to expose corn-yellow teeth and one gleaming gold incisor. "He's going to be late."

My heart stopped. My jaw dropped open.

The sergeant yawned, stretched, hauled in his legs in. "You look surprised, Fetisov?"

"I am," I admitted. "I must get this medicine to my wife." I opened my right palm and held out the taxol capsule for him to see.

He was enough over six feet to look me directly in the eye. He glanced at the capsule and placed both hands on the altar. He leaned forward until his eyes were beyond the place priests prepared the Eucharist now scattered with papers, files, and dirty ashtrays. He peered down at my gear. He sat down, picked up a ballpoint, and wrote partly with his pen and partly with his tongue as his eyebrows danced helping him write. I watched carefully as he wrote: *Riukzak* — backpack, *Chemodan* — suitcase, and *Inostrannoye palto* — foreign coat. No reference to money.

"I want the capsule and everything else," he said, slapping the altar. "Your wedding ring, sneakers, belt, and socks."

I was thunderstruck. I placed the capsule on the altar. "I must have this back," I said.

He shot me a look and motioned for everything else. I set them on the altar, never expecting to see them again.

I didn't.

The sergeant tore off a copy of the receipt, gave it to the Senator, and asked, "No wallet?"

"Oh." The Senator pulled it out of his fine coat pocket. "He has a few hundred rubles. Like most Americans, Fetisov travels on credit cards."

"That's a lie!" I blurted out. "There was *twenty hundred-dollar-bills* in there. Search him!"

The sergeant looked at the Senator. I think he winked. "It's Fetisov who's lying. He had two hundred thirty rubles, count it, sergeant."

The sergeant opened my wallet and looked at my credit cards and social security card. "What's this one?" he said, holding up my Florida driver's license. "It looks phony."

"Americans have driver's licenses with their pictures; it's a common form of identification to drive and to vote."

"Good idea," the sergeant said. He thumbed through the Rubles and set them on the altar. "You'll get your money back when you're released, Fetisov. You ever been in a Russian jail?"

I shook my head. "Never had the pleasure. Probably not the nicest people in there."

He smiled a fox-in-the-henhouse smile. "It will be a unique experience for you."

"I'm sure it will be, but it will be brief."

The Senator smiled an inverted smile and glanced at the wall clock: 3:10 a.m..

"I'm innocent," I said. "Now, I'd like to make my one phone call to James Collins."

The sergeant looked puzzled. "Who's he?"

"America's new Moscow *Chargé d'affaires*; he'll straighten this out."

The Senator shook his head derisively. "Your 'one phone call?' I don't think so. You'll be here until your trial, Fetisov. You watch too much TV. Write a letter after the trial."

"Trial?" I said, astonished. "What trial? What kind? A jury trial?" My mind flashed to my parents' Thanksgiving weekend conversation at the Plaza Hotel. Mom's mention of Solzhenitsyn had launched Dad into a tirade: *There've been no jury trials in Russia for seventy-five years! Since the nineteen-thirties, thirty-five million people were banished to the Gulags without trials. Few survived. Rule by fear enervates Russians.*

"Jury trial?" The Senator scoffed. "You'll face a Russian judge."

My heart sank. He said something, but it was drowned out by blood rushing in my ears.

"Let's have the belt, too," the sergeant sneered. "Belts aren't allowed." I drew a deep breath to steady my racing heart, yanked off the belt and set it on the desk. "No," I said, "it wouldn't look good for an American to hang himself awaiting trial."

"Get your smart ass up against the wall!" the sergeant jeered. He jabbed at a wall marked with foot-long, black-ink lines like a closet door chronicling a kid's growth.

"And wipe off that smirk," the Senator blurted. "It's picture taking time."

That prompted two KGB agents armed with pistols and vicious scowls to step closer, ready to rip out my heart if I gave him any lip. One growled, "Stand straight against the wall, gut in, shoulders back." The second agent said, "Hold your head level; eyes straight ahead."

"Gotcha." I stood barefoot on the icy flagstone, back against the X, and put on my stony look saved for my McDee-teenagers about to be axed for smoking pot on the job. I felt the color drain from my face.

"Height six feet, three inches," one guard said. "Weight about ninety-one kilos."

The sergeant took photos, full-face and profile, and fingerprinted me. He got black ink on his mitts and wiped them off with a rag soaked with kerosene stored in a Stoli bottle. He examined his fingers and scrubbed some more around a thumbnail. He did not offer me the rag. He pulled a prisoner list from a pile, added my name, and picked up a black indelible marker.

"Fetisov," he said, "this will be your third name." With the marker and help from his tongue, he tattooed 87-15.867 on the inside of my forearm. That jogged my curiosity.

"What's the eighty-seven before the dash for?" I asked, pointing.

"Blagoveshchensk's city-size ranking. The rest is the criminal count."

I wondered when Blago had started tallying criminals, last year or 1917.

The sergeant admired his printing and yelled, "Hey, you two, get your asses in gear!"

The sleeping guards moaned, stretched, and re-holstered their truncheons. The taller, burlier of the duo had the size and robustness of a lumberjack. He had matted red hair as snaky as Medusa's, and he loped more than walked. His partner, as short as Napoleon, had a large head, deep-set eyes, flat nose, cauliflower ears, and the odious, sadistic, pulp-faced look of a welterweight. He probably had five hundred way of being a brutal SOB and knew them all. Napoleon took two steps for every one Paul Bunyan took.

"Search him," the sergeant ordered.

"Strip!" Napoleon yelled and jabbed my gut with his cudgel.

I stripped down to my shorts.

"All the way!" Napoleon whacked me on the butt for encouragement.

I dropped my shorts. They fell to my ankles. I stepped out of them, and Napoleon pulled latex gloves from his pocket. I glanced down at my knockwurst, now the size of a cocktail wiener.

Napoleon stepped behind me and whacked my calves. "Bend over and spread 'em!"

I did. He thumped me across the butt, smashing my fingers. "Wider!"

I spread my cheeks wider. Napoleon did a full body search called a *soback-hik* — dog procedure — an ugly, graceless, hurtful, humiliating, anal-cavity-quest for drugs. He found none.

"Dress!" he growled and snapped off the gloves, tossing them at a waste-basket and missing.

I pulled on my clothes and held up my beltless jeans.

The sergeant printed my name in block letters on a file folder and slid my passports, airline tickets, credit cards, rubles, and wallet inside. He hung my L. L. Bean coat on the back of his chair. I figured I never see it again. I was right.

"Take Fetisov down to the *boxik* — holding cell," the sergeant ordered. The Senator smiled.

Napoleon gave me a fanged smile with all the warmth of a wolf snarl. He was Ivan the Terrible and Attila the Hun rolled into one. "That way!" he screamed and bludgeoned me. I stumbled around the end of the chancel.

In the rear of the monastery was the sacristy, the polygonal area where the choir once chanted and bearded priests robed in ecclesiastical splendor. It had the fusty odor of Grammy Locke's Beacon Hill attic. In its half-light, I noted a blood-stained door on the left, a grungy door on the right, dusty cassocks, yellowed-white surplices, and soiled caps. That gave me an escape idea. My pulse quickened as I thought about it: dress like a priest, kick the door's rotten lock off, and flee for Tequila Grill.

Napoleon bashed my right kidney. I howled and stumbled to the door on the right.

"Open it, idiot!" he screamed.

With one hand holding up my jeans, I pulled open the door and froze, wary as a spelunker squinting into a stygian blackness melting into the temple's gut, a bottomless cave. Napoleon thrashed my kidney again. I groaned and took the first step. The darkness smelled earthy and felt like I was stepping off the face of the earth. Napoleon hammered my neck. I cried out and took another step. The wood stairs creaked. The reek intensified. I groped for a handrail. None. Slowly, I tramped down into the barnyard stench. At the foot of the stairs, I felt hard-packed clay under my bare toes. Ten steps down the long darkness, a weak bulb emitted a dim glow. The noisome air was a chaos of odors: Fecal, rooty, clammy, urinal. Beyond the one bulb's glimmer, dimness dissolved into blackness.

Napoleon struck me again. Alternating hands were holding up my jeans, my right-hand fingers strummed slim, cold bars that felt like steel stalactites. I alternated hands, and my left-hand fingers felt huge, moist, timeworn stalagmites. Closer, the faint bulb was shrouded in a tapestry of spider webs and cast enough light to morph the stalagmites into refrigerator-sized granite blocks big enough to please King Khufu.

I heard a primal wail; a high-pitched shriek gorged with a loss, grief, defeat, and rage. In the far reaches of the sour darkness, a barred cell materialized bulging with outstretched arms, shaved skulls, and agonized faces, moaning in desolation and despair like a choir of Munch's *Scream of Nature* lookalikes.

"Where you from?" a skull shouted in accented Russian. "Me, Rīga. What's your city?"

"Born in Tver," I shouted; "living in — "

WHAM!

Napoleon bludgeoned my kidney so hard I keeled over, grasping my side and groaning. As the groan passed my lips, it took with it all my faith in hope, prayer, trust, and the goodness of the Christian God for putting me here. I never held those certainties again.

"Shut up!" he snarled. "No talking! No looking left or right! Hands behind your back!"

I rose, stooped, bent, and shuffled on into a sharp and growing latrine stench. Halfway to the skulls' cell, the dirt was urine-dark. Napoleon screamed, "Stop!" in front of a cubicle the size of a coffin. The reek was so nauseous, I barfed last night's burrito, splattering it onto the feces oozing over the doorsill.

Napoleon thumped the coffin with his baton. "This is your *boxik* — box — Fetisov."

Then, careful not to step in humanure, he elbowed me aside and from his belt unsnapped a brass key ring the size of a grapefruit. He unlocked the *boxik*; it made a rusty screech when he swung it out. A sharp, piercing, carbolic fragrance decanted. A knife-like thrust of foulness that burned my nostrils and watered my eyes. I had never smelled old shit, old urine, old blood, old vomit, and old pus — the years of human agony saturating the *boxik* floor and walls. Tears gushing from my eyes made the inside of the mummy pod a blur, but it appeared too short and too narrow for my frame.

"Inside!" Napoleon screamed with a clobber to my neck.

My arms flew out. My jeans fell. My head whacked doorframe. I dropped to my knees in the urine and feces. Blood flowed.

I twisted my head around and looked up at the little sadist. "It's too small! I can't fit!"

"Stoop and hunch you fucking idiot!" the lumberjack shrieked and booted me.

My hands skidded through the muck. I pushed up half standing and yanked up my jeans. I extended a leg and toed the floor of the box. Crusty. I stepped in. The glaze cracked. Cold, sticky, brown shit oozed between my toes. The hilarious little psychopath bashed me again. My forehead whacked the coffin frame. Blood clouded my eyes. I turned, swiped my eyes on my arm, and glared at them. I was real tired of being used as a punching bag. Napoleon's eyes were as calmly intent on killing me as an Amur tiger would have been.

The lumberjack looked brainless.

We make lots of choices in life, and it's easy to make lousy ones. Some men buckle when enduring sadistic abuse. Some men get annoyed and run. But all men dread being wedged into a coffin. That fear sprinted to my brain's threat center, the medulla gland, deep within the hypothalamus and triggered an involuntary response in my kidneys' adrenal glands. Instantly, my bloodstream flooded with epinephrine to combat the threat, and my heart raced, palms sweat, pupils dilate, and hair stood on end. My respiration bolted. Muscles energized as the fight-or-flight sensor kicked in. If you're human, you react. I reacted.

I wheeled around, smashed Napoleon's jaw with a right cross, and crushed a left hook into Bunyan's gut. He doubled over. I hit him with a right to his broad cheek. He fell backward, hooking my neck with an arm as he went down. We tangled. Out of a muddle of limbs, a bludgeon clunked my head. I slumped into the muck. Ooze clouded my eyes. Another blow landed behind my left ear. That was all I could recall.

When I was able to shake that off, I felt a gooey, fetid putridness on my face.

Strangely, instead of thinking of goo and goons, memories of Anastasia flooded my mind. Memories are the fuel that feeds our drive to stay alive. Memories of what was happening to her. Memories of my not showing up at the Charlotte Airport with her taxol. Memories of not being there for my sweet woman and comforting her. Memories of not being able to do anything about the exasperating FDA impaled on outdated rules that refuse to embrace change that is killing millions of women. Memories of Congress not passing laws to close our border or approve the gift of medicines' undergoing approval for life-threatened people — crazy — they're already dying, right?

"Ahhh!" Someone kicked my balls. Kicked again.

The kicks didn't get the results Napoleon wanted. He screamed, "Idiot, crawl into the box!"

I wiped shit off my face, swiped my hands on my jeans, and levered myself up. I pulled up my jeans and sidled in. It was impossible to stand. I slouched, chin on chest, legs in an S.

Napoleon rammed the door shut. "Haul your knee in, idiot!" he screeched.

The two guards joined forces and shoved until, finally, the lock clicked.

I twisted around. My right knee was bent at an odd angle. My bare feet cracked the feces crust. Squishiness seeped between my toes. That dredged up a reminiscence of a long-ago summer in Maine. As a boy, my pal, Dick, and I would lope barefoot through pastures dotted with cow pies at great-grandmother's farm on Moose Hill. We'd hoot with delightful at the same squishiness between our toes. I started laughing now. The laughter built, emanating from the depths of the primordial cranium and growing to an alarming frequency and intensity.

I heard Napoleon declare, "He's going nuts!"

That made me laugh even harder. After a while, I stopped laughing. The inside of the box was cave-black. The odor was overpowering. Emotions surged.

"How long will I be in here?" I yelled.

Silence.

"How long?!" I tried again.

Nothing.

I hunched over in the cramped blackness. It was impossible to sit or lay or sleep. Terrible thoughts haunted me, making me feel worse than not thinking at all. My life, once a circus of action, was locked in miserable suspension, a nightmare without meaning and purpose. I tried to focus on Anastasia. She had to have taxol. I had failed my quiet, decent, brave, beautiful wife. She had trusted me. My wife, with the delightfully oblique sense of humor and the manifest destiny to be a great mother and professor, had trusted good old reliable Troy Locke. She had to stop trusting me. Damn her for trusting me! I was furious at her. Furious at being here. Furious at the KGB. Furious at the FDA. I pounded the door and fumed and pounded some more.

After a long time, an old feeling seized me, a feeling experienced at high school football game kickoffs. Standing tense and anxious on the forty-yard line, I'd cross myself for divine support with the belief the sign-of-the-cross would provide succor. I crossed myself now. The darkness slowly abated. Life arose, thoughts of bright, joyous pasts and boundless futures fueled by my Calvinistic conscience Dad instilled, one of resilience and perseverance. I pounded on the steel door and only stopped when my hands were a swollen pulp. I thought of Houdini. How would that old Hungarian get out of this box? An escape plan formulated.

I twisted around. Wedged my back against the inner wall, braced a knee against the door latch and pushed with all I had. My body trembled. The door moved. The latch budged. But not quite enough. I rammed harder. It moved a fraction of an inch but not enough to avoid the latch. I tried again. Again. And stopped, panting and exhausted. This box would have stumped Harry Handcuff. Never in my twenty-two years had I felt more trapped. More so than being chest-deep in a sandy foxhole in Iraq with my dead buddy, Tinker, beside me, bullets whizzing overhead while I burrowed with bare hands to deepen the hole.

I juggled around, relaxed, and thought how stupid escape would be. I've always rationalizing my defeats. If I could have broken out of the box, I would have snuck upstairs, pulled on a surplus and cap, and snuck out the rear door. Barefoot, in -55° weather, lacking a hat and coat, I wouldn't last the five minutes it would take to get to Ivan's warehouse, wake the old guard, get in, and bury myself in a haystack to say nothing of making it to Slava's.

I slumped back, defeated, abandoned, and achingly desolate in the putridness.

I shook. And not entirely from frustration. I was freezing and famished and breathless and retching and felt like gnawing my way out. I started panting like Leftovers did chasing squirrels. I thought of him napping on a snug blanket, food and water at his side in Blowing Rock. I needed fresh air. Sultry, orange-blossom air would do. Air laced with a potpourri of tropical scents. This coffin's sewer air made me so sick I started to hyperventilate. My shoulders heaved. I puked. The last of last night's beer and burrito splattered down my front and onto my mucky feet. When I stopped retching, I wiped my mouth off and wiped my feet on the back of my jeans. I hollered for help. No one came. I holler more. Still no one. After a while, I decided that if I continued down this path, nurturing bitterness, I would become crazier than Captain Ahab in his endless pursuit of the white whale.

"Relax, rest," I said to myself aloud. In boot camp, I discovered a way to will myself to sleep. Squads would gather around and bet how long it would take mre to fall asleep. Usually, less than ninety seconds. Would it work now?

I closed my eyes and began the process, one body part at a time. Concentrated on my toes until they tinkled asleep. Move on to the left foot. Will it to sleep. When it grew numb, move up to the left ankle, left calf, left thigh, left hip, right toes, foot, calf, thigh, hip; left hand, left arm, right hand, right arm, neck, zonk.

This time, my body tingled all over, but I did not fade into the usual deep slumber.

My brain had other plans. It wanted to dwell on what I'd done so stupidly wrong to get caught. Cockiness was at the top of that list. I tried my damnedest to push cockiness aside and sleep, but my mind became even more analytical. In a bizarre way, it was a relief. In numbing my body for sleep, it had grown numb to the cold, and I felt myself depart from my surroundings. I was hermetically sealed from my filthy foul pod. Tolstoy said, *there are no conditions to which a person cannot grow accustomed.* It worked. I doubted Leo had this in mind. To find relief, I fiercely, actively, concentrated. I analyzed, dissected, and probed every hour of the last month in search of answers and prayed to God for the grace to accept my role.

Mom was dead. Nothing I could do about that. She'd left me an inheritance. Can't get to it. Dad was badly hurt and hopefully recovering. Nothing I could do about that. Nastia would die without taxol. Nothing I can do about that ... but I had to do something about that!

Finally, the trusty cerebrum slipped into gear. My cocky arrogance, thinking I could tilt against Soviet windmills, landed me here. Now I must think of a way out. I must talk to Nastia. I must find her more taxol. With the inheritance, we could buy more Chinese taxol. Would the KGB take an IOU on my bequest? Would they set me free? I had to get to a phone. I could give Anastasia power of attorney. She could get to the money, fly here with it and pay bribes, and make another taxol purchase. But *how* could I call her?

If I offered the sergeant a big chunk of money, he might let me use his phone. If I gave him thousands, maybe he'd spring me. Or would it be easier to bribe the judge? Or both? Bribes have greased the probity of Russian justice for millennia. A bribe was the way to go!

With that settled, I slumped back and relaxed. I braced my shoulders into the V of joining walls, jammed my knees against wall and door and bent my chin to chest. I tried again to will myself to sleep. My right arm suddenly scraped steel. I heard a tinny scratch. My Timex!

The booking sergeant had overlooked my watch. Bribe Napoleon to get to the sergeant. I pressed the stem. The phosphorescent face emitted a luminous 4:57. I'd been in the coffin one hour and forty-five minutes. I called out: Nothing. And then I tried not to look at the watch as the minutes dragged on. Though I failed to sleep, after a long time, I willed myself into an outer-body-like trance as patient as Gandhi. I accepted my plight. Dialed my mind back to Black Friday and relived every minute of every hour since. I was up to the Sergeant Foss's call about Mom's death, when, at 5:11 a.m., the need to urinate was so over-powering all thought ceased. When I couldn't hold it any longer, I arched out and let it go. Urine splattered my bare feet. Its sterile warmth washed the shit off the tops of my feet and toes. Five hours later, at 10:15 New Year's Eve morning — the day I'd planned to be in Charlotte with the taxol — intestinal cramps became so severe, I hunched over and dropped my jeans; they puddled around my ankles, and I let it go. There was not enough space to bend over and move them, and the urine-soaked jeans filled with crap. I was now bare-assed, cold, and wet. I started to shiver violently, but not hard enough to not feel lice crawling up my legs. Warm excrement is a lice magnet. I picked off the ones I could reach and pinched out their life. Those on my calves and back had a field day. Later, still S-wedged in freezing, ankle-deep muck, I must have dozed off a few times for that long day finally came to an end. Saturday, New Year's Eve Day 1991, ended.

The New Year began. Two hours into the first day of 1992, at 2:07 a.m. — when the sane world was washing out champagne flutes and sweeping up confetti — Napoleon opened my coffin's steel door. For twenty-three hours, I'd been stuffed inside. Like a mummy, I could not move, legs functionless. My clothes, sodden and soaked, were twisted around my ankles like handcuffs and heavy with excreta, my strength so weak I couldn't have broken a toothpick.

"Out!" Napoleon screamed.

"I can't move," I said.

Napoleon reached in and whacked my arm.

I grabbed my right leg, slid my foot through feces, and lifted it up and over the stoop. Setting it on urine-soaked dirt, I braced myself against the coffin wall, grasped the frame, and lifted my left foot out. I pushed off and unkinked my spine. I wiped feces from my hands onto my jeans and slowly, ever so slowly, I straightened. I arched my back. Spine knuckles snapped and popped like breakfast Rice Krispies in milk. I stomped my bare feet. Shit splattered. Napo-leon jumped back and cursed. I reached down and pulled up my cold, stiff, crap-heavy jeans. I felt a louse digging the back of my thigh, got a fingernail under it fierce head and yanked it out. The vicious little psychopath laughed and watched me study the vermin's broad, flat, body and grind it into the dirt.

The Timex bribe had crystallized in my mind, but was this the time to pitch it?

"You like the shit box, Fetisov?" Napoleon sneered, poking me, but not very hard.

"I've lived on a farm," I said. "What else you got?"

"A hot soapy shower, clean clothes, and a delicious breakfast."

"Sure," I said flatly, weary of broken promises and reached for my shit-heavy pants.

The felt coat had no buttons — prisoners swallow them, throw up, and land in sick bay. The floppy felt hat looked like a spineless bag. I stripped and threw my rancid clothes into a barrel marked Грязная Одежда — Dirty Clothes — but left on my waterproof Timex. I twisted the faucet and jumped out of the icy surge. The shower wasn't a shower at all. It was a chest-high lead-pipe gushing freezing water. I gulped some and started washing off shit, paying no heed to the brain, nervous system, anemia, and kidney problems encountered from lead poisoning. I darted in and out of the cold explosion, delighted to be scrubbing off urine, feces, and lice. Once rinsed reasonably clean, I extended my wrist into the blast and twisted it to wash the crap off the gold Timex, digging off the last flakes between links with dirty fingernails.

There were no towels. Dressing wet, I said, "I'd like talk to the sergeant; can you arrange it?"

Napoleon went bug-eyed. He laughed cynically. "Are you nuts?"

"No. I'll give you this Rolex if you arrange it." I rotated my wrist. The Timex gleamed. "Not many Rolexes in Blago."

Napoleon snatched my wrist, twisted it, and studied the Timex. "It's expensive, right?"

"Very!" I tapped the English letters TIMEX of the face, and spelled them out: "R-O-L-E-X!"

"I've heard of Rolex," the greedy little sadist said. "Gimme it, and I'll set up a meet."

"Good," I said and slipped off the bracelet. With both hands, I laid the newly-christened Rolex in his palms as if it were a crucifix made for Karol Jógef Wojtyla (aka John Paul II). Napoleon wiped it on his pant leg several times and slid it on his wrist. He twisted it this way and that, smiling covetously as it twinkled. I had completed the initial step in my scheme, felt like a conquering hero home from WWII, and finished dressing. We wound through warrens to a large, arched, brick-lined concave crowded with benches that would have made a superb wine cellar beneath Trump Plaza.

Three *zeks*[26] in gray prisoner clothes worked in the kitchen behind a four-foot serving line. One had the big, shaggy, bowl haircut, one was bald, and one's hair was long and frizzy and tied in a ponytail. They looked like the Three Stooges and had probably killed for these cushy jobs. Moe, the bowl-cut, held an oar-sized paddle and stirred what smelled like rotten cabbage in a 50-gallon gas cooker. Curly, bald with cranial tattoos, mixed yeast and molasses into a pasty, rye dough. Larry, frizzy-haired, was kneading black dough into ropey lengths, cutting it into foot-long sections and laying them in shoe-box-sized pans before setting them on the oven to rise.

Moe, obviously the head honcho, gave me a toothless smile. "Hungry?"

"I could eat a skunk," I said. "Ladle me some … ah, from the bottom, please."

"Yes, sir; anything you say, sir." Moe dropped the oar on the dirt floor, ran grimy fingers through his kinky thatch, and dipped deeply. He ladled out a heaping serving and slopped it into a coffee can and said something to Larry who picked up a rag, opened the oven, and yanked out a bread pan. He spooned out a glob of hot, sticky, black dough and banged it into my can. It covered a leaf of black cabbage. The odor radiating from the glob of half-baked dough reminded me of the yeasty scent in the Squire Shop a month ago and flooded my mouth with saliva.

"Five minutes," Napoleon said, slouching back, firing up a Marlboro, and admiring his Rolex.

"Utensils?" I said to Moe, and he gave me a nothing-I-can-do-about-it shoulder hunch.

With two fingers, I spooned up the hot dough, rolled it around on my tongue, chewed it, and swallowed. It tasted as good as a scoop of Ben and Jerry's ice cream. I wolfed down the whole glob, licked my fingers, and stirred the soup with a digit. The soup was thin, cold, and stunk. A black potato peel with a five-inch-long, withered eye floated to the top. A moldy frozen cabbage leaf sprinkled with sawdust followed. I said a silent prayer, picked up the can, and drank hungrily and spewed.

Moe laughed. "Not hungry enough, huh?" He came around the serving line, picked up my tin can, and dumped the slop back in the cooker. "You will be."

"Never," I said. I was wrong.

"Let's go," Napoleon said, and we wound through dark passages, climbed the dark stairs, and entered the sacristy, approaching another door stained with red fingerprints.

"Is this the sergeant's office?" I said, nodding at his Rolex and lifting my head questioningly.

"Sucker," Napoleon scoffed.

"You promised I could speak with him."

"Idiot!"

"Then take cash. I've got lots of money."

"Not in Russia you don't, and I don't take credit cards."

Napoleon opened the door and shoved me in. It looked like a doctor's office: examining table, bright lights, and tools. But it wasn't. It was an interrogation room. In the bastion of irrationality, my questioning began at 2:30 a.m., Sunday, January 1, 1992. It continued five, vicious hours that night and every night for the next two weeks. The term interrogation room doesn't depict the chamber accurately. It lacks the flavor of savagery and physical sadism the KGB dishes out. Four generations of viperine guards have learned how to kick kidneys, knee groins, ram night-sticks into solar plexuses, and shove pitiless shiv under prisoners' ribs without leaving a trace of blood in destroying organs without leaving a telltale bruise. My questioning began with a beating that left me unmarked, gasping, thrashing, and writhing, head-to-toe, and front-to-back. My questioning ended with a heartless, brutal, loathsome, steel-core-rubber-hosed-beatings that continued until I fell unconscious. In between, an extraordinarily unpleasant looking country recruit, bald as a brick, with dim cement-gray eyes, zits, pockmarks, dirty fingers, and a weak chin lashed me to the metal table with metal bands, then bound my head, arms, and legs. Once immobile, he tilted the table into a vertical position, placed a pencil between my forehead and a flood lamp and clicked on the lamp. I blinked. The blaze burned my eyes. When I closed my eyes, he belted my kidneys with a rubber mallet. Whenever I shifted, the pencil dropped, and I was kidney-whacked again, again, and again.

I soon got the message and held the pencil in place, praying the burning wouldn't blind me. The cornea is a clear window of tissue on the front of all eyeballs. It damages easily. When exposed to intense light, the eyeball will sunburn, and the cornea's cells blister and crack. The condition is known as photokeratitis and can appear within hours. My cornea didn't feel like it was burning. It felt like someone had torn out my eyeballs and scrubbed them with fine-grit sandpaper. The effect is usually temporary and dissipates within thirty-six hours. Long, repeated exposure will damage the retina. Those light-sensitive cells are located on the back of the eye and transmit images to the brain. Their damage is called solar retinopathy. Though not as painful as photokeratitis, its fallout can be permanent. The condition is usually reversible over time — a week, a month, a year — depending on the extent of the damage. In my case healing progressed steadily over the next three months, remained static for some months, and then slowly improved. I was nearly back to normal in six months when I enjoyed the surprise of a lifetime.

During the interrogations, without a flicker of emotion, interrogators asked me the same questions, over-and-over, to which I repeated the same answers. No, I was *not* in the drug trade. No, I did *not* belong to a smuggling cabal. No, my uncle did not know anything about my mission to China. No, I had no relatives in Russia taking part in a conspiracy. No, I have no Amur Region drug contacts. Yes, taxol *is* an unapproved drug for another few weeks, but it is *not* a narcotic. Yes, the American government will be approving taxol as a cure for breast and ovarian cancer. *Yes*, of course, that makes taxol an *unapproved and illegal drug but only for a few more weeks*! Yes, I brought taxol into Russia with twenty-thousand undeclared dollars. Yes, I paid bribes, including my watch, to vicious guards and the KGB boss who stole my last two thousand dollars. Yes, I purchased the illegal drug in China with undeclared money, but I did it to save my wife's life! She's dying of breast cancer; you must understand! May I, *please* make a phone call?"

"No calls." WHACK!

At eight, my first night's interrogation ended. Exhausted, depressed, defeated, frustrated, thwarted, hurting, and nearly sightless, guards hauled me away, legs banging behind, down the cellar stairs to a new hell. I recognized the smell of primitive earthiness, but they dragged me past my stinking coffin to the cage with the skull-like heads and skinny arms protruding. They dropped me. I hit the ground with a thud and turned my head enough to see guards unlocked the cell door and swing it out. One guard clubbed prisoners aside standing in the doorway, and they collapsed backwards in a wave like dominos. He kicked and shoved and cleared enough space to dump me inside. The cell door slammed. The lock clicked.

After a time, I pulled myself up. The cell, about twenty-by-forty feet, was filled with grimy, slat-thin, tattooed-faced men and the overpowering stench of excreta, sweat, and cigarettes that made my feeble eyes leak more. My body ached. Everything hurt: arms, hands, kidneys, belly, legs. There was no place to sit. Many of the prisoners raged and snarled like junkyard dogs. Slowly, painfully, using cell-bars as crutches, I elbowed my way through the horde, searching for a place to rest. I was five inches taller and thirty pounds heavier than most of the prisoners but never felt so isolated in my life. I didn't know a soul, and no one knew me.

As my eyes cleared, I made out the wall of granite blocks lined with bunks: four-tiered oak-planks built to last forever, like the pyramids in Giza, berths for sixteen men. The others slept on the dirt jammed together in an ideal breeding ground for tuberculosis, typhoid, and recidivism. There was a dull glow from light permeating snow through one high, horizontal, barred, cellar window. There was no water, no sink, no toilet, no toilet paper; there was a *parasha* — shit barrel — beneath the glowing window. Men stood, sat and slept without moving. I felt it wise to remain silent and did. I overheard mumbled conversations of successful rapes, robberies, murders, arsons, and heated complaints of skimpy rations of soup, bread, and *parasha* time, which, with barely any food to eat, was only seldom used. The cell was my home for the next two weeks.

Fortunately, at six-three and still two hundred pounds, I had the residual strength to demand, *and get,* a plank for three hours of sleep mornings after interrogation. When my sleep time was up, I commandeered a floor space beside the wall to avoid being stepped upon. Our food was served in tin cans three times a day: six, noon, and six. I missed breakfast due to questioning. Lunch was a cup of salt water, sometimes enriched with fish scales or beef innards and a hunk of black bread we craved. Dinner was rotten soup. There were no spoons, knives, or forks, but there was no need for them as there was no meat and not enough vegetables in the soup to require cutting. By the end of the second week, I had lost so much weight I looked like a scarecrow with a nascent beard, and I had grown as irritable as the other zeks.

Hungry men are belligerent men. Non-stop brawls flared over trivialities: matches, cigarettes, standing spots, sleeping spots, bunk time, and *parasha.* These incessant clashes lead to fierce attacks and desperate beating. No one interfered. Fights were painful but never fatal. There was also an unspoken code about sharing. When, rarely, food, clothing, cigarettes, paper, pencils, money, and stamps arrived in permitted parcels, one-tenth of the package was shared with the weakest *zeks*. I never saw shampoo, insect repellents, soap, or pesticides, which left our clothes crawling with lice and us scratching like edgy dogs.

At the end of my questioning the morning of January 13, 1992, my interrogator demanded that I give him a list of people who might want to send me parcels of permitted money, food, clothes, soap, stamps, and shampoo. I gave him Anastasia, Dad, Kahuna, and Ingrid's names and addresses.

I was allowed to sleep all that night of the 13-14th, and the next morning, at breakfast, Napoleon announced, "Fetisov, today's your trial day. Shower."

I smiled triumphantly. "At last!" I said. "A chance to tell my story."

I couldn't have been more wrong!

***

TWENTY-ONE

Amur Region Provincial Court, Blagoveschensk, Siberia
January 14, 1992

"Hurry up!" Napoleon snapped as I stepped out of the cell.

"What time does court begin?" I asked.

Napoleon looked at his 'Rolex.' "About nine. You've got two hours to eat and doll up."

Jeers, taunts, and catcalls followed me from the cell as the nasty little psycho and his Paul Bunyan-sized sidekick, snugly dressed in *shapki, valenki, perchatki, shineli, and pistolety* — hats, boots, gloves, greatcoats, and side arms — escorted me from the testosterone-saturated cell to the shower. That moldy relic of Stalinism had slimy lead pipes, rusty faucets, a feces-rimmed hole-in-the-floor, and a trough-sink. Fumes reeked so badly, I held my breath. There was no toilet paper, but I didn't need any; an unheralded benefit of a paltry diet made defecation once a week or less. I dug through a heap of 'washed' clothes — none for someone over six feet — and waited for those being ripped off a long corpse by a trustee. After stripping it nude, the trustee flung the clothes at me. A guard stabbed the deceased numerous times. Insurance. No one left the Popov Monastery alive.

I set aside the cold, stiff, woolen pants, shirt, and flannel footwraps and undressed. I tossed my licey clothes on the to-be-washed heap. Unlike my other shower three weeks earlier that was spent scrubbing off feces, in today's soap-less, icy jet, I darted in and out of the frigid blast, digging at crotch lice and scratching at dead skin, blisters, and festers clinging to loose skin hanging from my legs and arms. While I air-dried, I hacked off two-weeks of ruby stubble with a communal razor wired to a pipe. Still wet and shivering, I pulled on scratchy pants and shirt and swaddled my feet in flannel footrags, or *portyanki*. Bunyan dug through another pile and threw me a felt hat and a belted overcoat. Underwear would have been nice, bandages and ointments even better. I winced and hobble when the foot wraps bunched under the pads of my sore feet and the wool pants chafed bedbug sores. I wondered about the sanity of the martyred Thomas Becket in his hair shirt.

Showered, shaved, and dressed, I said, "Ready for truth to prevail."

Bunyan yanked my wrists behind my back and twisted them like he was tying a rope. Napoleon snapped on handcuff and wrestled leather mittens on my hands. We wound through the subterranean labyrinth to the staircase and up dark stairs to the sacristy, musty, dusty, and draped with cassocks, surplices, and the mildewed stench of unuse.

The duty sergeant, sitting at the altar-desk, was the same grumpy sergeant who had booked me weeks earlier. We snaked around the chancel, and he said in stentorian Russian, "Well, well, well if it's not Igor Vladimirovich. Your day for Russian justice, Americansky!"

"I hope they'll banish me from Russia for life," I said, referring to the traditional Czarist sentence for foreigners. My heart did not soar with optimism.

"Bank on it," he said derisively, and Napoleon gave me a shove.

I stumbled off the dais into the nave where agents in greatcoats and *shapkas*, earflaps down, smoked and studied files. In the Communist world, unemployment does not exist; men occupied every desk in the unheated sanctuary.

Outside, the day was still night, black and cold. Pollution obscured Venus, but dawn's first rays brightened the chemical smog in the east. I leaned against the church as my two escorts paused on the landing to chat, smoke, and exhale billows of formaldehyde, vinyl chloride, hydrogen cyanide, and 4,000 other chemicals into the air. As they gossiped, I watched a sliver of moon glow through the smudge and shivered when icy gusts rasped a jagged edge to the wind. But I gulped in the biting air hungrily, my first lung full of fresh air in weeks. The cold scorched my lungs, but not unpleasantly. Mucous dripped from my nose. I tried to wipe it off on my shoulder, but couldn't quite reach it, and it froze in stringy snotcicles. My eyes watered. My lashes froze. I curled up my bottom lip and huffed, but it did no good.

Disdainful of the bitter cold and snug in their thick outerwear, Bunyan lifted

Napoleon's wrist and glanced at his Rolex. Apparently still a few minutes early for court, they fired up five-cent-a-pack cigarettes again, hacked, coughed, spit, and continued their kibitz of Christmas week, the vodka swilled, the prostitutes laid. Neither attended church, but their wives had, and they guffawed at believers' futile prayers to a God gone AWOL.

For three weeks, I had been in the cold dark cell, and my flood lamp-burned eyes slowly grew accustomed to dawn's soft light. I discerned the vague outline of a hedgerow. Then, standing before us, dozens of fire-hydrant-shaped women in thick watchcaps and greatcoats so long they rested on their toes. The sky lightened, and the fire hydrants drifted closer. I distinguished faces and arms filled with packages. Beyond them, Monastery Lane was bordered by frozen birch trees that looked like skeletons standing at rigid attention and snow-covered fir boughs that had learned to bend in the wind. There were islands of brush in what used to be the monastery's lawns, and, to the south and China, thickets of pliable willows shimmered along the river bank. With hopeful eyes and noses as red as a drunk's, the women peered at us in silence over the tops of their scarves. Those in the rear edged forward. In the growing dawn's pervasive stillness, I heard the faint tinkling of boys' laughter. As the continence of night gave way to the luminosity of day, their silhouettes emerged shouldering hockey sticks that looked like rifles as they jostled down *Ulitsa Reeka.* Grandparents, stooped under the weight of years, waddled behind them like penguins.

A flock of the largest gray-and-black crows I'd ever seen swooped in to scratch for food. A scrawny black dog snuck toward them, belly to the ground, tail tense, tip twitching, ears pricked. Just as the mutt was about to pounce, the pigeons' wings flapped and fluttered off, their feathers trembling desultory snowflakes in the sunlight. With unrequited hope for breakfast lost, the dog slunk up onto the landing and sniffed me.

Napoleon said, "Watch," and he booted the dog over the heads of the first row of women. It hit the ground, yelped, and loped down *Monastyr Pereulok,* tail tucked between its legs, fearful look on his face when he glimpsed back over his shoulder. The women scowled at Napoleon. He laughed and took a final deep drag on his coffin nail.

Day lightened and brought the wind's sharpened intensity. Its bite reminded of my bitterly-stern, pushy, great-aunt, Harriet, a spinster and a capricious lady who comes and goes as she pleases and never knows how long she'd stay. I blinked several times in the sufficient light. On the river, boys hit slapshots in snow-free spots under the watchful eyes of elders, who, against better judgment, turned expectant eyes heavenly, seeking traces of an early spring. A lone girl pirouetted gracefully along the perimeter, casting shy eyes at the boys.

While my escorts smoked and gossiped, I studied the church. Seventy years of atheism had left it in appalling decay, a national tattoo that desecrated places of worship and left them in shameful decline or ludicrous use as repair shops, circuses, and prisons. Massive chunks of white-stucco clung to hanging lathes. In places, desk-sized slabs had broken off and crafted a stucco brim that rimmed the church. I could not see them but was certain the ornate Byzantine crosses had long ago been pilfered. The gilded onion domes listed drunkenly in flaky peels.

More women trudged down unplowed *Pereulok Monastyr* to the prison, bent over by the burdens of incarcerations and Christmas packages, plodding past birch trees as stiff and erect as West Point plebes and isosceles-shaped firs whose snowy arms swayed in the wind as if preening. At the end of the lane, across *Ulitsa Reeka,* there was enough light now to see Ivan's warehouse clearly. There was no sign of life. He'd fled to Egypt.

Except for Napoleon and Bunyan's chatter and wind whistling through nearby trees, there were no other sounds, and I relished the quiet amidst crumbling decay, the first near silence I had had since my arrest. In the cell, *zeks* argued endlessly, and this quiet gave me a few moments to think about the trial and Anastasia. Surely, the trial would be a kangaroo court, and I would be convicted. The judge would never listen to me, and I would probably get a slap on the wrist and a fine. I wondered how Anastasia was faring without the taxol I was to bring her. I wondered about the years I spent accumulating useless knowledge. Would philosophy help me if I was convicted? No. I would need new know-how, like rules of the criminal code, one that would define beyond doubt everything I would need to survive in jail if I were sentenced to a hellhole where honesty and caring are traded for toughness and an antithetical version of honor. I wondered if I could isolate within my mind the raw-edged sentiments needed to maintain a semblance of dignity in a crass life and survive brutal unknowns. I tried to recall what Elie Wiesel had said about surviving Auschwitz when his death was a certainty, but the night he spoke at Colby, I had dozed through most of his lecture.

An old woman stepped forward and pushed up her watchcap. Above her eyes, she had a square, weathered forehead. She tugged her scarf down. It exposed what looked like a badly wrinkled prune. She smiled at me from what was once her face. Her wide-set eyes and thick cheeks struggled to look happy.

"This is for my son," she said to me and meekly held up a package in mittened hands.

I jerked my head back several times, indicating my cuffed hands behind me. She understood.

To Napoleon, I said, "Why don't you take their packages?"

"We do," he said and sniggered. "Every three or four weeks. It's time to go."

He shoved me off the stoop and hopped down. I hit the ground, teetered, recovered, and followed Bunyan and Napoleon plowing through the women. Bunyan sent the old lady flying with the force of an NFL tackle clearing a path to the goal line.

From deep within her, the old woman pushed herself up, conjured the courage to follow us, and said, "Please take this torte to my son, Ivan Alexandrovich Bartniansky. I beg you, sir."

Napoleon flung his arm at the torte, sending it sailing like a saucer. It disappeared in a fluffy snowbank. His harsh response to an old woman's plea incited a verbal riot. "What about Slava Ivanovich Vsevolod, what have you done with him?" "Is Petor Arkadyich Trofim alive?" "Where is Sergei Dmitrich Yefim?" "Anatoly Ivanych Papp, what happened to him?"

Napoleon glared at them in silence, turned, and continued to the cop car. Having been bludgeoned for speaking, I remained silent and followed. The *Lada* was the ubiquitous blue-on-white of all Soviet police cars, crowned with a red bubble. In the dozen steps to the car, snow slithered through holes in my boots, wet my footrags, and froze my feet. Bunyan opened the *Lada's* rear door and shoved me belly-first into the minuscule space. I wrestled around and looked out the back window and shook my head at the wives, mothers, sisters, and girlfriends, all shackled immobile by totalitarianism.

Napoleon slammed my tinny door, opened his, and said, "That'll teach them."

Bunyan ground the starter until the dinky engine kicked over, jammed it into gear, and weaved around potholes down *Pereulok Monastyr*. We turned right on *Ulitsa Reeka* and left on *Prospekt Leninskaya* — Lenin Avenue — Blagoveshchensk's main drag. The six-lane avenue was bisected by tram tracks and bustled with bumper-to-bumper vans, trucks, and cars. There were *Ladas*, *Chaikas*, *Volgas* and more than a few mafia-owned Mercedes chauffeured by beefy bodyguards with sanctimonious owners perched in back wearing mink coats and displaying the arrogant confidence of wealthy criminals triumphant in Kremlin-backed support. Sidewalks were a beehive of activity, people hustling to work and babushkas pulling babies on sleds. After a sixteen-hour night waiting like winter bears for temperatures to rise out of the lethal range, they poured out of Stalinkas for fresh air with Shih-Tzus, Collies, Airedale Terriers, and a kinky-haired Cocker Spaniel whose golden booties matched its golden pelt.

Within minutes, we slid to a stop at the Amur Region Provincial Court, a gloomy, five-story, concrete edifice blackened by decades of industrial soot and one-hundred thirty-two years of exhaust fumes, thanks to Etienne Lenoir's gift to mankind of the internal combustion engine. My henchman escorted me up three flights of cold, dim stairs to an unmarked door and two new guards.

The courtroom was cold, dusky, and drab. Gray paint peeled down the walls; the windows were so grimy they appeared shuttered; the chairs were rusty, and three, cigarette-burned tables were stacked with papers and surrounded by six people. Incongruously, and in bizarre juxtaposition, above the judge's bench hung a colored photograph of Russia's first, last, and only democratically-elected president in one thousand years, the self-confident, rosy-cheeked, red-nosed, silver-haired Boris Nikolayvich Yeltsin. There soon appeared a short, squat, wattled judge with the sallow complexion of a Siberian and the slanty black eyes of a Mongol. He had big yellow horse-teeth when he spoke. At the two tables sat two lawyers in loose-fitting, black suits, yellowed-white shirts, and thin black ties. Guards shoved me to the table on the left, the defendant table, just like on Perry Mason. Completing the picture of Russian justice was a steno clerk, a fat, young woman with black hair, ends dyed red, sitting before the judge.

All conversation was in Russian.

I said to the guards, "I can't sit with my hands cuffed behind my back." They ignored me.

The defense lawyer, a gangly, pocked-faced man with a gray crew cut, cleared up my predicament with a silent palms-up gesture, indicating me to stand.

I shot him a baffled look. "I'm to stand during the trial? How about uncuff-ing me?"

"It's time for sentencing," he hissed through golden teeth.

My jaw dropped. "But there's been no trial; I haven't — "

He placed an index finger against his pallid lips and shushed, "Shhh."

"You call *this* Russian justice?"

I felt drained and defeated. I despised the system. I loathed the lawyer. Since my face always mirrored my emotions, I tried to wipe it clean. Being sentenced without a trial had to be one gigantic mistake. I told myself, *Easy does it; you'll get a chance to speak. Be cool, stay quiet.* But fate delights in the unexpected kick to the *cojones.*

I was looking for justice in a system devised by the Three Stooges, Marx, Engels, and Lenin.

The judge glared at me. In his stubby yellowed fingers, he twirled a flashy gavel — dark mahogany mallet, light oak handle. Abruptly he smashed it down on the sounding block. It sounded like a sledgehammer. The silence-shattering BANG echoed twice across the near-empty tribunal. I flinched. But I recovered quickly and rolled my shoulders back, eyes fixed on the far distance. At that moment, I saw Anastasia in her white wedding dress on the balcony at Canyon in Blowing Rock. She was gazing down at the multi-layered, blue-to-smoky, Blue Ridge Mountains sprawled out beneath her. I yearned to touch her, hold her, talk to her, and deep within my soul, I knew, at that very instant, I could not, and would not, ever again.

Without preamble, the judge adjusted his robe and asserted, in a high, squeaky voice, "The Russian Republic, Amur Region, Blagoveschensk Provincial Court, in accordance with Article Fifty-eight of the Criminal Code's Sections Two, Seven, Nine and Twelve, sentences you, Igor Vladimirovich Fetisov, also known as Troy Vladimirovich Locke of Blowing Rock, North Carolina, America, to five years deprivation of freedom in the corrective labor camp at Pevek, Russia, sentence to begin immediately, days granted for time served."

BANG!

My blood pressure soared. My heart thundered. I felt dizzy. Sick. I refocused my eyes from the far distance to the near distance and fixed them on the short, fat, robed, little weasel. I felt as alert and motionless as Michelangelo's David awaiting the approaching Goliath and craved his stone and sling. Once, playing middle linebacker at Watauga High, a pulling guard and fullback from Avery rammed through the center of our defensive and spiked me high and low, their helmets smashing into my chest and crotch. I hit the ground with enough force that the impact knocked every wisp of air from my lungs. I was unable to move, breathe, or speak. I was that paralyzed again. I wanted to scream but couldn't. The absurdity of a five-year sentence ricocheted around in my head. I tried to inhale and weaved. I felt my lawyer's steadying fingers on my shackled arm. I looked at him, eyes pleading for help. I tried to talk, but words wouldn't come.

"Shhh," my legal eagle cautioned again. "If you speak, you *will* get another five."

My eyebrows shot up at this fiasco. My anger turned to rage. Adrenaline charged through my body. I thought of Anastasia dying without the taxol. I thought how the lunar goddess of Communism was still pulling the tides of Russia's justice. Nothing had changed. Yeltsin's *"democratic"* Russia was the same old autocratic Russia.

"Your honor," I addressed the judge. "I have *not* stated my case." My voice was fury-swollen but respectful.

My lawyer whispered, "The evidence convicted you."

To my surprise, the judge said in a calm, shrill voice, "Mister Fetisov, you confessed to bringing undeclared money into Russia. You acknowledged purchasing an unregistered, illegal drug in China and smuggling it into Russia. You admitted leaving the Soviet Union without your father's permission in August 1974, years before he died, legless and handless on October 18, 1976, in Osh. Your confessions support your sentence. The five years will begin today, January 14, 1992, at" — he glanced up at the wall clock — "nine forty-five."

I was not surprised at the rationale. I was shocked at the revelation. "Papa died *when*?"

"Silence!" he ordered.

Every muscle in my body twitched from frustration at the lies and irrationalities. I was livid. Heartsick. Tired of being muzzled by an insane system in a country of violence, poverty, negligence, misinformation, overheated rhetoric, lies, and arbitrariness run by incompetents in an all-powerful bureaucracy that executes myriads of irrational laws. I had to tear off the rusty lock of bolshevism and let the truth out of its cage. The truth would exonerate me.

An icy rigidity took root deep within me. I brushed aside my advocate's caveat and began to speak, slowing and annunciating conscientiously, "Your honor, as a child my mother told me, *"Your Papa's life ended in Afghanistan before you were born.* She never told me he survived bedridden in Osh and unable to live a normal life. As for taxol, it is an *anti-cancer* drug for breast and ovarian cancers. It is *not* a narcotic. I bought it in China to save my wife's life because America has not yet approved it. Cancer is killing my wife right now, *today*. World scientists have studied taxol for thirty years. Clinical trials have concluded. America will be selling taxol within months. Taxol will save the lives of millions of women. Russia has the unique opportunity to lead the entire world in approving taxol for cancer today!"

"Silence!" the judge shouted. "You heard the sentence." With a sharp blow, he struck his ceremonial mallet against the sounding block again.

That WHAM was both a perceivable and symbolic punctuation that proclaimed the finality of the gavel-to-gavel gobbledygook. And by the luck and accidents governing life on earth, it plunged me compassless into *terra incognita*, thrown into an abyss where I'd blunder and lurch and always wonder what I was doing there.

The judge raised his gavel and let the mallet slide into his palm. He aimed the handle like a dagger at me and turned it to the door. "You — ," he said to the guards — "take Fetisov to the train. Now!" The judge scooped up his papers and vanished.

The guards, one tall and muscular with a hooked nose and beady eyes, one a little shorter and skinny as a scarecrow, snatched my arms, spun me around, and shoved me past the recording secretary. When she looked up, she wiped a tear from her eyes and started to speak.

"Write to my wife, please," I begged. "Let her know where and when I'm going."

"Shut up you dumb son-of-a-bitch," the thin guard snarled contemptuously.

He and his sidekick hauled me out the door and dragged me, stumbling, down the stairs. I tried to think of Anastasia but could only fixate on five years in jail. Five long years away from her. Five years irrevocably lost, never to be retrieved. Prison meant death for Anastasia, and images of her flashed through my brain, whirling tornadoes of fragmented memories. Would that be all I'd have left of her? Memories and sorrow and regret. I knew loss for the first time when Mom died.

Nothing had prepared me for the loss of life without Anastasia.

TWENTY-TWO

Blagoveshchensk to Vladivostok
January 14, 1992 – March 15, 1992

Gale-force winds pummeled Blagoveshchensk streets choked with waist-deep drifts that snow blowers cleaved into pristine canyons, burying corners under two-story mounds that artists molded into sculptures and kids in plastic wash-tubs swooped down and tumbled into muffled babushkas shoveling sidewalks. Tots wrapped in so many blankets they looked like cocoons rode in sleds pulled by grandparents. Workers, unfazed by yet another January blizzard battering Siberia, slogged to their wheels. Most Siberians jobs start at a civilized ten o'clock. Roadside cops waved batons to stop drivers, snarling traffic while extracting bribes for driving too fast, too slow, too close to the curb, too far from the curb, rebuff a bribe and go directly to jail. Cops have to eat, too, was famously explained to Dad by President Mikhail Gorbachev.

I had to clear my mind, calm fears and think.

The *Lada's* dinky engine strained mightily as we jarred over corduroy streets past gloomy office buildings. The weather sign on the SatCom Bank blinked minus 46° C, sounding even colder at minus 52° F when converted. Within blocks, the streets rotted to a jaw-rattling patchwork of potholes.

"Is the railroad station far?" I asked.

"Three kilometers north," the tall guard thundered. He was so towering tall his knees straddled the steering wheel; his elbows winged out like a seagull. He turned, shot me a malicious look, and blustered, "But you're going a *little* further north."

"Yeah," his cohort scoffed. "A thousand kilometers north of the Arctic Circle."

Knowing them implacable and incapable of changing anything, I remained silent and saw horrendous images of life in a top-of-the-world flash across my mind: Crumbling, Soviet-era building with no hot water, central heating, or indoor plumbing.

We slid to a stop in front of the railroad station. On the short drive, I had thought of an escape plan, figuring it had to be on the train, when the guard riding shotgun jumped out and yanked my door open.

"Get out!" he yelled at me.

I squirmed out of the backseat, stood, and, with hands cuffed behind my back, arched kinks out of my spine. The shameless homunculus booted me so hard I stumble into a line of babushkas in a threadbare overcoats and rubber boots selling tea to travelers from a row of steaming samovars. One helped me up. I thanked her. Inside the railroad station, it was marginally warmer from the body heat of seven dozen travelers and stupefied homeless dozing on benches or staring hungrily at pastry kiosks. I was preceded and followed by my two escorts. Wayfarers cast fleeting glances at me as we snaked through the sprawl of humanity and out the north exit to the platforms and furthest tracks' wood-slated cattle-car surrounded by six guards with AK-47s slung over their thick shoulders. They smoked and jabbered nonchalantly and appeared well-fed, laid-back, and toasty in their thick, blue, rabbit-hair *shapkas*, padded overcoats, and fur-lined boots with two-inch soles.

The sergeant of the guard, a tall, muscular, brut with piercing black eyes and a primitive, crusty manner watched me approach, staring silently like a feral child would. In that visceral, inert silence, everything seemed to slow down. Snowflakes seemed to individuate. Each flake became bigger and crystalline and drifted down beside the cattle car, as if in no hurry to reach the platform. Without uttering a word, he snatched my arm, spun me, unlocked my shackles, and tossed them to my escorts who were leaving.

"I heard yesterday you'd be here this morning," the sergeant snapped.

I yanked off the mittens, rubbed inflamed wrists, and poker-faced, "Before my trial, I'm shocked."

"Shut up," he growled and thumbed through a fat key ring.

He found the key, unlocked the cattle-car door, and rammed it over its icy track with a push and a kick from his nifty, fur-lined, blue boot. Duplicitously, he bent over from the waist and made a sweeping gesture with his arm, fingers raking snow. "*Entré vous, Americansky.*"

"*Merci beaucoup,*" I replied with identical balderdash, snout in the air, and stepped aboard, triggering a boot in the butt from him and a stony-eyed glare from prisoners I bowled over. I straightened, excused myself, and helped an old man up. I pulled on my mittens and looked for a place to sit. The door banged shut. The padlock clicked. The sergeant gave it a tug. Insurance.

Inside the cattle car, or *vagony*, it was dim, cold, windy, and standing-room only. It reeked of urine, feces, and smoke, part of the Soviet's *Gleichschaltung*[27] of Russian society. Of the one hundred-plus men in the *vagony,* most smoked. No one moved. No one spoke. The few who had heard my accent glared at me, menacing as pit bulls. At substantially over six feet, I was taller than everyone I could see, and, despite three weeks of rotten food, still, probably, the strongest. I was confident I could take on any two or three of these skeleton at once … but no more. I excused myself and sidled through the grimy, shivering bodies to take a spot beside a hole in the wooden siding near the rear. Within minutes, biting cold penetrated my overcoat, and I trembled violently. I tried to inch away from the hole. In that icy, gloomy isolation, my thoughts turned bitter at a lifetime of screw-ups that ended in this gigantic blooper. For the first time in my life, I knew, *really knew,* anguish. It sunk in. For *five years — eighteen hundred and twenty-five days,* I would be incarcerated. Life as I had known it was kaput. My life was now a collection of memories, memories no one could steal. That reality was of little comfort. I thought about my early years in Tver. Mom held three jobs to support us. I thought of my childhood infatuation with Nastia. I smiled thinking about my not wanting to leave for America. I thought of my school days in Blowing Rock and Boone, my college in Waterville, and the army and marriage and the manager's job at McDonald's. I wondered when the spark had first kindled my love for Nastia. Was it pushing her on a Tver swing or playing in the sandbox? With five years of nothing ahead of me but time, my mind roamed unhurriedly over the past, the days, months, and years. I must have been chuckling at some mental image when a *zek* huddled next to me scowled. He probably figured me deranged.

We waited hours in the bitter cold, grumbling, stomping feet, clapping hands, flaying bodies, anything to stimulate warmth. Men argued over space, cigarettes, insolent looks, snide remarks, and in what corner to make the toilet or *parasha.* John Harrington invented the flush toilet in 1596; it still hadn't made it to Blago 396 years later.

In mid-afternoon, daylight ebbed. Dimness became blackness at 3:30. Night brought an intensified cold parlayed by polar blasts piercing siding cracks. Hours later, a guard unlocked the cattle-car door and slid it open. A far-off platform light cast long weak shadows of several guards watching two *zeks* carrying a clattering box to the door. Behind them, two *zeks* tugged a cart that smelled yeasty.

"Stay inside the *vagony*!" a guard screamed. "Take one bowl from the box!"

The dishes ran out three men before me and two dozen other men, but we soon shared other zek-licked-out bowls, a timeworn Gulag tradition.

"Stay inside for bread!" another guard threatened. "Or you *will* be shot!"

The *zeks* pushing the bread cart jimmied it into the doorway after the bowls were gone, and I drooled at the smell of hot, yeasty, black rye. There was enough light to see that it had been hacked into (skimpy) half-pound chunks, just as regulations stipulated. It was laced with sawdust and hay, just as regulations did not stipulate. When it was my turn, I stuck out a mitten for the rye. Sawdust dusted my mitten like dandruff. I hefted it a couple times to test its weight. It felt light. No surprise. Rations were always light.

A gaunt prisoner shoved me aside and stepped out onto the platform to eye the cardboard box for the biggest hunk of black-bread. I stared at him, surprised, and nibbled my chunk. He pulled off a mitten and pointed a long, thin, grimy finger at a big end piece.

"That piece, please," he pleaded. "I'm starving."

The server gave him the indicated piece just as a guard whipped his AK-47 off his shoulder. He fired two rounds into the prisoner's chest at point-blank range. The prisoner dropped. Dead. Blood stained the snow. The guard raised his rifle and blasted skyward so he could tell his lieutenant he'd fired warning shots. Regulations apparently mandate warning shots.

I figured the execution would whip up passions; the *zeks* would bulldoze the guard. I was wrong. Unlike America where a cop-shootings set off riots and 24/7 media coverage, a corpse in a prisoners' *vagony* in Siberia did not slow down the bread line.

"Now, you filthy scum, stay inside or you *will* be shot, too!" the guard warned.

Zeks sidestepped the corpse as dispassionately as Americans sidestep starving sidewalk bums and heart attack victims who rarely trigger a glimpse. We reserve our rubbernecking for 100-car pileups and mass school shootings, guaranteed to draw whispered misinformation and inspire the talking heads.

I stood beside the door and watched sentient lice crawl to the crimson feast and felt a strange regret that the murder hadn't titillated any sympathy. The guard jabbed his bayonet deep into the corpse chest — no one escapes on his watch — and kicked it aside. The prized chunk of bread the man had died for fell out of his hand. Someone snatched it.

I heard a man complain the wagon lacked a stove to cook on, but no one seemed to care; bread was being served. Soup might arrive in the morning.

A professorial-looking prisoner shuffled up for his bread, and the trigger happy guard said, "Ivan Ivanovich" — all intellectuals were given that contemptuous nicknamed — "drag this stiff over there." He pointed his chin at the corpse and raised it at an overflowing trash bin worked by some ribby mongrels.

Ivan Ivanovich clenched his black-bread between horse-sized teeth and dragged the body to the Dumpster, leaving a bloody sitzmark as its tombstone. The mutts attack its nose and ears.

Shielding my bread with my crooked, left arm, I pushed through the car to the rear of the *vagony*, far from the site and coppery smell of blood. I pulled off both leather mittens and stuffed them in my pocket — mittens were prized by thieves — and palmed the bread to thaw it. When my palms grew numb, I held the chunk in my fingertips and huffed on it. As it thawed, sawdust sprinkled my hands. I wondered if I could digest sawdust or if it would sit in my stomach like the embalming elixir of the ancient Egyptians used to make mummies. They removed all the internal organs, except for the heart, salted the inside abundantly and stuffed the inside with sawdust like a Thanksgiving turkey.

The rye bread exuded a yeasty scent that sent my saliva glands working overtime. I clasped the frozen chunk between grimy fingers and began spinning it like a squirrel working an acorn, lathing off shaving. But chiseling with central incisors was exasperatingly slow, and my belly screamed for more, faster. I held the chunk to my lips and huffed on a corner until a thumb-nail-sized area turned spongy. The yeasty scent overpowered the sawdust's piney odor, and I nibbled off a hunk and rolled it around on my tongue. The scrumptious morsel was a textual delighted, a replenishing nourishment, a filet mignon. But, alas, rye bread gobbled in this fashion does not stop cravings, and my frontal cortex kicked in; reason reminded me of delayed gratification, and, when half-eaten, with great self-restraint, I squirreled the frozen half of my precious rye in my pocket. Tomorrow would be soup with no bread with it.

It was bitter cold. Long, stretched-out, arctic gusts wooed through siding cracks, drowning *zeks'* grumblings and all my thoughts except how to stay warm. As mutterings died down, the silence bore the soft music of a distant train. Minutes later the platform groaned. The *vagony* shook. Determined chugs smacked into us, a coupling. Steel wheels spun on steel rails. They spun again and caught. A slow rhythmic clicking began. Between slat cracks, I watched the platform pass, the station gate, signal disc, Stalinkas, long-forgotten wooden houses, and then Blagoveschensk's glow was snuffed out. The train's huffing escalated. A numbing cold skulked through the siding, tearing at bodies like an unseeable carnivore.

Northwest of Blagoveshchensk, the headlights of the occasional 18-wheeler roaring by on Amur 461 reminded me of my escape vow, *No one else but me can set me free*, and yanked on a slat so I could squeeze through. I planned to leap off the train, hail a truck and flee this lunacy. When the slat proved immovable, I yanked off my mittens, slid bare hands into the narrow space between them and tugged. No luck. I pushed men aside, stepped back, and kicked it hard. One broke. I pulled on my mittens, slid an arm through the hole, and tugged at the next rotten board. It broke. I put my shoulder against the slat below it and pushed until I trembled with exhaustion. It didn't budge. Felt-boot kicks didn't break it. After fifteen minutes of futility, I banged the broken boards back into place, gave up on this spot, and searched the length of the car, on both sides, for another likely rotten spot. Nothing. I resigned myself to failure, again, and moved to a small opening on the ice-slippery floor, squeezing in between bodies.

Dozens of *zeks* had watched my attempt, but no one offered to help, accepting their fate as unalterable. Without a word, I dropped to the floor and curled up with other bodies braided together like fornicating snakes. I longed for Anastasia, her warmth, her touch, her voice, and images of her cradled in my mind to a symphony of metallic-thumps of steel-on-steel and the rumble of stomachs and men's moans, groans, coughs, wheezes, sneezes, and farts.

I felt men brushing past to piss, steal hats and mittens, and exchange loot with truculent *Urkagans* — brutal, hardened criminals — for cigarettes. They'd opened for business next to the sliding door, announcing, "Four, hand-rolled cigarettes for a chunk of bread or pair of mittens; six for a hat; ten for a coat." I rose on an elbow and watched Ivan Ivanovich approach them. Bulked up in two overcoats, he traded the corpse's mittens and hat for a chunk of bread and a cigarette. Ivan wasn't your typical intellectual; he had had enough street smarts to strip the corpse bare.

On the floor, sleep wouldn't come. The culprits were the hard, frozen floor, the stench of unwashed bodies, and the nagging reminders of my lifetime of failures. Failure to escape Russia, secure the taxol, graduate from Colby, land a decent job, and even my failure to be decently wounded in Iraq. Being shot in the ass is a beggarly way to earn a purple heart. After a very long time, the clickity-clack cadence rocked me into oblivion, and I slept.

We arrived at Belorgorsk before dawn on day two (1,823 days to go). The train backed onto a siding; we waited all that day without food or water, breaking off sheets of ice coating slots to quench thirst. Arguments culminated in blows over cigarettes, straw, and a warmer spot to sleep. When a fierce *Urkagan*, a self-proclaimed murderer declared, "The left far-back-corner is our latrine," no one objected. Three frail men, huddled in that corner, butt-walked over a little.

Belorgorsk is at 51° north latitude. Daylight was five gloomy-hours long, and the temperature stayed far below freezing. We endured it in trembling silence, clinging together for warmth like widows lost in doom and despair. One old man spent his daylight picking up trampled stalks of straw. As the sun set about 3 p.m., he wedged into an opening next to the latrine, huddled over his fist of straw, ate the kernels, and sucked on the straw. When he finished, he flopped down on frozen urine to sleep. I pulled off a mitten, slid my hand into my pocket, and broke off pieces of bread for my one meal of the day. I ate every morsel and felt guilty for not sharing it with the straw-eater.

At sunrise morning three, I stepped over the straw-eater's corpse to use the latrine. When I finished, I picked up his weightlessness and laid it atop the others forming a cadaver-fence around the latrine. At noon, the cattle-car door slid open, and my heart skipped a beat. Two local *zeks* set a steamy tub of borscht in the doorway. Two other *zeks* put down a cardboard box of five-pound loaves of warm black bread cut into hefty chunks. The scent of hot vegetables and yeasty bread sent my saliva flooding. We scrambled for the doorway, shouting and shoving, and only stopped when a guard fired an AK-47 blast.

"One at a time!" he commanded. "Stay inside!"

We did. They gave us spoons. Those with spoons and soup tins lined up for portions, hovering over the borscht and black bread like mother hens over chicks. When my turn came, I noticed the hot tub had melted a crescent in the platform and hungrily said, "Dip deeply, please."

The server looked up at me, astonished. "*Americansky?*"

"*Da.*"

He shook his head, dug deeply, and filled my tin with beet slices, a hunk of pork, potato eyes, and one, small, green, cabbage leaf: Mana!

"Thank you," I said in English, knowing I'd never use English again for five years.

He gave me an empathetic look, reached in the cardboard box and produced a humongous chunk of warm black bread. I bit the rye and started chewing then slid the rest in my pocket for tomorrow. "Thank you very much," I muffled with a full mouth.

I returned to the latrine-end of the cattle-car and luxuriated in the fragrances, tastes, and textures of vegetables and meat, my first since our Christmas dinner in Blowing Rock. Soon after, in the weakening twilight, a train rumbled up, coupled with us, and we left for Vladivostok, nine-hundred miles southeast. Russia's southernmost city sits at 43° north latitude, like Portland, Maine, and the Trans-Siberian Express makes its 6,000-mile, ten-time-zones journey, Moscow to Vladivostok, (the distance from San Francisco to Shanghai), in seven days. The final leg, Belorgorsk to Vladivostok, takes the Trans-Siberian Express twenty-four hours. A Russian *Lada,* on notoriously appalling roads, makes it in 25 hours. Our odyssey took 61 days.

We spent weeks confined in overcrowded prisons in Birobiazhan, Khabarovsk, Lesozavodsk, and Ussuriysk awaiting trains with the willingness or the capacity to haul an ever-increasing number of *zeks* to the Pacific port for spring icebreakers' long slog north to the forests of Kolyma and mines of Pevek. Through those famished weeks we slept in our clothes, never showered, and ate once a day — and often less. We fought cold, lice, and starvation. Each city brought more prisoners, and as we increased, food portions shrunk and we grew hungrier. The little negligible quality there had been quickly dwindled as straw added to black bread helped bind the sawdust, and we brushed off the sawdust and masticated the chewy straw like goats. The pitiable soup waned to a concoction of mostly water laden with rotten potato peels, moldy cabbage leafs, fibrous beetroots occasionally enhanced with cockroach-infested fish and cattle innards, hair and scales. Skin ulcers, hair loss, festers, and diarrhea were common among us. Dozens starved en route, their bodies stripped of treasured clothes, their ribby cadavers stacked to cordon off the latrine. I saw thighs cannibalized but couldn't bring myself to join the feast.

All the prisons en route were crowded, cold, foul cornucopian clones putrid with feces, urine, death, and despair. Headcounts were taken twice a day, at dawn and twilight, and whenever we boarded cattle-cars. I preferred the freezing wagons to the icy prison cells as the train's rhythms, thankfully, quickly built to an allegro pace and mercifully dissipated the biting wind's stench of human waste and death. To avoid freezing, we sat and knelt huddled in knots or sprawled on the floor, spooned together, and floated on the quiet refuge of deflated dreams and looming misery. A few men relayed their stories, but most remained silent. I tried to face the loss of Anastasia and taxol by looking at it squarely, bracing myself solidly, realizing the full weight and implications of my five-year absence, the loss, hopelessness, and emptiness of the sentence for as far into the future as I could see.

Some petty squabbles, pushes, and shoves persisted over standing-room, sitting-room, denigrating looks, slander, bread portions, and cigarettes, but, mostly, silence prevailed. A few crazed souls muttered schizophrenic incomprehensibilities, but those waned as the days dragged on and the weakest perished. I recalled the isolation I'd felt the evening I'd taken the Moscow Metro jammed with commuters to Domodedovoskay for the night flight to Blagoveshchensk. This isolation-in-a-crowd was worse.

After a few attempts at conversations — my accent made men suspicious — I abandoned it and played the game, *What's My Line,* studying gaunt faces and torpid bodies in the rocking shadows, speculating on occupations, lives, and crimes as if I were Bennett Cerf. Once I developed a plausible scenario for a man, I'd move on to the next. This game took hours. When I finished with the men around me, I'd slid a hand along icy siding-slats, step over legs and arms, and wedge into another spot toward the rear with a new cast of contestants. At the latrine, the men presented a challenge. What possible crimes could a clutch of grandfathers have made to land them aboard this Orient Express? I was dwelling on that conundrum and dreaming up scenarios, when one of the men, a cordial-looking, white-bearded, white-haired, knavery-faced, old geezer with eyes that mirrored everything he had ever seen, smiled at me. He looked like a skinny Hemingway at eighty-five — had it not been for Ketchum. He sat with three others *zeks* next to the corpse-fence ringing the latrine. I watched him watch me for a time as he continued in a one-way, but respectful, conversation with a slat-thin, scraggily-bearded, vacant-eyed old man with a caulk-white face tattooed in Jesus scenes: Cross, Last Supper, and Lazarus rising. When I broke off a hunk of ice to wet my parched lips, he smiled again, brushed a mop of white hair off his eyes, and beckoned me to join him.

I was moved by his comity and pushed up off the floor. I slapped snow off my coat and took careful steps over legs and arms, swaying to the very rear of the rocking train as it plowed east over frost-heaved tracks. My lurching earned me snarls, growls, and scowls, but I made it to the old man's side without a blow, wondering if the feces and urine might make me gag. It didn't. The latrine corner was as odorless as a fall day. The stench of cadaverine and puterscene, the proteins formed from decomposing meat, radiates a nasty tang but not from frozen cadavers with little meat on their bones. Someday archeologists will probe these corpses and conclude, *For a civilized people, Russians ate like mice.*

With the toe of my boot, I nudged tattoo face's leg over and dropped down beside the old man. His feet were the size of snowshoes. This close, he appeared to be on the far side of eighty, but his eyes twinkled, and his smile engaged like that of a teenager. He pulled off a leather mitten and extended a long, thin, papery hand speckled with so many liver spots it looked like a brown trout.

I pulled off mine, and we shook. He said, "How nice it is to be studied by someone not stalking Pushkin intellectuals." *In English!*

I was flabbergasted. His English had a surprising European-Yiddish lilt, a legacy of his many Jewish classmates in Denmark I soon learned. He had also used the derogatory term mother used when she overdosed on Dad's philosophy and called him a Pushkin intellectual.

"English?" I said with a wide, crooked smile that cracked open interrogation wounds at the corners of my mouth. "How'd you know I spoke English, Mister — ?"

"Hanrik Severinovich Seeliganov," he said, smiling mischievously. "I thought you might get to me eventually in that game you've been playing. What may I call you?"

My head was still reeling in disbelief, but I managed, "Troy Locke."

Seeliganov tucked enough scraggly white locks under his felt hat to reveal intense blue eyes. "You have a strange name for a Russian, Mister Locke."

"Troy, please," I said. "You have a strange name for a Russian, Mister Seeliganov."

"Once upon a time, my surname didn't have the suffix." His eyes fixed on mine. "Locke wasn't your birth name." More a statement than a question.

"No, sir, I was born Igor Vladimirovich Fetisov and adopted as a kid. Last month I was a McDonald's manager; today I am a convicted felon bound for Pevek, wherever the hell that is."

"We both are destined there." Seeliganov paused for a moment. "Igor was your name before you were adopted and immigrated to America?"

"Immigrated and then adopted. How'd you know?"

"Locke is a British name. But your sun-bleached hair, tanned face, American accent, and casual mannerisms, unknown to Soviets, says American. I'll bet your step-father is English."

"Boy is he ever," I said and smiled to acknowledge his accuracy. "Do I detect a trace of Europe and Yiddish in your English; Dutch, perhaps?"

"Danish. Mama insisted on teaching me English."

Seeliganov's intelligent face sank into forgotten reflections and appeared on the verge of tears. But he shook that off, raked his frosty beard with stick fingers and said, "I didn't like this beard at first, but it grew on me."

I said, "Witty," but it was lost in steel-on-steel screeching as the train suddenly clattered to a long, jerky stop.

"A Cyclops-eyed, west-bound express will soon be barreling through; we going onto a siding," Hans said, grabbing an upright. His face was strained and wrinkled with the echoes of childhood. Once his balance was regained and the trained slowed, his face took on a look of expectancy as if he planned to disembark, but that look reverted to one of despondency, wretched in the knowledge that we were on this train to stay. His wretchedness almost made me bawl.

I touched his arm. "Tell me about Denmark, Hanrik."

He sighed, regaining control. "Call me Hans; that's what my parents called me, Hans."

Our train stopped. Hans paused for some seconds as Trans-Siberian Express whooshed by, and there was a far distant look in his eyes. When it was quiet again, he relaxed and said, "Long before World War Two and our arrest would be a good place to start. I was born the February the Tsar was overthrown."

"Nineteen-seventeen," I said. Troy Locke, historian.

Hans nodded. "We lived on a ten-acre farm near Copenhagen, a few kilometers across the Baltic Sea from Malmö, Sweden, and close to the bridge now going up to connect our countries. I was a happy child, tending animals, studying lessons, playing outside. My parents were teachers, Papa, French, math, Mama, English. Papa and I fished in the long Baltic summers." He smiled broadly. "I wish I'd remained a fishermen. When I was sixteen, we spent Christmas with my father's older brother, Thor. He'd married a Ukrainian girl and taught English and anthropology at Dnipro University in Odessa. That December, it was too cold to swim in the Black Sea, so we visited museums to see recently-recovered relics of the Black Sea Deluge — "

I threw up a hand. "Whoa, Hans! What's that?"

"Anthropologist and archeologists have new evidence of a breach in Istanbul's Bosporus Strait. It flooded the Black Sea five thousand years ago."

"Really?" I said skeptically. "Never heard of it."

"Long ago, both the Caspian and Black Seas were fresh-water lakes far below sea level. Today's Caspian Sea is still ninety feet below sea level. Scientists determined the Black Sea had been five hundred feet below sea level! The massive Bosporus Strait breach set off a years-long, cataclysmic inundation as the Mediterranean poured in and flooded the Black Sea basin."

"That's two thousand years before Homer. Is there any proof?"

"The first great work of world literature, The Epic of Gilgamesh, is one. It was carved on Mesopotamian clay tablets and dates back to that period. Those writers were certain the Black Sea flooding was the basis for their epic tales."

"I've never heard of that Epic, but literature is full of deluge stories."[28]

"Sure it is. But the Epic of Gilgamesh is a translation of wedge-shaped characters carved in clay and known as cuneiform. These were man's first recordings, long before the Noah's Ark story. A second, more convincing proof is the undersea explorations that discovered people lived far below the surface of the Black Sea on the shoreline of a small, freshwater, Black Sea."

"Interesting. So what happened during your family's Odessa holiday visit?"

"The last night we were there, we'd taken mineral baths in a plush spa, ate piping hot Ukrainian borscht and *varenyky* — dumplings — and the adults drank vodka-spiked and fruity *uzvar*. They gave me a sip. We'd a great time with Thor, his wife, and friends, but at two that morning, three Soviet agents pounded on Thor's door, waking us sleeping on the floor. They searched our belongings, wrote a search protocol, arrested Papa and Thor, and took them off. Without a trial, the brothers were sentenced to Kolyma for twenty years for plotting to subvert the Soviet Union."

I was incredulous. I grabbed his thin arm. "Whatever for, Hans?"

Hans looked grim. "For talking to their friends about life in Denmark. The other Ukrainian couples had asked about life in Denmark. Work, car, home, the usual questions with which foreigners pepper Soviets. One man, hearing my parents' salaries, was so envious he made us nervous. Another man, a shipbuilder, mentioned Stalin was confiscating foreigners' property and arresting them. Later, I overheard father and Uncle Thor whispering that he and Olga should leave with us at six in the morning. They had grown frightened and agreed. But — "

"One of your dinner guests squealed later?"

"Unfortunately, yes." Seeliganov leaned forward and rested his forearms on his knobby knees, fully possessed with his childhood horrors. "Mama, Olga, and I were arrested the next morning. They were sent to a labor camp in the Altai Mountains south of Barnaul, Siberia. I never saw them again. I was sent to an orphanage near Tolstoy's Yasnaya Polyana where my name was mongrelized, and I learned Russian. Since I was already fluent in two languages, I was assigned as a tourist guide on the estate. Mostly, though, I was the flock's watchdog. Tourists were rare, and I spent my days tending sheep and nights reading in Lev Nikolayevich's library. I loved reading and was self-taught."

I smiled. "Like Abe Lincoln. Did your Papa and Thor survive Kolyma?"

"Papa did. Thor didn't. The Gulag killed him." Hans looked at me with watery eyes. "Papa was freed after Khrushchev condemned Stalin and demolished his reputation in his secret speech in nineteen fifty-six, railing about Stalin's intolerance, brutality, abuse of power, repression, and physical annihilations of innocents. Khrushchev emptied the Gulags. Dad spent the next two years finding me and looking for my mother. He tried to get us exit visas for Denmark, but … " Seeliganov shook his head.

I gently squeezed his bony arm. "I'm sorry, Hans. What was the difference between your uncle and father; why didn't they both survive?"

"*Work*," Seeliganov said forcefully. "Papa took pride in the accomplishment of and dignity of daily work, no matter what he did or for whom he did it. Work saved his life. He worked fourteen- to sixteen-hour days, always filled his daily norm, and sometimes got a little extra bread with his gruel. Thor refused hard work, got starvation rations, and died the winter of thirty-four." I was silent for a while and then asked, "Suppose that'll be our fate, Hans?"

He grinned, exposing peat-stained teeth badly in need of a dentist. "Nah, we're too smart. We'll work hard in Pevek or freeze to death." He laughed. "Did you know Pevek is at seventy degrees north latitude, the northernmost of Russian towns, and freezing ten months a year?"

"No I didn't, but it sounds breathtaking."

Hans laughed. "Fortunately, the earth has a molten core that warms the mines. We'll have a warm place to work and sleep and enough food or we'd perish. The Kremlin wouldn't get its minerals mined otherwise."

"True," I said. "But how did Russia ever find precious minerals in such a hell hole?"

"History, Troy," Hans said. He chuckled. "Your ancestors were persistent.

In seventeen eighty-five, Catherine the Second commissioned Joseph Billings, an Englishman, to map eastern Siberian and the Alaskan coast. Billings found the settlement called Pevek by natives on a bay a few days sail west of the Pacific. The name Pevek comes from a variation of the *Chukchi* word, *Pagyt-kenay*, meaning smelly mountain. A battle fought on the site between the indigenous *Chukchi* and *Yukaghir* left hordes slaughtered. Neither tribe buried their dead and rotting flesh made a stench during the short summers when the victorious *Chukchi* pastured reindeer there."

"Sounds like Shangri-La," I said. "Why would a sane person live there?"

"Oh, there's been progress," Hans said with a flinty laugh. "Corpses are now tossed in open pits and buried in July when the permafrost thaws. In nineteen twenty-six, Soviet geologists discovered tin, gold, mercury, coal, and uranium in its mountains. Stalin arrested thousands, banished them to Pevek, and launched his mining program. At its peak, Pevek had twelve thousand miners, families, guards, but mostly prisoners."

"So," I said, "if we fulfill our daily norm and don't freeze to death we might make it?"

Hans studied me a long minute, and in his stoic imperturbable manner said, "You will, Troy. Me? I'm seventy-five, too old, too tired, and too frail."

I was about to refute that when a thug barreled through the prisoners, shoved a feeble old man aside, and pulled out his schlong. The old man fell on top of me, and I helped him up. The goon splattered urine on the pyramid of corpses and dribbled the last drops on the straw-eater's face. It froze instantaneously, giving the gray face a jaundiced tint. The thug put his horse back in the barn, buttoned up, and left, without so much as an 'excuse me.'

I said, "You *will* survive, Hans, I'll help you."

"You're kind," Hans said. "But if the cold doesn't get me the radon will."

I shot him a puzzled look. "Radon?"

"A colorless, odorless, radioactive gas that seeps into mines and cellars from decaying radium, thorium, and uranium. It causes twenty thousand lung cancer deaths a year."

"Never heard of it. Is it new? I'm surprised my geology prof never mentioned radon."

"New? It was discovered the year the French Revolution began."

"The year George Washington became our first president, seventeen eighty-nine."

"Educators sanitize the world for the young. Like gold, uranium's a heavy metal and the source of tremendous concentrated energy common in the earth's crust. Mine shafts are dug along tin, gold, copper, and silver veins. That exposes miners, us, to radioactive uranium and radon, and their charged particles cling to dust. When it's inhaled — " Hans shrugged.

And I finished his thought, "People die. Can't you mine gold and skip the uranium?"

"Impossible. Once an ore vein is located, shafts are sunk, and crosscuts dug horizontally at various levels to work it. Tunnels follow veins, some up, some down, some sideway. Most are later filled with tailings, the waste rock. Pray, we get latrine duty."

"But you're a professor, Hans, surely they'll find an academic niche to use you."

"Wrong. They're not interested in schooling, and I know nothing practical. You'll fare better you can cook."

I'd had enough of radon and guessing and changed the subject. "How'd you end here?"

Seeliganov grinned broadly. Deep crinkles formed around his eyes. His smile exposed gaps of several missing teeth. "On American Christmas Day, Mikhail Sergeyevich dissolved the Soviet Union and resigned, and I celebrated by giving a soapbox speech to celebrating Russians on the demise of Communism and birth of democracy. In it, I mentioned your First Amendment."

"The hands-off religion, free speech, and free press speech one?"

Hans nodded and clapped his mittened hands. "Yes, and they loved it."

"They'd never heard the litany of inalienable rights?"

"No, and I gave it at the Tomb of the Unknown Soldier."

"A propitious time and place to bury totalitarianism."

"Yes. But the antediluvian wizards guarding the Kremlin didn't agree. You might say, I had a landslide off my soapbox! The lackeys arrested me just as Tolstoy warned they would do in *Karenina: The danger lies not in the hydra of revolution, but in the tenacity of traditionalism, the holding back of progress by the Bolsheviks.*"

"Didn't you screamed for help?"

"It did no good." Hans tilted his head back and laughed until tears ran down his cheeks. "Those poor intolerant fools. The Cold War is over; Russia is a shell of its former self; corruption is rampant; everyone wears blue jeans and listens to Michael Jackson, and the ruling *côterie* take their jobs so seriously they ignore reality."

"Russia's not alone," I said. "America suffers from myopia, too. We act like world cops, but we can't afford to be. We're lousy at preventing wars and worse at concluding them."

Seeliganov gave that some thought. "Yes, America *was* dragged into World War One, World War Two, Korea, and Vietnam."

"All started with Democrats in the White House," I said.

"And ending with the abominations crafted at Versailles, Yalta, Potsdam, and Panmunjom with America fleeing Vietnam with its tail between its legs." Hans made a push-off motion with his hand. "But enough of that, how did *you* end up here?"

The train had gathered speed, and I started to half shout but couldn't. My throat was parched. I scraped ice off the siding and put it in my mouth. It melted, and I said, "It's a long story."

"We've nothing but time."

I began my story in sunny Florida and ended with my arrest, jail, trial, and Pevek sentence. In summary, I concluded, "Hans, the sorry truth is our Food and Drug Administration, known by its letters F-D-A, exercises control over all drug development in America; it holds life-and-death over millions of our people. In Anastasia's case, her breast cancer could not wait for taxol's approval. That wait has already killed forty thousand women a year for the thirty years while the FDA knew taxol was a cure for sixty-six percent of them. Fortunately, Chinese taxol is available to the world if women could buy it. Now I plan to sell Chinese taxol to the world."

Hans smiled and gently squeezed my arm. "Right after this nine hundred mile jaunt to Vladivostok, the four thousand miles icebreaker ride to Pevek, and five years in a mine."

I grimaced. "Yeah, there's that."

Seeliganov talked like my Dad, thought like him, and he became best friends. If I was Quixote, he was my sidekick, Sancho.

On March 15, 1992, the temperature inside the cattle car warmed noticeably and slat ice dripped down the siding. I stood and stretched and squinted through the slats at something unbelievable: water.

"Hans, look, there's *water*!" I yelled. Just then the train's C-hook couplings clattered and clanged as the train slowed, entering Vladivostok. "And apartment buildings, shops, cars, highways, factories, civilization!"

"I've been here when I work in the Sakhalin Islands. We're nine thousand kilometers from Moscow and home of Russia's Pacific Fleet. The city of six hundred thousand sits on the tip of the Muravyov-Amursky Peninsula, an eighteen-mile-long, seven-mile-wide headland known as *Haishenwai*, or Sea Cucumber Cliff, in Chinese."

"Are we close to China?"

"Less than one hundred miles to China and North Korea," Hans said.

"I wonder why Vladivostok isn't Chinese."

"It used to be. The Chinese ruled the region for centuries until they ceded it to Russia in eighteen sixty after the Qing Dynasty was defeated by the British in the Opium War." Hans stood. "You'd better stand too, or you'll get trampled."

After a two-month trek of wind-whipped blizzards crossing Siberia, the warm, salty air felt exalting. It brought every *zek* to his feet like a five-alarm fire drill. Men shoved and elbowed for a peek at the port city rolling over bay hills, looking like San Francisco's six thousand miles east.

"Troy," Hans said as we banged to a stop, "you're going to love the Vokzalnaya Railroad Station and think you've been there before."

"I've never been to Vladivostok. Impossible."

"It's a clone of Moscow's Yaroslavsky Rail Station, the busiest in Moscow."

"Haven't been there, either."

"Oh." Hans appeared surprised. "Well, take a look."

I peered through cracks and saw an impressive, yellow-plastered, sprawl of station. It had a metal-hipped, fairy-tale roof, gabled windows, pillars, reliefs, and glazed-ceramic images. The building was adorned with mosaics of birds, berries, and fruits. The *zeks* jammed the doorway like rush-hour metro commuters in Moscow's *Krasnaya Ploshad* — Red Square Station. Guards unlocked the doors and shouted, "Outside, you pigs! Line up four abreast!"

For twenty minutes, two thousands of us unloaded, weak and stiff as octogenarians. We hobbled and shuffled out of a string of cattle cars, formed a long, raggedy line, and traipsed through the railroad station. I admired the Japanese flagstone underfoot and the glazed images on the walls. Outside the front door, a restored steam engine stood beside a sign that read: *Here your majestic train ride ends after a 9,288 km journey from Moscow.* I glanced a final time at the station's long, gaudy stretch of yellow-plastered protrusions, gewgaws, sweeping arches, turrets, and showy reliefs, turned to Hans and said, "Looks like Claude Monet designed it."

"A bit much, isn't it?"

The Vokzalnaya Railroad Station's had the overall impression of — pick any building on the Champs-Élysées — a French edifice on overdrive.

In the parking lot were buses, vans, trucks, trams, motorcycles, taxis, bikes, and Japanese cars, all spewing thick, black, exhaust plumes that helped mask our fustiness. But we didn't need a ride to the transit camp, *Vtorya Rechka.* We walked.

"RIGHT TURN, MARCH!" a guard yelled, and the hodgepodge of scuzzy, ragged, starving *zeks* snaked north onto Aleutskaya Street and east on Svetlan-skaya. We plodded through districts crowded with apartments, markets, repair shops, jewelers, museums, hairdressers, office buildings, dry cleaners, banks, skyscrapers, churches, and the ubiquitous statue of Lenin on a round-about near McDonald's. Sidewalks were jammed. Markets were crowded. The air hung thick and vibrated with exhaust fumes from rumbling buses, wailing sirens, woofing dogs, and the clanging of a tall, gothic, Catholic Church bell.

Armies of babushkas swept the streets of rubbish, but even the stench of exhaust fumes fortified with garbage could not mask the stench of our bodies. It was a long, smelly march through a surprisingly modern city. Little kids pointed at us and wailed. Moms herded them to the far side of the sidewalks, far from the criminals.

The last quarter mile was a steep hill. The Vladivostok transit camp sat atop a broad knoll overlooking the city to the west and a foggy sweep of Pacific Ocean to the east. A purple-black pall spewed from a flotilla of exhaust stacks and hung immobile in the thick, damp air.

At the transit camp conditions worsened.

With its enormous prisoner population, the camp was a distinct nation, a world unto itself.

It had a caste system, code of conduct, and unique language — an amalgam of criminal slang, prison terms, and curses. For instance, stealing personal pos-sessions was acceptable; taking bread brought a swift and brutal death. Atop the camp's hierarchical caste reigned the hardened criminal, *urkagans,* then the street thugs — *ulichnyye bandity* — followed by political prisoners — *polit-zaklyuchennyye* — and trustees, or *pridurki.* At the bottom were goners, the *dokhodyagi,* men so weak from malnutrition and disease they scavenged garbage dumps strewn with decaying bodies and potato peelings to sustain their short journey to death. In the morning, the night's corpses were stacked at the barrack doors. They warmed enough on sunny days to reek before *dokhodyagi* dragged them to the dump.

Menacing *urkagans*, the thieves, rapists, and murderers, frightened the guards who warily entered the barracks in pairs for headcounts at reveille and bed-check. We socially friendly people, the bookkeepers, professors, barbers, bathhouse attendants, cooks, factory workers, students, shopkeepers, plumbers, electricians, and one McDonald's manager cowered to one side and kept tabs on the *urkagans*. And yet it was us, not the *urkagans*, who were despised by the camp guards. They had no fear of us having switchblades or shanks. They feared the written word: newspapers, letters, and cards, any trace of culture, knowledge, or rebellion that might seep through camp. Possessing a pencil and paper was a crime.

We ate three times a day: six, noon, and six, but as the number of *zeks* increased the gruel thinned, the spoiled vegetables were scarcer, and even the cockroach-infested innards disappeared. Extra sawdust laced the black bread, which Hans claimed had more glucose in it than a Snickers candy bar. He maintained, "The smaller your body shrinks, the bigger your brain grows. Starving increases cell tissues in the frontal-temporal lobes and hippocampus."

"Swell," I said. "I'll be Einstein then starve." I paused, scowling. "That's counterintuitive."

"It is. But for a million years, our ancestors' brains had to learn how to deal with starvation. Gluconeogenesis kept *Homo sapiens* alive. When food stopped, and it often did throughout our evolutionary history due to game migration and a host of other reasons, metabolism shifted, and new glucose molecules were created from amino acids taken from muscle protein to feed the brain. It gave mankind time to think of a way to find more food."

I laughed. "So we'll be a brainy weakling?"

"Not that either. After three days, your liver will crank up and use body fat to create brain fuel to preserve your muscle mass."

I smacked Hans on the back. "Smart, muscular, skinny, what every health nut dreams of."

We spent our transit camp days in the yard, talking politics and philosophy in small groups while watching, transfixed, by the hypnotic surf crashing in. When temperatures dropped below freezing, we huddled inside and continued talking. Beatings were common for trivial offenses. Staring at *urkagans*, objecting when *urkagans* stole clothes off your back or refusing to give them your bread. As one of the tallest and strongest *zeks*, I never had a problem and protected my friends.

At reveille, guards entered the barracks banging steel pipes on iron wheel rims and screaming, "Up you filthy pigs! Get your asses up!"

One morning when I climbed down from my fourth-tier plank, the man sleeping next to me didn't move. A guard reached up and beat him with a truncheon. He still didn't move.

"Might be dead," I said.

"Let's see." The guard pulled a hunting knife from his belt. He grasped the two-by-four bed post, swung onto the lower plank, and sunk his knife into the man's chest. He did not move. The guard snarled, "Haul him outside."

I climbed up the bed, grabbed the man's collar, and yanked, his heels thumped down. He didn't weigh ninety pounds. Rigor had set in; his body was mummy-stiff. His body fluids slicked my hand, and I lost my grip. His head whacked the cement floor, sounding like a baseball bat hitting a watermelon.

"This body is so stiff," I explained to the guard, "it means he probably died before midnight."

"Do I look like a wife who gives a shit? Haul his sorry dead ass out of here!"

For thirty long days, from the Ides of March to mid-April, we waited in the Vladivostok Hilton for the ice to break enough to reach Magadan, the Kolyma Region's *zek*-built capital of 150,000. Most prisoners were destined for its forest and mines and slow deaths.

I didn't know it at the time, but my luck was soon to change.

***

TWENTY-THREE

Leaving Vladivostok
April 16, 1992

At seven o'clock on a chilly, foggy, mid-April morning, a scraggly two thousands of us *zeks* shambled down the hill, overlooking the Pacific Ocean, to a sprawling shipyard shrouded in smog and clogged with ships. Crews in foul-weather gear slogged through the chemical miasma, readying dinghies, cutters, sloops, and one highly-restored wooden yacht whose varnish reflected the choking photochemical-haze brewed by ultraviolet radiation interaction on hydrocarbons, oxides, and nitrogen, or so claimed Hans. There was a single-funneled freighter with forests of booms and derricks on fore and aft decks, a sailboat on spring lines, two tankers, fishing boats, two container ships, a barge with dredging shovels resting amidship, and a sleek four-mast schooner with sails being unfurled. There was a visiting destroyer, flying the Union Jack, and a Russian submarine, heavily guarded, its periscope protruding from the conning tower. A football-sized field, our staging area, was across from three freighters and an icebreaker. We stopped there and were counted off in four unequal groups.

My band of 250 followed Sleepy, a yawning seaman, to the five-deck *N. S. Rossiya.* Sleepy stopped beside the gangway, scrubbed his eyes, and began, "You're boarding a 1988, *Arktika*-class, nuclear-powered icebreaker built in Saint Petersburg. It has a double-hull; its deck is four hundred eighty-five feet long, and it's one hundred eighty feet tall with a draft of thirty-six feet."

I noticed something odd — no davits projecting with lifeboats — and wormed my way to the front of the hodgepodge and shouted,

"Where're the lifeboats?"

Sleepy smiled slyly. "There ain't none on icebreakers. If the *Rossiya* sinks, skate."

"Right," I said as Hans came panting up beside me and grumbled, "He just might do that to yesterday."

I stared at the frail old man. "Are you losing your mind?"

"You'll see." He shot me a sardonic look. "When we get there."

"To yesterday?" I snapped my head to disperse his nonsense.

The bulk of prisoners shuffled past the *Rossiya* to three, oil-powered transports, sitting low in the water, provisioned, engines stoked, funnels smoking, ready to resupply *zeks* and wares to Magadan. Walking up the gangway, Sleepy came alive.

"The *Rossiya's* got a swimming pool, sauna, cinema, library, and gym" he bragged. "Its two nuclear reactors generates seventy-five thousand horsepower each, enough to drive its twelve-foot propellers twenty-four miles an hour, cruising, and twelve miles an hour in ten-foot ice."

"Impressive," I said. "How much uranium does it devour a day?"

"A pound, enough to power a small city. If we burned oil, we'd use a hundred tons a day."

"Doubly impressive!" I said. "What happens to the spent fuel rods and old reactors?"

Sleepy pointed at his feet. The Arctic Ocean is a vast nuclear dumping ground.

We stepped onto the icebreaker's main deck and followed the line to a dimly-lit labyrinth of companionways leading to the cargo hole. After months of close-quarter confinement, I needed fresh air not another enclosure and tapped Hans on the shoulder.

"Let's go aft and watch the *Dalstroi, Marilee,* and *Kapitan Daniliken* board," I said and so we did.

We dawdled on the fantail and were the last getting to the cargo bay to claim our berth, the cold, hard, steel deck. After a roll call, guards announced, "You're free to go topside. If you jump overboard and try to swim ashore, you'll find the water freezing, experience cold shock, cardiac arrest, hypothermia, and die."

Although exhausted and starving from the morning's march to the shipyard and lack of food, the rattle and clatter of the anchor chain scraping through hawse holes beaconed. We hurried to the starboard side and watched dock crews cast off mooring lines from the wharf's mushroom-shaped steel bollards bolted to the dock. Lines were stowed, starboard thrusters activated, and she pushed sideways away from the dock. The *Rossiya* vibrated all over like Leftovers did when shaking off a bath. Her propellers reversed, and the massive icebreaker backed slowly, creating a foamy froth under the fantail. She came about, nosed east into the channel, and we sailed from Vladivostok on noon's high tide. The *Rossiya* led the convoy in tandem south-southeast into an onshore breeze and mild chop from the incoming tide.

We went forward. With the wind in my face, I felt free. We turned and watched Vladivostok disappear and then, from the forepeak, high above the globular bow, we stared at towering cliffs pocked with a million nesting peregrines, soaring and dipping and filling beaks with insects for hatchlings. Geometry[29] tells us the horizon is a little more than three miles away for a person six feet tall before earth's curvature blocks your view. At the bow, three stories above the sea, we could see about twenty miles. It felt joyous to set eyes on green cliffs, leafy woods, and sandy beaches as we plowed toward Japan and the shore drifted by us. After a while, we were ordered to the mess for soup and bread, after the crew had eaten, of course. After lunch, most prisoners returned to the cargo hole for naps. But Hans and I opted for the bow and the smell of the ocean and the view of Russia's easternmost towns of Dunay and Nakhodka gliding by as we entered the Sea of Japan.

There, a light chop and five-foot rollers occasionally sent cold spray over the bow rail, which felt restorative against my beard. The day stayed mild, and Hans and I didn't mind the light shower plowing eastward, hats in hands, overcoats flapping, wetness dampening our grimy hair. Once out of the clasp of the Siberian landmass, the sky turned from colorless murk to a cerulean blue and the temperature notched up to sixty degrees. Gulag horrors evaporated with the vanishing Russian horizon.

"The Japanese Sapporo Island are three hundred miles due east," Hans said, pointing. "But once we're around the Russian headland — " he nodded over his left shoulder at the massive Russian cliffs sliding into the sea — "we'll bear north for the Nevelskoy Strait, a four-mile-wide narrow between Eurasia and the Sakhalin Islands."

"Will it take long to get there?" I asked as if time made a difference.

"A thousand miles? Four days, plus or minus. Depends on currents and ice."

A tall, thin, pimply-faced deckhand approached us and lit up. He looked sad and lonely. He must have been new as he offered us cigarettes. I thanked him and held up a palm. Hans took one and a light from a flimsy blue butane lighter the sailor cupped in his pallid hands.

"This is quite the ship," I said to him in Russian. "Much crew?"

"Yes," he replied. "One hundred thirty-eight. We work around the clock in three four-hour, on-and-off shifts." He paused, lost in despondency. "We left port a year ago, have two to go."

He took a deep drag off his cheap cigarette. I thought he was going to bawl. "You married?" I asked, spotting the ring on his right ring finger, the Russian way.

He nodded wretchedly. "It's a long time before I'll see Lena again."

"Two years *is* a long time. It'll be five for me."

He started to speak but stopped. Second thoughts. He slouched off: Don't speak to *zeks*.

Three times a day, we ate in the crew mess, on the main deck, aft of the bow, and never saw land again for the next four days. We never saw the swimming pool, sauna, cinema, library, and gym either. But the temperature held, and we breathed fresh air, and we walked back and forth on the rolling decks, free from harassment. Hans and I met a few other *zeks* banished to Pevek, but, for the most part, we avoided *zeks* and their disputes over cigarettes, stealing, and pettiness. At noon on the fourth day, the temperature dropped below freezing and stayed there. But after being cooped up for months in foul transit camps, cattle cars, and prison cells, the freedom of the vast sea was a magnet that temperature couldn't thwart. The food remained the same — gruel, soup, and black bread — but the *Rossiya* cooks served it hot and thick with unspoiled vegetables and real rye-flour black bread. Delicious! With better ingredients, I put on a few pounds and the extra padding made sleeping on the steel deck tolerable, although the constant engine whine and endless tossing of turbulent seas kept us half-awake dreading a *Titanic* fate.

In the Nevelskoy Strait, Hans said, "When I was here, the Kremlin planned a tunnel from the Sakhalin Islands to the mainland but later changed that to a bridge."

I looked from the island on our right to the shore on the left side. "So where is it?"

"Nothing happened, money. The abundance of fish, lumber, coal, oil, and gas here are still causing fights between Russia and Japan over the Sakhalin Islands as they have for centuries."

Once through the Nevelskoy Strait, we entered the Okhotsk Sea, and the Kamchatka Peninsula lay far to our northeast. The Kuril Islands, a fiery ring of volcano peaks, stretched from the Kamchatka Peninsula southwest to the Sakhalin Islands to our east, forming a break with the Pacific Ocean. Here the *Rossiya* went to work. We felt trembles beneath our feet as we shivered at the bow and peered through the icy mist at the icebreaker slashing two-foot ice crusts under its massive hull. Whenever it smashed ridges as thick as I was tall, it jarred my molars and sent us staggering.

"It's weird how quickly ice appeared," I remarked, observing the thickening ice.

"It's all the fresh water flowing in from the Amur River," Hans explained, pointing west. "It reduces the ocean's salinity, raises the freezing point from twenty-seven to thirty-two degrees, and leaves the Okhotsk Sea icebound from October to May."

I leaned over the rail and watched the *Rossiya*'s colossal bulbous bow batter through the ice pack. Her engines beat. Her propellers thrashed. In places, she heaved up onto solid ice, but her weight soon crushed great slabs into garage-sized chunks that tore at the hull and groaned and scraped against its steel plates until chewed into desk-sized chunks by twelve-foot propellers.

Though the outside temperature stayed far below freezing and the ice battle made restful sleep impossible and eating messy, the nuclear power plant kept the cargo hole toasty as we tossed around like popcorn popping. The first ice was one- or two-feet thick, and the reinforced bow cut through the ice blanket with ease. The further north we battered, the thicker the ice grew until it reached a constant six feet or more. Sometimes, the *Rossiya* would stop, reversed, moved astern, revived up, and lunged into ice ten or twelve feet thick, cracking 100-yard splinters in the glassy surface that looked like the San Andreas Fault had reached Asia. Once the convoy steamed through the icebreaker's channel, the ice would quickly congeal and refreeze into a solid mass. The icebreaker battered on; the 550-mile-leg to Magadan took three bronco-busting days.

We moored at Magadan's Nagaev Pier at eleven o'clock on the bitterly cold night of April 23, 1992. The twilight sky was awash in deep translucent shades of rose and pearl-gray. Magadan is on the same latitude as Stockholm and Anchorage, but it lacks their Gulf Stream and Pacific Current furnaces, and it remains refrigerated nine months a year by the sprawling Siberian landmass that spawns the Continental Climate.

When the steel hatch doors opened, guards prodded our silent, smelly hodgepodge of 250 illegal Tajiks, Uzbeks, Turks, Kirghizs, Azizs, one legal Russian, and one Russian/American dual-citizen down the ice-slick gangway to the dock. We scurried the last few steps like rats fleeing a sinking ship as most of the prisoners disembarked here, overjoyed to be leaving seasickness behind and anticipating a better life in the Arctic wilds where nature was its prison. They would work in the vast Magadan wildernesses, felling trees with axes or milling lumber into beams, planks, and boards at sawmills that dotted the planet's largest forest. For the *zeks* who accepted toil, work itself would be a lifesaver, and they might survive as Hans's father had. For those who resisted work, they would be fed less and starve to death.

The three transports disgorged their *zeks* who assembled in a parade area under a flood of spotlights. The men looked like a convention of beggars. Roll call started. Names were called and men shuffled forward for assignments. It was a long process, and we shivered in silent agony in the numbing gale as snow blanketed the hills and lashed elephant-sized boulders along the shoreline that cast foreboding shadows in the long low rays of a sleepless sun. At the end of roll call, guards repeatedly called out the names of three dozen *zeks* who hadn't responded, having died onboard and bodies dumped unceremoniously into the Okhotsk Sea, names never recorded.

A guard holding a megaphone and slapping a riding whip against his thigh struck some men to make space. He shouted through his bullhorn, "You will be run through a disinfecting shower for lice before joining your work crews! Remember your assignments! You will sleep under the stars until you build your barracks!"

Zeks stared in angor: *Build our own Gulag in this frozen wasteland?*

Hans and I and twenty-two others — two squads of twelve — were ordered back aboard the *Rossiya*. I worried, *if they had to build their barracks in this wasteland, what did Pevek hold in store for us?* With a sagging heart and real reluctance, I re-climbed the gangway and stood at the fantail, lofting three stories above the quay, pondering life at the top of the world and feeling very abandoned. A tall, thin man, Czechoslovakian by his accent, approached, leaned on the rail beside me, and introduced himself. Bernd Schröder. He was from a village near Karlovy Vary, a German spa town in western Czechoslovakia. His was a luckless story — the first of a dozen I heard over the next two weeks. In 1938, in Munich, Britain, France, and Italy agreed to allow the Nazis to annex Czechoslovakia's northwest mountain region known as Sudetenland. At Potsdam, Stalin, Truman, and Atlee's agreed to confiscate without compensation all of the Sudetenland, including Schröder's village. Schröder, his father, mother, and older sister, because of their German ethnicity, were banished to the Siberian Far East. His mother and sister died of pneumonia the first winter. He and his father were janitors in a cooking school; they stole food to survive until arrested and the father shot. Bernd was sentenced to thirty-years' hard labor. He'd been in a Gulag for eleven years and being transferred to Pevek to complete his sentence. As he'd talked, we watched the lucky *zeks* tramp into Magadan in an eerily-silent procession set in a grotesque, claustrophobic, monotony of gray: buildings, streets, trees, vehicles, and people. Kafkaesque.

Hours later, the *Rossiya* and three transports, off-loaded and refueled, cast off, bearing southeast into long, cold morning rays. The lengthening late-April day hovered at least ten degrees below freezing, and we wore everything we owned, as usual. Guards allowed us topside anytime during the final 4,500-mile leg north. Sometimes Hans, Schröder, and I stood at the bow and talked about work, family, and dreams. Sometimes we stared silently into the future over the vast and empty sea. And sometimes we stood at the stern, recalling childhood memories, eyes fixed on the transports plowing in our wake a mile apart laden with a year's supply of oil and staples for the ten thousand souls earning triple wages for living in Pevek. It takes nearly two miles to stop a ship their size and weight, but there was no northbound ship-traffic here, and we never made an emergency stop. Sailing to the Arctic was not cruising Miami to New York.

Three days after leaving Magadan, we sliced through the Kuril Islands, rounded the Kamchatka Peninsula, and headed north-northeast for the Bering Strait. An extra serving of black bread began: Arctic rations. The fourth night out, the gruel was so salty it made me crazy for water to drink; the fifth night the gruel was grease laden, and I became violently ill.

"I need the rail, *now*," I yelped to Hans, gagging and clutching my mouth. I slammed out the galley door, beelined for the rail, and spewed grease into the churning Pacific. I would have given a thousand dollars for a toothbrush, tube of Crest, and Scope, but I had to settle for spitting a million times. When my stomach calmed, I wiped off my mouth, took some deep breaths, and looked up off the stern at the Milky Way. Stars gleamed in abundance and shimmered in the strangely warm breeze, riding the Japanese current pushing us north. The current carries anything in its clutches from the southern Pacific to the Arctic. Maybe even the Kon-Tiki-like raft. I thought about Kennewick Man [30] with the morphological features of a Polynesian. Was he the origin of the projected-faced Eskimos? If he had arrived ten thousands of years ago, when the Bering Strait was underwater, Thor Heyerdahl was right.

Hans approached, hacking and spitting, too. I looked to see if he'd puke. He didn't. He'd eaten the same grease; the Russian digestive tract is acclimated to suety diets.

I nodded at Orion's Belt, which at this high latitude sat low in the west-southwest sky. "What's that constellation, Hans?"

Hans turned, gazed for a fraction of a sec and said, "Orion's Belt. Those three stars: Mintaka, Alnilam, and Alnitak are seven quadrillion miles — that's fifteen zeroes or a thousand light years — from here. They're four hundred thousand times more luminous than that thermonuclear furnace we call our sun, which is one star among stars more plentiful than grains of sand on earth."

I shook my head incredulously. "Good to know," I said.

He smiled. "Here's another. Know how wide the universe is?"

"Dad had mentioned something, but I forgot. Pretty wide, right?"

"Light travels six trillion miles a year, and the universe is one hundred fifty-six billion light-years wide."

"Big job for God to do in seven days."

Hans smiled and turned his face into the wind.

The icebreaker was doing twenty-six knots, pushed by the following sea. The breeze was dewy. I wiped moisture off my face and pointed low in the northern sky. "And that one?"

"Ah, come on," Hans said disparagingly. "The Big Dipper."

Above the merlot-dark ocean, heaven's dome was sprinkled with a zillion stars, twinkling, and flickering. Suddenly, all the stars in the north vanished. Great wavy green and purple sheets of aureoles Borealis swayed across the firmament, painting out the dome.

"That's a shame," Hans said. "That starlight traveled six trillion miles a year for a hundred thousand years for us to see. Now it gets blotted out by solar flares from a geomagnetic storm of high-energy electrons colliding with oxygen and nitrogen molecules."

I shook my head. "Yeah, it's a damn shame."

We stood lost in the phenomena's sublimity, and I would have stumbled trying to verbalize its magnificence. One pleasure in life is to be in the company of someone who can savor a natural spectacle of Beauty and Truth in silence and not feel compelled to talk. Silence lights our way and leaves us free to float on wonder. Why do men squabble about the universe's creation in futile arguments as fierce as those between liberals and conservatives and as fruitless as tea versus coffee? As a kid in Tver, Mom explained the northern lights: "When Whitey Fox chased a snow rabbit up Mount Elbrus,[31] he flicked his tail. It showered the sky with snowflakes that sparkle in the moonlight, and that light lead spirits to heaven. Listen and you'll hear the light crackle. Whistle and it will approach to hear your prayers."

I whistled a plangent dirge. The aurora seemed to approach, and I uttered a prayer.

Hans looked at me and smiled. He knew the fable.

The light show continued, and I thought of Mom and hoped she'd heard my prayer. I added prayers for Dad and Anastasia. The three crystallized into a single entity, my family, a compilation of love, caring, and kindness. One dead, one dying, and one in iffy shape that left me wallowing in loneliness. Like the aureoles Borealis that blotted out light from far-flung galaxies, mortality was stealing my family and abandoning me to an uncaring and indifferent world. I had felt loneliness in a desert foxhole, but not since Adam awaited Eve had another man felt the loneliness I felt. Maybe astronaut Michael Collins had, whizzing around the dark side of the moon for 48 minutes each lap, with no contact with Earth and only peering into the vast reaches of blackness while Armstrong and Aldrin hopped around like kangaroos on the lunar surface. If I'd gotten her the taxol, Anastasia and I would have spent the next fifty years forging careers and building lives: kids, houses, cars, vacations, retirement. But I'd failed. I thought of all my warts and failures and all the people I had offended and troubles I'd caused. Maybe, after serving my five years, I'll live on a mountaintop like Zarathustra and gaze down on an equatorial sea and smell the fecundity and feel the warmth and watch lush flowers bloom and children grow and dig in the earth and rest under warm winter's starry dome and soak up freedom saturated with love and peace. We delude ourselves. We become imprisoned in goals and standards constructed to keep our material, moral, ethical, religious, and financial benchmarks in check. We ladder-climbers forever go for the brass-ring — the Mercedes, country club, palatial home, tony community — a never-ending, ulcer-triggering, coronary-assured, money-grubbing quest for more. I do not need, nor do I want, more. A monk's cell is fine for me filled with yesterday's books, yesterday's clothes, and yesterday's music. Rat races are for rats.

The light show ended. After a silence, Hans cleared his throat. "Think she heard you?"

"A whisper overheard is not meant to be an aria heard," I said. "The Bible says she did."

One of his bushy white eyebrows shot up. "Do you believe it?"

"I hope it is right," I said with a shrug. "Is that your prelude to a philosophic chat?"

Hans stewed on that a minute, and then he swept his arm across the starry ribbon overhead and said, wonderingly, "Suppose there's life out there, Troy?"

"Who knows? Dad says there used to be water on Mars. Maybe there is."

"There's water on Jupiter and Europa, too. Comets are iceberg filled with organic molecules. With the universe's water, energy, and biology, you know what happens when organic molecules couple with water and an energy source?"

"You get life. So you think we're not alone. Where is everybody?"

"The Feruri Paradox," Hans said. "Somewhere in that vast array — " his arm swept over the dazzling dome — "of a trillion million stars is another planet with life, maybe like ours, maybe different, but life. Maybe they know of us. Maybe they don't. Maybe they're shrewder. Maybe they're naïver. Or maybe we're animals in their zoo. We know the iron in our blood and the calcium in our bones is forged from the stars. The water circulating in earth's rocks or those on Saturn's moon, Enceladus, or on some Goldilocks exoplanet, a thousand light years away has absorbed enough of our identical essential elements: sulfur, phosphorous, potassium, and sodium to support life if not create it."

"As Aristotle said of his Golden Mountain, 'If something can happen, given infinity, it will happen.'"

"Life's critical elements appear across the universe. New planets form daily. The Big Bang occurred thirteen point two billion years ago. And mankind, as we know it, has walked this planet for two hundred thousand years, a tiny fraction of the time earth was created four point five, four, three billion years ago. Consider it took a billion years for the earth to cool enough to support one-cell organisms. Those prolific cyanobacterial stromatolites, composed of Precambrian marine algae, were the stars of Earth's Life Show for the next *three— billion—years* until five hundred million years ago!"

"When the Cambrian Explosion occurred," I added.

"Exactly. When our terrestrial orb evolved all the familiar animal-parts: heads, tails, legs, arms. But even after the Cambrian Explosion, it took another *three* hundred million years for mammals to appear and another one hundred nine-six million years for upright Lucy to come down from the trees. Man has been on earth less than four seconds of a twenty-four-hour clock — four seconds out of eighty-six thousand four hundred seconds — a miniscule fraction of the time, exactly zero point zero, zero, zero, zero, four, six, two percent of that time."

"Nothing." I cocked my head, bewildered at his assertion.

"On a twenty-four-hour clock, each second equals fifty-two thousand eighty-three years. Fossils prove anatomically modern Homo sapiens appeared in Africa two hundred thousand years ago. Neanderthals disappeared fifty thousand years ago."

"One second ago on your clock," I said. "If God created earth four and a half billion years ago, or twenty-four hours ago on your clock, He waited until four seconds ago to conceive man and a second ago to fashion modern humans to replace Neanderthals. Where's that leave the Biblical promise of an afterlife for you?"

He looked at me compassionately. "Facts cannot be ignored. I have no religious belief, but as a caring human being, I have an unbounded love for my fellow man and an unbridled admiration for the beauty, harmony, and structure of the universe. I've dethroned myself of the conviction of man's centrality to it. If you wish to call the workings of the universe, God, I'll not quarrel with you, but know all beginnings have ends. Our solar system *will* end in the Big Crush, if we don't bring about our extinction first. The sun will gradually run out of hydrogen and helium in about three billion years. Our solar system will be swallowed up by the expanding sun or vaporize and freeze. Those colossal forces are indifferent to man's individual fate or rewarding good, punishing evil, and granting an afterlife. Man's fixation on his being the only species of the *eight million species on earth* with an afterlife is arrogant and preposterous, wishful thinking that makes us prisoners of our addictions. At birth, the spark of life is given to all living creatures, bringing animation to man, dogs, cats, apes, flies, cockroaches, lice, and amoebas. Why should heaven be the exclusive realm of man?"

"I guess it's just hope," I said.

Hans said, "Yes, a dream of enlightened man."

***

We'd been en route some days when, one mid-May morning, the mist cleared, and the sparkling sun cast shimmering reflections off the ice. Hans and I were leaning over the bow rail, watching the icebreaker do its job with the ease of a sharp knife cutting warm butter. The day was unusually warm and breezeless, which made my bushy red beard itch.

I said, "It feels as warm as a February morning in Miami Beach."

"It does," Hans said taking deep gulps of warm air. "But this, Troy, is the Bering Strait, and *that's* Alaska's Cape Prince of Wales." With a long thin finger, he pointed at serrated, snow-covered hills rimming the eastern horizon.

"So close to America yet so far." I looked east and west. "There's a spec rising there."

"That's a Russian island."

My head whipped back-and-forth. "No way! America's that close to Russia?"

"It grows even closer." Hans squinted ahead. "Know what time and day it is?"

I glanced up at the sun about twenty degrees above the horizon. "The sun doesn't rise high in the Arctic; I'd guess it's about ten o'clock Saturday morning the fifteenth of May."

Seeliganov laughed heartily. "For you it is! For me, it's ten Sunday morning the sixteenth."

I thought he'd flipped his lid. "Huh?"

"The International Dateline runs directly beneath us, splitting those two islands coming up." Hans pointed to the right and left over the vast, white, icy sprawl at twin rock piles.

"That's Big Diomede Island's to the port," he said. "It sits at one-hundred sixty-nine degree west longitude and is Russia's easternmost point; far from Kaliningrad's nineteen degrees west. Russians call it Ratmanov; sailors call it Tomorrow."

"Lemme guess. The smaller rock's Little Diomede?"

I indicated the rocky spec across the narrow slowly rising out of the whiteness about two miles east of Ratmanov. The icebreaker slowed to a walking pace.

"It is. Sailors call it Yesterday; it's American. Straight ahead you see ice swirling and breaking up. In winter, the Bering Sea is frozen solid. The native Inuits on Yesterday keep a runway shoveled off for their daily mail plane, and they can walk from America to Russia, in summer, swim. Mikhail Gorbachev wanted to build the second bridge between the continents," Hans said and laughed hardily. His breath stunk.

"Second bridge? Never heard of a first."

"The first was six hundred miles wide, formed seventy thousand years ago by the drop in ocean levels when the earth cooled, glaciers formed, and the Ice Age began. It disappeared thirteen thousand years ago as earth warmed, stranding the Siberians who'd move here."

"I bet Ronnie wasn't interested," I said.

"No, he certainly wasn't. But four years ago, Lynne Cox, an American, swam the two miles from Russia to America in two hours. Reagan and Gorbachev both congratulated her."

"I'll be damned," I said. "So that's what you meant in Vladivostok: 'skate to Yesterday?'"

"It is. A hundred Inuits live on Yesterday. They live on fish, seal, and polar bear. Look!" He pointed at a clearing at the base of a cliff. "Kids flying kites on the heliport."

"Amazing," I said. "They can't get them aloft in the on-shore breeze." In the sun's dazzling rays, a dozen kids were running zig-zags, trying to get their kites up, on a bare, basketball-sized area at the base of near-vertical cliffs where the island cliffs bluntly met the frozen sea. The *N. S. Rossiya* veered to the east to stay in the channel, smashing towards Yesterday, three hundred yards to starboard. I wondered: *Could I jump overboard and make it?*

"Hans," I said, "think there's helicopter service today?"

"Monday to Saturday. America tends to its people: mail, flights, housing, even a school."

The *Rossiya* plowed on. Small, white homes clinging to the bottom of jagged cliffs were distinguishable. Little Diomede looked as round as a cheesecake with sides rising vertically from the sea. The top of the island was windswept, flat, and sprinkled with ice-age boulders bathed in day's coppery light. There were no trees, no vegetation, nothing but ice. And snow.

I watched in thundering silence as a resolution took shape. The icebreaker rammed closer.

Under the bow, ice shattered by the ship's brute strength was bolstered by the Strait's warm currents. The ice to the east, toward Yesterday, looked steel-solid. *Surely it will hold me? I'll jump over the side and dash to Yesterday. We're getting close enough.*

The clatter from shattering bow-ice sounded like a demolishing derby. I had to shout at Hans to be heard. "Why's the ice rupturing and fracturing in front of us but not toward Yesterday?"

"The Arctic Ocean is a *cul-de-sac; a* warm water current, the Kuro-Siwo, sweeps through the Bering Strait at the rate of one million cubic meters a second," Hans said professorially.

"That volume of water, flowing at that speed, is called a Sverdrup," I said. "Dad gave me the lecture last November about the Gulf Stream. 'One Sverdrup equals the flow of all rivers on earth caused by the wind and the Coriolis Effect, the inertial force deflecting water to the right in this hemisphere.'" We were about a half mile from Yesterday.

"You make your father proud."

"Does all that warm water flooding the Arctic Ocean melt the ice cap?"

Hans smiled. "The 'Open Polar Sea' is a myth. But its fierce gyratory currents make it the most treacherous ocean on earth. High winds, extreme salinity, and the sea's shallowness cause the warm salty water to sink beneath the upper layer of snow, river, and rainwater ice to form currents that spin south off Norway to join the Global Conveyor Belt. Here it's no problem."

Beneath the chattering bow, the Kuro-Siwo current's ravenous swirls chomped off house-sized ice chunks that the icebreaker chewed through. In places, the ship slowed, geared down, and climbed the ice floe, cutting it into thick hunks. It demolished the mile-long landing strip for Little Diomede, the lifeline linking the isolated isle to the world, where miles made little difference, and, at the zenith of the midnight sun, hours made no difference. Your belly tells you the time.

We were three hundred yards from Yesterday. Starboard ice was solid to shore. Next to the heliport, a 30,000-gallon oil storage tank sat next to a generator building with electric wires protruding to utilities poles and houses. There were no streets, no cars, no trees, no parks, and no churches. I saw one snowmobile.

I heard whup, whup, whup, and looked up. Beating down the island's craggy side came a four-door Bell 206-B111 helicopter; it slowed, tilted its blades, hovered, and flared above the kids. They scrammed. The copter had an Alaskan state seal on its side — a circle of a yellow sky and a blue mountain. It hung there as immobile as a dragonfly. Its four, self-determined wings top the helicopter aeronautics. The dragonfly can fly upward, downward, forward, backward, *and upside down.* The rotor's downwash whipped up a maelstrom that blew the limp windsock into a rigid cone and obscured the red-cheeked kids dashing out of the whirlwind clutching their kites. The pilot gently lowered skids onto the pad and cut the engine. The effect was immediate. The rotors slowed. The snowstorm settled. The pilot threw open the door and stepped out. He ducked beneath the whirling blades that flapped his leather bomber jacket's fur collar.

He pulled a bag from his pocket.

The kids flung their kites aside and sprung, mittened hands darting out.

"That's the mailman and shuttle to the mainland," Hans said.

"He looks like the Candy Man," I said. "Suppose he's going right back?"

"I'm sure he is."

"Has Yesterday got cops?"

"They're in short supply and fly over once a month. No jail either."

"My kind of place," I said. "Looks like they adopted all the American civilization they wanted. Not much. They live like perennial doormats."

Hans laughed. "They'd disagree. It is the educated who have etched the planet with invisible property lines and peopled it with endless gods that keep us in perpetual wars."

We drew closer. The houses were clones, as though a builder from Nome flew over with one plan and a machine that spit out tiny, drab houses on stilts. Dark-skinned men with black almond eyes hacked stairs in the ice between houses. A woman armed with a shovel chased a polar bear cub from her garbage can. A kid in a red snowsuit and purple mittens slid down a slope and smacked into a girl clutching her kite. She jumped up, smiled, and waved at me. I returned her wave. A snowmobiler zoomed onto the heliport for the mail sack.

"Big Diomede's twenty-nine square kilometers of granite, quartz, and no vegetation," Hans said. "Little Diomede's one-tenth the size and same composition."

I was concentrating on escaping and felt the chill of fear. "The ice looks thick enough."

"I'm sure it is," Hans said.

I gave Hans a look that said, *Should I make a run for it?*

He nodded. His pale blue eyes said, *I'd never dissuade you.*

Without another word spoken, I whirled around and dashed amidship. The starboard railing, across from the nuclear reactors, was the lowest point on the icebreaker. I leaned over and looked down. Solid ice, twelve feet below, ice slabs pushing up the side like ski jumps. I'd drop, hit the ice-slope, slide five feet, spring up, and sprint two football field lengths to America and freedom.

I leaned over further and twisted my head around to see the bridgewing. Clear. The ship was noisily bucking ice with its weight crunching it into huge chunks that slid under the keel or up the side, cracking and snapping and scraping. The surface to Yesterday was as flat as an ice rink and snow-covered.

Hans pat my back. "Goodbye, my friend."

I yanked off my overcoat, gave it to him. "I'll see you in Moscow in ten years." With my body taut as a banjo string, I clenched the rail, wheeled both legs over like it was a Pommel Horse, and dropped to the length of my body. Clinging to the rail, I looked left and right — clear — and let go. My felt boots tobogganed down the slope. My legs twisted. I whacked a sharp edge. My knee throbbed. I ignored the pain, scrambled onto all fours, and, like a lightning bolt, sprinted. Elbows pumped. Knees lifted. The snow was ankle-deep. Heavy. My knee throbbed. I started to hobble. In twenty seconds, I'd covered half the distance. Hit slush. A six-inch pipe was spewing warm raw sewage on top of the ice. I was running in muck the color of molasses. Where was that 600-mile-wide Bering Strait land-bridge when you needed it?

Kids cheered. A fullback sailing for the goal line. A kid tugged on the pilot's arm. Pointed.

The pilot yanked off his aviator sunglasses and raised a hand to shade his eyes. I could almost hear his wonderment: *Why's a red-bearded bum fleeing a Russian icebreaker?*

"I'm an American!" I screamed at him. "Help! Help!"

"American?!" the pilot shot back.

"Troy Locke from Blowing Rock, North Carolina!"

"Gotcha!" He whirled around and dove into his chopper. Rotors spun. Kids scattered.

I heard a thunderous screech. A six-inch crack opened near my feet. Black water swirled ten feet below me. A crack zigzagged out fifty yards. Another screech. A rumble. The crevice widened. I leaped over it and glanced over my shoulder. The *Rossiya* had turned. It was coming at me. Splitting ice. I thought of Anastasia, of home and sprinted with all my might. I must get to Yesterday. I have to board that chopper. I had to get more taxol.

The copter's rotors roared. It lifted off. Dipped. Turned. At that very moment, my right knee buckled. I fell. I scrambled up. My knee throbbed. The pain was excruciating. Gasping, I dragged my right leg. On the heliport, the kids jumped up and down and cheered soundlessly, their voices lost in helicopter thrashing.

I'd made it ten yards when the chatter of fireworks blasted behind me. In front of me, a line of snow-puffs exploded. More chatter. More snow puffs. Automatic rifle fire.

I stopped, leaned down, hands on knees, panting. The helicopter was thirty yards off. It stopped. Hovered. I looked over my shoulders. A guard on the starboard bridgewing had an AK-47 aimed at my back. He raised it at the copter. The pilot nosed up and turned away.

The guard shouted, "*Kuda ty bezheesh?* — Going somewhere?"

"*Nyet*," I said and raised my arms. I kept on shuffling in baby steps toward Yesterday.

He fired an extended blast over my head and below the helicopter's skids. Every sixth round was a tracer that lit up like a laser.

The pilot got the message, U-turned, and whup, whup, whup back to Yesterday and America. I got the message and limped back to the *Rossiya* in dejected boot prints.

A deckhand threw a rope ladder over the side. Slowly and painfully, I climbed aboard to be greeted with rifle-butt blows to the kidneys. The guards, regaling themselves in the sport, laughed and joked until it grew tiresome, then Hans helped me to my feet. He threw my overcoat over my shoulders.

I hurt so much I couldn't move and leaned against the starboard rail and watched Yesterday drop below the horizon. The temperature dropped. The fog thickened. The transports at our stern drew closer, halving their one-mile gap. Cold west blasts whipped off the Siberian landmass and slammed the *Rossiya*. It pitched and heaved through the ice crust, its mighty bow doing a Herculean job. I was sick at heart and physically sick. Had I had anything in my stomach, I would have retched. Now, my list of failures had grown. Would it cost Anastasia her life? It was as if the blank pages of my future life had been written in invisible ink. All my fruitless acts were the magic glasses that should have made them visible to the puppeteer.

My silence, apparently, was disconcerting to Hans as he started a geography lesson. "We're nearing the top of the world where all the longitude lines converge."

"Really," I said with that familiar indifferent tone.

"Here all ocean currents: the Alaskan Stream, Aleutian North Slope, Bering Slope, and Kamchatka blast through the Bering Strait narrow and form the planet's weather patterns."

"Isn't that something?"

The deck quivered mounting the thickening ice. The *Rossiya* geared down to a brawny eight knots, just over nine mph, to prevent hull damage. It rammed aside house-sized ice-islands thicker than I was tall and capped with snow, their bottoms gnawed V-shaped by the hungry sea. For a while, I stared at the white plateau ahead, but I saw only my mountain of failures, the guilt that was a knife in my heart that left no peace, no joy, no pride; the ghosts that stomp through my sleepless nights. I went to the stern. Here the icy discards clutched together, drawn like iron filings to a magnet to coagulate into clusters that trailing transports maneuvered around but never left our wake, and I could hear the golden tones of Anastasia's voice again. In places, waves broke free from the following sea and crashed into the icebreaker's stern, and I would scamper backward. I asked a deckhand about our safety. He assured me there was an ice pilot aboard who determined the thickness of the ice and the speed the ship could safely maintain. I saw no evidence of him.

The unrelenting nuclear power plant drove slowly and steadily on into the never ending day. Sometimes, hammering north, the ice would smash into two pieces and fall in two chunks to port and starboard. Sometimes we climbed aboard it. Sometimes the ice seemed welded solid, and a colossal sheet would jump the bow intact, and we rammed beneath it. Eventually, the ice always slithered off one side or the other and slapped noisily onto its ice bed; its razor edges glinting in the wet sunlight.

The further the *Rossiya* plowed above the Arctic Circle the harder the brute worked. Bearing westward, it cut a wide swath around Cape Dezhnyou, the uppermost Cape of eastern Russia. We pitched and heaved in midnight sun's weak angling rays that dipped but never set, skimming the ice horizon to rise again. Overhead, circumpolar constellations winked like fireflies as they made their slow turn around Polaris that had shone like a channel marker for millennia for edgy navigators thankful for Zeus's affair with Callista for its birth.

Whenever I could, I left the hole to stare at the ice to our port. One day I was surprised to see the long shadow of a polar bear kneeling on an ice flow, seal-hunting in the dampened light. A pair of frisky cubs waited hungrily on shore. In the vast emptiness, they looked as misplaced as giraffes on Mars.

"Look at the white bears!" I said to Hans. "Mama and her babies."

"They're always white," Hans said, unfazed. "Lack of melanin pigment. It's the determinant of skin, feather, and fur color as it absorbs the UV radiation that's in short supply here. That's why the lynx, owl, wolf, fox, and polar bear stay white year round. Your reddish yellow hair is caused by the melanin pigment pheomelanin produced by your hair follicles."

"Glad I asked." That was more than I wanted to know but thought of an incongruity. "Why are the Inuits dark-skinned, black-haired, and black-eyed and not albinos?"

"The half-second since they arrived from Polynesia."

Stern ice swallowed Cape Dezhnyou as the *Rossiya* headed northwest into the Chukchi Sea and the journey's last four-hundred-mile leg. We were about as far north as you can put to sea, and the world was one continuous sunray strobing off ice twenty-four/seven mid-May to the first days of August. In places the ice grew ten- or twelve-feet thick. We stopped, reversed, and slammed ahead, smashing sheets into clusters, until, finally, just after midnight on Thursday, May 28, 1992, the icebreaker abruptly swung southeast into the broad reaches of Chaunskaya Bay, the gateway to the Pevek Gulag at 69.7° north latitude.

It was the beginning of Pevek's fifty-day summer and as cold as February in Blowing Rock. We were asleep in the ship's black hole. We awakened when the engines slowed, and the propellers started thrashing. Hans and I grabbed our blanket and pillow (our overcoat, hat, and mittens), wrestled them on, and rushed through the dim companionways topside to the bow rail. The sky was spotless. The midnight sun sat one-finger-width above the western horizon, dipping as if to set, but at the cusp of the summer solstice, it never does. The lazy furnace doesn't climb to the median, either, stopping at forty degrees. It made for bright days of enchantment and illumination that bring clarity and transparency to this long-frozen world, a binary existence where winter's sour dispositions, darkness, and shadows vanish.

Ground fog drifted down Pevek Mountain's steep, bleak slope sploshed with slope-mine tailings that had stolen the lives of countless *zeks* over six decades, deaths that immersed this lonely province in perpetual gloom. Finally, we approached the dock, and the *Rossiya* shifted gears. I felt the starboard engine slow, the port engine reverse. The massive icebreaker engines gargled quietly and nudged into bulkhead fenders lining the wharf-laden harbor on the lip of Chaunskaya Bay. The twelve-foot propellers fell silent after weeks of relentless thrashing. The beast stilled.

The welcomed stillness ended abruptly with a cacophony of hungry squawks of thousands of feathered scavengers. They dipped and soared in the crystal air, scooping up mosquitoes at a breakneck tempo, bickering over pilings, or plummeting like dive bombers to claw fish from the bay, brown-streaked with raw sewerage belching from sewer pipes in a fecal time bomb.

As if an alarm bell had gonged, young and old streamed from dreary buildings to behold the arrival of the annual supply ships, for the earth had tilted, the seasons had changed. Birds coupled. Chicks hatched. Life was going on, indifferent and uncaring.

"Those birds," Hans said, his arm roller-coasting after a flock wheeling through the sky, "are Willows, Ptarmigans, and Ravens that live here year round."

"How about those ducks, geese, and gulls paddling around?" I asked.

"They're Chinese peregrines. The Sandpipers are from Argentina; Terns from Antarctic."

"That's one very long way to fly!" I said, marveling at the irrepressible aves.

"Mating is an irresistible magnet," my insightful friend said. "Any distance is short for a honeymoon."

"I suppose … " Images of Anastasia, awaiting her honeymoon, filled my silver screen. I swatted mosquitoes and said to myself, *Our love is unaffected by distance* and my eyes blurred. I longed for her. I longed for our times together. I longed for all those things that would have to wait five long years … if she lived five years. I did not want to be here. I carried her, fresh and vivid, in my mind. The tone of her voice, the warmth of her lips, the proud way she carried her head. I had to stop thinking about her, or I would go crazy. I folded her memory between the pages of my mind and closed the book.

I sought relief by staring at the transports docking with mechanical precision. Bowlines were moored to dock-cleats, gangways lowered, hatches opened, cargo unleashed. The docks sprang alive. Longshoremen appeared, swinging aboard cranes, waving through clouds of mosquitoes. The permafrost's soggy ground is a perfect breeding place. Stevedores took their stations for offloading. Dogs appeared, pissing on pilings, sniffing one another, begging for handouts. A few yards away, a shop sign flashed 3° (37° Fahrenheit). Balmy!

Guards yelled, "Fall in!"

Quietly, we twenty-four formed a wavy line on the port deck. We were checked off and tramped down the gangway to terra firma to be recounted. Having been prisoners five months surviving on scant rations sloppily wolfed down in crowded prisons and rough seas, we were weak. Our sea legs wobbled when tentative feet hit the rigid dock that seemed to sway. Slowly and cautiously, I adjusted to motionlessness and clung to the dock rail.

Guards herded us aside for the captain and crew to pass. Pevek officials appeared with proffered vodka and cigarettes. One guard booted a scrawny mutt into the bay, talked and joked, blasé about the howling dog or our fleeing. Running meant instant execution.

I was still steadying myself against the rail, breathing deeply, absorbing spring's sweet fragrance and listening to peaceful bird songs— floating on midnight's radiance — when, oddly, I felt a bubbling spirit of blissful hope well up inside. It was an exultant elation, like the one I felt hearing the Marriage of Figaro Overture the first time that touched my soul with euphoria and carried me off on a flight of fancy. But my spiritual rhapsody was fleeting, and it was quickly grounded in a moroseness and the sulky reminder that this wasteland would be my prison for five years — if I survived the mine. Waves of loneliness shattered my ethereal joy. I felt my shoulders slump, my eyes blur, my heart cry out for Anastasia. Each time her face appeared in my mind, uncontrollable tears surfaced. I had to stop that or I'd never survive.

I took a deep breath, planted my feet firmly, eased my grip on the rail, and, weaving, began to pencil in my journal's blank pages. I will face the next five years, squarely, factually. I will be alone, wifeless, familyless, and countryless. I will survive. The five years will be one long, blurry emptiness. It will look like the fuzzy image of a far distance through the wrong end of a telescope. I can do it. I will do it. Bullshit.

I could never stand that much aloneness. And the mine toil? Life in a Gulag? Slaving in the Arctic five years? I thought about my wonderful mind and how it would atrophy. I thought about my wonderful body and how it would wither. I thought about dying and being tossed into a pit to be eaten by furry white scavengers, bones buried in permafrost some July to be exhumed in ten thousand years like the hairy mammoth.

I looked around. No one had died in route. All the *zeks* were gawking and waiting for a ride to the Gulag. My eyes ran over the solitary Pevekians and their bleak village of five-story buildings, warehouses — many abandoned — and the funereal mountain beyond. There was a store, a little onion-domed church, no bars, no discos, no theater. A drab life for quarantined Russians who see planes twice a month and supply ships once a year, a sad, neglected, cheerless town of a ten thousand souls living in desuetude and abandonment surrounded by a bay-front girdled with docks lined with rusty cranes and mountains of coal. Rising behind them, resting on stilts, were sour, five-story, precast-concrete *Stalinkas* bisected by a narrow gravel road. Beyond the apartments was a gravel soccer field splotched with puddles and alive with beer-guzzling boys playing midnight ball in shorts and T-shirts in near-freezing weather. A goalie booted the ball into a lingering snowbank and bellowed to his teammates. The field emptied as the clamoring teams sprinted for the docks. Trailing them galloped slim teenage girls in shorts and sweatshirts. Other than their clothes, the only colors were spring birds, shoots of tender grass, and clusters of purple crocuses at the base of footings sledged into the permafrost.

High up the icy mountain, a half-mile above Pevek, snow swirling at the barren summit nearly obfuscated the barbed-wire-manacled Gulag, five, low, stone buildings with six barred-windows to a side. My soon-to-be-home. The fence restraint wasn't much. Half the double-rows of poles lie frost-heaved on the rock-peppered earth leaving long gaps in the razor-wire under snowbanks that would make escape easy. If there were anywhere to which to escape. A truck pulled out of the Gulag. I heard the rusty metal-on-metal screech of dock cranes coming to life. Oxidized arms stretched over cargo holes to disgorge pallets of fresh potatoes, cabbage, carrots, cooking oil, flour, salt, sugar, vodka, frozen chicken legs (aka Bush legs), Marlboros, and clothing.

Hans inhaled deeply, pointed at a clump of imperial-looking crocuses at the foot of an apartment piling, and said, "Those certainly 'bring back the hour of splendor in the grass, of glory in the flower.'"

"Let's hope we find 'strength in what remains behind,'" I said, unmoved by the poet's message, for, at that very moment, waves of depression were sweeping over me. The culprit was that sweet, loving, redolent, orange-blossom-Thanksgiving weekend, those joyous, idealistic days with Anastasia and my parents eight months ago, before her cancer, before taxol, before prison. My heart ached. I wondered if I could ever muster the strength found in memories to face what lay ahead.

Hans placed his hand on my shoulder like a loving father. "Mother Nature is sparse here, but she's beautiful," he said. "It's all we have, Troy. Enjoy it."

Hans was right. I looked around. The midnight sun hung low in the sky on this enchanting white night when darkness never falls. The cool breeze skimming over the harbor settled on the village and ruffled grass shoots and swayed the long, slender, tubular crocuses. A sea lion's insistent barks penetrated the cheers and shouts and carnival atmosphere of hundreds of enthusiastic onlookers pouring out of *Stalinkas* to overfill Pevek's Main Street. The arrival of the annual supply ships was the highlight of the year generating a raucous gaiety that swelled as pallets unloaded in excitement only prolonged isolation could spawn. Anticipating packages from relatives and newly-stocked store shelves, great hoots went up as pallets swung onto the dock stenciled Пиво — Pivo, or beer — and Водка — Vodka. A few people glared at us with opprobrium, despite none of us having done anything punishable in a civilized society. Our presence was a presumption of guilt for taking the wheels abandoned by dead *zeks* or the handful who had completed their sentences, left long ago by wives and families, and choose to remain in Pevek as highly paid guards.

Vendors materialized with beer, vodka, and cigarettes. A late arrival sidled up to the dock selling hot, roasted kielbasa from a make-shift-grill that smelled so good my mouth flooded. A pack of dogs gathered, sniffing, tongues dripping with hope.

"I'd take another year to my sentence for a beer and kielbasa," Hans said, smacking his lips.

"Not me,' I said. "I've got five years and won't take another day for anything."

Hans looked around and shook his head. "These poor souls. They're paid triple wages to work in this wasteland with nothing to do, nowhere to go, and nothing to spend money on."

"Prisoners, too, huh?"

"*Troy!*" a familiar woman's voice shouted. "*Hey, Troy! Troy Locke!*"

I whirled around. My eyes swirling over the crowd.

"*It's me!*" she screamed. "*Over here!*"

There was only one person on earth with that voice.

***

TWENTY-FOUR

Pevek, Chukotka Autonomous Region, Russia
Thursday, May 28, 1992

"*Troy, Troy Locke, darling!*" the woman screamed again in English.

A thousand heads whipped around. I turned my shocked head to follow their eyes. My body was rooted under a Clydesdalean weight of awe and disbelief.

Hans elbowed me. "Over there, on the left, red beret, red sweater, blonde hair."

And there she was: *Anastasia*!

I was dumbfounded; speechless as a ventriloquist's dummy; my mind a muddle of delight and despair. Delight at the intoxicating pleasure of holding Nastia in my arms again, despair at the colossal waste of five years laying ahead like some satanic abyss. I tried to see through that miasma as my mind sprang into action, spawning hope. I had tried to accept the five-year sentence as a sensible man would, that is to say, dispassionately, beyond the reach of panic. But that was crap. The inevitable Gulag years laying ahead left me numb with fear and dread. I stood there staring at Anastasia with the glassy eyes of a dummy. She'd been standing on the dock of the bay. She pushed forward, elbowing past women in bathrobes and men in long-johns, her smile anxious and loving. I felt its magnetic heat drawing me to her.

"Well, come here!" she shouted, waving and jumping and elbowing through the crowd.

My reality began to reboot. I'd known Anastasia since I could crawl. We'd shared lives and love, powerful links, unaffected by distance or the passage of time, or so I had tried to convince myself. I had thought I could survive without physical contact with her, not feeling her warmth, seeing her incredible eyes, beamy smile, and tousling hair. I was wrong. My stomach ached for her. I felt dizzy, giddy, sweaty, and like the world's biggest fool.

Hans shoved me. "What are you waiting for, *go!*"

I bolted.

A rifle butt slammed into my gut so hard it knocked me on my can.

"One more step," the guard threatened in Russian, and in English, "*Go ahead, make my day!*"

"But that's my wife," I said, pushing up. "I haven't seen her in seven months."

"One step and you're dead!" He chambered a round.

"May she come onto the dock, please?"

"Yeah."

"Thanks," I said to him and to her, I yelled, "Come here, Nastia, I can't leave!"

Having witnessed the exchange, the crowd, mostly oldsters, split like the Red Sea. Anastasia sidled through with the confidence of Moses and stepped onto the end of the dock. I heard the *snick* of another guard chambering a round.

The first guard jabbed me. "One centimeter, you grimy son of a bitch, it's curtains."

"Yes, sir," I said and stood at rigid attention, eyes glued on the end of the dock now crammed with teenagers swilling beer and puffing cigarettes. Anastasia elbowed into that throng. Having earned her Ph.D. in Moscow jostling on and off the world's busiest Metro, she was not to be thwarted by a rowdy horde of Arctic teenagers. She broke through and galloped down the dock like a filly going for the wire. She stopped abruptly at the guard's side, unslung her canvas beach bag with the Miami scene from her shoulder, and holding it by its cotton-cords, reached in and pulled out a shiny red carton of Marlboros. The writing was in English.

"For you," Anastasia said in Russian, handing him the carton, "allowing me to see my husband."

He said, "*Spaseba bolshoi,*" and looked puzzled reading the warning. "What's this say?"

"It's the usual warning that smoking causes cancer."

"Not to me it don't! Me tough Russian."

Anastasia smiled sweetly. "Of course, you are."

I was floored. Russians know bribery greases the wheels of government, but Nastia had the presence of mind to plan an inducement before she'd left America. Maybe she'd greased other wheels as well. She spun around, gave me a killer smile, dropped the canvas bag, and levitated into my open arms. Her hands flew up and yanked my grungy face down to her anxious lips. We kissed long and hard. As her body pressed into mine, I felt weak-kneed; a bugle blast woke up my dopamine reserves from their long, lifeless sleep.

I gasped, pushing her away far enough to say, "How'd you ever find — "

"Oh, Troy," she swooned, "later."

She felt the charge of desire rushing through her body and tightened her grip around my neck. She pulled my head down and pressed her soft red lips into my beard. She sought and found my lips again. She pressed her body harder against mine. I could feel the warmth of her soft right breast through my coat. We kissed torturously. Forces within us awakened in a response that gentleness could never have roused. My fingers got busy. They tugged her hips. Stroked her hair. Lifted her chin on both sides of her face. Her knees trembled. She quivered all over, and still we kissed. The fleshy curve of her hips pressed into my long-forgotten loin and stirred something I hadn't felt in seven months.

"Whew!" she exclaimed, twisting away from our needy fog. With one hand holding her beret, the other stiff-arming me, she squealed, "Easy, tiger," and gave me the once over. "You look like hell, Locke! You're dirty and scrawny and stinky, but it's wonderful to — "

The crowd cheered and screamed, "*Potseloval yeyo opyat* — Kiss her again!"

Who was I to argue? I ran my palms along Anastasia's jawline, looked into her eyes and saw a sea of love. I drew her face to mine, and in the soft, chilly, midnight sun we kissed, softly, then passionately, demandingly. When we stopped, I saw a desperate urgency in her face, a look of hopelessness and self-incrimination. Was that the force that had driven her to find me?

"How did you ever find me in the middle of nowhere, Nastia?" I asked.

She pressed a finger against my lips. "One second." Tears clouded her pale blue eyes. Lines creased her brow. Mascara smudged her cheeks. "Just hold me."

I held her. Questions flared through my mind like fireworks. *How had she gotten here? What was happening with her breast cancer? How long could she stay? Would they let us be together? What was new with dad?*

After a minute, I whispered, "My dearest Nastenka, I've died a million deaths thinking of you. I'm heart-sick about the taxol. I tried, but — " I hunched my shoulders and shuttered uncontrollably. "Can you ever forgive me?"

"Of course," she said. "It wasn't your fault. The KGB's everywhere. Ivan explained."

"Thank God. So how *are* you? And Dad? Are you still playing Florence Nightingale or are you in Orlando teaching math? Tell me everything."

Anastasia lifted her face, sniffed, and wiped tears on the sleeve of her red sweater. "I'm okay. Ivan called from Hugarta the day he arrived in Egypt. He told us he'd fled after you were arrested. He explained about the taxol. Then a letter arrived in April from a Blagoveshchensk clerk. She said you'd been sentenced to five years in Pevek and would arrive in late May. And, shock of all shocks, you were on national TV a couple of weeks ago. An Alaskan helicopter pilot told Anderson Cooper about seeing you fleeing from a Russian icebreaker in the Bering Strait. So, after my ASU math finals were graded — I quit teaching in Orlando as soon as I landed the ASU math job — I flew here. Dad is okay; he's up to two-laps-a-day around Bass Lake."

"Maybe I'll be swapped for a Russian spy."

"Don't count on it. On the way here, I stopped in Tver and visited my parents for a week, and now … *here I am*!" She started jitterbugging.

"Here you are, indeed!" I said, reaching for her waist, pulling her to me.

Anastasia leaned back and puffed a strand of hair away. "There's a plane to Pevek twice a month. I've been right here waiting for you for six nightless days."

I smiled. "Lots of ice to break through. How'd you come, Moscow and Blagoveshchensk?"

"Delta to Moscow, Aeroflot to Irkutsk, Magadan, and Pevek."

"And Dad, how's he?"

"He's driving, plans to teach this fall, and he has a girlfriend," she said with disapproval.

"The grad students who attended our wedding a year ago? That tall busty blonde?"

Anastasia stepped back and shot me a squinted-eyed look. "How'd you know that?"

"Men have a nose for that kinda stuff."

"I'd better not find you sniffing around Arctic dollies, buster." She looked at me, sniffed, and wrinkled her nose. "But I'm safe. What woman would want a man as skinny as a stick who stinks like a skunk? Don't you eat, shower, or brush your teeth?"

"Nah," I grinned. "One of the joys of being a convict's we don't do any of that stuff."

Hans, standing quietly nearby, coughed. I turned to see him smiling broadly at our banter. With a head nod, I asked him to step over. I said, "Excuse me, Hans. Nastia, this is my good friend Professor Hansel Seeliganov. Hans is a proponent of democracy banished to Pevek for ten years."

Anastasia extended her hand and a pleasant smile. As they shook, Hans said in Danish-accented English, "Your husband and I have survived on prisoners' fare, Anastasyia — " he pronounced it the Russian way, five syllables — "rotten potato-cabbage soup and chunks of black bread. As for personal hygiene, well, suffice it to say our icebreaker was not the Queen Mary."

Anastasia looked intrigued. "Your accent sounds like a variation of German, so how in the world did you end up here?"

"I was born in Denmark," Hans explained. "And the Danish and Swedish languages were derived from the East Norse dialect, which is heavy in German. As to this excursion to the Arctic" he grinned; his eyes twinkled, "my family — Dad, Mom, and I — were arrested, when I was a boy, while we vacationed at the Black Sea. We were banished to three different labor camps. I spent my youth at Yasnaya Polyana, attended school there, and, after college, taught at Moscow University."

I snapped my fingers. "Say, Nastia, maybe you took one of his classes."

Seeliganov laughed. "Anastasyia, Troy has told me endless tales about you. I taught geology; you studied astrophysics, and I regret to say we never met. I'm in Pevek mainly because I *believed* Yeltsin wanted democracy. On Christmas day, after Gorbachev resigned, I stood on a soapbox outside the Kremlin and faced a grim, suspicious, frightened crowd waiting with silent expectation with eyes gazing hopefully at the fortress. It felt like the Speakers Corner in Hyde Park, and I outlined truths about democracy point-by-point. Unfortunately, the truth was Boris Nikolayevich wanted no part of democracy. He preferred the totalitarian world of silence, lethargy, high walls, and dark dens for his greedy comrades. But enough of that, you're *brave* to have journey alone all the way to the top of the world."

"Thank you, Hans," Anastasia said. "Stupid might be closer. Leaving the unrestrained freedoms of America to return to a world of distrust, malice, deceit and lies is crazy."

I heard a truck approach. "Guys," I said, panicky, "I think that's our truck. Nastia, have you had chemo? When do you leave? Tell me everything, quickly!"

"Chemo? Not yet. Taxol's still not sold. Congress's holding hearings to revise their deal. Tree-huggers are still outraged. The media is still blasting the NCI."

"Typical Congress," I said, "nothing's changed. Do you think they'll let me see you?"

The truck stopped, backed up, parting the crowd; the driver swung down and lit a smoke.

"I'll tell you tomorrow," Anastasia said and glanced at her watch. "No, today at eight."

I thought she was loony. "Love, at eight o'clock, I'll be up there." I pointed at the Gulag.

"No you won't," she said cunningly.

"What do you mean?" I said. "I'm a prisoner."

"Darling, this may be Yeltsin's new Russia, but it's still the same old corrupt Russia it's always been. I called on the Gulag commandant yesterday. For a carton of Marlboros, a liter of Johnny Walker, and one thousand dollars, I bought you a four-day furlough!"

I yelped, "I don't believe it! *Four days for us alone, no way*!?"

"It's the truth. Five hundred yesterday bought it; five hundred in four days is insurance."

I laced my fingers into hers and gave her a great big smooch. "You're un-believable!"

"And you stink," she said. "While you get checked in up there, I'll find a bar of soap, razor, shaving cream, shampoo, and that barrel of champagne and bucket of caviar you promised me last Thanksgiving. Pevek isn't Paris, but we're having a honeymoon, darling!"

Hans stepped back and stared at Nastia. "You're shrewd. Conjugal visits have always been allowed in Russia, but you were wise to withhold half your money. Bureaucrats lie."

"Four days," I exclaimed. "Is there a hotel and a call center?"

"Yes, both," Nastia said. "I've called Dad twice. It's sixteen hours earlier in Blowing Rock. Here it's just after midnight; there it's just after eight yester-day morning."

"Gotcha," I said and suddenly worried. The opportunity of having a four-day honeymoon would have made the old Troy Locke ecstatic, but it left me overwhelmed with doubt. Would I be man enough? Starvation rations had stripped fifty pounds off my frame, and I hadn't had an erection since Christmas in Blowing Rock. The flaccid muscle was comatose. I pulled Anastasia close and nuzzled my lips to her ear. "Awakening Cupid's arrow will be a challenge."

"Oh, poo." Anastasia nuzzled into my beard and whispered, "I'll get it working, Mother Nature taught us how." She pointed to an unpainted *Stalinka*. "Our boudoir is on the third floor of that apartment building … the corner unit with the light on."

"Looks like the Waldorf Astoria," I said.

Hans said, "I'm so proud of you, Nastia. Was the commandant the usual tedious, inflexible, greedy-eyed vulture they all are?"

"Yes, but ten, new hundred-dollar-bills waved in his face did the trick."

"And your room, is it adequate?"

"Soviet luxury," Nastia replied with a shrug. "Toilet, shower, couch-bed, hot plate, frig."

"The Taj Mahal," I said. "My first hot shower and shave in six months, I can't wait."

Anastasia wrinkled her nose. "Me either."

"And food?" Hans said.

"Adequate. There are two cafes in town and one at the airport well-stocked with sausage, ham, cheese, pastries, vodka, and tons of canned stuff."

The truck driver flicked his cigarette into the bay, came around the rear of the duce-and-a-half, dropped the tailgate, and tied back the flap.

"All aboard!" he yelled.

Guards herded us aboard, jabbing with their rifles butts held at port-arms.

"Seven hours!" I said to Nastia, dawdling to be the last aboard to get the rear seat. Once in, I stuck my head out under the flap and yelled, "How'll I find you?"

"I'll be the lady in red with a basket of goodies at the bottom of Gulag Hill!"

The driver yanked the flap down. It smacked my face and hid Nastia. He climbed into the cab, cranked it up, and when the truck lurched, I poked my head out to wave at Nastia.

She blew me a kiss.

"What a delightfully clever woman," Hans said.

"Yes," I beamed, "she is."

I yanked the stiff canvas flap back again but couldn't spot her as the truck had rumbled around a corner. I dropped the flap and slouched, praying things worked out.

The truck banged bottom on Pevek's pot-hole streets filled with voices of young men warbling beer songs. Those faded as the truck geared down for the crawl up Gulag Hill. I wanted to jump out, rush to Anastasia, and hold her in my arms. But fleeing was pointless. Where could we hide high above the Arctic Circle?

The Arctic Circle is a shifting, imaginary line circumscribing the top of the earth. Fluctuating tidal forces — the result of variable lunar orbits — drift the circle northward forty-nine feet a year from its current position of 66.5622° north latitude. Above the unstable circle, summer sun never sets and winter sun never rises for at least 24 continuous hours. Hollywood showcases Arctic escapes. They are fantasies. The Tiaga, a globe-circling, boreal forest of spruce, fir, larch, and bogs in southern Siberia, above the Arctic Circle, diminishes to a near-lifeless biome of lichen, moss, miniscule flowers, and thin grasses hurriedly sprout during its ephemeral growing season. Nature is its own Maginot Line.

I lifted the rear flap and looked at the rolling mountains above Pevek. They reminded me of Salzburg. The winter-cold breeze resulted from air drifting over the ice-sculpted mountains. But it felt clean and refreshing against my grungy face, and my heart sang with rekindled joy. I felt like a von Trapp and wanted to belt out *The Hills Are Alive With the Sound of Music* though I was, in fact, watching peregrines swoop through bug-clouds to feed their young. All earth's eight million species have families and feed and care for their young unless they're caged like parakeets or *zeks*. Later that six-week-summer, tromping back to the Gulag mornings after our twelve-hour night shift, we witnessed a favorite pastime of guards. Stake naked slackers to the permafrost and watch mosquitoes' kamikaze their frail bodies and siphon blood until they were unconscious.

The truck ground to a stop inside the compound a half-mile above Pevek. We climbed down and looked around. The Gulag was five, low, rock, barracks and four smaller buildings on a snow-covered, four-acre shelf etched into the mountainside that looked a Vermont barnyard fenced in by two rows of razor wire with a no man's land in between. Watchtowers with powerful searchlights stood at the four corners keeping an eye on a mess hall, gatehouse, parcel building, infirmary, tool shack, and the five, long, squat, cattle-sheds with six barred-windows to a side. To one side stood a windowless, brick box: solitary confinement. During my five-year incarceration, the quintet of stone barracks grew to an octet, for deep beneath this barren wasteland was a mother lode of precious minerals. *Zeks* built the new Gulags from tailings hand-carried two miles at the end of every shift despite our endless battle with hunger and fatigue. During those five years, one-in-three *zeks* died of malnutrition, exhaustion, scurvy, pellagra, infections, tuberculosis, and unbelievable cruelty.

Four rows of two-foot-wide, quadruple-tiered, planks (bunks), two down each wall and two, end-to-end, down the center, lined our barrack's forty- by eighty-foot interior. The two narrow passageways were crowded with stools (oil-barrels hacksawed in half), one oil-barrel-coal-burning stove, and a crude *parasha* — shit bucket — next to the door beside my planks. A stooped-back, wrinkly-faced, old orderly, Dimitri Ivanovich, who'd been in the Gulag nineteen years and kept the coal fires stoked and shit bucket emptied, introduced himself to us and assigned planks. As the only American, Dimitri had probably been instructed to assign me the worse bunk: the lowest plank beside the door and *parasha*. *Urkagans*, hardened criminals, fought for and claimed the warmest planks midway down the barracks next to the stove. Gulag life was harsh and the mortality high, and within six months, I received two Christmas presents. The first was a plank far from the door and the *parasha* on the fourth tier near a window with a view of Pevek when I scraped off the soot and ice. The second was a lifesaver.

It was after one o'clock in the morning when exhausted and starved, I crawled onto my plank and closed my eyes, oblivious to the fecal odor. Naturally, I was so excited about seeing Anastasia sleep would not come. Intoxicating pictures of her raced through my mind. And the men grunting into the bucket and cursing for lack of TP didn't bother me as the hours dragged on. I must have dozed off as I awoke cold. Someone had taken my hat and overcoat — my covers. Just before reveille that sun-bright, first night, Dimitri Ivanovich returned with an armful of coats and hats. He opened the door by my feet and announced our coats and hats had numbers sewn. Gulag artists paint numbers on stamp-sized scraps of white cloth that are sewn on outerwear.

When Dimitri kicked the Gulag door shut, the stack of black coats and felt hats teetered. He grit his two teeth, steadied the load by bearing down with his stubbly chin, lost control, and dumped it beside the *parasha*. The hats and coats hit the frozen dirt with a muffled thud that sent out rollers of stench waves.

"You're Fetisov, the American, right?" Dimitri asked me.

"That's me, Igor Vladimirovich Fetisov," I said, sitting up.

"Not anymore. You're number four eighty-nine."

The old man spoke in the distinctive Old Russian that accented the unstressed o and the explosive g heard in Arkhangelsk. He started pawing through the stack with liver-spotted hands laced with blue veins and stopped when he found my coat and hat.

"Here you go, four eighty-nine," he said with an upside-down smile.

"Thanks, Dimitri Ivanovich," I said, glancing at the 85 sewn on his hat. "Or should I say eighty-five?"

His rheumy eyes glittered. "In the barrack, we keep our names, Igor Vladimirovich. Now listen, the sergeant of the guard said you may leave after breakfast. I'll come get you."

"Thanks, Dimitri Ivanovich," I said. "My wife's here; she flew in from America and — "

"I know," he interrupted. "She paid the commandant five thousand dollars for your honeymoon. The Gulag has no secrets."

"I believe you, but start a new rumor, your ransom number's too high." My stomach growled. "Say, when's breakfast and what's served?"

"Breakfast is in two hours; it's Siberian oatmeal," he said, straight-faced. Boiled hay mush.

I stood and put an arm around his thin shoulders. "Dimitri Ivanovich, I lived on that in Vladivostok, I'll wait and eat with my wife."

"I would, too, if I had a wife." Later, he told me his wife divorced him fifteen years ago.

With no sleep, I zombied through roll-call, skipped eating, and gave my chunk of black bread to Hans. After breakfast, the prisoners were divided into squads and left for their assignments, and I hurried back to the barracks to doll up for my honeymoon. I ran my fingers through grimy hair — this was not our week to bathe — and dressed in the same grimy woolen pants, shirt, and overcoat I'd worn every day since leaving Blago and waited for Dimitri.

When he hobbled in, we hustled out into the bright nippy June morning. The sun had risen to a stingy twenty-five degrees above the horizon, and snowing had stopped.

At the gate, Dimitri talked to the guard who jabbed me in the chest, warning, "Four days, Fetisov. Be back in ninety-six hours, that's midnight in four days or it will be solitary."

"You bet," I whooped, wanting to slap him on the back.

I hurried out the gate without looking back. The town of Pevek, a half-mile below, looked like monopoly houses on the edge of Chaunskaya Bay. Far beyond, across miles of bay-ice, the horizon's cleavage glinted where white ice met blue sky. I hoisted the skirt of my overcoat and ran down the beaten path. My boots made snow-puffs with every step and snow weaseled into holes of my soles, but I didn't care. Within minutes, I spotted a red beret and blonde hair in the long soft rays of the early sun. Anastasia was watching a violent soccer game. The breeze floating up the hill carried shouts and cheers and the smell beer. I yelled then screamed, and she finally looked up, spotted me, and started running. We ran into each other's arms and kissed and hugged and both started talking at once.

I held up a hand. "You first, Nastia. My last five months is one sentence long."

"When you didn't return to Blowing Rock," she gasped, "do you want to hear all this?"

"You bet."

"Dad and I figured something was wrong. Two days later, Uncle Ivan's called from Egypt and told us what had happened. I was a day late returning the rental car to Charlotte and getting back to Orlando but started teaching high school math at Boone High on East Kaley in Orlando. But teaching wasn't what I did."

"Slow down. What did you do if you didn't teach?"

"Refereed," she snapped in a spiteful holophrasm. "I hated the sass, fighting, and disrespect and started prowling around for a college job. I landed one at ASU and am staying in your old room until I find a place."

"Why don't you stay there until I get out?"

"It's a little awkward, eating Cheerios with your dad's live-in."

"That old hound," I said, unsurprised.

"That's the one," Anastasia said. "She's the one that came to your mom's funeral," and she sniffed me. "My God you look terrible and stink. Why didn't you shower before leaving?"

"Not our week to shower. You look good enough for both of us. Now, unless you're totally into that soccer mêlée, what say we buy some bubbly and beeline for the *boudoir*?"

"I thought you'd never ask."

Our honeymoon suite was a tiny, rental room in a dingy apartment building. It was hot and as dull as a monk's cell. As I stripped, Anastasia stuffed my filthy woolens in a garbage bag and set them in the hall outside the door for the maid to launder. She washed her hands and laid out some new duds for me.

"While you shower, scrub, and shave, I'll start on the ham and eggs," she said and kissed me.

The tub had a hand-held shower. I brushed my teeth and soaped and shampooed ... three times.

When the stink disappeared, I lathered my beard, shaved, and re-brushed and flossed my teeth and gargled some Listerine. The bath towel, a Soviet-see-through the size of a dishcloth, was clean but unabsorbent, so I dried out sprawled out on the foldout bed feasting on ham and eggs, yeast bread, cheese, butter, coffee, Stolichnaya with orange juice, milk (powdered), and *Krasny Okyabr* chocolates.

Unsure how my system would take the goodies, I took small bites between slow, deep kisses.

"I'm worried, Nastia, about Cupid's arrow. It hasn't worked since last Christmas."

"Then we'd better rest after you eat," she said. "You look exhausted."

"I am."

After we had finished eating, we cuddled, belly-to-belly and toes-to-toes. She fiddled and stroked and started breathing hard as she always did.

It was useless.

"Cut it out, Nastia, it's no good. I'm finished. Let's sleep."

"Of course, darling." Her hands stayed busy. She descended ever so slowly with a busy tongue. Fantasies floated through my mind.

Then she said, "Well, well, well, what's this?"

I inhaled sharply. "I don't recognize it."

Trusting you'll excuse me from the unnecessary chore relating how the influx of protein, minerals, and vitamins steeped in love for the next ninety-six hours worked its magic, I'll skip that denouement. Let me conclude by saying we made plans for Anastasia to return at Christmas, six months off, which, on that last night together, June 4, 1992, seemed like a light year away. On that night, neither of us knew, or could have guessed we had just had our last time together *ever*! Neither of us would have been able to have endured that knowledge had it been known, and at 11:30 that sunny night I left our bed for the Gulag whistling and day-dreaming about a Christmas honeymoon in Pevek. Symptoms of my nervous excitement, brought on by an overdose of an experge-facient soon passed and my Gulag life shaped my world again.

TWENTY-FIVE

Gulag 17, Pevek, Chukotka Autonomous Region, Russia
June 5, 1992

The clunk of the Gulag's sliding door bolt whacking its stop jarred me awake. The screech of iron-on-iron hinges popped my eyes open. A bright, icy blast whistled into the darkness. A gravelly voice shouted, "*Podni mite svoi zad sploshnye nary!* — Get your scummy asses off the planks!"

Reveille.

When I pulled the bottom of my black felt overcoat off my face, the ice-caked fringe scraped my nose. My plank creaked when I rolled to take a look and squinted into the glare flooding the doorway at two silhouettes. Guards.

One, tall and reedy, held the door for the second, short and stocky.

Both wore *shapki, valenki, perchatki, shineli, and pistolety* — hats, boots, gloves, greatcoats and side arms. In one hand, the tall guard had the servile task of a Uriah Heep, holding a chain that suspended a Lada-sized wheel rim. The short guard smacked it with a lug wrench. Ear-splitting bongs echoed down the long, cold barracks squalid with body odors and latrine stench that I could never accept.

I blinked. My eyes slowly adjusted to June's unrationed light pouring into our oasis overflowing with bodies: one-hundred-plus *zeks* sprawled out on planks, shivering under overcoats, scratching lice, moaning at bed sores, coughing, sneezing, and farting. A phlegmy light leaked through six windows smudged with finger-thick coal dust inside and thicker ice outside.

Daylight streaming through the door glinted off the small round eyes and nostril hairs of the short guard. He had a large head, deep-set eyes, and the long-snouted chinlessness of a pig. He clanged the rim again. The pair acted like they were two hours from the Stone Age. The shorter man elbowed his obsequious cohort and aimed the lug wrench at Krasnoperov, a barefoot *zek* from Orel, relieving himself at the *parasha* next to my feet.

The tall guard had the snarling, omnivorous look of a wild beast. He grit his teeth and rammed the door into the *parasha.* Krasnoperov arched backward, limboing, aiming for the punchbowl sliding my way. The short guard grunted something, and the tall guard clicked on a switch. An 80-foot string of weak light bulbs flickered to life. Their wavering intensity, dull-to-dim-to-dull, re-minded me of the first workable incandescent bulb at the Edison Museum in Fort Myers showcasing Tom's brainchild of 1879. They cast just enough light to make icicles dangling from ceiling rafters sparkle like tinsel, and snow-piping festooning wall cracks glisten like icing squeezed from pastry bags.

The pig guard swiveled, shoved Krasnoperov, still-pissing, aside and rushed at me.

Instinctively, I contracted into the fetal position. He whacked my calf with the stainless steel baton and erupted in a full-throated, stridulous snarl, "*Vastavij zhopa* — Up asshole!"

I grasped my calf and thought: *Not like yesterday's wake-up romps with Nastia. This cruel son of a bitch probably spent his free time breaking bricks with the edge of his hand.*

Pig squinted at the newly-painted number 489 on my overcoat. It stood out too well. Jet-black on a white patch. Artists brush numbers painted on rags stitched by tailors to the front and back of hats and overcoats. Numbers are easier for identification than bothersome names, especially when ID'ing corpses. He sneered at me, elbowed his chum, and spoke in Russian.

"Hey, Shakalov, ain't four eighty-nine the guy they talked about?" They spoke Russian.

"Yeah," Shakalov said. "The American."

Pig jabbed me in the kidneys. *"On your feet, Four Eighty-Nine!"*

I pulled my bare feet out of my coat sleeves, swung them to the earthen floor, and stood, fully dressed, that is to say, barefoot, wool pants, and shirt over candy-striped long-johns, long-sleeved T-shirt, and a vest. I glanced down warily at the repugnant little sadist. The soles of my feet felt warm in the urine-damp dirt.

"Open your shirt and drop your pants!" Pig yelled.

I loosened the rope around my waist. My wool pants shot down with a scratchy whoosh to puddle around my feet. Pig's eyes blazed with dollar signs. He smiled at Shakalov grinning knowingly. They'd never seen peppermint-striped long-johns. Nastia had brought them from home. I opened my wool shirt and exposed the padded vest and long-sleeved T-shirt she'd purchased in Pevek's thriving black market.

More dollar signs lit Pig's beady eyes. "Not approved, four-eighty-nine! Take 'em off!"

He started whacking me to hasten my disrobing. Guards searched *zeks* for civvies worn under Gulag issue, selling them on the black market. Kleptocracy's tender.

"Two days solitary confinement," Shakalov growled, sticking out his hand for my warm duds.

"Starting next week," Pig amended. "Today you're burying stiffs. And write a confession to the commandant about why you violated Gulag dress code!"

"Yes, sir," I said, pulling off my nifty underwear. Goose-bumps pimpled my body like measles. I relinquished my forbidden attire into Shakalov's greedy paws. His eyes gleamed like a jackal eyeing a rodent as he juggled the treasure, sticking it under the arm suspending the chain and wheel rim. With his sly, shifty eyes and stealthy manner his name suited him.[32]

I pulled on my scratchy woolens, wrapped my arms around my chest for warmth, and plunked down on my bunk, two, knee-high, ten-inch-planks, lowest of a tier of four, beside the *parasha*. The man directly above me, and Hans, above him, were silent as church mice during my rousting. The man on the top plank, closest to God, mumbled prayers, his head a foot from the frosty ceiling-headers, haloed with snow like crown-moldings.

A squall whistled into the barracks and flash-froze Krasnoperov's puddle.

Pig turned and shouted above the blast, "You newly-arrived are squad forty-one and forty-two! Here's our welcoming gift: You eat first today!"

Late last night, Hans, describing the rituals and routines of Gulag life, had warned, "At our achingly painful reveille you'll meet two malicious schomos."

I had returned at 11:52 from my four-day honeymoon, beating the curfew, but just barely, and bearing gifts. Nastia had sewn a kangaroo pouch into the inside lining of my overcoat—*zeks*' pants, shirts, and coats were virtually pocketless — and I'd stuffed it with a kielbasa and bottle of *Baltika* for Hans, a small, canned, Polish ham, and a bag of sugar-coated rye cookies for Bondarev and

Yesipov, unfortunates I'd befriended on the icebreaker. Luckily, the gate guard never stepped out of his cozy hut to frisk me in June's, cold, bright midnight with a temperature of 23°, according to the thermometer nailed to the leeward side of a pole, out of the wind.

Dimitri Ivanovich claimed, "At sixty-five below zero *zeks* don't have to work," adding, witheringly, "that sheltered gage has never been that low in my nineteen years here."

Jackal, the tall guard, Shakalov, skinny enough to stand in a cornfield and scare crows, carried an AK-47 and gored *zeks* with its muzzle. Pig ping-ponged the lug wrench, bouncing it off the tire rim and whacking *zeks* as toothless and scrawny as Auschwitz survivors.

Across from my plank, Ivan, a tall, gaunt, old-timer with deeply-carved, horror-disfigured eye sockets, atrophied legs, and one rag-bound foot glared at Pig. Ivan's simian brow of dried, cracked skin was as tattooed as an Egyptian obelisk with barbed-wire hieroglyphics that denoted a long sentence. He stretched out prehensile toes, grasped his other foot-rag, and coughed so hard it sounded as if he were hacking out the last of his lungs. He spit at Pig — missed — and yanked his overcoat over his bristly head shaved bald during the May shower.

Pig spun around and struck his bare foot with a vicious blow. "*Vastavij zhopa* — Up asshole!"

Ivan didn't flinch. He didn't scream. He pulled his overcoat down to expose a toothless snarl and eyes blaring with defiance. While sitting on the throne gumming a chunk of ham last night, Ivan, who suffered anemia, scurvy, and diarrhea so badly he perched on the *parasha* often, told his story. A Tartar from Ufa,[33] he'd worked at the rich Bashneft Oil refinery until sentenced to twenty years for selling a can of gas he had collected from a dripping pipe to support his family. His wife, a janitor, sent him a package once a year.

Pig smashed his foot again. "Three days in the hole! Water to eat!"

Ivan's leg flew up in silent agony. The foot has many frangible parts. Twenty-six bones, thirty-three joints, and over one hundred tendons, ligaments, and muscles. Pig broke something.

Ivan shrugged and raised an eyebrow indifferently that shot up the end of his barbed-wire-tattoo. He was already starving to death; his expression said, *So what?*

Zeks tattoo themselves with images of Christ, monasteries, fortresses, swastikas, and military insignias for symbolic proclamations of social rank and political contempt. Using needles and razors, they painfully etch tattoos into the dermis and packed it with a urine- and blood-soot-paste. Infections are common, deaths not uncommon.

Everyone was up, putting on dry footrags and grim faces.

Pig's syncopated BONG — AHH, BONG — AHH filled the barracks. What fun. He flayed like a goose-stepping drum major with his silver baton, striking men and thumping the rim to the middle of the barracks.

Hans leaned over the edge of his plank. "Pig's the schmo; Jackal's a schnook." He didn't need to explain the Yiddish distinction between jerk and gullible stupidity. "It's time to eat, let's go."

"Steak and eggs, I can hardly wait," I said, rubbing my leg and noting a spot of blood on my pants, not from Pig's blow.

The bunk swayed. Hans's long, grimy barefoot toed for the edge of my plank, climbing down from his third-tier perch. Its wobble did not disrupt Bashir Beridze, the top-bunked-Grozny paladin trumpeting prayers with fervor and a Chechen accent. Elshan Orujov, the Azerbaijani on the second plank over me, yelled, "Hey, Beridze, shut the hell up with that Muslim shit!"

Bashir kept on praying. I wondered if anyone heard his clarion call. To me, robotic passions demonstrably displayed by the devout are repulsive. Moral certitude is either the waving of the weaks' white flag of surrender to life's demands or the fundamentalists' waving of the red flag of warning of life's imminent annihilation by those of similar convictions. My assessment may be unjust, but I associate both religious and secular zeal with pathology and serve up the billions of slain pagans, heretics, witches, and unbelievers from centuries of crusades, inquisitions, reformations, exterminations, purges, and revolutions as corroboration.

I closed my eyes and skated out of that thought into dreamy reflections of Anastasia and listened to the snowshoe-slaps of Hans's bare feet on frozen earth. When I opened my eyes, Hans had sidled past Pig reading a clip board and was grumbling at the stove, searching for his *valenki* drying in orbits of others circling the red-hot coal-drum like an asteroid belt around a luminous sun.

Hans padded back to the plank and pulled down two sets of *portyanki* — footrags — from countless others draped over crossbeams like dirty noodles the length of the barracks. They add a sour stench to air thick with a smoke-urine-feces fragrance clinging to everything just the way the air at McDonald's is anointed with French fry grease. Hans wrapped his feet: Newer rags first, stringy tatters on top, next to his boots, wide enough for another ten thicknesses of rags.

"Did you sleep well?" Hans asked, nodding at the overflowing *parasha*.

"Sure," I said, "dreaming of us living on a Caribbean Island."

"Is Anastasyia returning?"

"At Christmas. You gotta love Soviet conjugal visits."

Hans studied my buoyancy. "High expectations lead to heartbreak," he warned. "I never expect anything and am never disappointed."

I shrugged, fingered the bloody tear in my pants and felt the planks for a nail. Finding it, I pulled off a mitten, got fingernails under its ragged head, and worked the two-inch offender out. I had a thought and etched a hash mark in the stone next to my plank: Day One in Shangri-La.

Day One endured, unchanged and unaffected, for five years, although it took me several months to accept life's new normal. In the Gulag, little things, trifles, were given arbitrary, absolute, importance. Animate objects of little innate worth because of their essentialness in sustaining life validated their importance and need to risk life and limb to defend. A can for your ladle of watery porridge, a plastic cup for water, a boot lace, a match, a sock, a hat all became more valuable than gold and defended at all cost.

On each one of the next eighteen hundred and twenty-six days, I scratched hash-marks in sets of five, four verticals lines slashed by a diagonal. The day I left seven rows were covering the wall next to my plank: the final scratch, seventh row, fifth grouping: day 1826.

While we awaited breakfast call, scrawny, crippled, tortured *zeks* smoked and muttered to themselves or one another. Already dressed — we all slept in all our clothes — men groaned and moaned and dug at bedsores and scratch at lice while wrapping their feet in *portyanki*. They found and pulled on their *valenki* and wedged spoons inside boots — if they had one. Men, whose felt boots had disintegrated, tied on tire-tread-sandals, known as *chetezes*, after the Cheliabinsk Tractor Plant.[34]

In the middle of the barracks, Jackal booted aside the remaining *valenki* drying in orbits around the stove, clearing a path for Pig, who finished studying his clipboard. He drum-rolled the red-hot surface, raising an acrid plume of dust.

"Stand up and listen scumbags!" he yelled. We stood. "You *should stop* loafing!" he shouted. "You *ought to stop* killing yourselves! You *have to stop* missing your quotas ... or" — DRUM ROLL — "it's half-rations for all!"

Pig's diktat produced a chorus of growls and a weary look from me. He'd used the phrase, ты должен остановить — TY DOLZHENM OSTANOVIT.

The word, должен — *dolzhenm* — resonates a particular deference in *spoken* Russian, conveying several different meanings. It can mean you *must* stop, *have* to stop, *ought* to stop, and *should* stop. I translated *dolzhenm* the three ways to illustrate the point. *Dolzhenm* use also illustrates the limitations of Russian's thin, 150,000-word vocabulary; English has a lexicon of one million words. Understanding Russian inflection is central to grasping Russian, and that, Anglophiles, is an epanalepsis.

To avoid mines and escape torture, Pig was referring to *zeks'* proclivity for swallowing wire to induce internal bleeding and escape work even though self-mutilation sometimes led to death. When sufficient blood passed, *zeks* were rewarded a week in the infirmary to clear up "gastric infections." Other men, suffering doom after bed-check, would jimmy open the Gulag door and slink into the Arctic frig for the long cold sleep.

After the half-ration threat, our shepherds stomped the length of the barracks and slammed out for the next wakeup. Our five, squat, flat-roofed, rock barracks, anchored to the mountainside by the weight of their stone, were held together by mortar crumbling so badly that snow-laden wind howled through cracks not chinked with coal chunks or caulked with footrags too stringy to wear. The four-tiered bunk swayed when men moved. Orujov, the Aziz, and Beridze, the Chechen, climbed down for their morning toilet and quest for *valenki*.

"Once we're mining, we'll help fulfill that quota," Hans said optimistically.

"If we survive burying decaying corpses," said Yesipov, a former East German Stasi guard with a snaky smile. His face had been slashed from earlobe to bottom lip during interrogation after an arrest for attempting to escape East Berlin. He was nabbed wedged in a Lada's mini-trunk on October 15, 1989 — 25 days before the Wall fell freeing all East Germans.

"Yesipov," Hans said, biliously, "grave-digging is our primer course for mining."

"Sure it is," Yesipov replied derisively. "Hacking permafrost under an endless sun is exactly like digging mines in tunnels as black as Africa a quarter-mile below the earth's surface."

Ten minutes after reveille, the cook's assistant summoned squads 41 and 42 to the mess, and we filed out into a nippy June morning. It was so cold my nostrils froze into crusty passages that I had to twitch to open. With heads bent, hands clasped behind backs and *valenki* squeaking in fresh snow, we advanced to a trio of guards. One stood with a clipboard and ballpoint pen, another stood rigidly with a rifle at port arms, the third, the duty officer, scowled.

"Halt!" Clipboard shouted. "Sound off!"

One-by-one we stopped two paces in front of him, stood at attention, and shouted our last name, first name, patronymic, sentence, and profession. Clipboard checked us off his list under the watchful eye of the lieutenant. Then we shuffled through new snow, across the compound, to a second checkpoint next to the mess hall. Two more guards — clipboard and rifle — and a lieutenant — scowling — ordered identical recitations. Once our two squads of twelve were checked off, the two officers compared their counts. A miss-count earned them a *zek's* life.

The mess hall, a low, wide, windowless, stone shoebox with seating for eighty on four rows of planks lined with benches. It smelled like a bakery in a smokers' lounge. Its gritty walls, smoke-stained ceiling, and earthen floor greasy with mashed fish bones and rotten innards added to the aroma. Table planks were set on oil barrels and stretched from the entrance to the serving line. We hustled to the front and the mouth-watering aroma of hot yeast bread. From a cardboard box stenciled, **презервативы**—PREZERVATIVY, condoms, I fished out a tin bowl, fingernailed off gunk, and held it out for my breakfast, a top-ladled scoop of watery *grechikha kasha* — buckwheat porridge — with fish bones and a chunk of warm *chornee klebph* — black bread. I sat close to the kitchen's warmth and hefted the bread up-and-down a few times in my hand to guess its weight. It was far below the regulation quarter-pound, but Gulag bread always was. I'd had skimpier. I sniffed the bread and nibbled a little crust without too much sawdust.

Hans watched me weighing the chunk. "Those Kremlin fools are inescapable."

"Phantoms always are," I said. "Forget them, let's eat." My suggestion didn't register.

"The Kremlin created a *Nutrient Guide*, a recipe book for all five hundred Gulags."

"And you're shocked that no one follows their Bible?"

Hans shook his head. "No, just discouraged. Russians accept fraud, stupidity, brutality, and futility and allow tyrants to build the insane system to govern themselves."

"It *would* be discouragingly tragic, Hans, if it weren't so ridiculously hilarious."

"There's a very thin line between comedy and tragedy in Russia."

Dobrolynbov, a lifer from Veronezh, slurped from his bowl, wiped his mouth on his sleeve, squashed his bread flat as a pita then growled, "Their *Guide* says Arctic ration are one kilo — " two and a quarter pounds — "of fish, meat, oil, fat, vegetables, and bread *every* day."

I laughed at the fiction. "I've never seen that much food in a week in six months."

"I've never seen that much in *any month* in my twelve years," Dobrolynbov said.

He slurped some more fishy porridge. "Sip it slowly, friend; the mind is tricked into thinking the belly's being filled."

"I'll try that," I said. "Nothing else works."

Like most prisoners, Dobrolynbov's wife had dumped him, and he never received a package.

Breakfast was silent, *zeks* locked in memories of pancakes and eggs with wives and girlfriends. Before he ate, I saw a man pray. Another crossed himself. Most Soviets had forgotten how. Ten minutes later, after drinking the porridge and wolfing down a hunk of bread, the usual brambling ensued over cigarettes, space, and poppycock. Squads rotated in, pushing and shoving and glaring at us for our seats. Men licked their bowls to the length of their tongues then wiped them clean with bread crusts arched as perfectly as spatulas for the job. Sogginess was nibbled off, and dry crusts squirreled into slits in overcoats for later. A haze settled over the room. Men who had received packages pulled out cigarettes from secret caches and fired up. A few lucky bummed smokes. Orujov, the Azerbaijani, scoured the earthen floor, slick with suet, spit, and fish bones, for butts. He carefully extracted tobacco shreds from butts and rolled them in a paper scrap.

All too soon Vladimir Zyryanov, our squad leader, gathered us in a corner for grave-digging assignments and got grim looks but no groans. Burying winter's dead meant we ate in the mess three times a day. A luckier two were assigned the snow-shoveling brigade. The luckiest man got guard-house mopping duty, which meant a warm place to work, bones tossed on the floor to gnaw on, and longer butts to smoke. The unlucky mass trudged to the coal mine three miles north for twelve hours of digging with a chunk of bread and bowl of warm, salty water for lunch at the canteen.

Zyryanov had been a Saratov coalminer and had served four of his twenty years. He stood an inch over my six-three, had a scared eye socket, broken nose, and the cauliflower ears of a boxer. As he spoke, he scratched his three-week stubble that set off an avalanche of sawdust crumbs snowing onto his overcoat. He was explaining our assignments when a fish bone snagged between my lateral incisor and canine tooth. I'm sure you've experienced similar minutiae, but this triviality became an event so incredible I credit it with saving my life. I had tried to tongue out the bone and then suck at it, and probably would have gotten it, given time, but the table's planks were splinter-rich, and I broke off a sliver and was digging at the bone when Zyryanov said, "Let's get to work!"

He'd never asked us to go into the cold until the last possible moment, and we stood as he did. Just as I rose, a guard approached. He'd been watching me and smiling evilly at my digging at the fishbone snagged in my teeth. His smile broadened, exposing mossy-green teeth stained from a lifetime of smoking and drinking minimally-oxidized, Chinese, green tea — *Camellia sinensis* — popular in the Middle Kingdom since Homer.[35]

"Got some steak caught in your teeth, Americansky?" he scoffed.

"No, sir," I replied. "It's caviar."

He laughed. "Sure it is."

"Sir," Hans said. "Fetisov's a famous chef at the prestigious McDonald's restaurants."

The guard squinted, searching memory. "Didn't they opened a place in Moscow?"

"They did," Hans said. "On Pushkin Square, January thirty-first, nineteen-eighty-nine. Perhaps the Gulag could use Fetisov's gastronomic talents?"

The guard gave that some thought. "Hey now, that's a good idea. I'll mention it." He jabbed me with his AK-47. "In the meantime, Americansky, you're going to love burying stiffs."

It took six months for the seed Hans planted to flower. But flower it did. It saved our lives.

Eighty men leaving at once clogged the doorway, giving Beridze time to kneel in the mud beside the table and thank Allah for breakfast. Orujov, the Azerbaijani, took the small butts, sliced them open with a grimy fingernail, and shook tobacco shreds onto a scrap of paper that he rolled into a cigarette. He dragged the red head of a kitchen match over the table plank, and the reactive phosphorus ignited the potassium chlorate, casting a pleasant, but fleeting, smell that masked the mess hall and body stench for all of two seconds.

Orujov said to me, "There's nothing like a smoke after breakfast."

I looked at him disgustedly. "Don't you worry about TB?"

"When you're here four years," he said, "you'll be divorced and grubbing for smokes, too."

I shook my head and my heart filled with love for Anastasia. "Never happen."

Weeks later, while hauling coal in sleighs to the conveyor belt, the Aziz told me his story. He'd been a Soviet army sergeant and fought in Afghanistan eight years. In a fierce firefight, he'd run out of ammo and was captured by the mujahideen. He escaped in 1987, made it back to his unit, and was arrested and convicted of treason for having been captured — twenty years for being a POW and not hand-fought to the death, a heartless — but still prevailing — doctrine Stalin initiated in WW II.

"Outside stragglers!" a guard yelled at us.

I pulled my hat down over my ears but didn't tie the string. I tightened the rope around the waist of my black overcoat and steeled myself for the necropolis. Last in line, I stared at the shuffling black overcoats filing out like Carpenter Ants, inborn with divisions of labor, and squeaked across the new snow to the tool shed.

"Form two columns for body search and number check!" a guard yelled.

With June's cold wind howling, we pulled opened coats and shirts for patting down. Bread crusts and cigarette butts were okay. Pencils, pens, newspapers, paper or civilian clothes — sometimes swapped at breakfast — were confiscated. Orujov was threatened with solitary confinement if he didn't have his number 473 repainted by Gulag artists *today*. Numbers had to be easily visible from an unspecified distance. By the time inspection finished, the sun had risen a few degrees, and the temperature had nudged up to the freezing point. I was anxious to get to work. Doing nothing for six months is brutal. Probably why so many Sunshine State retirees croak the relaxing winter they arrive.

Armed with chisels, hammers, adzes, shovels, and one, homemade wheelbarrow, we trudged to the rear of the Gulag, and for the next three days, we hacked permafrost, expanding the cemetery in fifteen-hour marathons, gaining a few yards every day. We broke for ten-minute dinners and suppers, longer for headcounts and body searches. We stole everything from corpses' pockets as we buried them, though there wasn't much, most bodies had been stripped bare for clothes. Whenever someone stopped to use a corner of the resting place as a latrine, whippings and lashings were generously bestowed. To endure the gruesome task, my mind fixed on Anastasia or wandered to an idiotic dream of escape. I nicknamed our Gulag, Gulag 17, after the 1953 Academy Award winner, *Stalag 17*, starring Bill Beedle (aka William Holden), as the enterprising cynic Sefton. Unlike Sefton, who bartered with the Germans and escaped through Austria, I never considered chiseling through one hundred yards of permafrost to liberty. The Arctic is not Austria. High above the boreal Tiaga, lichen, moss, grass, and tiniest of flowers will not support human life, and is as proficient at exterminating it as a guillotine.

Late on the third night, guards ordered, "Bury bodies!"

All through the witching hours, we pried frozen corpses from shoulder-high stacks insulating the Gulag's wall and threw them into the pit. When frozen together like Siamese twins, we tossed pairs in and stomped down protruding arms and legs. We finished burying the withered bodies in the greedy lodestone under brittle globs of permafrost about 3:00 a.m.

After two hours of sleep, the banging of the lug wrench on the tire iron awakened us. The day was bright, cold, and snowy. After breakfast, Zyryanov assigned us to the graveyard shift at the coal mine. Work began that evening at seven; snow shoveling filled our day. We finished shoveling Gulag snow at 3:30 and flopped onto our planks, exhausted. I traded my last two *mazevozky pri-aniki* — honey-rye cookies — for paper and pencil and wrote Anastasia. When finished, I took three, ten-ruble notes, stashed in my foot-rag, and set the letter and money into the trembling, translucent hands of Dimitri Ivanovich. He mailed the letter to Nastia. She received it five months later, and her reply, dated that same day, November 22, 1992, was received the following June 1st, three hundred sixty days for the round trip.

It was the first, last, and the only letter received from my love; she chitchatted about teaching at ASU and Dad. Withholding the best for last, she explained she could not make the journey to Pevek at Christmas as she was heavy with child and I would be a father on March 5, 1993 — which meant: *I was already a father*! But of what? A boy or a girl?

She swore she would return to Pevek in June 1993 with our child. She did not. I waited the entire anxious month for her, convinced something dreadful had happened.

It had. But I get ahead of myself.

During the endless days of that abbreviated summer, the three-mile hike to the mineshaft evenings soon turned bitter cold, and yet I remained buoyant, thrilled about Anastasia returning at Christmas. After a skimpy supper of *gre-chikha kasha*, we assembled by the barracks in pairs for headcount. We marched past the guard shack, located between the inner and outer fences, where sentries stared out windows at us as they warmed themselves, drank tea and smoked.

We tramped beneath the Gulag's fading entrance sign proclaiming *Labor is Honor, Glory, and Heroism*. The proclamation, our *raison d'être*, lacked the one essential that I came to appreciate as the months dragged on and quote psychiatrist Thomas Szasz, *Work is the greatest analgesic, soporific, stimulant, tranquilizer, narcotic and to some extent antibiotic — the closest thing to a genuine panacea — known to medicine*. How true!

In pairs, side-by-side, and paced a non-threatening five steps between pairs, we formed two stretched-out columns up the mountain. With backs bent, shoulders hunched, heads lowered, lungs gasping, pace funeral, young *zeks* talked despite guards' warnings, "No talking! March in line! Hands behind you! Eyes fixed ahead!"

For the first fifty yards, guards screamed, "March in step!" but soon the natural shelf the Gulag set on steepened, sleet fell, and walking became perilous. The backs of our black overcoats frosted with ice. Bent over, grunting, heads down, knuckling the ground, we looked like silverback gorillas. With eyes fixed on the heels of the man in front of me, I prayed for the naked crest and plodded up the well-trodden path, smoothed by decades of slogging.

Guards barked, "Keep up! Hands behind your backs! No talking or it is isolation!"

The cowering tapered off as the mountain steepened, air thinned, and it extracted its tolls on legs and lungs. At the summit, winds howled, and temperatures plunged. Ice-pellets slashed faces, watered eyes, and blurred vision. With freezing bodies racked with exhaustion, my mind plunged into depths of despair. I clung to the dream of the chunk of warm bread and a ladle of hot water at midnight dinner and maybe snatching a second chunk of bread if the cook wasn't looking.

To escape insanity from hunger and hardship, I made myself think of the future after Gulag 17. I vowed to live a humble, moral, creative life of tolerance, harmony, and friendship. With my inheritance, Nastia and I would build a fine home and fill it with kids. She would teach college math, and I would launch Carlos O'Brien's Mexican restaurants. In spare time, I would research taxol, find a reliable Chinese supplier, start a lab to explore broadening its usages, and market the drug worldwide to cancer clinics. I began a mental, alphabetical list of all countries I could think of, and, oddly, trudging through the snow, I forgot my cold feet and the snow weaseling through sole holes in my boots. Compiling the list took days and weeks, and I asked Hans for his help. When I put the A's in alphabetical order, I committed them to memory. The A's we remembered were: Afghanistan, Albania, Algeria, American Samoa, Andorra, Angola, Anguilla, Antigua, Argentina, Armenia, Aruba, Australia, Austria, and Azerbaijan. The B's: Bahamas, Bahrain, Bangladesh....

Along the mountain peaks, at this latitude and altitude, neither bushes nor grass grew. Only rocks and lacerating winds. We leaned into North wind and made slow, stiff, shambling, stumbling progress. We fell. Hands bled. Faces stung. Men cursed. Gulag old-hands, like magicians, pulled secreted rags from caches sewn in their overcoats' seams to wrap their faces, leaving only sunken eyes exposed that cast a death pallor like Halloween zombies. Guards dressed in fur hats and thick greatcoats that brushed the tops of their fur-lined boots were not allowed to cover their faces. For once, we were the lucky ones.

Looking over my left shoulder at the foot of Pevek Mountain, a thick layer of coal-smog blurred the town sprawled out along the lip of Chaunskaya Bay. Long rays of night sun punched through the crepuscular wreath and cast dancing shadows of cavorting footballers, too young to worry about the epidemic of respiratory ailments that lay ahead of them for playing in coal-smog-air thicker than an airport's smoking lounge.

Up peaks and down gullies we shuffled. One pair of guards was twenty feet in front of each twelve-man squad. Another pair of guards trailed twenty feet behind. Both pairs as suspicious as Roman sentries. In each duo, one guard carried an AK-47 at port arms, ready to blast, the other wrestled a leashed and snarling long-haired German Shepherd, straining to attack.

June's solstice was summer's apex. By September's equinox, dark winter had set in. The sun dropped below the horizon for thirty minutes on the second night of August. After that, days telescoped, nights snowballed, and summer shriveled to winter. By the end of August, every *zek* had scrounged tattered rags to bind his face. With ends tucked in, we looked like Egyptian mummies ready for the afterlife. Often, after a long night shouldering the wheel, guards halted us on the return to our planks, and, despite being weary and anxious for food and rest, we restacked stone-pyramids to shoulder-height and strung rope between them to mark the ridge for winter's all-black days. In November, our restacked markers proved as reliable as crosshairs in a transit, stumbling through blackness to work the mine and barracks to sleep, our lives bet on rocks, ropes, and dogs.

The hikes to and from the mine were gruesome.

The mine was a horror.

***

TWENTY-SIX
Gulag 17's Coal Mine
June 8, 1992

Under a splotchy, cement-gray sky, red-fringed in the long rays, we tramped through wafered-coal outcroppings down Pevek Mountain's North Slope aimed like Basset Hounds honing in on our target, the stench of rotten eggs radiating from the mine shaft. In this land of northern lights and midnight sun, the bright night's cold breeze carried the faint hum of Russian strategic bombers high overhead aimed for Alaska, probably to shadow F-22s. Closer to the mine, the air teemed with the grating sound of a relentless conveyor belt and the metronomic striking of a smithy at work, sharpening augers and chisels. Around the compound were quiescent spotlights positioned to shine, in seven weeks when the sun dropped below the horizon for the first time since May on blacksmith shop, mess hall, equipment shed, generator shack, office, infirmary, guard house, garage, and testing lab.

After another headcount, squad leader Vladimir Zyryanov yelled, "Gather round."

We cold, hungry, dirty dozen huddled together, more for warmth than his lecture, and the stench of our bodies was overpowered by the putrid rotten-egg reek.

"This mine," Zyryanov said, "began as a surface slope mine and followed a seam far into the mountain. When the coal ran out, we dug vertical shafts down and a series of horizontal seams off it. The lab over there — " he pointed — "tests for coal moisture, ash, sulfur, volatile gasses, and fixed carbon. Now, line up at the equipment shed beside the lab, and I'll assign tools."

We shuffled through an inch of new snow across the compound for tools. My tool was a horse-collar. Hans a small shovel. Orujov and Beridze wide shovels. The other eight *zeks* got pickaxes, hammers, chisels, and augers. Each man was issued two alligator clips and a 5-Watt, hands-free, miners-cap-lamp riveted to two frayed straps, one for encircling the head, the other for going over the crown. A four-foot wire dangled from the light plugged into a battery the size of a pack of cigarettes. Steel-toed boots, hard hats, gas detectors, safety glasses, ear protectors, and portable respirators would have been nice, but this was mining the way Romans had in the days of Julius Caesar.

Zyryanov leaned against the equipment shed and tugged off his felt boots. "Take your boots off," he ordered. "Hook the lamps to your hats with the clips; tie them tight with your *portyanki*. Switch them on when we enter the mine."

I sat on a dirty snowbank and clipped the cap-lamp to my felt hat. I pulled off my boots, unwrapped the footrags, and used them to secure the lamp and two straps around my head. The light wobbled. I yanked the foot rags tighter and slid the battery and wire under my overcoat belt and into a pocket. My feet were freezing and hastily pulled my boots back on.

"Single file!" Zyryanov shouted.

I stepped directly behind him, and Hans squeezed in behind me. The other ten fell in with guards taking up the rear. In a few minutes, we snaked around huge piles of coal, and the horse-collar was chafing my neck. I grit my teeth and lifted it with both hands to ease the rawness.

Beyond pyramids of shiny, black, anthracite, we enter the mine through a twenty-foot opening crowded with a four-foot conveyer belt, noisily spewing coal, and a seven-foot exhaust fan, roaring like a jet engine and choking the air with the noisomeness of rotten eggs. I dropped one side of my horse-collar, held my nose, and tailed Zyryanov down the steep slope.

Around a few corners, the racket lessened enough to be heard. I tapped his broad shoulder. "What's that rotten stink?"

He stopped and turned. His eyes glittered in my lamplight and said, "Hydrogen-sulfide."

"Oh." I had no idea what hydrogen-sulfide was, and he didn't explain.

As the slope steepened, my lamp played off layers of rock Hans identified as sedimentary, metamorphic, and igneous. One six-foot-thick granite strata was swirled with marble and studded with a sparkling inter-grown-cluster of clear, six-sided, quartz crystals glimmering like diamonds. The fist-sized finger-cluster protruded and looked as if it could easily be broken off for a great paper weight, but for … Around a couple more bends and down a seven-degree slope, the fan howl dwindled to a soft, steady whoosh, like an evening breeze through mountain-top pines. The stink intensified.

Zyryanov stopped and faced the squad. As men caught up, his lamp played off anxious faces sniffing the air like wary dogs.

"Those quartz crystals back there were formed in hot, granite, hydrothermal veins," he said. "Don't touch them! They are a display. We sell crystals to Samsung for computer chips. That rotten egg stink is hydrogen sulfide, a color-less, poisonous gas caused by the breakdown of organic matter. It *will* kill you and it *will* explode. And before some smartass asks, we don't have canaries. There is *no* smoking in the mine! *None!* A flame will set it off." He looked at twelve terrified faces. "Other than that you're safe. Mostly."

Hans, slouching against a granite wall, hands on knees, breathing hard, looked up and raised a hand. "But, Volva, what about floods, cave-ins, rockfalls, and a roof collapse?"

"Ahh, there are always those," Zyryanov said, gesticulating with a throw-away motion.

I looked around in the dark foulness and asked, "Where are we digging?"

He pointed between his feet. "Three hundred feet straight down."

"Elevators?"

He gave me a dry smile.

Hans grabbed my arm. I turned around. My light shone on spooky eyes. In a Rod Serling voice, he said, "You're about to enter the ancient world of mega-fauna and dinosaurs."

"Oh, boy," I said. "Big ferns and giant lizards."

I turned to follow Zyryanov and stumbled over some tailings. Hans grabbed my arm helpfully and said, "Actually, lizard's a misnomer."

I wasn't ready for a lecture and said, determinedly, "I read dinosaur meant terrible lizard."

"It does," Hans agreed. "But they weren't lizards at all. They're ectothermic reptiles who basked in the sun or slumbered in the shade for thermoregula-tion."

"Good God, Hans," I said, "ectothermic?"

"Greek for *ektós, thermós* — outside, hot — the Arctic was a hot steamy swamp until — "

I said, "I know, I know. Until the Chicxulub meteor snuff lizards sixty-five million years ago in the Fifth Extinction!"

Hans lectured, "Since life began on Earth, five mass extinctions have exceeded its normal death rate. The most recent, the Cretaceous–Paleogene extinction occurred 65 million years ago, was a mass extinction of animal and plants within a geologically short period of time claimed to have been caused by a meteor striking earth and leaving a hole one-hundred-ten miles in diameter and twelve miles deep adjacent to the Yucatan Peninsula. In the past half-billion years, there have been five major events when over half of earth's animal species have died out. There'll be another. Nuke."

"Isn't that something," I sniped. I had an overwhelming case of claustrophobia and my friend thought it time to babble.

"Here's the 'elevator'," Zyryanov shouted, and we closed ranks, bumping into one another, and almost pushing me down the shaft. I grabbed the rickety rung between two two-by-four sides to avoid certain death.

With headlamps bobbing like erratic fireflies on a series of wobbly handmade ladders, we followed Zyryanov down three hundred feet of layered rock, stopping just below five feet of rose-granite in a dark, dank hall arched with coal-barrier-roof-pillars ten feet high. The pillars formed a series of excavated rooms that extended beyond the reach of our cap-lamps and looked as endless as those in the Hermitage.[36] Except for men sloshing in orange water or yelping when they smacked their heads on overhangs, three-hundred feet into the earth's twenty-five-mile crust was thunderingly silent. And warm!

"Leave your overcoats by the ladder," Zyryanov said, "it stays a constant fifty-five degrees."

"Not constant, Vova," Hans corrected. "The earth warms one and one-half degrees every hundred feet to its core, which is about eleven thousand degrees, hotter than the sun's surface."

Zyryanov shot him a look. "Thanks, professor, my fact for the day."

Without skipping a beat, he assigned jobs. "Seeliganov you're the belt cleaner/scooper (scooping coal onto the belt that fell off). Orujov and Beridze, you're fillers (shoveling coal from the face into coal-sleighs). Ivan and Igor (me), you're coal haulers (pulling coal-sleighs to the conveyor belt just as 70,000 pit-ponies had in Britain in George Washington's day). The rest of you chisel and auger the face. You two," he said to Ivan and me, "hook your collar to those sleigh chains and start hauling as soon as you're full."

The acrid air filled with the bongs and whacks of pickaxers chiseling coal off the seam's ten-foot face and the clunks of fillers shoveling chunks into our sleighs.

When my sleigh was full, I shouted to the squad leader, "Where the conveyor, Vova?"

Zyryanov pointed into a pitch-black tunnel. "Two hundred meters that way!"

The coal-sleigh was the size of my childhood Radio Flyer, a red steel wagon with four wheels and high wooden-staked sides I zipped down Chestnut Street on in Blowing Rock. This 'Radio Flyer' had runners instead of steel wheels with hooks at the tip that attached to the chains hooked to my collar. I took my overcoat from the heap beside the ladder, rolled it around the horse collar for padding, shouldered into my pit-pony harness, and, head down, dragged it out of the pillared room into blackness. The squad vanished. My cap-lamp threw a puny beam onto the floor strewn with broken pickaxe handles, tattered boots, puddles, trenches, and tailings. The rotten egg stench lessened. Warm air carried the stink upward; the rumble of the conveyor belt grew louder. I tried to visualize the enormous weight and compression forces of the North American Tectonic Plate sliding into the eastern Siberia's Eurasian Plate that had crushed ancient plants into coal as hard as steel. Was the plate-shifting finished?

My shoulders scraped outcroppings. My boots snagged and tore on jagged-edged tailings. My head whacked low ceilings, but I rammed shoulders into the pony collar and tried not to dwell on cave-ins. I felt like a horseless Paul Revere in this black night. In places, the going got so rough, so wet, and so steep, it forced me to crawl, crab, and slosh, but I finally reached the rackety conveyor belt. Hans shoveled coal muffs raining down on him.

I tugged the coal sleigh up a ramp, heaved up an end, and dumped it onto the conveyor.

Then I plopped down to rest and leaned against the edge of granite that felt like a knife. I was cold, my feet were wet, and everything ached. Hans tossed his shovel and plunked down beside me. The belt kept grumbling and spitting muffs, obliging us to shout.

"Hard to imagine how old this place is;" Hans yelled, "I'd guess Carboniferous Period of the Paleozoic Era, three-hundred-sixty million years, give or take." He flipped his hand.

"Before the Dinosaurs?" I asked.

Hans nodded. "Oh, long before."

"Suppose we'll hit dino bones?"

Hans elbowed me. "Not a chance. The lithosphere's sixty-two-mile-thick."

"Good to know we're safe," I said. "Here comes Zyryanov, I'm better giddy-up." And on that cherry note, I shouldered into my pit-pony fetter and disappeared into the tunnel.

We worked twelve-hour nights, six nights a week, breaking for a midnight lunch at the canteen, a room at the mine entrance that held thirty men at a seating. The food was always the same: a chunk of black bread and a cup of warm salted watery soup ladled from a pot sitting on the coal stove. My nights of hauling coal continued, unchanging, for six months. Cold, filth, exhaustion, and hunger were constant companions. The loss of liberties and the enforcement of restraints on everything made our days a zombie-like continuum of work, beatings, pitiable food, and insufficient sleep. The beatings dished out by vicious guards quelled any appetite for retribution, and we lived in silence. I took no part in arguments and the hopeless gossip that Yeltsin's democracy would soon commute our sentences.

When guards blew whistles at 7:00 a.m., signaling the end of the work night, the pounding of sledgehammers, the clanging of pickaxes, the grunts of exertion ceased, and quiet set in, and the labored strains of wretched men climbing flimsy ladders began. Outside, roll call began in the cold blackness. Men became hysterical as icy blasts whipped overcoats, turned fingers white through holes in mittens, made feet stomp in stiffened boots, and lashed tears from eyes. We huddled and shivered and grumbled and swore and waited for stragglers. A correct roll call might take three or four attempts and thirty or forty minutes before ordered to "March!" Then into the blackness where we followed the dogs in knee deep snow and trudged three miles along ridgelines clotted with refrigerator-sized boulders, moguls Aspen skiers would die for, and frozen corpses.

At the Gulag, after another head count and body search, it was porridge, bread, and sleep.

Too soon sleep ended and the barracks came alive with the usual poppycock: arguments over cigarette butts, space, freedom, and dirty looks. Men played chess with pieces hammered from granite shards or played poker with cards made of layered paper glued together with a bread-and-water paste and characters painted in a blood-soot dye. A few men spent those precious hours formulating crazy plans of escape. Others mended coats, foot rags, and felt boots. Twice a month we took soapless showers in icy water and once a month we changed our clothes. Silly arguments never stopped over the latest rumor of freedom: *My cousin wrote that Yeltsin was freeing all non-felon political prisoners next month.* Sure. There were even arguments over the value of the new 1992 kopek and Ruble, which no one had even seen, but claimed it was struck with a double-headed eagle over the *Банк России* — Bank Russia — legend.

Time passed slowly. By November, the days had eclipsed into twenty-four-hour blackness, and the endless regimen of roll calls, porridge, black bread, tramping to work and tramping to sleep became an endless rut of hunger, cold, and exhaustion. With never enough rest, never enough food, and with yesterday like today, like tomorrow, life became a teaspoon-paced cycle of maddening sameness, severity, and dashed illusions in the cold, fetid air of sweat, rot, and death both in the Gulag and below ground in the labyrinthine of catacombs.

Summer evening three-mile slogs to the mine turned bitter cold in mid-August. The little Arctic vegetation turned brown, frost hit, snow fell, and all the clement sweetness of the ephemeral summer vanished. In autumn's shivering treks to and from the mine, I longed for the mosquitoes of summer, though lice, Carpenter Ants, and bedbugs were year-round companions. We plucked them off bodies, coats, hats, mittens, pants, footrags, and shirts. Ants thrive on bedbugs. A female bedbug lays 500 eggs in her ten-month life. Her eggs hatch in seven days, and since the parasites prefer body-heat to stove-heat, they breed, molt, shed skin, and thrive on human flesh.

As the months dragged on, death and starvation claimed the lives of dozens and the cherished top plank in the middle of the barracks, near the stove, far from the *parasha,* and somewhat freer of bedbugs and ants became vacant and the craving of most men. I grabbed it.

Twice a day, during group toilet and at midnight lunch, and twice a month during three-minute showers, I sometimes found scraps of paper with news of the outside world and hastily read it. Sometimes tidbits were scribbled on shower walls: Yeltsin's shock therapy had set off hyperinflation, desperation, depression, and millions of unemployed; the end of the Cold War had cost the country 25% of its industrial output; one-in-five jobs across Russia had been lost; half of Russian cities had one-industry employers, and many had pink-slipped everyone; in 1993, half the country was living on $25 a month and wages were falling; male life expectancy had plunged to age 56; the cost of medicine had skyrocketed. This news always led to long debates and gave rise to speculation, hopes, and dreams that never materialized.

Six months of dragging coal sleds to the conveyor withered my line-backer-sized-frame to that of a Kenyan marathoner. In mid-December, I fell sick and was unable to pull the sleigh; on Christmas Day 1992, I was reassigned to the pick-axe crew. The following day, the McDonald's seed Hans had planted the prior June flowered into a Christmas cactus more glorious than the spidery-legged, lipstick-red cactus at the Briarpatch we swooped under that Black Friday thirteen months before. Hans had said I was a culinary expert. I had reinforced it daily when guards screamed at us to report. We'd bellow our family name, given name, patronymic, year of birth, article of violation, length of sentence, and trade: *Fetisov, Igor, Vladimirovich, 1969, Article 58, five years, restaurateur*!

And so it came to pass, on the day after Christmas, while shuffling through the chow-line the Gulag 17's head cook, Ivan Shelpov, a tall, tattooed skeleton of thirty-two, serving twenty years for selling drugs to Tver middle schoolers, keeled over with abdominal pains in his swollen belly and spewed from both ends. Shelpov had washed dishes in a Novosibirsk restaurant and knew a spoon from a mop and little else. He missed vomiting into the porridge tub by a couple of inches, but his diarrhea splattered six feet of line, which didn't slow down the hungry. He died fifteen minutes later; prognosis: Acute ptomaine poisoning. His assistant said Ivan had been gorging himself for a week on canned horse meat from Osh, Kyrgyzstan.

His premature departure to the big kitchen in the sky awakened my Lady Luck. We dragged Shelpov's corpse to the heap behind the barracks and returned to eat. The Gulag commandant appeared and anointed *moi*, the McDee major domo, Gulag *Schlockmeister*. What a lifesaving Christmas present! Who would have ever dreamed my burger savvy would be the springboard to Gulag head cook? But then, who'd have dreamed three weeks later America would inaugurate a tomcatting, draft-dodging, Arkansas governor, 46, its 42nd president.

As Gulag head cook seven hundred miles north of the Arctic Circle, I was given the authority to appoint my staff. I requested Hans and kept Shelpov's assistant as a handyman. We kept the kitchen clean, the food hot, and, whenever guards weren't watching, we'd feast on their leftovers, sucking the marrow from guards' discarded pork, beef, and chicken bones. Over the next fifty-two months, we made bread, porridge, and soup and purloined enough pilfered bones to fill out our baggy pants. The only family contact I had in all those lonely months was receiving a few letters: one from Anastasia, a wedding announcement from Kahuna and Ingrid, two from Dad, and one from my mother-in-law, Oksana, with details about the birth and care of our baby, Nastia.

Dad's last letter was the news of Anastasia's death.

***

TWENTY-SEVEN

Gulag 17, Pevek, Chukotka Autonomous Region, Russia
January 2, 1997

"*Dobroe utro; i kak* Troy *eto prekraenoye utro*? — Good morning; and how's Troy this beautiful morning?" Hans Seeliganov caroled, clambering down from his third-tier plank, below my plank.

I wondered if my old friend wanted the truth. Six days over my five-year sentence, I was depressed, disheartened, and discouraged and certainly not ready to pop open my eyes and head for the kitchen singing Hi Ho, Hi Ho, It's Off to Work We Go. I laid there, eyes closed, nursing an acute case of megrims and listening to my jolly friend shamble to the stove and rifle through the ring of boots. I glanced down. The stove was so hot, the middle of the inky barracks glowed as red as Amsterdam's *Rossebuurt* district.

"Did you croak?" Hans brayed sunnily, slapping his boots together to knock off the ice.

"*Nyet, nyet,*" I said. "I'm okay, Hans."

I rolled onto my back and stared up at the rafters. An icicle hung like a dagger two inches from my nose. Was it portentous?

"It's time to rise and shine and behold the glory of the morning," Hans prodded in English.

"Yeah, right. Another all-black morning only an Eskimo could love."

"Ahh, but this could be your *lucky* morning." Hans acted as if he had a secret.

"Sure it could. If the former Chargé d'affaires and newly-crowned American puppeteer acts on the letter I wrote the ambassador from Blagoveschensk trial five years ago."

"Collins will, Troy! Get the fireworks ready!"

That sounded strange. How would Hans know anything about the ambassador?

"Fireworks," I lamented, "why didn't I think of it?" I'd never seen Hans so cocky.

"Help comes to those who believe," Hans entreated.

I broke off the icicle, sat up, and heaved it at the barrel stove. "Here's your fireworks!"

The ice-dagger hit the red-hot stove, shattered, hissed but didn't exude the effluvium of 4th of July cordite. It spooked Hans, and he jumped, slipped, and hit the frozen earth hard. Fully dressed, except for his feet, he was always first to hit the dirt mornings, tiptoeing around frozen puddles for his boots before other *zeks* tramped them in the melting pools. The spill didn't faze him. Always even-tempered, he pushed himself up, yawned, enjoyed a slow, languorous stretch, and bent down to pull on his boots, putting one foot on his knee, teetering and pulling on a boot.

He chuckled. "You know, it's reprehensible, Yeltsin's democracy just isn't getting the job done. Tens of millions of Russians are unemployed. There's no work in monotowns.[37] Half of Russia lives on twenty-five dollars a month. Our Gulag's half empty and two are shuttered. I say enough of Boris!" His voice hit a high-octane pitch. "We need Stalin!"

Old friends now, we enjoyed jesting at Gulag lunacy, safely expressed in English. "At least Joe kept the Gulags full," I agreed, wondering why he'd changed the subject. Hans's goofy cynicism made my clock run backward into the throes of *déjà vu.* I realized, with a small pang, I was now a twenty-seven-year-old widower and father of a little girl I'd never seen. Five years ago, I was a carefree, newlywed, McDonald's manager galloping off on a white stallion, seeking taxol for my maiden in distress, and now I'm far from all the aches of home. Since then, I'd been *poisoned with deep grief that came in battalions,* to paraphrase the Bard. Mother had been killed, Anastasia had died, Dad's heart had given out, and I was imprisoned. The one flickering candle in all that darkness came with the birth of our daughter. And she had learned to crawl, walk, and talk while the earth made four laps around the sun and I had hauled coal and made black bread and porridge.

With little news from the outside world filtering into the Gulag, I did not know then how those five years saw G. H. W. Bush lose reelection to the playboy from Arkansas, or Panamanian President and drug lord-narco-kleptocracy-king Noriega jailed for forty years, or Czechoslovakia split in two, or the European Union formed, or South Africa adopt majority rule.

I rolled over, scratched my stone calendar with my old secret nail. I tallied the hash marks: 1,832. Seven days over my five-year sentence. Did Russian justice exist or was it an oxymoron?

I heard a rusty squeal and felt a blast of frigid air rush into the Gulag. Too dark to see, the temperature always plunged when the north door opened. If it closed quickly, which it did, it indicated a trustee. Guards always left the door open. Shivering, I squinted into the blackness and saw the familiar stooped and hunchbacked shape of Dimitri Ivanovich Popov, a lifer, known by his diminutive, Dema. He shuffled to the stove's red glow. He kept the *parasha* emptied and the coal fires stoked twenty-four/seven, sleeping in catnaps like a dog. Dema stopped beneath my plank and looked up. His face was lined with so many wrinkles it looked like a roadmap. His rheumy blue eyes glowed with excitement. The old buzzard was bursting with news.

"*Chto proiskhodit* — What's happening — Dema Ivanovich?" I said and prayed.

With one boot on, Hans hopped over and sang out, "It appears Dema has a secret."

"Good news, perhaps," I said, curious as to how Hans would know.

The old man had never heard spoken English and stared at us as if he were insane.

"Must be, Dema Ivanovich looks as if he's going to explode," Hans observed.

I climbed down, careful not to step on mittened fingers, and elbowed between Dema and a gaggle of *zeks* searching for their *valenki*. Locke, the protector of the old and infirmed.

Davayte poslushayem yego — Let's hear it — Dema," I encouraged.

Dema squared his frail shoulders and said in Russian, "Fetisov, you're to report to the commandant at eleven this morning." He looked around conspiratorially and leaned in close. His breath stunk. His clothes reeked. He grasped my hand in his withered paws. "When I mopped his floor last night I saw your plane ticket. Pevek to Magadan to Moscow *today*!"

My heart leaped!

"*Mazel tov!*" Hans cried.

I grabbed Dema frail arms, hoisted him up, and kissed his furrowed cheeks.

Hans said, "See? Wishes *do* come true!"

I set Dema down and danced around the stove, hands over my head, booting *valenki*, yelping like I'd scored the Super Bowl's winning touchdown. When I finished my victory lap, I said, "How'd you know, Hans?"

"One of the benefits of old age is nocturia. I met Dema at the punchbowl last night."

Dema yanked my arm and insisted, "You must cook this morning."

"Of course, Dimitri Ivanovich. We will, and it'll be the best damn food you've ever eaten!" I yelped in Russian and to Hans, in English, "Partner, you'll be head cook mañana."

"I can hardly wait," Hans said.

"Ah, come on, Hans, it'll save your life. You'll be with your daughter before you know it!"

I was beyond excited, yanked on my boots, tightened the belt around my overcoat, and we hurried into the frigid blackness that, today, felt as crisp and fresh as a good apple. The sky was ablaze with a trillion stars. The sun was a blushing promise beneath the earth's tilted axis. It had set in November and wouldn't rise for two more weeks and then for only thirty-four minutes, and I'd be long gone!

Every day we made black bread, porridge, and soup, and every day we followed the same three recipes, like airline pilots running through checkoff lists that assured safety. Little could be done to enhance the taste or the food or help. McDees had prepared me for dealing with incompetent help. But Hans, who had been starving in the mines for seven months and couldn't lift a teaspoon when I promoted him, caught on fast.

We tromped through knee-deep snow to the guard shack for the storeroom keys, then to the storeroom, loaded the sled — a sheet of plywood with ropes looped through holes — with cartons of sunflower oil and three forty-kilo bags of buckwheat for porridge.

"Stuff three cans of the diced pears under the *grechka,* Hans. Say, why are you looking so chipper? I'm the one getting out."

"You getting out means I'm halfway through my ten years," he said. "I'd write Yeltsin and plead for a release, but censors wouldn't mail the letter."

"Boris has been out sick — heart — for six months. Write him a letter; I'll mail it in Moscow."

"And one to my daughter?"

"Of course."

We dragged the sled across the compound. *Zeks* were stomping and shivering and straggling out of the barracks for reveille's thirty-five-minute roll call. Guards always beat the last *zeks* coming outside, and I found myself humming, *Hi Ho, Hi Ho, It's Off to Work I Go* like I was one of Snow White's dwarfs. A blizzard kicked up and peppered us with ice crystals. I laughed out loud. It only magnified my joy. I unlocked the kitchen door, fired up the two-drawer pizza oven, and Hans started reheating bread and calling out the recipe to me.

"Dump in three bags of buckwheat," he said. "Turn on the electric cooker and dough hook."

I did and watched the hook slowly break-up the flour and clumps of straw and grapefruit-size balls of sawdust, warming it by fiction. "Done," I said.

"Add four buckets of snow, two handfuls of salt, and bring the porridge to a boil," Hans said.

The black bread Hans was reheating smelled yeasty, and we looked around — safe — and helped ourselves to some. Then we began slicing the warm, five-pound-loaves into quarter-pound chunks. "The porridge is boiling," I said.

"Turn it down to simmer before serving," Hans said without glancing at the checklist. "Add the pears. Hey, they're not on my list." He acted surprised.

When the prisoners stomped in, Hans passed out bread, and I spooned out gruel into bowls for those with bowls. Men without bowls waited for those that did to lick them clean. After breakfast, the *zeks* left for work, and, again, Hans and I trudged across the compound to the guard shack for keys. A rising half-moon hung on the western horizon low enough to throw long shadows off Pevek buildings at the foot of Pevek Mountain. Back in the kitchen, I didn't have to glance at the recipe and started cooking lunch. I warmed a big can of powdered milk on the stove and added three tablespoons of yeast and sugar to work. Hans tore off a brittle yellow requisition slip, blew off the dust, and sat on the kitchen floor to write his letters. I thought of my little Anastasia as I washed out the cooker with melted snow, wondering if she had started nursery school. I dumped in three forty-kilo-bags of rye flour, salt, and brown sugar and turned on the dough hook and let the dry ingredients mix for five minutes. She had probably started school and was taking ballet like her Mom had. All Russian girls dream of being the next Anna Pavlova. I added some water, molasses, and yeast.

Hans wrote in bursts, stopping, reflecting, and writing quickly. In the time it took the dough to mix, Hans finished writing and reread the letters. His tongue peeked out from between his lips to help his effort crossing out a word, adding another. I shut off the dough hook and punched the dough. It was as big and spongy as a giant beach ball. Little Anastasia had never seen an ocean. That would be fun, building sand castles. I added the sunflower oil and turned the machine on. I wondered if I'd have to get her a visa to leave Russia . Hans stopped fiddling and gave me the letters. He scribbled addresses. I stuffed them in my pocket, removed the dough hook, and covered the tub with a cloth. We set the tub next to the stove where it would rise to twice its size. I wondered if little Anastasia would recognize me. I wondered how Tver had changed in five years. And America.

While the dough expanded, we oiled dozens of loaf pans. Then we hoisted the tub and dumped the dough onto the lightly floured table, deflated it, and cut the big glob into two parts. We each kneaded half. When it felt just right, we sliced the dough into two-foot lengths, pressed them — seam-side down — into bread tins and popped out the air. We set the bread tins around the stove to rise again. At ten thirty we were feeding the bread into the pizza oven and had the lunch soup made: water, meal, and horse innards.

"While you're flipping the bread out of the pans to cool on racks," I said, pulling on my overcoat, "I'm going to the barracks to get ready to leave."

Hans smiled. "That won't take long."

"Please, memorize this." I gave him my Blowing Rock address, a hug, and headed to the bath house. Crossing the compound, I looked down at Pevek. A half moon had risen just enough to cast spider-leg-shadows off dock cranes rimming Chaunskaya Bay. Pevek wasn't much. Lots of vacancies in sad building on a spit of land at the edge of the iced-over bay. In my fifty-four months at the Gulag, I never returned to Pevek after those four glorious days with Anastasia. I'd relived those four days and her death a million times, more after our baby was born and Anastasia's breast cancer had metastasized uncontrollably.

In the Gulag shower, I never grew accustomed to slipping and skipping on ice-covered planks in freezing water. It is done fast. In those moments, I made plans to take little Anastasia to a Caribbean Island. Visions of steamy cascades of tropical rain flooded my mind, always out of reach here. Once hosed down, I shaved off my beard and cut my hair with the communal razor, all the time wondering if I could fit into little Nastia's life. Could she make the transition to America? Would the islands be a better place to raise her than Blowing Rock?

She had lived with her grandmother in a little apartment in Tver, 150 miles north of Moscow. Would she be ready to leave the only home she had ever known to rattle around in a big house in a North Carolina mountain village with two traffic lights? The Blowing Rock house was a hollow cage that only hope, love, and expectations could recast as a caring and accepting nest. Could the village help instill in her a feeling of belonging? Would it? Could I help the transition? I had doubts. How can a four-year-old, without knowing a word of English, ever connect to a small, isolated, Appalachian hamlet where people still claim, "We ain't got no foreigners here." Even so picturesque a village as Blowing Rock, glittering with wealth, privilege, luxury, and power, was only a joyous interlude for weekend flatlanders. They scoffed-up second homes at bargain-basement prices in an economically depressed county lacking a soul and purpose other than perpetuating the myth of the bucolic splendor of living on mountain tops with hundred-mile views and a nearby university.

At Mom's funeral, I had felt utterly alone in Blowing Rock, even when walking down crowded Main Street on a sunny afternoon. Survival there meant earning your living elsewhere, or, for locals, being a professor, doctor, lawyer, or landed gentry. Everyone else sold real estate, flipped burgers, or subsisted on food stamps. Would it be wiser to start life anew as one, paradoxically, both an emigrant and an immigrant?

Dema came into the bath house and set down a washed, damp, set of clothes on the stool. I wrapped foot-rags around my feet and pulled on the scratchy shirt and pants and my old boots. Wearing underwear again would be a treat. I took the two letters out of my grungy pants pocket, slid them into my washed ones, pulled on a felt hat and padded overcoat, and returned to the barracks for a few cherished things, letters and a faded, lined, and wrinkled photograph of Anastasia with our baby with Dad at Bass Lake. I'd never shared it with a soul. Anastasia had mailed it. With my secret nail, I had dug a wall crevice beside my plank. Since I had nothing else, there was nothing to pack. I looked around the void, climbed the four sleeping-planks, lifted the fourth-tier plank next to the wall, and slid out a brick-sized rock it had taken me two weeks to dig free. I pulled out the four letters and one picture, the only source of comfort I'd had for five years. On the reverse side of the picture, Nastia had written, *Your family, Bass Lake, July 4, 1993*. The picture, taken a few weeks before Anastasia died, showed the three of them sitting under a sugar maple on a quilt Grammy Locke had knit. A picnic basket and grill, tilting on the lush green slope running down to Bass Lake. Behind them, the hillside was a radiant, pink profusion of wild rhododendron blooms winding up through the oaks and maples below Moses Cone's mansion. In the checkered shade of one ancient maple, Anastasia was cuddling our baby who, in plump little fingers, warily held out the mushy remains of a hot dog bun to a Canadian gander. She had four inches of curly blonde hair and mustard on her pink cheeks as she tormented the gander. Leftovers, ears pinned back, body tense, fangs displayed, was guarding her, ready to spring. I could almost hear him growl. The gander was squawking, his black head and long neck stretched out so far it exposed his white chinstrap as he honked and hissed and flapped his six-foot brown wings, demandingly. Canadian geese are monogamous and mate for life. His mate waited patiently behind him, two goslings under foot. Anastasia wore a kerchief snugged tightly around her hairless head. She looked haggard and exhausted but contented. Dad looked pale and fragile and exhausted. The baby looked like a handful and a half.

The picture was all I had of my past life. It was as powerful an emollient as midazolam would have been in easing my pain and helping me cope with my losses. I had long since come to terms with Mom's death, but Anastasia's death still gave me nightmares. I could not imagine life without her. Dad looked thin and weak, but he was teaching "fulltime" — that's nine hours a week — or had been the last time I received the second letter from him two years ago. Had he died? Probably.

In my twenty-seventh year now, I'd been incarcerated five years, and it was from barren Pevek I would begin my homeward odyssey. Turbo-jet on Yakootiya Airlines to the Sokol Airport in Magadan, an icebound city of 90,000 one thousand miles to the southwest. I'd skip Blagoveshchensk, another thousand miles southwest — and still in Siberia! — and fly directly to Moscow, train to Tver, and visit my mother-in-law, the only family I had, and meet my little girl and bring her home.

Mom was killed a month before I left five years ago. My once-a-year, June-letters from Dad stopped two years ago, and I worried his heart might have given out. My June letter of 1993 that Anastasia had written on October 18, 1992, told me she was pregnant. Dad had written two letters. The first said Anastasia's cancer had reappeared with viciousness and our daughter, also named Anastasia, had been born on March 5, 1993, at the Watauga Medical Center in Boone. His later letter said Anastasia had died, her ashes buried in Blowing Rock beside mother, and that Oksana, Nastia's mother, had come to America to pick up the baby who was soon to be four years old. Oksana was raising our child in Tver until I was released.

I had no desire to live in Russia. I'd pick her up and bring her back to Blowing Rock and then make plans. I had to phone Oksana and tell her I was freed and on my way. I worried about little Anastasia; she knew only Russian, but I consoled myself with the faith little kids pick up languages fast. I did. She would too. I wondered if she would fight leaving the only home she'd ever known.

Dema stomped into the barracks. "It's time. Follow me to the Commandant's office."

"You bet," I said.

I had said goodbye to my friends, and with a buoyant heart, I followed Dema, slogging through the snow to the small, stone, Gulag office by the main gate. We stomped off snow onto the cement floor and entered the warm outer office, smaller than a one-car garage.

Dema said, "Wait," and pushed aside a tarpaulin and entered the inner office. He reappeared and held the tarpaulin aside. "Enter."

I ducked under his sweaty armpit and entered the Gulag's inner sanctum. A weak light shown from a dusty bulb above the plywood desk of the commandant, a tall, thin, unshaven man of forty. He sat in an armless chair before a scattered of files and an overfilled ashtray fashioned from a herring can. I stood at rigid attention, hands stiffly at my thighs, eyes fixed on a glossy, red-nosed Yeltsin on the wall behind the commandant. There were no windows, no chairs, and three wooden boxes crammed with files. Spartan.

He looked at me without speaking, his scowling eyes asking the usual question.

"Fetisov, Igor, Vladimirovich," I said. "Article fifty-eight, five years, restaurateur, reporting as ordered, sir," repeating the unasked question.

The commandant thumbed through a stack of papers, licked his thumb when he came to a mimeographed sheet and studied it a moment. "You've finished your sentence, Fetisov," he announced, tilting back in his chair. He lit a Marlboro, inhaled deeply, exhaled, and studied me. He pawed through some more papers, found a face-down one, licked his thumb again, turned it over and signed it. A man makes a special flourish when signing his name, but I couldn't make out his upside-down hen-scratching written in Russian. He kept the original and gave me a carbon copy. Since the Gulag had no property desk, and I wore everything I owned, I didn't need to sign for belongings.

The muscles in his neck bulged with the effort as he picked up an airline ticket to Moscow and some Rubles. He did not mention the exchange rate. "Take the supply truck to the airport," he said. "Dismissed!" A jealous look accompanied his bark.

I stepped backed one pace, said, "*Spaseba*, Commandant; *dosvedana*," turned and fled. Instantly, my mind filled with one goal: Get my little girl and bring her home.

In the outer office, Dema was mopping the cement floor with dirty water and a dirtier mop. I said goodbye to him and tightened the belt on my buttonless overcoat. And at noon on the bitter-cold, black, blizzardy day of January 2, 1997, I bound out of the Gulag main office, humming *Born Free as The Wind Blows* into the howling wind and galloped the few steps to the main gate, proudly holding my papers up for the guards to read. They already knew and motioned me through, pointing at a truck, idling roughly, coughing and eructing thick black smoke. Trucks are never shut off in winter.

I brushed a foot of snow off the running board, stepped up, and climbed into the cab.

The truck driver cocked his chin at me. "You Fetisov?" he asked in Russian.

"I am, indeed; Igor Fetisov," I replied to the big, ruddy-faced man. "And you?"

"I'm your ride, Ivan Smirnov."

Smirnov had plump sausage-like fingers and a basketball belly protruding from his open overcoat. He wore a *shapka*, earflaps up, fur-lined boots to his knees covered with snow that was puddling on the floor pan. He levered himself around and eyed me head to toe. The inside of the cab was warm, almost hot. I yanked off my hat.

"A lousy day to go home, ain't it?" Smirnov said, turning on the headlights. "Fifty-eight below zero, wind blowing like hell."

"A beautiful day to go home," I countered.

"Want a real cigarette?" he asked, shaking out a Marlboro from his pack and extending it.

I held up a hand. "No, thanks, never need them. I appreciate the ride to the airport."

"Don't thank me till we get there. The road is shitty; we gotta make it first."

Smirnov's basketball belly kept the steering wheel at arm's length, and he had to stretch to grind the shifter into four-wheel low as he depressed the clutch. Dashboard lights glowed off his fleshy skin, splotchy and freckled in places but mostly concealed by his bushy mustache and two-week stubble. His long snarled eyebrows needed braiding. His eyes were hard. I was glad he was ordered to drive me to the airport, and I didn't have to ask for a lift.

"Americansky ain't ya?" he asked through tobacco-stained teeth and popped the clutch. The headlights reamed a fuzzy tunnel into the blizzard.

"Ye-es," I said as the truck jerked forward.

The engine strained through swirling snow and hit unplowed snowbanks serving as speed-bumps that kept us from flying down the precipice to Pevek. The hamlet was a faint scatter of fireflies twinkling at the base of a white ribbon uncoiling westward. It looked like an impressionistic charcoal LeRoy Neiman might have sketched of the Little Nell Run on Aspen Mountain with the village of Aspen nestled at its base.

"Noon and barely any lights on in the village," I said. "What gives?"

Smirnov shrugged but didn't reply. The strong, silent type.

I was overjoyed to be free! And yet my freedom was dulled, not by the black, numbing, cold, but by pondering the fate of all the *zeks* I left behind, their long, wretched years ahead. One-in-three would die of malnutrition, exhaustion, scurvy, pellagra, infections, or tuberculosis, the scourge of Russian Gulags.

Wind blasts furrowed thigh-high snow gullies in the road, and it took us a slow, cautious twenty minutes to crawl down to Pevek and an hour to plow the 16 km to the airport. But I arrived two hours early for the four o'clock flight to Moscow, delighted to be early and savor the taste of freedom. I'd order scrambled eggs, sausage, toast, pancakes, and pastries, then read a newspaper, talk to ordinary people, sit on a toilet, wash my hands in hot, soapy water, look in a mirror, buy a toothbrush and brush my teeth.

Two weeks before, during our three-minute shower, I'd stared into floor ice and saw the reflection of an unrecognizable face. It was an old man's face, skeletal, wrinkled, and puddled with black circles beneath eyes and Santa's white hair. At the time, I wondered if my hair had turned white overnight as the unhappy Marie Antoinette's had the night before she walked to the guillotine. Perhaps my skimpy diet had caused the melanin pigment in my hair follicles to stop producing. Regardless, kids would take one look at me and scream, "Ghoul!"

Pevek International Airport sets on the edge of the North American Continental Shelf five feet above the Arctic Sea. Twice-a-month flights roar in over thick sheets of ice. The terminal, a three-story, concrete box, extended the length of a football field, its upper floors cantilevered out, handy for spearing sea lions. Lights flickered from second- and third-floor windows of the workers' dorm. To the rear, rising four stories above it, was the air control tower, and, beyond it, beacons glowed red down a mile-and-a-half runway with the capacity to land thirty planes an hour. The two, monthly, commercial flights arriving presented no separation problems for controllers, although random landings of Tupolov Tu-95s, the four-engine, swept-wing, turboprop-powered, strategic bombers that buzzed Alaska probably kept them awake.

Smirnov geared down and stopped in the middle of the shoebox at a narrow door in a portico boarded up with five 4- x 8-foot sheets of plywood. I glanced at my ticket, PWE to SVO, two airport codes I would never forget. Like many Americans, my mind was cluttered with BOS, JFK, DCA, MIA, DAL, DEN and SFO. To that, I added the codes for Pevek and Sheremetyevo.

I thanked the driver — he grunted — and I hopped down. No one was shoveling snow, but there was no need to shovel snow. The noon storm was as proficient as a snow-blower. I heard the drone of a plane overhead and looked up at contrails aimed east. I wished I was on it; Anchorage was only two hours away. I yanked on PIA's main door. It didn't budge. I hoisted a leg, braced a boot, and tugged with both hands. The ice cracked around the bottom of the door, and it screeched open. I stepped into an airlock, stood in the heat until sweat broke out all over me for the first time in five years, and pulled off my hat and mittens.

The second door opened to a barn-like space, and I took my first breath of freedom. It smelled like stale smoke and spilled beer and looked abandoned. A row of vacant shops had signs: Аренда — For Rent — in dusty windows. They gave the cavities an inexpressibly forlorn and defeated look. *Build it and they will come* may fill a ballpark in an Iowa corn field, but it is not enough of a draw to fill empty shops 700 miles north of the Arctic Circle with locals. PIA was not a five-star gateway to luxury brand shops, galleries, theaters, and sleep pods. It was a silent, crumbling dive suited for grabbing a newspaper, beer, and sand-wich, which was fine with me.

Across the way, a woman in a Yakootiya Airlines uniform sat perched on a stool at the ticket counter. I headed over. She glanced up, yawned, and said, "*Vernis' v tri* — Come back at three o'clock," and bent back over to read her seedy tabloid. Its headline screamed: *Yeltsin Ready for Battle*! No one admits reading tabloids. They sell millions every week.

"Thank you, is there a phone call center here?" I asked hopefully.

Without looking up, she pointed past the line of vacant shops.

I hustled down, paid a ransom, and called my mother-in-law, Oksana, in Tver. It was 2:00 p.m., January 2, 1997, in Pevek and 5:00 a.m. the same day in Tver, and 8:00 p.m. yesterday, New Year's Day, in Blowing Rock, NC. Oksana was excited to hear my voice and thrilled I'd be at their home late that same day. I wanted to speak to little Anastasia, but she was asleep. My three minutes were up too soon, and the line went dead before I could say goodbye.

I wandered past Passport Control, barricaded and vacant and looked for a bathroom when I detected the unfamiliar whiff of real food. My juices flowed. No, that's not accurate: my juices gushed, surged, and cascaded. I drooled.

At the far end of the barn-like terminal, weak spotlights played on a café sign Оазис — Oasis — with flashing signs, пиво — *pivo*, beer — next to a six-foot bottle of Жигулёвское — Zhigulyovskoye. The beer was once the second most popular Soviet beverage, after vodka, produced by 700 breweries. There was a scattered of red plastic chairs, Formica tables, and counter seats. Behind the counter worked two women. My stomach growled. I figured I'd scarf my way through a banquet, sluiced it down with a bit of the old nasty, and satiate my five-year hunger while searching for my sense of humor.

The cook, in back, was a short, stout, florid woman with a parrot-like nose. She wore a sleeveless dress and had tucked her gray hair under a babushka. Shielding her, neck-to-knees, was a white apron smudged with beef blood or beet juice. Sweat dripped off her beak and sizzled on the stovetop where she stood stirring a pot the same size as her copious derriere. She stopped, ladled out some, and slurped noisily; it sounded delicious and smelled even better.

Her compatriot, a tall, thin, lithe, young woman was filling a display case with square slabs of gingerbread pastries oozing with jam and *pastila* confections, a fruit puree, honey and whipped egg-white yummy. She heard the cook slurp and straightened. Her name tag said Tatyana.

She turned and said, "*Pakhnet khorosho, Ol'ga* — Smells good, Olga."

The heavenly odor emanating from Olga's spoon smelled like braised ham and fried onions. I salivated, but what ex-con wouldn't? Those bouquets had not pierced my proboscis for five years. I swung aboard a counter seat, set down my felt hat and leather mittens, and picked up an Аленка — Alenka — chocolate bar from a display next to the register.

Аленка is not the best Russian chocolate, but it was the only Russian chocolate at PIA. I unwrapped it, took a big, heavenly bite, and with a mouth full garbled, in Russian, "What're you pushing today, Tanya?"

I wanted to tell her she was the only woman I'd spoken to in five years, feeling a little of the old satyriasis curse, but quickly felt mortified, embarrassed, and humiliated: A widower about to fetch an unknown daughter eyeing new merchandise.

"Nothing special," Tatyana replied and looked me over warily.

"I'll have four eggs over easy, a platter of all-beef sausages, stack of light rye toast slathered with butter and strawberry jam, oh, and a big glass of cold milk."

Her mouth dropped open. Her hands flew to her hips. "Who do you think you are, mister, some czarevitch about to ascend the throne? We've got powdered eggs, powdered milk, canned-ham, and black bread." She licked jam off her fingers. "And these yummies."

Her dark blue eyes zeroed in knowingly on my overcoat, hacked-off hair, and stubbly face.

"Oh, okay," I said disappointedly. "What's that Olga's stirring?"

"Borscht. Try it, you could use a good meal, but don't eat too much too fast."

"Thank you," I said pleasantly. "And some real black bread and butter, please."

Tanya smiled. "Sure."

A sharp-featured girl of eighteen or nineteen, she wore a wedding band on her right-hand, ring-finger, the Russian way. "Did you just get out?" she asked. She set a huge loaf of black bread on the cutting board and sliced off three thick slabs.

"Is it that easy to spot?" I asked.

"Those swanky French duds and fat face gave you away." Tanya smiled and set silverware and a tub of butter on the counter beside my bread.

I dug in. Between mouthfuls, I said, "Does your borscht have carrots, beets, cabbage, meat, dill, and scallions? I want the real thing, not some mystery construal like I've eaten for five years, five days, three hours, and thirty-two minutes."

She smiled. "Everything except scallions. We're still using last summer's onions. One bowl of borscht, Olga!" she said over her shoulder and to me, "You speak good Russian, but you have a strange accent."

"Not many Americans in the Arctic. Have you been in Pevek long, Tanya?"

"Three years. I'm waiting for my husband. He has two more years to go. I live upstairs, work here, and see him once a year for two nights. More I cannot afford. Bribes. Do you go to America now?"

"After I pick up my daughter in Tver."

"You're married?"

"I was. My wife died. Her mother has raised our daughter since she was a baby."

"We don't have kids. Maybe you know my husband, Vladislav Pavlovich?"

"No, I'm afraid not. He must have been in another barrack. What was his crime?"

"Poaching a deer. We had no food, no jobs, and were hungry. Vlad went to the forest, killed a small buck, and got arrested. Are you sure you don't know him?"

"Never heard of him." That was a lie. I knew Vlad. Everyone did. The arrival of a handsome young man from Samara for a petty crime was instant news, especially for the criminals. He'd been "adopted" by a gangster and housed in his upper bunk. I did not want to burden his wife with his fate and changed the subject.

"I heard it's been hard for Yeltsin to transition to democracy, lots of people unemployed."

"It has been," she said. "Just like me."

Customers started to filter in, and between them she told me about Yeltsin's shock therapy. Consumer prices skyrocketed starting in early 1992; a deep credit crunch shut down industries and brought a long depression, worse than the 1930s. His reforms devastated living standards, especially retirees and those on welfare. Russia's GDP fell fifty percent and wiped out vast sectors of the economy. Inequality and unemployment catapulted. Incomes plummeted. Hyperinflation, caused by the Central Bank's loose monetary policy, obliterated personal savings and plunged tens of millions into poverty. To jump-start the economy, Yeltsin's launched a program of free vouchers, giving away state business in a mass privatization to all Russians with vouchers bearing a nominal value of 10,000 rubles. But the purchase of shares in state enterprises was a flop. A wealthy few oligarchs bought people's vouchers for kopeks on the ruble and gained control of former state companies for practically nothing.

When Tanya finished, she asked me for my story. I told her. You have heard this before, and I won't relay it again. She was moved to tears. As passengers began arriving for the four o'clock flight, I left and bought the latest newspaper, a *Pravda,* dated December 24, 1996, and read all the news the Kremlin saw fit to print.

After receiving my boarding pass, I had a whore's bath in heavenly hot water in the men's room. I took a look at myself in a mirror for the first time in five years: I looked like a snow maiden who'd been on a never-ending run to Iditarod. Dark-ringed eyes in a pale, skeletal face with a grubby shave and hacked hair.

Pravda wrote President Yeltsin had declared himself "Battle Ready" and had returned to work after a six-month absence battling heart disease. Cardiologist Michael DeBakey advised him to lay off the vodka. Other tidbits: Newt Gingrich was in tax trouble over a college course he taught, an explosion in Houston killed 9; Sweden, Austria, Switzerland, and Italy rejected new nuclear reactors as did the people in Kostroma, Russia in their first-ever referendum with images of 10-year-old Chernobyl fresh in their minds. Steve Jobs returned to turn around Apple, and Jim Kelly threw two TD passes in the final minutes of a wild-card game, beating the Chiefs 20-9.

The eighty-four-passenger Tupolev, Tu-134 turbo-jet bumped down the snow-packed runway at two-thirty. With its wings attached to the fuselage's underbelly, it gave the plane a low, swept-winged look. Its dual-jets were in the rear, high above the wings. Twenty-six glum faces got off — home for the Christmas holiday in Pevek. An ancient gas-tanker pulled up to refuel the plane.

Fifty-two of us boarded at 3:30 p.m.. At 4:00 the turbo-jet fired up, engines roared, and the jet rocked back-and-forth like a car stuck in a snowdrift. The captain ordered everyone off. He, the copilot, navigator, and a crew of five joined us. Empty, the Tupolev Tu-134 weighs thirty tons. While sitting at the gate, its hot tires had melted the ice, and the plane had settled three inches. Fortunately, the wings were low enough for us to reach, and we rocked the big jet out of its holes. We turned it around, pointed it at the runway, and reboarded.

The flight to Moscow and refueling stops were long and uneventful. I stared out the window into blackness, overcome with delight at leaving Gulag thievery, hardships, beatings, and death; overjoyed with jittery excitement about the future with my daughter. I thought about the trans-Siberian connector train from Blagoveshchensk to Belorgorsk and on to Birobiazhan, Khabarovsk, Vyazemskaya, Guberovo, Ruzhino, Ussuriysk, and Vladivostok. I thought about the long icebreaker slog to Pevek and my failed escape at Yesterday. I thought about the horrible years in the Gulag. There are not a lot of places to which I never want to return. Pevek topped the list. I wondered about Yeltsin's caviar style democracy and how it had changed life for little Anastasia. Sometimes late at night, I'd wept over my two Anastasias. Sometimes I wondered if I'd ever take another wife, certain I'd never be able to share myself again in return for another woman offering her vulnerabilities, hopes, fears, trust, and love. In the Gulag, I knew solitude. I would forever prefer desolation and isolation to making another relationship leap. My goal now was to mesh being a father with the plan I had settled on. The word plan was not accurate. It was more than a plan. A campaign would be closer. It gave my life purpose and meaning. Raise my daughter and develop a world market for taxol, now trademarked Taxol®,[38] and do it from some warm, isolated, tropical island.

At times, I felt the compulsion to return to the mountains of North Carolina as strong as the one that pulls Monarch butterflies thousands of miles, over generations, to the Oyamel Fir Forests of Mexico's central mountains to lay their eggs and start life anew. But I knew I must leave my childhood home and start life anew.

As these forces ebbed and flowed within my being, I found myself bursting with a fizzy excitement at the thought of seeing my baby. Holding her. Making a tropical home. And, as if in celestial celebration, my plane's starboard window came ablaze with luminous, green shimmerings. Gyrating curtains, in a spectrum of colors: orange, red, and violet to blue and yellow and green, sky-high folds discoing over the white tundra like strobe lights on a floor of towheads. Zeus had heard of my release and flung arrows into the earth's atmosphere to emit an electromagnetic light show.

And then I slept.

With poverty at an all-time high in Russia, my Gulag finery attracted no attention arriving at Domodedova — Sheremetyevo was snowed in, and we diverted to DME. With my dearth of luggage, I breezed through security, boarded a heated bus to the Domodedova Metro, disembarked at Komsomolskaya, and ran to the Leningradsky Train Station across the square. In twenty minutes, I was aboard a train to Tver and slept. It was a 'balmy' -27° outside, according to a weather sign outside the train station in Tver when I jumped into a cab. The driver had the heat cranked to broil, and I sweat for the first time in five years. We slammed over pot-holed streets in the city center and whizzed across the double-spanned Starovolzhsky Bridge over the Volga, Europe's longest and largest river. My heart was racing at the left on Gorkgo, right on Skyortsova-Stepanova; it galloped when we turned up the three blocks to my mother-in-law's nine-story apartment building. I pulled out my dwindling wad of rubles, paid, got out, and looked around. Nothing had changed. Few working lights, gungy buildings, babushkas shoveling snow at 10:30 p.m. I had a thought and popped into the first-floor grocery. Stolichnaya Elite was $40; Stolichnaya Blue Label: $2. I counted my rubles and bought M & Ms for Nastia instead.

It was still the same day I had left Pevek. I stuffed the M & Ms in my overcoat and dashed through the snow to the rear of the building, its entrance. Up three-step stoop. Press Oksana's buzzer. She buzzed me in.

The stairwell was closet dark. It smelled like a honkytonk's men's room: a rancid fog of urine, beer, and dirty ashtrays. I felt for the banister. It was rough. Boys still carved their names in it just as I had. I stumbled over a sleeping drunk. Six stairs later, I was at the first level. One overhead lights worked; it exposed a scummy tile floor and dirty plaster walls etched with graffiti in fifty years of paint layers. The outer coat was olive-green over blue, brown, black, and gray — like Schliemann's archeological dig at Troy that revealed its many reincarnations. A pack of teenagers yacked, smoked and drank beer. One was pissing in the elevator. The foulness hung there and would never disappear.

The kids heard me stumble and sneered at my Gulag rags. "Get lost, Pops," one snarled.

I growled, "Get the hell out of here or you're dead; five more years in the Gulag won't bother me one fucking bit!" They scattered, tripping over the drunk rushing outside.

I stepped into the elevator. It smelled like the Gulag's honey pot. I held my breath for the slow, wheezing, eight-story rise. When it stopped, I gulped some stale air, wiped my boots on the concrete landing, and dashed up to the ninth floor.

There were four apartments. The door on the front left flew open. Oksana stepped into the hall, weeping and laughing and throwing open her arms. She wore a tatty, flannel robe over a long, gray nightgown; feet thrust in frayed pink slippers. She was a short, thin woman, thick through the hips. Her head was held erect on a strong neck, and her long, blonde hair, now silvered and fine, was drawn up and twirled in a loose chignon at the nape of her neck. We embraced, traded cheek kisses and started talking at the same time.

"You first," I said in Russian.

"You're here! You're here!" she exclaimed, kissing me again and again.

"Finally. How are you, Oksana? How's my baby?"

"I'm fine. Little Nastia's growing like dacha weeds."

She pushed me out to arms' length, looked at my Gulag regalia and shook her head. "What a site!" She sniffed. "What a smell!" She kissed both my cheeks again. "You're as skinny as my father was after his twenty years in Kolyma. Smell like he did, too."

"No hot shower, no soap for five years," I explained.

"We'll fix that. Come in, come in."

Oksana tugged me through the two steel doors, double-bolted them, and said, "You get in the shower and brush your teeth then put on the things I set out for you. I'll fix food."

"You bought me clothes? You shouldn't have — "

"It was nothing. They're from the secondhand shop."

A widow now, Oksana's pension was $100 per month. Her apartment was my wife's childhood home and about the size of a three-car garage. Opposite the entryway, the kitchenette was jammed with a two-burner stove, mini-frig, tiny sink, and small table. There was a toilet closet and a tiny room with a bathtub and handheld shower. There were two narrow bedrooms — one with its door closed — and a sliver of a living room crowded with a China cabinet, dining room table, TV, three chairs, and a pull-out couch where I would sleep.

The hot shower was breathtaking. I scrubbed and hosed off three times and brushed my teeth with a new toothbrush and Crest for the first time in five years. What a delight! I dressed in the soft, clean, second-hand clothes and returned to the living/dining/bedroom for happy catching up, devouring baked ham, fried fish, cheese, fresh cucumbers, tomatoes, pears, and apples, all washed down with Stolichnaya Blue Label mixed with Turkish OJ, a Russian mimosa.

Our laughter finally woke Nastia. Her bedroom door squeaked open and a little head peeked out, long blonde curls falling over clown red cheeks and pastel blue eyes.

I smiled at my little four-year-old and said, "Hi Anastasyia."

She scrubbed her eyes and studied me. Anastasyia wore pink booted-PJs and was buffing her right cheek with a Linus blanket. She cautiously shuffled over to grandma, never taking her eyes off me, and crawled into her lap.

"This is your daddy, Nastenka. Remember? I told you this morning he was coming."

Nastia nuzzled a second, found the desired spot, and looked at me some more. Then she looked at the wedding pictures of her Mom and me, stuffed behind the China cabinet's cherry trim. She was confused, probably my white hair and pasty skin now versus my strawberry-blond hair and tanned face then.

She pointed a finger at me and then the pictures, questioningly. "Are you that man?"

"I am, Anastasyia," I replied. "My hair has changed colors."

And then she stuck out her tongue at me. *Her father*! I gave her a phony gasp and smiled.

"Why is your hair whiter than babushka's?" she asked shyly.

"I've been worrying a long time about you."

"Worrying turns hair white?"

"It can. I've been gone since before you were born."

Anastasyia held up four, plump, little fingers. "I'm four," she said. "You're a big girl. Say — " I held up a little, yellow bag of M&Ms with peanuts — "know what this is?"

She stared at the yellow bag and shook her head back-and-forth, spinning out those long blonde curls.

I rattled the bag. "Marbles?" Nastia guessed.

"Guess again," I said.

Oksana said, "With our economy, we don't have money for candy."

Nastia's eyes sprung open at the word candy.

She slinked out of babushka's lap and moseyed my way. I tore open a corner of the M&Ms and poured some colorful nuggets into my palm. Nastia darted over, grabbed one, and popped it in her mouth. She crunched it, looked up at grandma, and smiled. She rushed back, snatched an M&M for both hands, and returned to babushka's lap.

***

The next three weeks were a joy. We got to know each other, and I rejoined the world. Anastasyia was truly a delight and the image of her Mom. A few bags of M&Ms, two Snickers, and heartfelt love earned her trust. Mornings while she slept, I took care of business. I called Francesca Villafuerte (our next door neighbor in Blowing Rock who had kept Leftovers) and arranged for a house-keeper to clean the long-vacant house since my stepdad had died. I called Marlene LaPointe, my Boone lawyer, and got the details on my inheritance. Marlene transferred funds from her escrow account into my checking account at the State Employees Credit Union. We discussed selling the house, and she suggested a broker. Anita Roy, now manager of SECU, transferred ten thousand dollars to the Bank of Tver, the largest privately-owned bank in the Tver Region so I could begin to repay Oksana for her years of caring for Nastia and purchase our passports and airline tickets.

Anastasyia and I spent our days visiting museums, the circus — five times! — and walking the snowy paths through Central Park to eat at Milano's (her first pizza). She "Loved it!" A new grocery store in a new mall sold Kraft's Macaroni & Cheese and she "Loved it," too. She roared with laughter at the Dr. Seuss's *Happy Birthday to You* book. The intensity of her laughter reminded me of her Mom. She went wild with a box of 64 Crayola crayons and the *Mermaid and Princesses Coloring Book*. The police certified Nastia's American birth certificate (after three trips and many days of waiting), and finally approved her to be added to my new Russian passport — kids are included in parents' Russian passport. Once the passports were in hand, we trained to Moscow for four days at the Aerostar Hotel, applying for and receiving two new American passports. Between waits at the U. S. Embassy, I introduced her to Americana: we feasted on Baskin Robin's ice cream, McDonald's cheeseburgers and fries, T.G.I. Friday's cheesecake, and visited the 50-acre Moscow Zoo on Big Gruzinskaya Street for popcorn and to see new animals.

With heartfelt thanks, hugs, and teary goodbyes, we left Russia January 31, 1997, and arrived at Kennedy International Airport at two p.m. where Anastasyia saw her first Americans.

"They look just like everyone else," she said in Russian.

"People don't wear signs," I agreed. "But I know they're Americans. Look at them. Do you see a difference?"

"They joke a lot. Russians never laugh."

There was a frail old black lady with thin white hair who smiled at us. Two rough biker dudes ignored us. A pleasant, chubby, middle-aged teacher said, "Hello." A bespectacled silver-haired accountant-type with three giggly teenagers looked too flustered to speak. A beat-up, rheumy-eyed alcoholic, smiled, and graciously and modestly gave us her seat. A wild-haired hippie in a cracked and torn leather jacket was in his own world. An academic donning a beret was reading a book. A stout businessman wearing an expensive overcoat was arguing with someone. A skinny twenty-something in a thick sheepskin coat, architect glasses, and torn jeans, said, "Aren't you a cutie pie," and I explained to Anastasyia what he said and she smiled at him. Everyone listened carefully to a gate change announcement, and I knew they were Americans. Our casual, free, deindustrialized citizens.

In Blowing Rock, the empty house had been cleaned, and my old room made up with pink curtains and matching bedspread (thanks to Mrs. V). Nastia couldn't believe the size of her room. I moved into the big, lonely, master suite. The next morning, Nastia met Mrs. V and Leftovers, now a little gray around the muzzle. And just as I had two decades earlier, Nastia started school at Blowing Rock Elementary that week with her vast ten-word English vocabulary, which grew at a phenomenal rate, though we always spoke Russian at home, but never in public, unless we had secrets to share.

Weekdays, I walked Anastasia to school: down Chestnut Street to Main, north two blocks to Morris, and down two blocks. While she learned, I scouted for a building, read, and worked out at the Wellness Center in Boone to regain my strength. With the village's tourists gone, hopeful real estate agents eagerly help me purchased a vacant building for my first Carlos O'Brien's Mexican Restaurant, not far from the Outback Steak House on SR 321. On Saturdays, we attended Rocket basketball games and cheered at hockey-like scores, often 5 to 2 or less. Evenings we read, looked at old Tver photo albums, and played word games. Sundays, after church, we'd snip a spray of fir from an evergreen that ringed the house, drive to the cemetery, lay it on her Mom's grave, and say prayers to two women she'd never know and had only seen in pictures. For fun, we drove to Appalachian Mountain to ski and ice skate or hiked around Bass Lake with Leftovers who never tired of chasing squirrels and Canadian geese. Evenings we read children's English books and followed the printed and spoken words read by actors. At spring break in March, we flew to Saint Monique in the West Indies to begin to fulfill my Gulag dream. Anastasyia, who I always addressed as Nastia, quickly become Ana to her classmates—five-year-olds couldn't get their tongues around a five-syllable name, and, soon, Ana was speaking flawless English.

During vacation, we flew from Charlotte to Miami, changed to a British West Indies (BEEWEE) flight to Saint Monique, and arrived at 6:00 p.m. just as the big red ball of sun dropped into the western Caribbean. Eight hundred miles north of the equator, nights and days stay 12-hours long year round. We taxied to the Calabash Hotel on the island's west side for a week of sand, sun, surf, house-hunting, and non-stop questions. Nastia's curiosity began at breakfast and didn't stop until she rechecked the southern sky ablaze with unfamiliar stars and laid her head on her pillow at seven. The first morning, she kangarooed into my room at 6:10, bounced up onto my bed, and proclaimed, "Daddy, the sun's up, the sun's up! Get up!"

I was still groggy from yesterday's long travel and the tumbler of red rum punch they give check-ins. "Slip out of your PJs and into shorts and a T-shirt,"

I said. "I'll be ready in a flash."

Nastia flew out of my bedroom and rummaged through her suitcase. I showered quickly and heard her slam out the door as I started to shave. Five minutes later, she burst into the bathroom, her eyes as big as bagels.

"*Daddy!*" she exploded. "A man's behind our cottage with a *gun!*"

"Honey," I soothed, "he's the security guard. Lots of burglaries here."

"But why's he at our place? Nobody can steal our stuff our door's locked and open windows are barred."

"Thieves use long bamboo poles with hooks to snatch purses."

Nastia folded her arms over her chest defiantly. "You haven't bought me a purse."

"Aren't you lucky? You'll never be robbed."

She scowled at me exactly like her Mom would have. "What's for breakfast? Not Cheerios and peanut butter toast again?"

"Nah, you're in luck. It'll be a West Indian breakfast. Scrambled eggs, ham, goat, and lots of fruits you've never seen before."

"No Cheerios?"

"No Cheerios."

"What's that bing-bonging noise, Daddy?"

"Steel drums. The band practices at sunrise before it gets too hot."

"What's a steel drum?"

"A long time ago, French planters bought African slaves here to raise sugarcane. Evenings, the slaves made music banging on the bottoms of big oil cans with sticks. Today, they use pan drums. They look like the ends of oil drums."

"If you bang a drum it'll make music?"

"If you hit it in the right place."

"Can I have an old oil drum, Daddy? Can I please?"

"After breakfast, we'll look. Come on, let's eat."

Our breakfast was a tropical feast served on the Calabash's open porch by island waitresses. They swayed to the pings of steel drums and delivered platters of eggs, sausage, meats, toasted rolls, and multi-colored fruit: mangoes, guava, passion fruit, starfruit, pawpaw, custard apples (that look like hand-grenades and taste like custard), coconuts, and pineapples. After breakfast, we changed into bathing suits. Nastia scampered out of the bathroom in a bikini splashed with a brilliant hibiscus, pink flip-flops, and aqua-tinted sunglasses. We slathered on sunscreen, locked up, and head down a crushed shell walkway winding through manicured grass splotched with vibrant flower beds in rainbows of color.

Nastia darted to a clump of flowers and stopped. "We only have azaleas and rhododendrons in Blowing Rock, Daddy, what's that spiky red one called that looks like a cat's fat tail."

"That's an Alpinia, Nastia."

She laughed and bent down to sniff the exotic red foliage and said to the flower, "You've got a funny name, Mister Alpinia!"

I knelt down beside her, put an arm around her narrow shoulder. "My Dad told me long ago the Alpinia is named after an Italian man who studied them. It's in the Ginger Lily family."

"Is that a lily, too?" she asked, pointing at a purple daylily.

"It is. And that's a Bleeding Heart, and that's a Chrysanthemum."

"How about the one with a red bloom as big as your face?"

"That's a hibiscus like the ones on your bathing suit. Let's run to the beach before it gets hot."

"Okay," Ana yelped and darted for the black sand just beyond a hedge of sea grapes.

I jogged after her and stopped at the shore. The beautiful, warm, sunny scene was spectacular, and apricity enveloped me like a dog-hair sweater. I pointed right and left. "North or south, kiddo?"

"The steel drums are that way." She pointed north.

The rising sun casting long, curving shadows of royal palms over the soft black sand and lazy splashes of the still-sleepy Caribbean.

"What's that big green ice cream cone there?" She pointed about a mile ahead. "Why's the sand black? It looks like pepper, but I don't sneeze."

Nastia pulled off her flip flops and dug her toes in up to her ankle, raised her foot, and let the black sand trickle down through her toes.

"That cone thing is a big piton, or peak, called Mount Pelée. It's the core of an old volcano, and this black sand came from that volcano's lava a long, long time ago."

"My teacher said lava is red."

"It is. But when red lava cools it turns black; rains and tides made it into fine, black sand."

"Then why is that sand down there white?"

"Limestone. A long, long time ago this island sank into the sea. It was covered with shells, and they got squashed and turned into limestone. Then the island rose when the earth's Atlantic Plate ducked under the Caribbean Plate, and the limestone weathered to white sand."

"Oh. What are all those knife-looking trees? They don't grow in Blowing Rock."

"They're palm trees, Nastia; there are over three hundred different kinds of palms."

"That's a lot. What's that tree with the reddish-orange flowers kids are squirting with?"

"A tulip tree. The cup-shaped flower holds water for birds or water fights."

"And those two trees? One with little green footballs, the other with big green ones."

"Avocado and papaya, Sweetheart," I said.

My head was growing fuzzy. "Want to swim?"

"Yeah!" She took off, skid to a stop, swooped down, and picked up a shell. "What's this great, big, twisty, pink thing?"

"A snail's shell; it's called a conch. People eat the meat, cut a hole in the small end of the shell, and blow into it. It makes a low trumpet sound."

"Can I try it? Daddy, look!" she screamed. "That thing's coming right at me!"

Nastia pointed at a crab the size of a salad plate with its big claw up, snapping.

"That's a crab," I said. "Kick sand at him."

She did. It darted away.

"Does it snow here?" Nastia asked, wonderingly.

"Never," I said.

"Does it get cold?"

"Never ever."

"Can we live here, Daddy?"

"I don't see why not."

And for the next week, we swam, hiked, and explored property for sale. We found an incredible spot, and I purchased it. Over the next two years, we spent June in Tver, visiting relatives, and December, July, and August in Saint Monique transforming an old French fort into an island home. And did those years whiz by! While Anastasia finished two years of elementary school in Blowing Rock, I got Carlos O'Brien's Mexican Restaurant Numero Uno up and running. Old and new friends filled our lives. Kahuna, Ingrid, and their daughter, Kaarina, came up to ski the first two winters; the next year they were divorced. I figured we'd never see them again. I was wrong. We kept the house in Blowing Rock for summers and winter skiing, and, in August that year, we moved to Saint Monique. Nastia enrolled in the international school for expats and a few locals, and I launched Carlos O'Brien's II and my Taxol business.

And our world took an astonishing turn.

***

TWENTY-EIGHT

Saint Monique, Leeward Islands
June 3, 2001

Our home stood high on the side of a great coned piton, tucked on the back of a deep, grassy shelf studded with mango, papaya, and coconut palm fruit trees there for the taking. Bougainvillea swirled around their mossy trunks like purple petticoats, and the air hung thick and smelled turfy. Old-timers called our lap of land Lena's Leap, and when trade-winds soughed up its sheer face, the sylvan air whispered secrets of Lena and her long-ago sailor. The house, once a seventeenth-century fort, stood with its windows flung open to catch the cooling breeze of sunny days and the starry warmth of winter nights. Its hand-hued blocks blended in with the lichen-gray ledge and hedge that sheltered it and faced a tranquil curve of a beryl sea and Martinique's meringuey peaks.

Above the fortress, prehistoric forests rose, sprawling green tarpaulins spiked with mist-draped peaks that faded in drizzly blurs to haze from view and onto the canvas of island Van Goghs. From the volcanic black-sand beach a half-mile below, time-worn steps led up a ropy lava flow, noble foot-holes stabbed by the Sun King's foot soldiers during his 72-year reign. The stairs continued 2,013 more steps—Nastia has counted—to the top of Mount Pelée's soundless peak where a stone bench, brackish with mariners' tears, faced the echoing sea. That space-pillared crown, at 3,000 meters the island's highest point, was sledged level, rock blocked, a mighty fortress built. Its ramparts bore peepholes for Louis XIV's riflemen, and, on the leeward side, a hidden door that repelled yesterday's pirates — now locked — repulsed today's pilgrims. The only things higher were comma-sized red-tail hawks spiraling on land-baked updrafts that looked like curly mobiles hung from heaven.

Behind our home, springs gushed over a 120-foot-high sheer ledge like a mini Yosemite. Half its flow, funneled into a pipe, powered a high-head hydro-turbine, its electricity stored in battery banks to power pumps, lights, fans, water heater, refrigerator, stove, and computers. The turbine's discharge water topped off our cistern before merging with the waterfall at ledge's edge before cascading to the ocean. Hydropower is a function of gravity and flow rate. Every 2.31 feet of vertical drop between the inlet and turbine produced one pound of pressure per-square-inch (psi) gained. Our 120-foot vertical drop, or head, to the turbine, produced 51.95 psi, and with its 45-gallon-a-minute flow generated 11 kilowatts per hour[39] — kWh. Our highly-efficient, 18-cubic-foot refrigerator and four-burner stove used about 2 kWh per day. We never ran out of power.

With East Africa eight hours ahead of Saint Monique, six o'clock's dawn always found me working on my Taxol business before waking Nastia. My desk was a picnic table, my office the seaside edge of the parade grounds where I could soak up the beauty of the day engulfed in smells as earthy as poi, and sip rich, black coffee under thick green leaves quelling the leaping sun. I'd fire up the computer, link to a satellite, and spread the news of inexpensive Taxol to a needful world while far below me, the cradle of the sea, now calm as a morning lake, tried to rock itself free. Having reestablished my deal with Zhou and the Hande Company in Kunming at a sale price one-tenth that of BMS, I did all advertising, merchandising, and sales to poor clinics and hospitals via the Internet. BMS was chalking up billion dollar sales — thanks to the congressional gift of a monopoly to the world's richest 65 countries — leaving me selling Taxol to the list I'd memorized in the Gulag, but I soon switched from that list — too geographically sprawling — and concentrated on Africa's half billion women.

It was distressing to learn that Kenya, a country of 26 million, had a vast need for Taxol, but little money to buy even my cheap Taxol for Nairobi's seven hospitals: Women's, M. P. Shah, Mater, Kijabe Mission, Kenyatta National, and the Coast Province General Hospital in Mombasa — but I kept grinding away. It was tormenting to learn that poorer countries, like Malawi, a country of 10 million, had one pathologist and one oncologist (an expatriate from North Carolina) who did limited chemotherapy for a very wary government. The few cancer patients who had had the money to buy Taxol had died. Most had been injected at the last-stage of advanced cancer when likely to die, and no amount of explaining changed the government's mind. So I plodded on, contacting hospitals and clinics across the Dark Continent's villages and cities, selling Taxol whenever convincing explanations and low price met an urgent need. Far below my desk, I watched great cloud shadows skim over the stupendous sea and cheer delightfully when I made a sale, prolonging a woman's life as I was unable to do for Anastasia.

During dawn's working hours, large thoughts often floated down, indicative of the area's propensity to induce sprawling reveries. One of these was to use my restaurant profits to expand my Taxol effort. I hired two, bright, local, high school graduates. They hiked up the stairs from Tivoli at dawn five days a week and joined me in the airy office, quickly mastering the science of Taxol and principles of marketing.

Lena's Leap was the quietest places in the world — except at dawn — when cicadae tuned their chorus for the day and brilliantly plumed birds swooped in for a raucous breakfast of soft mangoes. On Saturdays, island children bubbling with village gossip scampered up the banisterless stairs to shinnied up my fruit trees and pick a basket full for Saturday's market. Those plunderers, and occasionally their mothers, I rarely saw a father, were happy and mild-mannered, despite their prison of poverty, living in the timeless rhythms of a pickled life that preserved them from the mayhem and lunacy of our wired world, delighted, finally, to control their destiny, freed by parliament in 1976 of the dogged English and that colonial joyride. Naturally, tourists decried their lives as *devoid of information*, the oxygen of modern life that penetrates rice curtains, iron curtains but never reaches most Saint Moniqueans.

My halcyon days were a counterpoint to inescapable cantina nights. Being on stage four hours (5 - 9 p.m.) seven nights a week at Carlos O'Brien's II never left me ravenous for riotous outings to offset the onsets of occasion doldrums. Unfettered with America's labor laws, Nastia was our weekend hostess and loved it. Days, while she was in school, I was in constant activities, selling Chinese taxol or promoting a low-interest microloan program to the island poor that had quickly grown. Some days, my Gulag-shaped inclinations toward cerebral hobbies were rampant, and I secluded myself on our piton like Zarathustra, reading, painting, or blowing my trumpet. Some days, unhurried and alone under my pedestal of blue, I'd reminiscence on the Gulag's long trudges to the coal mine and climb Mount Pelée's summit — better than an hour on a Stairmaster — and gaze at wind-bent, bonsai-sized trees that stayed wet as a frog's belly and reflect on those frozen-slog memories. Most days, though, I sold Taxol and helped farmers plant and harvest cash crops for tourist hotels.

Afternoons, after Nastia's return from school, urgency disappeared and time measured timeless, life's tick-tock gone. We'd exercise our minds in stretched-out reading in the green-fingered shadows of quivering palms or explore the island. During summer's wet season when thunder ripped the gummy silence and rain pelted the vast and empty sea, tourists fled, and we withdrew to Blowing Rock and Carlos O'Brien's I.

Occasionally, I would grow restless in my bassinet of quietude after an evening making license plates, and, with the conviction of a death-row inmate after his last supper, pace my ancient patio and formulate plans as complex as Kasparov's end games for dealing with this new life. *The need for a woman, you ask.* Well, maybe. Sometime. But later. Much later. *Surely,* you ask, *embosomed to the point of anesthetization in solitary confinement caused you to miss the bedlam and mayhem cluttering our changing world?* Never! Yes, I missed friendships. But mostly I missed my wife, Anastasia, in this English-speaking world of tourists and dark-skinned natives who spoke unfathomable patois.

I've always found my best ideas germinate in dark, quiet nooks away from the blaze of streetlights, as, I am sure you have as well. The absolute perfect place for the propagation of such logistics is under a firmament thick with stars. So, on my ancient parade grounds, I'd hoof with a *zek's* zeal over the expanse of flagstone big enough to drill a company of French Foreign Legion renegades, and feel mailed resolve grow as back-and-forth I'd go, watching the occasional cruise ship twinkling by, mending plans on the uneven stones and rocky past high above the Caribbean's salty tang, far from the Gulag's grisly memories. And, yes, sometimes my crows' nest felt constrictive, mobbed with yesterday's ghosts and today's dreams. I would think of yesterday's reckless seafarers who had braved these wild seas in rickety boats and squandered the treasure of life stealing these island specs from Aborigines, replacing them with torrents of Africans whose descendants I employed. Was I any better? Was I doing the right thing, providing jobs for Taxol merchandisers, restaurant employees, or credit for truck gardeners in the Information Age? Was I just one more Ugly American exploiting Africans as white men have learned to do so well for so long? Was I but an opportunist chaining a drowsy population to stasis while the world spun by? Was I acting fast enough? I *must* act faster. Do more! Oh, Lord, give me patience while I do your work, and I mean right damn now!

Some days in my nature-brimming cranny, I found comfort reciting Wordsworth or blasting the silence with my trumpet like Chuck Mangione, or, like a long-dead sentry, peer into the unfixed future through crenelled battlements beneath scaly bronze cannons resting on rusty iron cradles as the sea pedaled toward tomorrow. There were no enemies out there now, only the dorsal fins of sloops billowing by from unknown places on and off the edge of my world. Dry season days arched cloudless and powder-blue above rippled stripes in turquoise and indigo, foamy where the sea collapsed to nibble at Saint Monique's sandy cuff. Far below, topless tourists sprawled out between paisley umbrellas, lotion-greased bodies sown like oily paired rice, frying on the skillet-hot sand before cooling in the coiling surf. And, yes, some days the old binoculars were hauled out to watch eager nymphs at play. Nights, late, when nature was asleep, I'd switch on BBC as it danced over the vast drink and drowned my world in the tragicomedies of ended lives and ended hopes, always in slow, polite Queen's English, which allowed ample time for the message to worm in deeply.

Days I spent like this, solitude devoured by aspirations and whims as unstructured as free verse.

Nights, like a bat, I worked.

Carlos O'Brien's II was a clone of its Blowing Rock brother: same menu, same food, better staff. Islanders work harder and never griped. Business in Saint Monique was good, never great, due to the rainy season's dearth of tourists. Wages of three dollars an hour were three times the country's minimum wage, if locals could even find a job, which two out of three couldn't. On Saturday, market day, Nastia and I would jeep down our piton to the quaint, seaside village and capital, Tivoli, for brunch and weekly shopping for vegetables for home and restaurant.

With never a drape drawn or a sash shut, the May Saturday morning that changed our lives forever began with the usual murmur of rustling fronds drifting through open jalousies, the jubilation of birds, and the laughter of Dubois kids wanting a lift to town. Their clatter grew louder as dappled light melted through the foliage and languid dawn seeped down our piton.

I heard a thud. Another. Coconuts thumping grass. Far off, the air was awash with a growl, a metallic drone, which set the air trembling. I opened an eye. Using it as a gauge, I plotted the precise point where the sun rose through the mango tree and cast a long shadow across my uncanny lens. Positioning my eye at the exact horizontal angle, I shot an azimuth, which gave me the hour of the day, accurate to within a minute of Greenwich sidereal time. The mango tree acted as a gigantic gnomon on my internal sundial and calibrated for variations in longitude and deviations in solar meridians to achieve this nifty feat. It was six-thirty-two.

"Hi ya, Daddy," Nastia sang out, dancing into my bedroom, face sparkling with eagerness as she sprinkled gold dust about. She pounced on my bed and threw her sticky arms around my neck. She had that sweaty kid smell when she nuzzled my neck and dampened my T-shirt.

"Wanna smooch?" she whooped.

"I always want a smooch from my favorite girl," I rejoiced and gave her a big hug.

She giggled and kissed my cheek lovingly. "Daddy, I'm your only girl."

Nastia placed a sticky palm on my chest and pushed out to arm's length. She brushed aside wisps of blonde hair and gave me a squinted eyed look and a snarky faux scowl that reminded me so much of her Mom tears clouded my eyes.

"Know something?" she chirped.

I felt like sobbing and shook my head. "Not much. What-cha got?"

"I want a sister."

My eyes sprung open. "Whoa, kiddo, that takes a wife!"

"I know, silly. I can help you find one." Deadly serious.

"I told you, 'No Hansa, she hitched to that turbaned brute.'" This was something I did not want to discuss. "Is that racket the DuBois kids?"

"Of course, it's Saturday morning. Shine showed me how to climb a coconut tree, and we picked coconuts and mangoes! Aren't you proud of me?"

"I'm always proud of you, Nastenka. It's good to have a second skill in life."

"Shine's up in the mango tree now tossing them down to~for the market. And nobody's got 'clonked in the head.' What's that growly noise?"

"Bulldozers; they're widening the gap to the mainland to build stilt houses."

"I forgot. Hansa told me that last Saturday while you were at the Post Office."

"Where Gwen told me the same news."

With the impatience of famished larvae, yellow, carbon-tongued Caterpillars were ripping into the rain forest older than Homer, dropping maple-shaped mahoganies and elm-tall flamboyants that snapped like toothpicks in the scuffle to make room for a population growing exponentially, six to the harried mother. Gwen, the postmistress, was the single mother of four and had saved enough money to build her first stilt home. Nastia loved her. I wondered if she were the wife candidate.

Nastia smiled slyly. "Gwen isn't married, Daddy."

"No, I don't believe she is; but don't go getting any ideas."

"*Ana!*" a girl yelled as she poked her head in my bedroom window. "Hi, Mister Troy. Ana come help carry coconuts to the jeep. Shine won't help!"

Nastia darted to the window, leaned out, and yelled, "Shine, help Doreen or else!"

"*Or else what*?!" a muffled voice replied from the tree top.

"Or else you'll walk to town; that's what!" Nastia screamed.

"Honey," I said, "is that any way to treat Shine?"

"Shine's a brat."

"Many boys are," I said and threw off the sheet. I straightened my shorts and went to the window to take a look. The brat was in the very top of the mango's airy cage pitching mangoes to his sisters, aiming for their kinky black heads thick with ribbons. With dozer racket and kids' racket a certainty, I surrendered.

"Nastia, scram," I said. "Tell Shine to bail out of the tree; I'll be ready in ten minutes."

"Want me to fix coffee, Daddy?" Her eyes were as wide as a Spaniel's, anxious to please.

I kissed her on the forehead. "No thanks, Nastuska, I'll wait for Hansa's."

I zipped through a hot shower and shaved, slipped on fresh underwear, thanking the Lord I was out of the Gulag, and pulled on red shorts, a tank-top that looked like Betsy Ross had made it, and sandals, ready for town and our regular breakfast at our usual spot, Islan Deelits. We always ate before hitting the market for the week's onions, lettuce, garlic, tomatoes, and chili peppers, that way you skip buying chips, peanuts, and beer. The bistro was run by proprietor, Hansa Purandara, whose name rolls off your tongue like a harp glissando, and her long-time live-in, Indiana Jones Cumarasami, father of three of her growing pride.

"Come on, gang!" I shouted, backing out the plank front door and twisting the key to lock it.

There was a telltale giggle from behind a ten-foot-tall poinsettias hedge. Aficionados ready to pounce. I glanced over my shoulder at animated faces peeking through the crimson blaze, wearing big grins and fresh clothes. I turned. They sprang, bouncing and yowling, as frisky as kittens.

"Morn'n, morn'n, Mista Troy!" Shine yelled, black eyes sparkling, missing teeth embossing a jack-o-lateen smile, sticky hand latching onto mine. Shine, a handsome kid, looked like a stove-blackened version of Michael Jackson at six balancing a basket of mangoes on his head.

"Come on, Daddy," Nastia cried darting over to me. "Hurry up; I'm starved." She snatched my other hand and tugged.

"Okay, okay," I said to her and to Shine, "that basket looks heavy; need help?"

"Shit no. It ain't heavy for me." The shit came out SHE-EAT in heavy patois.

Shine ducked a swat coming from Doreen, twelve, his older sister, for that serving of profanity. With no after-school programs, fatherless boys wiled away their afternoons at the rum shop, learning the ways of the world in a strange catechism of alcohol, drugs, and reggae. Nastia had picked up a fair amount of his vocabulary but saved it for stubbed toes and scraped knees.

The Jeep, stored in a one-car garage behind the house, was built next to the ledge and turbine.

"Good morning girls," I said. "How's the DuBois trio this morning?"

They sang out, "We's fine, Mista Troy!" in *a cappella* with smiles as sweet as baklava.

"And your new brothers?"

"The twins are fine and getting fat!" exclaimed the smallest girl, Regina, four-years-old.

She had a soft smile, brown face, and the high, wide cheekbones and slanty eyes of a Carib, the Lesser Antilles indigenous people. Regina always reminded me of Song Lin's wife, Mim. Her ancestors probably arrived via the busy Bering Strait Bridge Hans mentioned.

Shine pressed in tight, wobbling under his load. "We's can lorry to town with ya, caint we's, Mista Troy?"

"Of course, you can, Shine," Nastia butted in, "if you're good."

"I's always good."

Shine's short-sleeved white shirt was pressed and clean except for mango juice. His red tie and gray shorts were frayed around the edges. He wore nothing on his feet and owned no shoes. His three sisters had a gazillion mauve ribbons tied in tiny bows at the ends of Medusa braids and wore pink dresses, stiff with starch. They carried their lacy white socks and red plastic shoes molded in China. Doreen was tall, slender, and an attractive, light-skinned mulatto, like her mother. Her father was a French volunteer teacher here on a two-year assignment. The middle sister, Moreen, eight, thin and anemic, was striking and bore a strong resemblance to her East Indian father, the executive secretary to the Prime Minister, who moonlighted repairing Jeeps. There was an erudite air about Moreen radiating from her straight back, high head, and noble carriage more than from the droll book, *Red Rum Punch,* she carried. The third girl, Regina, had the features of an Asian — the four kids were a biologic melting pot.

With her frilly white socks, Doreen dabbed perspiration off her forehead and steered her half-sisters out of the hard-edged sun to cool under a mahogany tree, pausing while I opened the garage door. Moreen shivered and slipped on a sweater. Regina sucked her thumb and swayed. When I flung the doors open wide, the hinges squawked like something alive, and the kids scrambled for the back seats. Doreen won, springing over the tailgate and gliding onto the seat in one graceful movement.

"Hey, no fair, Dore!" Shine griped, planting his feet and struggling to balance his load.

"Hey nothing, sit in front with Ana," Doreen ordered, with more than a trace of *parler vous* in her voice. Tivoli's schools still used teaching volunteers from France; a two-year commitment college grads can substitute for the draft and slaying of Serbs or Iraqis or whoever today's U. N. peacekeepers are protecting.

"Come on, Shine," I said. "Hop in front with Nastia and me."

"Crap," he whined. His fat under-lip quivered. "I wants to sits in back. I's can't see nothing up front. Why's ya let dem sit back there and not me?" Shine stood rooted behind the jeep.

I threw my hands up. "I provide the ride. You provide the buns. Mind Doreen or walk."

Shine remained motionless.

"And keep on swearing," Doreen warned, shaking a finger, "and you *will* go straight to hell. I'm telling Father Shannon!" Doreen reached around the roll bar and cuffed him again.

"Father Shannon can kiss my ass," Shine blurted.

"Shine," Nastia said gravely, "God doesn't approve of swearing. It's a mortal sin."

"How would you know?" Shine said.

"Cause I heard babushka tell *dedushka.*"

Shine's face screwed up in a bamboozled look. "Whooo?"

"My grandma and grandpa. She knows all that God stuff."

"It is *not* a mortal, Ana," Moreen corrected sedulously, snuffing and shivering. "Saying A-S-S is a venial sin, serious but temporal unless Shine persists, and then he *is* doomed. That's what Father Shannon says, *and priests know.*"

Shine's profanity was not taken lightly by his scholarly sister. He climbed aboard, riding shotgun.

"Thank God for Father Shannon," I said, wondering when the parish priest would spend his time teaching birth control instead of paving paths to hell with the sanctity of a drop of sperm. "All set gang?"

I glanced in the rearview mirror and cranked up the chariot. The three girls were squirming in search of comfort in the minuscule space Chrysler calls a backseat. Shine wiped a crocodile tear from his eye, set the basket of mangoes on the floorboard, and said, "Goose this motha, Mista Troy!" That earned him another swat.

I nodded at Shine's mangoes. "They ripe?"

"They sure is." Shine's long black eyelashes fluttered with sincerity. He picked up a yellowish-red one and squeezed it. It split open and his fingers left a little orange indentations in the soft flesh that exuded a sweet fresh odor. Shine wiped his fingers on his pants.

"I'm freezing. May I use your towel, Mister Troy?" Moreen asked, sniffling. It was 80°.

"Sure, Moe, it's in my scuba bag. Slip on the fins too, they'll keep your tootsies warm."

She giggled and burrowed into the dive bag. "You always joke, Mister Troy."

Doreen tapped me on the shoulder. "We're taking Shine to Father Shannon's catechism class. He needs it bad, bad." She reached over the seat and jabbed a finger into Shine's side.

"I hate de fag!" Shine exploded.

The Sacred Heart Catholic Church was a one-man-band run by a porky, gay drunk, Dale Shannon, who, by his own admission, was inferior in learning to no one in the West Indies. He claims to have read the complete abridged works of St. Augustine. At Carlos O'Brien's II, the good Father cries for Ireland when inebriated and mumbles Latin gobbledygook when only tipsy.

I nosed the Jeep onto the crushed-shell drive, crossed Lena's Leap, and eased into a canopy of trees in dozens of shades of green tumbling down the piton. It quickly became as steep as a toboggan run and as wavy as a string, leaving your breath behind. I slowed at the waterfall cascading off a ledge where the DuBois clan showered. Their home, a two-room stilt-hut, sat close to the road at a corkscrewed in a stand of coconut palms. Chirping birds radiated a peace-of-the-ages kind of feeling.

"Kick this goddamn hotrod, Mista Troy!" Shine squealed. "Go fast as hell. There's Ma!"

"Shine!" Doreen exclaimed, "Enough!" and swung at his head. He ducked. Her blow — fairly hard — hit my left shoulder. Right-hand driving is SOP in British protectorates, and I wasn't expecting to be hit and swerved. I avoided a black-bellied sheep, straining at the end of his tether, but nailed a rooster whose red feathers went flying.

Shine screamed, "Look at Ma's big tits, Mista Troy!"

Ma, a gorgeous mulatto of 28, sat on her front stoop, tending her roadside fruit stand and nursing a pair of Adonis twins. She beamed. Her vigorous hand flapping yanked dark nipples from puckered mouths. Her breasts were, indeed, remarkable. And, I confess, I had one of those lustful, libidinous lapses ... but only for a sec, I assure you. All the excitement caused one of her baby boys to pee straight up like a park fountain.

Shine tallyhoed. What fun!

Tamarind bushes, heavy with tasty pods, leaned into the road, and woodpeckers tap-tap-tapped at their delectable contents. Soon the suburbs began. Little shacks set on mini-yards like buttons in buttonholes, porches east-facing to snatch refreshing breezes.

Down a ways and around a hairpin curve, the gap was gashed with bulldozer tracks and across the road laid burning trees, pungent with oily fumes. A thrill of Third World driving is the absence of caution signs, blinking lights, and twelve-dollar-an-hour flaggers.

"Mama could use that wood to cook," Moreen said, her voice, in my face mask, sounded like she was in a cave.

"If she had a man to saw it and a mule to haul it," Shine said. "Which she don't."

For most Saint Moniqueans, every meal was a picnic, cooking outdoors on wood fires.

The rainforest, lumpy as tapioca, ended, and, rolling out before us was a quarter-mile jetty and a boiling black sand beach swaying with coconut palms. A white woman drifted on a red float under cerulean skies stacked with Rembrandt clouds that looked like angels might float out from behind them at any second. Tourist couples strolled along the tide line with distant sailboats barely brushed in. A pod of dolphin arched in a tidal eddy, outwitting baitfish. Behind us, monkeys chattered. Long ago, planters, puffed with rum riches, paid more for the African monkeys' great grandparents than they had for the slaves.

Sad environs surrounded the entrance to Tivoli. Rodney Bay yachts lay motionless on glassy water tied to red-and-white mooring cans strung together like party favors. Royal palms ringed the horseshoe-shaped harbor, and a bright, red pier and thatched-roof boathouse stood on the far side. It was early; boat traffic was light. My sloop sparkled.

"There's *On Business!*" Shine sang. "Why you keep it in such a stinky frigg'n place?"

"SHINE!" Doreen fumed, bashing him hard for the f-word.

He shrieked. "Well, it *do* smell like crap, Dore!"

"This is the only mooring on the island," I said. "You'd better watch your tongue, Shine, or she'll take off your head."

Shine was right. The harbor was sludgy and rancid. When engineers spliced a link from the mainland to our piton, they failed miserably. Lacking cross-tides, the breakwater created a barrier that trapped the harbor's feces from flushing tides. Devoid of oxygen, the harbor mushed up, and its bottom turned squishy as cow flaps. When ancient sentries swam the channel to take their post on the piton, they crossed teal waters teeming with mahi-mahi and grouper. The kids were quiet, and my thoughts wandered back to Pevek and its frozen bay and then jerked back to now as we chattered across the plank bridge over the chocolate-brown Victoria River, the weedy, windy, open sewer that glided through Shantytown, the gateway to Tivoli.

I slowed to a crawl. Shantytown was a ghetto. Lean men missing teeth from chewing sugarcane, smoked and drank rum while women head-carried wares to market in baskets of hand-woven palm fronds. Children head-carried five-gallon pails of water from the village pipe without spilling a drop. Punchy strains of reggae drifted through huts thrown up with driftwood that looked as if it had washed up on the beach from square-rigged Spanish galleons. Houses stood on stilts to escape the reach of storm tides. A woman with arms the size of thighs held a machete and lopped off a rooster's head in one quick chop. She held up her work for inspection and dropped it. The fowl, headless as Ichabod Crane's nemesis, ran. Dead is not always dead. Chanticleer ran in circles spurting blood before a hut with a roof sparkling with recycled ingenuity: tin cans sliced open, hammered flat, and thatched into metal shingles. A boy in pursuit of the fowl snatched his leg. Wings flapped. Feathers flew. Blood splattered.

And the rooster succumbed to take his pot-ready place.

In the next yard, a woman scrubbing underwear on a rock by the river rose and draped them over a hedge to dry. Bare-naked kids chased goats in a cacophony of trilling laryngeal bleats of maaa, maaa. Despite the rickety appearance of this ghetto, no house had blown down since Hurricane Janet blew through fifty years earlier. Around a corner, Shantytown gave way to the wood frame and cement-block buildings of the capital, Tivoli, now besieged by reggae's insistent throbs. At sea level, the heat was pervasive, but it acted like a starter's gun for the Dubois kids.

I slowed, and Shine grabbed the mango basket and swung out a leg. Moreen unwrapped the towel and whipped off my diving mask. Regina stood with a foot on the tailgate. Doreen stretched her long legs, ready to alight before I rolled to a stop on Rue de Versailles, Main Street.

Over her shoulder, Moreen said, "Thanks, Mister Troy" and jumped out. The others followed.

I parked in front of the restaurant, stepped out, and started twirling my keys.

Nastia jumped out of the sleigh and said, "Let's eat first, Daddy. I'm starved."

"You go on in. Order the usual. I'll run to the Post Office and be right back."

Rue de Versailles was blanketed with the ashy smells of chimneys clearing their throats from cooking breakfast. The din of Bob Marley's, *Get Up* marched down the street, thumping my cochlea like a smithy at work. *Get Up* was one of the reggae king's calls to arms recorded in Jamaica before he died at thirty-six. *Get up, Get up. Stand up for your rights!* is its entire alias.

My stomach growled, and I hurried over palm shadows splayed across the mucky street. Marley became deafening. In the timeless generational music-quarrel, I wondered if young Ludwig's key thumping bashed his mother's tympanic membranes. Probably not. Beethoven's clavichord soothed, his harmonies were sweet, his chord progression gradual. Today's dementias was teamed with horrific videos and it's killing us, beaming its idiocy at our unlicked cubs like some spaceship gone wacko. Maybe Ludwig's deafness was a blessing.

Out of the lee, a high-pressure breeze kicked up as cool and refreshing as a tumbler of ice tea on an August afternoon. Main Street runs fifty yards in from, and parallel to, cliffs running above the Atlantic shore. Bamboo creaked leaning out of the wind. Marley was replaced by the joyous chatter of kids at play in the cemetery in the heart of town. In fresh dirt the size of a pillow, two boys drew circles for marbles in the little newly-spaded grave. A gaggle of girls played hopscotch beside a mausoleum. A peculiar characteristic of the West Indies is they do not find some dreary spot on the outskirt of town to lay their dead. Here, the dearly departed are inextricably grounded in everyday life. I was thinking about Anastasia and Mom when a voice directly beside me boomed, "Morn'n, Morn'n, Mister Troy."

I jumped. "Good morning, Darien," I said.

In the soft umbrage of the post office's west side, a thin, wrinkled, white-haired, black man stood snipping the crown of another thin, wrinkled, white-haired, black man seated on a stump. Darien Pope, the capital's barber, also used his stump as a dentist's chair. A wind gush blew white hair onto the wooden stairs of the chink-walled post office creaking on its stilts.

"Busy, Darien?" I asked.

"Somewhat. You figure on a shearing afta breakfast?" He chuckled. "You've got mail."

"Do I, now?" I bound up the board stairs, which sprang under my weight like a trampoline and brought a bobbing Gwen Castoguay into view. Her head was bent over a folder of stamps, counting. Gwen's black shoulders gleamed like a swimmer's between spaghetti straps of pink cotton and a dress that hugged her torso. She licked a long pink finger and raised her eyes from the mish-mash of stamp sheets. Tall, lean, and stately, Gwen's left cheek was sculpted with a deep dimple that moved as her lips moved. My eyes followed her right hand from left breast to right hip, helping her smooth her dress.

She smiled broadly. "Morn'n, Morn'n, Mister Troy." Her perfect white teeth flashed white against raven skin. "You got mail."

"*Buenos dias*, Gwen. *¿Qué tal?*" I said, affably, yanking my eyes back from their marathon.

The woman had the carriage, face, and body of Janet Jackson. *Why, Lord, do you plague me with these loose, licentious, lascivious thoughts?*

"*Bastante bien, gracias*, Troy," Gwen bubbled in return.

She studied Spanish weekends at the college and continued, "*Tengo una carta para usted.*" As she spun on bare feet, her dress flared pleasantly, unmasking strong thighs. "D'is one's sure been 'round for weeks!" She reached into a pigeonhole marked W (Whitey?) withdrew two letters, one from Moscow, probably my Gulag friend Hans's daughter, the other a grayish-violet envelope and sniffed it. "That one sure does *smell goood.*" She chuckled and gave me the tardy dispatch.

I studied it. "Look at those postmarks! Ecuador, Peru, Antigua. It's circled the hemisphere. *Gracias.* " I stepped into rays spilling through the door, tilted the envelope to catch the sun, and examined it. The paper appeared more reddish-purple than violet. Mauve meant personal. It was torn and bore no return address. That meant non-conformist. The postmark was obliterated by cancellations. The envelope was handwritten: *Not* a bill. Blue fountain pen ink meant traditionalist. I pried open a corner and sniffed the inside. The odor was faintly familiar. I re-examined the writing. The capitals T and L in my name appeared to be carefully drawn, like a kid might do, more scrawled than cursive, more like drawn by someone who picked up English late in life. Like Ingrid. My heart skipped a beat. I wanted to boogie around the counter and plant a smackeroo on Gwen's lips. I didn't, of course, Yankee rectitude stifled the feeling — a Dad trait. We chatted a minute, and I said goodbye and headed for the restaurant thinking how I missed marriage or the cozier aspects of the sacrament. I was going to read this after breakfast.

But then I got curious.

***

TWENTY-NINE

A Surprise Visit
June 3, 2001

I paused, sweating, near the Post Office. A ribby donkey yoked to a substantial cart sluggishly clomped by. Squinting north and south, I saw no black cats and struck off down Rue de Versailles for Islan Deelits. I'd planned to read the mystery letters at breakfast, but curiosity won. I tore open one end of the envelopes, huffed, and extracted the obscurity. Hans wanted to visit America this summer. He'd been freed and was home. Fantastic!

The second letter's salutation began: Dear Restaurateur. I flipped to page two. The valediction read: Divorcee on Wheels, Ingrid.

I started reading and was whistling the Beach Boy's *Get Around*, but I had the good sense to keep an eye on the street like the point man on a foot patrol looking for land mines. Tivoli's main drag was a zoo of cats, dogs, goats, sheep, geese, chickens, pigs, partridges in a palm tree, and kids coaxing homemade kites into the breathless air. I skimmed the letter and stopped abruptly when I stepped on a pig oinking delightedly, cooling in the mud like a subterranean reptile.

Across the street, the Dubois kids worked the open-air market and quibbled with customers over coconut prices. There was a string of stalls hawking used clothes, fresh fruits, and vegetables. Skinned and quartered sheep buzzed with flies at bloodied counters. Stall-owners argued over carcasses of this and that being unloaded from the abattoir pickup. Market day always reminded me of cave dwellers squabbling over wooly mammoth cadavers, shooing flies and bickering for the filet. I spotted a bench and sat to read Ingrid's letter, smoothing out the wrinkles on my hairy leg, and rereading it word-for-word. A warm glow set in.

Dear Restaurateur,

I wish I could express this eloquently, but my brain is feeble, and this pen feels like a chisel. Everything I say will sound trite or stupid. I've sat here in Winter Park's sticky weather for two months. Today, it's grayer than a sidewalk and looks more like Helsinki in February than Florida in April, and it makes me sad. I'm draggy, snap at Kaarina too often, and feel like a marionette with strings plucked by the divorce. Thank God for Kaarina.

Did you know I went nonstop from high school at 16, to Rollins, to marriage, to work, to having a baby with never a break? I never took time off to thumb around Europe. I, the fast-tracked, organized, regimented, D-U-L-L Ingrid! Unless I do something different, Troy, I'm going to positively absolutely die! I don't want to end life at twenty-seven as a divorcee with a kid and an empty photo album. Who cares about me anymore? Only Kaarina.

So I'm cutting loose — and, by God, I've already started! I don't know if I've the stamina to finish, but I'm giving it my best shot. Down at that joint in Winter Park Anastasia and I used to frequent after tennis, I sipped an excellent margarita and finalized my plan. Yes, I know you'll want to know: The food was hot and spicy, but the service was terrible! Don't bimbos know single women can leave hefty tips?

Here's The Plan:

Step One: I quit my job

I've wanted to do something different with my life for a long time. And that, dear friend, includes digging around the roots of my Finnish family tree. Like your hopscotching version of life — minus the Gulag, of course — mine begins the first of May. You'll think I'm loony, but of late my life has been joyless and friendless. Anastasia's death and our split are black clouds that have been shadowing me for too long, and I'm sick and tired of being sick and tired. Don't get me wrong; the cool tennis-set consoled me at first, but things changed fast. Funny, there were so many of Kahuna's soul mates initially — to the point of nausea — but now my phone never rings. And there's no one here to fix broken stuff. I feel as isolated as Doctor Zhivago Anastasia used to talk about. Funny, too, how all our old friends disappeared; no one invites me anywhere anymore. No one cares how I'm doing or if I'm doing. Hint, hint! It's like being a latchkey kid who comes home with the gold star pinned to her blouse, but Mom's not there with a love pat, cookie, and glass of milk. Life is for giving and living and looking ahead. Guess that's why He gave us eyes looking forward and not fly-eyes. So, here's my solution, dear friend —

Step two: A trip to Finland and the Islands

We're off to Finland for a month, and when I return, I'm coming down, unasked, to visit. You've blabbered to me about how you and little Anastasia's love your queenless fort on your Leeward Island. I've gotta see the finished product. It's been years since Kahuna and I were down and saw it after you first bought it. I'm sure the rebuilt fort is a metaphor of you: Austere, chaste, unpretentious, straightforward, and peaceful. So tidy up your guestroom, this camp follower and her kid have booked a trip down June 5 on L.I.A.T. My condo has a sales contract pending. Every cent of that money will go into the stock market. I'm leaving the For Sale sign up, though, until the deal's signed, sealed, and delivered and the money's parked at Fidelity. Except for the smallest of mementos, most of our honeymoon relics have been hauled to Good Will, and I may ditch my VW for a red Mustang convertible and drive to Miami for the flight with the top down and 'Born to be Wild' blaring on the stereo.

That, Troy, my dear, is the old news.

Step three: Ingrid's new lease on life

The new news is — DRUM ROLL — If Finland looks promising, Kaarina and I will move back and restart life. Finland's electronics, information, and communication companies are looking for whiz kids like me. I've made some contacts, and in the month we're there, I'll have scads of interviews and, undoubtedly, offers. This means I really will be doing something about those things I've yakked about forever. Don't think I'm loony. For two years since the divorce, I've felt like a death row captive awaiting the chair. I can't go on like this. I need to discover more about me and my role in life. I may just wander around that land of midnight sun, toss out my net, and skim in life's bounty. Some of my colleagues were taking a pool on how long I'll stay! Anyway, it's a great time to do it and stop moping around Winter Park.

Kaarina and I will stay with my parents and brothers who think it's great that I'm returning. My bitchy sisters-in-law think I'm deranged. In a way, I hate going, but I need family ... friends for sure AND THAT IS A HINT! Then I'll fly down with Kaarina for a visit with you and little Anastasia for a few days before we head back to Finland — maybe. I'm guessing the attire in Saint Monique is

T-shirts, shorts, and bathing suits. We won't bring much. Oh, and thanks for all your cheery cards and letter. If all that tranquility hasn't driven you daffy, FAX me at 863-297-7015. We arrive on Leeward Islands Air Transport at 7:30 p.m. June 5th.

Divorcee on Wheels

Shocked? I was blown away. Ingrid and her daughter would be here in two days!

I folded the letter, jimmied it back into the envelope, and high tailed it to the restaurant to discuss it with Nastia.

A hundred yards from Islan Deelits, the punishment of reggae's redundancy swarmed over me like the sledging sun, and any hope of a tranquil chat with Nastia was lost to steel drums hammering from Kingdom Come amplifiers the size of refrigerators.

Islan Deelits was a tacky little pink board-building on three-foot stilts. I swung through the door into cool dimness and wondered what would happen to the business if the restaurant ever cleared up and advertised. Without it, Islan Deelits *mañana* was as obscure as a mole's in this paradise of fickle tourists dreading salmonella, botulism, and cholera.

"Over here, Daddy," Nastia chimed from one of six tables in the blue shadows. "Did we get mail?"

"Yeap," I replied, blinking to adjust my eyes to the dimness. "One took a month to get here, look at all the postmarks."

I set the mauve envelope beside a bowl of sliced mangoes, soursop, and papaya. Nastia snapped it up, studied the envelope, sniffed it, and squealed, "Wow! Where's Peru?"

"In South America. Wipe off your hands. Did you order?"

Nastia wiped her hands on her shorts. "Yeap, I told Hansa 'the usual,' like you said."

"Good girl." I kissed the top of her head and slid into the wooden booth.

Nastia pulled the letter out of its envelope, poked out her tongue from the side of her mouth for help and read.

I smelled cordon bleu scents and heard two voices meandering in from the kitchen as I looked around the unsunned walls. Two corners held hallowed religious *objets d'art:* Mary, the Blessed Virgin, knelt in one corner, eyes downcast, concentrating on the afterlife; Brahma, the creator in the Hindu's supreme triad, glared from the other, planning tomorrows for all he was worth. Across the table, Nastia was smiling and tracing Ingrid's cursive with a long, slender finger as I fingernailed termite trenches in the seat and glanced out the window. Islan Deelits had expanded. Two tables baked in the sharp-edged sun for dining *alfresco* with an excellent view of the market's bloody offerings. Lean men wearing hand-me-downs stood in a triangle of building shade and appeared to be hung from clotheslines. The streets scene spoke eloquently. In this land of plenty and breathtaking beauty, there were far too many bare-bottomed urchins and cripples with curable ailments. The bicycle was a recent introduction. The washing machine had yet to appear. And, for 99.9% of the residents, the information highway was as far off as Sagittarius.

When Nastia turned to page two, I asked, "So, what do you think?"

"I'm excited," Nastia exclaimed, "but cursive's hard to read."

"Take all the time you need, Sweetie."

"A voice sang out from the kitchen, "That you, Troy?"

"It is, indeed, Hansa," I said. "Hungry as a wolf and dying for a cup of coffee."

As if by magic the enthusiastic *femme fatale*, Hansa Purandare, appeared with a steaming coffee pot and an old cup. With the innate lure of gravity, she swayed up to the table all smiles and teeth, rolled up in a gaily-colored sari that exposed her copper midriff and deep cleavage.

"Troy, you look scrawny," she jived. "You been lost at sea?"

She fluttered her eyelashes lubriciously and poured my coffee, patting her long black locks.

Nastia looked up from her cursive struggle and smiled slyly. "Hansa, Daddy's going to look for a wife so I can have a sister."

"Hey," I objected. "Just one minute young lady!"

Hansa chucked. "I thought your Daddy liked bachelorhood, Anastasia."

"Nope. He promised to find me a sister, and Daddy never lies."

"Okay, okay you two, lay off; I enjoy the celibacy of my monkhood," I proclaimed. Then I huffed on the coffee and took a sip, trying not to stare overtly at Hansa's soft curves and statuesqueness. The Purandare family had been in Saint Monique seven generations, arriving the year after the Brits emancipated slaves in 1834. That was also the year of the worse famine in West Indian history. Short of workers, the resourceful English shipped from India thousands of indentured servants to replace the emaciated Africans. Today, the Indians were the islands merchants, doctors, and lawyers—unlike the Africans, who the Brits never permitted to read, marry, or attend church.

Hansa slid silverware onto the table and dished me a beguiling look. "Anastasia ordered the usual for you; okay?"

"It is," I acknowledged.

Nastia dropped the letter. "Daddy!" she exploded, "Ingrid and Kaarina are coming in two days!"

"Exciting, huh?" I huffed on my coffee again and sipped some. "Do you like Kaarina?"

"I do, I do! She'd make a super sister. Unless you marry Hansa 'because she's not really married, just living with that turbaned brute,'" Nastia parroted. Who said the apple doesn't fall close to the tree?

Hansa tilted her head back and laughed heartily.

"Sweetheart, I'll marry your Daddy, but do you like boys?"

"I hate boys!" Nastia blurted.

Hansa scowled. "Too bad for us. I guess I'd better stay here in this coop." Hansa leaned over and kissed Nastia's cheek and gave her a sun-bright smile. "Honey, you sure need a mother, but I can't be her. I've got a man and three boys and —" Hansa lowered her eyes until her long curly lashes rested on smooth copper cheeks, turned sideward, and pulled her sari snug. Below her ample breasts pouched the slightest curve of a growing cocoon —"I don't know what this is."

I gave her my reprehensible look, totally inexcusable I assure you. "Pregnant again? Well, we don't want some naggy old witch with a bunch of boys anyway, do we Nastia?"

"No boys for sure."

"Would you hit me again with coffee and go see about our food, please? We've lots to do."

"Yes, sir, right away, sir," Hansa said, topping off my cup. She wangled her head side-to-side, the Indian way, and with one arm overhead, breasts swinging, and hips swaying like a hula's, headed for the kitchen.

"Daddy," Nastia began deadly serious, "we do have a lot to do to. We don't have sheets or towels for the guest room, and I need stuff for Kaarina and me to play with."

"You mean like a hula hoop, dolls, and a monopoly game?"

"Exactly!"

"Sweetie, how about showing Kaarina how to climb palm trees and pick mangoes and hike to the top of our piton and swim in water salty enough to sit in?"

Nastia considered that all of two seconds and exclaimed, "Great idea! But what about nights?"

"You'll be so tired you'll sleep."

Hansa bustled out of the kitchen, emanating great smells, clangs, and bangs, and vivaciously attacked the dining room, straightening, wiping, and tidying, trying to stay ahead of the open windows and dry season dust.

Within minutes, our breakfast appeared proudly borne overhead by a clone of Indiana Jones. This Indiana wore khaki shorts and shirt, epaulets on, sleeves hacked off to display sculptured biceps. Armored with the cockiness good looks given the illiterate, he cackled up to the table, eyes twinkling, teeth sparkling, and made salutations. Indiana was an inch taller than my seventy-five inches, black bearded, and looked exactly like Harrison Ford except for better incisors and skin the tea-color of Michael Jackson's before his bleach jobs. He deftly hefted a basket of toast and *beignets* (fluffy donuts dusted with powdered sugar), and, the cynosure, an enormous mahogany platter heaped with lip-smacking victuals. I thanked God I wasn't at the Gulag.

With the panache of the consummate *maître d'*, Indiana slid the plenitude onto the altar, jerked his hand aloft, and exclaimed, "*Voilá!*" He stood silent, awaiting a pat.

Nastia dove for a *beignet*. I boosted one jungly eyebrow skeptically. "What kinda heartburn's this?"

Indiana put on a pretended hurt look, pulled a rag from his belt, and dabbed at a speck of splatter on the platter.

I sniffed. It passed the smell test. I couldn't help myself and stuck a finger into the lobster and coconut milk sauce smothering a broiled conch and licked it. The heavenly taste was a blend of Creole/Cajun heritage as compelling as champagne and caviar. I sniffed around the platter some more, its stringy wisps of steam rising from the lobster and well-charred, gizzard-burning sausage-casings laying on a bed of sweet onion rings flawlessly encircling three easy-over eggs confettied with sautéed diced onions, toasted garlic, parsley, and enough hot red chili to scorch my uvula. Fried green tomatoes, crusty with cheesy-herbal breadcrumbs, and a rainbow of fruit: yellow paw-paw, red cashew apple, green carambola, white guava, and orange mango slices gilded the edges of our repast. A wicker basket held a Mount Everest of freshly baked, thickly sliced, butter-drenched, yeast toast Hansa had baked. I'd given her Mom's recipe for yeast bread, and Hansa now sold yeast rolls and cinnamon buns to all the island hotels daily.

Nastia gobbled down her first beignet, picked up a second, and looked at me.

I scowled. She set it down, and she started on her lobster and said "Ummm," and plowed on.

Indiana and I bantered for a minute as the room filled with the pungent aroma of fresh lobster hot off mahogany coals smothered with capers and sweet onions. Three years ago, I'd given a bushel of Vidalia seed onions to Thomas Roberts, a dauntless farmer and coached him how to plant them: lots of cow manure, spaced five inches apart, watered daily if it didn't rain. Thomas harvested them when their tops yellowed and dried them in mesh bags. He tilled and planted and weeded and watered religiously, and now he pedaled them to every eatery in Saint Monique (letting twenty percent of his onions flower and go to seed for the next planting — onions are biennial). He made enough money with his unique onions to buy a beat-up pickup. The poor don't need handouts; they need credit and an idea.

Indiana cleared his throat, hovered and leaned forward.

In the restaurant's twilight, I picked up the salt shaker, banged loose a few grains of rock-like deliquescence, and sprinkled the eggs. I sliced off a hunk of the conch, dipped it in the golden yolk, and positioned it carefully on my tongue, rolling it around like a sommelier at a wine tasting — but this could not be spit out.

"Umm," I said as hot deliciousness filled my mouth. Never had I tasted anything as essential to my life as this big tender chunk of gastropod mollusk. I raised my voice, "Ahh, acceptable."

"Ahh come on, Troy," Indiana scoffed. "You can do better than that."

"The donuts are really yummy," Nastia muttered through a mouth full of lobster.

I chewed some more and elevated my "Umm" to "DELECTABLE!" and swallowed.

Breakfast did, indeed, smell great and taste marvelous, and right then and there I decided to marry an island cook. I'd get big and fat; she'd have babies galore, and we'd live to be one hundred. But it was a fleeting fantasy. *What Colby alum would ever marry a native unable to decipher Kant's Categorical Imperative?* We devoured the repast — except for one big half of the second lobster for the doggy bag — and I looked around the empty restaurant and belched.

Nastia yelped, "*Daddy!*"

I shoved the platter aside and said, "We've got to fax Ingrid. You go out and play with Hansa's boys, and I'll write a reply."

She did. I rubbed my belly like Henry VIII, picked up Ingrid's oft-canceled letter and extracted the two pages. A trace of Ingrid's Opium scent weaved past the lobster scent. After she and Kahuna spent a March vacation with me in Saint Monique in 1997 — two months after I had been freed from the Gulag and bought the fortress — Kaarina and Nastia had played while my guests poo-pooed my fort plan. They'd trashed it, in fact, and now she had invited herself down. Finns *are* inscrutable.

I mulled over my recent jag of lonely, pitiful, sorrowful depression and reckoned I'd probably have jumped off Lena's Leap if not for my six-year-old. Nastia was a bouncing, giggling, laughing bundle of joy all day, every day. Seeing Ingrid and Kaarina would be the highlight of our year.

I pinched my arm. I was awake. Savoring the moment, I said, "Thank you, Lord."

Since today was June 3rd, Ingrid would be here in two days. I had to get the fax to her now! Her sarcasm about my letter-writing flops stung, but I stood guilty as charged. I would never earn a black belt in letter writing. In fact, I rarely wrote anyone. Over my five years in the Gulag, my life, according to Dad, 'was a scrapbook of three, one-paragraph letters from the Arctic.'

Hansa refilled my cup, her exquisite face screwing up in a puzzle. "Something's wrong? You look spooky." She cocked her head to one side like a robin looking for worms.

"It's nothing. I'm just thinking about stuff. An old friend is coming down."

"An old female friend?"

"Yes." I felt my face flush.

"When?" I detected a hint of jealousy in her voice.

"Day after tomorrow." I pushed aside the empty plates. "Have you paper and pencil?"

"Sure." She scurried off to get writing stuff, and I fished the wallet out of my very tight trunks. Hansa was back in a flash and gave me a 100-Watt, pre-tip smile. Competition makes the world go round.

"How much?" I inquired.

She scowled. "You know how much it is for two meals. Same as it always is."

"Astronomical!" I grumbled and peeled off two lovely little Hamilton, which, incredibly, covered the cost of our meals and a one hundred percent tip. "What're you grinning about, woman?"

"Oh, nothing," Hansa said, giving me a long, quizzical look. She took our dishes and switched those fertile hips toward the kitchen.

I looked out the window. Nastia's legs were wrapped around a palm tree, two-stories above Island Deelits, wrestling a coconut loose. I tried to fathom Ingrid's motive for wanting to return to a place that she had put down. Maybe she'd gone over the edge. Or maybe she just couldn't stand life without Anastasia and me around. I may not be the world's greatest of catch, but neither am I some impecunious ape. Of course, all that would be sorted out soon enough. Maybe it was a heavenly intervention.

Charles Henry, a delightful old codger with a hoary crown and prune skin, witchdoctor by repute, told me our piton's dreamy listlessness began the night the Carib maiden, Lena, swan-dived off my jagged ledge in a lovers' quarrel. *She returns often,* he claimed. I do not doubt him. Once, as a boy, I had a vision at the Moose Hill Cemetery while at Grandma Locke's Maine farm. I have lived in this bewildering place of bewitching superstitions long enough to appreciate others often have, and some still do. Perhaps the philter was planetary, living so close to shooting stars, imbibing the lacy Milky Way, soaking up the energy from nearby galaxies that seem closer here, far from the ambient light and deafening wail of civilization.

"Write," I told myself.

My Dear Ingrid, began the wordsmith, paused to watch the kids out the open window, smell the ocean, and sip coffee.

Neither the wide sea's tranquility nor this lumpy isle's viridity has done us in, though we're touched by your concern. It would be Nastia and my great pleasure to have you and Kaarina as our houseguest for a stay of indeterminate length. Do not bring more clothes than you can comfortably carry in one hand. No dresses, shoes, hats, umbrellas, lotions, or other sundry First World paraphernalia. We have all the stuff you'll need.

With my flawless logic, ever keen to the feminine plight, I detected a touch of blue funk in your epistle about life's roulette wheel. Forget not that within your cheerless brain rests an escape valve: It forgets. Time helps. I know with the divorce you have your reasons, but giving up on life in America to hole up in Finland! Surely you jest! You are no longer a starry-eyed co-ed. (But then again you never were.)

Come down. Look around. Share the excitement of pure air, moon grins,

more stars than you can count, and soak up some of our sun, rum, and
serenity.

BUT DO NOT FLEE TO A LIFE IN A COUNTRY OF AVOWED
SOCIALISTS!

I read it over, tinkered here and there, and signed it, *Restaurateur*.

I stepped outside onto the porch and stretched. A five-minute deluge had cooled the air, pockmarked Main Street, and chased Nastia and her pals from palm heights. Pigs cooled in mud holes. Hens scratched. Cosmos, Tivoli's glassy-eyed Rasta sporting knee-long dreadlocks and wearing a bamboo suit, clicked and clacked up the porch, towing a mangy sheep and two mangier goats. Wearing wood is about as appealing to me as mining Gulag coal is. Nonchalantly, Cosmos tipped over the garbage barrel to let his flock forage.

"Hi, Cosmos," I said to him and to Nastia, shouted, "Come on, Nasty, we gotta fax a letter!"

Nastia trotted to my side beaming. "Shine's gonna sell my coconuts for me," she yelped. "I'll be rolling in dough!"

"You keeping all the loot?"

"Nope. I'm giving him a ten percent commission, like you do in your Taxol business, Daddy." Right then, she looked so much like her Mom it took my breath away.

"Come on," I said, "we've gotta get to the Ramada Inn." I wiped a tear from my cheek before she spotted it. "They have the only fax machine in Saint Monique."

"Then we'll go to Saint George's for sheets and towels?" asked my little housekeeper.

"And the big grocery store to restock the larder."

"Do you think they'll stay a long time, Daddy? Maybe Ingrid could help you in the Taxol business or be a waitress. She told me she was a waitress in college."

"She was. We've sure got lots of opportunities for her, huh?"

"I've got a funny feeling they'll stay," Anastasia said. "Don't you, Daddy?"

"You're rarely wrong," I said. "Jump in."

She wasn't.

REQUIESCAT

Strew on her roses, roses,
And never a spray of yew!
In quiet she reposes;
Ah, would that I did too!
Her mirth the world required;
She bathed it in smiles of glee.
But her heart was tired, tired,
And now they let her be....

Matthew Arnold

FOOTNOTES

1 Henry, 06/28/1491-01/28/1547, was King at 18 and had the ample energy for tennis and dalliances with consorts who were divorced, beheaded, died/divorced, beheaded, and survived.

2 СССР, or Союз Советских Социалистических Республик, Union of Soviet Socialist Republics.

3 Joseph Stalin, was born 12/18/1878 in Gori, Georgia, as Ioseb Besarionis dze Jughashivili; he died 03/5/1953.

4 In *Only One Year*, Stálina explains why she took her mother's name, Allilueva, soon after her father's death.

5 An acronym for Glavnoe Upravlenie Ispravitel'no-Trudovykh Lagerei, Main Administration of Corrective Labor Camp; it is a term largely unknown until Aleksandr Solzhenitsyn's The Gulag Archipelago, 1918-1965 (1973) likened the forced labors camps, where some 30-40 million perished, to an island chain extending across the Soviet Union.

6 Openness in speech

7 Economic and political reconstruction

8 Here's your fact for the day: When flying into Moscow's Sheremetyevo, it appears Шереме́тьево.

9 Olyushka, Olya, and Olenka are tender diminutives for Olga.

10 The infamous, 8-story, Neo-Baroque, 1898, yellow-brick-façaded Moscow jail feared by millions of innocent victims of Stalin's purges located at 2 Dzerzhinsky Square. Feliks Dzerzhinsky headed the CHEKA, an acronym for All-Russian Extraordinary Commission for the Suppression of Counterrevolution and Sabotage, the predecessor of the KGB. Today it is the home of the FSB, (Federalnaya Sduzhba Bespasnos), watchdogs of domestic happenings.

11 The first match, held July 9, 1877, was the same year Edison invented the phonograph and Queen Victoria was proclaimed Empress of India.

12 She referred to the Orange County Convention Center, a seven-million-square-foot edifice that draws one million delegates annually with an economic impact of $1.9 billion.

13 Formed in March 1933, the Civilian Conservation Corps, or CCC, was one of FDR's first New Deal programs. Three million men, under army control, served in public works projects, building 800 parks, planting 3 billion trees, and promoting environmental conservation and good citizenship through strenuous outdoor labor that, coincidently, helped the army prepare disciplined young men for WWII.

14 A drab, black, knee-high, felt boot made of wool, the valenki has been a staple for generations of Russians to protect against harsh cold, worn either as inner or outer footwear and often paired with rain boots to keep dry.

15 Russian for New City from the Old Russian: Новъ and Городъ.

16 Mikoyan MiG-29—Микоян МиГ-29—developed by Mikoyan during the 1970s to counter the American Falcon fighters, McDonnell Douglas F-15 and General Dynamics F-16.

17 In 1904, the Trans-Siberian Railroad's 5,870 miles of spurs were joined, linking Moscow to Vladivostok, an incredible feat at the time—to put it into perspective, it is about the same distance (6,252 miles) from L.A. to London. The 60-mile spur, Belogorsk to Blagoveschensk, was completed by Gulag inmates in 1949.

18 The traditional steamed buns filled with ground pork, vegetables, eggs, or bean paste eaten for breakfast.

19 外国人

20 Translated as the supreme ultimate fist.

21 He had made a joke. Chainik, the Russian word for a teapot, sounds similar to the English word Chinese.

22 The Russian word for Chinese, Kutaey when pronounced with a long ending, Kutaėcy, means fucking Chinese.

23 Zhanna, or Жанна, is the Russian equivalent of Jeanne; Zha, Jean, is one of its diminutives.

24 In the six-month Battle of Stalingrad (8/23/1942 – 2/2/1943), Nazi Germany fought the Soviet Union in close-quarter combat in one of the bloodiest clashes in the history of warfare. Much of the city was reduced to rubble. It was WWII's most strategically decisive battle, a turning point in the European theater. Soviets captured tens of thousands of Germans, banished them to Siberia, and never permitted them to return home at war's end.

25 VE, or Victory in Europe, May 8, 1945.

26 An abbreviation of the present participle of the Russian заключенный, or ZAKlyuchennyy, prisoner.

27 The enforcement of standardization and the elimination of all opposition within the political, economic, and cultural institutions of a state. From German Gleichschalten (to bring into line), from gleich (same) + schalten (to switch, turn). Used by the Nazi regime and Soviets for totalitarian control.

28 The flood or deluge myth is a common narrative of a deity or deities who destroyed civilization, often in an act of divine retribution that is widespread among cultures. Some are the Mesopotamian flood stories, Hindu religious books from India, Puranas, the Deucalion in Greek mythology, Genesis flood narrative of Noah's Ark, and in thelore of the K'iche' and Maya peoples in Mesoamerica, the Lac Courte Oreilles Ojibwa tribe of Native Americans in North America, the Muisca people, and Cañari Confederation, in South America.

29 The earth curves about 8 inches a mile, but it does not take 9 miles to curve 72 inches. To illustrate, look at the Pythagorean Theorem using 6 feet for the curvature. Here is Harley's diagram with the 1 in the diagram replaced by x, since in this case the distance is unknown.

The theorem of Pythagoras: a2 = 39632 + x2 = 15705369 + x2 Solving for x: x2 = a2 − 15705369, and must be 3963 miles + 6 feet (Let's say the men are actually 6'3", so their eyes are six feet above ground.). Thus a = 3963.001136 miles, x2 = 15705378 - 15705369 = 9, x = 3 miles

30 The name given to the skeleton of a 55-year-old, slender, Paleoindian man found on a bank of the Columbia River in Kennewick, Washington. DNA tests show he dates to 9,400 B.C.E. and resembles a Polynesian.

31 Located in the Kabardio-Balkariya Region, Russia's highest mountain is 5,642 meters, or 18,510.5 feet tall.

32 Shakal—шакал—means jackal in Russian.

33 Ufa, Уфа, the capital of the Bashkortostan Republic in Central Russia, is the home of Bashneft Oil Company. It produces LPG and 156 million barrels of gasoline, diesel, fuel oil and petrochemicals a year.

34 Chelyabinsk Tractor Plant—Челябинский тракторный завод, or Chelyabinskiy traktornyy zavod, (abbreviated ЧТЗ, ChTZ), a wealthy and storied showcase of Soviet industry established in 1933 in that Ural Mountain city and famed for its WW II tanks.

35 Tea, Russia's de facto national beverage since Mongolian ruler, Altyn Khan, gifted Tsar Michael I 250 pounds of tea leaves in 1638.

36 Saint Petersburg's Baroque-façade-style Winter Palace, one of four built on the same spot over the last two centuries, has 1,500 rooms and halls.

37 Or, моногородов, one-industry cities; half of Russia's largest cities had one employer.

38 To the shock of scientists and surprise of no one, BMS successfully patented Taxol, a natural substance, another congressional gift.

39 A kWh calculation: head in feet (120) x flow in gallons per minute (45) ÷ by a factor of 12.

ABOUT THE AUTHOR

Ceylon Barclay, former President of Worldwide Marketing for Chinese Taxol extractor, Great Wall Pharmaceutical Company, has spent the last thirty-five years launching and advancing economic projects in global hot spots, including China, Russia, Sri Lanka, Nicaragua, Kenya, and Grenada. Along the way, he has written several books and served as President of Friends of the Upper Volga Institute with Mikhail Gorbachev. He studied philosophy at Colby College, aesthetics at the University of Miami Graduate School, and lives in the mountains of North Carolina with his wife, a Russian professor.

Ceylon Barclay (left) with former Soviet statesman Mikhail Gorbachev.

The legal system ignored him,
then setenced him to death ....

A Date with the
EXECUTIONER

A true story
told by
Ellen Smith

boldventurepress.com